JULES VERNE

JULES VERNE

AROUND THE WORLD IN EIGHTY DAYS

20,000 LEAGUES UNDER THE SEA

LONGMEADOW PRESS

Around the World in Eighty Days was first published in 1873
20,000 Leagues Under the Sea was first published in 1864

Published exclusively for Waldenbooks in 1984 by

Octopus Books Limited
59 Grosvenor Street
London W1

Copyright © 1984 arrangement
Octopus Books Limited

Illustrations: Mary Evans Picture Library

ISBN 0 681 28759 4

Printed by Kingsport Press, USA

CONTENTS

CONTENTS

AROUND THE WORLD
IN EIGHTY DAYS

Chapter One

In which Phileas Fogg and Passepartout accept each other, the one as Master, the other as Servant.

MR. PHILEAS FOGG LIVED, in 1872, at No. 7, Saville Row, Burlington Gardens, the house in which Sheridan died in 1814. He was one of the most noticeable members of the Reform Club, though he seemed always to avoid attracting attention; an enigmatical personage, about whom little was known, except that he was a polished man of the world. People said that he resembled Byron, – at least that his head was Byronic; but he was a bearded, tranquil Byron, who might live on a thousand years without growing old.

Certainly an Englishman it was more doubtful whether Phileas Fogg was a Londoner. He was never seen on 'Change, nor at the Bank, nor in the counting-rooms of the 'City'; no ships ever came into London docks of which he was the owner; he had no public employment; he had never been entered at any of the Inns of Court, either at the Temple, or Lincoln's Inn, or Gray's Inn; nor had his voice ever resounded in the Court of Chancery, or in the Exchequer, nor the Queen's Bench, or the Ecclesiastical Courts. He certainly was not a manufacturer; nor was he a merchant or a gentleman farmer. His name was strange to the scientific and learned societies, and he never was known to take part in the sage deliberations of the Royal Institution or the London Institution, the Artisan's Association or the Institution of Arts and Sciences. He belonged, in fact, to none of the numerous societies which swarm in the English capital, from the Harmonic to that of the Entomologists, founded mainly for the purpose of abolishing pernicious insects.

Phileas Fogg was a member of the Reform, and that was all.

The way in which he got admission to this exclusive club was simple enough.

He was recommended by the Barings, with whom he had an open credit. His checks were regularly paid at sight from his account current, which was always flush.

Was Phileas Fogg rich? Undoubtedly. But those who knew him best could not imagine how he had made his fortune, and Mr. Fogg was the last person to whom to apply for the information. He was not lavish, nor, on the contrary, avaricious; for whenever he knew that money was needed for a noble, useful, or benevolent purpose, he supplied it quietly and sometimes anonymously. He was, in short, the least communicative of men. He talked very little and seemed all the more mysterious for his taciturn manner. His daily habits were quite open to observation; but whatever he did was so exactly the same thing that he had always done before, that the wits of the curious were fairly puzzled.

Had he travelled? It was likely, for no one seemed to know the world more familiarly; there was no spot so secluded that he did not appear to have an intimate acquaintance with it. He often corrected, with a few clear words, the thousand conjectures advanced by members of the club as to lost and unheard-of travellers, pointing out the true probabilities, and seeming as if gifted with a sort of second sight, so often did events justify his predictions. He must have travelled everywhere, at least in the spirit.

It was at least certain that Phileas Fogg had not absented himself from London for many years. Those who were honoured by a better acquaintance with him than the rest, declared that nobody could pretend to have ever seen him anywhere else. His sole pastimes were reading the papers and playing whist. He often won at this game, which, as a silent one, harmonized with his nature; but his winnings never went into his purse, being reserved as a fund for his charities. Mr. Fogg played, not to win, but for the sake of playing. The game was in his eyes a contest, a struggle with a difficulty, yet a motionless, unwearying struggle, congenial to his tastes.

Phileas Fogg was not known to have either wife or children, which may happen to the most honest people; either relatives or near friends, which is certainly more unusual. He lived alone in his house in Saville Row, whither none penetrated. A single domestic sufficed to serve him. He breakfasted and dined at the club, at hours mathematically fixed, in the same room, at the same table, never taking his meals with other members, much less bringing a guest with him; and went home at exactly midnight, only to retire at once to bed. He never used the cosy chambers which the Reform provides for its favoured members. He passed ten hours out of the twenty-four in Saville Row, either in sleeping or making his toilet. When he chose to take a walk it was with a regular step in the entrance hall with its mosaic flooring, or in the circular gallery with its dome supported by twenty red porphyry Ionic columns, and illumined by blue painted windows. When he breakfasted or dined all the resources of the club – its kitchens and pantries, its buttery and dairy – aided to crowd his table with their most succulent stores; he was served by the gravest waiters, in dress coats, and shoes with swan-skin soles, who proffered the viands in special porcelain, and on the finest linen; club decanters, of a lost mould, contained his sherry, his port, and his cinnamon-spiced claret; while his beverages were refreshingly cooled with ice, brought at great cost from the American lakes.

If to live in this style is to be eccentric, it must be confessed that there is something good in eccentricity!

The mansion in Saville Row, though not sumptuous, was exceedingly comfortable. The habits of its occupant were such as to demand but little from the sole domestic, but Phileas Fogg required him to be almost superhumanly prompt and regular. On this very 2nd of October he had dismissed James Forster, because that luckless youth had brought him shaving-water at eighty-four degrees Fahrenheit instead of eighty-six; and he was awaiting his successor, who was due at the house between eleven and half-past.

Phileas Fogg was seated squarely in his armchair, his feet close together like those of a grenadier on parade, his hands resting on his knees, his body straight, his head erect; he was steadily watching a complicated clock which indicated the hours, the minutes, the seconds, the days, the months, and the years. At exactly half-past eleven Mr. Fogg would, according to his daily habit, quit Saville Row, and repair to the Reform.

A rap at this moment sounded on the door of the cosy apartment where Phileas Fogg was seated, and James Forster, the dismissed servant, appeared.

'The new servant,' said he.

A young man of thirty advanced and bowed.

'You are a Frenchman, I believe,' asked Phileas Fogg, 'and your name is John?'

'Jean, if monsieur pleases,' replied the newcomer, 'Jean Passepartout, a surname which has clung to me because I have a natural aptness for going out of one business into another. I believe I'm honest, monsieur, but, to be outspoken, I've had several trades. I've been an itinerant singer, a circus-rider, when I used to vault like Leotard, and dance on a rope like Blondin. Then I got to be a professor of gymnastics, so as to make better use of my talents; and then I was a sergeant fireman at Paris, and assisted at many a big fire. But I quitted France five years ago, and, wishing to taste the sweets of domestic life, took service as a valet here in England. Finding myself out of place, and hearing that Monsieur Phileas Fogg was the most exact and settled gentleman in the United Kingdom, I have come to monsieur in the hope of living with him a tranquil life, and forgetting even the name of Passepartout.'

'Passepartout suits me,' responded Mr. Fogg. 'You are well recommended to me; I hear a good report of you. You know my conditions?'

'Yes, monsieur.'

'Good. What time is it?'

'Twenty-two minutes after eleven,' returned Passepartout, drawing an enormous silver watch from the depths of his pocket.

'You are too slow,' said Mr. Fogg.

'Pardon me, monsieur, it is impossible——'

'You are four minutes too slow. No matter; it's enough to mention the error. Now from this moment, twenty-nine minutes after eleven, a.m., this Wednesday, October second, you are in my service.'

Phileas Fogg got up, took his hat in his hand, put it on his head with an automatic motion, and went off without a word.

Passepartout heard the street door shut once; it was his new master going out. He heard it shut again; it was his predecessor, James Forster, departing in his turn. Passepartout remained alone in the house in Saville Row.

Chapter Two

In which Passepartout is convinced that he has at last found his ideal.

'..ITH,' MUTTERED PASSEPARTOUT, somewhat flurried, 'I've seen people at Madame Tussaud's as lively as my new master!'

Madam Tussaud's 'people,' let it be said, are of wax, and are much visited in London; speech is all that is wanting to make them human.

During his brief interview with Mr. Fogg, Passepartout had been carefully observing him. He appeared to be a man about forty years of age, with fine, handsome features, and a tall, well-shaped figure; his hair and whiskers were light, his forehead compact and unwrinkled, his face rather pale, his teeth magnificent. His countenance possessed in the highest degree what physiognomists call 'repose in action,' a quality of those who act rather than talk. Calm and phlegmatic, with a clear eye, Mr. Fogg seemed a perfect type of that English composure which Angelica Kauffmann has so skilfully represented on canvas. Seen in the various phases of his daily life, he gave the idea of being perfectly well-balanced, as exactly regulated as a Leroy chronometer. Phileas Fogg was, indeed, exactitude personified, and this was betrayed even in the expression of his very hands and feet; for in men, as well as in animals, the limbs themselves are expressive of the passions.

He was so exact that he was never in a hurry, was always ready, and was economical alike of his steps and his motions. He never took one step too many, and always went to his destination by the shortest cut; he made no superfluous gestures, and was never seen to be moved or agitated. He was the most deliberate person in the world, yet always reached his destination at the exact moment.

He lived alone, and so to speak, outside of every social relation; and as he knew that in this world account must be taken of friction, and that friction retards, he never rubbed against anybody.

As for Passepartout, he was a true Parisian of Paris. Since he had abandoned his own country for England, taking service as a valet, he had in vain searched for a master after his own heart, Passepartout was by no means one of those pert dunces depicted by Molière, with a bold gaze and a nose held high in the air; he was an honest fellow, with a pleasant face, lips a trifle protruding, soft-mannered and serviceable, with a good round head, such as one likes to see on the shoulders of a friend. His eyes were blue, his complexion rubicund, his figure almost portly and well-built, his body muscular and his physical powers fully developed by the exercises of younger days. His brown hair was somewhat tumbled; for while the ancient sculptors are said to have known eighteen methods of arranging Minerva's tresses, Passepartout was familiar with but one of dressing his own: three strokes of a large-tooth comb completed his toilet.

It would be rash to predict how Passepartout's lively nature would agree with Mr. Fogg. It was impossible to tell whether the new servant would turn out as absolutely methodical as his master required: experience alone could solve the question. Passepartout had been a sort of vagrant in his early years, and now yearned for repose; but so far he had failed to find it, though he had already served in ten English houses. But he could not take root in any of these; with chagrin he found his masters invariably whimsical and irregular, constantly running about the country, or on the look-out for adventure. His last master, young Lord Longferry, Member of Parliament, after passing his nights in the Haymarket taverns, was too often brought home in the morning on policemen's shoulders. Passepartout, desirous of respecting the gentleman whom he served, ventured a mild remonstrance on such conduct; which being ill-received, he took his leave. Hearing that Mr. Phileas Fogg was looking for a servant, and that his life was one of unbroken regularity, that he neither travelled nor stayed from home overnight, he felt sure that this would be the place he was after. He presented himself, and was accepted, as has been seen.

At half-past eleven, then, Passepartout found himself alone in the house in Saville Row. He began its inspection without delay, scouring it from cellar to garret. So clean, well-arranged, solemn a mansion pleased him; it seemed to him like a snail's shell, lighted and warmed by gas, which sufficed for both these purposes. When Passepartout reached the second story he recognised at once the room which he was to inhabit, and he was well satisfied with it. Electric bells and speaking tubes afforded communication with the lower stories; while on the mantel stood an electric clock, precisely like that in Mr. Fogg's bedchamber, both beating the same second at the same instant. 'That's good, that'll do,' said Passepartout to himself.

He suddenly observed, hung over the clock, a card which, upon inspection, proved to be a programme of the daily routine of the house. It comprised all that was required of the servant, from eight in the morning, exactly at which hour Phileas Fogg rose, till half-past eleven, when he left the house for the Reform club, – all the details of service, the tea and toast at twenty-three minutes past eight, the shaving-water at thirty-seven minutes past nine, and the toilet at twenty minutes before ten. Everything was regulated and foreseen that was to be done from half-past eleven a.m. till midnight, the hour at which the methodical gentleman retired.

Mr. Fogg's wardrobe was amply supplied and in the best taste. Each pair of trousers, coat, and vest bore a number, indicating the time of year and season at which they were in turn to be laid out for wearing; and the same system was applied to the master's shoes. In short, the house in Saville Row, which must have been a very temple of disorder and unrest under the illustrious but dissipated Sheridan, was cosiness, comfort, and method idealized. There was no study, nor were there books, which would have been quite useless to Mr. Fogg; for at the Reform two libraries, one of general literature and the other of law and politics, were at his service. A moderate-sized safe stood in his bedroom, constructed so as to defy fire as well as burglars; but Passepartout found neither arms nor hunting weapons anywhere; everything betrayed the most tranquil and peaceable habits.

Having scrutinized the house from top to bottom, he rubbed his hands, a broad smile overspread his features, and he said joyfully, 'this is just what I wanted! Ah, we shall get on together, Mr. Fogg and I! What a domestic and regular gentleman! A real machine; well, I don't mind serving a machine.'

Chapter Three

In which a conversation takes place which seems likely to cost Phileas Fogg dear.

PHILEAS FOGG, HAVING shut the door of his house at half-past eleven, and having put his right foot before his left five hundred and seventy-five times, and his left foot before his right five hundred and seventy-six times, reached the Reform Club, an imposing edifice in Pall Mall, which could not have cost less than three millions. He repaired at once to the dining-room, the nine windows of which open upon a tasteful garden, where the trees were already gilded with an autumn colouring; and took his place at the habitual table, the cover of which had already been laid for him. His breakfast consisted of a side-dish, a broiled fish with Reading sauce, a scarlet slice of roast beef garnished with mushrooms, a rhubarb and gooseberry tart, and a morsel of Cheshire cheese, the whole being washed down with several cups of tea, for which the Reform is famous. He rose at thirteen minutes to one, and directed his steps towards the large hall, a sumptuous apartment adorned with lavishly-framed paintings. A flunkey handed him an uncut *Times*, which he proceeded to cut with a skill which betrayed familiarity with this delicate operation. The perusal of this paper absorbed Phileas Fogg until a quarter before four, whilst the *Standard*, his next task, occupied him till the dinner hour. Dinner passed as breakfast had done, and Mr. Fogg reappeared in the reading-room and sat down to the *Pall Mall* at twenty minutes before six. Half-an-hour later several members of the Reform came in and drew up to the fireplace, where a coal fire was steadily burning. They were Mr. Fogg's usual partners at whist: Andrew Stuart, an engineer; John Sullivan and Samuel Fallentin, bankers; Thomas Flanagan, a brewer; and Gauthier Ralph, one of the Directors of the Bank of England; – all rich and highly respectable personages, even in a club which comprises the princes of English trade and finance.

'Well, Ralph,' said Thomas Flanagan, 'what about that robbery?'

'Oh,' replied Stuart; 'the bank will lose the money.'

'On the contrary,' broke in Ralph, 'I hope we may put our hands on the robber. Skilful detectives have been sent to all the principal ports of America and the Continent, and he'll be a clever fellow if he slips through their fingers.'

'But have you got the robber's description?' asked Stuart.

'In the first place, he is no robber at all,' returned Ralph, positively.

'What! a fellow who makes off with fifty-five thousand pounds, no robber?'

'No.'

'Perhaps he's a manufacturer, then.'

'The *Daily Telegraph* says that he is a gentleman.'

It was Phileas Fogg, whose head now emerged from behind his newspapers, who made this remark. He bowed to his friends, and entered into the conversation. The affair which formed its subject, and which was town talk, had occurred three days before at the Bank of England. A package of bank-notes, to the value of fifty-five thousand pounds, had been taken from the principal cashier's table, that functionary being at the moment engaged in registering the receipt of three shillings and sixpence. Of course he could not have his eyes everywhere. Let it be observed that the Bank of England reposes a touching confidence in the honesty of the public. There are neither guards nor gratings to protect its treasures; gold, silver, bank-notes are freely exposed, at the mercy of the first comer. A keen observer of English customs relates that, being in one of the rooms of the Bank one day, he had the curiosity to examine a gold ingot weighing some seven or eight pounds. He took it up, scrutinized it, passed it to his neighbour, he to the next man, and so on until the ingot, going from hand to hand, was transferred to the end of a dark entry; nor did it return to its place for half-an-hour. Meanwhile, the cashier had not so much as raised his head. But in the present instance things had not gone so smoothly. The package of notes not being found when five o'clock sounded from the ponderous clock in the 'drawing office,' the amount was passed to the account of profit and loss. As soon as the robbery was discovered, picked detectives hastened off to Liverpool, Glasgow, Havre, Suez, Brindisi, New York, and other ports, inspired by the proffered reward of two thousand pounds, and five per cent. on the sum that might be recovered. Detectives were also charged with narrowly watching those who arrived at or left London by rail, and a judicial examination was at once entered upon.

There were real grounds for supposing, as the *Daily Telegraph* said, that the thief did not belong to a professional band. On the day of the robbery a well-dressed gentleman of polished manners, and with a well-to-do air, had been observed going to and fro in the paying-room, where the crime was committed. A description of him was easily procured and sent to the detectives; and some hopeful spirits, of whom Ralph was one, did not despair of his apprehension. The papers and clubs were full of the affair, and everywhere people were discussing the probabilities of a successful pursuit; and the Reform Club was especially agitated, several of its members being Bank officials.

Ralph would not concede that the work of the detectives was likely to be in vain, for he thought that the prize offered would greatly stimulate their zeal and activity. But Stuart was far from sharing this confidence; and as they placed themselves at the whist-table, they continued to argue the matter. Stuart and Flanagan played together, while Phileas Fogg had Fallentin for his partner. As the game proceeded the conversation ceased, excepting between the rubbers, when it revived again.

'I maintain,' said Stuart, 'that the chances are in favour of the thief, who must be a shrewd fellow.'

'Well, but where can he fly to?' asked Ralph. 'No country is safe for him.'

'Pshaw!'

'Where could he go, then?'

'Oh, I don't know that. The world is big enough.'

'It was once,' said Phileas Fogg, in a low tone. 'Cut, sir,' he added, handing the cards to Thomas Flanagan.

The discussion fell during the rubber, after which Stuart took up its thread. 'What do you mean by "once"? Has the world grown smaller?'

'Certainly,' returned Ralph. 'I agree with Mr. Fogg. The world *has* grown smaller, since a man can now go round it ten times more quickly than a hundred years ago. And that is why the search for this thief will be more likely to succeed.'

'And also why the thief can get away more easily.'

'Be so good as to play, Mr. Stuart,' said Phileas Fogg.

But the incredulous Stuart was not convinced, and when the hand was finished, said eagerly: 'You have a strange way, Ralph, of proving that the world has grown smaller. So, because you can go round it in three months——'

'In eighty days,' interrupted Phileas Fogg.

'That is true, gentlemen,' added John Sullivan. 'Only eighty days, now that the section between Rothal and Allahabad, on the Great Indian Peninsula Railway, has been opened. Here is the estimate made by the *Daily Telegraph*:—

From London to Suez *viâ* Mont Cenis and Brindisi, by rail and steamboats..	7	days
From Suez to Bombay, by steamer......................................	13	,,
From Bombay to Calcutta, by rail	3	,,
From Calcutta to Hong Kong, by steamer	13	,,
From Hong Kong to Yokohama (Japan), by steamer	6	,,

From Yokohama to San Francisco, by steamer .... 22 ,,
From San Francisco to New York, by rail .... 7 ,,
From New York to London, by steamer and rail .... 9 ,,

Total... 80 days.

'Yes, in eighty days!' exclaimed Stuart, who in his excitement made a false deal. 'But that doesn't take into account bad weather, contrary winds, shipwrecks, railway accidents, and so on.'

'All included,' returned Phileas Fogg, continuing to play despite the discussion.

'But suppose the Hindoos or Indians pull up the rails,' replied Stuart; 'suppose they stop the trains, pillage the luggage-vans, and scalp the passengers!'

'All included,' calmly retorted Fogg; adding, as he threw down the cards, 'Two trumps.'

Stuart, whose turn it was to deal, gathered them up, and went on: 'You are right theoretically, Mr. Fogg, but practically——'

'Practically also, Mr. Stuart.'

'I'd like to see you do it in eighty days.'

'It depends on you. Shall we go?'

'Heaven preserve me! But I would wager four thousand pounds that such a journey, made under these conditions, is impossible.'

'Quite possible, on the contrary,' returned Mr. Fogg.

'Well, make it then!'

'The journey round the world in eighty days?'

'Yes.'

'I should like nothing better.'

'When?'

'At once. Only I warn you that I shall do it at your expense.'

'It's absurd!' cried Stuart, who was beginning to be annoyed at the persistency of his friend. 'Come, let's go on with the game.'

'Deal over again, then,' said Phileas Fogg. 'There's a false deal.'

Stuart took up the pack with a feverish hand; then suddenly put them down again.

'Well, Mr. Fogg,' said he, 'it shall be so; I will wager the four thousand on it.'

'Calm yourself, my dear Stuart,' said Fallentin. 'It's only a joke.'

'When I say I'll wager,' returned Stuart, 'I mean it.'

'All right,' said Mr. Fogg; and turning to the others continued: 'I have a deposit of twenty thousand at Baring's which I will willingly risk upon it.'

'Twenty thousand pounds!' cried Sullivan. 'Twenty thousand pounds, which you would lose by a single accidental delay!'

'The unforeseen does not exist,' quietly replied Phileas Fogg.

'But, Mr. Fogg, eighty days are only the estimate of the least possible time in which the journey can be made.'

'A well-used minimum suffices for everything.'

'But, in order not to exceed it, you must jump mathematically from the trains upon the steamers, and from the steamers upon the trains again.'

'I will jump – mathematically.'

'You are joking.'

'A true Englishman doesn't joke when he is talking about so serious a thing as a wager,' replied Phileas Fogg, solemnly. 'I will bet twenty thousand pounds against anyone who wishes, that I will make the tour of the world in eighty days or less; in nineteen hundred and twenty hours, or a hundred and fifteen thousand two hundred minutes. Do you accept?'

'We accept,' replied Messrs. Stuart, Fallentin, Sullivan, Flanagan, and Ralph, after consulting each other.

'Good,' said Mr. Fogg. 'The train leaves for Dover at a quarter before nine. I will take it.'

'This very evening?' asked Stuart.

'This very evening,' returned Phileas Fogg. He took out and consulted a pocket almanac, and added, 'As to-day is Wednesday, the second of October, I shall be due in London, in this very room of the Reform Club, on Saturday, the twenty-first of December, at a quarter before nine p.m.; or else the twenty thousand pounds, now deposited in my name at Baring's, will belong to you, in fact and in right, gentlemen. Here is a cheque for the amount.'

A memorandum of the wager was at once drawn up and signed by the six parties, during which Phileas Fogg preserved a stoical composure. He certainly did not bet to win, and had only staked the twenty thousand pounds, half of his fortune, because he foresaw that he might have to expend the other half to carry out this difficult, not to say unattainable, project. As for his antagonists, they seemed much agitated; not so much by the value of their stake, as because they had some scruples about betting under conditions so difficult to their friend.

The clocks struck seven, and the party offered to suspend the game so that Mr. Fogg might make his preparations for departure.

'I am quite ready now,' was his tranquil response. 'Diamonds are trumps: be so good as to play, gentlemen.'

Chapter Four

In which Phileas Fogg astounds Passepartout, his servant.

HAVING WON TWENTY GUINEAS at whist, and taken leave of his friends, Phileas Fogg, at twenty-five minutes past seven, left the Reform Club.

Passepartout, who had conscientiously studied the programme of his duties, was more than surprised to see his master guilty of the inexactness of appearing at this unaccustomed hour; for, according to rule, he was not due in Saville Row until precisely midnight.

Mr. Fogg repaired to his bedroom, and called out, 'Passepartout!'

Passepartout did not reply. It could not be he who was called; it was not the right hour.

'Passepartout!' repeated Mr. Fogg, without raising his voice.

Passepartout made his appearance.

'I've called you twice,' observed his master.

'But it is not midnight,' responded the other, showing his watch.

'I know it; I don't blame you. We start for Dover and Calais in ten minutes.'

A puzzled grin overspread Passepartout's round face; clearly he had not comprehended his master.

'Monsieur is going to leave home?'

'Yes,' returned Phileas Fogg. 'We are going round the world.'

Passepartout opened wide his eyes, raised his eyebrows, held up his hands, and seemed about to collapse, so overcome was he with stupefied astonishment.

'Round the world!' he murmured.

'In eighty days,' responded Mr. Fogg. 'So we haven't a moment to lose.'

'But the trunks?' gasped Passepartout, unconsciously swaying his head from right to left.

'We'll have no trunks; only a carpet-bag, with two shirts and three pairs of stockings for me, and the same for you. We'll buy our clothes on the way. Bring down my mackintosh and travelling-cloak, and some stout shoes, though we shall do little walking. Make haste!'

Passepartout tried to reply, but could not. He went out, mounted to his own room, fell into a chair, and muttered: 'That's good, that is! And I, who wanted to remain quiet!'

He mechanically set about making the preparations for departure. Around the world in eighty days! Was his master a fool! No. Was this a joke, then? They were going to Dover; good. To Calais; good again. After all, Passepartout, who had been away from France five years, would not be sorry to set foot on his native soil again. Perhaps they would go as far as Paris, and it would do his eyes good to see Paris once more. But surely a gentleman so chary of his steps would stop there; no doubt, – but, then, it was none the less true that he was going away, this so domestic person hitherto!

By eight o'clock Passepartout had packed the modest carpet-bag, containing the wardrobes of his master and himself; then, still troubled in mind, he carefully shut the door of his room, and descended to Mr. Fogg.

Mr. Fogg was quite ready. Under his arm might have been observed a red-bound copy of 'Bradshaw's Continental Railway Steam Transit and General Guide,' with its time-tables showing the arrival and departure of steamers and railways. He took the carpet-bag, opened it, and slipped into it a goodly roll of Bank of England notes, which would pass wherever he might go.

'You have forgotten nothing?' asked he.

'Nothing, monsieur.'

'My mackintosh and cloak?'

'Here they are.'

'Good. Take this carpet-bag,' handing it to Passepartout. 'Take good care of it, for there are twenty thousand pounds in it.'

Passepartout nearly dropped the bag, as if the twenty thousand pounds were in gold, and weighed him down.

Master and man then descended, the street-door was double-locked, and at the end of Saville Row they took a cab and drove rapidly to Charing Cross. The cab stopped before the railway station at twenty minutes past eight. Passepartout jumped off the box and followed his master, who, after paying the cabman, was about to enter the station, when a poor beggar-woman, with a child in her arms, her naked feet smeared with mud, her head covered with a wretched bonnet, from which hung a tattered feather, and her shoulders shrouded in a ragged shawl, approached, and mournfully asked for alms.

Mr. Fogg took out the twenty guineas he had just won at whist, and handed them to the beggar, saying, 'Here, my good woman. I'm glad that I met you'; and passed on.

Passepartout had a moist sensation about the eyes; his master's action touched his susceptible heart.

Two first-class tickets for Paris having been speedily purchased, Mr. Fogg was crossing the station to the train, when he perceived his five friends of the Reform.

'Well, gentlemen,' said he, 'I'm off, you see; and if you will examine my passport when I get back, you will be able to judge whether I have accomplished the journey agreed upon.'

'Oh, that would be quite unnecessary, Mr. Fogg,' said Ralph politely. 'We will trust your word, as a gentleman of honour.'

'You do not forget when you are due in London again?' asked Stuart.

'In eighty days; on Saturday, the twenty-first of December, 1872, at a quarter before nine p.m. Good-bye, gentlemen.'

Phileas Fogg and his servant seated themselves in a first-class carriage at twenty minutes before nine; five minutes later the whistle screamed, and the train slowly glided out of the station.

The night was dark, and a fine, steady rain was falling. Phileas Fogg, snugly ensconced in his corner, did not open his lips. Passepartout, not yet recovered from his stupefaction, clung mechanically to the carpet-bag, with its enormous treasure.

Just as the train was whirling through Sydenham, Passepartout suddenly uttered a cry of despair.

'What's the matter?' asked Mr. Fogg.

'Alas! In my hurry – I – I forgot——'

'What?'

'To turn off the gas in my room!'

'Very well, young man,' returned Mr. Fogg, coolly; 'it will burn – at your expense.'

Chapter Five

In which a new species of funds, unknown to the moneyed men, appears on 'Change.

PHILEAS FOGG RIGHTLY suspected that his departure from London would create a lively sensation at the West End. The news of the bet spread through the Reform Club, and afforded an exciting topic of conversation to its members. From the Club it soon got into the papers throughout England. The boasted 'tour of the world' was talked about, disputed, argued with as much warmth as if the subject were another Alabama claim. Some took sides with Phileas Fogg, but the large majority shook their heads and declared against him; it was absurd, impossible, they declared, that the tour of the world could be made, except theoretically and on paper, in this minimum of time, and with the existing means of travelling. *The Times, Standard, Morning Post,* and *Daily News,* and twenty other highly respectable newspapers scouted Mr. Fogg's project as madness; the *Daily Telegraph* alone hesitatingly supported him. People in general thought him a lunatic, and blamed his Reform Club friends for having accepted a wager which betrayed the mental aberration of its proposer.

Articles no less passionate than logical appeared on the question, for geography is one of the pet subjects of the English; and the columns devoted to Phileas Fogg's venture were eagerly devoured by all classes of readers. At first some rash individuals, principally of the gentler sex, espoused his cause, which became still more popular when the *Illustrated London News* came out with his portrait, copied from a photograph in the Reform Club. A few readers of the *Daily Telegraph* even dared to say, 'Why not, after all? Stranger things have come to pass.'

At last a long article appeared, on the 7th of October, in the bulletin of the Royal Geographical Society, which treated the question from every point of view, and demonstrated the utter folly of the enterprise.

Everything, it said, was against the travellers, every obstacle imposed alike by man and by nature. A miraculous agreement of the times of departure and arrival, which was impossible, was absolutely necessary to his success. He might, perhaps, reckon on the arrival of trains at the designated hours, in Europe, where the distances were relatively moderate; but when he calculated upon crossing India in three days, and the United States in seven, could he rely beyond misgiving upon accomplishing his task? There were accidents to machinery, the liability of trains to run off the line, collisions, bad weather, the blocking up by snow, – were not all these against Phileas Fogg? Would he not find himself, when travelling by steamer in winter, at the mercy of the winds and fogs? Is it uncommon for the best ocean steamers to be two or three days behind time? But a single delay would suffice to fatally break the chain of communication; should Phileas Fogg once miss, even by an hour, a steamer, he would have to wait for the next, and that would irrevocably render his attempt vain.

This article made a great deal of noise, and being copied into all of the papers, seriously depressed the advocates of the rash tourist.

Everybody knows that England is the world of betting men, who are of a higher class than mere gamblers; to bet is in the English temperament. Not only the members of the Reform, but the general public, made heavy wagers for or against Phileas Fogg, who was set down in the betting books as if he were a race-horse. Bonds were issued, and made their appearance on 'Change; 'Phileas Fogg bonds' were offered at par or at a premium, and a great business was done in them. But five days after the article in the bulletin of the Geographical Society appeared, the demand began to subside: 'Phileas Fogg' declined. They were offered by packages, at first of five, then of ten, until at last nobody would take less than twenty, fifty, a hundred!

Lord Albemarle, an elderly paralytic gentleman, was now the only advocate of Phileas Fogg left. This noble lord, who was fastened to his chair, would have given his fortune to be able to make the tour of the world, if it took ten years; and he bet five thousand pounds on Phileas Fogg. When the folly as well as the uselessness of the adventure was pointed out to him, he contented himself with replying, 'If the thing is feasible, the first to do it ought to be an Englishman.'

The Fogg party dwindled more and more, everybody was going against him, and the bets stood a hundred and fifty and two hundred to one; and a week after his departure an incident occurred which deprived him of backers at any price.

The commissioner of police was sitting in his office at nine o'clock one evening, when the following telegraphic despatch was put into his hands:—

Suez to London

ROWAN, COMMISSIONER OF POLICE, SCOTLAND YARD:
I've found the bank robber, Phileas Fogg. Send without delay warrant of arrest to Bombay.

FIX, Detective.

The effect of this despatch was instantaneous. The polished gentleman disappeared to give place to the bank robber. His photograph, which was hung with those of the rest of the members at the Reform Club, was minutely examined, and it betrayed, feature by feature, the description of the robber which had been provided to the police. The mysterious habits of Phileas Fogg were recalled; his solitary ways, his sudden departure; and it seemed clear that, in undertaking a tour round the world on the pretext of a wager, he had had no other end in view than to elude the detectives, and throw them off his track.

Chapter Six

In which Fix, the detective, betrays a very natural impatience.

THE CIRCUMSTANCES UNDER which this telegraphic despatch about Phileas Fogg was sent were as follows:—

The steamer Mongolia, belonging to the Peninsular and Oriental Company, built of iron, of two thousand eight hundred tons burden, and five hundred horse-power, was due at eleven o'clock a.m. on Wednesday, the 9th of October, at Suez. The Mongolia plied regularly between Brindisi and Bombay *via* the Suez Canal, and was one of the fastest steamers belonging to the company, always making more than ten knots an hour between Brindisi and Suez, and nine and a half between Suez and Bombay.

Two men were promenading up and down the wharves, among the crowd of natives and strangers who were sojourning at this once straggling village – now, thanks to the enterprise of M. Lesseps, a fast-growing town. One was the British consul at Suez, who, despite the prophecies of the English Government, and the unfavourable predictions of Stephenson, was in the habit of seeing from his office window, English ships daily passing to and fro on the great canal, by which the old roundabout route from England to India by the Cape of Good Hope was abridged by at least a half. The other was a small, slight-built personage, with a nervous, intelligent face, and bright eyes peering out from under eyebrows which he was incessantly twitching. He was just now manifesting unmistakable signs of impatience, nervously pacing up and down, and unable to stand still for a moment. This was Fix, one of the detectives who had been despatched from England in search of the bank robber; it was his task to narrowly watch every passenger who arrived at Suez, and to follow up all who seemed to be suspicious characters, or bore a resemblance to the description of the criminal, which he received two days before from the police headquarters at London. The detective was evidently inspired by the hope of obtaining the splendid reward which would be the prize of success, and awaited with a feverish impatience, easy to understand, the arrival of the steamer Mongolia.

'So you say, consul,' asked he for the twentieth time, 'that this steamer is never behind time?'

'No, Mr. Fix,' replied the consul. 'She was bespoken yesterday at Port Said, and the rest of the way is of no account to such a craft.' I repeat that the Mongolia has been in advance of the time required by the company's regulations, and gained the prize awarded for excess of speed.'

'Does she come directly from Brindisi?'

'Directly from Brindisi; she takes on the Indian mails there, and she left there Saturday at five p.m. Have patience, Mr. Fix; she will not be late. But really I don't see how, from the description you have, you will be able to recognize your man, even if he is on board the Mongolia.'

'A man rather feels the presence of these fellows, consul, than recognizes them. You must have a scent for them, and a scent is like a sixth sense which combines hearing, seeing, and smelling. I've arrested more than one of these gentlemen in my time, and if my thief is on board, I'll answer for it, he'll not slip through my fingers.'

'I hope so, Mr. Fix, for it was a heavy robbery.'

'A magnificent robbery, consul; fifty-five thousand pounds! We don't often have such windfalls. Burglars are getting to be so contemptible nowadays! A fellow gets hung for a handful of shillings!'

'Mr Fix,' said the consul, 'I like your way of talking, and hope you'll succeed; but I fear you will find it far from easy. Don't you see, the description which you have there has a singular resemblance to an honest man?'

'Consul,' remarked the detective, dogmatically, 'great robbers *always* resemble honest folks. Fellows who have rascally faces have only one course to take, and that is to remain honest; otherwise they would be arrested offhand. The artistic thing is, to unmask honest countenances; it's no light task, I admit, but a real art.'

Mr. Fix evidently was not wanting in a tinge of self-conceit.

Little by little the scene on the quay became more animated; sailors of various nations, merchants, shipbrokers, porters, fellahs, bustled to and fro as if the steamer were immediately expected. The weather was clear, and slightly chilly. The minarets of the town loomed above the houses in the pale rays of the sun. A jetty pier, some two thousand yards long, extended into the roadstead. A number of fishing-smacks and coasting boats, some retaining the fantastic fashion of ancient galleys, were discernible on the Red Sea.

As he passed among the busy crowd, Fix, according to habit, scrutinized the passers-by with a keen, rapid glance.

It was now half-past ten.

The steamer doesn't come!' he exclaimed, as the port clock struck.

'She can't be far off now,' returned his companion.

'How long will she stop at Suez?'

'Four hours; long enough to get in her coal. It is thirteen hundred and ten miles from Suez to Aden, at the other end of the Red Sea, and she has to take in a fresh coal supply.'

'And does she go from Suez directly to Bombay?'

'Without putting in anywhere.'

'Good,' said Fix. 'If the robber is on board he will no doubt get off at Suez, so as to reach the Dutch or French colonies in Asia by some other route. He ought to know that he would not be safe an hour in India, which is English soil.'

'Unless,' objected the consul, 'he is exceptionally shrewd. An English criminal, you know, is always better concealed in London than anywhere else.'

This observation furnished the detective food for thought, and meanwhile the consul went away to his office. Fix, left alone, was more impatient than ever, having a presentiment that the robber was on board the Mongolia. If he had indeed left London intending to reach the New World he would naturally take the route *viâ* India, which was less watched and more difficult to watch than that of the Atlantic. But Fix's reflections were soon interrupted by a succession of sharp whistles, which announced the arrival of the Mongolia. The porters and fellahs rushed down the quay, and a dozen boats pushed off from the shore to go and meet the steamer. Soon her gigantic hull appeared passing along between the banks, and eleven o'clock struck as she anchored in the road. She brought an unusual number of passengers, some of whom remained on deck to scan the picturesque panorama of the town, while the greater part disembarked in the boats, and landed on the quay.

Fix took up a position, and carefully examined each face and figure which made its appearance. Presently one of the passengers, after vigorously pushing his way through the importunate crowd of porters, came up to him and politely asked if he could point out the English consulate, at the same time showing a passport which he wished to have *visaed*. Fix instinctively took the passport, and with a rapid glance read the description of its bearer. An involuntary motion of surprise nearly escaped him, for the description in the passport was identical with that of the bank robber which he had received from Scotland Yard.

'Is this your passport?' asked he.

'No, it's my master's.'

'And your master is——'

'He stayed on board.'

'But he must go to the consul's in person, so as to establish his identity.'

'Oh, is that necessary?'

'Quite indispensable.'

'And where is the consulate?'

'There, on the corner of the square,' said Fix, pointing to a house two hundred steps off.

'I'll go and fetch my master, who won't be much pleased, however, to be disturbed.'

The passenger bowed to Fix, and returned to the steamer.

Chapter Seven

Which once more demonstrates the uselessness of passports as aids to detectives

THE DETECTIVE PASSED down the quay, and rapidly made his way to the consul's office, where he was at once admitted to the presence of that official.

'Consul,' said he, without preamble, 'I have strong sense for believing that my man is a passenger on the Mongolia.' And he narrated what had just passed concerning the passport.

'Well, Mr. Fix,' replied the consul; 'I shall not be sorry to see the rascal's face; but perhaps he won't come here, – that is, if he is the person you suppose him to be. A robber doesn't quite like to leave traces of his flight behind him; and, besides, he is not obliged to have his passport countersigned.'

'If he is as shrewd as I think he is, consul, he will come.'

'To have his passport *visaed*?'

'Yes. Passports are only good for annoying honest folks, and aiding in the flight of rogues. I assure you it will be quite the thing for him to do; but I hope you will not *visa* the passport.'

'Why not? If the passport is genuine I have no right to refuse.'

'Still, I must keep this man here until I can get a warrant to arrest him from London.'

'Ah, that's your look-out. But I cannot——'

The consul did not finish his sentence, for as he spoke a knock was heard at the door, and two strangers entered, one of whom was the servant whom Fix had met on the quay. The other, who was his master, held out his passport with the request that the consul would do him the favour to *visa* it. The consul took the document and carefully read it, whilst Fix observed, or rather devoured, the stranger with his eyes from a corner of the room.

'You are Mr. Phileas Fogg?' said the consul, after reading the passport.

'I am.'

'And this man is your servant?'

'He is; a Frenchman, named Passepartout.'

'You are from London?'

'Yes.'

'And you are going——'

'To Bombay.'

'Very good, sir. You know that a *visa* is useless, and that no passport is required?'

'I know it, sir,' replied Phileas Fogg; 'but I wish to prove, by your *visa*, that I came by Suez.'

'Very well, sir.'

The consul proceeded to sign and date the passport, after which he added his official seal. Mr. Fogg paid the customary fee, coldly bowed, and went out, followed by his servant.

'Well?' queried the detective.

'Well, he looks and acts like a perfectly honest man,' replied the consul.

'Possibly; but that is not the question. Do you think, consul, that this phlegmatic gentleman resembles, feature by feature, the robber whose description I have received?'

'I concede that; but then, you know, all descriptions——'

'I'll make certain of it,' interrupted Fix. 'The servant seems to me less mysterious than the master; besides, he's a Frenchman, and can't help talking. Excuse me for a little while consul.'

Fix started off in search of Passepartout.

Meanwhile Mr. Fogg, after leaving the consulate, repaired to the quay, gave some orders to Passepartout, went off to the Mongolia in a boat, and descended to his cabin. He took up his note-book, which contained the following memoranda:-

Left London, Wednesday, October 2nd, at 8.45 p.m.

Reached Paris, Thursday, October 3rd, at 7.20 a.m.

Left Paris, Thursday, at 8.40 a.m.

Reached Turin by Mont Cenis, Friday, October 4th, at 6.35 a.m.

Left Turin, Friday, at 7.20 a.m.

Arrived at Brindisi, Saturday, October 5th, at 4 p.m.

Sailed on the Mongolia, Saturday, at 5 p.m.

Reached Suez, Wednesday, October 9th, at 11 a.m.

Total of hours spent, 158½; or, in days, six days and a half.

These dates were inscribed in an itinerary divided into columns, indicating the month, the day of the month, and the day for the stipulated and actual arrivals at each principal point, – Paris, Brindisi, Suez, Bombay, Calcutta, Singapore, Hong Kong, Yokohama, San Francisco, New York, and London, – from the 2nd of October to the 21st of December; and giving a space for setting down the gain made or the loss suffered on arrival at each locality. This methodical record thus contained an account of everything needed, and Mr. Fogg always knew whether he was behindhand or in advance of his time. On this Friday, October 9th, he noted his arrival at Suez, and observed that he had as yet neither gained nor lost. He sat down quietly to breakfast in his cabin, never once thinking of inspecting the town, being one of those Englishmen who are wont to see foreign countries through the eyes of their domestics.

Chapter Eight

In which Passepartout talks rather more, perhaps, than is prudent.

FIX SOON REJOINED PASSEPARTOUT, who was lounging and looking about on the quay, as if he did not feel that he, at least, was obliged not to see anything.

'Well, my friend,' said the detective, coming up with him, 'is your passport *visaed?*'

'Ah, it's you, is it, monsieur?' responded Passepartout. 'Thanks, yes, the passport is all right.'

'And you are looking about you?'

'Yes; but we travel so fast that I seem to be journeying in a dream. So this is Suez?'

'Yes.'

'In Egypt?'

'Certainly, in Egypt.'

'And in Africa?'

'In Africa?'

'In Africa!' repeated Passepartout. 'Just think, monsieur, I had no idea that we should go farther than Paris; and all that I saw of Paris was between twenty minutes past seven and twenty minutes before nine in the morning, between the Northern and the Lyons stations, through the windows of a car, and in a driving rain! How I regret not having seen once more Père la Chaise and the circus in the Champs Elysées!'

'You are in a great hurry, then?'

'I am not, but my master is. By the way, I must buy some shoes and shirts. We came away without trunks, only with a carpet-bag.'

'I will show you an excellent shop for getting what you want.'

'Really, monsieur, you are very kind.'

And they walked off together, Passepartout chatting volubly as they went along.

'Above all,' said he; 'don't let me lose the steamer.'

'You have plenty of time; it's only twelve o'clock.'

Passepartout pulled out his big watch. 'Twelve!' he exclaimed; 'why it's only eight minutes before ten.'

'Your watch is slow.'

'My watch? A family watch, monsieur, which has come down from my great-grandfather! It doesn't vary five minutes in the year, it's a perfect chronometer, look you.'

'I see how it is,' said Fix. 'You have kept London time, which is two hours behind that of Suez. You ought to regulate your watch at noon in each country.'

'I regulate my watch? Never!'

'Well, then, it will not agree with the sun.'

'So much the worse for the sun, monsieur. The sun will be wrong, then!'

And the worthy fellow returned the watch to its fob with a defiant gesture. After a few minutes' silence, Fix resumed: 'You left London hastily, then?'

'I rather think so! Last Friday at eight o'clock in the evening, Monsieur Fogg came home from his club, and three-quarters of an hour afterwards we were off.'

'But where is your master going?'

'Always straight ahead. He is going round the world.'

'Round the world?' cried Fix.

'Yes, and in eighty days! He says it is on a wager; but, between us, I don't believe a word of it. That wouldn't be common sense. There's something else in the wind.'

'Ah! Mr. Fogg is a character, is he?'

'I should say he was.'

'Is he rich?'

'No doubt, for he is carrying an enormous sum in brand-new bank-notes with him. And he doesn't spare the money on the way, either: he has offered a large reward to the engineer of the Mongolia if he gets us to Bombay well in advance of time.'

'And you have known your master a long time?'

'Why no; I entered his service the very day we left London.'

The effect of these replies upon the already suspicious and excited detective may be imagined. The hasty departure from London soon after the robbery; the large sum carried by Mr. Fogg; his eagerness to reach distant countries; the pretext of an eccentric and foolhardy bet, – all confirmed Fix in his theory. He continued to pump poor Passepartout, and learned that he really knew little or nothing of his master, who lived a solitary existence in London, was said to be rich, though no one knew whence came his riches, and was mysterious and impenetrable in his affairs and habits. Fix felt sure that Phileas Fogg would not land at Suez, but was really going on to Bombay.

'Is Bombay far from here?' asked Passepartout.

'Pretty far. It is a ten days' voyage by sea.'

'And in what country is Bombay?'

'India.'

'In Asia.'

'Certainly.'

'The deuce! I was going to tell you – there's one thing that worries me – my burner!'

'What burner?'

'My gas-burner, which I forgot to turn off, and which is at this moment burning – at my expense. I have calculated, monsieur, that I lose two shillings every four and twenty hours, exactly sixpence more than I earn; and you will understand that the longer our journey——'

Did Fix pay any attention to Passepartout's trouble about the gas? It is not probable. He was not listening, but was cogitating a project. Passepartout and he had now reached the shop, where Fix left his companion to make his purchases, after recommending him not to miss the steamer, and hurried back to the consulate. Now that he was fully convinced Fix had quite recovered his equanimity.

'Consul,' said he, 'I have no longer any doubt. I have spotted my man. He passes himself off as an odd stick, who is going round the world in eighty days.'

'Then he's a sharp fellow,' returned the consul, 'and counts on returning to London after putting the police of the two continents off his track.'

'We'll see about that,' replied Fix.

'But are you not mistaken?'

'I am not mistaken.'

'Why was this robber so anxious to prove, by the visa, that he had passed through Suez?'

'Why? I have no idea; but listen to me.'

He reported in a few words the most important parts of his conversation with Passepartout.

'In short,' said the consul, 'appearances are wholly against this man. And what are you going to do?'

'Send a despatch to London for a warrant of arrest to be despatched instantly to Bombay, take passage on board the Mongolia, follow my rogue to India, and there, on English ground, arrest him politely, with my warrant in my hand, and my hand on his shoulder.'

Having uttered these words with a cool, careless air, the detective took leave of the consul, and repaired to the telegraph office, whence he sent the despatch which we have seen to the London police office. A quarter of an hour later found Fix, with a small bag in his hand, proceeding on board the Mongolia; and ere many moments longer, the noble steamer rode out at full steam upon the waters of the Red Sea.

Chapter Nine

In which the Red Sea and the Indian Ocean prove propitious to the designs of Phileas Fogg.

THE DISTANCE BETWEEN Suez and Aden is precisely thirteen hundred and ten miles, and the regulations of the company allow the steamers one hundred and thirty-eight hours in which to traverse it. The Mongolia, thanks to the vigorous exertions of the engineer, seemed likely, so rapid was her speed, to reach her destination considerably within that time. The greater part of the passengers from Brindisi were bound for India – some for Bombay, others for Calcutta by way of Bombay, the nearest route thither, now that a railway crosses the Indian peninsula. Among the passengers was a number of officials and military officers of various grades, the latter being either attached to the regular British forces, or commanding the Sepoy troops and receiving high salaries ever since the central government has assumed the powers of the East India Company: for the sub-lieutenants get 280*l.*, brigadiers, 2400*l.*, and generals of division, 4,000*l.* What with the military men, a number of rich young Englishmen on their travels, and the hospitable efforts of the purser, the time passed quickly on the Mongolia. The best of fare was spread upon the cabin tables at breakfast, lunch, dinner, and the eight o'clock supper, and the ladies scrupulously changed their toilets twice a day; and the hours were whiled away, when the sea was tranquil, with music, dancing, and games.

But the Red Sea is full of caprice, and often boisterous, like most long and narrow gulfs. When the wind came from the African or Asian coast the Mongolia, with her long hull, rolled fearfully. Then the ladies speedily disappeared below; the pianos were silent; singing and dancing suddenly ceased. Yet the good ship ploughed straight on, unretarded by wind or wave, towards the straits of Bab-el-Mandeb. What was Phileas Fogg doing all this time? It might be thought that, in his anxiety, he would be constantly watching the changes of the wind, the disorderly raging of the billows – every chance, in short, which might force the Mongolia to slacken her speed, and thus interrupt his journey. But if he thought of these possibilities, he did not betray the fact by any outward sign.

Always the same impassible member of the Reform Club, whom no incident could surprise, as unvarying as the ship's chronometers, and seldom having the curiosity even to go upon the deck, he passed through the memorable scenes of the Red Sea with cold indifference; did not care to recognize the historic towns and villages which, along its borders, raised their picturesque outlines against the sky; and betrayed no fear of the dangers of the Arabic Gulf, which the old historians always spoke of with horror, and upon which the ancient navigators never ventured without propitiating the gods by ample sacrifices. How did this eccentric personage pass his time on the Mongolia? He made his four hearty meals every day, regardless of the most persistent rolling and pitching on the part of the steamer; and he played whist indefatigably, for he had found partners as enthusiastic in the game as himself. A tax-collector, on the way to his post at Goa; the Rev. Decimus Smith, returning to his parish at Bombay; and a brigadier-general of the English army, who was about to rejoin his brigade at Benares, made up the party, and, with Mr. Fogg, played whist by the hour together in absorbing silence.

As for Passepartout, he, too, had escaped seasickness, and took his meals conscientiously in the forward cabin. He rather enjoyed the voyage, for he was well fed and well lodged, took a great interest in the scenes through which they were passing, and consoled himself with the delusion that his master's whim would end at Bombay. He was pleased, on the day after leaving Suez, to find on deck the obliging person with whom he had walked and chatted on the quays.

'If I am not mistaken,' said he, approaching this person with his most amiable smile, 'you are the gentleman who so kindly volunteered to guide me at Suez?'

'Ah! I quite recognize you. You are the servant of the strange Englishman——'

'Just so, Monsieur——'

'Fix.'

'Monsieur Fix,' resumed Passepartout, 'I'm charmed to find you on board. Where are you bound?'

'Like you, to Bombay.'

'That's capital! Have you made this trip before?'

'Several times. I am one of the agents of the Peninsula Company.'

'Then you know India?'

'Why – yes,' replied Fix, who spoke cautiously.

'A curious place, this India?'

'Oh, very curious. Mosques, minarets, temples, fakirs, pagodas, tigers, snakes, elephants! I hope you will have ample time to see the sights.'

'I hope so, Monsieur Fix. You see, a man of sound sense ought not to spend his life jumping from a steamer upon a railway train, and from a railway train upon a steamer again, pretending to make the tour of the world in eighty days! No; all these gymnastics, you may be sure, will cease at Bombay.'

'And Mr. Fogg is getting on well?' asked Fix, in the most natural tone in the world.

'Quite well, and I too. I eat like a famished ogre; it's the sea air.'

'But I never see your master on deck.'

'Never; he hasn't the least curiosity.'

'Do you know, Mr. Passepartout, that this pretended tour in eighty days may conceal some secret errand – perhaps a diplomatic mission?'

'Faith, Monsieur Fix, I assure you I know nothing about it, nor would I give half-a-crown to find out.'

After this meeting, Passepartout and Fix got into the habit of chatting together, the latter making it a point to gain the worthy man's confidence. He frequently offered him a glass of whisky or pale ale in the steamer bar-room, which Passepartout never failed to accept with graceful alacrity, mentally pronouncing Fix the best of good fellows.

Meanwhile the Mongolia was pushing forward rapidly; on the 13th, Mocha, surrounded by its ruined walls whereon date-trees were growing, was sighted, and on the mountains beyond were espied vast coffee-fields. Passepartout was ravished to behold this celebrated place, and thought that, with its circular walls and dismantled fort, it looked like an immense coffee cup and saucer. The following night they passed through the Strait of Bab-el-Mandeb, which means in Arabic 'The Bridge of Tears,' and the next day they put in at Steamer Point, north-west of Aden harbour, to take in coal. This matter of fuelling steamers is a serious one at such distances from the coal mines; it costs the Peninsular Company some eight hundred thousand pounds a year. In these distant seas, coal is worth three or four pounds sterling a ton.

The Mongolia had still sixteen hundred and fifty miles to traverse before reaching Bombay, and was obliged to remain four hours at Steamer Point to coal up. But this delay, as it was foreseen, did not affect Phileas Fogg's programme; besides, the Mongolia, instead of reaching Aden on the morning of the 15th, when she was due, arrived there on the evening of the 14th, a gain of fifteen hours.

Mr. Fogg and his servant went ashore at Aden to have the passport again *visaed*; Fix, unobserved, followed them. The *visa* procured, Mr. Fogg returned on board to resume his former habits; while Passepartout, according to custom, sauntered about among the mixed population of Somanlis, Banyans, Parsees, Jews, Arabs, and Europeans who comprise the twenty-five thousand inhabitants of Aden. He gazed with wonder upon the fortifications which make this place the Gibraltar of the Indian Ocean, and the vast cisterns where the English engineers were still at work, two thousand years after the engineers of Solomon.

'Very curious, *very* curious,' said Passepartout to himself, on returning to the steamer. 'I see that it is by no means useless to travel, if a man wants to see something new.' At six p.m. the Mongolia slowly moved out of the roadstead, and was soon once more on the Indian Ocean. She had a hundred and sixty-eight hours in which to reach Bombay, and the sea was favourable, the wind being in the north-west, and all sails aiding the engine. The steamer rolled but little, the ladies, in fresh toilets, reappeared on deck, and the singing and dancing were resumed. The trip was being accomplished most successfully, and Passepartout was enchanted with the congenial companion which chance had secured him in the person of the delightful Fix. On Sunday, October 20th, towards noon, they came in sight of the Indian coast: two hours later the pilot came on board. A range of hills lay against the sky in the horizon, and soon the rows of palms which adorn Bombay came distinctly into view. The steamer entered the road formed by the islands in the bay, and at half-past four she hauled up at the quays of Bombay.

Phileas Fogg was in the act of finishing the thirty-third rubber of the voyage, and his partner and himself having, by a bold stroke, captured all thirteen of the tricks, concluded this fine campaign with a brilliant victory.

The Mongolia was due at Bombay on the 22nd; she arrived on the 20th. This was a gain to Phileas Fogg of two days since his departure from London, and he calmly entered the fact in the itinerary, in the column of gains.

Chapter Ten

In which Passepartout is only too glad to get off with the loss of his shoes

EVERYBODY KNOWS THAT the great reversed triangle of land, with its base in the north and its apex in the south, which is called India, embraces fourteen hundred thousand square miles, upon which is spread unequally a population of one hundred and eighty millions of souls. The British Crown exercises a real and despotic dominion over the larger portion of this vast country, and has a governor-general stationed at Calcutta, governors at Madras, Bombay, and in Bengal, and a lieutenant-governor at Agra.

But British India, properly so called, only embraces seven hundred thousand square miles, and a population of from one hundred to one hundred and ten millions of inhabitants. A considerable portion of India is still free from British authority; and there are certain ferocious rajahs in the interior who are absolutely independent. The celebrated East India Company was all-powerful from 1756, when the English first gained a foothold on the spot where now stands the city of Madras, down to the time of the great Sepoy insurrection. It gradually annexed province after province, purchasing them of the native chiefs, whom it seldom paid, and appointed the governor-general and his subordinates, civil and military. But the East India Company has now passed away, leaving the British possessions in India directly under the control of the Crown. The aspect of the country, as well as the manners and distinctions of race, is daily changing.

Formerly one was obliged to travel in India by the old cumbrous methods of going on foot or on horseback, in palanquins or unwieldy coaches; now, fast steamboats ply on the Indus and the Ganges, and a great railway, with branch lines joining the main line at many points on its route, traverses the peninsula from Bombay to Calcutta in three days. This railway does not run in a direct line across India. The distance between Bombay and Calcutta, as the bird flies, is only from one thousand to eleven hundred miles; but the deflections of the road increase this distance by more than a third.

The general route of the Great Indian Peninsula Railway is as follows:– Leaving Bombay, it passes through Salcette, crossing to the continent opposite Tannah, goes over the chain of the Western Ghauts, runs thence north-east as far as Burhampoor, skirts the nearly independent territory of Bundelcund, ascends to Allahabad, turns thence eastwardly, meeting the Ganges at Benares, then departs from the river a little, and, descending south-eastward by Burdivan and the French town of Chandernagor, has its terminus at Calcutta.

The passengers of the Mongolia went ashore at half-past four p.m.; at exactly eight the train would start for Calcutta.

Mr. Fogg, after bidding good-bye to his whist partners, left the steamer, gave his servant several errands to do, urged it upon him to be at the station prompt at eight, and, with his regular step, which beat to the second, like an astronomical clock, directed his steps to the passport office. As for the wonders of Bombay – its famous city hall, its splendid library, its forts and docks, its bazaars, mosques, synagogues, its Armenian churches, and the noble pagoda on Malebar Hill with its two polygonal towers – he cared not a straw to see them. He would not deign to examine even the masterpieces of Elephanta, or the mysterious hypogea, concealed south-east from the docks, or those fine remains of Buddhist architecture, the Kanherian grottoes of the island of Salcette.

Having transacted his business at the passport office, Phileas Fogg repaired quietly to the railway station, where he ordered dinner. Among the dishes served up to him, the landlord especially recommended a certain giblet of 'native rabbit,' on which he prided himself.

Mr. Fogg accordingly tasted the dish, but, despite its spiced sauce, found it far from palatable. He rang for the landlord, and on his appearance, said, fixing his clear eyes upon him, 'Is this rabbit, sir?'

'Yes, my lord,' the rogue boldly replied, 'rabbit from the jungles.'

'And this rabbit did not mew when he was killed?'

'Mew, my lord! What, a rabbit mew! I swear to you——'

'Be so good, landlord, as not to swear, but remember this: cats were formerly considered, in India, as sacred animals. That was a good time.'

'For the cats, my lord?'

'Perhaps for the travellers as well!'

After which Mr. Fogg quietly continued his dinner. Fix had gone on shore shortly after Mr. Fogg, and his first destination was the head quarters of the Bombay police. He made himself known as a London detective, told his business at Bombay, and the position of affairs relative to the supposed robber, and nervously asked if a warrant had arrived from London. It had not reached the office; indeed, there had not yet been time for it to arrive. Fix was sorely disappointed, and tried to obtain an order of arrest from the director of the Bombay police. This the director refused, as the matter concerned the London office, which alone could legally deliver the warrant. Fix did not insist, and was fain to resign himself to await the arrival of the important document; but he was determined not to lose sight of the mysterious rogue as long as he stayed in Bombay. He did not doubt for a moment, any more than Passepartout, that Phileas Fogg would remain there, at least until it was time for the warrant to arrive.

Passepartout, however, had no sooner heard his master's orders on leaving the Mongolia, than he saw at once that they were to leave Bombay as they had done Suez and Paris, and that the journey would be extended at least as far as Calcutta, and perhaps beyond that place. He began to ask himself if this bet that Mr. Fogg talked about was not really in good earnest, and whether his fate was not in truth forcing him, despite his love of repose, around the world in eighty days!

Having purchased the usual quota of shirts and shoes, he took a leisurely promenade about the streets, where crowds of people of many nationalities – Europeans, Persians with pointed caps, Banyas with round turbans. Sindes with square bonnets, Parsees with black mitres, and long-robed Armenians – were collected. It happened to be the day of a Parsee festival. These descendants of the sect of Zoroaster – the most thrifty, civilized, intelligent, and austere of the East Indians, among whom are counted the richest native merchants of Bombay – were celebrating a sort of religious carnival, with processions and shows, in the midst of which Indian dancing-girls, clothed in rose-coloured gauze, looped up with gold and silver, danced airily, but with perfect modesty, to the sound of viols and the clanging of tambourines. It is needless to say that Passepartout watched these curious ceremonies with staring eyes and gaping mouth, and that his countenance was that of the greenest booby imaginable.

Unhappily for his master, as well as himself, his curiosity drew him unconsciously farther off than he intended to go. At last, having seen the Parsee carnival wind away in the distance, he was turning his steps towards the station, when he happened to espy the splendid pagoda on Malebar Hill, and was seized with an irresistible desire to see its interior. He was quite ignorant that it is forbidden to Christians to enter certain Indian temples, and that even the faithful must not go in without first leaving their shoes outside the door. It may be said here that the wise policy of the British Government severely punishes a disregard of the practices of the native religions.

Passepartout, however, thinking no harm, went in like a simple tourist, and was soon lost in admiration of the splendid Brahmin ornamentation which everywhere met his eyes, when of a sudden he found himself sprawling on the sacred flagging. He looked up to behold three enraged priests, who forthwith fell upon him, tore off his shoes, and began to beat him with loud, savage exclamations. The agile Frenchman was soon upon his feet again, and lost no time in knocking down two of his long-gowned adversaries with his fists and a vigorous application of his toes; then, rushing out of the pagoda as fast as his legs could carry him, he soon escaped the third priest by mingling with the crowd in the streets.

At five minutes before eight, Passepartout, hatless, shoeless, and having in the squabble lost his package of shirts and shoes, rushed breathlessly into the station.

Fix, who had followed Mr. Fogg to the station, and saw that he was really going to leave Bombay, was there, upon the platform. He had resolved to follow the supposed robber to Calcutta, and farther, if necessary. Passepartout did not

observe the detective, who stood in an obscure corner; but Fix heard him relate
his adventures in a few words to Mr. Fogg.

'I hope that this will not happen again,' said Phileas Fogg, coldly, as he got
into the train. Poor Passepartout, quite crestfallen, followed his master without
a word. Fix was on the point of entering another carriage, when an idea struck
him which induced him to alter his plan.

'No, I'll stay,' muttered he. 'An offence has been committed on Indian soil.
I've got my man.'

Just then the locomotive gave a sharp screech, and the train passed out into
the darkness of the night.

Chapter Eleven

*In which Phileas Fogg secures a curious means of conveyance at a fabulous
price.*

THE TRAIN HAD STARTED punctually. Among the passengers were a number of
officers, Government officials, and opium and indigo merchants, whose business
called them to the eastern coast. Passepartout rode in the same carriage with his
master, and a third passenger occupied a seat opposite to them. This was Sir
Francis Cromarty, one of Mr. Fogg's whist partners on the Mongolia, now on his
way to join his corps at Benares. Sir Francis was a tall, fair man of fifty, who had
greatly distinguished himself in the last Sepoy revolt. He made India his home,
only paying brief visits to England at rare intervals; and was almost as familiar as
a native with the customs, history and character of India and its people. But
Phileas Fogg, who was not travelling, but only describing a circumference, took
no pains to inquire into these subjects; he was a solid body, traversing an orbit
around the terrestrial globe, according to the laws of rational mechanics. He was
at this moment calculating in his mind the number of hours spent since his
departure from London, and, had it been in his nature to make a useless
demonstration, would have rubbed his hands for satisfaction. Sir Francis
Cromarty had observed the oddity of his travelling companion – although the
only opportunity he had for studying him had been while he was dealing the
cards, and between two rubbers – and questioned himself whether a human
heart really beat beneath this cold exterior, and whether Phileas Fogg had any
sense of the beauties of nature. The brigadier-general was free to mentally
confess, that, of all the eccentric persons he had ever met, none was comparable
to this product of the exact sciences.

Phileas Fogg had not concealed from Sir Francis his design of going round the
world, nor the circumstances under which he set out; and the general only saw
in the wager a useless eccentricity and a lack of sound commonsense. In the way
this strange gentleman was going on, he would leave the world without having
done any good to himself or anybody else.

An hour after leaving Bombay the train had passed the viaducts and the island
of Salcette, and had got into the open country. At Callyan they reached the

junction of the branch line which descends towards south-eastern India by
Kandallah and Pounah; and, passing Pauwell, they entered the defiles of the
mountains, with their basalt bases, and their summits crowned with thick and
verdant forests. Phileas Fogg and Sir Francis Cromarty exchanged a few words
from time to time, and now Sir Francis, reviving the conversation, observed,
'Some years ago, Mr. Fogg, you would have met with a delay at this point which
would probably have lost you your wager.'

'How so, Sir Francis?'

'Because the railway stopped at the base of these mountains, which the
passengers were obliged to cross in palanquins or on ponies to Kandallah, on the
other side.'

'Such a delay would not have deranged my plans in the least,' said Mr. Fogg. 'I
have constantly foreseen the likelihood of certain obstacles.'

'But, Mr. Fogg,' pursued Sir Francis, 'you run the risk of having some difficulty
about this worthy fellow's adventure at the pagoda.' Passepartout, his feet
comfortably wrapped in his travelling-blanket, was sound asleep, and did not
dream that anybody was talking about him. 'The Government is very severe
upon that kind of offence. It takes particular care that the religious customs of
the Indians should be respected, and if your servant were caught——'

'Very well, Sir Francis,' replied Mr. Fogg; 'if he had been caught he would
have been condemned and punished, and then would have quietly returned to
Europe. I don't see how this affair could have delayed his master.'

The conversation fell again. During the night the train left the mountains
behind, and passed Nassik, and the next day proceeded over the flat, well-
cultivated country of the Khandeish, with its straggling villages, above which
rose the minarets of the pagodas. This fertile territory is watered by numerous
small rivers and limpid streams, mostly tributaries of the Godavery.

Passepartout, on waking and looking out, could not realize that he was
actually crossing India in a railway train. The locomotive, guided by an English
engineer and fed with English coal, threw out its smoke upon cotton, coffee,
nutmeg, clove, and pepper plantations, while the steam curled in spirals around
groups of palm-trees, in the midst of which were seen picturesque bungalows,
viharis (a sort of abandoned monasteries), and marvellous temples enriched by
the exhaustless ornamentation of Indian architecture. Then they came upon
vast tracts extending to the horizon, with jungles inhabited by snakes and tigers,
which fled at the noise of the train; succeeded by forests penetrated by the
railway, and still haunted by elephants which, with pensive eyes, gazed at the
train as it passed. The travellers crossed, beyond Malligaum, the fatal country so
often stained with blood by the sectaries of the goddess Kali. Not far off rose
Ellora, with its graceful pagodas, and the famous Aurungabad, capital of the
ferocious Aureng-Zeb, now the chief town of one of the detached provinces of
the kingdom of the Nizam. It was thereabouts that Feringhea, the Thuggee
chief, king of the stranglers, held his sway. These ruffians, united by a secret
bond, strangled victims of every age in honour of the goddess Death, without
ever shedding blood; there was a period when this part of the country could
scarcely be travelled over without corpses being found in every direction. The
English Government has succeeded in greatly diminishing these murders,
though the Thuggees still exist, and pursue the exercise of their horrible rites.

At half-past twelve the train stopped at Burhampoor, where Passepartout was able to purchase some Indian slippers, ornamented with false pearls, in which, with evident vanity, he proceeded to incase his feet. The travellers made a hasty breakfast and started off for Assurghur, after skirting for a little the banks of the small river Tapty, which empties into the Gulf of Cambray, near Surat.

Passepartout was now plunged into absorbing reverie. Up to his arrival at Bombay, he had entertained hopes that their journey would end there; but now that they were plainly whirling across India at full speed, a sudden change had come over the spirit of his dreams. His old vagabond nature returned to him; the fantastic ideas of his youth once more took possession of him. He came to regard his master's project as intended in good earnest, believed in the reality of the bet, and therefore in the tour of the world, and the necessity of making it without fail within the designated period. Already he began to worry about possible delays, and accidents which might happen on the way. He recognized himself as being personally interested in the wager, and trembled at the thought that he might have been the means of losing it by his unpardonable folly of the night before. Being much less cool-headed than Mr. Fogg, he was much more restless, counting and recounting the days passed over, uttering maledictions when the train stopped, and accusing it of sluggishness, and mentally blaming Mr. Fogg for not having bribed the engineer. The worthy fellow was ignorant that, while it was possible by such means to hasten the rate of a steamer, it could not be done on the railway.

The train entered the defiles of the Sutpour Mountains, which separate the Khandeish from Bundelcund, towards evening. The next day Sir Francis Cromarty asked Passepartout what time it was; to which, on consulting his watch, he replied that it was three in the morning. This famous timepiece, always regulated on the Greenwich meridian, which was now some seventy-seven degrees westward, was at least four hours slow. Sir Francis corrected Passepartout's time, whereupon the latter made the same remark that he had done to Fix; and upon the general insisting that the watch should be regulated in each new meridian, since he was constantly going eastward, that is in the face of the sun, and therefore the days were shorter by four minutes for each degree gone over, Passepartout obstinately refused to alter his watch, which he kept at London time. It was an innocent delusion which could harm no one.

The train stopped, at eight o'clock, in the midst of a glade some fifteen miles beyond Rothal, where there were several bungalows, and workmen's cabins. The conductor, passing along the carriages, shouted, 'Passengers will get out here!'

Phileas Fogg looked at Sir Francis Cromarty for an explanation; but the general could not tell what meant a halt in the midst of this forest of dates and acacias.

Passepartout, not less surprised, rushed out and speedily returned, crying: 'Monsieur, no more railway!'

'What do you mean?' asked Sir Francis.

'I mean to say that the train isn't going on.'

The general at once stepped out, while Phileas Fogg calmly followed him, and they proceeded together to the conductor.

'Where are we?' asked Sir Francis.

'At the hamlet of Kholby.'

'Do we stop here?'

'Certainly. The railway isn't finished.'

'What! not finished?'

'No. There's still a matter of fifty miles to be laid from here to Allahabad, where the line begins again.'

'But the papers announced the opening of the railway throughout.'

'What would you have, officer? The papers were mistaken.'

'Yet you sell tickets from Bombay to Calcutta,' retorted Sir Francis, who was growing warm.

'No doubt,' replied the conductor; 'but the passengers know that they must provide means of transportation for themselves from Kholby to Allahabad.'

Sir Francis was furious. Passepartout would willingly have knocked the conductor down, and did not dare to look at his master.

'Sir Francis,' said Mr. Fogg, quietly, 'we will, if you please, look about for some means of conveyance to Allahabad.'

'Mr. Fogg, this is a delay greatly to your disadvantage.'

'No, Sir Francis; it was foreseen.'

'What! You knew that the way——'

'Not at all; but I knew that some obstacle or other would sooner or later arise on my route. Nothing, therefore, is lost. I have two days, which I have already gained, to sacrifice. A steamer leaves Calcutta for Hong Kong at noon, on the 25th. This is the 22nd, and we shall reach Calcutta in time.'

There was nothing to say to so confident a response.

It was but true that the railway came to a termination at this point. The papers were like some watches, which have a way of getting too fast, and had been premature in their announcement of the completion of the line. The greater part of the travellers were aware of this interruption, and leaving the train, they began to engage such vehicles as the village could provide – four-wheeled palkigharis, waggons drawn by zebus, carriages that looked like perambulating pagodas, palanquins, ponies, and what not.

Mr. Fogg and Sir Francis Cromarty, after searching the village from end to end, came back without having found anything.

'I shall go afoot,' said Phileas Fogg.

Passepartout, who had now rejoined his master, made a wry grimace, as he thought of his magnificent, but too frail Indian shoes. Happily he too had been looking about him, and, after a moment's hesitation, said, 'Monsieur, I think I have found a means of conveyance.'

'What?'

'An elephant! An elephant that belongs to an Indian who lives but a hundred steps from here.'

'Let's go and see the elephant,' replied Mr. Fogg.

They soon reached a small hut, near which, enclosed within some high palings, was the animal in question. An Indian came out of the hut, and, at their request, conducted them within the enclosure. The elephant, which its owner had reared, not for a beast of burden, but for warlike purposes, was half domesticated. The Indian had begun already, by often irritating him, and feeding him every three months on sugar and butter, to impart to him a ferocity not in his nature, this method being often employed by those who train the Indian elephants for battle. Happily, however, for Mr. Fogg, the animal's instruction in this direction had not gone far, and the elephant still preserved his natural gentleness. Kiouni – this was the name of the beast – could doubtless travel rapidly for a long time, and, in default of any other means of conveyance, Mr. Fogg resolved to hire him. But elephants are far from cheap in India, where they are becoming scarce; the males, which alone are suitable for circus shows, are much sought, especially as but few of them are domesticated. When, therefore, Mr. Fogg proposed to the Indian to hire Kiouni, he refused point-blank. Mr. Fogg persisted, offering the excessive sum of ten pounds an hour for the loan of the beast to Allahabad. Refused. Twenty pounds? Refused also. Forty pounds? Still refused. Passepartout jumped at each advance; but the Indian declined to be tempted. Yet the offer was an alluring one, for, supposing it took the elephant fifteen hours to reach Allahabad, his owner would receive no less than six hundred pounds sterling.

Phileas Fogg, without getting in the least flurried, then proposed to purchase the animal outright, and at first offered a thousand pounds for him. The Indian, perhaps thinking he was going to make a great bargain, still refused.

Sir Francis Cromarty took Mr. Fogg aside, and begged him to reflect before he went any further; to which the gentleman replied that he was not in the habit of acting rashly, that a bet of twenty thousand pounds was at stake, that the elephant was absolutely necessary to him, and that he would secure him if he had to pay twenty times his value. Returning to the Indian, whose small, sharp eyes, glistening with avarice, betrayed that with him it was only a question of how great a price he could obtain, Mr. Fogg offered first twelve hundred, then fifteen hundred, eighteen hundred, two thousand pounds. Passepartout, usually so rubicund, was fairly white with suspense.

At two thousand pounds the Indian yielded.

What a price, good heaven!' cried Passepartout, 'for an elephant!'

It only remained now to find a guide, which was comparatively easy. A young Parsee, with an intelligent face, offered his services, which Mr. Fogg accepted, promising so generous a reward as to materially stimulate his zeal. The elephant was led out and equipped. The Parsee, who was an accomplished elephant driver, covered his back with a sort of saddle-cloth, and attached to each of his flanks some curiously uncomfortable howdahs.

Phileas Fogg paid the Indian with some bank-notes which he extracted from the famous carpet-bag, a proceeding that seemed to deprive poor Passepartout of his vitals. Then he offered to carry Sir Francis to Allahabad, which the brigadier gratefully accepted, as one traveller the more would not be likely to fatigue the gigantic beast. Provisions were purchased at Kholby, and while Sir Francis and Mr. Fogg took the howdahs on either side, Passepartout got astride the saddle-cloth between them. The Parsee perched himself on the elephant's neck, and at nine o'clock they set out from the village, the animal marching off through the dense forest of palms by the shortest cut.

Chapter Twelve

In which Phileas Fogg and his companions venture across the Indian forests, and what ensued.

IN ORDER TO SHORTEN the journey, the guide passed to the left of the line where the railway was still in process of being built. This line, owing to the capricious turnings of the Vindhia Mountains, did not pursue a straight course. The Parsee, who was quite familiar with the roads and paths in the district, declared that they would gain twenty miles by striking directly through the forest.

Phileas Fogg and Sir Francis Cromarty, plunged to the neck in the peculiar howdahs provided for them, were horribly jostled by the swift trotting of the elephant, spurred on as he was by the skilful Parsee; but they endured the discomfort with true British phlegm, talking little, and scarcely able to catch a glimpse of each other. As for Passepartout, who was mounted on the beast's back, and received the direct force of each concussion as he trod along, he was very careful, in accordance with his master's advice, to keep his tongue from between his teeth, as it would otherwise have been bitten off short. The worthy fellow bounced from the elephant's neck to his rump, and vaulted like a clown on a spring-board; yet he laughed in the midst of his bouncing, and from time to time took a piece of sugar out of his pocket, and inserted it in Kiouni's trunk, who received it without in the least slackening his regular trot.

After two hours the guide stopped the elephant, and gave him an hour for rest, during which Kiouni, after quenching his thirst at a neighbouring spring, set to devouring the branches and shrubs round about him. Neither Sir Francis nor Mr. Fogg regretted the delay, and both descended with a feeling of relief. 'Why, he's made of iron!' exclaimed the general, gazing admiringly on Kiouni.

'Of forged iron,' replied Passepartout, as he set about preparing a hasty breakfast.

At noon the Parsee gave the signal of departure. The country soon presented a very savage aspect. Copses of dates and dwarf-palms succeeded the dense forests; then vast, dry plains, dotted with scanty shrubs, and sown with great blocks of syenite. 'All this portion of Bundelcund, which is little frequented by travellers, is inhabited by a fanatical population, hardened in the most horrible practices of the Hindoo faith. The English have not been able to secure complete dominion over this territory, which is subjected to the influence of rajahs, whom it is almost impossible to reach in their inaccessible mountain fastnesses. The travellers several times saw bands of ferocious Indians, who, when they perceived the elephant striding across country, made angry and threatening motions. The Parsee avoided them as much as possible. Few animals were observed on the route; even the monkeys hurried from their path with contortions and grimaces which convulsed Passepartout with laughter.

In the midst of his gaiety, however, one thought troubled the worthy servant. What would Mr. Fogg do with the elephant, when he got to Allahabad? Would he carry him on with him? Impossible! The cost of transporting him would make him ruinously expensive. Would he sell him, or set him free? The estimable beast certainly deserved some consideration. Should Mr. Fogg choose to make him, Passepartout, a present of Kiouni, he would be very much embarrassed; and these thoughts did not cease worrying him for a long time.

The principal chain of the Vindhias was crossed by eight in the evening, and another halt was made on the northern slope, in a ruined bungalow. They had gone nearly twenty-five miles that day, and an equal distance still separated them from the station of Allahabad.

The night was cold. The Parsee lit a fire in the bungalow with a few dry branches, and the warmth was very grateful. The provisions purchased at Kholby sufficed for supper, and the travellers ate ravenously. The conversation, beginning with a few disconnected phrases, soon gave place to loud and steady snores. The guide watched Kiouni, who slept standing, bolstering himself against the trunk of a large tree. Nothing occurred during the night to disturb the slumberers, although occasional growls from panthers and chatterings of monkeys broke the silence; the more formidable beasts made no cries or hostile demonstration against the occupants of the bungalow. Sir Francis slept heavily, like an honest soldier overcome with fatigue. Passepartout was wrapped in uneasy dreams of the bouncing of the day before. As for Mr. Fogg, he slumbered as peacefully as if he had been in his serene mansion in Saville Row.

The journey was resumed at six in the morning; the guide hoped to reach Allahabad by evening. In that case, Mr. Fogg would only lose a part of the forty-eight hours saved since the beginning of the tour. Kiouni, resuming his rapid gait, soon descended the lower spurs of the Vindhias, and towards noon they passed by the village of Kallenger, on the Cani, one of the branches of the Ganges. The guide avoided inhabited places, thinking it safer to keep to the open country, which lies along the first depressions of the basin of the great river. Allahabad was now only twelve miles to the north-east. They stopped under a clump of bananas, the fruit of which, as healthy as bread and as succulent as cream, was amply partaken of and appreciated.

At two o'clock the guide entered a thick forest which extended several miles; he preferred to travel under cover of the woods. They had not as yet had any unpleasant encounters, and the journey seemed on the point of being successfully accomplished, when the elephant, becoming restless, suddenly stopped.

It was then four o'clock.

'What's the matter?' asked Sir Francis, putting out his head.

'I don't know, officer,' replied the Parsee, listening attentively to a confused murmur which came through the thick branches.

The murmur soon became more distinct; it now seemed like a distant concert of human voices accompanied by brass instruments. Passepartout was all eyes and ears. Mr. Fogg patiently waited without a word. The Parsee jumped to the ground, fastened the elephant to a tree, and plunged into the thicket. He soon returned, saying,——

'A procession of Brahmins is coming this way. We must prevent their seeing us, if possible.'

The guide unloosed the elephant and led him into a thicket, at the same time asking the travellers not to stir. He held himself ready to bestride the animal at a moment's notice, should flight become necessary; but he evidently thought that the procession of the faithful would pass without perceiving them amid the thick foliage, in which they were wholly concealed.

The discordant tones of the voices and instruments drew nearer, and now droning songs mingled with the sound of the tambourines and cymbals. The head of the procession soon appeared beneath the trees, a hundred paces away; and the strange figures who performed the religious ceremony were easily distinguished through the branches. First came the priests, with mitres on their heads, and clothed in long lace robes. They were surrounded by men, women, and children, who sang a kind of lugubrious psalm, interrupted at regular intervals by the tambourines and cymbals; while behind them was drawn a car with large wheels, the spokes of which represented serpents entwined with each other. Upon the car, which was drawn by four richly caparisoned zebus, stood a hideous statue with four arms, the body coloured a dull red, with haggard eyes, dishevelled hair, protruding tongue, and lips tinted with betel. It stood upright upon the figure of a prostrate and headless giant.

Sir Francis, recognizing the statue, whispered, 'The goddess Kali; the goddess of love and death.'

'Of death, perhaps,' muttered back Passepartout, 'but of love – that ugly old hag? Never!'

The Parsee made a motion to keep silence.

A group of old fakirs were capering and making a wild ado round the statue; these were striped with ochre, and covered with cuts whence their blood issued drop by drop – stupid fanatics, who, in the great Indian ceremonies, still throw themselves under the wheels of Juggernaut. Some Brahmins, clad in all the sumptuousness of Oriental apparel, and leading a woman who faltered at every step, followed. This woman was young, and as fair as a European. Her head and neck, shoulders, ears, arms, hands, and toes, were loaded down with jewels and gems, – with bracelets, earrings, and rings, while a tunic bordered with gold, and covered with a light muslin robe betrayed the outline of her form.

The guards who followed the young woman presented a violent contrast to her, armed as they were with naked sabres hung at their waists, and long damascened pistols, and bearing a corpse on a palanquin. It was the body of an old man, gorgeously arrayed in the habiliments of a rajah, wearing, as in life, a turban embroidered with pearls, a robe of tissue of silk and gold, a scarf of cashmere sewed with diamonds, and the magnificent weapons of a Hindoo prince. Next came the musicians and a rearguard of capering fakirs, whose cries sometimes drowned the noise of the instruments; these closed the procession.

Sir Francis watched the procession with a sad countenance, and, turning to the guide, said, 'A suttee.'

The Parsee nodded, and put his fingers to his lips. The procession slowly wound under the trees, and soon its last ranks disappeared in the depths of the wood. The songs gradually died away; occasionally cries were heard in the distance, until at last all was silence again.

Phileas Fogg had heard what Sir Francis said, and, as soon as the procession had disappeared, asked: 'What is a "suttee"?'

'A suttee,' returned the general, 'is a human sacrifice, but a voluntary one. The woman you have just seen will be burned to-morrow at the dawn of the day.'

'Oh, the scoundrels!' cried Passepartout, who could not repress his indignation.

'And the corpse?' asked Mr. Fogg.

'Is that of the prince, her husband,' said the guide; 'an independent rajah of Bundelcund.'

'Is it possible,' resumed Phileas Fogg, his voice betraying not the least emotion, 'that these barbarous customs still exist in India, and that the English have been unable to put a stop to them?'

'These sacrifices do not occur in the larger portion of India,' replied Sir Francis; 'but we have no power over these savage territories, and especially here in Bundelcund. The whole district north of the Vindhias is the theatre of incessant murders and pillage.'

'The poor wretch!' exclaimed Passepartout, 'to be burned alive!'

'Yes,' returned Sir Francis, 'burned alive. And if she were not, you cannot conceive what treatment she would be obliged to submit to from her relatives. They would shave off her hair, feed her on a scanty allowance of rice, treat her with contempt; she would be looked upon as an unclean creature, and would die in some corner, like a scurvy dog. The prospect of so frightful an existence drives these poor creatures to the sacrifice much more than love or religious fanaticism. Sometimes, however, the sacrifice is really voluntary, and it requires the active interference of the Government to prevent it. Several years ago, when I was living at Bombay, a young widow asked permission of the governor to be burned along with her husband's body; but, as you may imagine, he refused. The woman left the town, took refuge with an independent rajah, and there carried out her self-devoted purpose.'

While Sir Francis was speaking, the guide shook his head several times, and now said: 'The sacrifice which will take place to-morrow at dawn is not a voluntary one.'

'How do you know?'

'Everybody knows about this affair in Bundelcund.'

'But the wretched creature did not seem to be making any resistance,' observed Sir Francis.

'That was because they had intoxicated her with fumes of hemp and opium.'

'But where are they taking her?'

'To the pagoda of Pillaji, two miles from here; she will pass the night there.'

'And the sacrifice will take place——'

'To-morrow, at the first light of dawn.'

The guide now led the elephant out of the thicket, and leaped upon his neck. Just at the moment that he was about to urge Kiouni forward with a peculiar whistle, Mr. Fogg stopped him, and, turning to Sir Francis Cromarty, said, 'Suppose we save this woman.'

'Save the woman, Mr. Fogg!'

'I have yet twelve hours to spare; I can devote them to that.'

'Why, you are a man of heart!'

'Sometimes,' replied Phileas Fogg, quietly; 'when I have the time.'

Chapter Thirteen

In which Passepartout receives a new proof that fortune favours the brave.

THE PROJECT WAS A BOLD one, full of difficulty, perhaps impracticable. Mr. Fogg was going to risk life, or at least liberty, and therefore the success of his tour. But he did not hesitate, and he found in Sir Francis Cromarty an enthusiastic ally.

As for Passepartout, he was ready for anything that might be proposed. His master's idea charmed him; he perceived a heart, a soul, under that icy exterior. He began to love Phileas Fogg.

There remained the guide: what course would he adopt? Would he not take part with the Indians? In default of his assistance, it was necessary to be assured of his neutrality.

Sir Francis frankly put the question to him.

'Officers,' replied the guide, 'I am a Parsee, and this woman is a Parsee. Command me as you will.'

'Excellent,' said Mr. Fogg.

'However,' resumed the guide; 'it is certain, not only that we shall risk our lives, but horrible tortures, if we are taken.'

'That is foreseen,' replied Mr. Fogg. 'I think we must wait till night before acting.'

'I think so,' said the guide.

The worthy Indian then gave some account of the victim, who, he said, was a celebrated beauty of the Parsee race, and the daughter of a wealthy Bombay merchant. She had received a thoroughly English education in that city, and, from her manners and intelligence, would be thought a European. Her name was Aouda. Left an orphan, she was married against her will to the old rajah of Bundelcund; and, knowing the fate that awaited her, she escaped, was retaken, and devoted by the rajah's relatives, who had an interest in her death, to the sacrifice from which it seemed she could not escape.

The Parsee's narrative only confirmed Mr. Fogg and his companions in their generous design. It was decided that the guide should direct the elephant towards the pagoda of Pillaji, which he accordingly approached as quickly as possible. They halted, half-an-hour afterwards, in a copse, some five hundred feet from the pagoda, where they were well concealed; but they could hear the groans and cries of the fakirs distinctly.

They then discussed the means of getting at the victim. The guide was familiar with the pagoda of Pillaji, in which, as he declared, the young woman was imprisoned. Could they enter any of its doors while the whole party of Indians was plunged in a drunken sleep or was it safer to attempt to make a hole in the walls? This could only be determined at the moment and the place themselves; but it was certain that the abduction must be made that night, and not when, at break of day, the victim was led to her funeral pyre. Then no human intervention could save her.

As soon as night fell, about six o'clock, they decided to make a reconnaissance around the pagoda. The cries of the fakirs were just ceasing; the Indians were in the act of plunging themselves into the drunkenness caused by liquid opium mingled with hemp, and it might be possible to slip between them to the temple itself.

The Parsee, leading the others, noiselessly crept through the wood, and in ten minutes they found themselves on the banks of a small stream, whence, by the light of the rosin torches, they perceived a pyre of wood, on the top of which lay the embalmed body of the rajah, which was to be burned with his wife. The pagoda, whose minarets loomed above the trees in the deepening dusk, stood a hundred steps away.

'Come!' whispered the guide.

He slipped more cautiously than ever through the brush, followed by his companions; the silence around was only broken by the low murmuring of the wind among the branches.

Soon the Parsee stopped on the borders of the glade, which was lit up by the torches. The ground was covered by groups of the Indians, motionless in their drunken sleep; it seemed a battle-field strewn with the dead. Men, women, and children lay together.

In the background, among the trees, the pagoda of Pillaji loomed indistinctly. Much to the guide's disappointment, the guards of the rajah, lighted by torches, were watching at the doors and marching to and fro with naked sabres; probably the priests, too, were watching within.

The Parsee, now convinced that it was impossible to force an entrance to the temple, advanced no farther, but led his companions back again. Phileas Fogg and Sir Francis Cromarty also saw that nothing could be attempted in that direction. They stopped, and engaged in a whispered colloquy.

'It is only eight now,' said the brigadier, 'and these guards may also go to sleep.'

'It is not impossible,' returned the Parsee.

They lay down at the foot of a tree, and waited.

The time seemed long; the guide ever and anon left them to take an observation on the edge of the wood, but the guards watched steadily by the glare of the torches, and a dim light crept through the windows of the pagoda.

They waited till midnight; but no change took place among the guards, and it became apparent that their yielding to sleep could not be counted on. The other plan must be carried out; an opening in the walls of the pagoda must be made. It remained to ascertain whether the priests were watching by the side of their victim as assiduously as were the soldiers at the door.

After a last consultation, the guide announced that he was ready for the attempt, and advanced, followed by the others. They took a roundabout way, so as to get at the pagoda on the rear. They reached the walls about half-past twelve, without having met anyone; here there was no guard, nor were there either windows or doors.

The night was dark. The moon, on the wane, scarcely left the horizon, and was covered with heavy clouds; the height of the trees deepened the darkness.

It was not enough to reach the walls; an opening in them must be accomplished, and to attain this purpose the party only had their pocket-knives.

Happily the temple walls were built of brick and wood, which could be penetrated with little difficulty; after one brick had been taken out, the rest would yield easily.

They set noiselessly to work, and the Parsee on one side and Passepartout on the other began to loosen the bricks so as to make an aperture two feet wide. They were getting on rapidly, when suddenly a cry was heard in the interior of the temple, followed almost instantly by other cries replying from the outside. Passepartout and the guide stopped. Had they been heard? Was the alarm being given? Common prudence urged them to retire, and they did so, followed by Phileas Fogg and Sir Francis. They again hid themselves in the wood, and waited till the disturbance, whatever it might be, ceased, holding themselves ready to resume their attempt without delay. But awkwardly enough, the guards now appeared at the rear of the temple, and there installed themselves, in readiness to prevent a surprise.

It would be difficult to describe the disappointment of the party, thus interrupted in their work. They could not now reach the victim; how, then, could they save her? Sir Francis shook his fists, Passepartout was beside himself, and the guide gnashed his teeth with rage. The tranquil Fogg waited, without betraying any emotion.

'We have nothing to do but to go away,' whispered Sir Francis.

'Nothing but to go away,' echoed the guide.

'Stop,' said Fogg. 'I am only due at Allahabad to-morrow before noon.'

'But what can you hope to do?' asked Sir Francis. 'In a few hours it will be daylight, and——'

'The chance which now seems lost may present itself at the last moment.'

Sir Francis would have liked to read Phileas Fogg's eyes.

What was this cool Englishman thinking of? Was he planning to make a rush for the young woman at the very moment of the sacrifice, and boldly snatch her from her executioners?

This would be utter folly, and it was hard to admit that Fogg was such a fool. Sir Francis consented, however, to remain to the end of this terrible drama. The guide led them to the rear of the glade, where they were able to observe the sleeping groups.

Meanwhile Passepartout, who had perched himself on the lower branches of a tree, was resolving an idea which had at first struck him like a flash, and which was now firmly lodged in his brain.

He had commenced by saying to himself, 'What folly!' and then he repeated, 'Why not, after all? It's a chance – perhaps the only one; and with such sots!' Thinking thus, he slipped, with the suppleness of a serpent, to the lowest branches, the ends of which bent almost to the ground.

The hours passed, and the lighter shades now announced the approach of day, though it was not yet light. This was the moment. The slumbering multitude became animated, the tambourines sounded, songs and cries arose; the hour of the sacrifice had come. The doors of the pagoda swung open, and a bright light escaped from its interior, in the midst of which Mr. Fogg and Sir Francis espied the victim. She seemed, having shaken off the stupor of intoxication, to be striving to escape from her executioner. Sir Francis's heart throbbed; and convulsively seizing Mr. Fogg's hand, found in it an open knife. Just at this moment the crowd began to move. The young woman had again fallen into a stupor caused by the fumes of hemp, and passed among the fakirs, who escorted her with their wild, religious cries.

Phileas Fogg and his companions, mingling in the rear ranks of the crowd, followed; and in two minutes they reached the banks of the stream, and stopped fifty paces from the pyre, upon which still lay the rajah's corpse. In the semi-obscurity they saw the victim, quite senseless, stretched out beside her husband's body. Then a torch was brought, and the wood, soaked with oil, instantly took fire.

At this moment Sir Francis and the guide seized Phileas Fogg, who, in an instant of mad generosity, was about to rush upon the pyre. But he had quickly pushed them aside, when the whole scene suddenly changed. A cry of terror arose. The whole multitude prostrated themselves, terror-stricken, on the ground.

The old rajah was not dead, then, since he rose of a sudden, like a spectre, took up his wife in his arms, and descended from the pyre in the midst of the clouds of smoke, which only heightened his ghostly appearance.

Fakirs and soldiers and priests, seized with instant terror, lay there with their faces on the ground, not daring to lift their eyes and behold such a prodigy.

The inanimate victim was borne along by the vigorous arms which supported her, and which she did not seem in the least to burden. Mr. Fogg and Sir Francis stood erect, the Parsee bowed his head, and Passepartout was, no doubt, scarcely less stupefied.

The resuscitated rajah approached Sir Francis and Mr. Fogg, and, in an abrupt tone, said, 'Let us be off!'

It was Passepartout himself, who had slipped upon the pyre in the midst of the smoke and, profiting by the still overhanging darkness, had delivered the young woman from death! It was Passepartout who, playing his part with a happy audacity, had passed through the crowd amid the general terror.

A moment after all four of the party had disappeared in the woods, and the elephant was bearing them away at a rapid pace. But the cries and noise, and a ball which whizzed through Phileas Fogg's hat, apprised them that the trick had been discovered.

The old rajah's body, indeed, now appeared upon the burning pyre; and the priests, recovered from their terror, perceived that an abduction had taken place. They hastened into the forest, followed by the soldiers, who fired a volley after the fugitives; but the latter rapidly increased the distance between them, and ere long found themselves beyond the reach of the bullets and arrows.

Chapter Fourteen

In which Phileas Fogg descends the whole length of the beautiful Valley of the Ganges without ever thinking of seeing it.

THE RASH EXPLOIT HAD been accomplished; and for an hour Passepartout laughed gaily at his success. Sir Francis pressed the worthy fellow's hand, and his master said, 'Well done!' which, from him, was high commendation; to which Passepartout replied that all the credit of the affair belonged to Mr. Fogg. As for him, he had only been struck with a 'queer' idea; and he laughed to think that for a few moments he, Passepartout, the ex-gymnast, ex-sergeant fireman, had been the spouse of a charming woman, a venerable, embalmed rajah! As for the young Indian woman, she had been unconscious throughout of what was passing, and now, wrapped up in a travelling-blanket, was reposing in one of the howdahs.

The elephant, thanks to the skilful guidance of the Parsee, was advancing rapidly through the still darksome forest, and, an hour after leaving the pagoda, had crossed a vast plain. They made a halt at seven o'clock, the young woman being still in a state of complete prostration. The guide made her drink a little brandy and water, but the drowsiness which stupefied her could not yet be shaken off. Sir Francis, who was familiar with the effects of the intoxication produced by the fumes of hemp, reassured his companions on her account. But he was more disturbed at the prospect of her future fate. He told Phileas Fogg that, should Aouda remain in India, she would inevitably fall again into the hands of her executioners. These fanatics were scattered throughout the country, and would, despite the English police, recover their victim at Madras, Bombay, or Calcutta. She would only be safe by quitting India for ever.

Phileas Fogg replied that he would reflect upon the matter.

The station at Allahabad was reached about ten o'clock, and the interrupted line of railway being resumed, would enable them to reach Calcutta in less than twenty-four hours. Phileas Fogg would thus be able to arrive in time to take the steamer which left Calcutta the next day, October 25th, at noon, for Hong Kong.

The young woman was placed in one of the waiting-rooms of the station, whilst Passepartout was charged with purchasing for her various articles of toilet, a dress, shawl, and some furs; for which his master gave him unlimited credit. Passepartout started off forthwith, and found himself in the streets of Allahabad, that is, the 'City of God,' one of the most venerated in India, being built at the junction of the two sacred rivers, Ganges and Jumna, the waters of which attract pilgrims from every part of the peninsula. The Ganges, according to the legends of the Ramayana, rises in heaven, whence owing to Brahma's agency, it descends to the earth.

Passepartout made it a point, as he made his purchases, to take a good look at the city. It was formerly defended by a noble fort, which had since become a state prison; its commerce has dwindled away, and Passepartout in vain looked about him for such a bazaar as he used to frequent in Regent Street. At last he came upon an elderly, crusty Jew, who sold second-hand articles, and from whom he purchased a dress of Scotch stuff, a large mantle, and a fine otter-skin pelisse, for which he did not hesitate to pay seventy-five pounds. He then returned triumphantly to the station.

The influence to which the priests of Pillaji had subjected Aouda began gradually to yield, and she became more herself, so that her fine eyes resumed all their soft Indian expression.

When the poet-king, Ucaf Uddaul, celebrates the charms of the queen of Ahmehnagara, he speaks thus:—

'Her shining tresses, divided in two parts, encircle the harmonious contour of her white and delicate cheeks, brilliant in their glow and freshness. Her ebony brows have the form and charm of the bow of Kama, the god of love, and beneath her long silken lashes the purest reflection and a celestial light swim, as in the sacred lakes of Himalaya, in the black pupils of her great clear eyes. Her teeth, fine, equal, and white, glitter between her smiling lips like dewdrops in a passion-flower's half-enveloped breast. Her delicately formed ears, her vermilion hands, her little feet, curved and tender as the lotus-bud, glitter with the brilliancy of the loveliest pearls of Ceylon, the most dazzling diamonds of Golconda. Her narrow and supple waist, which a hand may clasp around, sets forth the outline of her rounded figure and the beauty of her bosom, where youth in its flower displays the wealth of its treasures, and beneath the silken folds of her tunic she seems to have been modelled in pure silver by the godlike hand of Vicvarcarma, the immortal sculptor.'

It is enough to say, without applying this poetical rhapsody to Aouda, that she was a charming woman, in all the European acceptation of the phrase. She spoke English with great purity, and the guide had not exaggerated in saying that the young Parsee had been transformed by her bringing up.

The train was about to start from Allahabad, and Mr. Fogg proceeded to pay the guide the price agreed upon for his service, and not a farthing more; which astonished Passepartout, who remembered all that his master owed to the guide's devotion. He had, indeed, risked his life in the adventure at Pillaji, and if he should be caught afterwards by the Indians, he would with difficulty escape their vengeance. Kiouni, also, must be disposed of. What should be done with the elephant, which had been so dearly purchased? Phileas Fogg had already determined this question.

'Parsee,' said he to the guide, 'you have been serviceable and devoted. I have paid for your service, but not for your devotion. Would you like to have this elephant? He is yours.'

The guide's eyes glistened.

'Your honour is giving me a fortune!' cried he.

'Take him, guide,' returned Mr. Fogg, 'and I shall still be your debtor.'

'Good!' exclaimed Passepartout; 'take him, friend. Kiouni is a brave and faithful beast.' And, going up to the elephant, he gave him several lumps of sugar, saying, 'Here, Kiouni, here, here.'

The elephant grunted out his satisfaction, and, clasping Passepartout around the waist with his trunk, lifted him as high as his head. Passepartout, not in the least alarmed, caressed the animal, which replaced him gently on the ground.

Soon after, Phileas Fogg, Sir Francis Cromarty, and Passepartout, installed in a carriage with Aouda, who had the best seat, were whirling at full speed towards Benares. It was a run of eighty miles, and was accomplished in two hours. During the journey, the young woman fully recovered her senses. What was her astonishment to find herself in this carriage, on the railway, dressed in European habiliments, and with travellers who were quite strangers to her! Her companions first set about fully reviving her with a little liquor, and then Sir Francis narrated to her what had passed, dwelling upon the courage with which Phileas Fogg had not hesitated to risk his life to save her, and recounting the happy sequel of the venture, the result of Passepartout's rash idea. Mr. Fogg said nothing; while Passepartout, abashed, kept repeating that 'it wasn't worth telling.'

Aouda pathetically thanked her deliverers, rather with tears than words; her fine eyes interpreted her gratitude better than her lips. Then, as her thoughts strayed back to the scene of the sacrifice, and recalled the dangers which still menaced her, she shuddered with terror.

Phileas Fogg understood what was passing in Aouda's mind, and offered, in order to reassure her, to escort her to Hong Kong, where she might remain safely until the affair was hushed up – an offer which she eagerly and gratefully accepted. She had, it seems, a Parsee relation, who was one of the principal merchants of Hong Kong, which is wholly an English city, though on an island on the Chinese coast.

At half-past twelve the train stopped at Benares. The Brahmin legends assert that this city is built on the site of the ancient Casi, which, like Mahomet's tomb, was once suspended between heaven and earth; though the Benares of to-day, which the Orientalists call the Athens of India, stands quite unpoetically on the solid earth. Passepartout caught glimpses of its brick houses and clay huts, giving an aspect of desolation to the place, as the train entered it.

Benares was Sir Francis Cromarty's destination, the troops he was rejoining being encamped some miles northward of the city. He bade adieu to Phileas Fogg, wishing him all success, and expressing the hope that he would come that way again in a less original but profitable fashion. Mr. Fogg lightly pressed him by the hand. The parting of Aouda, who did not forget what she owed to Sir Francis, betrayed more warmth; and, as for Passepartout, he received a hearty shake of the hand from the gallant general.

The railway, on leaving Benares, passed for a while along the valley of the Ganges. Through the windows of their carriage the travellers had glimpses of the diversified landscape of Behar, with its mountains clothed in verdure, its fields of barley, wheat, and corn, its jungles peopled with green alligators, its neat villages and its still thickly-leaved forests. Elephants were bathing in the waters of the sacred river, and groups of Indians, despite the advanced season and chilly air, were performing solemnly their pious ablutions. These were fervent Brahmins, the bitterest foes of Buddhism, their deities being Vishnu, the solar god, Shiva, the divine impersonation of natural forces, and Brahma, the supreme ruler of priests and legislators. What would these divinities think of India, anglicized as it is to-day, with steamers whistling and scudding along the Ganges, frightening the gulls which float upon its surface, the turtles swarming along its banks, and the faithful dwelling upon its borders?

The panorama passed before their eyes like a flash, save when the steam concealed it fitfully from the view; the travellers could scarcely discern the fort of Chupenie, twenty miles south-westward from Benares, the ancient stronghold of the rajahs of Behar; or Ghazipur and its famous rose-water factories; or the tomb of Lord Cornwallis, rising on the left bank of the Ganges; the fortified town of Buxar, or Patna, a large manufacturing and trading place, where is held the principal opium market of India; or Monghir, a more than European town, for it is as English as Manchester or Birmingham, with its iron foundries, edge-tool factories, and high chimneys puffing clouds of black smoke heavenward.

Night came on; the train passed on at full speed, in the midst of the roaring of the tigers, bears, and wolves which fled before the locomotive; and the marvels of Bengal, Golconda, ruined Gour, Murshedabad, the ancient capital, Burdwan, Hugly, and the French town of Chandernagor, where Passepartout would have been proud to see his country's flag flying, were hidden from their view in the darkness.

Calcutta was reached at seven in the morning, and the packet left for Hong Kong at noon; so that Phileas Fogg had five hours before him.

According to his journal, he was due at Calcutta on the 25th of October, and that was the exact date of his actual arrival. He was therefore neither behindhand nor ahead of time. The two days gained between London and Bombay had been lost, as has been seen, in the journey across India. But it is not to be supposed that Phileas Fogg regretted them.

Chapter Fifteen

In which the bag of bank-notes disgorges some thousands of pounds more.

THE TRAIN ENTERED THE station, and Passepartout, jumping out first, was followed by Mr. Fogg, who assisted his fair companion to descend. Phileas Fogg intended to proceed at once to the Hong Kong steamer, in order to get Aouda comfortably settled for the voyage. He was unwilling to leave her while they were still on dangerous ground.

Just as he was leaving the station a policeman came up to him, and said, 'Mr. Phileas Fogg?'

'I am he.'

'Is this man your servant?' added the policeman, pointing to Passepartout.

'Yes.'

'Be so good, both of you, as to follow me.'

Mr. Fogg betrayed no surprise whatever. The policeman was a representative of the law, and law is sacred to an Englishman. Passepartout tried to reason about the matter, but the policeman tapped him with his stick, and Mr. Fogg made him a signal to obey.

'May this young lady go with us?' asked he.

'She may,' replied the policeman.

Mr. Fogg, Aouda, and Passepartout were conducted to a 'palki-gari,' a sort of four-wheeled carriage, drawn by two horses, in which they took their places and were driven away. No one spoke during the twenty minutes which elapsed before they reached their destination. They first passed through the 'black town,' with its narrow streets, its miserable, dirty huts and squalid population; then through the 'European town,' which presented a relief in its bright brick mansions, shaded by cocoanut-trees and bristling with masts, where, although it was early morning, elegantly dressed horsemen and handsome equipages were passing back and forth.

The carriage stopped before a modest-looking house, which, however, did not have the appearance of a private mansion. The policeman having requested his prisoners – for so, truly, they might be called – to descend, conducted them into a room with barred windows, and said: 'You will appear before Judge Obadiah at half-past eight.'

He then retired, and closed the door.

'Why, we are prisoners!' exclaimed Passepartout, falling into a chair.

Aouda, with an emotion she tried to conceal, said to Mr. Fogg: 'Sir, you must leave me to my fate! It is on my account that you receive this treatment; it is for having saved me!'

Phileas Fogg contented himself with saying that it was impossible. It was quite unlikely that he should be arrested for preventing a suttee. The complainants would not dare present themselves with such a charge. There was some mistake. Moreover, he would not in any event abandon Aouda, but would escort her to Hong Kong.

'But the steamer leaves at noon!' observed Passepartout, nervously.

'We shall be on board by noon,' replied his master, placidly.

It was said so positively, that Passepartout could not help muttering to himself, 'Parbleu, that's certain! Before noon we shall be on board.' But he was by no means reassured.

At half-past eight the door opened, the policeman appeared, and, requesting them to follow him, led the way to an adjoining hall. It was evidently a court-room, and a crowd of Europeans and natives already occupied the rear of the apartment.

Mr. Fogg and his two companions took their places on a bench opposite the desks of the magistrate and his clerk. Immediately after, Judge Obadiah, a fat, round man, followed by the clerk, entered. He proceeded to take down a wig which was hanging on a nail, and put it hurriedly on his head.

'The first case,' said he; then, putting his hand to his head, he exclaimed, 'Heh! This is not my wig!'

'No, your worship,' returned the clerk, 'it is mine.'

'My dear Mr. Oysterpuff, how can a judge give a wise sentence in a clerk's wig?'

The wigs were exchanged.

Passepartout was getting nervous, for the hands on the face of the big clock over the judge seemed to go round with terrible rapidity.

'The first case,' repeated Judge Obadiah.

'Phileas Fogg?' demanded Oysterpuff.

'I am here,' replied Mr. Fogg.

'Passepartout?'

'Present!' responded Passepartout.

'Good,' said the judge. 'You have been looked for, prisoners, for two days on the trains from Bombay.'

'But of what are we accused?' asked Passepartout, impatiently.

'You are about to be informed.'

'I am an English subject, sir,' said Mr. Fogg, 'and I have the right——'

'Have you been ill-treated?'

'Not at all.'

'Very well; let the complainants come in.'

A door was swung open by order of the judge and three Indian priests entered.

'That's it,' muttered Passepartout; 'these are the rogues who were going to burn our young lady.'

The priests took their places in front of the judge, and the clerk proceeded to read in a loud voice, a complaint of sacrilege against Phileas Fogg and his servant, who were accused of having violated a place held consecrated by the Brahmin religion.

'You hear the charge?' asked the judge.

'Yes sir,' replied Mr. Fogg, consulting his watch, 'and I admit it.'

'You admit it?'

'I admit it, and I wish to hear these priests admit, in their turn, what they were going to do at the pagoda of Pillaji.'

The priests looked at each other; they did not seem to understand what was said.

'Yes,' cried Passepartout, warmly; 'at the pagoda of Pillaji, where they were on the point of burning their victim.'

The judge stared with astonishment, and the priests were stupefied.

'What victim?' said Judge Obadiah. 'Burn whom? In Bombay itself?'

'Bombay?' cried Passepartout.

'Certainly. We are not talking of the pagoda of Pillaji, but of the pagoda of Malebar Hill, at Bombay.'

'And as a proof,' added the clerk, 'here are the desecrator's very shoes, which he left behind him.'

Whereupon he placed a pair of shoes on his desk.

'My shoes!' cried Passepartout, in his surprise permitting this imprudent exclamation to escape him.

The confusion of master and man, who had quite forgotten the affair at Bombay, for which they were now detailed at Calcutta, may be imagined.

Fix, the detective, had foreseen the advantage which Passepartout's escapade gave him, and, delaying his departure for twelve hours, had consulted the priests of Malebar Hill. Knowing that the English authorities dealt very severely with this kind of misdemeanour, he promised them a goodly sum in damages, and sent them forward to Calcutta by the next train. Owing to the delay caused by the rescue of the young widow, Fix and the priests reached the Indian capital before Mr. Fogg and his servant, the magistrates having been already warned by a despatch to arrest them should they arrive. Fix's disappointment when he learned that Phileas Fogg had not made his appearance in Calcutta, may be imagined. He made up his mind that the robber had stopped somewhere on the route and taken refuge in the southern provinces. For twenty-four hours Fix watched the station with feverish anxiety; at last he was rewarded by seeing Mr. Fogg and Passepartout arrive, accompanied by a young woman, whose presence he was wholly at a loss to explain. He hastened for a policeman; and this was how the party came to be arrested and brought before Judge Obadiah.

Had Passepartout been a little less preoccupied, he would have espied the detective ensconced in a corner of the court-room, watching the proceedings with an interest easily understood; for the warrant had failed to reach him at Calcutta, as it had done at Bombay and Suez.

Judge Obadiah had unfortunately caught Passepartout's rash exclamation, which the poor fellow would have given the world to recall.

'The facts are admitted?' asked the judge.

'Admitted,' replied Mr. Fogg, coldly.

'Inasmuch,' resumed the judge, 'as the English law protects equally and sternly the religions of the Indian people, and as the man Passepartout has admitted that he violated the sacred pagoda of Malebar Hill, at Bombay, on the 20th of October, I condemn the said Passepartout to imprisonment for fifteen days and a fine of three hundred pounds.'

'Three hundred pounds!' cried Passepartout, startled at the largeness of the sum.

'Silence!' shouted the constable.

'And inasmuch,' continued the judge, 'as it is not proved that the act was done by the connivance of the master with the servant, and as the master in any case must be held responsible for the acts of his paid servant, I condemn Phileas Fogg to a week's imprisonment and a fine of one hundred and fifty pounds.'

Fix rubbed his hands softly with satisfaction; if Phileas Fogg could be detained in Calcutta a week, it would be more than time for the warrant to arrive. Passepartout was stupefied. This sentence ruined his master. A wager of twenty thousand pounds lost, because he, like a precious fool, had gone into the abominable pagoda!

Phileas Fogg, as self-composed as if the judgement did not in the least concern him, did not even lift his eyebrows while it was being pronounced. Just as the clerk was calling the next case, he rose, and said, 'I offer bail.'

'You have that right,' returned the judge.

Fix's blood ran cold, but he resumed his composure when he heard the judge announce that the bail required for each prisoner would be one thousand pounds.

'I will pay it at once,' said Mr. Fogg, taking a roll of bank-bills from the carpet-bag, which Passepartout had by him, and placing them on the clerk's desk.

'The sum will be restored to you upon your release from prison,' said the judge. 'Meanwhile, you are liberated on bail.'

'Come!' said Phileas Fogg to his servant.

'But let them at least give me back my shoes!' cried Passepartout, angrily.

'Ah, these are pretty dear shoes!' he muttered, as they were handed to him. 'More than a thousand pounds apiece; besides, they pinch my feet.'

Mr. Fogg, offering his arm to Aouda, then departed, followed by the crestfallen Passepartout. Fix still nourished hopes that the robber would not, after all, leave the two thousand pounds behind him, but would decide to serve out his week in jail, and issued forth on Mr. Fogg's traces. That gentleman took a carriage, and the party were soon landed on one of the quays.

The Rangoon was moored half a mile off in the harbour, its signal of departure hoisted at the mast-head. Eleven o'clock was striking; Mr. Fogg was an hour in advance of time. Fix saw them leave the carriage and push off in a boat for the steamer, and stamped his feet with disappointment.

'The rascal is off, after all!' he exclaimed. 'Two thousand pounds sacrificed! He's as prodigal as a thief! I'll follow him to the end of the world if necessary; but at the rate he is going on, the stolen money will soon be exhausted.'

The detective was not far wrong in making this conjecture. Since leaving London, what with travelling expenses, bribes, the purchase of the elephant, bails, and fines, Mr. Fogg had already spent more than five thousand pounds on the way and the percentage of the sum recovered from the bank robber, promised to the detectives, was rapidly diminishing.

Chapter Sixteen

In which Fix does not seem to understand in the least what is said to him.

THE RANGOON – ONE OF the Peninsular and Oriental Company's boats plying in the Chinese and Japanese seas – was a screw steamer, built of iron, weighing about seventeen hundred and seventy tons, and with engines of four hundred horse-power. She was as fast, but not as well fitted up, as the Mongolia, and Aouda was not as comfortably provided for on board of her as Phileas Fogg could have wished. However, the trip from Calcutta to Hong Kong only comprised some three thousand five hundred miles, occupying from ten to twelve days, and the young woman was not difficult to please.

During the first days of the journey Aouda became better acquainted with her protector, and constantly gave evidence of her deep gratitude for what he had done. The phlegmatic gentleman listened to her, apparently at least, with coldness, neither his voice nor his manner betraying the slightest emotion; but he seemed to be always on the watch that nothing should be wanting to Aouda's comfort. He visited her regularly each day at certain hours, not so much to talk himself as to sit and hear her talk. He treated her with the strictest politeness, but with the precision of an automaton, the movements of which had been arranged for this purpose. Aouda did not quite know what to make of him, though Passepartout had given her some hints of his master's eccentricity, and made her smile by telling her of the wager which was sending him round the world. After all, she owed Phileas Fogg her life, and she always regarded him through the exalting medium of her gratitude.

Aouda confirmed the Parsee guide's narrative of her touching history. She did, indeed, belong to the highest of the native races of India. Many of the Parsee merchants have made great fortunes there by dealing in cotton; and one of them, Sir Jametsee Jeejeebhoy, was made a baronet by the English government. Aouda was a relative of this great man, and it was his cousin, Jeejeeh, whom she hoped to join at Hong Kong. Whether she would find a protector in him she could not tell; but Mr. Fogg essayed to calm her anxieties, and to assure her that everything would be mathematically – he used the very word – arranged. Aouda fastened her great eyes, 'clear as the sacred lakes of the Himalaya,' upon him; but the intractable Fogg, as reserved as ever, did not seem at all inclined to throw himself into this lake.

The first few days of the voyage passed prosperously, amid favourable weather and propitious winds, and they soon came in sight of the great Andaman, the principal of the islands in the Bay of Bengal, with its picturesque Saddle Peak, two thousand four hundred feet high, looming above the waters. The steamer passed along near the shores, but the savage Papuans, who are in the lowest scale of humanity, but are not, as has been asserted, cannibals, did not make their appearance.

The panorama of the islands, as they steamed by them, was superb. Vast forests of palms, arecs, bamboo, teakwood, of the gigantic mimosa, and tree-like ferns covered the foreground, while behind, the graceful outlines of the mountains were traced against the sky; and along the coasts swarmed by thousands the precious swallows whose nests furnish a luxurious dish to the tables of the Celestial Empire. The varied landscape afforded by the Andaman Islands was soon passed, however, and the Rangoon rapidly approached the Straits of Malacca, which give access to the China seas.

What was detective Fix, so unluckily drawn on from country to country, doing all this while. He had managed to embark on the Rangoon at Calcutta without being seen by Passepartout, after leaving orders that, if the warrant should arrive, it should be forwarded to him at Hong Kong; and he hoped to conceal his presence to the end of the voyage. It would have been difficult to explain why he was on board without awaking Passepartout's suspicions, who thought him still at Bombay. But necessity impelled him, nevertheless, to renew his acquaintance with the worthy servant, as will be seen.

All the detective's hopes and wishes were now centred on Hong Kong; for the steamer's stay at Singapore would be too brief to enable him to take any steps there. The arrest must be made at Hong Kong, or the robber would probably escape him for ever. Hong Kong was the last English ground on which he would set foot; beyond, China, Japan, America offered to Fogg an almost certain refuge. If the warrant should at last make its appearance at Hong Kong, Fix could arrest him and give him into the hands of the local police, and there would be no further trouble. But beyond Hong Kong, a simple warrant would be of no avail; an extradition warrant would be necessary, and that would result in delays and obstacles, of which the rascal would take advantage to elude justice.

Fix thought over these probabilities during the long hours which he spent in his cabin, and kept repeating to himself, 'Now, either the warrant will be at Hong Kong, in which case I shall arrest my man, or it will not be there; and this time it is absolutely necessary that I should delay his departure. I have failed at Bombay, and I have failed at Calcutta: if I fail at Hong Kong, my reputation is lost. Cost what it may, I *must succeed*! But how shall I prevent his departure, if that should turn out to be my last resource?'

Fix made up his mind that, if worst came to worst, he would make a confidant of Passepartout, and tell him what kind of a fellow his master really was. That Passepartout was not Fogg's accomplice, he was very certain. The servant, enlightened by his disclosure, and afraid of being himself implicated in the crime, would doubtless become an ally of the detective. But this method was a dangerous one, only to be employed when everything else had failed. A word from Passepartout to his master would ruin all. The detective was therefore in a sore strait. But suddenly a new idea struck him. The presence of Aouda on the Rangoon, in company with Phileas Fogg, gave him new material for reflection.

Who was this woman? What combination of events had made her Fogg's travelling companion? They had evidently met somewhere between Bombay and Calcutta; but where? Had they met accidentally, or had Fogg gone into the interior purposely in quest of this charming damsel? Fix was fairly puzzled. He asked himself whether there had not been a wicked elopement; and this idea so impressed itself upon his mind that he determined to make use of the supposed intrigue. Whether the young woman were married or not, he would be able to create such difficulties for Mr. Fogg at Hong Kong, that he could not escape by paying any amount of money.

But could he even wait till they reached Hong Kong? Fogg had an abominable way of jumping from one boat to another, and, before anything could be effected, might get full under weigh again for Yokohama.

Fix decided that he must warn the English authorities, and signal the Rangoon before her arrival. This was easy to do, since the steamer stopped at Singapore, whence there is a telegraphic wire to Hong Kong. He finally resolved, moreover, before acting more positively, to question Passepartout. It would not be difficult to make him talk; and, as there was no time to lose, Fix prepared to make himself known.

It was now the 30th of October, and on the following day the Rangoon was due at Singapore.

Fix emerged from his cabin and went on deck. Passepartout was promenading up and down in the forward part of the steamer. The detective rushed forward with every appearance of extreme surprise, and exclaimed, 'You here, on the Rangoon?'

'What, Monsieur Fix, are you on board?' returned the really astonished Passepartout, recognizing his crony of the Mongolia. 'Why, I left you at Bombay, and here you are, on the way to Hong Kong! Are you going round the world too?'

'No, no,' replied Fix; 'I shall stop at Hong Kong – at least for some days.'

'Hum!' said Passepartout, who seemed for an instant perplexed. 'But how is it I have not seen you on board since we left Calcutta?'

'Oh, a trifle of seasickness, – I've been staying in my berth. The Gulf of Bengal does not agree with me as well as the Indian Ocean. And how is Mr. Fogg?'

'As well and as punctual as ever, not a day behind time! But, Monsieur Fix, you don't know that we have a young lady with us.'

'A young lady?' replied the detective, not seeming to comprehend what was said.

Passepartout thereupon recounted Aouda's history, the affair at the Bombay pagoda, the purchase of the elephant for two thousand pounds, the rescue, the arrest and sentence of the Calcutta court, and the restoration of Mr. Fogg and himself to liberty on bail. Fix, who was familiar with the last events, seemed to be equally ignorant of all that Passepartout related; and the latter was charmed to find so interested a listener.

'But does your master propose to carry this young woman to Europe?'

'Not at all. We are simply going to place her under the protection of one of her relatives, a rich merchant at Hong Kong.'

'Nothing to be done there,' said Fix to himself, concealing his disappointment. 'A glass of gin, Mr. Passepartout?'

'Willingly, Monsieur Fix. We must at least have a friendly glass on board the Rangoon.'

Chapter Seventeen

Showing what happened on the voyage from Singapore to Hong Kong.

THE DETECTIVE AND PASSEPARTOUT met often on deck after this interview, though Fix was reserved, and did not attempt to induce his companion to divulge any more facts concerning Mr. Fogg. He caught a glimpse of that mysterious gentleman once or twice; but Mr. Fogg usually confined himself to the cabin, where he kept Aouda company, or according to his inveterate habit, took a hand at whist.

Passepartout began very seriously to conjecture what strange chance kept Fix still on the route that his master was pursuing. It was really worth considering why this certainly very amiable and complacent person, whom he had first met at Suez, had then encountered on board the Mongolia, who disembarked at Bombay, which he announced as his destination, and now turned up so unexpectedly on the Rangoon, was following Mr. Fogg's tracks step by step. What was Fix's object? Passepartout was ready to wager his Indian shoes – which he religiously preserved – that Fix would also leave Hong Kong at the same time with them, and probably on the same steamer.

Passepartout might have cudgelled his brain for a century without hitting upon the real object which the detective had in view. He could never have imagined that Phileas Fogg was being tracked as a robber around the globe. But as it is in human nature to attempt the solution of every mystery, Passepartout suddenly discovered an explanation of Fix's movements, which was in truth far from unreasonable. Fix, he thought, could only be an agent of Mr. Fogg's friends at the Reform Club, sent to follow him up, and to ascertain that he really went round the world as had been agreed upon.

'It's clear!' repeated the worthy servent to himself, proud of his shrewdness. 'He's a spy sent to keep us in view! That isn't quite the thing, either, to be spying Mr. Fogg, who is so honourable a man! Ah, gentlemen of the Reform, this shall cost you dear!'

Passepartout, enchanted with his discovery, resolved to say nothing to his master, lest he should be justly offended at this mistrust on the part of his adversaries. But he determined to chaff Fix, when he had the chance, with mysterious allusions, which, however, need not betray his real suspicions.

During the afternoon of Wednesday, October 30th, the Rangoon entered the Strait of Malacca, which separates the peninsula of that name from Sumatra.

The mountainous and craggy islets intercepted the beauties of this noble island from the view of the travellers. The Rangoon weighed anchor at Singapore the next day at four a.m., to receive coal, having gained half a day on the prescribed time of her arrival. Phileas Fogg noted this gain in his journal, and then, accompanied by Aouda, who betrayed a desire for a walk on shore, disembarked.

Fix, who suspected Mr. Fogg's every movement, followed them cautiously, without being himself perceived; while Passepartout, laughing in his sleeve at Fix's manœuvres, went about his usual errands.

The island of Singapore is not imposing in aspect, for there are no mountains; yet its appearance is not without attractions. It is a park chequered by pleasant highways and avenues. A handsome carriage, drawn by a sleek pair of New Holland horses, carried Phileas Fogg and Aouda into the midst of rows of palms with brilliant foliage, and of clove-trees whereof the cloves form the heart of a half-open flower. Pepper plants replaced the prickly hedges of European fields; sago-bushes, large ferns with gorgeous branches, varied the aspect of this tropical clime; while nutmeg-trees in full foliage filled the air with a penetrating perfume. Agile and grinning bands of monkeys skipped about in the trees, nor were tigers wanting in the jungles.

After a drive of two hours through the country, Aouda and Mr. Fogg returned to the town, which is a vast collection of heavy-looking, irregular houses, surrounded by charming gardens rich in tropical fruits and plants; and at ten o'clock they re-embarked, closely followed by the detective, who had kept them constantly in sight.

Passepartout, who had been purchasing several dozen mangoes – a fruit as large as good-sized apples, of a dark-brown colour outside and a bright red within, and whose white pulp, melting in the mouth, affords gourmands a delicious sensation – was waiting for them on deck. He was only too glad to offer some mangoes to Aouda, who thanked him very gracefully for them.

At eleven o'clock the Rangoon rode out of Singapore harbour, and in a few hours the high mountains of Malacca, with their forests inhabited by the most beautifully-furred tigers in the world, were lost to view. Singapore is distant some thirteen hundred miles from the island of Hong Kong, which is a little English colony near the Chinese coast. Phileas Fogg hoped to accomplish the journey in six days, so as to be in time for the steamer which would leave on the 6th of November for Yokohama, the principal Japanese port.

The Rangoon had a large quota of passengers, many of whom disembarked at Singapore, among them a number of Indians, Ceylonese, Chinamen, Malays, and Portuguese, mostly second-class travellers.

The weather, which had hitherto been fine, changed with the last quarter of the moon. The sea rolled heavily, and the wind at intervals rose almost to a storm, but happily blew from the south-west, and thus aided the steamer's progress. The captain as often as possible put up his sails, and under the double action of steam and sail the vessel made rapid progress along the coasts of Anam and Cochin China. Owing to the defective construction of the Rangoon, however, unusual precautions became necessary in unfavourable weather; but the loss of time which resulted from this cause, while it nearly drove Passepartout out of his senses, did not seem to affect his master in the least. Passepartout blamed the captain, the engineer, and the crew, and consigned all who were connected with the ship to the land where the pepper grows. Perhaps the thought of the gas, which was remorselessly burning at his expense in Saville Row, had something to do with his hot impatience.

'You are in a great hurry, then,' said Fix to him one day, 'to reach Hong Kong?'

'A very great hurry!'

'Mr. Fogg, I suppose, is anxious to catch the steamer for Yokohama?'

'Terribly anxious.'

'You believe in this journey around the world, then?'

'Absolutely. Don't you, Mr. Fix?'

'I? I don't believe a word of it.'

'You're a sly dog!' said Passepartout, winking at him.

This expression rather disturbed Fix, without his knowing why. Had the Frenchman guessed his real purpose? He knew not what to think. But how could Passepartout have discovered that he was a detective? Yet, in speaking as he did, the man evidently meant more than he expressed.

Passepartout went still further the next day; he could not hold his tongue.

'Mr. Fix,' said he, in a bantering tone; 'shall we be so unfortunate as to lose you when we get to Hong Kong?'

'Why,' responded Fix, a little embarrassed, 'I don't know; perhaps ——'

'Ah, if you would only go on with us! An agent of the Peninsular Company, you know, can't stop on the way! You were only going to Bombay, and here you are in China. America is not far off, and from America to Europe is only a step.'

Fix looked intently at his companion, whose countenance was as serene as possible, and laughed with him. But Passepartout persisted in chaffing him by asking him if he made much by his present occupation.

'Yes, and no,' returned Fix; 'there is good and bad luck in such things. But you must understand that I don't travel at my own expense.'

'Oh, I am quite sure of that!' cried Passepartout, laughing heartily.

Fix, fairly puzzled, descended to his cabin and gave himself up to his reflections. He was evidently suspected; somehow or other the Frenchman had found out that he was a detective. But had he told his master? What part was he playing in all this: was he an accomplice or not? Was the game, then, up? Fix spent several hours turning these things over in his mind, sometimes thinking that all was lost, then persuading himself that Fogg was ignorant of his presence, and then undecided what course it was best to take.

Nevertheless, he preserved his coolness of mind, and at last resolved to deal plainly with Passepartout. If he did not find it practicable to arrest Fogg at Hong Kong, and if Fogg made preparations to leave that last foothold of English territory, he, Fix, would tell Passepartout all. Either the servant was the accomplice of his master, and in this case the master knew of his operations, and he should fail; or else the servant knew nothing about the robbery, and then his interest would be to abandon the robber.

Such was the situation between Fix and Passepartout. Meanwhile Phileas Fogg moved about above them in the most majestic and unconscious indifference. He was passing methodically in his orbit around the world, regardless of the lesser stars which gravitated around him. Yet there was near by what the astronomers would call a disturbing star, which might have produced an agitation in this gentleman's heart. But no! the charms of Aouda failed to act, to Passepartout's great surprise; and the disturbances, if they existed, would have been more difficult to calculate than those of Uranus which led to the discovery of Neptune.

It was every day an increasing wonder to Passepartout, who read in Aouda's eyes the depths of her gratitude to his master. Phileas Fogg, though brave and gallant, must be, he thought, quite heartless. As to the sentiment which this journey might have awakened in him, there was clearly no trace of such a thing; while poor Passepartout existed in perpetual reveries.

One day he was leaning on the railing of the engine-room, and was observing the engine, when a sudden pitch of the steamer threw the screw out of the water. The steam came hissing out of the valves; and this made Passepartout indignant.

'The valves are not sufficiently charged!' he exclaimed. 'We are not going. Oh, these English! If this was an American craft, we should blow up, perhaps, but we should at all events go faster!'

Chapter Eighteen

In which Phileas Fogg, Passepartout, and Fix go each about his business.

THE WEATHER WAS BAD during the latter days of the voyage. The wind, obstinately remaining in the north-west, blew a gale, and retarded the steamer. The Rangoon rolled heavily, and the passengers became impatient of the long, monstrous waves which the wind raised before their path. A sort of tempest arose on the 3rd of November, the squall knocking the vessel about with fury, and the waves running high. The Rangoon reefed all her sails, and even the rigging proved too much, whistling and shaking amid the squall. The steamer was forced to proceed slowly, and the captain estimated that she would reach Hong Kong twenty hours behind time, and more if the storm lasted.

Phileas Fogg gazed at the tempestuous sea, which seemed to be struggling especially to delay him, with his habitual tranquillity. He never changed countenance for an instant, though a delay of twenty hours, by making him too late for the Yokohama boat, would almost inevitably cause the loss of the wager. But this man of nerve manifested neither impatience nor annoyance; it seemed as if the storm were a part of his programme, and had been foreseen. Aouda was amazed to find him as calm as he had been from the first time she saw him.

Fix did not look at the state of things in the same light. The storm greatly pleased him. His satisfaction would have been complete had the Rangoon been forced to retreat before the violence of wind and waves. Each delay filled him with hope, for it became more and more probable that Fogg would be obliged to remain some days at Hong Kong; and now the heavens themselves became his allies, with the gusts and squalls. It mattered not that they made him sea-sick — he made no account of this inconvenience; and whilst his body was writhing under their effects, his spirit bounded with hopeful exultation.

Passepartout was enraged beyond expression by the unpropitious weather.

Everything had gone so well till now! Earth and sea had seemed to be at his master's service; steamers and railways obeyed him; wind and steam united to speed his journey. Had the hour of adversity come? Passepartout was as much excited as if the twenty thousand pounds were to come from his own pocket. The storm exasperated him, the gale made him furious, and he longed to lash the obstinate sea into obedience. Poor fellow! Fix carefully concealed from him his own satisfaction, for, had he betrayed it, Passepartout could scarcely have restrained himself from personal violence.

Passepartout remained on deck as long as the tempest lasted, being unable to remain quiet below, and taking it into his head to aid the progress of the ship by lending a hand with the crew. He overwhelmed the captain, officers, and sailors, who could not help laughing at his impatience, with all sorts of questions. He wanted to know exactly how long the storm was going to last; whereupon he was referred to the barometer, which seemed to have no intention of rising. Passepartout shook it, but with no perceptible effect; for neither shaking nor maledictions could prevail upon it to change its mind.

On the 4th, however, the sea became more calm, and the storm lessened its violence; the wind veered southward, and was once more favourable. Passepartout cleared up with the weather. Some of the sails were unfurled, and the Rangoon resumed its most rapid speed. The time lost could not, however, be regained. Land was not signalled until five o'clock on the morning of the 6th; the steamer was due on the 5th. Phileas Fogg was twenty-four hours behindhand, and the Yokohama steamer would, of course, be missed.

The pilot went on board at six, and took his place on the bridge, to guide the Rangoon through the channels to the port of Hong Kong. Passepartout longed to ask him if the steamer had left for Yokohama; but he dared not, for he wished to preserve the spark of hope, which still remained, till the last moment. He had confided his anxiety to Fix, who – the sly rascal! – tried to console him by saying that Mr. Fogg would be in time if he took the next boat; but this only put Passepartout in a passion.

Mr. Fogg, bolder than his servant, did not hesitate to approach the pilot, and tranquilly ask him if he knew when a steamer would leave Hong Kong for Yokohama.

'At high tide tomorrow morning,' answered the pilot.

'Ah!' said Mr. Fogg, without betraying any astonishment.

Passepartout, who heard what passed, would willingly have embraced the pilot, while Fix would have been glad to twist his neck.

'What is the steamer's name? asked Mr. Fogg.

'The Carnatic.'

'Ought she not to have gone yesterday?'

'Yes, sir; but they had to repair one of her boilers, and so her departure was postponed till tomorrow.'

'Thank you,' returned Mr. Fogg, descending mathematically to the saloon.

Passepartout clasped the pilot's hand and shook it heartily in his delight, exclaiming, 'Pilot, you are the best of good fellows!'

The pilot probably does not know to this day why his responses won him this enthusiastic greeting. He remounted the bridge, and guided the steamer through the flotilla of junks, tankas, and fishing boats which crowd the harbour of Hong Kong.

At one o'clock the Rangoon was at the quay, and the passengers were going ashore.

Chance had strangely favoured Phileas Fogg, for, had not the Carnatic been forced to lie over for repairing her boilers, she would have left on the 6th of November, and the passengers for Japan would have been obliged to await for a week the sailing of the next steamer. Mr. Fogg was, it is true, twenty-four hours behind his time; but this could not seriously imperil the remainder of his tour.

The steamer which crossed the Pacific from Yokohama to San Francisco made a direct connection with that from Hong Kong, and it could not sail until the latter reached Yokohama; and if Mr. Fogg was twenty-four hours late on reaching Yokohama, this time would no doubt be easily regained in the voyage of twenty-two days across the Pacific. He found himself, then, about twenty-four hours behindhand, thirty-five days after leaving London.

The Carnatic was announced to leave Hong Kong at five the next morning. Mr. Fogg had sixteen hours in which to attend to his business there, which was to deposit Aouda safely with her wealthy relative.

On landing, he conducted her to a palanquin, in which they repaired to the Club Hotel. A room was engaged for the young woman, and Mr. Fogg, after seeing that she wanted for nothing, set out in search of her cousin Jeejeeh. He instructed Passepartout to remain at the hotel until his return, that Aouda might not be left entirely alone.

Mr. Fogg repaired to the Exchange, where, he did not doubt, everyone would know so wealthy and considerable a personage as the Parsee merchant. Meeting a broker, he made the inquiry, to learn that Jeejeeh had left China two years before, and, retiring from business with an immense fortune, had taken up his residence in Europe – in Holland, the broker thought, with the merchants of which country he had principally traded. Phileas Fogg returned to the hotel, begged a moment's conversation with Aouda, and, without more ado, apprised her that Jeejeeh was no longer at Hong Kong, but probably in Holland.

Aouda at first said nothing. She passed her hand across her forehead, and reflected a few moments. Then, in her sweet, soft voice, she said: 'What ought I to do, Mr. Fogg?'

'It is very simple,' responded the gentleman. 'Go on to Europe.'

'But I cannot intrude——'

'You do not intrude, nor do you in the least embarrass my project. Passepartout!'

'Monsieur.'

'Go to the Carnatic, and engage three cabins.'

Passepartout, delighted that the young woman, who was very gracious to him, was going to continue the journey with them, went off at a brisk gait to obey his master's order.

Chapter Nineteen

In which Passepartout takes a too great interest in his master, and what comes of it.

HONG KONG IS AN ISLAND which came into the possession of the English by the treaty of Nankin, after the war of 1842; and the colonizing genius of the English has created upon it an important city and an excellent port. The island is situated at the mouth of the Canton River, and is separated by about sixty miles from the Portuguese town of Macao, on the opposite coast. Hong Kong has beaten Macao in the struggle for the Chinese trade, and now the greater part of the transportation of Chinese goods finds its depôt at the former place. Docks, hospitals, wharves, a Gothic cathedral, a Government house, macadamized streets give to Hong Kong the appearance of a town in Kent or Surrey transferred by some strange magic to the antipodes.

Passepartout wandered, with his hands in his pockets, towards the Victoria port, gazing as he went at the curious palanquins and other modes of conveyance, and the groups of Chinese, Japanese, and Europeans who passed to and fro in the streets. Hong Kong seemed to him not unlike Bombay, Calcutta and Singapore, since, like them, it betrayed everywhere the evidence of English supremacy. At the Victoria port he found a confused mass of ships of all nations: English, French, American and Dutch, men-of-war and trading vessels, Japanese and Chinese junks, sempas, tankas and flower-boats, which formed so many floating parterres. Passepartout noticed in the crowd a number of the natives who seemed very old and were dressed in yellow. On going into a barber's to get shaved he learned that these ancient men were all at least eighty years old, at which age they are permitted to wear yellow, which is the Imperial colour. Passepartout, without exactly knowing why, thought this very funny.

On reaching the quay where they were to embark on the Carnatic, he was not astonished to find Fix walking up and down. The detective seemed very much disturbed and disappointed.

'This is bad,' muttered Passepartout, 'for the gentlemen of the Reform Club!' He accosted Fix with a merry smile, as if he had not perceived that gentleman's chagrin. The detective had, indeed, good reasons to inveigh against the bad luck which pursued him. The warrant had not come! It was certainly on the way, but as certainly it could not now reach Hong Kong for several days; and this being the last English territory on Mr. Fogg's route, the robber would escape, unless he could manage to detain him.

'Well, Monsieur Fix,' said Passepartout, 'have you decided to go on with us as far as America?'

'Yes,' returned Fix, through his set teeth.

'Good!' exclaimed Passepartout, laughing heartily. 'I knew you could not persuade yourself to separate from us. Come and engage your berth.'

They entered the steamer office and secured cabins for four persons. The clerk, as he gave them the tickets, informed them that, the repairs on the Carnatic having been completed, the steamer would leave that very evening, and not next morning as had been announced.

'That will suit my master all the better,' said Passepartout. 'I will go and let him know.'

Fix now decided to make a bold move; he resolved to tell Passepartout all. It seemed to be the only possible means of keeping Phileas Fogg several days longer at Hong Kong. He accordingly invited his companion into a tavern which caught his eye on the quay. On entering, they found themselves in a large room handsomely decorated, at the end of which was a large camp-bed furnished with cushions. Several persons lay upon this bed in a deep sleep. At the same tables which were arranged about the room some thirty customers were drinking English beer, porter, gin, and brandy; smoking, the while, long red clay pipes stuffed with little balls of opium mingled with essence of rose. From time to time one of the smokers, overcome with the narcotic, would slip under the table, whereupon the waiters, taking him by the head and feet, carried and laid him upon the bed. The bed already supported twenty of these stupefied sots.

Fix and Passepartout saw that they were in a smoking-house haunted by those wretched, cadaverous, idiotic creatures, to whom the English merchants sell every year the miserable drug called opium, to the amount of one million four hundred thousand pounds – thousands devoted to one of the most despicable vices which afflict humanity! The Chinese Government has in vain attempted to deal with the evil by stringent laws. It passed gradually from the rich, to whom it was at first exclusively reserved, to the lower classes, and then its ravages could not be arrested. Opium is smoked everywhere, at all times, by men and women, in the Celestial Empire; and, once accustomed to it, the victims cannot dispense with it, except by suffering horrible bodily contortions and agonies. A great smoker can smoke as many as eight pipes a day; but he dies in five years. It was in one of these dens that Fix and Passepartout, in search of a friendly glass, found themselves. Passepartout had no money, but willingly accepted Fix's invitation in the hope of returning the obligation at some future time.

They ordered two bottles of port, to which the Frenchman did ample justice, while Fix observed him with close attention. They chatted about the journey, and Passepartout was especially merry at the idea that Fix was going to continue it with them. When the bottles were empty, however, he rose to go and tell his master of the change in the time of the sailing of the Carnatic.

Fix caught him by the arm, and said, 'Wait a moment.'

'What for, Mr. Fix?'

'I want to have a serious talk with you.'

'A serious talk!' cried Passepartout, drinking up the little wine that was left in the bottom of his glass. 'Well, we'll talk about it tomorrow; I haven't time now.'

'Stay! What I have to say concerns your master.'

Passepartout, at this, looked attentively at his companion. Fix's face seemed to have a singular expression. He resumed his seat.

'What is it that you have to say?'

Fix placed his hand upon Passepartout's arm, and, lowering his voice, said, 'You have guessed who I am?'

'Parbleu!' said Passepartout, smiling.

'Then I'm going to tell you everything——'

'Now that I know everything, my friend! Ah! that's very good. But go on, go on. First, though, let me tell you that those gentlemen have put themselves to a useless expense.'

'Useless!' said Fix. 'You speak confidently. It's clear that you don't know how large the sum is.'

'Of course I do,' returned Passepartout. 'Twenty thousand pounds.'

'Fifty-five thousand!' answered Fix, pressing his companion's hand.

'What!' cried the Frenchman. 'Has Monsieur Fogg dared – fifty-five thousand pounds! Well, there's all the more reason for not losing an instant,' he continued, getting up hastily.

Fix pushed Passepartout back in his chair, and resumed: 'Fifty-five thousand pounds; and if I succeed, I get two thousand pounds. If you'll help me, I'll let you have five hundred of them.

'Help you?' cried Passepartout, whose eyes were standing wide open.

'Yes; help me keep Mr. Fogg here for two or three days.'

'Why, what are you saying? Those gentlemen are not satisfied with following my master and suspecting his honour, but they must try to put obstacles in his way! I blush for them!'

'What do you mean?'

'I mean that it is a piece of shameful trickery. They might as well waylay Mr. Fogg and put his money in their pockets!'

'That's just what we count on doing.'

'It's a conspiracy, then,' cried Passepartout, who became more and more excited as the liquor mounted in his head for he drank without perceiving it. 'A real conspiracy! And gentlemen, too. Bah!'

Fix began to be puzzled.

'Members of the Reform Club!' continued Passepartout. 'You must know, Monsieur Fix, that my master is an honest man, and that, when he makes a wager, he tries to win it fairly!'

'But who do you think I am?' asked Fix, looking at him intently.

'Parbleu! An agent of the members of the Reform Club, sent out here to interrupt my master's journey. But, though I found you out some time ago, I've taken good care to say nothing about it to Mr. Fogg.'

'He knows nothing, then?'

'Nothing,' replied Passepartout, again emptying his glass.

The detective passed his hand across his forehead, hesitating before he spoke again. What should he do? Passepartout's mistake seemed sincere, but it made his design more difficult. It was evident that the servant was not the master's accomplice, as Fix had been inclined to suspect.

'Well,' said the detective to himself, 'as he is not an accomplice, he will help me.'

He had no time to lose: Fogg must be detained at Hong Kong, so he resolved to make a clean breast of it.

'Listen to me,' said Fix abruptly. 'I am not, as you think, an agent of the members of the Reform Club——'

'Bah!' retorted Passepartout, with an air of raillery.

'I am a police detective, sent out here by the London office.'

'You, a detective?'

'I will prove it. Here is my commission.'

Passepartout was speechless with astonishment when Fix displayed this document, the genuineness of which could not be doubted.

'Mr. Fogg's wager,' resumed Fix, 'is only a pretext, of which you and the gentlemen of the Reform are dupes. He had a motive for securing your innocent complicity.'

'But why?'

'Listen. On the 28th of last September a robbery of fifty-five thousand pounds was committed at the Bank of England by a person whose description was fortunately secured. Here is this description; it answers exactly to that of Mr. Phileas Fogg.'

'What nonsense!' cried Passepartout, striking the table with his fist. 'My master is the most honourable of men!'

'How can you tell? You know scarcely anything about him. You went into his service the day he came away; and he came away on a foolish pretext, without trunks, and carrying a large amount in bank-notes. And yet you are bold enough to assert that he is an honest man!'

'Yes, yes,' repeated the poor fellow, mechanically.

'Would you like to be arrested as his accomplice?'

Passepartout, overcome by what he had heard, held his head between his hands, and did not dare to look at the detective. Phileas Fogg, the saviour of Aouda, that brave and generous man, a robber! And yet how many presumptions there were against him! Passepartout essayed to reject the suspicions which forced themselves upon his mind; he did not wish to believe that his master was guilty.

'Well, what do you want of me?' said he, at last, with an effort.

'See here,' replied Fix; 'I have tracked Mr. Fogg to this place, but as yet I have failed to receive the warrant of arrest for which I sent to London. You must help me to keep him here in Hong Kong——'

'I! But I——'

'I will share with you the two thousand pounds reward offered by the Bank of England.'

'Never!' replied Passepartout, who tried to rise, but fell back, exhausted in mind and body.

'Mr. Fix,' he stammered; 'even should what you say be true – if my master is really the robber you are seeking for – which I deny – I have been, am, in his service; I have seen his generosity and goodness; and I will never betray him – not for all the gold in the world. I come from a village where they don't eat that kind of bread!'

'You refuse?'

'I refuse.'

'Consider that I've said nothing,' said Fix; 'and let us drink.'

'Yes; let us drink!'

Passepartout felt himself yielding more and more to the effects of the liquor. Fix, seeing that he must, at all hazards, be separated from his master, wished to entirely overcome him. Some pipes full of opium lay upon the table. Fix slipped one into Passepartout's hand. He took it, put it between his lips, lit it, drew several puffs, and his head, becoming heavy under the influence of the narcotic, fell upon the table.

'At last!' said Fix, seeing Passepartout unconscious. 'Mr. Fogg will not be informed of the Carnatic's departure; and, if he is, he will have to go without his cursed Frenchman!

And, after paying his bill, Fix left the tavern.

Chapter Twenty

In which Fix comes face to face with Phileas Fogg.

WHILE THESE EVENTS WERE passing at the opium-house, Mr. Fogg, unconscious of the danger he was in of losing the steamer, was quietly escorting Aouda about the streets of the English quarter, making the necessary purchases for the long voyage before them. It was all very well for an Englishman like Mr. Fogg to make the tour of the world with a carpet-bag; a lady could not be expected to travel comfortably under such conditions. He acquitted his task with characteristic serenity, and invariably replied to the remonstrances of his fair companion, who was confused by his patience and generosity,—

'It is in the interest of my journey — a part of my programme.'

The purchases made, they returned to the hotel, where they dined at a sumptuously served *table-d'hôte*; after which Aouda, shaking hands with her protector after the English fashion, retired to her room for rest. Mr. Fogg absorbed himself throughout the evening in the perusal of the *Times* and *Illustrated London News*.

Had he been capable of being astonished at anything, it would have been not to see his servant return at bed-time. But, knowing that the steamer was not to leave for Yokohama until the next morning, he did not disturb himself about the matter. When Passepartout did not appear the next morning to answer his master's bell, Mr. Fogg, not betraying the least vexation, contented himself with taking his carpet bag, calling Aouda, and sending for a palanquin.

It was then eight o'clock; at half-past nine, it being then high tide, the Carnatic would leave the harbour. Mr. Fogg and Aouda got into the palanquin, their luggage being brought after on a wheelbarrow, and half-an-hour later stepped upon the quay whence they were to embark. Mr. Fogg then learned that the Carnatic had sailed the evening before. He had expected to find not only the steamer, but his domestic, and was forced to give up both; but no sign of disappointment appeared on his face, and he merely remarked to Aouda, 'It is an accident, madam; nothing more.'

At this moment a man who had been observing him attentively approached. It was Fix, who, bowing, addressed Mr. Fogg: 'Were you not, like me, sir, a passenger by the Rangoon, which arrived yesterday?'

'I was, sir,' replied Mr. Fogg coldly. 'But I have not the honour——'

'Pardon me; I thought I should find your servant here.'

'Do you know where he is, sir?' asked Aouda anxiously.

'What!' responded Fix, feigning surprise. 'Is he not with you?'

'No,' said Aouda. 'He has not made his appearance since yesterday. Could he have gone on board the Carnatic without us?'

'Without you, madam?' answered the detective. 'Excuse me, did you intend to sail in the Carnatic?'

'Yes, sir.'

'So did I, madam, and I am excessively disappointed. The Carnatic, its repairs being completed, left Hong Kong twelve hours before the stated time, without any notice being given; and we must now wait a week for another steamer.'

As he said 'a week' Fix felt his heart leap for joy. Fogg detained at Hong Kong a week! There would be time for the warrant to arrive, and fortune at last favoured the representative of the law. His horror may be imagined when he heard Mr. Fogg say, in his placid voice, 'But there are other vessels besides the Carnatic, it seems to me, in the harbour of Hong Kong.'

And, offering his arm to Aouda, he directed his steps toward the docks in search of some craft about to start. Fix, stupefied, followed; it seemed as if he were attached to Mr. Fogg by an invisible thread. Chance, however, appeared really to have abandoned the man it had hitherto served so well. For three hours Phileas Fogg wandered about the docks, with the determination, if necessary, to charter a vessel to carry him to Yokohama; but he could only find vessels which were loading or unloading, and which could not therefore set sail. Fix began to hope again.

But Mr. Fogg, far from being discouraged, was continuing his search, resolved not to stop if he had to resort to Macao, when he was accosted by a sailor on one of the wharves.

'Is your honour looking for a boat?'

'Have you a boat ready to sail?'

'Yes, your honour; a pilot-boat – No. 43 – the best in the harbour.'

'Does she go fast?'

'Between eight and nine knots the hour. Will you look at her?'

'Yes.'

'Your honour will be satisfied with her. Is it for a sea excursion?'

'No; for a voyage.'

'A voyage?'

'Yes; will you agree to take me to Yokohama?'

The sailor leaned on the railing, opened his eyes wide, and said, 'Is your honour joking?'

'No. I have missed the Carnatic; and I must get to Yokohama by the 14th at the latest to take the boat for San Francisco.'

'I am sorry,' said the sailor; 'but it is impossible.'

'I offer you a hundred pounds per day, and an additional reward of two hundred pounds if I reach Yokohama in time.'

'Are you in earnest?'

'Very much so.'

The pilot walked away a little distance, and gazed out to sea, evidently struggling between the anxiety to gain a large sum and the fear of venturing so far. Fix was in mortal suspense.

Mr. Fogg turned to Aouda and asked her, 'You would not be afraid, would you, madam?'

'Not with you, Mr. Fogg,' was her answer.

The pilot now returned, shuffling his hat in his hands.

'Well, your honour,' replied he; 'I could not risk myself, my men, or my little boat of scarcely twenty tons on so long a voyage at this time of year. Besides, we could not reach Yokohama in time, for it is sixteen hundred and sixty miles from Hong Kong.'

'Only sixteen hundred,' said Mr. Fogg.

'It's the same thing.'

Fix breathed more freely.

'But,' added the pilot; 'it might be arranged another way.'

Fix ceased to breathe at all.

'How?' asked Mr. Fogg.

'By going to Nagasaki, at the extreme south of Japan, or even to Shanghai, which is only eight hundred miles from here. In going to Shanghai we should not be forced to sail wide of the Chinese coast, which would be a great advantage, as the currents run northward, and would aid us.'

'Pilot,' said Mr. Fogg. 'I must take the American steamer at Yokohama, and not at Shanghai or Nagasaki.'

'Why not?' returned the pilot. 'The San Francisco steamer does not start from Yokohama. It puts in at Yokohama and Nagasaki, but it starts from Shanghai.'

'You are sure of that?'

'Perfectly.'

'And when does the boat leave Shanghai?'

'On the 11th, at seven in the evening. We have, therefore, four days before us, that is ninety-six hours; and in that time, if we had good luck and a south-west wind, and the sea was calm, we could make those eight hundred miles to Shanghai.'

'And you could go——'

'In an hour; as soon as provisions could be got aboard and the sails put up.'

'It is a bargain. Are you the master of the boat?'

'Yes; John Bunsby, master of the Tankadere.'

'Would you like some earnest-money?'

'If it would not put your honour out——'

'Here are two hundred pounds on account. Sir,' added Phileas Fogg, turning to Fix, 'if you would like to take advantage——'

'Thanks, sir; I was about to ask the favour.'

'Very well. In half-an-hour we shall go on board.'

'But poor Passepartout?' urged Aouda, who was much disturbed by the servant's disappearance.

'I shall do all I can to find him,' replied Phileas Fogg.

While Fix, in a feverish, nervous state, repaired to the pilot-boat the others directed their course to the police-station at Hong Kong. Phileas Fogg there gave Passepartout's description, and left a sum of money to be spent in the search for him. The same formalities having been gone through at the French consulate, and the palanquin having stopped at the hotel for the luggage, which had been sent back there, they returned to the wharf.

It was now three o'clock; and pilot-boat No. 43, with its crew on board, and its provisions stored away, was ready for departure.

The Tankadere was a neat little craft of twenty tons, as gracefully built as if she were a racing yacht. Her shining copper sheathing, her galvanized ironwork, her deck, white as ivory, betrayed the pride taken by John Bunsby in making her presentable. Her two masts leaned a trifle backward; she carried brigantine, foresail, storm-jib, and standing-jib, and was well rigged for running before the wind; and she seemed capable of brisk speed, which, indeed, she had already proved by gaining several prizes in pilot-boat races. The crew of the Tankadere was composed of John Bunsby, the master, and four hardy mariners, who were familiar with the Chinese seas. John Bunsby himself, a man of forty-five or thereabouts, vigorous, sunburnt, with a sprightly expression of the eye, and energetic and self-reliant countenance, would have inspired confidence in the most timid.

Phileas Fogg and Aouda went on board, where they found Fix already installed. Below deck was a square cabin, of which the walls bulged out in the form of cots, above a circular divan; in the centre was a table provided with a swinging lamp. The accommodation was confined but neat.

'I am sorry to have nothing better to offer you,' said Mr. Fogg to Fix, who bowed without responding.

The detective had a feeling akin to humiliation in profiting by the kindness of Mr. Fogg.

'It's certain,' thought he, 'though rascal as he is, he is a polite one!'

The sails and the English flag were hoisted at ten minutes past three. Mr. Fogg and Aouda, who were seated on deck, cast a last glance at the quay, in the hope of espying Passepartout. Fix was not without his fears lest chance should direct the steps of the unfortunate servant, whom he had so badly treated, in this direction; in which case an explanation the reverse of satisfactory to the detective must have ensued. But the Frenchman did not appear, and, without doubt, was still lying under the stupefying influence of the opium.

John Bunsby, master, at length gave the order to start, and the Tankadere, taking the wind under her brigantine, foresail, and standing-jib, bounded briskly forward over the waves.

Chapter Twenty-One

In which the master of the Tankadere runs great risk of losing a reward of two hundred Pounds.

THIS VOYAGE OF EIGHT HUNDRED MILES was a perilous venture, on a craft of twenty tons, and at that season of the year. The Chinese seas are usually boisterous, subject to terrible gales of wind, and especially during the equinoxes; and it was now early November.

It would clearly have been to the master's advantage to carry his passengers to Yokohama, since he was paid a certain sum per day; but he would have been rash to attempt such a voyage, and it was imprudent even to attempt to reach Shanghai. But John Bunsby believed in the Tankadere, which rode on the waves like a seagull; and perhaps he was not wrong.

Late in the day they passed through the capricious channels of Hong Kong, and the Tankadere, impelled by favourable winds, conducted herself admirably.

'I do not need, pilot,' said Phileas Fogg, when they got into the open sea, 'to advise you to use all possible speed.'

'Trust me, your honour. We are carrying all the sail the wind will let us. The poles would add nothing, and are only used when we are going into port.'

'It's your trade, not mine, pilot, and I confide in you.'

Phileas Fogg, with body erect and legs wide apart, standing like a sailor, gazed without staggering at the swelling waters. The young woman, who was seated aft, was profoundly affected as she looked out upon the ocean, darkening now with the twilight, on which she had ventured in so frail a vessel. Above her head rustled the white sails, which seemed like great white wings. The boat, carried forward by the wind, seemed to be flying in the air.

Night came. The moon was entering her first quarter, and her insufficient light would soon die out in the mist on the horizon. Clouds were rising from the east, and already overcast a part of the heavens.

The pilot had hung out his lights, which was very necessary in these seas crowded with vessels bound landward; for collisions are not uncommon occurrences, and, at the speed she was going the least shock would shatter the gallant little craft.

Fix, seated in the bow, gave himself up to meditation. He kept apart from his fellow-travellers, knowing Mr. Fogg's taciturn tastes; besides, he did not quite like to talk to the man whose favours he had accepted. He was thinking, too, of the future. It seemed certain that Fogg would not stop at Yokohama, but would at once take the boat for San Francisco; and the vast extent of America would insure him impunity and safety. Fogg's plan appeared to him the simplest in the world. Instead of sailing directly from England to the United States, like a common villain, he had traversed three-quarters of the globe, so as to gain the American continent more surely; and there, after throwing the police off his track, he would quietly enjoy himself with the fortune stolen from the bank. But, once in the United States what should he, Fix, do? Should he abandon this man? No, a hundred times no! Until he had secured his extradition, he would not lose sight of him for an hour. It was his duty, and he would fulfil it to the end. At all events, there was one thing to be thankful for; Passepartout was not with his master; and it was above all important, after the confidences Fix had imparted to him, that the servant should never have speech with his master.

Phileas Fogg was also thinking of Passepartout, who had so strangely disappeared. Looking at the matter from every point of view, it did not seem to him impossible that, by some mistake, the man might have embarked on the Carnatic at the last moment; and this was also Aouda's opinion, who regretted very much the loss of the worthy fellow to whom she owed so much. They might then find him at Yokohama; for if the Carnatic was carrying him thither, it would be easy to ascertain if he had been on board.

A brisk breeze arose about ten o'clock; but, though it might have been prudent to take in a reef, the pilot, after carefully examining the heavens, let the craft remain rigged as before. The Tankadere bore sail admirably, as she drew a great deal of water, and everything was prepared for high speed in case of a gale.

Mr. Fogg and Aouda descended into the cabin at midnight, having been already preceded by Fix, who had lain down on one of the cots. The pilot and crew remained on deck all night.

At sunrise the next day, which was November 8th, the boat had made more than one hundred miles. The log indicated a mean speed of between eight and nine miles. The Tankadere still carried all sail, and was accomplishing her greatest capacity of speed. If the wind held as it was, the chances would be in her favour. During the day she kept along the coast, where the currents were favourable; the coast, irregular in profile, and visible sometimes across the clearings, was at most five miles distant. The sea was less boisterous, since the wind came off land – a fortunate circumstance for the boat, which would suffer, owing to its small tonnage, by a heavy surge on the sea.

The breeze subsided a little towards noon, and set in from the south-west. The pilot put up his poles, but took them down again within two hours, as the wind freshened up anew.

Mr. Fogg and Aouda, happily unaffected by the roughness of the sea, ate with a good appetite, Fix being invited to share their repast, which he accepted with secret chagrin. To travel at this man's expense and live upon his provisions was not palatable to him. Still, he was obliged to eat, and so he ate.

When the meal was over, he took Mr. Fogg apart, and said, 'Sir,' – this 'sir' scorched his lips, and he had to control himself to avoid collaring this gentleman,' – 'sir, you have been very kind to give me a passage on this boat. But, though my means will not admit of my expending them as freely as you, I must ask to pay my share——'

'Let us not speak of that, sir,' replied Mr. Fogg.

'But, if I insist——'

'No, sir,' repeated Mr. Fogg, in a tone which did not admit of a reply. 'This enters into my general expenses.'

Fix, as he bowed, had a stifled feeling, and going forward, where he ensconced himself, did not open his mouth for the rest of the day.

Meanwhile they were progressing famously, and John Bunsby was in high hope. He several times assured Mr. Fogg that they would reach Shanghai in time; to which that gentleman responded that he counted upon it. The crew set to work in good earnest, inspired by the reward to be gained. There was not a sheet which was not tightened, not a sail which was not vigorously hoisted; not a lurch could be charged to the man at the helm. They worked as desperately as if they were contesting in a Royal Yacht regatta.

By evening, the log showed that two hundred and twenty miles had been accomplished from Hong Kong, and Mr. Fogg might hope that he would be able to reach Yokohama without recording any delay in his journal; in which case, the only misadventure which had overtaken him since he left London would not seriously affect his journey.

The Tankadere entered the Straits of Fo-Kien, which separate the island of Formosa from the Chinese coast, in the small hours of the night, and crossed the Tropic of Cancer. The sea was very rough in the straits, full of eddies formed by the counter currents, and the chopping waves broke her course, whilst it became very difficult to stand on deck.

At daybreak the wind began to blow hard again, and the heavens seemed to predict a gale. The barometer announced a speedy change, the mercury rising and falling capriciously; the sea also, in the south-east, raised long surges which indicated a tempest. The sun had set the evening before in a red mist, in the midst of the phosphorescent scintillations of the ocean.

John Bunsby long examined the threatening aspect of the heavens muttering indistinctly between his teeth. At last he said in a low voice to Mr. Fogg, 'Shall I speak out to your honour?'

'Of course.'

'Well, we are going to have a squall.'

'Is the wind north or south?' asked Mr. Fogg quietly.

'South. Look! a typhoon is coming up.'

'Glad it's a typhoon from the south, for it will carry us forward.'

'Oh, if you take it that way,' said John Bunsby, 'I've nothing more to say.' John Bunsby's suspicions were confirmed. At a less advanced season of the year the typhoon, according to a famous meteorologist, would have passed away like a luminous cascade of electric flame; but in the winter equinox, it was to be feared that it would burst upon them with great violence.

The pilot took his precautions in advance. He reefed all sail, the polemasts were dispensed with; all hands went forward to the bows. A single triangular sail, of strong canvas, was hoisted as a storm-jib, so as to hold the wind from behind. Then they waited.

John Bunsby had requested his passengers to go below; but this imprisonment in so narrow a space, with little air, and the boat bouncing in the gale, was far from pleasant. Neither Mr. Fogg, Fix, nor Aouda consented to leave the deck.

The storm of rain and wind descended upon them towards eight o'clock. With but its bit of sail, the Tankadere was lifted like a feather by a wind, an idea of whose violence can scarcely be given. To compare her speed to four times that of a locomotive going on full steam would be below the truth.

The boat scudded thus northward during the whole day, borne on by monstrous waves, preserving always, fortunately, a speed equal to theirs. Twenty times she seemed almost to be submerged by these mountains of water which rose behind her; but the adroit management of the pilot saved her. The passengers were often bathed in spray, but they submitted to it philosophically. Fix cursed it, no doubt; but Aouda, with her eyes fastened upon her protector, whose coolness amazed her, showed herself worthy of him, and bravely weathered the storm. As for Phileas Fogg, it seemed just as if the typhoon were a part of his programme.

Up to this time the Tankadere had always held her course to the north; but towards evening the wind, veering three-quarters, bore down from the north-west. The boat, now lying in the trough of the waves, shook and rolled terribly; the sea struck her with fearful violence. At night the tempest increased in violence. John Bunsby saw the approach of darkness and the rising of the storm with dark misgivings. He thought awhile, and then asked his crew if it was not time to slacken speed. After a consultation he approached Mr. Fogg, and said, 'I think your honour, that we should do well to make for one of the ports on the coast.'

'I think so too.'

'Ah!' said the pilot. 'But which one?'

'I know of but one,' returned Mr. Fogg tranquilly.

'And that is——'

'Shanghai.'

The pilot, at first, did not seem to comprehend; he could scarcely realize so much determination and tenacity. Then he cried, 'Well – yes! Your honour is right. To Shanghai!'

So the Tankadere kept steadily on her northward track.

The night was really terrible; it would be a miracle if the craft did not founder. Twice it would have been all over with her if the crew had not been constantly on the watch. Aouda was exhausted, but did not utter a complaint. More than once Mr. Fogg rushed to protect her from the violence of the waves.

Day reappeared. The tempest still raged with undiminished fury; but the wind now returned to the south-east. It was a favourable change, and the Tankadere again bounded forward on this mountainous sea, though the waves crossed each other, and imparted shocks and counter-shocks which would have crushed a craft less solidly built. From time to time the coast was visible through the broken mist, but no vessel was in sight. The Tankadere was alone upon the sea.

There were some signs of a calm at noon, and these became more distinct as the sun descended toward the horizon. The tempest had been as brief as terrific. The passengers, thoroughly exhausted, could now eat a little, and take some repose.

The night was comparatively quiet. Some of the sails were again hoisted, and the speed of the boat was very good. The next morning at dawn they espied the coast, and John Bunsby was able to assert that they were not one hundred miles from Shanghai. A hundred miles, and only one day to traverse them! That very evening Mr. Fogg was due at Shanghai, if he did not wish to miss the steamer to Yokohama. Had there been no storm, during which several hours were lost, they would be at this moment within thirty miles of their destination.

The wind grew decidedly calmer, and happily the sea fell with it. All sails were now hoisted, and at noon the Tankadere was within forty-five miles of Shanghai. There remained yet six hours in which to accomplish that distance. All on board feared that it could not be done, and everyone – Phileas Fogg, no doubt, excepted – felt his heart beat with impatience. The boat must keep up an average of nine miles an hour, and the wind was becoming calmer every moment! It was a capricious breeze, coming from the coast, and after it passed the sea became smooth. Still, the Tankadere was so light, and her fine sails caught the fickle zephyrs so well, that, with the aid of the current, John Bunsby found himself at six o'clock not more than ten miles from the mouth of Shanghai River. Shanghai itself is situated at least twelve miles up the stream. At seven they were still three miles from Shanghai. The pilot swore an angry oath; the reward of two hundred pounds was evidently on the point of escaping him. He looked at Mr. Fogg. Mr. Fogg was perfectly tranquil; and yet his whole fortune was at this moment at stake.

At this moment, also, a long black funnel crowned with wreaths of smoke, appeared on the edge of the waters. It was the American steamer, leaving for Yokohama at the appointed time.

'Confound her!' cried John Bunsby, pushing back the rudder with a desperate jerk.

'Signal her!' said Phileas Fogg quietly.

A small brass cannon stood on the forward deck of the Tankadere, for making signals in the fogs. It was loaded to the muzzle; but just as the pilot was about to apply a red-hot coal to the touchhole, Mr. Fogg said, 'Hoist your flag!'

The flag was run up at half-mast, and, this being the signal of distress, it was hoped that the American steamer, perceiving it, would change her course a little, so as to succour the pilot-boat.

'Fire!' said Mr. Fogg. And the booming of the little cannon resounded in the air.

Chapter Twenty-Two

In which Passepartout finds out that, even at the Antipodes, it is convenient to have some money in one's pocket.

THE CARNATIC, SETTING sail from Hong Kong at half-past six on the 7th of November, directed her course at full steam towards Japan. She carried a large cargo and a well-filled cabin of passengers. Two state-rooms in the rear were, however, unoccupied, – those which had been engaged by Phileas Fogg.

The next day a passenger with a half-stupefied eye, staggering gait, and disordered hair, was seen to emerge from the second cabin, and to totter to a seat on deck.

It was Passepartout; and what had happened to him was as follows:— Shortly after Fix left the opium den, two waiters had lifted the unconscious Passepartout, and had carried him to the bed reserved for the smokers. Three hours later, pursued even in his dreams by a fixed idea, the poor fellow awoke, and struggled against the stupefying influence of the narcotic. The thought of a duty unfulfilled shook off his torpor, and he hurried from the abode of drunkenness. Staggering and holding himself up by keeping against the walls, falling down and creeping up again, and irresistibly impelled by a kind of instinct, he kept crying out, 'The Carnatic! the Carnatic!'

The steamer lay puffing alongside the quay, on the point of starting. Passepartout had but few steps to go; and, rushing upon the plank, he crossed it, and fell unconscious on the deck, just as the Carnatic was moving off. Several sailors, who were evidently accustomed to this sort of scene, carried the poor Frenchman down into the second cabin, and Passepartout did not wake until they were one hundred and fifty miles from China. Thus he found himself the next morning on the deck of the Carnatic, and eagerly inhaling the exhilarating sea-breeze. The pure air sobered him. He began to collect his senses, which he found a difficult task; but at last he recalled the events of the evening before, Fix's revelation, and the opium-house.

'It is evident,' said he to himself, 'that I have been abominably drunk! What will Mr. Fogg say? At least I have not missed the steamer, which is the most important thing.'

Then, as Fix occurred to him:— 'As for that rascal, I hope we are well rid of him, and that he has not dared, as he proposed, to follow us on board the Carnatic. A detective on the track of Mr. Fogg, accused of robbing the Bank of England! Pshaw! Mr. Fogg is no more a robber than I am a murderer.'

Should he divulge Fix's real errand to his master? Would it do to tell the part the detective was playing? Would it not be better to wait until Mr. Fogg reached

London again, and then impart to him that an agent of the metropolitan police had been following him round the world, and have a good laugh over it? No doubt; at least, it was worth considering. The first thing to do was to find Mr. Fogg, and apologize for his singular behaviour.

Passepartout got up and proceeded, as well as he could with the rolling of the steamer, to the after-deck. He saw no one who resembled either his master or Aouda. 'Good!' muttered he; 'Aouda has not got up yet, and Mr. Fogg has probably found some partners at whist.'

He descended to the saloon. Mr. Fogg was not there. Passepartout had only, however, to ask the purser the number of his master's state-room. The purser replied that he did not know any passenger by the name of Fogg.

'I beg your pardon,' said Passepartout persistently. 'He is a tall gentleman, quiet, and not very talkative, and has with him a young lady——'

'There is no young lady on board,' interrupted the purser. 'Here is a list of the passengers; you may see for yourself.'

Passepartout scanned the list, but his master's name was not upon it. All at once an idea struck him.

'Ah! am I on the Carnatic?'

'Yes.'

'On the way to Yokohama?'

'Certainly.'

Passepartout had for an instant feared that he was on the wrong boat; but, though he was really on the Carnatic, his master was not there.

He fell thunderstruck on a seat. He saw it all now. He remembered that the time of sailing had been changed, that he should have informed his master of that fact, and that he had not done so. It was his fault, then, that Mr. Fogg and Aouda had missed the steamer. Yes, but it was still more the fault of the traitor who, in order to separate him from his master, and detain the latter at Hong Kong, had inveigled him into getting drunk! He now saw the detective's trick; and at this moment Mr. Fogg was certainly ruined, his bet was lost, and he himself perhaps arrested and imprisoned! At this thought Passepartout tore his hair. Ah, if Fix ever came within his reach, what a settling of accounts there would be!

After his first depression, Passepartout became calmer, and began to study his situation. It was certainly not an enviable one. He found himself on the way to Japan, and what should he do when he got there? His pocket was empty; he had not a solitary shilling – not so much as a penny. His passage had fortunately been paid for in advance; and he had five or six days in which to decide upon his future course. He fell to at meals with an appetite, and ate for Mr. Fogg, Aouda, and himself. He helped himself as generously as if Japan were a desert, where nothing to eat was to be looked for.

At dawn on the 13th the Carnatic entered the port of Yokohama. This is an important way-station in the Pacific, where all the mail-steamers, and those carrying travellers between North America, China, Japan, and the Oriental islands, put in. It is situated in the bay of Yeddo, and at but a short distance from that second capital of the Japanese Empire, and the residence of the Tycoon, the civil Emperor, before the Mikado, the spiritual Emperor, absorbed his office in his own. The Carnatic anchored at the quay near the custom-house, in the midst of a crowd of ships bearing the flags of all nations.

Passepartout went timidly ashore on this so curious territory of the Sons of the Sun. He had nothing better to do than, taking chance for his guide, to wander aimlessly through the streets of Yokohama. He found himself at first in a thoroughly European quarter, the houses having low fronts, and being adorned with verandas, beneath which he caught glimpses of neat peristyles. This quarter occupied, with its streets, squares, docks and warehouses, all the space between the 'promontory of the Treaty' and the river. Here, as at Hong Kong and Calcutta, were mixed crowds of all races, – Americans and English, Chinamen and Dutchmen, mostly merchants ready to buy or sell anything. The Frenchman felt himself as much alone among them as if he had dropped down in the midst of Hottentots.

He had, at least, one resource, – to call on the French and English consuls at Yokohama for assistance. But he shrank from telling the story of his adventures, intimately connected as it was with that of his master: and, before doing so, he determined to exhaust all other means of aid. As chance did not favour him in the European quarter, he penetrated that inhabited by the native Japanese, determined, if necessary, to push on to Yeddo.

The Japanese quarter of Yokohama is called Benten, after the goddess of the sea, who is worshipped on the islands round about. There Passepartout beheld beautiful fir and cedar groves, sacred gates of a singular architecture, bridges half hid in the midst of bamboos and reeds, temples shaded by immense cedar-trees, holy retreats where were sheltered Buddhist priests and sectaries of Confucius, and interminable streets, where a perfect harvest of rose-tinted and red-cheeked children, who looked as if they had been cut out of Japanese screens, and who were playing in the midst of short-legged poodles and yellowish cats, might have been gathered.

The streets were crowded with people. Priests were passing in processions, beating their dreary tambourines; police and custom-house officers with pointed hats encrusted with lac, and carrying two sabres hung to their waists; soldiers, clad in blue cotton with white stripes, and bearing guns; the Mikado's guards, enveloped in silken doublets, hauberks, and coats of mail; and numbers of military folk of all ranks – for the military profession is as much respected in Japan as it is despised in China – went hither and thither in groups and pairs. Passepartout saw, too, begging friars, long-robed pilgrims, and simple civilians, with their warped and jet-black hair, big heads, long busts, slender legs, short stature, and complexions varying from copper colour to a dead white, but never yellow, like the Chinese, from whom the Japanese widely differ. He did not fail to observe the curious equipages, – carriages and palanquins, barrows supplied with sails, and litters made of bamboo; nor the women, – whom he thought not especially handsome, – who took little steps with their little feet, whereon they wore canvas shoes, straw sandals, and clogs of worked wood, and who displayed tight-looking eyes, flat chests, teeth fashionably blackened, and gowns crossed with silken scarfs, tied in an enormous knot behind, – an ornament which the modern Parisian ladies seem to have borrowed from the dames of Japan.

Passepartout wandered for several hours in the midst of this motley crowd, looking in at the windows of the rich and curious shops, the jewellery establishments glittering with quaint Japanese ornaments, the restaurants decked with streamers and banners, the tea-houses, where the odorous beverage was being drunk with 'saki,' a liquor concocted from the fermentation of rice, and the comfortable smoking-houses, where they were puffing, not opium, which is almost unknown in Japan, but a very fine, stringy tobacco. He went on till he found himself in the fields, in the midst of vast rice plantations. There he saw dazzling camelias expanding themselves, with flowers which were giving forth their last colours and perfumes, not on bushes, but on trees; and within bamboo enclosures, cherry, plum, and apple trees, which the Japanese cultivate rather for their blossoms than their fruit, and which queerly-fashioned grinning scarecrows protected from the sparrows, pigeons, ravens, and other voracious birds. On the branches of the cedars were perched large eagles; amid the foliage of the weeping willows were herons, solemnly standing on one leg; and on every hand were crows, ducks, hawks, wild birds, and a multitude of cranes, which the Japanese consider sacred, and which to their minds symbolize long life and prosperity.

As he was strolling alone, Passepartout espied some violets among the shrubs.

'Good!' said he; 'I'll have some supper.'

But, on smelling them, he found that they were odourless.

'No chance there,' thought he.

The worthy fellow had certainly taken good care to eat as hearty a breakfast as possible before leaving the Carnatic; but as he had been walking about all day, the demands of hunger were becoming importunate. He observed that the butchers' stalls contained neither mutton, goat, nor pork; and knowing also that it is a sacrilege to kill cattle, which are preserved solely for farming, he made up his mind that meat was far from plentiful in Yokohama, – nor was he mistaken; and in default of butcher's meat, he could have wished for a quarter of wild boar or deer, a partridge, or some quails, some game or fish, which, with rice, the Japanese eat almost exclusively. But he found it necessary to keep up a stout heart, and to postpone the meal he craved till the following morning. Night came, and Passepartout re-entered the native quarter, where he wandered through the streets, lit by vari-coloured lanterns, looking on at the dancers who were executing skilful steps and boundings, and the astrologers who stood in the open air with their telescopes. Then he came to the harbour, which was lit up by the rosin torches of the fishermen, who were fishing from their boats.

The streets at last became quiet, and the patrol, the officers of which, in their splendid costumes, and surrounded by their suites, Passepartout thought seemed like ambassadors, succeeded the bustling crowd. Each time a company passed, Passepartout chuckled, and said to himself: 'Good! another Japanese embassy departing for Europe!'

Chapter Twenty-Three

In which Passepartout's nose becomes outrageously long.

THE NEXT MORNING POOR, jaded, famished Passepartout said to himself that he must get something to eat at all hazards, and the sooner he did so the better. He might, indeed, sell his watch; but he would have starved first. Now or never he must use the strong, if not melodious voice which nature had bestowed upon him. He knew several French and English songs, and resolved to try them upon the Japanese, who must be lovers of music, since they were for ever pounding their cymbals, tam-tams, and tambourines, and could not but appreciate European talent.

It was, perhaps, rather early in the morning to get up a concert, and the audience, prematurely aroused from their slumbers, might not, possibly pay their entertainer with coin bearing the Mikado's features. Passepartout therefore decided to wait several hours; and, as he was sauntering along, it occurred to him that he would seem rather too well dressed for a wandering artist. The idea struck him to change his garments for clothes more in harmony with his project; by which he might also get a little money to satisfy the immediate cravings of hunger. The resolution taken, it remained to carry it out.

It was only after a long search that Passepartout discovered a native dealer in old clothes, to whom he applied for an exchange. The man liked the European costume, and ere long Passepartout issued from his shop accoutred in an old Japanese coat, and a sort of one-sided turban, faded with long use. A few small pieces of silver, moreover, jingled in his pocket.

'Good!' thought he. 'I will imagine I am at the Carnival!'

His first care, after being thus 'Japanesed,' was to enter a tea-house of modest appearance, and upon half a bird and a little rice, to breakfast like a man for whom dinner was as yet a problem to be solved.

'Now,' thought he, when he had eaten heartily, 'I mustn't lose my head. I can't sell this costume again for one still more Japanese. I must consider how to leave this country of the Sun, of which I shall not retain the most delightful of memories, as quickly as possible.'

It occurred to him to visit the steamers which were about to leave for America. He would offer himself as a cook or servant, in payment of his passage and meals. Once at San Francisco, he would find some means of going on. The difficulty was, how to traverse the four thousand seven hundred miles of the Pacific which lay between Japan and the New World.

Passepartout was not the man to let an idea go begging, and directed his steps towards the docks. But, as he approached them, his project, which at first had seemed so simple, began to grow more and more formidable to his mind. What need would they have of a cook or servant on an American steamer, and what confidence would they put in him, dressed as he was? What references could he give?

As he was reflecting in this wise, his eyes fell upon an immense placard which a sort of clown was carrying through the streets. This placard, which was in English, read as follows:—

ACROBATIC JAPANESE TROUPE,
HONOURABLE WILLIAM BATULCAR, PROPRIETOR,
LAST REPRESENTATIONS,
PRIOR TO THEIR DEPARTURE TO THE UNITED STATES,
OF THE
LONG NOSES! LONG NOSES!
UNDER THE DIRECT PATRONAGE OF THE GOD TINGOU!
GREAT ATTRACTION!

'The United States!' said Passepartout; 'that's just what I want!'

He followed the clown, and soon found himself once more in the Japanese quarter. A quarter of an hour later he stopped before a large cabin, adorned with several clusters of streamers, the exterior walls of which were designed to represent, in violent colours and without perspective, a company of jugglers.

This was the Honourable William Batulcar's establishment. That gentleman was a sort of Barnum, the director of a troupe of mountebanks, jugglers, clowns, acrobats, equilibrists, and gymnasts, who, according to the placard, was giving his last performances before leaving the Empire of the Sun for the States of the Union.

Passepartout entered and asked for Mr. Batulcar, who straightway appeared in person.

'What do you want?' said he to Passepartout, whom he at first took for a native.

'Would you like a servant, sir?' asked Passepartout.

'A servant!' cried Mr. Batulcar, caressing the thick grey beard which hung from his chin. 'I already have two who are obedient and faithful, have never left me, and serve me for their nourishment, – and here they are,' added he, holding out his two robust arms, furrowed with veins as large as the strings of a bass-viol.

'So I can be of no use to you?'

'None.'

'The devil! I should so like to cross the Pacific with you!'

'Ah!' said the Honourable Mr. Batulcar. 'You are no more a Japanese than I am a monkey! Why are you dressed up in that way?'

'A man dresses as he can.'

'That's true. You are a Frenchman, aren't you?'

'Yes; a Parisian of Paris.'

'Then you ought to know how to make grimaces?'

'Why,' replied Passepartout, a little vexed that his nationality should cause this question; 'we Frenchmen know how to make grimaces, it is true, – but not any better than the Americans do.'

'True. Well, if I can't take you as a servant, I can as a clown. You see, my friend, in France they exhibit foreign clowns, and in foreign parts French clowns.'

'Ah!'

'You are pretty strong, eh?'

'Especially after a good meal.'

'And you can sing?'

'Yes,' returned Passepartout, who had formerly been wont to sing in the streets.

'But can you sing standing on your head, with a top spinning on your left foot, and a sabre balanced on your right?'

'Humph! I think so,' replied Passepartout, recalling the exercises of his younger days.

'Well, that's enough,' said the Honourable William Batulcar.

The engagement was concluded there and then.

Passepartout had at last found something to do. He was engaged to act in the celebrated Japanese troupe. It was not a very dignified position, but within a week he would be on his way to San Francisco.

The performance, so noisily announced by the Honourable Mr. Batulcar, was to commence at three o'clock, and soon the deafening instruments of a Japanese orchestra resounded at the door. Passepartout, though he had not been able to study or rehearse a part, was designated to lend the aid of his sturdy shoulders in the great exhibition of the 'human pyramid,' executed by the Long Noses of the god Tingou. This 'great attraction' was to close the performance.

Before three o'clock the large shed was invaded by the spectators, comprising Europeans and natives, Chinese and Japanese, men, women and children, who precipitated themselves upon the narrow benches and into the boxes opposite inside, and were vigorously performing on their gongs, tam-tams, flutes, bones, tambourines, and immense drums.

The performance was much like all acrobatic displays; but it must be confessed that the Japanese are the first equilibrists in the world.

One, with a fan and some bits of paper, performed the graceful trick of the butterflies and the flowers; another traced in the air, with the odorous smoke of his pipe, a series of blue words, which composed a compliment to the audience; while a third juggled with some lighted candles, which he extinguished successively as they passed his lips, and relit again without interrupting for an instant his juggling. Another reproduced the most singular combinations with a spinning-top; in his hands the revolving tops seemed to be animated with a life of their own in their interminable whirling; they ran over pipe-stems, the edges of sabres, wires, and even hairs stretched across the stage; they turned around on the edges of large glasses, crossed bamboo ladders, dispersed into all the corners, and produced strange musical effects by the combination of their various pitches of tone. The jugglers tossed them in the air, threw them like shuttlecocks with wooden battledores, and yet they kept on spinning; they put them into their pockets, and took them out still whirling as before.

It is useless to describe the astonishing performances of the acrobats and gymnasts. The turning on ladders, poles, balls, barrels, &c., was executed with wonderful precision.

But the principal attraction was the exhibition of the Long Noses, a show to which Europe is as yet a stranger.

The Long Noses form a peculiar company, under the direct patronage of the god Tingou. Attired after the fashion of the Middle Ages, they bore upon their shoulders a splendid pair of wings; but what especially distinguished them was the long noses which were fastened to their faces, and the uses which they made of them. These noses were made of bamboo, and were five, six, and even ten feet long, some straight, others curved, some ribboned, and some having imitation warts upon them. It was upon these appendages, fixed tightly on their real noses, that they performed their gymnastic exercises. A dozen of these sectaries of Tingou lay flat upon their backs, while others, dressed to represent lightning-rods, came and frolicked on their noses, jumping from one to another, and performing the most skilful leapings and somersaults.

As a last scene, a 'human pyramid' had been announced, in which fifty Long Noses were to represent the Car of Juggernaut. But, instead of forming a pyramid by mounting each other's shoulders, the artists were to group themselves on top of the noses. It happened that the performer who had hitherto formed the base of the Car had quitted the troup, and as, to fill this part, only strength and adroitness were necessary, Passepartout had been chosen to take his place.

The poor fellow really felt sad when – melancholy reminiscence of his youth! – he donned his costume, adorned with vari-coloured wings, and fastened to his natural feature a false nose six feet long. But he cheered up when he thought that this nose was winning him something to eat.

He went upon the stage, and took his place beside the rest who were to compose the base of the Car of Juggernaut. They all stretched themselves on the floor, their noses pointing to the ceiling. A second group of artists disposed themselves on these long appendages, then a third above these, then a fourth, until a human monument reaching to the very cornices of the theatre soon arose on top of the noses. This elicited loud applause in the midst of which the orchestra was just striking up a deafening air, when the pyramid tottered, the balance was lost, one of the lower noses vanished from the pyramid, and the human monument was shattered like a castle built of cards!

It was Passepartout's fault. Abandoning his position, clearing the footlights without the aid of his wings, and clambering up to the right-hand gallery, he fell at the feet of one of the spectators, crying, 'Ah, my master! my master!'

'You here?'

'Myself.'

'Very well; then let us go to the steamer, young man!'

Mr. Fogg, Aouda, and Passepartout passed through the lobby of the theatre to the outside, where they encountered the Honourable Mr. Batulcar, furious with rage. He demanded damages for the 'breakage' of the pyramid; and Phileas Fogg appeased him by giving him a handful of bank-notes.

At half-past six, the very hour of departure, Mr. Fogg and Aouda, followed by Passepartout, who in his hurry had retained his wings, and nose six feet long, stepped upon the American steamer.

Chapter Twenty-Four

During which Mr. Fogg and party cross the Pacific Ocean.

WHAT HAPPENED WHEN THE pilot-boat came in sight of Shanghai will be easily guessed. The signals made by the Tankadere had been seen by the captain of the Yokohama steamer, who, espying the flag at half-mast, had directed his course towards the little craft. Phileas Fogg, after paying the stipulated price of his passage to John Bunsby, and rewarding that worthy with the additional sum of five hundred and fifty pounds, ascended the steamer with Aouda and Fix; and they started at once for Nagasaki and Yokohama.

They reached their destination on the morning of the 14th of November. Phileas Fogg lost no time in going on board the Carnatic, where he learned, to Aouda's great delight – and perhaps to his own, though he betrayed no emotion – that Passepartout, a Frenchman, had really arrived on her the day before.

The San Francisco steamer was announced to leave that very evening, and it became necessary to find Passepartout, if possible, without delay. Mr. Fogg applied in vain to the French and English consuls, and, after wandering through the streets a long time, began to despair of finding his missing servant. Chance, or perhaps a kind of presentiment, at last led him into the Honourable Mr. Batulcar's theatre. He certainly would not have recognized Passepartout in the eccentric mountebank's costume; but the latter, lying on his back, perceived his master in the gallery. He could not help starting, which so changed the position of his nose as to bring the 'pyramid' pell-mell upon the stage.

All this Passepartout learned from Aouda, who recounted to him what had taken place on the voyage from Hong Kong to Shanghai on the Tankadere, in company with one Mr. Fix.

Passepartout did not change countenance on hearing this name. He thought that the time had not yet arrived to divulge to his master what had taken place between the detective and himself; and in the account he gave of his absence, he simply excused himself for having been overtaken by drunkenness, in smoking opium at a tavern in Hong Kong.

Mr. Fogg heard this narrative coldly, without a word; and then furnished his man with funds necessary to obtain clothing more in harmony with his position. Within an hour the Frenchman had cut off his nose and parted with his wings, and retained nothing about him which recalled the sectary of the god Tingou.

The steamer which was about to depart from Yokohama to San Francisco belonged to the Pacific Mail Steamship Company, and was named the General Grant. She was a large paddle-wheel steamer of two thousand five hundred tons, well equipped and very fast. The massive walking-beam rose and fell above the deck; at one end a piston-rod worked up and down; and at the other was a connecting-rod which, in changing the rectilinear motion to a circular one, was directly connected with the shaft of the paddles. The General Grant was rigged with three masts, giving a large capacity for sails, and thus materially aiding the steam power. By making twelve miles an hour, she would cross the ocean in twenty-one days. Phileas Fogg was therefore justified in hoping that he would reach San Francisco by the 2nd of December, New York by the 11th, and London on the 20th, – thus gaining several hours on the fatal date of the 21st of December.

There was a full complement of passengers on board, among them English, many Americans, a large number of Coolies on their way to California, and several East Indian officers, who were spending their vacation in making the tour of the world. Nothing of moment happened on the voyage; the steamer, sustained on its large paddles, rolled but little, and the Pacific almost justified its name. Mr. Fogg was as calm and taciturn as ever. His young companion felt herself more and more attached to him by other ties than gratitude; his silent but generous nature impressed her more than she thought; and it was almost unconsciously that she yielded to emotions which did not seem to have the least effect upon her protector. Aouda took the keenest interest in his plans, and became impatient at any incident which seemed likely to retard his journey.

She often chatted with Passepartout, who did not fail to perceive the state of the lady's heart; and, being the most faithful of domestics, he never exhausted his eulogies of Phileas Fogg's honesty, generosity, and devotion. He took pains to calm Aouda's doubts of a successful termination of the journey, telling her that the most difficult part of it had passed, and now they were beyond the fantastic countries of Japan and China, and were fairly on their way to civilized places again. A railway train from San Francisco to New York, and a transatlantic steamer from New York to Liverpool, would doubtless bring them to the end of this impossible journey round the world within the period agreed upon.

On the ninth day after leaving Yokohama, Phileas Fogg had traversed exactly one half of the terrestrial globe. The General Grant passed, on the 23rd of November, the one hundred and eightieth meridian, and was at the very antipodes of London. Mr. Fogg had, it is true, exhausted fifty-two of the eighty days in which he was to complete the tour, and there were only twenty-eight left. But, though he was only half-way by the difference of the meridians, he had really gone over two-thirds of the whole journey; for he had been obliged to make long circuits from London to Aden, from Aden to Bombay, from Calcutta to Singapore, and from Singapore to Yokohama. Could he have followed without deviation the fiftieth parallel, which is that of London, the whole distance would only have been about twelve thousand miles; whereas he would be forced, by the irregular methods of locomotion, to traverse twenty-six thousand, of which he had, on the 23rd of November, accomplished seventeen thousand five hundred. And now the course was a straight one, and Fix was no longer there to put obstacles in their way!

It happened also, on the 23rd of November, that Passepartout made a joyful discovery. It will be remembered that the obstinate fellow had insisted on keeping his famous family watch at London time, and on regarding that of the countries he had passed through as quite false and unreliable. Now, on this day, though he had not changed the hands, he found that his watch exactly agreed with the ship's chronometers. His triumph was hilarious. He would have liked to know what Fix would say if he were aboard!

'The rogue told me a lot of stories,' repeated Passepartout, 'about the meridians, the sun, and the moon! Moon, indeed! moonshine more likely! If one listened to that sort of people, a pretty sort of time one would keep! I was sure that the sun would some day regulate itself by my watch!'

Passepartout was ignorant that, if the face of his watch had been divided into twenty-four hours, like the Italian clocks, he would have no reason for exultation; for the hands of his watch would then, instead of as now indicating nine o'clock in the morning, indicate nine o'clock in the evening, that is the twenty-first hour after midnight, – precisely the difference between London time and that of the one hundred and eightieth meridian. But if Fix had been able to explain this purely physical effect, Passepartout would not have admitted, even if he had comprehended it. Moreover, if the detective had been on board at that moment, Passepartout would have joined issue with him on a quite different subject, and in an entirely different manner.

Where was Fix at that moment?

He was actually on board the General Grant.

On reaching Yokohama, the detective, leaving Mr. Fogg, whom he expected to meet again during the day, had repaired at once to the English consulate, where he at last found the warrant of arrest. It had followed him from Bombay, and had come by the Carnatic, on which steamer he himself was supposed to be. Fix's disappointment may be imagined when he reflected that the warrant was now useless. Mr. Fogg had left English ground, and it was now necessary to procure his extradition!

'Well,' thought Fix, after a moment of anger, 'my warrant is not good here, but it will be in England. The rogue evidently intends to return to his country, thinking he has thrown the police off his track. Good! I will follow him across the Atlantic. As for the money, Heaven grant there may be some left! But the fellow has already spent in travelling, rewards, trials, bail, elephants, and all sorts of charges, more than five thousand pounds. Yet, after all, the Bank is rich!'

His course decided on, he went on board the General Grant, and was there when Mr. Fogg and Aouda arrived. To his utter amazement, he recognized Passepartout, despite his theatrical disguise. He quickly concealed himself in his cabin, to avoid an awkward explanation, and hoped – thanks to the number of passengers – to remain unperceived by Mr. Fogg's servant.

On that very day, however, he met Passepartout face to face on the forward deck. The latter, without a word, made a rush for him, grasped him by the throat, and, much to the amusement of a group of Americans, who immediately began to bet on him, administered to the detective a perfect volley of blows, which proved the great superiority of French over English pugilistic skill.

When Passepartout had finished, he found himself relieved and comforted. Fix got up in a somewhat rumpled condition, and, looking at his adversary, coldly said, 'Have you done?'

'For this time – yes.'

'Then let me have a word with you.'

'But I——'

'In your master's interest.'

Passepartout seemed to be vanquished by Fix's coolness, for he quietly followed him, and they sat down aside from the rest of the passengers.

'You have given me a thrashing,' said Fix. 'Good. I expected it. Now, listen to me. Up to this time I have been Mr. Fogg's adversary. I am now in his game.'

'Aha!' cried Passepartout; 'you are convinced he is an honest man?'

'No,' replied Fix coldly, 'I think him a rascal. Sh! don't budge, and let me speak. As long as Mr. Fogg was on English ground, it was for my interest to detain him there until my warrant of arrest arrived. I did everything I could to keep him back. I sent the Bombay priests after him, I got you intoxicated at Hong Kong, I separated you from him, and I made him miss the Yokohama steamer.'

Passepartout listened, with closed fists.

'Now,' resumed Fix, 'Mr. Fogg seems to be going back to England. Well, I will follow him there. But hereafter I will do as much to keep obstacles out of his way as I have done up to this time to put them in his path. I've changed my game, you see, and simply because it was for my interest to change it. Your interest is the same as mine; for it is only in England that you will ascertain whether you are in the service of a criminal or an honest man.'

Passepartout listened very attentively to Fix, and was convinced that he spoke with entire good faith.

'Are we friends?' asked the detective.

'Friends? – no,' replied Passepartout; 'but allies, perhaps. At the least sign of treason, however, I'll twist your neck for you.'

'Agreed,' said the detective quietly.

Eleven days later, on the 3rd of December, the General Grant entered the bay of the Golden Gate, and reached San Francisco.

Mr. Fogg had neither gained nor lost a single day.

Chapter Twenty-Five

In which a slight glimpse is had of San Francisco.

IT WAS SEVEN IN THE morning when Mr. Fogg, Aouda, and Passepartout set foot upon the American continent, if this name can be given to the floating quay upon which they disembarked. These quays, rising and falling with the tide, thus facilitate the loading and unloading of vessels. Alongside them were clippers of all sizes, steamers of all nationalities, and the steamboats, with several decks rising one above the other, which ply on the Sacramento and its tributaries. There were also heaped up the products of a commerce which extends to Mexico, Chile, Peru, Brazil, Europe, Asia, and all the Pacific islands.

Passepartout, in his joy on reaching at last the American continent, thought he would manifest it by executing a perilous vault in fine style; but, tumbling upon some worm-eaten planks, he fell through them. Put out of countenance by the manner in which he thus 'set foot' upon the New World, he uttered a loud cry, which so frightened the innumerable cormorants and pelicans that are always perched upon these movable quays, that they flew noisily away.

Mr. Fogg, on reaching shore, proceeded to find out at what hour the first train left for New York, and learned that this was at six o'clock p.m.; he had, therefore, an entire day to spend in the Californian capital. Taking a carriage at a charge of three dollars, he and Aouda entered it, while Passepartout mounted the box beside the driver, and they set out for the International Hotel.

From his exalted position Passepartout observed with much curiosity the wide streets, the low, evenly ranged houses, the Anglo-Saxon Gothic churches, the great docks, the palatial wooden and brick warehouses, the numerous conveyances, omnibuses, horse-cars, and upon the side-walks, not only Americans and Europeans, but Chinese and Indians. Passepartout was surprised at all he saw. San Francisco was no longer the legendary city of 1849 – a city of banditti, assassins, and incendiaries, who had flocked hither in crowds in pursuit of plunder; a paradise of outlaws, where they gambled with gold-dust, a revolver in one hand and a bowie-knife in the other: it was now a great commercial emporium.

The lofty tower of its City Hall overlooked the whole panorama of the streets and avenues, which cut each other at right angles, and in the midst of which appeared pleasant, verdant squares, while beyond appeared the Chinese quarter, seemingly imported from the Celestial Empire in a toy-box. Sombreros and red shirts and plumed Indians were rarely to be seen; but there were silk hats and black coats everywhere worn by a multitude of nervously active, gentlemanly-looking men. Some of the streets – especially Montgomery Street, which is to San Francisco what Regent Street is to London, the Boulevard des Italiens to Paris, and Broadway to New York – were lined with splendid and spacious stores, which exposed in their windows the products of the entire world.

When Passepartout reached the International Hotel, it did not seem to him as if he had left England at all.

The ground floor of the hotel was occupied by a large bar, a sort of restaurant freely open to all passers-by, who might partake of dried beef, oyster soup, biscuits, and cheese, without taking out their purses. Payment was made only for the ale, porter, or sherry which was drunk. This seemed 'very American' to Passepartout. The hotel refreshment-rooms were comfortable, and Mr. Fogg and Aouda, installing themselves at a table, were abundantly served on diminutive plates by negroes of darkest hue.

After breakfast, Mr. Fogg, accompanied by Aouda, started for the English consulate to have his passport *visaed*. As he was going out, he met Passepartout, who asked him if it would not do well, before taking the train, to purchase some dozens of Enfield rifles and Colt's revolvers. He had been listening to stories of attacks upon the trains by the Sioux and Pawnees. Mr. Fogg thought it a useless precaution, but told him to do as he thought best, and went on to the consulate.

He had not proceeded two hundred steps, however, when, 'by the greatest chance in the world,' he met Fix. The detective seemed wholly taken by surprise. What! Had Mr. Fogg and himself crossed the Pacific together, and not met on the steamer! At least Fix felt honoured to behold once more the gentleman to whom he owed so much, and as his business recalled him to Europe, he should be delighted to continue the journey in such pleasant company.

Mr. Fogg replied that the honour would be his; and the detective – who was determined not to lose sight of him – begged permission to accompany them in their walk about San Francisco – a request which Mr. Fogg readily granted.

They soon found themselves in Montgomery Street, where a great crowd was collected; the side-walks, street, horse-car rails, the shop-doors, the windows of the houses, and even the roofs, were full of people. Men were going about carrying large posters, and flags and streamers were floating in the wind; while loud cries were heard on every hand.

'Hurrah for Camerfield!'

'Hurrah for Mandiboy!'

It was a political meeting; at least so Fix conjectured, who said to Mr. Fogg, 'Perhaps we had better not mingle with the crowd. There may be danger in it.'

'Yes,' returned Mr. Fogg; 'and blows, even if they are political, are still blows.'

Fix smiled at this remark; and in order to be able to see without being jostled about, the party took up a position on the top of a flight of steps situated at the upper end of Montgomery Street. Opposite them, on the other side of the street, between a coal wharf and a petroleum warehouse, a large platform had been erected in the open air, towards which the current of the crowd seemed to be directed.

For what purpose was this meeting? What was the occasion of this excited assemblage? Phileas Fogg could not imagine. Was it to nominate some high official – a governor or member of Congress? It was not improbable, so agitated was the multitude before them.

Just at this moment there was an unusual stir in the human mass. All the hands were raised in the air. Some, tightly closed, seemed to disappear suddenly in the midst of the cries – an energetic way, no doubt, of casting a vote. The crowd swayed back, the banners and flags wavered, disappeared an instant, then reappeared in tatters. The undulations of the human surge reached the steps, while all the heads floundered on the surface like a sea agitated by a squall. Many of the black hats disappeared, and the greater part of the crowd seemed to have diminished in height.

'It is evidently a meeting,' said Fix, 'and its object must be an exciting one. I should not wonder if it were about the Alabama, despite the fact that that question is settled.'

'Perhaps,' replied Mr. Fogg simply.

'At least, there are two champions in presence of each other, the Honourable Mr. Camerfield and the Honourable Mr. Mandiboy.'

Aouda, leaning upon Mr. Fogg's arm, observed the tumultuous scene with surprise, while Fix asked a man near him what the cause of it all was. Before the man could reply, a fresh agitation arose; hurrahs and excited shouts were heard; the staffs of the banners began to be used as offensive weapons; and fists flew about in every direction. Thumps were exchanged from the tops of the carriages and omnibuses which had been blocked up in the crowd. Boots and shoes went whirling through the air, and Mr. Fogg thought he even heard the crack of revolvers mingling in the din. The rout approached the stairway, and flowed over the lower step. One of the parties had evidently been repulsed; but the mere lookers-on could not tell whether Mandiboy or Camerfield had gained the upper hand.

'It would be prudent for us to retire,' said Fix, who was anxious that Mr. Fogg should not receive any injury, at least until they got back to London. 'If there is any question about England in all this, and we were recognized, I fear it would go hard with us.'

'An English subject——' began Mr. Fogg.

He did not finish his sentence; for a terrific hubbub now arose on the terrace behind the flight of steps where they stood, and there were frantic shouts of, 'Hurrah for Mandiboy! Hip, hip, hurrah!'

It was a band of voters coming to the rescue of their allies, and taking the Camerfield forces in flank. Mr. Fogg, Aouda, and Fix found themselves between two fires; it was too late to escape. The torrent of men, armed with loaded canes and sticks, was irresistible. Phileas Fogg and Fix were roughly hustled in their attempts to protect their fair companion; the former, as cool as ever, tried to defend himself with the weapons which nature has placed at the end of every Englishman's arm, but in vain. A big brawny fellow with a red beard, flushed face, and broad shoulders, who seemed to be the chief of the band, raised his clenched fist to strike Mr. Fogg, whom he would have given a crushing blow, had not Fix rushed in and received it in his stead. An enormous bruise immediately made its appearance under the detective's silk hat, which was completely smashed in.

'Yankee!' exclaimed Mr. Fogg, darting a contemptuous look at the ruffian.

'Englishman!' returned the other. 'We will meet again!'

'When you please.'

'What is your name?'

'Phileas Fogg. And yours?'

Colonel Stamp Proctor.'

The human tide now swept by, after returning Fix, who speedily got upon his feet again, though with tattered clothes. Happily, he was not seriously hurt. His travelling overcoat was divided into two unequal parts, and his trousers resembled those of certain Indians, which fit less compactly than they are easy to put on. Aouda had escaped unharmed, and Fix alone bore marks of the fray in his black and blue bruise.

'Thanks,' said Mr. Fogg to the detective, as soon as they were out of the crowd.

'No thanks are necessary,' replied Fix; 'but let us go.'

'Where?'

'To a tailor's.'

Such a visit was, indeed, opportune. The clothing of both Mr. Fogg and Fix was in rags, as if they had themselves been actively engaged in the contest between Camerfield and Mandiboy. An hour after, they were once more suitably attired, and with Aouda returned to the International Hotel.

Passepartout was waiting for his master, armed with half-a-dozen six-barrelled revolvers. When he perceived Fix, he knit his brows; but Aouda having, in a few words, told him of their adventure, his countenance resumed its placid expression. Fix evidently was no longer an enemy, but an ally; he was faithfully keeping his word.

Dinner over, the coach which was to convey the passengers and their luggage to the station drew up to the door. As he was getting in, Mr. Fogg said to Fix, 'You have not seen this Colonel Proctor again?'

'No.'

'I will come back to America to find him,' said Phileas Fogg calmly. 'It would not be right for an Englishman to permit himself to be treated in that way, without retaliating.'

The detective smiled, but did not reply. It was clear that Mr. Fogg was one of those Englishmen who, while they do not tolerate duelling at home, fight abroad when their honour is attacked.

At a quarter before six the travellers reached the station, and found the train ready to depart. As he was about to enter it, Mr. Fogg called a porter, and said to him: 'My friend, was there not some trouble to-day in San Francisco?'

'It was a political meeting, sir,' replied the porter.

'But I thought there was a great deal of disturbance in the streets.'

'It was only a meeting assembled for an election.'

'The election of a general-in-chief, no doubt?' asked Mr. Fogg.

'No, sir; of a justice of the peace.'

Phileas Fogg got into the train, which started off at full speed.

Chapter Twenty-Six

In which Phileas Fogg and party travel by the Pacific Railroad.

'FROM OCEAN TO OCEAN,' – so say the Americans; and these four words compose the general designation of the 'great trunk line' which crosses the entire width of the United States. The Pacific Railroad is, however, really divided into two distinct lines: the Central Pacific, between San Francisco and Ogden, and the Union Pacific, between Ogden and Omaha. Five main lines connect Omaha with New York.

New York and San Francisco are thus united by an uninterrupted metal ribbon, which measures no less than three thousand seven hundred and eighty-six miles. Between Omaha and the Pacific the railway crosses a territory which is still infested by Indians and wild beasts, and a large tract which the Mormons, after they were driven from Illinois in 1845, began to colonize.

The journey from New York to San Francisco consumed, formerly, under the most favourable conditions, at least six months. It is now accomplished in seven days.

It was in 1862 that, in spite of the Southern Members of Congress, who wished a more southerly route, it was decided to lay the road between the forty-first and forty-second parallels. President Lincoln himself fixed the end of the line at Omaha, in Nebraska. The work was at once commenced, and pursued with true American energy; nor did the rapidity with which it went on injuriously affect its good execution. The road grew, on the prairies, a mile and a half a day. A locomotive, running on the rails laid down the evening before, brought the rails to be laid on the morrow, and advanced upon them as fast as they were put in position.

The Pacific Railroad is joined by several branches in Iowa, Kansas, Colorado, and Oregon. On leaving Omaha, it passes along the left bank of the Platte River as far as the junction of its northern branch, follows its southern branch, crosses the Laramie territory and the Wahsatch Mountains, turns the Great Salt Lake, and reaches Salt Lake City, the Mormon capital, plunges into the Tuilla Valley, across the American Desert, Cedar and Humboldt Mountains, the Sierra Nevada, and descends, *viâ* Sacramento, to the Pacific – its grade, even on the Rocky Mountains, never exceeding one hundred and twelve feet to the mile.

Such was the road to be traversed in seven days, which would enable Phileas Fogg – at least, so he hoped – to take the Atlantic steamer at New York on the 11th for Liverpool.

The car which he occupied was a sort of long omnibus on eight wheels, and with no compartments in the interior. It was supplied with two rows of seats, perpendicular to the direction of the train on either side of an aisle which conducted to the front and rear platforms. These platforms were found throughout the train, and the passengers were able to pass from one end of the train to the other. It was supplied with saloon cars, balcony cars, restaurants, and smoking cars; theatre cars alone were wanting, and they will have these some day.

Books and news dealers, sellers of edibles, drinkables, and cigars, who seemed to have plenty of customers, were continually circulating in the aisles.

The train left Oakland station at six o'clock. It was already night, cold and cheerless, the heavens being overcast with clouds which seemed to threaten snow. The train did not proceed rapidly; counting the stoppages, it did not run more than twenty miles an hour, which was a sufficient speed, however, to enable it to reach Omaha within its designated time.

There was but little conversation in the car, and soon many of the passengers were overcome with sleep. Passepartout found himself beside the detective; but he did not talk to him. After recent events, their relations with each other had grown somewhat cold; there could no longer be mutual sympathy or intimacy between them. Fix's manner had not changed; but Passepartout was very reserved, and ready to strangle his former friend on the slightest provocation.

Snow began to fall an hour after they started, a fine snow, however, which happily could not obstruct the train; nothing could be seen from the windows but a vast, white sheet, against which the smoke of the locomotive had a greyish aspect.

At eight o'clock a steward entered the car and announced that the time for going to bed had arrived; and in a few minutes the car was transformed into a dormitory. The backs of the seats were thrown back, bedsteads carefully packed were rolled out by an ingenious system, berths were suddenly improvised, and each traveller had soon at his disposition a comfortable bed, protected from curious eyes by thick curtains. The sheets were clean and the pillows soft. It only remained to go to bed and sleep – which everybody did – while the train sped on across the State of California.

The country between San Francisco and Sacramento is not very hilly. The Central Pacific, taking Sacramento for its starting-point, extends eastward to meet the road from Omaha. The line from San Francisco to Sacramento runs in a north-easterly direction, along the American River, which empties into San Pablo Bay. The one hundred and twenty miles between these cities were accomplished in six hours, and towards midnight, while fast asleep, the travellers passed through Sacramento; so that they saw nothing of that important place, the seat of the State government, with its fine quays, its broad streets, its noble hotels, square, and churches.

The train, on leaving Sacramento, and passing the junction, Roclin, Auburn, and Colfax, entered the range of the Sierra Nevada. Cisco was reached at seven in the morning; and an hour later the dormitory was transformed into an ordinary car, and the travellers could observe the picturesque beauties of the mountain region through which they were steaming. The railway track wound in and out among the passes, now approaching the mountain sides, now suspended over precipices, avoiding abrupt angles by bold curves, plunging into narrow defiles, which seemed to have no outlet. The locomotive, its great funnel emitting a weird light, with its sharp bell, and its cow-catcher extended like a spur, mingled its shrieks and bellowings with the noise of torrents and cascades, and twined its smoke among the branches of the gigantic pines.

There were few or no bridges or tunnels on the route. The railway turned around the sides of the mountains, and did not attempt to violate nature by taking the shortest cut from one point to another.

The train entered the State of Nevada through the Carson Valley about nine o'clock, going always north-easterly; and at midday reached Reno, where there was a delay of twenty minutes for breakfast.

From this point the road, running along Humboldt River, passed northward for several miles by its banks; then it turned eastward, and kept by the river until it reached the Humboldt Range, nearly at the extreme eastern limit of Nevada.

Having breakfasted, Mr. Fogg and his companions resumed their places in the car, and observed the varied landscape which unfolded itself as they passed along: the vast prairies, the mountains lining the horizon, and the creeks with their frothy, foaming streams. Sometimes a great herd of buffaloes, massing together in the distance, seemed like a movable dam. These innumerable multitudes of ruminating beasts often form an insurmountable obstacle to the passage of the trains; thousands of them have been seen passing over the track for hours together, in compact ranks. The locomotive is then forced to stop and wait till the road is once more clear.

This happened, indeed, to the train in which Mr. Fogg was travelling. About twelve o'clock a troop of ten or twelve thousand head of buffalo encumbered the track. The locomotive, slackening in speed, tried to clear the way with its cow-catcher; but the mass of animals was too great. The buffaloes marched along with a tranquil gait, uttering now and then deafening bellowings. There was no use of interrupting them, for, having taken a particular direction, nothing can moderate and change their course; it is a torrent of living flesh which no dam could contain.

The travellers gazed on this curious spectacle from the platforms; but Phileas Fogg, who had the most reason of all to be in a hurry, remained in his seat, and waited philosophically until it should please the buffaloes to get out of the way.

Passepartout was furious at the delay they occasioned and longed to discharge his arsenal of revolvers upon them.

'What a country!' cried he. 'Mere cattle stop the trains, and go by in a procession, just as if they were not impeding travel! Parbleu! I should like to know if Mr. Fogg foresaw *this* mishap in his programme! And here's an engineer who doesn't dare to run the locomotive into this herd of beasts!'

The engineer did not try to overcome the obstacle, and he was wise. He would have crushed the first buffaloes, no doubt, with the cow-catcher; but the locomotive, however powerful, would soon have been checked, the train would inevitably have been thrown off the track, and would then have been helpless.

The best course was to wait patiently, and regain the lost time by greater speed when the obstacle was removed. The procession of buffaloes lasted three full hours, and it was night before the track was clear. The last ranks of the herd were now passing over the rails, while the first had already disappeared below the southern horizon.

It was eight o'clock when the train passed through the defiles of the Humboldt Range, and half-past nine when it penetrated Utah, the region of the Great Salt Lake, the singular colony of the Mormons.

Chapter Twenty-Seven

In which Passepartout undergoes, at a speed of twenty miles an hour, a course of Mormon history.

DURING THE NIGHT OF the 5th of December, the train ran south-easterly for about fifty miles; then rose an equal distance in a north-easterly direction, towards the Great Salt Lake.

Passepartout, about nine o'clock, went out upon the platform to take the air. The weather was cold, the heavens grey, but it was not snowing. The sun's disc, enlarged by the mist, seemed an enormous ring of gold, and Passepartout was amusing himself by calculating its value in pounds sterling, when he was diverted from this interesting study by a strange-looking personage who made his appearance on the platform.

This personage, who had taken the train at Elko, was tall and dark, with black moustaches, black stockings, a black silk hat, a black waistcoat, black trousers, a white cravat, and dogskin gloves. He might have been taken for a clergyman. He went from one end of the train to the other, and affixed to the door of each car a notice written in manuscript.

Passepartout approached and read one of these notices, which stated that Elder William Hitch, Mormon missionary, taking advantage of his presence on train No. 48, would deliver a lecture on Mormonism in car No. 117, from eleven to twelve o'clock; and that he invited all who were desirous of being instructed concerning the mysteries of the religion of the 'Latter Day Saints' to attend.

'I'll go,' said Passepartout to himself. He knew nothing of Mormonism except the custom of polygamy, which is its foundation.

The news spread quickly through the train, which contained about one hundred passengers, thirty of whom, at most, attracted by the notice, ensconced themselves in car No. 117. Passepartout took one of the front seats. Neither Mr. Fogg nor Fix cared to attend.

At the appointed hour Elder William Hitch rose, and, in an irritated voice, as if he had already been contradicted, said, 'I tell you that Joe Smith is a martyr, that his brother Hiram is a martyr; and that the persecutions of the United

States government against the prophets will also make a martyr of Brigham Young. Who dares to say the contrary?'

No one ventured to gainsay the missionary, whose excited tone contrasted curiously with his naturally calm visage. No doubt his anger arose from the hardships to which the Mormons were actually subjected. The government had just succeeded, with some difficulty, in reducing these independent fanatics to its rule. It had made itself master of Utah, and subjected that territory to the laws of the Union, after imprisoning Brigham Young on a charge of rebellion and polygamy. The disciples of the prophet had since redoubled their efforts, and resisted, by words at least, the authority of Congress. Elder Hitch, as is seen, was trying to make proselytes on the very railway trains.

Then, emphasizing his words with his loud voice and frequent gestures, he related the history of the Mormons from Biblical times: how that, in Israel, a Mormon prophet of the tribe of Joseph published the annals of the new religion, and bequeathed them to his son Mormon; how, many centuries later, a translation of this precious book, which was written in Egyptian, was made by Joseph Smith, Junior, a Vermont farmer, who revealed himself as a mystical prophet in 1825; and how, in short, the celestial messenger appeared to him in an illuminated forest, and gave him the annals of the Lord.

Several of the audience, not being much interested in the missionary's narrative, here left the car; but Elder Hitch, continuing his lecture, related how Smith, Junior, with his father, two brothers, and a few disciples, founded the church of the 'Latter Day Saints,' which, adopted not only in America, but in England, Norway and Sweden, and Germany, counts many artisans, as well as men engaged in the liberal professions, among its members; how a colony was established in Ohio, a temple erected there at a cost of two hundred thousand dollars, and a town built at Kirkland; how Smith became an enterprising banker, and received from a simple mummy showman a papyrus scroll written by Abraham and several famous Egyptians.

The Elder's story became somewhat wearisome, and his audience grew gradually less, until it was reduced to twenty passengers. But this did not disconcert the enthusiast, who proceeded with the story of Joseph Smith's bankruptcy in 1837, and how his ruined creditors gave him a coat of tar and feathers; his reappearance some years afterwards, more honourable and honoured than ever, at Independence, Missouri, the chief of a flourishing colony of three thousand disciples, and his pursuit thence by outraged Gentiles, and retirement into the Far West.

Ten hearers only were now left, among them honest Passepartout, who was listening with all his ears. Thus he learned that, after long persecutions, Smith reappeared in Illinois, and in 1839 founded a community at Nauvoo, on the Mississippi, numbering twenty-five thousand souls, of which he became mayor, chief justice, and general-in-chief; that he announced himself, in 1843, as a candidate for the Presidency of the United States; and that finally, being drawn into ambuscade at Carthage, he was thrown into prison, and assassinated by a band of men disguised in masks.

Passepartout was now the only person left in the car, and the Elder, looking him full in the face, reminded him that, two years after the assassination of Joseph Smith, the inspired prophet, Brigham Young, his successor, left Nauvoo for the banks of the Great Salt Lake, where, in the midst of that fertile region, directly on the route of the emigrants who crossed Utah on their way to California, the new colony, thanks to the polygamy practised by the Mormons, had flourished beyond expectation.

'And this,' added Elder William Hitch, 'this is why the jealousy of Congress has been aroused against us! Why have the soldiers of the Union invaded the soil of Utah? Why has Brigham Young, our chief, been imprisoned, in contempt of all justice? Shall we yield to force? Never! Driven from Vermont, driven from Illinois, driven from Ohio, driven from Missouri, driven from Utah, we shall yet find some independent territory on which to plant our tents. And you, my brother,' continued the Elder, fixing his angry eye upon his single auditor, 'will you not plant yours there, too, under the shadow of our flag?'

'No!' replied Passepartout courageously, in his turn retiring from the car, and leaving the Elder to preach to vacancy.

During the lecture the train had been making good progress, and towards half-past twelve it reached the north-west border of the Great Salt Lake. Thence the passengers could observe the vast extent of this interior sea, which is also called the Dead Sea, and into which flows an American Jordan. It is a picturesque expanse, framed in lofty crags in large strata, encrusted with white salt, – a superb sheet of water, which was formerly of larger extent than now, its shores having encroached with the lapse of time, and thus at once reduced its breadth and increased its depth.

The Salt Lake, seventy miles long and thirty-five wide, is situated three miles eight hundred feet above the sea. Quite different from Lake Asphaltite, whose depression is twelve hundred feet below the sea, it contains considerable salt, and one quarter of the weight of its water is solid matter, its specific weight being 1170, and, after being distilled, 1000. Fishes are of course unable to live in it, and those which descend through the Jordan, the Weber, and other streams, soon perish.

The country around the lake was well cultivated, for the Mormons are mostly farmers; while ranches and pens for domesticated animals, fields of wheat, corn, and other cereals, luxuriant prairies, hedges of wild rose, clumps of acacias and milk-wort, would have been seen six months later. Now the ground was covered with a thin powdering of snow.

The train reached Ogden at two o'clock, where it rested for six hours. Mr. Fogg and his party had time to pay a visit to Salt Lake City, connected with Ogden by a branch road; and they spent two hours in this strikingly American town, built on the pattern of other cities of the Union, like a chequer-board, 'with the sombre sadness of right angles,' as Victor Hugo expresses it. The founder of the City of the Saints could not escape from the taste for symmetry which distinguishes the Anglo-Saxons. In this strange country, where the people are certainly not up to the level of their institutions, everything is done 'squarely,' – cities, houses, and follies.

The travellers, then, were promenading, at three o'clock, about the streets of the town built between the banks of the Jordan and the spurs of the Wahsatch Range. They saw few or no churches, but the prophet's mansion, the court-house, and the arsenal, blue-brick houses with verandas and porches, surrounded by gardens bordered with acacias, palms, and locusts. A clay and pebble wall, built in 1853, surrounded the town; and in the principal street were the market and several hotels adorned with pavilions. The place did not seem thickly populated. The streets were almost deserted, except in the vicinity of the Temple, which they only reached after having traversed several quarters surrounded by palisades. There were many women, which was easily accounted for by the 'peculiar institution' of the Mormons; but it must not be supposed that all the Mormons are polygamists. They are free to marry or not, as they please; but it is worth noting that it is mainly the female citizens of Utah who are anxious to marry, as, according to the Mormon religion, maiden ladies are not admitted to the possession of its highest joys. These poor creatures seemed to be neither well off nor happy. Some – the more well-to-do, no doubt – wore short, open black silk dresses, under a hood or modest shawl; others were habited in Indian fashion.

Passepartout could not behold without a certain fright these women, charged, in groups, with conferring happiness on a single Mormon. His common sense pitied, above all, the husband. It seemed to him a terrible thing to have to guide so many wives at once across the vicissitudes of life, and to conduct them, as it were, in a body to the Mormon paradise, with the prospect of seeing them in the company of the glorious Smith, who doubtless was the chief ornament of that delightful place, to all eternity. He felt decidedly repelled from such a vocation, and he imagined – perhaps he was mistaken – that the fair ones of Salt Lake City cast rather alarming glances on his person. Happily, his stay there was but brief. At four the party found themselves again at the station, took their places in the train, and the whistle sounded for starting. Just at the moment, however, that the locomotive wheels began to move, cries of 'Stop! stop!' were heard.

Trains, like time and tide, stop for no one. The gentleman who uttered the cries was evidently a belated Mormon. He was breathless with running. Happily for him, the station had neither gates nor barriers. He rushed along the track, jumped on the rear platform of the train, and fell exhausted into one of the seats.

Passepartout, who had been anxiously watching this amateur gymnast, approached him with lively interest, and learned that he had taken flight after an unpleasant domestic scene.

When the Mormon had recovered his breath, Passepartout ventured to ask him politely how many wives he had; for, from the manner in which he had decamped, it might be thought that he had twenty at least.

'One, sir,' replied the Mormon, raising his arms heavenward, – 'one, and that was enough!'

Chapter Twenty-Eight

In which Passepartout does not succeed in making anybody listen to reason.

THE TRAIN, ON LEAVING Great Salt Lake at Ogden, passed northward for an hour as far as Weber River, having completed nearly nine hundred miles from San Francisco. From this point it took an easterly direction towards the jagged Wahsatch Mountains. It was in the section included between this range and the Rocky Mountains that the American engineers found the most formidable difficulties in laying the road, and that the government granted a subsidy of forty-eight thousand dollars per mile, instead of sixteen thousand allowed for the work done on the plains. But the engineers, instead of violating nature, avoided its difficulties by winding around, instead of penetrating the rocks. One tunnel only, fourteen thousand feet in length, was pierced in order to arrive at the great basin.

The track up to this time had reached its highest elevation at the Great Salt Lake. From this point it described a long curve, descending towards Bitter Creek Valley, to rise again to the dividing ridge of the waters between the Atlantic and the Pacific. There were many creeks in this mountainous region, and it was necessary to cross Muddy Creek, Green Creek, and others, upon culverts.

Passepartout grew more and more impatient as they went on, while Fix longed to get out of this difficult region, and was more anxious than Phileas Fogg himself to be beyond the danger of delays and accidents, and set foot on English soil.

At ten o'clock at night the train stopped at Fort Bridger station, and twenty minutes later entered Wyoming Territory, following the valley of Bitter Creek throughout. The next day, December 7th, they stopped for a quarter of an hour at Green River station. Snow had fallen abundantly during the night, but, being mixed with rain, it had half melted, and did not interrupt their progress. The bad weather, however, annoyed Passepartout; for the accumulation of snow, by blocking the wheels of the cars, would certainly have been fatal to Mr. Fogg's tour.

'What an idea!' he said to himself. 'Why did my master make this journey in winter? Couldn't he have waited for the good season to increase his chances?'

While the worthy Frenchman was absorbed in the state of the sky and the depression of the temperature, Aouda was experiencing fears from a totally different cause.

Several passengers had got off at Green River, and were walking up and down the platforms; and among these Aouda recognized Colonel Stamp Proctor, the same who had so grossly insulted Phileas Fogg at the San Francisco meeting. Not wishing to be recognized, the young woman drew back from the window, feeling much alarm at her discovery. She was attached to the man who, however coldly, gave her daily evidences of the most absolute devotion. She did not

comprehend, perhaps, the depth of the sentiment with which her protector
inspired her, which she called gratitude, but which, though she was unconscious
of it, was really more than that. Her heart sank within her when she recognized
the man whom Mr. Fogg desired, sooner or later, to call to account for his
conduct. Chance alone, it was clear, had brought Colonel Proctor on this train;
but there he was, and it was necessary, at all hazards, that Phileas Fogg should
not perceive his adversary.

Aouda seized a moment when Mr. Fogg was asleep to tell Fix and Passepartout
whom she had seen.

'That Proctor on this train!' cried Fix. 'Well, reassure yourself, madam; before
he settles with Mr. Fogg, he has got to deal with me! It seems to me that I was
the more insulted of the two.'

'And besides,' added Passepartout, 'I'll take charge of him, colonel as he is.'

'Mr. Fix,' resumed Aouda, 'Mr. Fogg will allow no one to avenge him. He said
that he would come back to America to find this man. Should he perceive
Colonel Proctor, we could not prevent a collision which might have terrible
results. He must not see him.'

'You are right, madam,' replied Fix; 'a meeting between them might ruin all.
Whether he were victorious or beaten, Mr. Fogg would be delayed, and——'

'And,' added Passepartout, 'that would play the game of the gentlemen of the
Reform Club. In four days we shall be in New York. Well, if my master does not
leave this car during those four days, we may hope that chance will not bring
him face to face with this confounded American. We must, if possible, prevent
his stirring out of it.'

The conversation dropped. Mr. Fogg had just woke up, and was looking out of
the window. Soon after Passepartout, without being heard by his master or
Aouda, whispered to the detective, 'Would you really fight for him?'

'I would do anything,' replied Fix, in a tone which betrayed determined will,
'to get him back living to Europe!'

Passepartout felt something like a shudder shoot through his frame, but his
confidence in his master remained unbroken.

Was there any means of detaining Mr. Fogg in the car, to avoid a meeting
between him and the colonel? It ought not to be a difficult task, since that
gentleman was naturally sedentary and little curious. The detective, at least,
seemed to have found a way; for, after a few moments, he said to Mr. Fogg,
'These are long and slow hours, sir, that we are passing on the railway.'

'Yes,' replied Mr. Fogg; 'but they pass.'

'You were in the habit of playing whist,' resumed Fix, 'on the steamers.'

'Yes; but it would be difficult to do so here. I have neither cards nor partners.'

'Oh, but we can easily buy some cards, for they are sold on all the American
trains. And as for partners, if madam plays——'

'Certainly, sir,' Aouda quickly replied; 'I understand whist. It is part of an
English education.'

'I myself have some pretensions to playing a good game. Well, here are three
of us, and a dummy——'

'As you please, sir,' replied Phileas Fogg, heartily glad to resume his favourite
pastime – even on the railway.

Passepartout was despatched in search of the steward, and soon returned with
two packs of cards, some pins, counters, and a shelf covered with cloth.

The game commenced. Aouda understood whist sufficiently well, and even received some compliments on her playing from Mr. Fogg. As for the detective, he was simply an adept, and worthy of being matched against his present opponent.

'Now,' thought Passepartout, 'we've got him. He won't budge.'

At eleven in the morning the train had reached the dividing ridge of the waters at Bridger Pass, seven thousand five hundred and twenty-four feet above the level of the sea, one of the highest points attained by the track in crossing the Rocky Mountains. After going about two hundred miles, the travellers at last found themselves on one of those vast plains which extend to the Atlantic, and which nature has made so propitious for laying the iron road.

On the declivity of the Atlantic basin the first streams, branches of the North Platte River, already appeared. The whole northern and eastern horizon was bounded by the immense semicircular curtain which is formed by the southern portion of the Rocky Mountains, the highest being Laramie Peak. Between this and the railway extended vast plains, plentifully irrigated. On the right rose the lower spurs of the mountainous mass which extends southward to the sources of the Arkansas River, one of the great tributaries of the Missouri.

At half-past twelve the travellers caught sight for an instant of Fort Halleck, which commands that section; and in a few more hours the Rocky Mountains were crossed. There was reason to hope, then, that no accident would mark the journey through this difficult country. The snow had ceased falling, and the air became crisp and cold. Large birds, frightened by the locomotive, rose and flew off in the distance. No wild beast appeared on the plain. It was a desert in its vast nakedness.

After a comfortable breakfast, served in the car, Mr. Fogg and his partners had just resumed whist, when a violent whistling was heard, and the train stopped. Passepartout put his head out of the door, but saw nothing to cause the delay; no station was in view.

Aouda and Fix feared that Mr. Fogg might take it into his head to get out; but that gentleman contented himself with saying to his servant, 'See what is the matter.'

Passepartout rushed out of the car. Thirty or forty passengers had already descended, amongst them Colonel Stamp Proctor.

The train had stopped before a red signal which blocked the way. The engineer and conductor were talking excitedly with a signal-man, whom the station-master at Medicine Bow, the next stopping place, had sent on before. The passengers drew around and took part in the discussion, in which Colonel Proctor, with his insolent manner, was conspicuous.

Passepartout, joining the group, heard the signal-man say, 'No! you can't pass. The bridge at Medicine Bow is shaky, and would not bear the weight of the train.'

This was a suspension-bridge thrown over some rapids, about a mile from the place where they now were. According to the signal-man, it was in a ruinous condition, several of the iron wires being broken; and it was impossible to risk the passage. He did not in any way exaggerate the condition of the bridge. It may be taken for granted that, rash as the Americans usually are, when they are prudent there is good reason for it.

Passepartout, not daring to apprise his master of what he heard, listened with set teeth, immovable as a statue.

'Hum!' cried Colonel Proctor; 'but we are not going to stay here, I imagine, and take root in the snow?'

'Colonel,' replied the conductor, 'we have telegraphed to Omaha for a train, but it is not likely that it will reach Medicine Bow in less than six hours.'

'Six hours!' cried Passepartout.

'Certainly,' returned the conductor. 'Besides, it will take us as long as that to reach Medicine Bow on foot.'

'But it is only a mile from here,' said one of the passengers.

'Yes, but it's on the other side of the river.'

'And can't we cross that in a boat?' asked the colonel.

'That's impossible. The creek is swelled by the rains. It is a rapid, and we shall have to make a circuit of ten miles to the north to find a ford.'

The colonel launched a volley of oaths, denouncing the railway company and the conductor; and Passepartout, who was furious, was not disinclined to make common cause with him. Here was an obstacle, indeed, which all his master's bank-notes could not remove.

There was a general disappointment among the passengers, who, without reckoning the delay, saw themselves compelled to trudge fifteen miles over a plain covered with snow. They grumbled and protested, and would certainly have thus attracted Phileas Fogg's attention if he had not been completely absorbed in his game.

Passepartout found that he could not avoid telling his master what had occurred, and, with hanging head he was turning towards the car, when the engineer – a true Yankee, named Forster – called out, 'Gentlemen, perhaps there is a way, after all, to get over.'

'On the bridge?' asked a passenger.

'On the bridge.'

'With our train?'

'With our train.'

Passepartout stopped short, and eagerly listed to the engineer.

'But the bridge is unsafe,' urged the conductor.

'No matter,' replied Forster; 'I think that by putting on the very highest speed we might have a chance of getting over.'

'The devil!' muttered Passepartout.

But a number of the passengers were at once attracted by the engineer's proposal, and Colonel Proctor was especially delighted, and found the plan a very feasible one. He told stories about engineers leaping their trains over rivers without bridges, by putting on full steam; and many of those present avowed themselves of the engineer's mind.

'We have fifty chances out of a hundred of getting over,' said one.

'Eighty! ninety!'

Passepartout was astounded, and, though ready to attempt anything to get over Medicine Creek, thought the experiment proposed a little too American. 'Besides,' thought he, 'there's still a more simple way, and it does not even occur to any of these people! Sir,' said he aloud to one of the passengers, 'the engineer's plan seems to me a little dangerous, but——'

'Eight chances!' replied the passenger, turning his back on him.

'I know it,' said Passepartout, turning to another passenger, 'but a simple idea——'

'Ideas are no use,' returned the American, shrugging his shoulders, 'as the engineer assures us that we can pass.'

'Doubtless,' urged Passepartout, 'we can pass, but perhaps it would be more prudent——'

'What! Prudent!' cried Colonel Proctor, whom this word seemed to excite prodigiously. 'At full speed, don't you see, at full speed!'

'I know – I see,' repeated Passepartout; 'but it would be, if not more prudent, since that word displeases you, at least more natural——'

'Who! What! What's the matter with this fellow?' cried several.

The poor fellow did not know to whom to address himself.

'Are you afraid?' asked Colonel Proctor.

'I afraid! Very well; I will show these people that a Frenchman can be as American as they!'

'All aboard!' cried the conductor.

'Yes, all aboard!' repeated Passepartout, and immediately. 'But they can't prevent me from thinking that it would be more natural for us to cross the bridge on foot, and let the train come after!'

But no one heard this sage reflection, nor would anyone have acknowledged its justice. The passengers resumed their places in the cars. Passepartout took his seat without telling what had passed. The whist-players were quite absorbed in their game.

The locomotive whistled vigorously; the engineer, reversing the steam, backed the train for nearly a mile – retiring, like a jumper, in order to take a longer leap. Then, with another whistle, he began to move forward; the train increased its speed, and soon its rapidity became frightful; a prolonged screech issued from the locomotive; the piston worked up and down twenty strokes to the second. They perceived that the whole train, rushing on at the rate of a hundred miles an hour, hardly bore upon the rails at all.

And they passed over! It was like a flash. No one saw the bridge. The train leaped, so to speak, from one bank to the other, and the engineer could not stop it until it had gone five miles beyond the station. But scarcely had the train passed the river, when the bridge, completely ruined, fell with a crash into the rapids of Medicine Bow.

Chapter Twenty-Nine

In which certain incidents are narrated which are only to be met with on American railroads.

THE TRAIN PURSUED ITS course, that evening, without interruption, passing Fort Saunders, crossing Cheyenne Pass, and reaching Evans Pass. The road here attained the highest elevation of the journey, eight thousand and ninety-one feet above the level of the sea. The travellers had now only to descend to the Atlantic by limitless plains, levelled by nature. A branch of the 'grand trunk' led off southward to Denver, the capital of Colorado. The country round about is rich in gold and silver, and more than fifty thousand inhabitants are already settled there.

Thirteen hundred and eighty-two miles had been passed over from San Francisco, in three days and three nights; four days and nights more would probably bring them to New York. Phileas Fogg was not as yet behindhand.

During the night Camp Walbach was passed on the left; Lodge Pole Creek ran parallel with the road, marking the boundary between the territories of Wyoming and Colorado. They entered Nebraska at eleven, passed near Sedgwick, and touched at Julesburg, on the southern branch of the Platte River.

It was here that the Union Pacific Railroad was inaugurated on the 23rd of October, 1867, by the chief engineer, General Dodge. Two powerful locomotives, carrying nine cars of invited guests, amongst whom was Thomas C. Durant, vice-president of the road, stopped at this point; cheers were given, the Sioux and Pawnees performed an imitation Indian battle, fireworks were let off, and the first number of the *Railway Pioneer* was printed by a press brought on the train. Thus was celebrated the inauguration of this great railroad, a mighty instrument of progress and civilisation, thrown across the desert, and destined to link together cities and towns which do not yet exist. The whistle of the locomotive, more powerful than Amphion's lyre, was about to bid them rise from American soil.

Fort McPherson was left behind at eight in the morning, and three hundred and fifty-seven miles had yet to be traversed before reaching Omaha. The road followed the capricious windings of the southern branch of the Platte River, on its left bank. At nine the train stopped at the important town of North Platte, built between the two arms of the river, which rejoin each other around it and form a single artery, – a large tributary whose waters empty into the Missouri a little above Omaha.

The one hundred and first meridian was passed.

Mr. Fogg and his partners had resumed their game; no one – not even the dummy – complained of the length of the trip. Fix had begun by winning several guineas, which he seemed likely to lose; but he showed himself a not less eager whist-player than Mr. Fogg. During the morning, chance distinctly favoured that gentleman. Trumps and honours were showered upon his hands.

Once, having resolved on a bold stroke, he was on the point of playing a spade, when a voice behind him said, 'I should play a diamond.'

Mr. Fogg, Aouda, and Fix raised their heads, and beheld Colonel Proctor.

Stamp Proctor and Phileas Fogg recognized each other at once.

'Ah! it's you, is it, Englishman?' cried the colonel; 'it's you who are going to play a spade!'

'And who plays it,' replied Phileas Fogg coolly, throwing down the ten of spades.

'Well, it pleases me to have it diamonds,' replied Colonel Proctor, in an insolent tone.

He made a movement as if to seize the card which had just been played, adding, 'You don't understand anything about whist.'

'Perhaps I do, as well as another,' said Phileas Fogg, rising.

'You have only to try, son of John Bull,' replied the colonel.

Aouda turned pale, and her blood ran cold. She seized Mr. Fogg's arm and gently pulled him back. Passepartout was ready to pounce upon the American, who was staring insolently at his opponent. But Fix got up, and going to Colonel Proctor said, 'You forget that it is I with whom you have to deal, sir; for it was I whom you not only insulted, but struck!'

'Mr. Fix,' said Mr. Fogg, 'pardon me, but this affair is mine, and mine only. The colonel has again insulted me, by insisting that I should not play a spade, and he shall give me satisfaction for it.'

'When and where you will,' replied the American, 'and with whatever weapon you choose.'

Aouda in vain attempted to retain Mr. Fogg; as vainly did the detective endeavour to make the quarrel his. Passepartout wished to throw the colonel out of the window, but a sign from his master checked him. Phileas Fogg left the car, and the American followed him upon the platform.

'Sir,' said Mr. Fogg to his adversary, 'I am in a great hurry to get back to Europe, and any delay whatever will be greatly to my disadvantage.'

'Well, what's that to me?' replied Colonel Proctor.

'Sir,' said Mr. Fogg, very politely; 'after our meeting at San Francisco, I determined to return to America and find you as soon as I had completed the business which called me to England.'

'Really!'

'Will you appoint a meeting for six months hence?'

'Why not ten years hence?'

'I say six months,' returned Phileas Fogg; 'and I shall be at the place of meeting promptly.'

'All this is an evasion,' cried Stamp Proctor. 'Now or never!'

'Very good. You are going to New York?'

'No.'

'To Chicago?'

'No.'

'To Omaha?'

'What difference is it to you? Do you know Plum Creek?'

'No,' replied Mr. Fogg.

'It's the next station. The train will be there in an hour, and will stop there ten minutes. In ten minutes several revolver-shots could be exchanged.'

'Very well,' said Mr. Fogg. 'I will stop at Plum Creek.'

'And I guess you'll stay there too,' added the American insolently.

'Who knows?' replied Mr. Fogg, returning to the car as coolly as usual. He began to reassure Aouda, telling her that blusterers were never to be feared, and begged Fix to be his second at the approaching duel, a request which the detective could not refuse. Mr. Fogg resumed the interrupted game with perfect calmness.

At eleven o'clock the locomotive's whistle announced that they were approaching Plum Creek station. Mr. Fogg rose, and, followed by Fix, went out upon the platform. Passepartout accompanied him, carrying a pair of revolvers. Aouda remained in the car, as pale as death.

The door of the next car opened, and Colonel Proctor appeared on the platform, attended by a Yankee of his own stamp as his second. But just as the combatants were about to step from the train, the conductor hurried up, and shouted, 'You can't get off, gentlemen!'

'Why not?' asked the colonel.

'We are twenty minutes late, and we shall not stop.'

'But I am going to fight a duel with this gentleman.'

'I am sorry,' said the conductor; 'but we shall be off at once. There's the bell ringing now.'

The train started.

'I'm really very sorry, gentlemen,' said the conductor. 'Under any other circumstances I should have been happy to oblige you. But, after all, as you have not had time to fight here, why not fight as we go along?'

'That wouldn't be convenient, perhaps, for this gentleman,' said the colonel, in a jeering tone.

'It would be perfectly so,' replied Phileas Fogg.

'Well, we are really in America,' thought Passepartout, 'and the conductor is a gentleman of the first order!'

So muttering, he followed his master.

The two combatants, their seconds, and the conductor passed through the cars to the rear of the train. The last car was only occupied by a dozen passengers, whom the conductor politely asked if they would not be so kind as to leave it vacant for a few moments, as two gentlemen had an affair of honour to settle. The passengers granted the request with alacrity, and straightway disappeared on the platform.

The car, which was some fifty feet long, was very convenient for their purpose. The adversaries might march on each other in the aisle, and fire at their ease. Never was duel more easily arranged. Mr. Fogg and Colonel Proctor, each provided with two six-barrelled revolvers, entered the car. The seconds, remaining outside, shut them in. They were to begin firing at the first whistle of the locomotive. After an interval of two minutes, what remained of the two gentlemen would be taken from the car.

Nothing could be more simple. Indeed, it was all so simple that Fix and Passepartout felt their hearts beating as if they would crack. They were listening for the whistle agreed upon, when suddenly savage cries resounded in the air, accompanied by reports which certainly did not issue from the car where the duellists were. The reports continued in front and the whole length of the train. Cries of terror proceeded from the interior of the cars.

Colonel Proctor and Mr. Fogg, revolvers in hand, hastily quitted their prison, and rushed forward where the noise was most clamorous. They then perceived that the train was attacked by a band of Sioux.

This was not the first attempt of these daring Indians, for more than once they had waylaid trains on the road. A hundred of them had, according to their habit, jumped upon the steps without stopping the train, with the ease of a clown mounting a horse at full gallop.

The Sioux were armed with guns, from which came the reports, to which the passengers, who were almost all armed, responded by revolver-shots.

The Indians had first mounted the engine, and half stunned the engineer and stoker with blows from their muskets. A Sioux chief, wishing to stop the train, but not knowing how to work the regulator, had opened wide instead of closing the steam-valve, and the locomotive was plunging forward with terrific velocity.

The Sioux had at the same time invaded the cars, skipping like enraged monkeys over the roofs, thrusting open the doors, and fighting hand to hand with the passengers. Penetrating the baggage-car, they pillaged it, throwing the trunks out of the train. The cries and shots were constant.

The travellers defended themselves bravely; some of the cars were barricaded, and sustained a siege, like moving forts, carried along at a speed of a hundred miles an hour.

Aouda behaved courageously from the first. She defended herself like a true heroine with a revolver, which she shot through the broken windows whenever a savage made his appearance. Twenty Sioux had fallen mortally wounded to the ground, and the wheels crushed those who fell upon the rails as if they had been worms. Several passengers, shot or stunned, lay on the seats.

It was necessary to put an end to the struggle, which had lasted for ten minutes, and which would result in the triumph of the Sioux if the train was not stopped. Fort Kearney station, where there was a garrison, was only two miles distant; but, that once passed, the Sioux would be masters of the train between Fort Kearney and the station beyond.

The conductor was fighting beside Mr. Fogg, when he was shot and fell. At the same moment he cried, 'Unless the train is stopped in five minutes, we are lost!'

'It shall be stopped,' said Phileas Fogg, preparing to rush from the car.

'Stay, monsieur,' cried Passepartout; 'I will go.'

Mr. Fogg had not time to stop the brave fellow, who, opening a door unperceived by the Indians, succeeded in slipping under the car; and while the struggle continued, and the balls whizzed across each other over his head, he made use of his old acrobatic experience, and with amazing agility worked his way under the cars, holding on to the chains, aiding himself by the brakes and edges of the sashes, creeping from one car to another with marvellous skill, and thus gaining the forward end of the train.

There, suspended by one hand between the baggage-car and the tender, with the other he loosened the safety chains; but, owing to the traction, he would never have succeeded in unscrewing the yoking-bar, had not a violent concussion jolted this bar out. The train, now detached from the engine, remained a little behind, whilst the locomotive rushed forward with increased speed.

Carried on by the force already acquired, the train still moved for several minutes; but the brakes were worked, and at last they stopped, less than a hundred feet from Kearney station.

The soldiers of the fort, attracted by the shots, hurried up; the Sioux had not expected them, and decamped in a body before the train entirely stopped.

But when the passengers counted each other on the station platform several were found missing; among others the courageous Frenchman, whose devotion had just saved them.

Chapter Thirty

In which Phileas Fogg simply does his duty.

THREE PASSENGERS – including Passepartout – had disappeared. Had they been killed in the struggle? Were they taken prisoners by the Sioux? It was impossible to tell.

There were many wounded, but none mortally. Colonel Proctor was one of the most seriously hurt; he had fought bravely, and a ball had entered his groin. He was carried into the station with the other wounded passengers, to receive such attention as could be of avail.

Aouda was safe; and Phileas Fogg, who had been in the thickest of the fight, had not received a scratch. Fix was slightly wounded in the arm. But Passepartout was not to be found, and tears coursed down Aouda's cheeks.

All the passengers had got out of the train, the wheels of which were stained with blood. From the tyres and spokes hung ragged pieces of flesh. As far as the eye could reach on the white plain behind, red trails were visible. The last Sioux were disappearing in the south, along the banks of Republican River.

Mr. Fogg, with folded arms, remained motionless. He had a serious decision to make. Aouda, standing near him, looked at him without speaking, and he understood her look. If his servant was a prisoner, ought he not to risk everything to rescue him from the Indians? 'I will find him, living or dead.' said he quietly to Aouda.

'Ah, Mr. – Mr. Fogg!' cried she, clasping his hands and covering them with tears.

'Living,' added Mr. Fogg, 'if we do not lose a moment.'

Phileas Fogg, by this resolution, inevitably sacrificed himself; he pronounced his own doom. The delay of a single day would make him lose the steamer at New York, and his bet would be certainly lost. But as he thought, 'It is my duty,' he did not hesitate.

The commanding officer of Fort Kearney was there. A hundred of his soldiers had placed themselves in a position to defend the station, should the Sioux attack it.

'Sir,' said Mr. Fogg to the captain, 'three passengers have disappeared.'

'Dead?' asked the captain.

'Dead or prisoners; that is the uncertainty which must be solved. Do you propose to pursue the Sioux?'

'That's a serious thing to do, sir,' returned the captain. 'These Indians may retreat beyond the Arkansas, and I cannot leave the fort unprotected.'

'The lives of three men are in question, sir,' said Phileas Fogg.

'Doubtless; but can I risk the lives of fifty men to save three?'

'I don't know whether you can, sir; but you ought to do so.'

'Nobody here,' returned the other, 'has a right to teach me my duty.'

'Very well,' said Mr. Fogg, coldly. 'I will go alone.'

'You, sir!' cried Fix, coming up; 'you go alone in pursuit of the Indians?'

'Would you have me leave this poor fellow to perish – him to whom every one present owes his life? I shall go.'

'No, sir, you shall not go alone,' cried the captain, touched in spite of himself. 'No! you are a brave man. Thirty volunteers!' he added, turning to the soldiers.

The whole company started forward at once. The captain had only to pick his men. Thirty were chosen, and an old sergeant placed at their head.

'Thanks, captain,' said Mr. Fogg.

'Will you let me go with you?' asked Fix.

'Do as you please, sir. But if you wish to do me a favour, you will remain with Aouda. In case anything should happen to me——'

A sudden pallor overspread the detective's face. Separate himself from the man whom he had so persistently followed step by step! Leave him to wander about in this desert! Fix gazed attentively at Mr. Fogg, and, despite his suspicions and of the struggle which was going on within him, he lowered his eyes before that calm and frank look.

'I will stay,' said he.

A few moments after, Mr. Fogg pressed the young woman's hand, and, having confided to her his precious carpet-bag, went off with the sergeant and his little squad. But, before going, he had said to the soldiers, 'My friends, I will divide five thousand dollars among you, if we save the prisoners.'

It was then a little past noon.

Aouda retired to a waiting-room, and there she waited alone, thinking of the simple and noble generosity, the tranquil courage of Phileas Fogg. He had sacrificed his fortune, and was now risking his life, all without hesitation, from duty, in silence.

Fix did not have the same thoughts, and could scarcely conceal his agitation. He walked feverishly up and down the platform, but soon resumed his outward composure. He now saw the folly of which he had been guilty in letting Fogg go alone. What! This man, whom he had just followed around the world, was permitted now to separate himself from him! He began to accuse and abuse himself, and, as if he were director of police, administered to himself a sound lecture for his greenness.

'I have been an idiot!' he thought, 'and this man will see it. He has gone, and won't come back! But how is it that I, Fix, who have in my pocket a warrant for his arrest, have been so fascinated by him? Decidedly, I am nothing but an ass!'

So reasoned the detective, while the hours crept by all too slowly. He did not know what to do. Sometimes he was tempted to tell Aouda all; but he could not doubt how the young woman would receive his confidences. What course should he take? He thought of pursuing Fogg across the vast white plains; it did not seem impossible that he might overtake him. Footsteps were easily printed on the snow! But soon, under a new sheet, every imprint would be effaced.

Fix became discouraged. He felt a sort of insurmountable longing to abandon the game altogether. He could now leave Fort Kearney station, and pursue his journey homeward in peace.

Towards two o'clock in the afternoon, while it was snowing hard, long whistles were heard approaching from the east. A great shadow, preceded by a wild light, slowly advanced, appearing still larger through the mist, which gave it a fantastic aspect. No train was expected from the east, neither had there been time for the succour asked for by telegraph to arrive; the train from Omaha to San Francisco was not due till the next day. The mystery was soon explained.

The locomotive, which was slowly approaching with deafening whistles, was that which, having been detached from the train, had continued its route with such terrific rapidity, carrying off the unconscious engineer and stoker. It had run several miles, when, the fire becoming low for want of fuel, the steam had slackened; and it had finally stopped an hour after, some twenty miles beyond Fort Kearney. Neither the engineer nor the stoker was dead, and, after remaining for some time in their swoon, had come to themselves. The train had then stopped. The engineer, when he found himself in the desert, and the locomotive without cars, understood what had happened. He could not imagine how the locomotive had become separated from the train; but he did not doubt that the train left behind was in distress.

He did not hesitate what to do. It would be prudent to continue on to Omaha, for it would be dangerous to return to the train, which the Indians might still be engaged in pillaging. Nevertheless, he began to rebuild the fire in the furnace; the pressure again mounted, and the locomotive returned, running backwards to Fort Kearney. This it was which was whistling in the mist.

The travellers were glad to see the locomotive resume its place at the head of the train. They could now continue the journey so terribly interrupted.

Aouda, on seeing the locomotive come up, hurried out of the station, and asked the conductor, 'Are you going to start?'

'At once, madam.'

'But the prisoners – our unfortunate fellow-travellers——'

'I cannot interrupt the trip,' replied the conductor. 'We are already three hours behind time.'

'And when will another train pass here from San Francisco?'

'To-morrow evening, madam.'

'To-morrow evening! But then it will be too late! We must wait——'

'It is impossible,' responded the conductor. 'If you wish to go, please get in.'

'I will not go,' said Aouda.

Fix had heard this conversation. A little while before, when there was no prospect of proceeding on the journey, he had made up his mind to leave Fort Kearney; but now that the train was there, ready to start, and he had only to take his seat in the car, an irresistible influence held him back. The station platform burned his feet, and he could not stir. The conflict in his mind again began; anger and failure stifled him. He wished to struggle on to the end.

Meanwhile the passengers and some of the wounded, among them Colonel Proctor, whose injuries were serious, had taken their places in the train. The buzzing of the overheated boiler was heard, and the steam was escaping from the valves. The engineer whistled, the train started, and soon disappeared, mingling its white smoke with the eddies of the densely falling snow.

The detective had remained behind.

Several hours passed. The weather was dismal, and it was very cold. Fix sat motionless on a bench in the station; he might have been thought asleep. Aouda, despite the storm, kept coming out of the waiting-room, going to the end of the platform, and peering through the tempest of snow, as if to pierce the mist which narrowed the horizon around her, and to hear, if possible, some welcome sound. She heard and saw nothing. Then she would return, chilled through, to issue out again after the lapse of a few moments, but always in vain.

Evening came, and the little band had not returned. Where could they be? Had they found the Indians, and were they having a conflict with them, or were they still wandering amid the mist? The commander of the fort was anxious, though he tried to conceal his apprehensions. As night approached, the snow fell less plentifully, but it became intensely cold. Absolute silence rested on the plains. Neither flight of bird nor passing of beast troubled the perfect calm.

Throughout the night Aouda, full of sad forebodings, her heart stifled with anguish, wandered about on the verge of the plains. Her imagination carried her far off, and showed her innumerable dangers. What she suffered through the long hours it would be impossible to describe.

Fix remained stationary in the same place, but did not sleep. Once a man approached and spoke to him, and the detective merely replied by shaking his head.

Thus the night passed. At dawn the half-extinguished disc of the sun rose above a misty horizon; but it was now possible to recognize objects two miles off. Phileas Fogg and the squad had gone southward; in the south all was still vacancy. It was then seven o'clock.

The captain, who was really alarmed, did not know what course to take.

Should he send another detachment to the rescue of the first? Should he sacrifice more men, with so few chances of saving those already sacrificed? His hesitation did not last long, however. Calling one of his lieutenants, he was on the point of ordering a reconnaissance, when gunshots were heard. Was it a signal? The soldiers rushed out of the fort, and half-a-mile off they perceived a little band returning in good order.

Mr. Fogg was marching at their head, and just behind him were Passepartout and the other two travellers, rescued from the Sioux.

They had met and fought the Indians ten miles south of Fort Kearney. Shortly before the detachment arrived, Passepartout and his companions had begun to struggle with their captors, three of whom the Frenchman had felled with his fists, when his master and the soldiers hastened up to their relief.

All were welcomed with joyful cries. Phileas Fogg distributed the reward he had promised to the soldiers, whilst Passepartout, not without reason, muttered to himself, 'It must certainly be confessed that I cost my master dear!'

Fix, without saying a word, looked at Mr. Fogg, and it would have been difficult to analyse the thoughts which struggled within him. As for Aouda, she took her protector's hand and pressed it in her own, too much moved to speak.

Meanwhile, Passepartout was looking about for the train; he thought he should find it there, ready to start for Omaha, and he hoped that the time lost might be regained.

'The train! the train!' cried he.

'Gone,' replied Fix.

'And when does the next train pass here?' said Phileas Fogg.

'Not till this evening.'

'Ah!' returned the impassible gentleman quietly.

Chapter Thirty-One

In which Fix the detective considerably furthers the interests of Phileas Fogg.

PHILEAS FOGG FOUND HIMSELF twenty hours behind time. Passepartout, the involuntary cause of this delay, was desperate. He had ruined his master!

At this moment the detective approached Mr. Fogg, and, looking him intently in the face, said—

'Seriously, sir, are you in great haste?'

'Quite seriously.'

'I have a purpose in asking,' resumed Fix. 'Is it absolutely necessary that you should be in New York on the 11th, before nine o'clock in the evening, the time that the steamer leaves for Liverpool?'

'It is absolutely necessary.'

'And, if your journey had not been interrupted by these Indians, you would have reached New York on the morning of the 11th?'

'Yes; with eleven hours to spare before the steamer left.'

'Good! you are therefore twenty hours behind. Twelve from twenty leaves eight. You must regain eight hours. Do you wish to try to do so?'

'On foot?' asked Mr. Fogg.

'No; on a sledge,' replied Fix. 'On a sledge with sails. A man has proposed such a method to me.'

It was the man who had spoken to Fix during the night, and whose offer he had refused.

Phileas Fogg did not reply at once; but Fix having pointed out the man, who was walking up and down in front of the station, Mr. Fogg went up to him. An instant after, Mr. Fogg and the American, whose name was Mudge, entered a hut built just below the fort.

There Mr. Fogg examined a curious vehicle, a kind of frame on two long beams, a little raised in front like the runners of a sledge, and upon which there was room for five or six persons. A high mast was fixed on the frame, held firmly by metallic lashings, to which was attached a large brigantine sail. This mast held an iron stay upon which to hoist a jib-sail. Behind, a sort of rudder served to guide the vehicle. It was, in short, a sledge rigged like a sloop. During the winter, when the trains are blocked up by the snow, these sledges make extremely rapid journeys across the frozen plains from one station to another. Provided with more sail than a cutter, and with the wind behind them, they slip over the surface of the prairies with a speed equal if not superior to that of the express trains.

Mr Fogg readily made a bargain with the owner of this landcraft. The wind was favourable, being fresh, and blowing from the west. The snow had hardened, and Mudge was very confident of being able to transport Mr. Fogg in a few hours to Omaha. Thence the trains eastward run frequently to Chicago and

New York. It was not impossible that the lost time might yet be recovered; and such an opportunity was not to be rejected.

Not wishing to expose Aouda to the discomforts of travelling in the open air, Mr. Fogg proposed to leave her with Passepartout at Fort Kearney, the servant taking upon himself to escort her to Europe by a better route and under more favourable conditions. But Aouda refused to separate from Mr. Fogg, and Passepartout was delighted with her decision; for nothing could induce him to leave his master while Fix was with him.

It would be difficult to guess the detective's thoughts. Was his conviction shaken by Phileas Fogg's return, or did he still regard him as an exceedingly shrewd rascal, who, his journey round the world completed, would think himself absolutely safe in England? Perhaps Fix's opinion of Phileas Fogg was somewhat modified; but he was nevertheless resolved to do his duty, and to hasten the return of the whole party to England as much as possible.

At eight o'clock the sledge was ready to start. The passengers took their places on it, and wrapped themselves up closely in their travelling-cloaks. The two great sails were hoisted, and under the pressure of the wind the sledge slid over the hardened snow with a velocity of forty miles an hour.

The distance between Fort Kearney and Omaha, as the birds fly, is at most two hundred miles. If the wind held good, the distance might be traversed in five hours; if no accident happened the sledge might reach Omaha by one o'clock.

What a journey! The travellers, huddled close together, could not speak for the cold, intensified by the rapidity at which they were going. The sledge sped on as lightly as a boat over the waves. When the breeze came skimming the earth the sledge seemed to be lifted off the ground by its sails. Mudge, who was at the rudder, kept in a straight line, and by a turn of his hand checked the lurches which the vehicle had a tendency to make. All the sails were up, and the jib was so arranged as not to screen the brigantine. A topmast was hoisted, and another jib, held out to the wind, added its force to the other sails. Although the speed could not be exactly estimated, the sledge could not be going at less than forty miles an hour.

'If nothing breaks,' said Mudge, 'we shall get there!'

Mr. Fogg had made it for Mudge's interest to reach Omaha within the time agreed on, by the offer of a handsome reward.

The prairie, across which the sledge was moving in a straight line, was as flat as a sea. It seemed like a vast frozen lake. The railroad which ran through this section ascended from the south-west to the north-west by Great Island, Columbus, an important Nebraska town, Schuyler, and Fremont, to Omaha. It followed throughout the right bank of the Platte River. The sledge, shortening this route, took a chord of the arc described by the railway. Mudge was not afraid of being stopped by the Platte River, because it was frozen. The road, then, was quite clear of obstacles, and Phileas Fogg had but two things to fear, – an accident to the sledge, and a change or calm in the wind.

But the breeze, far from lessening its force, blew as if to bend the mast, which, however, the metallic lashings held firmly. These lashings, like the chords of a stringed instrument, resounded as if vibrated by a violin bow. The sledge slid along in the midst of a plaintively intense melody.

'Those chords give the fifth and the octave.' said Mr. Fogg.

These were the only words he uttered during the journey. Aouda, cosily packed in furs and cloaks, was sheltered as much as possible from the attacks of the freezing wind. As for Passepartout, his face was as red as the sun's disk when it sets in the mist, and he laboriously inhaled the biting air. With his natural buoyancy of spirits, he began to hope again. They would reach New York on the evening, if not on the morning, of the 11th, and there were still some chances that it would be before the steamer sailed for Liverpool.

Passepartout even felt a strong desire to grasp his ally, Fix, by the hand. He remembered that it was the detective who procured the sledge, the only means of reaching Omaha in time; but, checked by some presentiment, he kept his usual reserve. One thing, however, Passepartout would never forget, and that was the sacrifice which Mr. Fogg had made, without hesitation, to rescue him from the Sioux. Mr. Fogg had risked his fortune and his life. No! His servant would never forget that!

While each of the party was absorbed in reflections so different, the sledge flew fast over the vast carpet of snow. The creeks it passed over were not perceived. Fields and streams disappeared under the uniform of whiteness. The plain was absolutely deserted. Between the Union Pacific road and the branch which unites Kearney with Saint Joseph it formed a great uninhabited island. Neither village, station, nor fort appeared. From time to time they sped by some phantom-like tree, whose white skeleton twisted and rattled in the wind. Sometimes flocks of wild birds rose, or bands of gaunt, famished, ferocious prairie-wolves ran howling after the sledge. Passepartout, revolver in hand, held himself ready to fire on those which came too near. Had an accident then happened to the sledge, the travellers, attacked by these beasts, would have been in the most terrible danger; but it held on its even course, soon gained on the wolves, and ere long left the howling band at a safe distance behind.

About noon Mudge perceived by certain landmarks that he was crossing the Platte River. He said nothing, but he felt certain that he was now within twenty miles of Omaha. In less than an hour he left the rudder and furled his sails, whilst the sledge, carried forward by the great impetus the wind had given it, went on half a mile further with its sails unspread.

It stopped at last, and Mudge, pointing to a mass of roofs white with snow, said: 'We have got there!'

Arrived! Arrived at the station which is in daily communication, by numerous trains, with the Atlantic seaboard!

Passepartout and Fix jumped off, stretched their stiffened limbs, and aided Mr. Fogg and the young woman to descend from the sledge. Phileas Fogg generously rewarded Mudge, whose hand Passepartout warmly grasped, and the party directed their steps to the Omaha railway station.

The Pacific Railroad proper finds its terminus at this important Nebraska town. Omaha is connected with Chicago by the Chicago and Rock Island Railroad, which runs directly east, and passes fifty stations.

A train was ready to start when Mr. Fogg and his party reached the station, and they only had time to get into the cars. They had seen nothing of Omaha; but Passepartout confessed to himself that this was not to be regretted, as they were not travelling to see the sights.

The train passed rapidly across the State of Iowa, by Council Bluffs, Des Moines, and Iowa City. During the night it crossed the Mississippi at Davenport, and by Rock Island entered Illinois. The next day, which was the

10th, at four in the evening, it reached Chicago, already risen from its ruins, and more proudly seated than ever on the borders of its beautiful Lake Michigan.

Nine hundred miles separated Chicago from New York; but trains are not wanting at Chicago. Mr. Fogg passed at once from one to the other, and the locomotive of the Pittsburg, Fort Wayne, and Chicago Railway left at full speed, as if it fully comprehended that that gentleman had not time to lose. It traversed Indiana, Ohio, Pennsylvania, and New Jersey like a flash, rushing through towns with antique names, some of which had streets and car-tracks, but as yet no houses. At last the Hudson came into view; and at a quarter-past eleven in the evening of the 11th, the train stopped in the station on the right bank of the river, before the very pier of the Cunard line.

The China, for Liverpool, had started three-quarters of an hour before!

Chapter Thirty-Two

In which Phileas Fogg engages in a direct struggle with bad fortune.

THE CHINA, IN LEAVING, seemed to have carried off Phileas Fogg's last hope. None of the other steamers were able to serve his projects. The Pereire, of the French Transatlantic Company, whose admirable steamers are equal to any in speed and comfort, did not leave until the 14th; the Hamburg boats did not go directly to Liverpool or London, but to Havre; and the additional trip from Havre to Southampton would render Phileas Fogg's last efforts of no avail. The Inman steamer did not depart till the next day, and could not cross the Atlantic in time to save the wager.

Mr. Fogg learned all this in consulting his 'Bradshaw,' which gave him the daily movements of the transatlantic steamers.

Passepartout was crushed; it overwhelmed him to lose the boat by three-quarters of an hour. It was his fault, for, instead of helping his master, he had not ceased putting obstacles in his path! And when he recalled all the incidents of the tour, when he counted up the sums expended in pure loss and on his own account, when he thought that the immense stake, added to the heavy charges of this useless journey, would completely ruin Mr. Fogg, he overwhelmed himself with bitter self-accusations. Mr. Fogg, however, did not reproach him; and, on leaving the Cunard pier, only said: 'We will consult about what is best to-morrow. Come.'

The party crossed the Hudson in the Jersey City ferry-boat, and drove in a carriage to the St. Nicholas Hotel, on Broadway. Rooms were engaged, and the night passed, briefly to Phileas Fogg, who slept profoundly, but very long to Aouda and the others, whose agitation did not permit them to rest.

The next day was the 12th of December. From seven in the morning of the 12th, to a quarter before nine in the evening of the 21st, there were nine days, thirteen hours, and forty-five minutes. If Phileas Fogg had left in the China, one of the fastest steamers on the Atlantic, he would have reached Liverpool, and then London, within the period agreed upon.

Mr. Fogg left the hotel alone, after giving Passepartout instructions to await his return, and inform Aouda to be ready at an instant's notice. He proceeded to the banks of the Hudson, and looked about among the vessels moored or anchored in the river, for any that were about to depart. Several had departure signals, and were preparing to put to sea at morning tide; for in this immense and admirable port there is not one day in a hundred that vessels do not set out for every quarter of the globe. But they were mostly sailing vessels, of which, of course, Phileas Fogg could make no use.

He seemed about to give up all hope, when he espied, anchored at the Battery, a cable's length off at most, a trading vessel, with a screw, wellshaped, whose funnel, puffing a cloud of smoke, indicated that she was getting ready for departure.

Phileas Fogg hailed a boat, got into it, and soon found himself on board the Henrietta, iron-hulled, wood-built above. He ascended to the deck, and asked for the captain, who forthwith presented himself. He was a man of fifty, a sort of sea-wolf, with big eyes, a complexion of oxidized copper, red hair and thick neck, and a growling voice.

'The captain?' asked Mr. Fogg.

'I am the captain.'

'I am Phileas Fogg, of London.'

'And I am Andrew Speedy, of Cardiff.'

'You are going to put to sea?'

'In an hour.'

'You are bound for——'

'Bordeaux.'

'And your cargo?'

'No freight. Going in ballast.'

'Have you any passengers?'

'No passengers. Never have passengers. Too much in the way.'

'Is your vessel a swift one?'

'Between eleven and twelve knots. The Henrietta, well known.'

'Will you carry me and three other persons to Liverpool?'

'To Liverpool? Why not to China?'

'I said Liverpool.'

'No!'

'No?'

'No. I am setting out for Bordeaux, and shall go to Bordeaux.'

'Money is no object?'

'None.'

The captain spoke in a tone which did not admit of a reply.

'But the owners of the Henrietta——' resumed Phileas Fogg.

'The owners are myself,' replied the captain. 'The vessel belongs to me.'

'I will freight it for you.'

'No.'

'I will buy it of you.'

'No.'

Phileas Fogg did not betray the least disappointment; but the situation was a grave one. It was not at New York as at Hong Kong, nor with the captain of the

Henrietta as with the captain of the Tankadere. Up to this time money had smoothed away every obstacle. Now money failed.

Still, some means must be found to cross the Atlantic on a boat, unless by balloon, – which would have been venturesome, besides not being capable of being put in practice. It seemed that Phileas Fogg had an idea, for he said to the captain, 'Well, will you carry me to Bordeaux?'

'No, not if you paid me two hundred dollars.'

'I offer you two thousand.'

'Apiece?'

'Apiece.'

And there are four of you?'

'Four.'

Captain Speedy began to scratch his head. There were eight thousand dollars to gain, without changing his route; for which it was well worth conquering the repugnance he had for all kinds of passengers. Besides, passengers at two thousand dollars are no longer passengers, but valuable merchandise. 'I start at nine o'clock,' said Captain Speedy, simply. 'Are you and your party ready?'

'We will be on board at nine o'clock,' replied, no less simply, Mr. Fogg.

It was half-past eight. To disembark from the Henrietta, jump into a hack, hurry to the St. Nicholas, and return with Aouda, Passepartout, and even the inseparable Fix, was the work of a brief time, and was performed by Mr. Fogg with the coolness which never abandoned him. They were on board when the Henrietta made ready to weigh anchor.

When Passepartout heard what this last voyage was going to cost, he uttered a prolonged 'Oh!' which extended throughout his vocal gamut.

As for Fix, he said to himself that the Bank of England would certainly not come out of this affair well indemnified. When they reached England, even if Mr. Fogg did not throw some handfuls of bank-bills into the sea, more than seven thousand pounds would have been spent!

Chapter Thirty-Three

In which Phileas Fogg shows himself equal to the occasion.

AN HOUR AFTER, THE HENRIETTA passed the lighthouse which marks the entrance of the Hudson, turned the point of Sandy Hook, and put to sea. During the day she skirted Long Island, passed Fire Island, and directed her course rapidly eastward.

At noon the next day, a man mounted the bridge to ascertain the vessel's position. It might be thought that this was Captain Speedy. Not the least in the world. It was Phileas Fogg, Esquire. As for Captain Speedy, he was shut up in his cabin under lock and key, and was uttering loud cries, which signified an anger at once pardonable and excessive.

What had happened was very simple. Phileas Fogg wished to go to Liverpool, but the captain would not carry him there. Then Phileas Fogg had taken passage for Bordeaux, and, during the thirty hours he had been on board, had so shrewdly managed with his bank-notes that the sailors and stokers, who were only an occasional crew, and were not on the best terms with the captain, went over to him in a body. This was why Phileas Fogg was in command instead of Captain Speedy; why the captain was a prisoner in his cabin; and why, in short, the Henrietta was directing her course towards Liverpool. It was very clear, to see Mr. Fogg manage the craft, that he had been a sailor.

How the adventure ended will be seen anon. Aouda was anxious, though she said nothing. As for Passepartout, he thought Mr. Fogg's manœuvre simply glorious. The captain had said 'between eleven and twelve knots,' and the Henrietta confirmed his prediction.

If, then – for there were 'ifs' still – the sea did not become too boisterous, if the wind did not veer round to the east, if no accident happened to the boat or its machinery, the Henrietta might cross the three thousand miles from New York to Liverpool in the nine days, between the 12th and the 21st of December. It is true that, once arrived, the affair on board the Henrietta, added to that of the Bank of England, might create more difficulties for Mr. Fogg than he imagined or could desire.

During the first days, they went along smoothly enough. The sea was not very unpropitious, the wind seemed stationary in the north-east, the sails were hoisted, and the Henrietta ploughed across the waves like a real transatlantic steamer.

Passepartout was delighted. His master's last exploit, the consequences of which he ignored, enchanted him. Never had the crew seen so jolly and dexterous a fellow. He formed warm friendships with the sailors, and amazed them with his acrobatic feats. He thought they managed the vessel like gentlemen, and that the stokers fired up like heroes. His loquacious good-humour infected every one. He had forgotten the past, its vexations and delays. He only thought of the end, so nearly accomplished; and sometimes he boiled over with impatience, as if heated by the furnaces of the Henrietta. Often, also, the worthy fellow revolved around Fix, looking at him with a keen, distrustful eye; but he did not speak to him, for their old intimacy no longer existed.

Fix, it must be confessed, understood nothing of what was going on. The conquest of the Henrietta, the bribery of the crew, Fogg managing the boat like a skilled seaman, amazed and confused him. He did not know what to think. For, after all, a man who began by stealing fifty-five thousand pounds might end by stealing a vessel; and Fix was not unnaturally inclined to conclude that the Henrietta, under Fogg's command, was not going to Liverpool at all, but to some part of the world where the robber, turned into a pirate, would quietly put himself in safety. The conjecture was at least a plausible one, and the detective began to seriously regret that he had embarked in the affair.

As for Captain Speedy, he continued to howl and growl in his cabin; and Passepartout, whose duty it was to carry him his meals, courageous as he was, took the greatest precautions. Mr. Fogg did not seem even to know that there was a captain on board.

On the 13th they passed the edge of the Banks of Newfoundland, a dangerous locality; during the winter, especially, there are frequent fogs and heavy gales of wind. Ever since the evening before the barometer, suddenly falling, had indicated an approaching change in the atmosphere; and during the night the temperature varied, the cold became sharper, and the wind veered to the south-east.

This was a misfortune. Mr. Fogg, in order not to deviate from his course, furled his sails and increased the force of the steam; but the vessel's speed slackened, owing to the state of the sea, the long waves of which broke against the stern. She pitched violently, and this retarded her progress. The breeze little by little swelled into a tempest, and it was to be feared that the Henrietta might not be able to maintain herself upright on the waves.

Passepartout's visage darkened with the skies, and for two days the poor fellow experienced constant fright. But Phileas Fogg was a bold mariner, and knew how to maintain headway against the sea; and he kept on his course, without even decreasing his steam. The Henrietta, when she could not rise upon the waves, crossed them, swamping her deck, but passing safely. Sometimes the screw rose out of the water, beating its protruding end, when a mountain of water raised the stern above the waves; but the craft always kept straight ahead.

The wind, however, did not grow as boisterous as might have been feared; it was not one of those tempests which burst, and rush on with a speed of ninety miles an hour. It continued fresh, but, unhappily, it remained obstinately in the south-east, rendering the sails useless.

The 16th of December was the seventy-fifth day since Phileas Fogg's departure from London, and the Henrietta had not yet been seriously delayed. Half of the voyage was almost accomplished, and the worst localities had been passed. In summer, success would have been well-nigh certain. In winter, they were at the mercy of the bad season. Passepartout said nothing; but he cherished hope in secret, and comforted himself with the reflection that, if the wind failed them, they might still count on the steam.

On this day the engineer came on deck, went up to Mr. Fogg, and began to speak earnestly with him. Without knowing why – it was a presentiment, perhaps – Passepartout became vaguely uneasy. He would have given one of his ears to hear with the other what the engineer was saying. He finally managed to catch a few words, and was sure he heard his master say, 'You are certain of what you tell me?'

'Certain, sir,' replied the engineer. 'You must remember that, since we started, we have kept up hot fires in all our furnaces, and though we had coal enough to go on short steam from New York to Bordeaux, we haven't enough to go with all steam from New York to Liverpool.'

'I will consider,' replied Mr. Fogg.

Passepartout understood it all; he was seized with mortal anxiety. The coal was giving out! 'Ah, if my master can get over that,' muttered he, 'he'll be a very famous man!' He could not help imparting to Fix what he had overheard.

'Then you believe that we really are going to Liverpool?'

'Of course.'

'Ass!' replied the detective, shrugging his shoulders and turning on his heel.

Passepartout was on the point of vigorously resenting the epithet, the reason of which he could not for the life of him comprehend; but he reflected that the unfortunate Fix was probably very much disappointed and humiliated in his self-esteem, after having so awkwardly followed a false scent around the world, and refrained.

And now what course would Phileas Fogg adopt? It was difficult to imagine.

Nevertheless he seemed to have decided upon one, for that evening he sent for the engineer, and said to him, 'Feed all the fires until the coal is exhausted.'

A few moments after, the funnel of the Henrietta vomited forth torrents of smoke. The vessel continued to proceed with all steam on; but on the 18th, the engineer, as he had predicted, announced that the coal would give out in the course of the day.

'Do not let the fires go down,' replied Mr. Fogg. 'Keep them up to the last. Let the valves be filled.'

Towards noon Phileas Fogg, having ascertained their position, called Passepartout, and ordered him to go for Captain Speedy. It was as if the honest fellow had been commanded to unchain a tiger. He went to the poop, saying to himself, 'He will be like a madman!'

In a few moments, with cries and oaths, a bomb appeared on the poopdeck. The bomb was Captain Speedy. It was clear that he was on the point of bursting. 'Where are we?' were the first words his anger permitted him to utter. Had the poor man been apoplectic, he could never have recovered from his paroxysm of wrath.

'Where are we?' he repeated, with purple face.

'Seven hundred and seven miles from Liverpool,' replied Mr. Fogg, with imperturbable calmness.

'Pirate!' cried Captain Speedy.

'I have sent for you, sir—'

'Pickaroon!'

'—Sir,' continued Mr. Fogg, 'to ask you to sell me your vessel.'

'No! By all the devils, no!'

'But I shall be obliged to burn her.'

'Burn the Henrietta!'

'Yes; at least the upper part of her. The coal has given out.'

'Burn my vessel!' cried Captain Speedy, who could scarcely pronounce the words. 'A vessel worth fifty thousand dollars!'

'Here are sixty thousand,' replied Phileas Fogg, handing the captain a roll of bank bills. This had a prodigious effect on Andrew Speedy. An American can scarceley remain unmoved at the sight of sixty thousand dollars. The captain forgot in an instant his anger, his imprisonment, and all his grudges against his passenger. The Henrietta was twenty years old; it was a great bargain. The bomb would not go off after all. Mr. Fogg had taken away the match.

'And I shall still have the iron hull,' said the captain in a softer tone.

'The iron hull and the engine. Is it agreed?'

'Agreed.'

And Andrew Speedy, seizing the bank-notes, counted them and consigned them to his pocket.

During this colloquy, Passepartout was as white as a sheet, and Fix seemed on the point of having an apoplectic fit. Nearly twenty thousand pounds had been expended, and Fogg left the hull and engine to the captain, that is, near the whole value of the craft! It was true, however, that fifty-five thousand pounds had been stolen from the bank.

When Andrew Speedy had pocketed the money, Mr. Fogg said to him, 'Don't let this astonish you, sir. You must know that I shall lose twenty thousand pounds, unless I arrive in London by a quarter before nine on the evening of the

21st of December. I missed the steamer at New York, and as you refused to take me to Liverpool——'

'And I did well!' cried Andrew Speedy; 'for I have gained at least forty thousand dollars by it!' He added, more sedately. 'Do you know one thing, Captain——'

'Fogg.'

'Captain Fogg, you've got something of the Yankee about you.'

And, having paid his passengers what he considered a high compliment, he was going away, when Mr. Fogg said, 'The vessel now belongs to me?'

'Certainly, from the keel to the truck of the masts, – all the wood, that is.'

'Very well. Have the interior seats, bunks, and frames pulled down, and burn them.'

It was necessary to have dry wood to keep the steam up to the adequate pressure, and on that day the poop, cabins, bunks, and the spare deck were sacrificed. On the next day, the 19th of December, the masts, rafts, and spars were burned; the crew worked lustily, keeping up the fires. Passepartout hewed, cut, and sawed away with all his might. There was a perfect rage of demolition.

The railings, fittings, the greater part of the deck, and top sides disappeared on the 20th, and the Henrietta was now only a flat hulk. But on this day they sighted the Irish coast and Fastnet Light. By ten in the evening they were passing Queenstown. Phileas Fogg had only twenty-four hours more in which to get to London; that length of time was necessary to reach Liverpoool with all steam on. And the steam was about to give out altogether!

'Sir,' said Captain Speedy, who was now deeply interested in Mr. Fogg's project, 'I really commiserate you. Everything is against you. We are only opposite Queenstown.'

'Ah,' said Mr. Fogg, 'is that place where we see the lights Queenstown?'

'Yes.'

'Can we enter the harbour?'

'Not under three hours. Only at high tide.'

'Stay,' replied Mr. Fogg calmly, without betraying in his features that by a supreme inspiration he was about to attempt once more to conquer ill-fortune.

Queenstown is the Irish port at which the transatlantic steamers stop to put off the mails. These mails are carried to Dublin by express trains always held in readiness to start; from Dublin they are sent to Liverpool by the most rapid boats, and thus gain twelve hours on the Atlantic steamers.

Phileas Fogg counted on gaining twelve hours in the same way. Instead of arriving at Liverpool the next evening by the Henrietta, he would be there by noon, and would therefore have time to reach London before a quarter before nine in the evening.

The Henrietta entered Queenstown Harbour at one o'clock in the morning, it then being high tide; and Phileas Fogg, after being grasped heartily by the hand by Captain Speedy, left that gentleman on the levelled hulk of his craft, which was still worth half what he had sold it for.

The party went on shore at once. Fix was greatly tempted to arrest Mr. Fogg on the spot; but he did not. Why? What struggle was going on within him? Had he changed his mind about 'his man'? Did he understand that he had made a grave mistake? He did not, however, abandon Mr. Fogg. They all got upon the train, which was just ready to start, at half-past one; at dawn of day they were in

Dublin; and they lost no time in embarking on a steamer which, disdaining to rise upon the waves, invariably cut through them.

Phileas Fogg at last disembarked on the Liverpool quay, at twenty minutes past twelve, December 21st. He was only six hours distant from London.

But at this moment Fix came up, put his hand upon Mr. Fogg's shoulder and, showing his warrant, said, 'You are really Phileas Fogg?'

'I am.'

'I arrest you in the Queen's name!'

Chapter Thirty-Four

In which Phileas Fogg at last reaches London.

PHILEAS FOGG WAS IN PRISON. He had been shut up in the Custom House, and he was to be transferred to London the next day.

Passepartout, when he saw his master arrested, would have fallen upon Fix had he not been held back by some policemen. Aouda was thunderstruck at the suddenness of an event which she could not understand. Passepartout explained to her how it was that the honest and courageous Fogg was arrested as a robber. The young woman's heart revolted against so heinous a charge, and when she saw that she could attempt or do nothing to save her protector, she wept bitterly.

As for Fix, he had arrested Mr. Fogg because it was his duty, whether Mr. Fogg were guilty or not.

The thought then struck Passepartout, that he was the cause of this new misfortune! Had he not concealed Fix's errand from his master? When Fix revealed his true character and purpose, why had he not told Mr. Fogg? If the latter had been warned, he would no doubt have given Fix proof of his innocence, and satisfied him of his mistake; at least, Fix would not have continued his journey at the expense and on the heels of his master, only to arrest him the moment he set foot on English soil. Passepartout wept till he was blind, and felt like blowing his brains out.

Aouda and he had remained, despite the cold, under the portico of the Custom House. Neither wished to leave the place; both were anxious to see Mr. Fogg again.

That gentleman was really ruined, and that at the moment when he was about to attain his end. This arrest was fatal. Having arrived at Liverpool at twenty minutes before twelve on the 21st of December, he had till a quarter before nine that evening to reach the Reform Club, that is, nine hours and a quarter; the journey from Liverpool to London was six hours.

If anyone, at this moment, had entered the Custom House, he would have found Mr. Fogg seated, motionless, calm, and without apparent anger, upon a wooden bench. He was not, it is true, resigned; but this last blow failed to force him into an outward betrayal of any emotion. Was he being devoured by one of

those secret rages, all the more terrible because contained, and which only burst
forth, with an irresistible force, at the last moment? No one could tell. There he
sat, calmly waiting – for what? Did he still cherish hope? Did he still believe,
now that the door of this prison was closed upon him, that he would succeed?

However that may have been, Mr. Fogg carefully put his watch upon the
table, and observed its advancing hands. Not a word escaped his lips, but his
look was singularly set and stern. The situation, in any event, was a terrible one,
and might be thus stated: If Phileas Fogg was honest he was ruined; if he was a
knave, he was caught.

Did escape occur to him? Did he examine to see if there were any practicable
outlet from his prison? Did he think of escaping from it? Possibly; for once he
walked slowly around the room. But the door was locked, and the window
heavily barred with iron rods. He sat down again, and drew his journal from his
pocket. On the line where these words were written, 'December 21st, Saturday,
Liverpool,' he added, '80th day, 11.40 a.m.,' and waited.

The Custom House clock struck one. Mr. Fogg observing his watch was two
hours too fast.

Two hours! Admitting that he was at this moment taking an express train, he
could reach London and the Reform Club by a quarter before nine, P.M. His
forehead slightly wrinkled.

At thirty-three minutes past two he heard a singular noise outside, then a
hasty opening of doors. Passepartout's voice was audible, and immediately after
that of Fix. Phileas Fogg's eyes brightened for an instant.

The door swung open, and he saw Passepartout, Aouda, and Fix, who hurried
towards him.

Fix was out of breath, and his hair was in disorder. He could not speak. 'Sir,'
he stammered, 'Sir – forgive me – a most – unfortunate resemblance – robber
arrested three days ago – you – are free!'

Phileas Fogg was free! He walked to the detective, looked him steadily in the
face, and with the only rapid motion he had ever made in his life, or which he
ever would make, drew back his arms, and with the precision of a machine,
knocked Fix down.

'Well hit! cried Passepartout. 'Parbleu! that's what you might call a good
application of English fists!'

Fix, who found himself on the floor, did not utter a word. He had only
received his deserts. Mr. Fogg, Aouda, and Passepartout left the Custom
House without delay, got into a cab, and in a few moments descended at the
station.

Phileas Fogg asked if there was an express train about to leave for London. It
was forty minutes past two. The express train had left thirty-five minutes before.

Phileas Fogg then ordered a special train.

There were several rapid locomotives on hand; but the railway arrangements
did not permit the special train to leave until three o'clock.

At that hour Phileas Fogg, having stimulated the engineer by the offer of a
generous reward, at last set out towards London with Aouda and his faithful
servant.

It was necessary to make the journey in five hours and a half; and this would
have been easy on a clear road throughout. But there were forced delays, and
when Mr. Fogg stepped from the train at the terminus, all the clocks in London

were striking ten minutes before nine.[1]

Having made the tour of the world, he was behindhand five minutes. He had lost the wager!

[1] A somewhat remarkable eccentricity on the part of the London clocks! – TRANSLATOR.

Chapter Thirty-Five

In which Phileas Fogg does not have to repeat his orders to Passepartout twice.

THE DWELLERS IN SAVILLE ROW would have been surprised, the next day, if they had been told that Phileas Fogg had returned home. His doors and windows were still closed; no appearance of change was visible.

After leaving the station, Mr. Fogg gave Passepartout instructions to purchase some provisions, and quietly went to his domicile.

He bore his misfortune with his habitual tranquillity. Ruined! And by the blundering of the detective! After having steadily traversed that long journey, overcome a hundred obstacles, braved many dangers, and still found time to do some good on his way, to fail near the goal by a sudden event which he could not have foreseen, and against which he was unarmed; it was terrible! But a few pounds were left of the large sum he had carried with him. There only remained of his fortune the twenty thousand pounds deposited at Barings, and this amount he owed to his friends of the Reform Club. So great had been the expense of his tour, that, even had he won, it would not have enriched him; and it is probable that he had not sought to enrich himself, being a man who rather laid wagers for honour's sake than for the sake proposed. But this wager totally ruined him.

Mr. Fogg's course, however, was fully decided upon; he knew what remained for him to do.

A room in the house in Saville Row was set apart for Aouda, who was overwhelmed with grief at her protector's misfortune. From the words which Mr. Fogg dropped, she saw that he was meditating some serious project.

Knowing that Englishmen governed by a fixed idea sometimes resort to the desperate expedient of suicide, Passepartout kept a narrow watch upon his master, though he carefully concealed the appearance of so doing.

First of all, the worthy fellow had gone up to his room, and had extinguished the gas burner, which had been burning for eighty days. He had found in the letter-box a bill from the gas company, and he thought it more than time to put a stop to this expense, which he had been doomed to bear.

The night passed. Mr. Fogg went to bed, but did he sleep? Aouda did not once close her eyes. Passepartout watched all night, like a faithful dog, at his master's door.

Mr. Fog called him in the morning, and told him to get Aouda's breakfast, and a cup of tea and a chop for himself. He desired Aouda to excuse him from breakfast and dinner, as his time would be absorbed all day in putting his affairs to rights. In the evening he would ask permission to have a few moments' conversation with the young lady.

Passepartout, having received his orders, had nothing to do but obey them. · He looked at his imperturbable master, and could scarcely bring his mind to leave him. His heart was full, and his conscience tortured by remorse; for he accused himself more bitterly than ever of being the cause of the irretrievable disaster. Yes! if he had warned Mr. Fogg, and had betrayed Fix's projects to him, his master would certainly not have given the detective passage to Liverpool, and then——

Passepartout could hold in no longer.

'My master! Mr. Fogg!' he cried, 'why do you not curse me? It was my fault that——'

'I blame no one,' returned Phileas Fogg, with perfect calmness. 'Go!'

Passepartout left the room, and went to find Aouda, to whom he delivered his master's message.

'Madam,' he added, 'I can do nothing myself – nothing! I have no influence over my master; but you, perhaps——'

'What influence could I have?' replied Aouda. 'Mr. Fogg is influenced by no one. Has he ever understood that my gratitude to him is overflowing? Has he ever read my heart? My friend, he must not be left alone an instant! You say he is going to speak with me this evening?'

'Yes, madam; probably to arrange for your protection and comfort in England.'

'We shall see,' replied Aouda, becoming suddenly pensive.

Throughout this day (Sunday) the house in Saville Row was as if uninhabited, and Phileas Fogg, for the first time since he had lived in that house, did not set out for his club when Westminster clock struck half-past eleven.

Why should he present himself at the Reform? His friends no longer expected him there. As Phileas Fogg had not appeared in the saloon on the evening before (Saturday, the 21st of December, at a quarter before nine), he had lost his wager. It was not even necessary that he should go to his bankers for the twenty thousand pounds; for his antagonists already had his cheque in their hands, and they had only to fill it out and send it to Barings to have the amount transferred to their credit.

Mr. Fogg, therefore, had no reason for going out, and so he remained at home. He shut himself up in his room, and busied himself putting his affairs in order. Passepartout continually ascended and descended the stairs. The hours were long for him. He listened at his master's door, and looked through the keyhole, as if he had a perfect right so to do, and as if he feared that something terrible might happen at any moment. Sometimes he thought of Fix, but no longer in anger. Fix, like all the world, had been mistaken in Phileas Fogg, and had only done his duty in tracking and arresting him; while he, Passepartout——. This thought haunted him, and he never ceased cursing his miserable folly.

Finding himself too wretched to remain alone, he knocked at Aouda's door, went into her room, seated himself, without speaking, in a corner, and looked ruefully at the young woman. Aouda was still pensive.

About half-past seven in the evening Mr. Fogg sent to know if Aouda would receive him, and in a few moments he found himself alone with her.

Phileas Fogg took a chair, and sat down near the fireplace, opposite Aouda. No emotion was visible on his face. Fogg returned was exactly the Fogg who had gone away; there was the same calm, the same impassibility.

He sat several minutes without speaking; then, bending his eyes on Aouda, 'Madam,' said he, 'will you pardon me for bringing you to England?'

'I, Mr. Fogg!' replied Aouda, checking the pulsations of her heart.

'Please let me finish,' returned Mr. Fogg. 'When I decided to bring you far away from the country which was so unsafe for you, I was rich, and counted on putting a portion of my fortune at your disposal; then your existence would have been free and happy. But now I am ruined.'

'I know it, Mr. Fogg,' replied Aouda; 'and I ask you in my turn, will you forgive me for having followed you, and – who knows? – for having, perhaps, delayed you, and thus contributed to your ruin?'

'Madam, you could not remain in India, and your safety could only be assured by bringing you to such a distance that your persecutors could not take you.'

'So, Mr. Fogg,' resumed Aouda, 'not content with rescuing me from a terrible death, you thought yourself bound to secure my comfort in a foreign land?'

'Yes, madam; but circumstances have been against me. Still, I beg to place the little I have left at your service.'

'But what will become of you, Mr. Fogg?'

'As for me, madam,' replied the gentleman, coldly, 'I have need of nothing.'

'But how do you look upon the fate, sir, which awaits you?'

'As I am in the habit of doing.'

'At least,' said Aouda, 'want should not overtake a man like you. Your friends——'

'I have no friends, madam.'

'Your relatives——'

'I have no longer any relatives.'

'I pity you, then, Mr. Fogg, for solitude is a sad thing, with no heart to which to confide your griefs. They say, though, that misery itself, shared by two sympathetic souls may be borne with patience.'

'They say so, madam.'

'Mr. Fogg,' said Aouda, rising and seizing his hand, 'do you wish at once a kinswoman and friend? Will you have me for your wife?'

Mr. Fogg, at this, rose in his turn. There was an unwonted light in his eyes, and a slight trembling of his lips. Aouda looked into his face. The sincerity, rectitude, firmness, and sweetness of this soft glance of a noble woman, who could dare all to save him to whom she owed all, at first astonished, then penetrated him. He shut his eyes for an instant, as if to avoid her look. When he opened them again, 'I love you!' he said, simply. 'Yes, by all that is holiest, I love you, and I am entirely yours!'

'Ah!' cried Aouda, pressing his hand to her heart.

Passepartout was summoned and appeared immediately. Mr. Fogg still held Aouda's hand in his own; Passepartout understood, and his big, round face became so radiant as the tropical sun at its zenith.

Mr. Fogg asked him if it was not too late to notify the Reverend Samuel Wilson, of Marylebone Parish, that evening.

Passepartout smiled his most genial smile, and said, 'Never too late.'

It was five minutes past eight.

'Will it be for to-morrow, Monday?'

'For to-morrow, Monday,' said Mr. Fogg, turning to Aouda.

'Yes; for to-morrow, Monday,' she replied.

Passepartout hurried off as fast as his legs could carry him.

Chapter Thirty-Six

In which Phileas Fogg's name is once more at a premium on 'Change.

IT IS TIME TO RELATE what a change took place in English public opinion, when it transpired that the real bank-robber, a certain James Strand, had been arrested, on the 17th of December, at Edinburgh. Three days before, Phileas Fogg had been a criminal, who was being desperately followed up by the police; now he was an honourable gentleman, mathematically pursuing his eccentric journey round the world.

The papers resumed their discussion about the wager; all those who had laid bets, for or against him, revived their interest, as if by magic; the 'Phileas Fogg bonds' again became negotiable, and many new wagers were made. Phileas Fogg's name was once more at a premium on 'Change.

His five friends of the Reform Club passed these three days in a state of feverish suspense. Would Phileas Fogg, whom they had forgotten, reappear before their eyes! Where was he at this moment? The 17th of December, the day of James Strand's arrest, was the seventy-sixth since Phileas Fogg's departure, and no news of him had been received. Was he dead? Had he abandoned the effort, or was he continuing his journey along the route agreed upon? And would he appear on Saturday, the 21st of December, at a quarter before nine in the evening, on the threshold of the Reform Club saloon?

The anxiety in which, for three days, London society existed, cannot be described. Telegrams were sent to America and Asia for news of Phileas Fogg. Messengers were despatched at the house in Saville Row morning and evening. No news. The police were ignorant of what had become of the detective, Fix, who had so unfortunately followed up a false scent. Bets increased, nevertheless, in number and value. Phileas Fogg, like a racehorse, was drawing near his last turning-point. The bonds were quoted, no longer at a hundred below par, but at twenty, at ten, and at five; and paralytic old Lord Albermarle bet even in his favour.

A great crowd was collected in Pall Mall and the neighbouring streets on Saturday evening; it seemed like a multitude of brokers permanently established around the Reform Club. Circulation was impeded, and everywhere disputes, discussions, and financial transactions were going on. The police had great difficulty in keeping back the crowd, and as the hour when Phileas Fogg was due approached, the excitement rose to its highest pitch.

The five antagonists of Phileas Fogg had met in the great saloon of the club. John Sullivan and Samuel Fallentin, the bankers, Andrew Stuart, the engineer,

Gauthier Ralph, the director of the Bank of England, and Thomas Flanagan, the brewer, one and all waited anxiously.

When the clock indicated twenty minutes past eight, Andrew Stuart got up, saying, 'Gentlemen, in twenty minutes the time agreed upon between Mr. Fogg and ourselves will have expired.'

'What time did the last train arrive from Liverpool?' asked Thomas Flanagan.

'At twenty-three minutes past seven,' replied Gauthier Ralph; 'and the next does not arrive till ten minutes before twelve.'

'Well, gentlemen,' resumed Andrew Stuart, 'if Phileas Fogg had come in the 7.23 train, he would have got here by this time. We can, therefore, regard the bet as won.'

'Wait; don't let us be too hasty,' replied Samuel Fallentin. 'You know that Mr. Fogg is very eccentric. His punctuality is well known; he never arrives too soon, or too late; and I should not be surprised if he appeared before us at the last minute.'

'Why,' said Andrew Stuart nervously, 'if I should see him, I should not believe it was he.'

'The fact is,' resumed Thomas Flanagan, 'Mr. Fogg's project was absurdly foolish. Whatever his punctuality, he could not prevent the delays which were certain to occur; and a delay of only two or three days would be fatal to his tour.'

'Observe, too,' added John Sullivan, 'that we have received no intelligence from him, though there are telegraphic lines all along his route.'

'He has lost, gentlemen,' said Andrew Stuart, – 'he has a hundred times lost! You know, besides, that the 'China' – the only steamer he could have taken from New York to get here in time – arrived yesterday. I have seen a list of the passengers, and the name of Phileas Fogg is not among them. Even if we admit that fortune had favoured him, he can scarcely have reached America. I think he will be at least twenty days behindhand, and that Lord Albermarle will lose a cool five thousand.'

'It is clear,' replied Gauthier Ralph; 'and we have nothing to do but to present Mr. Fogg's cheque at Barings to-morrow.'

At this moment, the hands of the club clock pointed twenty minutes to nine.

'Five minutes more,' said Andrew Stuart.

The five gentlemen looked at each other. Their anxiety was becoming intense; but, not wishing to betray it, they readily assented to Mr. Fallentin's proposal of a rubber.

'I wouldn't give up my four thousand of the best,' said Andrew Stuart, as he took his seat, 'for three thousand nine hundred and ninety-nine.'

The clock indicated eighteen minutes to nine.

The players took up their cards, but could not keep their eyes off the clock. Certainly, however secure they felt, minutes had never seemed so long to them!

'Seventeen minutes to nine,' said Thomas Flanagan, as he cut the cards which Ralph handed to him.

Then there was a moment of silence. The great saloon was perfectly quiet; but the murmurs of the crowd outside were heard, with now and then a shrill cry. The pendulum beat the seconds, which each player eagerly counted, as he listened, with mathematical regularity.

'Sixteen minutes to nine!' said John Sullivan, in a voice which betrayed his emotion.

One minute more, and the wager would be won. Andrew Stuart and his partners suspended their game. They left their cards, and counted the seconds.

At the fortieth second, nothing. At the fiftieth, still nothing.

At the fifty-fifth, a loud cry was heard in the street, followed by applause, hurrahs, and some fierce growls.

The players rose from their seats.

At the fifty-seventh second the door of the saloon opened; and the pendulum had not beat the sixtieth second when Phileas Fogg appeared, followed by an excited crowd who had forced their way through the club doors, and in his calm voice, said, 'Here I am, gentlemen!'

Chapter Thirty-Seven

In which it is shown that Phileas Fogg gained nothing by his tour around the world, unless it were happiness.

YES; PHILEAS FOGG IN person.

The reader will remember that at five minutes past eight in the evening – about five and twenty hours after the arrival of the travellers in London – Passepartout had been sent by his master to engage the services of the Reverend Samuel Wilson in a certain marriage ceremony, which was to take place the next day.

Passepartout went on his errand enchanted. He soon reached the clergyman's house, but found him not at home. Passepartout waited a good twenty minutes, and when he left the reverend gentleman, it was thirty-five minutes past eight. But in what a state he was! With his hair in disorder, and without his hat, he ran along the street as never man was seen to run before, overturning passers-by, rushing over the sidewalk like a waterspout.

In three minutes he was in Saville Row again, and staggered breathlessly into Mr. Fogg's room.

He could not speak.

'What is the matter?' asked Mr. Fogg.

'My master!' gasped Passepartout, – 'marriage – impossible——'

'Impossible?'

'Impossible – for tomorrow'

'Why so?'

'Because tomorrow – is Sunday!'

'Monday,' replied Mr. Fogg.

'No – today – is Saturday.'

'Saturday? Impossible!'

'Yes, yes, yes, yes!' cried Passepartout. 'You have made a mistake of one day! We arrived twenty-four hours ahead of time; but there are only ten minutes left!'

Passepartout had seized his master by the collar, and was dragging him along with irresistible force.

Phileas Fogg, thus kidnapped, without having time to think, left his house, jumped into a cab, promised a hundred pounds to the cabman, and, having run over two dogs and overturned five carriages, reached the Reform Club.

The clock indicated a quarter before nine when he appeared in the great saloon.

Phileas Fogg had accomplished the journey round the world in eighty days!

Phileas Fogg had won his wager of twenty thousand pounds!

How was it that a man so exact and fastidious could have made this error of a day? How came he to think that he had arrived in London on Saturday, the twenty-first day of December, when it was really Friday, the twentieth, the seventy-ninth day only from his departure?

The cause of the error is very simple.

Phileas Fogg had, without suspecting it, gained one day on his journey, and this merely because he had travelled constantly *eastward*; he would, on the contrary, have lost a day had he gone in the opposite direction, that is, *westward*.

In journeying eastward he had gone towards the sun, and the days therefore diminished for him as many times four minutes as he crossed degrees in this direction. There are three hundred and sixty degrees on the circumference of the earth; and these three hundred and sixty degrees, multiplied by four minutes, gives precisely twenty-four hours – that is, the day unconsciously gained. In other words, while Phileas Fogg, going eastward, saw the sun pass the meridian *eighty* times, his friends in London only saw it pass the meridian *seventy-nine* times. This is why they awaited him at the Reform Club on Saturday, and not Sunday, as Mr. Fogg thought.

And Passepartout's famous family watch, which had always kept London time, would have betrayed this fact, if it had marked the days as well as the hours and minutes!

Phileas Fogg, then had won the twenty thousand pounds; but as he had spent nearly nineteen thousand on the way, the pecuniary gain was small. His object was, however, to be victorious, and not to win money. He divided the one thousand pounds that remained between Passepartout and the unfortunate Fix, against whom he cherished no grudge. He deducted, however, from Passepartout's share the cost of the gas which had burned in his room for nineteen hundred and twenty hours, for the sake of regularity.

That evening, Mr. Fogg, as tranquil and phlegmatic as ever, said to Aouda: 'Is our marriage still agreeable to you?'

'Mr. Fogg,' replied she, 'it is for me to ask that question. You were ruined, but now you are rich again?'

'Pardon me, madam; my fortune belongs to you. If you had not suggested our marriage, my servant would not have gone to the Reverend Samuel Wilson's, I should not have been apprised of my error, and——'

'Dear Mr. Fogg!' said the young woman.

'Dear Aouda!' replied Phileas Fogg.

It need not be said that the marriage took place forty-eight hours after, and that Passepartout, glowing and dazzling, gave the bride away. Had he not saved her, and was he not entitled to this honour?

The next day, as soon as it was light, Passepartout rapped vigorously at his master's door. Mr. Fogg opened it, and asked, 'What's the matter, Passepartout?'

'What is it, sir? Why, I've just this instant found out——'

'What?'

'That we might have made the tour of the world in only seventy-eight days.'

'No doubt,' returned Mr. Fogg, 'by not crossing India. But if I had not crossed India, I should not have saved Aouda; she would not have been my wife, and——'

Mr. Fogg quietly shut the door.

Phileas Fogg had won his wager, and had made his journey around the world in eighty days. To do this he had employed every means of conveyance – steamers, railways, carriages, yachts, trading-vessels, sledges, elephants. The eccentric gentleman had throughout displayed all his marvellous qualities of coolness and exactitude. But what then? What had he really gained by all this trouble? What had he brought back from this long and weary journey?

Nothing, say you? Perhaps so; nothing but a charming woman, who, strange as it may appear, made him the happiest of men!

Truly, would you not for less than that make the tour around the world?

20,000 LEAGUES UNDER THE SEA

Chapter One

A Floating Reef

IN THE YEAR 1866 THE whole maritime population of Europe and America was excited by a mysterious and inexplicable phenomenon. This excitement was not confined to merchants, common sailors, sea-captains, shippers, and naval officers of all countries, but the governments of many states on the two continents were deeply interested.

The excitement was caused by an enormous 'something' that ships were often meeting. It was a long, spindle-shaped, and sometimes phosphorescent object, much larger and more rapid than a whale.

The different accounts that were written of this object in various log-books agreed generally as to its structure, wonderful speed, and the peculiar life with which it appeared endowed. If it was a cetacean it surpassed in bulk all those that had hitherto been classified; neither Cuvier, Lacepède, M. Dumeril, nor M. de Quatrefages would have admitted the existence of such a monster, unless he had seen it with his own scientific eyes.

By taking the average of observations made at different times – rejecting the timid estimates that assigned to this object a length of 200 feet, as well as the exaggerated opinions which made it out to be a mile in width and three in length – we may fairly affirm that it surpassed all the dimensions allowed by the ichthyologists of the day, if it existed at all. It did exist, that was undeniable, and with that leaning towards the marvellous that characterizes humanity, we cannot wonder at the excitement it produced in the entire world.

On the 20th of July, 1866, the steamer Governor Higgenson, of the Calcutta and Burnach Steam Navigation Company, met this moving mass five miles off the east coast of Australia. Captain Baker thought at first that he was in the presence of an unknown reef; he was preparing to take its exact position, when two columns of water, projected by the inexplicable object, went hissing up a hundred and fifty feet into the air. Unless there was an intermittent geyser on the reef, the Governor Higgenson had to do with some aquatic mammal, unknown till then, which threw out columns of water mixed with air and vapour from its blowholes.

A similar occurrence happened on the 23rd of July in the same year to the Columbus, of the West India and Pacific Steam Navigation Company, in the Pacific Ocean. It was, therefore, evident that this extraordinary cetaceous creature could transport itself from one place to another with surprising velocity, seeing there was but an interval of three days between the two observations, separated by a distance of more than 700 nautical leagues.

Fifteen days later, two thousand leagues from the last place it was seen at, the Helvetia, of the *Compagnie Nationale*, and the Shannon, of the Royal Mail Steamship Company, sailing to windward in that part of the Atlantic between the United States and Europe, each signalled the monster to the other in 42° 15′ N. lat. and 60° 35′ W. long. As the Shannon and Helvetia were of smaller dimensions than the object, though they measured 300 feet over all, the minimum length of the mammal was estimated at more than 350 feet. Now the largest whales, those that are found in the seas round the Aleutian, Kulammak, and Umgullich Islands, are never more than sixty yards long, if so long.

These accounts arrived one after another; fresh observations made on board the transatlantic ship Le Pereire, the running foul of the monster by the Etna, of the Inman line; a report drawn up by the officers of the French frigate La Normandie; a very grave statement made by the ship's officers of the Commodore FitzJames on board the Lord Clyde, deeply stirred public opinion. In light-hearted countries jokes were made on the subject; but in grave and practical countries like England, America, and Germany, much attention was paid to it.

In all the great centres the monster became the fashion; it was sung about in the cafés, scoffed at in the newspapers, and represented at all the theatres. It gave opportunity for hoaxes of every description. In all newspapers short of copy imaginary beings reappeared, from the white whale, the terrible 'Moby Dick' of the Northern regions, to the inordinate 'kraken,' whose tentacles could fold round a vessel of 500 tons burden and drag it down to the depths of the ocean. The accounts of ancient times were reproduced: the opinions of Aristotle and Pliny, who admitted the existence of these monsters, and the Norwegian tales about Bishop Pontoppidan, those of Paul Heggede, and lastly the report of Mr Harrington, whose good faith could not be put in question when he affirmed that, being on board the Castillian, in 1857, he saw this enormous serpent which until then had only frequented the seas of the old *Constitutionnel* newspaper.

Then broke out the interminable polemics of believers and disbelievers in learned societies and scientific journals. The 'question of the monster' inflamed all minds. The journalists who professed to be scientific, at strife with those who professed to be witty, poured out streams of ink during this memorable controversy; some even two or three drops of blood, for they wandered from the sea serpent to the most offensive personalities.

For six months the war went on with different success. To the leading articles of the Geographical Institute of Brazil, the Berlin Royal Academy of Science, the British Association, the Washington Smithsonian Institution, to the discussions of *The Indian Archipelago*, to the *Cosmos* of the Abbé Moigno, Petermann's *Mitheilungen*, the scientific chronicles of the best newspapers of the civilized world, the smaller newspapers answered with great animation. Their witty writers, parodying a saying of Linnaeus, quoted by the adversaries of the monster, sustained that, in fact, 'Nature did not make fools,' and adjured their contemporaries not to give the lie to Nature by admitting the existence of 'krakens,' sea serpents, 'Moby Dicks,' and other elucubrations of delirious sailors. Lastly, in an article of a much-dreaded satirical journal, the most liked of its contributions hurried over the whole ground, reached the monster, like Hippolytus gave his his finishing blow, and killed him in the midst of a universal burst of laughter. Wit had conquered science.

During the first months of the year 1867 the question seemed to be buried out of sight and mind, when some fresh facts brought it again before the notice of the public. It had then changed from a scientific problem to be solved to a real and serious danger to be avoided. The question took another phase. The monster again became an island or rock. On the 5th of March, 1867, the Moravian, of the Montreal Ocean Company, being, during the night, in 27° 30' lat. and 72° 15' long., struck her starboard quarter on a rock which no chart gave in that point. She was then going at the rate of thirteen knots under the combined efforts of the wind and her 400 horse power. Had it not been for the more than ordinary strength of the hull in the Moravian she would have been broken by the shock, and have gone down with the 237 passengers she was bringing from Canada.

The accident happened about 5 a.m. at daybreak. The officers on watch hurried aft and looked at the sea with the most scrupulous attention. They saw nothing except what looked like a strong eddy, three cables' length off, as if the waves had been violently agitated. The bearings of the place were taken exactly, and the Moravian went on her way without apparent damage. Had she struck on a submarine rock of some enormous fragment of wreck? They could not find out, but during the examination made of the ship's bottom when under repair it was found that part of her keel was broken.

This fact, extremely grave in itself, would perhaps have been forgotten, like so many others, if three weeks afterwards it had not happened again under identical circumstances, only, thanks to the nationality of the ship that was this time victim of the shock, and the reputation of the company to which the vessel belonged, the circumstance was immensely commented upon.

Everyone knows the name of the celebrated shipowners Cunard and Co. This intelligent company founded, in 1840, a postal service between Liverpool and Halifax, with three wooden vessels and an engine of 400 horse power, gauging 1,162 tons. Eight years afterwards the stock of the company increased to four vessels of 650 horse power and 1,820 tons, and two years later they had two more boats, superior in power and tonnage. In 1853 the Cunard Company, whose privilege of carrying the mails had just been renewed, added successively to their stock the Arabia, Persia, China, Scotia, Java, and Russia, all vessels of first-rate speed, and the largest which, next to the Great Eastern, had ever ploughed the seas. Thus, then, in 1867 the company possessed twelve vessels, eight with paddles and four with screws.

I give these brief details to show the importance of this maritime transport company, known in the entire world by its intelligent administration. No enterprise of transmarine navigation has been conducted with more skill; no business affair has been crowned with more success. During the last twenty-six years the Cunard vessels have crossed the Atlantic more than two thousand times, and no voyage has ever failed, no letter, man, nor vessel has ever been lost. Notwithstanding the powerful competition of France, passengers still choose the Cunard route in preference to every other, as is apparent from an examination of the official documents of late years. This understood, no one will be astonished at the commotion caused by the accident that happened to one of its finest steamers.

On the 13th April, 1867, by a smooth sea and favourable breeze, the Cunard steamer Scotia was in 15° 12' long. and 45° 37' lat. She was going at the rate of thirteen knots an hour under the pressure of her 1,000 horse power.

At 4.17 p.m., as the passengers were assembled at dinner in the great saloon, a slight shock was felt on the hull of the Scotia, on her quarter a little aft of the paddle.

The Scotia had not struck anything, but had been struck by some sharp and penetrating rather than blunt surface. The shock was so slight that no one on board would have been uneasy at it had it not been for the carpenter's watch, who rushed upon deck, calling out—— 'She is sinking! she is sinking!'

At first the passengers were much alarmed, but Captain Anderson hastened to reassure them by telling them the danger could not be imminent as the ship was divided into seven compartments by strong divisions, and could with impunity brave any leak.

Captain Anderson went down immediately into the hold and found that a leak had sprung in the fifth compartment, and the sea was rushing in rapidly. Happily there were no boilers in this compartment, or the fires would have been at once put out. Captain Anderson ordered the engines to be immediately stopped, and one of the sailors dived to ascertain the extent of the damage. Some minutes after it was ascertained that there was a large hole about two yards in diameter in the ship's bottom. Such a leak could not be stopped, and the Scotia, with her paddles half submerged, was obliged to continue her voyage. She was then 300 miles from Cape Clear, and after three days' delay, which caused great anxiety in Liverpool, she entered the company's docks.

The engineers then proceeded to examine her in the dry dock, where she had been placed. They could scarcely believe their eyes; at two yards and a half below water-mark was a regular rent in the shape of an isosceles triangle. The place where the piece had been taken out of the iron plates was so sharply defined that it could not have been done more neatly by a punch. The perforating instrument that had done the work was of no common stamp, for after having been driven with prodigious force, and piercing an iron plate one and three-eighths of an inch thick, it had been withdrawn by some wonderful retrograde movement.

Such was the last fact, and it again awakened public opinion on the subject. After that all maritime disasters which could not be satisfactorily accounted for were put down to the account of the monster. All the responsibility of the numerous wrecks annually recorded at Lloyd's was laid to the charge of this fantastic animal, and they usually amount to 3,000, of which 200 are lost by unknown causes.

Thanks to the 'monster,' communication between the two continents became more and more difficult; the public loudly demanded that the seas should be rid of the formidable cetacean at any price.

Chapter Two

For and Against

AT THE PERIOD WHEN THESE events were happening I was returning from a scientific expedition into the disagreeable region of Nebraska, in the United States. In my quality of Assistant Professor in the Paris Museum of Natural History, the French Government had attached me to that expedition. I arrived at New York, loaded with precious collections made during six months in Nebraska, at the end of March. My departure from France was fixed for the beginning of May. Whilst I waited and was occupying myself with classifying my mineralogical, botanical, and zoological riches, the incident happened to the Scotia.

I was perfectly acquainted with the subject which was the question of the day, and it would have been strange had I not been. I had repeatedly read all the American and European papers without being any the wiser as to the cause. The mystery puzzled me, and I hesitated to form any conclusion.

When I arrived at New York the subject was hot. The hypothesis of a floating island or reef, which was supported by incompetent opinion, was quite abandoned, for unless the shoal had a machine in its stomach, how could it change its position with such marvellous rapidity? For the same reason the idea of a floating hull or gigantic wreck was given up.

There remained, therefore, two possible solutions of the enigma which created two distinct parties; one was that the object was a colossal monster, the other that it was a submarine vessel of enormous motive power. This last hypothesis, which, after all, was admissible, could not stand against inquiries made in the two hemispheres. It was hardly probable that a private individual should possess such a machine. Where and when had he caused it to be built, and how could he have kept its construction secret? Certainly a government might possess such a destructive engine, and it was possible in these disastrous times, when the power of weapons of war has been multiplied, that, without the knowledge of others, a state might possess so formidable a weapon. After the chassepots came the torpedoes, and after the torpedoes the submarine rams, and after them – the reaction. At least, I hope so.

But the hypothesis of a war machine fell before the declaration of different governments, and as the public interest suffered from the difficulty of transatlantic communication, their veracity could not be doubted. Besides, secrecy would be even more difficult to a government than to a private individual. After inquiries made in England, France, Russia, Prussia, Spain, Italy, America, and even Turkey, the hypothesis of a submarine monitor was definitely rejected.

On my arrival at New York, several persons did me the honour of consulting me about the phenomenon in question. I had published in France a quarto work in two volumes, called *The Mysteries of the Great Submarine Grounds*. This book made some sensation in the scientific world, and gained me a special reputation in this rather obscure branch of Natural History. As long as I could deny the reality of the fact I kept to a decided negative, but I was soon driven into a corner, and was obliged to explain myself categorically. The Honourable Pierre Aronnax, Professor in the Paris Museum, was asked by the *New York Herald* to give his opinion on the matter. I subjoin an extract from the article which I published on the 30th of April:——

'After having examined the different hypotheses one by one, and all other suppositions being rejected, the existence of a marine animal of excessive strength must be admitted.

'The greatest depths of the ocean are totally unknown to us. What happens there? What beings can live twelve or fifteen miles below the surface of the sea? We can scarcely conjecture what organization of these animals is. However the solution of the problem submitted to me may affect the form of the dilemma, we either know all the varieties of beings that people our planet or we do not. If we do not know them all – if there are still secrets of ichthyology for us – nothing is more reasonable than to admit the existence of fishes or cetaceans of an organization suitable to the strata inaccessible to soundings, which for some reason or other come up to the surface at intervals.

'If, on the contrary, we do know all living species, we must of course look for the animal in question amongst the already classified marine animals, and in that case I should be disposed to admit the existence of a gigantic narwhal.

'The common narwhal, or sea-unicorn, is often sixty feet long. This size is increased five or tenfold, and a strength in proportion to its size being given to the cetacean, and its offensive arms being increased in the same proportion, you obtain the animal required. It will have the proportions given by the officers of the Shannon, the instrument that perforated the Scotia, and the strength necessary to pierce the hull of the steamer.

'In fact, the narwhal is armed with a kind of ivory sword or halberd, as some naturalists call it. It is the principal tusk, and is as hard as steel. Some of these tusks have been found imbedded in the bodies of whales, which the narwhal always attacks with success. Others have been with difficulty taken out of ships' bottoms, which they pierced through and through like a gimlet in a barrel. The Museum of the Paris Faculty of Medicine contains one of these weapons, two and a quarter yards in length and fifteen inches in diameter at the base.

'Now suppose this weapon to be ten times stronger, and its possessor ten times more powerful, hurl it at the rate of twenty miles an hour, and you obtain a shock that might produce the catastrophe required. Therefore, until I get fuller information, I shall suppose it to be a sea-unicorn of colossal dimensions, armed, not with a halberd, but with a spur like ironclads or battering rams, the massiveness and motive power of which it would possess at the same time. This inexplicable phenomenon may be thus explained, unless something exists over and above anything ever conjectured, seen, or experienced, which is just possible.'

The last words were cowardly on my part, but I wished up to a certain point to cover my dignity as professor, and not to give too much cause of laughter to the Americans, who laugh well when they do laugh. I reserved myself a loophole of escape, and, in fact, admitted the existence of the monster.

My article was well received, and provoked much discussion amongst the public. It rallied a certain number of partisans. The solution which it proposed left freedom to the imagination. The human mind likes these grand conceptions of supernatural beings. Now the sea is precisely their best instrument of transmission, the only medium in which these giants, by the side of which terrestrial animals, elephants or rhinoceri, are but dwarfs, can breed and develop. The liquid masses transport the largest known species of mammalia, and they perhaps contain molluscs of enormous size, crustaceans frightful to contemplate, such as lobsters more than a hundred yards long, or crabs weighing two hundred tons. Why should it not be so? Formerly, terrestrial animals, contemporaries of the geological epochs, quadrupeds, quadrumans, reptiles, and birds, were constructed in gigantic moulds. The Creator had thrown them into a colossal mould which time has gradually lessened. Why should not the sea in its unknown depths have kept there vast specimens of the life of another age – the sea which never changes, whilst the earth changes incessantly? Why should it not hide in its bosom the last varieties of these Titanic species, whose years are centuries, and whose centuries are millenniums?

But I am letting myself be carried away by reveries which are no longer such to me. A truce to chimeras which time has changed for me into terrible realities. I repeat, opinion was then made up as to the nature of the phenomenon, and the public admitted without contestation the existence of the prodigious animal which had nothing in common with the fabulous sea serpents.

But if some people saw in this nothing but a purely scientific problem to solve, others more positive, especially in America and England, were of opinion to purge the ocean of this formidable monster, in order to reassure transmarine communications.

The *Shipping and Mercantile Gazette*, *Lloyd's List*, the *Packet Boat*, and *Revue Maritime et Coloniale*, all papers devoted to insurance companies who threatened to raise their rate of premium, were unanimous on this point. Public opinion having declared its verdict, the United States were first in the field, and preparations for an expedition to pursue the narwhal were at once begun in New York. A very fast frigate, the Abraham Lincoln, was put in commission, and the arsenals were opened to Captain Farragut, who actively hastened the arming of his frigate.

But, as generally happens, from the moment it was decided to pursue the monster, the monster was not heard of for two months. It seemed as if this unicorn knew about the plots that were being weaved for it. It had been so much talked of, even through the Atlantic Cable! Would-be wits pretended that the cunning fellow had stopped some telegram in its passage, and was now using the knowledge for his own benefit.

So when the frigate had been prepared for a long campaign, and furnished with formidable fishing apparatus, they did not know where to send her to. Impatience was increasing with the delay, when on 2nd July it was reported that a steamer of the San Francisco line, from California to Shanghai, had met with the animal three weeks before in the North Pacific Ocean.

The emotion caused by the news was extreme, and twenty-four hours only were granted to Captain Farragut before he sailed. The ship was already victualled and well stocked with coal. The crew were there to a man, and there was nothing to do but to light the fires.

Three hours before the Abraham Lincoln left Brooklyn Pier I received the following letter:

To M. ARONNAX, Professor of the Paris Museum,
Fifth Avenue Hotel,
New York.

SIR,——If you would like to join the expedition of the Abraham Lincoln, the United States Government will have great pleasure in seeing France represented by you in the enterprise. Captain Farragut has a cabin at your disposition.

Faithfully yours,
J.B. HOBSON,
Secretary of Marine.

Chapter Three

As Monsieur Pleases

THREE SECONDS BEFORE the arrival of J.B. Hobson's letter I had no more idea of pursuing the unicorn than of attempting the North-West Passage. Three seconds after having read the secretary's letter I had made up my mind that ridding the world of this monster was my veritable vocation and the single aim of my life.

But I had just returned from a fatiguing journey, and was longing for rest in my own little place in the Jardin des Plantes amongst my dear and precious collections. But I forgot all fatigue, repose and collections, and accepted without further reflection the offer of the American Government.

'Besides,' I said to myself, 'all roads lead back to Europe, and the unicorn may be amiable enough to draw me towards the French coast. This worthy animal may allow itself to be caught in European seas for my especial benefit, and I will not take back less than half a yard of its halberd to the Natural History Museum.'

But in the meantime the narwhal was taking me to the North Pacific Ocean, which was going to the antipodes on the road to France.

'Conseil!' I called in an impatient tone. 'Conseil!'

Conseil was my servant, a faithful fellow who accompanied me in all my journeys, a brave Dutchman I had great confidence in; he was phlegmatic by nature, regular from principle, zealous from habit, showing little astonishment at the varied surprises of life, very skilful with his hands, apt at any service, and, in spite of his name, never giving any counsel, even when not asked for it.

By dint of contact with the world of *savants* in our Jardin des Plantes, Conseil had succeeded in knowing something. He was a specialist, well up in the classification of Natural History, but his science stopped there. As far as practice was concerned, I do not think he could have distinguished a cachalot from a whale. And yet what a brave fellow he was!

Conseil had followed me during the last ten years wherever science had directed my steps. He never complained of the length or fatigue of a journey, or of having to pack his trunk for any country, however remote, whether China or Congo. He went there or elsewhere without questioning the wherefore. His health defied all illness, and he had solid muscles, but no nerves – not the least appearance of nerves – of course I mean in his mental faculties. He was thirty years old, and his age to that of his master was as fifteen is to twenty. May I be excused for saying that I was forty?

But Conseil had one fault. He was intensely formal, and would never speak to me except in the third person, which was sometimes irritating.

'Conseil!' I repeated, beginning my preparations for departure with a feverish hand.

Certainly, I was certain of this faithful fellow. Usually I did not ask him if it was or was not convenient for him to accompany me on my travels; but this time an expedition was in question which might be a very long and hazardous one, in pursuit of an animal capable of sinking a frigate like a nutshell! There was matter for reflection even to the most impassive man in the world. What would Conseil say?

'Conseil!' I called for the third time.

Conseil appeared.

'Did monsieur call me?' said he on entering.

'Yes, my boy. Get yourself and me ready to start in two hours.'

'As it pleases monsieur,' answered Conseil calmly.

'There is not a minute to lose. Pack up all my travelling utensils, as many coats, shirts and socks as you can get in. Make haste!'

'And monsieur's collections?' asked Conseil.

'We will see to them presently.'

'What, the archiotherium, the hyrachotherium, the oreodons, the cheropotamus, and monsieur's other skins?'

'They will stay at the hotel.'

'And the live babiroussa of monsieur's?'

'They will feed it during our absence. Besides, I will give orders to have our menagerie forwarded to France.'

'We are not going back to Paris, then?' asked Conseil.

'Yes – certainly we are,' answered I evasively; 'but by making a curve.'

'The curve that monsieur pleases.'

'Oh, it is not much; not so direct a route, that's all. We are going in the Abraham Lincoln.'

'As it may suit monsieur.'

'You know about the monster, Conseil – the famous narwhal. We are going to rid the seas of it. The author of the Great Submarine Grounds cannot do otherwise than embark with Commander Farragut. A glorious mission, but – dangerous too. We don't know where we are going to. Those animals may be very capricious! But we will go, whether or no! We have a captain who will keep his eyes open.'

'As monsieur does I will do,' answered Conseil.

'But think, for I will hide nothing from you. It is one of those voyages from which people do not always come back.'

'As monsieur pleases.'

A quarter of an hour afterwards our trunks were ready. Conseil had packed them by sleight of hand, and I was sure nothing would be missing, for the fellow classified shirts and clothes as well as he did birds or mammals.

The hotel lift deposited us in the large vestibule of the first floor. I went down the few stairs that led to the ground floor. I paid my bill at the vast counter, always besieged by a considerable crowd. I gave the order to send my cases of stuffed animals and dried plants to Paris (France). I opened a sufficient credit for the babiroussa, and, Conseil following me, I sprang into a vehicle.

The vehicle, at fifteen shillings the course, descended Broadway as far as Union-square, went along Fourth-avenue to its junction with Bowery-street, then along Katrin-street, and stopped at the thirty-fourth pier. There the Katrin ferry-boat transported us, men, horses and vehicle, to Brooklyn, the great annex of New York, situated on the left bank of East River, and in a few minutes we arrived at the quay opposite which the Abraham Lincoln was pouring forth clouds of black smoke from her two funnels.

Our luggage was at once sent on board, and we soon followed it. I asked for Captain Farragut. One of the sailors conducted me to the poop, where I found myself in the presence of a pleasant-looking officer, who held out his hand to me.

'Monsieur Pierre Aronnax?' he said.

'Himself,' replied I. 'Do I see Captain Farragut?'

'In person. You are welcome, professor. Your cabin is ready for you.'

I bowed, and leaving the commander to his duties, went down to the cabin which had been prepared for me.

The Abraham Lincoln had been well chosen and equipped for her new destination. She was a frigate of great speed, furnished with overheating apparatus that allowed the tension of the steam to reach seven atmospheres. Under that pressure the Abraham Lincoln reached an average speed of eighteen miles and three-tenths an hour good speed, but not enough to wrestle with the gigantic cetacean.

The interior arrangements of the frigate were in keeping with her nautical qualities. I was well satisfied with my cabin, which was situated aft, and opened on the wardroom.

'We shall be comfortable here,' said I to Conseil.

'Yes, as comfortable as a hermit crab in a crumpet-shell.'

I left Conseil to stow our luggage away, and went up on deck in order to see the preparations for departure. Captain Farragut was just ordering the last moorings to be cast loose, so that had I been one quarter of an hour later the frigate would have started without me, and I should have missed this extraordinary, supernatural, and incredible expedition, the true account of which may well be received with some incredulity.

But Commander Farragut did not wish to lose either a day or an hour before scouring the seas in which the animal had just been signalled. He sent for his engineer.

'Is the steam full on?' asked the captain.

'Yes, captain,' replied the engineer.

'Go ahead then,' cried Farragut.

The Abraham Lincoln was soon moving majestically amongst a hundred ferry-boats and tenders loaded with spectators, past the Brooklyn quay, on which, as well as on all that part of New York bordering-the East River, crowds of spectators were assembled. Thousands of handkerchiefs were waved above the compact mass, and saluted the Abraham Lincoln until she reached the Hudson at the point of that elongated peninsula which forms the town of New York.

Then the frigate followed the coast of New Jersey, along the right bank of the beautiful river covered with villas, and passed between the forts, which saluted her with their largest guns. The Abraham Lincoln acknowledged the salutation by hoisting the American colours three times, their thirty-nine stars shining resplendent from the mizen peak; then modifying her speed to take the narrow channel marked by buoys and formed by Sandy Hook Point, she coasted the long sandy shore, where several thousand spectators saluted her once more.

Her escort of boats and tenders followed her till she reached the light boat, the two lights of which mark the entrance to the New York Channel.

Three o'clock was then striking. The pilot went down into his boat and rejoined the little schooner which was waiting under lee, the fires were made up, the screw beat the waves more rapidly, and the frigate coasted the low yellow shore of Long Island. At 8 p.m., after having lost sight in the north west of the lights on Fire Island, she ran at full steam on to the dark waters of the Atlantic.

Chapter Four

Ned Land

CAPTAIN FARRAGUT WAS a good seaman, worthy of the frigate he was commanding. His ship and he were one. He was the soul of it. No doubt arose in his mind on the question of the cetacean, and he did not allow the existence of the animal to be disputed on board. He believed in it like certain simple souls believe in the Leviathan – by faith, not by sight. The monster existed, and he had sworn to deliver the seas from it. He was a sort of Knight of Rhodes, a second Dieudonné de Gozon going to meet the serpent which was desolating his island. Either Captain Farragut would kill the narwhal or the narwhal would kill Captain Farragut – there was no middle course.

The officers on board shared the opinion of their chief. It was amusing to hear them talking, arguing, disputing and calculating the different chances of meeting whilst they kept a sharp look-out over the vast extent of ocean. More than one took up his position on the crosstrees who would have cursed the duty as a nuisance at any other time. Whilst the sun described its diurnal circle the rigging was crowded with sailors who could not keep in place on deck. And nevertheless the Abraham Lincoln was not yet ploughing with her stern the suspected waters of the Pacific.

As to the crew, all they wanted was to meet the unicorn, harpoon it, haul it on board, and cut it up. Captain Farragut had offered a reward of 2,000 dollars to the first cabin-boy, sailor, or officer who should signal the animal. I have already said that Captain Farragut had carefully provided all the tackle necessary for taking the gigantic cetacean. A whaler would not have been better furnished. We had every known engine, from the hand harpoon to the barbed arrow of the blunderbuss and the explosive bullets of the deck-gun. On the forecastle lay a perfect breechloader very thick at the breech and narrow in the bore, the model of which had been in the Paris Exhibition of 1867. This precious weapon, of American make, could throw with ease a conical projectile, weighing nine pounds, to a mean distance of ten miles. Thus the Abraham Lincoln not only possessed every means of destruction, but, better still, she had on board Ned Land, the king of harpooners.

Ned Land was a Canadian of uncommon skill, who had no equal in his perilous employment. He possessed ability, sangfroid, audacity, and subtleness to a remarkable degree, and it would have taken a sharp whale or a singularly wily cachalot to escape his harpoon. He was about forty years of age, tall (more than six feet high), strongly built, grave, and taciturn, sometimes violent, and very passionate when put out. His person, and especially the power of his glance, which gave a singular expression to his face, attracted attention.

I believe that Captain Farragut had done wisely in engaging this man. He was worth all the rest of the ship's company as far as his eye and arm went. I could not compare him to anything better than a powerful telescope which would be a cannon always ready to fire as well.

Ned Land was a descendant of French Canadians, and although he was so little communicative, he took a sort of liking to me. My nationality, doubtless, attracted him. It was an occasion for him to speak and for me to hear that old language of Rabelais which is still in use in some Canadian provinces. The family of the harpooner came originally from Quebec, and already formed a tribe of hardy fishermen when that town belonged to France. Little by little Ned Land acquired a liking for talk, and I was delighted to hear the recital of his adventures in the Polar Seas. He related his fishing expeditions and combats with great natural poetry. It was like listening to an epic poem of the time of Homer, an Iliad about hyperborean regions.

I now depict this brave companion as I knew him afterwards, for we are old friends united in that unchangeable friendship which is born and cemented in mutual danger. Ah, brave Ned, I only hope I may live a hundred years more to remember you longer.

Now what was Ned Land's opinion on the subject of this marine monster? I must acknowledge that he hardly believed in the narwhal, and that he was the only one on board who did not share the universal conviction.

One magnificent evening, three weeks after our departure, on the 30th of July, the frigate was abreast of Cape Blanc, thirty miles to leeward of the Patagonian coast. We had crossed the tropic of Capricorn, and the Straits of Magellan lay less than 700 miles to the south. Another week and the Abraham Lincoln would be ploughing the waters of the Pacific.

Seated on the poop, Ned Land and I were talking on all sorts of subjects, looking at that mysterious sea whose greatest depths have remained till now inaccessible to the eye of man. I brought the conversation naturally to the subject of the giant unicorn, and discussed the different chances of success in our expedition. Then seeing that Ned Land let me go on talking without saying anything himself, I pressed him more closely.

'Well, Ned,' I said to him, 'are you not yet convinced of the existence of the cetacean we are pursuing? Have you any particular reasons for being so incredulous?'

The harpooner looked at me for some minutes before replying, struck his forehead with a gesture habitual to him, shut his eyes as if to collect himself, and said at last——

'Perhaps I have, M. Aronnax.'

'Yet you, Ned, are a whaler by profession. You are familiar with the great marine mammalia, and your imagination ought easily to accept the hypothesis of enormous cetaceans. You ought to be the last to doubt in such circumstances.'

'That is what deceives you, sir,' answered Ned. 'It is not strange that common people should believe in extraordinary comets, or the existence of antediluvian monsters peopling the interior of the globe, but no astronomer or geologist would believe in such chimeras. The whaler is the same. I have pursued many cetaceans, harpooned a great number, and killed some few; but however powerful or well armed they were, neither their tails nor their defences could ever have made an incision in the iron plates of a steamer.'

'Yet, Ned, it is said that ships have been bored through by the tusk of a narwhal.'

'Wooden ships, perhaps,' answered the Canadian, 'though I have never seen it, and until I get proof to the contrary I deny that whales, cachalots, or sea-unicorns could produce such an effect.'

'Listen to me, Ned.'

'No, sir, no; anything you like but that – a gigantic poulp, perhaps?'

'No, that can't be. The poulp is only a mollusc; its flesh has no more consistency than its name indicates.'

'Then you really do believe in this cetacean, sir?' said Ned.

'Yes, Ned. I repeat it with a conviction resting on the logic of facts. I believe in the existence of a mammal, powerfully organized, belonging to the branch of vertebrata, like whales, cachalots, and dolphins, and furnished with a horn tusk, of which the force of penetration is extreme.'

'Hum!' said the harpooner, shaking his head like a man who will not let himself be convinced.

'Remark, my worthy Canadian,' I continued, 'if such an animal exists and inhabits the depths of the ocean, it necessarily possesses an organization the strength of which would defy all comparison.'

'Why must it have such an organization?' asked Ned.

'Because it requires an incalculable strength to keep in such deep water and resist its pressure. Admitting that the pressure of the atmosphere is represented by that of a column of water thirty-two feet high. In reality the column of water would not be so high, as it is sea-water that is in question, and its density is greater than that of fresh water. When you dive, Ned, as many times thirty-two feet of water as there are above you, so many times does your body support a pressure equal to that of the atmosphere – that is to say, 15lbs. for each square inch of its surface. It hence follows that at 320 feet this pressure equals that of 10 atmospheres; at 3,200 feet, 100 atmospheres; and at 32,000 feet, 1,000 atmospheres – that is, about six and a half miles, which is equivalent to saying that if you can reach this depth in the ocean, each square inch of the surface of your body would bear a pressure of 14,933⅓lbs. Do you know how many square inches you have on the surface of your body?'

'I have no idea, Aronnax.'

'About 6,500; and as in reality the atmospheric pressure is about 15lbs to the square inch, your 6.500 square inches support at this minute a pressure of 97,500 lbs.'

'Without my perceiving it?'

'Yes; and if you are not crushed by such a pressure, it is because the air penetrates the interior of your body with equal pressure, and there is a perfect equilibrium between the interior and exterior pressure, which thus neutralize each other, and allow you to bear it without inconvenience. But it is another thing in water.'

'Yes, I understand,' answered Ned, becoming more attentive, 'because I am in water, but it is not in me.'

'Precisely, Ned; so that at 32 feet below the surface of the sea you would undergo a pressure of 97,500 lbs; at 320 feet, 975,000 lbs; and at 32,000 ft the pressure would be 97,500,000 lbs – that is to say, you would be crushed as flat as a pancake.'

'The devil!' exclaimed Ned.

'If vertebrata can maintain themselves in such depths, especially those whose surface is represented by millions of square inches, it is by hundreds of millions of pounds we must estimate the pressure they bear. Calculate, then, what must be the resistance of their bony structure and the strength of their organization to withstand such a pressure.'

'They must be made of iron plate eight inches thick like ironclads!' said Ned.

'Yes, and think what destruction such a mass could cause if hurled with the speed of an express against the hull of a ship.'

Ned would not give in.

'Have I not convinced you?' I said.

'You have convinced me of one thing, sir, which is, that if such animals do exist at the bottom of the sea they must be as strong as you say.'

'But if they do not exist, Mr Obstinate, how do you account for the Scotia's accident?'

'Because it is——' began Ned hesitatingly.

'Go on!'

'Because – it is not true!' answered the Canadian, repeating, without knowing it, a celebrated answer of Arago.

But this answer proved the obstinacy of the harpooner and nothing else. That day I did not press him further. The accident to the Scotia was undeniable. The hole existed so really that they were obliged to stop it up, and I do not think that the existence of a hole can be more categorically demonstrated. Now the hole had not made itself, and since it had not been done by submarine rocks or submarine machines, it was certainly due to the perforating tool of an animal.

Now, in my opinion, and for all the reasons previously deduced, this animal belonged to the embranchment of the vertebrata, to the class of mammals, to the group of pisciforms, and, finally, to the order of cetaceans. As to the family in which it took rank, whale, cachalot, or dolphin, as to the genus of which it formed a part, as to the species in which it would be convenient to put it, that was a question to be elucidated subsequently. In order to solve it the unknown monster must be dissected; to dissect it, it must be taken, to take it, it must be harpooned – which was Ned Land's business – to harpoon it, it must be seen – which was the crew's business – and to see it, it must be encountered – which was the business of hazard.

Chapter Five

At Random

THE VOYAGE OF THE ABRAHAM LINCOLN for some time was marked by no incident. At last a circumstance happened which showed off the wonderful skill of Ned Land and the confidence that might be placed in him.

On the 30th of June the frigate, being then off the Falkland Islands, spoke some American whalers, who told us they had not met with the narwhal. But one of them, the captain of the Munroe, knowing that Ned Land was on board the Abraham Lincoln, asked for his help in capturing a whale they had in sight. Captain Farragut, desirous of seeing Ned Land at work, allowed him to go on board the Munroe, and fortune favoured our Canadian so well, that instead of one whale he harpooned two with a double blow, striking one right in the heart, and capturing the other after a pursuit of some minutes.

Certainly if the monster ever had Ned Land to deal with I would not bet in its favour.

The frigate skirted the south-east coast of America with extraordinary rapidity. On the 3rd of July we were at the opening of the Straits of Magellan, off Cape Vierges. But Captain Farragut did not wish to take this sinuous passage, but worked the ship for the doubling of Cape Horn.

The crew agreed with him unanimously. And certainly it was not possible that we should meet the narwhal in so narrow a pass.

On the 6th of July, about 3 p.m., we doubled, fifteen miles to the south, the solitary island to which some Dutch sailors gave the name of their native town, Cape Horn. The next day the frigate was in the Pacific.

'Keep a sharp look-out!' cried all the sailors.

Both eyes and telescopes, a little dazzled certainly by the thought of 2,000 dollars, never had a minute's rest. Day and night they observed the surface of the ocean; and even nyctalops, whose faculty of seeing in the darkness increased their chances fifty per cent, would have had to keep a sharp look-out to win the prize.

I myself, who thought little about the money, was not, however, the least attentive on board. I was constantly on deck, giving but few minutes to my meals, and indifferent to either rain or sunshine. Now leaning over the sea on the forecastle, now on the taffrail, I devoured with greedy eyes the soft foam which whitened the sea as far as those eyes could reach! How many times have I shared the emotion of the officers and crew when some capricious whale raised its black back above the waves! The deck was crowded in a minute. The companion ladders poured forth a torrent of officers and sailors, each with heaving breast and troubled eye watching the cetacean. I looked and looked till I was nearly blind, whilst Conseil, always calm, kept saying to me——

'If monsieur did not keep his eyes open so much he would see more.'

But vain excitement! The Abraham Lincoln would modify her speed, run down the animal signalled, which always turned out to be a simple whale or common cachalot, and disappeared amidst a storm of execration.

In the meantime the weather remained favourable. The voyage was being accomplished under the best conditions. It was then the bad season in the southern hemisphere, for the July of that zone corresponds with the January of Europe, yet the sea was so calm that the eye could scan a vast circumference.

Ned Land always showed the most tenacious incredulity; he even affected not to examine the seas except during his watch, unless a whale was in sight; and yet his marvellous power of vision might have been of great service. But eight hours out of the twelve the obstinate Canadian read or slept in his cabin.

'Bah!' he would answer; 'there is nothing. M. Aronnax; and even if there is an animal, what chance have we of seeing it? Are we not going about at random? I will admit that the beast has been seen again in the North Pacific, but two months have already gone by since that meeting, and according to the temperament of your narwhal it does not like to stop long enough in the same quarter to grow mouldy. It is endowed with a prodigious faculty of moving about. Now, you know as well as I do, professor, that Nature makes nothing inconsistent, and would not give to a slow animal the faculty of moving rapidly if it did not want to use it. Therefore, if the beast exists, it is far enough off now.'

I did not know what to answer to that. We were evidently going along blindly. But how were we to do otherwise? Our chances, too, were very limited. In the meantime no one yet doubted of our success, and there was not a sailor on board who would have bet against the narwhal and against its early apparition.

On the 20th of July the tropic of Capricorn was crossed at 105° longitude, and the 27th of the same month we crossed the equator on the 110th meridian. These bearings taken, the frigate took a more decided direction westward, and entered the central seas of the Pacific. Captain Farragut rightly thought that it was better to frequent the deep seas, and keep at a distance from continents or islands, which the animal had always seemed to avoid approaching. 'Doubtless because there was not enough water for him there,' said the boatswain. The frigate, therefore, passed at a good distance from the Society, Marquesas, and Sandwich Islands, crossed the tropic of Cancer by 132° longitude, and made for the seas of China.

We were at last on the scene of the last frolics of the monster; and the truth was, no one lived really on board. Hearts beat frightfully fast, and laid down the seeds of future aneurisms. The entire crew were under the influence of such nervous excitement as I could not give the idea of. They neither ate nor slept. Twenty times a day some error of estimation, or the optical delusion of a sailor perched on the yards, caused intolerable frights; and these emotions, twenty times repeated, kept us in a state of erethismus too violent not to cause an early reaction.

And, in fact, the reaction was not slow in coming. For three months – three months, each day of which lasted a century – the Abraham Lincoln ploughed all the waters of the North Pacific, running down all the whales signalled, making sharp deviations from her route, veering suddenly from one tack to another, and not leaving one point of the Chinese or Japanese coast unexplored. And yet nothing was seen but the immense waste of waters – nothing that resembled a gigantic narwhal, nor a submarine islet, nor a wreck, nor a floating reef, nor anything at all supernatural.

The reaction, therefore, began. Discouragement at first took possession of all minds, and opened a breach for incredulity. A new sentiment was experienced on board, composed of three-tenths of shame and seven-tenths of rage. They called themselves fools for being taken in by a chimera, and were still more furious at it. The mountains of arguments piled up for a year fell down all at once, and all everyone thought of was to make up the hours of meals and sleep which they had so foolishly sacrificed.

With the mobility natural to the human mind, they threw themselves from one excess into another. The warmest partisans of the enterprise became finally its most ardent detractors. The reaction ascended from the depths of the vessel, from the coal-hole, to the officers' wardroom, and certainly, had it not been for very strong determination on the part of Captain Farragut, the head of the frigate would have been definitely turned southward.

However, this useless search could be no further prolonged. The Abraham Lincoln had nothing to reproach herself with, having done all she could to succeed. No crew of the American Navy had ever shown more patience or zeal; its want of success could not be imputed to it. There was nothing left to do but to return.

A represention in this sense was made to the commander. The commander kept his ground. The sailors did not hide their dissatisfaction, and the service suffered from it. I do not mean that there was revolt on board, but after a reasonable period of obstinacy the commander, Farragut, like Columbus before him, asked for three days' patience. If in the delay of three days the monster had not reappeared, the man at the helm should give three turns of the wheel and the Abraham Lincoln should make for the European seas.

This promise was made on the 2nd of November. Its first effect was to rally the spirits of the ship's company. The ocean was observed with renewed attention.

Two days past. The frigate kept up steam at half-pressure. Large quantities of bacon were trailed in the wake of the ship, to the great satisfaction of the sharks. The frigate lay to, and her boats were sent in all directions, but the night of the 4th of November passed without unveiling the submarine mystery.

The next day, the 5th of November, was the last of the delay.

The frigate was then in 31° 15'N. latitude and 136° 42'E. longitude. Japan lay less than 200 miles to leeward. Eight bells had just struck as I was leaning over the starboard side. Conseil, standing near me, was looking straight in front of him. The crew, perched in the ratlins, were keeping a sharp look-out in the approaching darkness. Officers with their night-glasses swept the horizon.

Looking at Conseil, I saw that the brave fellow was feeling slightly the general influence – at least it seemed to me so. Perhaps for the first time, his nerves were vibrating under the action of a sentiment of curiosity.

'Well, Conseil,' said I, 'this is your last chance of pocketing 2,000 dollars.'

'Will monsieur allow me to tell him that I never counted upon the reward, and if the Union had promised a hundred thousand dollars it would never be any the poorer.'

'You are right, Conseil. It has been a stupid affair, after all. We have lost time and patience, and might just as well have been in France six months ago.'

'Yes, in monsieur's little apartments, classifying monsieur's fossils, and monsieur's babiroussa would be in its cage in the Jardin des Plantes, attracting all the curious people in Paris.'

'Yes, Conseil, and besides that we shall get well laughed at.'

'Certainly,' said Conseil tranquilly. 'I think they will laugh at monsieur. And I must say——'

'What, Conseil?'

'That it will serve monsieur right! When one has the honour to be a *savant* like monsieur, one does not expose——'

Conseil did not finish his compliment. In the midst of general silence Ned Land's voice was heard calling out——

'Look out there! The very thing we are looking for – on our weather beam!'

Chapter Six

With All Steam On

AT THIS CRY THE ENTIRE crew rushed towards the harpooner. Captain, officers, masters, sailors, and cabin-boys, even the engineers left their engines, and the stokers their fires. The order to stop her had been given, and the frigate was only moving by her own momentum. The darkness was then profound, and although I knew the Canadian's eyes were very good, I asked myself what he could have seen, and how he could have seen it. My heart beat violently.

But Ned Land was not mistaken, and we all saw the object he was pointing to.

At two cables' length from the Abraham Lincoln on her starboard quarter, the sea seemed to be illuminated below the surface. The monster lay some fathoms below the sea, and threw out the very intense but inexplicable light mentioned in the reports of several captains. This light described as immense and much-elongated oval, in the centre of which was condensed a focus the overpowering brilliancy of which died out by successive gradations.

'It is only an agglomeration of phosphoric particles,' cried one of the officers.

'No, sir,' I replied with conviction. 'Never did pholas or salpae produce such a light as that. That light is essentially electric. Besides – see! look out! It moves – forward – on to us!'

A general cry rose from the frigate.

'Silence!' called out the captain. 'Up with the helm! Reverse the engines!'

The frigate thus tried to escape, but the supernatural animal approached her with a speed double her own.

Stupefaction, more than fear, kept us mute and motionless. The animal gained upon us. It made the round of the frigate, which was then going at the rate of fourteen knots, and enveloped her with its electric ring like luminous dust. Then it went two or three miles off, leaving a phosphoric trail like the steam of an express locomotive. All at once, from the dark limits of the horizon, where it went to gain its momentum, the monster rushed towards the frigate with frightful rapidity, stopped suddenly at a distance of twenty feet, and then went out, not diving, for its brilliancy did not die out by degrees, but all at once as if turned off. Then it reappeared on the other side of the ship, either going round her or gliding under her hull. A collision might have occurred at any moment, which might have been fatal to us.

I was astonished at the way the ship was worked. She was being attacked instead of attacking; and I asked Captain Farragut the reason. On the captain's generally impassive face was an expression of profound astonishment.

'M. Aronnax,' he said, 'I do not know with how formidable a being I have to deal, and I will not imprudently risk my frigate in the darkness. We must wait for daylight, and then we shall change parts.'

'You have no longer any doubt, captain, of the nature of the animal?'

'No, sir. It is evidently a gigantic narwhal, and an electric one too.'

'Perhaps,' I added, 'we can no more approach it than we could a gymnotus or a torpedo.'

'It may possess as great blasting properties, and if it does it is the most terrible animal that ever was created. That is why I must keep on my guard.'

All the crew remained up that night. No one thought of going to sleep. The Abraham Lincoln, not being able to compete in speed, was kept under half-steam. On its side the narwhal imitated the frigate, let the waves rock it at will, and seemed determined not to leave the scene of combat.

Towards midnight, however, it disappeared, dying out like a large glow-worm. At seven minutes to one in the morning a deafening whistle was heard, like that produced by a column of water driven out with extreme violence.

The captain, Ned Land, and I were then on the poop, peering with eagerness through the profound darkness.

'Ned Land,' asked the commander, 'have you often heard whales roar?'

'Yes, captain, often; but never such a whale as I earned two thousand dollars by sighting.'

'True, you have a right to the prize; but tell me, is it the same noise they make?'

'Yes, sir; but this one is incomparably louder. It is not to be mistaken. It is certainly a cetacean there in our seas. With your permission, sir, we will have a few words with him at daybreak.'

'If he is in a humour to hear them, Mr Land,' said I, in an unconvinced tone.

'Let me get within a length of four harpoons,' answered the Canadian, 'and he will be obliged to listen to me.'

'But in order to approach him,' continued the captain, 'I shall have to put a whaler at your disposition.'

'Certainly, sir.'

'But that will be risking the lives of my men.'

'And mine too,' answered the harpooner simply.

About 2 a.m. the luminous focus reappeared, no less intense, about five miles to the windward of the frigate. Notwithstanding the distance and the noise of the wind and sea, the loud strokes of the animal's tail were distinctly heard, and even its panting breathing. When the enormous narwhal came up to the surface to breathe, it seemed as if the air rushed into its lungs like steam in the vast cylinders of a 2,000 horse-power engine.

'Hum!' thought I, 'a whale with the strength of a cavalry regiment would be a pretty whale!'

Until daylight we were all on the *qui-vive*, and then the fishing-tackle was prepared. The first mate loaded the blunderbusses, which throw harpoons the distance of a mile, and long duck-guns with explosive bullets, which inflict mortal wounds even upon the most powerful animals. Ned Land contented himself with sharpening his harpoon – a terrible weapon in his hands.

At 6 a.m. day began to break, and with the first glimmer of dawn the electric light of the narwhal disappeared. At 7 a.m. a very thick sea-fog obscured the atmosphere, and the best glasses could not pierce it.

I climbed the mizenmast and found some officers already perched on the mast heads.

At 8 a.m. the mist began to clear away. Suddenly, like the night before, Ned Land's voice was heard calling——

'The thing in question on the port quarter!'

All eyes were turned towards the point indicated. There, a mile and a half from the frigate, a large black body emerged more than a yard above the waves. Its tail, violently agitated, produced a considerable eddy. Never did caudal appendage beat the sea with such force. An immense track, dazzlingly white, marked the passage of the animal, and described a long curve.

The frigate approached the cetacean, and I could see it well. The accounts of it given by the Shannon and Helvetia had rather exaggerated its dimensions, and I estimated its length at 150 feet only. As to its other dimensions, I could only conceive them to be in proportion.

Whilst I was observing it, two jets of vapour and water sprang from its vent-holes and ascended to a height of fifty yards, thus fixing my opinions as to its way of breathing. I concluded definitely that it belonged to the vertebrate branch of mammalia, order of cetaceans, family . . . Here I could not decide. The order of cetaceans comprehends three families – whales, cachalots, and dolphins – and it is in this last that narwhals are placed.

The crew were waiting impatiently for their captain's orders. Farragut, after attentively examining the animal, had the chief engineer called.

'Is your steam up, sir?' asked the captain.

'Yes, captain,' answered the engineer.

'Then make up your fires and put on all steam.'

Three cheers greeted this order. The hour of combat had struck. Some minutes afterwards the funnels of the frigate were giving out torrents of black smoke, and the deck shook under the trembling of the boilers.

The Abraham Lincoln, propelled by her powerful screw, went straight at the animal, who let her approach to within half a cable's length, and then, as if disdaining to dive, made a little attempt at flight, and contented itself with keeping its distance.

This pursuit lasted about three-quarters of an hour, without the frigate gaining four yards on the cetacean. It was quite evident she would never reach it at that rate.

The captain twisted his beard impatiently.

'Ned Land!' called the captain, 'do you think I had better have the boats lowered?'

'No, sir,' answered Ned Land, 'for that animal won't be caught unless it chooses.'

'What must be done, then?'

'Force steam if you can, captain, and I, with your permission, will post myself under the bowsprit, and if we get within a harpoon length I shall hurl one.'

'Very well, Ned,' said the captain. 'Engineer, put on more pressure.'

Ned Land went to his post, the fires were increased, the screw revolved forty-three times a minute, and the steam poured out of the valves. The log was heaved, and it was found that the frigate was going eighteen miles and five-tenths an hour. But the animal went eighteen and five-tenths an hour too.

During another hour the frigate kept up that speed without gaining a yard. It was humiliating for one of the quickest vessels in the American navy. The crew began to get very angry. The sailors swore at the animal, who did not deign to answer them. The captain not only twisted his beard, he began to gnaw it too. The engineer was called once more.

'Have you reached your maximum of pressure?' asked the captain.

'Yes, sir.'

The captain order him to do all he could without absolutely blowing up the vessel, and coal was at once piled up on the fires. The speed of the frigate increased. Her masts shook again. The log was again heaved, and this time she was making nineteen miles and three-tenths.

'All steam on!' called out the captain.

The engineer obeyed. The manometer marked ten degrees. But the cetacean did the nineteen miles and three-tenths as easily as the eighteen and five-tenths.

What a chase! I cannot describe the emotion that made my whole being vibrate again. Ned Land kept his post, harpoon in hand. The animal allowed itself to be approached several times. Sometimes it was so near that the Canadian raised his hand to hurl the harpoon, when the animal rushed away at a speed of at least thirty miles an hour, and even during our maximum of speed it bullied the frigate, going round and round it.

A cry of fury burst from all lips. We were not further advanced at twelve o'clock than we had been at eight. Captain Farragut then made up his mind to employ more direct means.

'Ah!' said he, 'so that animal goes faster than my ship! Well, we'll see if he'll go faster than a conical bullet. Master, send your men to the forecastle.'

The forecastle gun was immediately loaded and pointed. It was fired, but the ball passed some feet above the cetacean, which kept about half a mile off.

'Let someone else have a try!' called out the captain. 'Five hundred dollars to whomsoever will hit the beast!'

An old gunner with a grey beard – I think I see now his calm face as he approached the gun – put it into position and took a long aim. A loud report followed and mingled with the cheers of the crew.

The bullet reached its destination; it struck the animal, but, gliding off the rounded surface, fell into the sea two miles off.

'Malediction!' cried the captain; 'that animal must be clad in six-inch iron plates. But I'll catch it, if I have to blow up my frigate!'

It was to be hoped that the animal would be exhausted, and that it would not be indifferent to fatigue like a steam-engine. But the hours went on, and it showed no signs of exhaustion.

It must be said, in praise of the Abraham Lincoln, that she struggled on indefatigably. I cannot reckon the distance we made during this unfortunate day at less than 300 miles. But night came on and closed round the heaving ocean.

At that minute I believed our expedition to be at an end, and that we should see the fantastic animal no more.

I was mistaken, for at 10.50 p.m., the electric light reappeared, three miles windward to the frigate, as clear and intense as on the night before.

The narwhal seemed motionless. Perhaps, fatigued with its day's work, it was sleeping in its billowy cradle. That was a chance by which the captain resolved to profit.

He gave his orders. The Abraham Lincoln was kept up at half-steam, and advanced cautiously so as not to awaken her adversary. It is not rare to meet in open sea with whales fast asleep, and Ned Land had harpooned many a one in that condition. The Canadian went back to his post under the bowsprit.

The frigate noiselessly approached, and stopped at two cables' length from the animal. No one breathed. A profound silence reigned on deck. We were not 1,000 feet from the burning focus, the light of which increased and dazzled our eyes.

At that minute, leaning on the forecastle bulwark, I saw Ned Land below me, holding the martingale with one hand and with the other brandishing his terrible harpoon, scarcely twenty feet from the motionless animal.

All at once he threw the harpoon, and I heard the sonorous stroke of the weapon, which seemed to have struck a hard body.

The electric light suddenly went out, and two enormous water-spouts fell on the deck of the frigate, running like a torrent from fore to aft, upsetting men, and breaking the lashing of the spars.

A frightful shock followed. I was thrown over the rail before I had time to stop myself, and fell into the sea.

Chapter Seven

A Whale of an Unknown Species

ALTHOUGH I WAS SURPRISED by my unexpected fall, I still kept a very distinct impression of my sensations. I was at first dragged down to a depth of about twenty feet. I was a good swimmer without any pretensions to equal Byron or Edgar Poe, both masters in the art, and this plunge did not make me lose my presence of mind. Two vigorous kicks brought me back to the surface.

My first care was to look for the frigate. Had the crew seen me disappear? Had the Abraham Lincoln veered round? Would the captain have a boat lowered?

Might I hope to be saved?

The darkness was profound. I perceived a black mass disappearing in the east, the beacon lights of which were dying out in the distance. It was the frigate. I gave myself up.

'Help! help!' cried I, swimming towards the frigate with desperate strokes.

My clothes embarrassed me. The water glued them to my body. They paralysed my movements. I was sinking.

'Help!' rang out again in the darkness.

This was the last cry I uttered. My mouth filled with water. I struggled not to be sucked into the abyss.

Suddenly my clothes were seized by a vigorous hand, and I felt myself brought back violently to the surface of the water, and I heard – yes, I heard these words uttered in my ear.

'If monsieur will have the goodness to lean on my shoulder, monsieur will swim much better.'

I seized the arm of my faithful Conseil.

'You!' I cried – 'you!'

'Myself,' answered Conseil, 'at monsieur's service.'

'Did the shock throw you into the sea too?'

'No; but being in the service of monsieur, I followed him.'

The worthy fellow thought that quite natural.

'What about the frigate?' I asked.

'The frigate!' answered Conseil, turning on his back; 'I think monsieur will do well not to count upon the frigate.'

'Why?'

'Because, as I jumped into the sea, I heard the man at the helm call out, "The screw and the rubber are broken."'

'Broken?'

'Yes, by the monster's tusk. It is the only damage she has sustained. I think; but without the helm she can't do anything for us.'

'Then we are lost!'

'Perhaps,' answered Conseil tranquilly. 'In the meantime we have still several hours before us, and in several hours many things may happen.'

The imperturbable sangfroid of Conseil did me good. I swam more vigorously, but, encumbered by my garments, which dragged me down like a leaden weight, I found it extremely difficult to keep up. Conseil perceived it.

'Will monsieur allow me to make a slit?' said he. And, slipping an open knife under my clothes, he slit them rapidly from top to bottom. Then he quickly helped me off with them whilst I swam for both. I rendered him the same service, and we went on swimming near each other.

In the meantime our situation was none the less terrible. Perhaps our disappearance had not been remarked, and even if it had the frigate could not tack without her helm. Our only chance of safety was in the event of the boats being lowered.

The collision had happened about 11 p.m. About 1 a.m. I was taken with extreme fatigue, and all my limbs became stiff with cramp. Conseil was obliged to keep me up, and the care of our preservation depended upon him alone. I heard the poor fellow breathing hard, and knew he could not keep up much longer.

'Let me go! Leave me!' I cried.

'Leave monsieur? Never!' he answered. 'I shall drown with him.'

Just then the moon appeared through the fringe of a large cloud that the wind was driving eastward. The surface of the sea shone under her rays. I lifted my head and saw the frigate. She was five miles from us, and only looked like a dark mass, scarcely distinguishable. I saw no boats.

I tried to call out, but it was useless at that distance. My swollen lips would not utter a sound. Conseil could still speak, and I heard him call out 'Help!' several times.

We suspended our movements for an instant and listened. It might be only a singing in our ears, but it seemed to me that a cry answered Conseil's.

'Did you hear?' I murmured.

'Yes, yes!'

And Conseil threw another despairing cry into space. This time there could be no mistake. A human voice answered ours. Was it the voice of some other victim of the shock, or a boat hailing us in the darkness? Conseil made a supreme effort, and leaning on my shoulder whilst I made a last struggle for us both, he raised himself half out of the water, and I heard him shout. Then my strength was exhausted, my fingers slipped, my mouth filled with salt water, I went cold all over, raised my head for the last time, and began to sink.

At that moment I hit against something hard, and I clung to it in desperation. Then I felt myself lifted up out of the water, and I fainted – I soon came to, thanks to the vigorous friction that was being applied to my body, and I half-opened my eyes.

'Conseil!' I murmured.

'Did monsieur ring?' answered Conseil.

Just then, by the light of the moon that was getting lower on the horizon, I perceived a face that was not Conseil's, but which I immediately recognized.

'Ned!' I cried.

'The same, sir, looking after his prize,' replied the Canadian.

'Were you thrown into the sea when the frigate was struck?'

'Yes, sir, but, luckier than you. I soon got upon a floating island.'

'An island?'

'Yes, or if you like better, on our giant narwhal.'

'What do you mean, Ned?'

'I mean that I understand now why my harpoon did not stick into the skin, but was blunted.'

'Why, Ned, why?'

'Because the beast is made of sheet-iron plates.'

I wriggled myself quickly to the top of the half-submerged being or object on which we had found refuge. I struck my foot against it. It was evidently a hard and impenetrable body, and not the soft substance which forms the mass of great marine mammalia. But this hard body could not be a bony carapace like that of antediluvian animals. I could not even class it amongst amphibious reptiles, such as tortoises and alligators, for the blackish back that supported me was not scaly but smooth and polished.

The blow produced a metallic sound, and, strange as it may appear, seemed caused by being struck on riveted plates. Doubt was no longer possible. The animal, monster, natural phenomenon that had puzzled the entire scientific world, and misled the imagination of sailors in two hemispheres, was, it must be acknowledged, a still more astonishing phenomenon, a phenomenon of man's making. The discovery of the existence of the most fabulous and mythological being would not have astonished me in the same degree. It seems quite simple that anything prodigious should come from the hand of the Creator, but to find the impossible realized by the hand of man was enough to confound the imagination.

We were lying upon the top of a sort of submarine boat, which looked to me like an immense steel fish. Ned Land's mind was made up on that point, and Conseil and I could only agree with him.

'But then,' said I, 'this apparatus must be a locomotive machine, and a crew inside of it to work it.'

'Evidently,' replied the harpooner, 'and yet for the three hours that I have inhabited this floating island it has not given sign of life.'

'The vessel has not moved?'

'No, M. Aronnax. It is cradled in the waves, but it does not move.'

'We know, without the slightest doubt, however, that it is endowed with great speed, and as a machine is necessary to produce the speed, and a mechanician to guide it, I conclude from that that we are saved.'

'Hum,' said Ned Land in a reserved tone of voice.

At that moment, and as if to support my arguments, a boiling was heard at the back of the strange apparatus, the propeller of which was evidently a screw, and it began to move. We only had time to hold on to its upper part, which emerged about a yard out of the water. Happily its speed was not excessive.

'As long as it moves horizontally,' murmured Ned Land, 'I have nothing to say. But if it takes into its head to plunge I would not give two dollars for my skin!'

The Canadian might have said less still. It therefore became urgent to communicate with whatever beings were shut up in the machine. I looked on its surface for an opening, a panel, a 'man-hole,' to use the technical expression; but the lines of bolts, solidly fastened down on the joints of the plates, were clear and uniform.

Besides, the moon then disappeared and left us in profound obscurity. We were obliged to wait till daybreak to decide upon the means of penetrating to the interior of this submarine boat.

Thus, then, our safety depended solely upon the caprice of the mysterious steersmen who directed this apparatus, and if they plunged we were lost! Unless that happened I did not doubt the possibility of entering into communication with them. And it was certain that unless they made their own air they must necessarily return from time to time to the surface of the ocean to renew their provision of breathable molecules. Therefore there must be an opening which put the interior of the boat into communication with the atmosphere.

As to the hope of being saved by Captain Farragut, that had to be completely renounced. We were dragged westward, and I estimated that our speed, relatively moderate, attained twelve miles an hour. The screw beat the waves with mathematical regularity, sometimes emerging and throwing the phosphorescent water to a great height.

About 4 a.m. the rapidity of the apparatus increased. We resisted with difficulty this vertiginous impulsion, when the waves beat upon us in all their fury. Happily Ned touched with his hand a wide balustrade fastened on to the upper part of the iron top, and we succeeded in holding on to it solidly.

At last this long night slipped away. My incomplete memory does not allow me to retrace all the impressions of it. A single detail returns to my mind. During certain lullings of the sea and wind, I thought several times I heard vague sounds, a sort of fugitive harmony produced by far-off chords. What, then, was the mystery of this submarine navigation, of which the entire world vainly sought the explanation? What beings lived in this strange boat? What mechanical agent allowed it to move with such prodigious speed?

When daylight appeared the morning mists enveloped us, but they soon rose, and I proceeded to make an attentive examination of the sort of horizontal platform we were on, when I felt myself gradually sinking.

'Mille diables!' cried Land, kicking against the sonorous metal, 'open inhospital creatures!'

But it was difficult to make oneself heard amidst the deafening noise made by the screw. Happily the sinking ceased.

Suddenly a noise like iron bolts violently withdrawn was heard from the interior of the boat. One of the iron plates was raised, a man appeared, uttered a strange cry, and disappeared immediately.

Some moments after eight strong fellows, with veiled faces, silently appeared, and dragged us down into their formidable machine.

Chapter Eight

Mobilis in Mobili

THIS ABDUCTION, SO BRUTALLY executed, took place with the rapidity of lightning. I do not know what my companions felt at being introduced into this floating prison; but, for my own part, a rapid shudder froze my very veins. With whom had we to do? Doubtless with a new species of pirates, who made use of the sea in a way of their own.

The narrow panel had scarcely closed upon me when I was enveloped by profound darkness. My eyes, dazzled by the light outside, could distinguish nothing. I felt my naked feet touch the steps of an iron ladder. Ned Land and Conseil, firmly held, followed me. At the bottom of the ladder a door opened and closed again immediately with a sonorous bang.

We were alone. Where? I neither knew nor could I imagine. All was darkness, and such absolute darkness, that after some minutes I had not been able to make out even those faint glimmers of light which float in the darkest nights.

Meanwhile, Ned Land, furious at this manner of proceeding, gave free course to his indignation.

'The people here equal the Scotch in hospitality!' he cried. 'They could not be worse if they were cannibals. I shouldn't be surprised if they were, but I declare they shan't eat me without my protesting!'

'Calm yourself, friend Ned; calm yourself,' answered Conseil tranquilly. 'Don't get into a rage beforehand. We aren't on the spit yet.'

'No, but we're in the oven. This hole's as dark as one. Happily my 'bowie-knife' is still on me, and I shall see well enough to use it. The first of these rascals that lays his hands on me——'

'Don't get irritated, Ned,' then said I to the harpooner, 'and do not compromise yourself by useless violence. Who knows that we are not overheard? Let us rather try to make out where we are.'

I groped my way about. When I had gone about five steps I came to an iron wall made of riveted plates. Then turning, I knocked against a wooden table, near which were several stools. The flooring of this prison was hidden under thick phormium matting, which deadened the noise of our footsteps. The walls revealed no traces of either door or window. Conseil, going round the reverse way, met me and we returned to the centre of the room, which measured about twenty feet by ten. As to its height, Ned Land, notwithstanding his tall stature, could not measure it.

Half an hour passed away without bringing any change in our position, when from the extreme of obscurity our eyes passed suddenly to the most violent light. Our prison was lighted up all at once – that is to say, it was filled with a luminous matter so intense that at first I could not bear its brilliancy. I saw from its whiteness and intensity that it was the same electric light that shone around the submarine boat like a magnificent phosphoric phenomenon. After having involuntarily closed my eyes I opened them again, and saw the luminous agent was escaping from a polished half-globe, which was shining in the top part of the room.

'Well, we can see at last!' cried Ned Land, who, with his knife in hand, held himself on the defensive.

'Yes,' answered I, risking the antithesis, 'but the situation is none the less obscure.'

'Let monsieur have patience,' said the impassible Conseil.

The sudden lighting of the cabin had allowed me to examine its least details. It only contained the table and five stools. The invisible door seemed hermetically closed. No noise reached our ears. All seemed dead in the interior of this machine. Was it moving, or was it motionless on the surface of the ocean, or deep in its depths? I could not guess.

However, the luminous globe was not lighted without a reason. I hoped that the men of the crew would soon show themselves, and my hope was well founded. A noise of bolts and bars being withdrawn was heard, the door opened, and two men appeared. One was short in stature, vigorously muscular, with broad shoulders, robust limbs, large head, abundant black hair, thick moustache, and all his person imprinted with that southern vivacity which characterizes the Provençal inhabitants of France.

The second deserves a more detailed description. I read at once his dominant qualities on his open face – self-confidence, because his head was firmly set on his shoulders, and his black eyes looked round with cold assurance – calmness, for his pale complexion announced the tranquillity of his blood – energy, demonstrated by the rapid contraction of his eyebrows; and lastly, courage, for his deep breathing denoted vast vital expansion. I felt involuntarily reassured in his presence, and augured good from it. He might be of any age from thirty-five to fifty. His tall stature, wide forehead, straight nose, clear-cut mouth, magnificent teeth, taper hands, indicated a highly-nervous temperament. This man formed certainly the most admirable type I had ever met with. One strange detail was that his eyes, rather far from each other, could take in nearly a quarter of the horizon at once. This faculty – I verified it later on – was added to a power of vision superior even to that of Ned Land. When the unknown fixed an object he frowned, and his large eyelids closed round so as to contract the range of his vision, and the result was a look that penetrated your very soul. With it he pierced the liquid waves that looked so opaque to us as if he read to the very depths of the sea.

The two strangers had on caps made from the fur of the sea-otter, sealskin boots, and clothes of a peculiar texture, which allowed them great liberty of movement.

The taller of the two – evidently the chief on board – examined us with extreme attention without speaking a word. Then he turned towards his companion, and spoke to him in a language I could not understand. It was a sonorous, harmonious, and flexible idiom, of which the vowels seemed very variously accented.

The other answered by shaking his head and pronouncing two or three perfectly incomprehensible words. Then, from his looks, he seemed to be questioning me directly.

I answered in good French that I did not understand his language, but he did not seem to know French, and the situation became very embarrassing.

'If monsieur would relate his story,' said Conseil, 'these gentlemen may understand some words of it.'

I began the recital of my adventures, articulating clearly all my syllables, without leaving out a single detail. I gave our names and qualities. The man with the soft, calm eyes listened to me calmly, and even politely, with remarkable attention. But nothing in his face indicated that he understood me. When I had done he did not speak a single word.

There still remained one resource – that of speaking English. Perhaps they would understand that almost universal language. I knew it, and German too, sufficiently to read it correctly, but not to speak it fluently.

'It is your turn now, Land,' I said to the harpooner. 'Make use of your best English, and try to be more fortunate than I.'

Ned did not need urging, and began the same tale in English, and ended by saying what was perfectly true, that we were half-dead with hunger. To his great disgust, the harpooner did not seem more intelligible than I. Our visitors did not move a feature. It was evident that they neither knew the language of Arago nor Faraday. I was wondering what to do next, when Conseil said to me——

'If monsieur will allow me, I will tell them in German.'

'What! do you know German?' I cried.

'Like a Dutchman, sir.'

'Well, do your best, old fellow.'

And Conseil, in his tranquil voice, told our story for the third time, but without success.

I then assembled all the Latin I had learnt at school, and told my adventures in that dead language. Cicero would have stopped his ears and sent me to the kitchen, but I did the best I could with the same negative result.

After this last attempt the strangers exchanged a few words in their incomprehensible language, and went away without a gesture that could reassure us. The door closed upon them.

'It is infamous!' cried Ned Land, who broke out again for the twentieth time. 'What! French, English, German, and Latin are spoken to those rascals, and not one of them has the politeness to answer.'

'Calm yourself, Ned,' said I to the enraged harpooner; 'anger will do no good.'

'But do you know, professor,' continued our irascible companion, 'that it is quite possible to die of hunger in this iron cage?'

'Bah!' exclaimed Conseil; 'with exercising a little philosophy we can still hold out a long while.'

'My friends,' said I, 'we must not despair. We have been in worse situations before now. Do me the pleasure of waiting before you form an opinion of the commander and crew of this vessel.'

'My opinion is already formed,' answered Ned Land. 'They are rascals——'

'Well, and of what country?'

'Of Rascaldom!'

'My worthy Ned, that country is not yet sufficiently indicated on the map of the world, and I acknowledge that the nationality of those two men is difficult to determine. Neither English, French, nor German, that is all we can affirm. However, I should be tempted to admit that the commander and his second were born under low latitudes. There is something meridional in them. But are they Spaniards, Turks, Arabians, or Indians? Their physical type does not allow me to decide; as to their language, it is absolutely incomprehensible.'

'That is the disadvantage of not knowing every language,' answered Conseil, 'or the disadvantage of not having a single language.'

'That would be of no use,' answered Ned Land. 'Do you not see that those fellows have a language of their own – a language invented to make honest men who want their dinners despair? But in every country in the world, to open your mouth, move your jaws, snap your teeth and lips, is understood. Does it not mean in Quebec as well as the Society Islands, in Paris as well as the antipodes, "I am hungry – give me something to eat?"'

'Oh,' said Conseil, 'there are people so unintelligent——'

As he was saying these words the door opened, and a steward entered. He brought us clothes similar to those worn by the two strangers, which we hastened to don.

Meanwhile the servant – dumb and deaf too in all appearance – had laid the cloth for three.

'This is something like,' said Conseil, 'and promises well.'

'I'll bet anything there's nothing here fit to eat,' said the harpooner. 'Tortoise liver, fillets of shark, or beafsteak from a sea-dog, perhaps!'

'We shall soon see,' said Conseil.

The dishes with their silver covers were symmetrically placed on the table. We had certainly civilized people to deal with, and had it not been for the electric light which inundated us I might have imagined myself in the Adelphi Hotel in Liverpool or the Grand Hotel in Paris. There was neither bread nor wine, nothing but pure fresh water, which was not at all to Ned Land's taste. Amongst the dishes that were placed before us I recognized several kinds of fish delicately cooked; but there were some that I knew nothing about, though they were delicious. I could not tell to what kingdom their contents belonged. The dinner service was elegant and in perfect taste; each piece was engraved with a letter and motto of which the following is a facsimile:

Mobilis in Mobile
N.

Mobile in a mobile element! The letter N was doubtless the initial of the enigmatical person who commanded at the bottom of the sea.

Ned and Conseil did not observe so much. They devoured all before them, and I ended by imitating them.

But at last even our appetite was satisfied, and we felt overcome with sleep. A natural reaction after the fatigue of the interminable night during which we had struggled with death.

My two companions lay down on the carpet, and were soon fast asleep. I did not go so soon, for too many thoughts filled my brain; too many insoluble questions asked me for a solution; too many images kept my eyes open. Where were we? What strange power was bearing us along? I felt, or rather I thought I felt, the strange machine sinking down to the lowest depths of the sea. Dreadful nightmares took possession of me. I saw a world of unknown animals in these mysterious asylums, amongst which the submarine boat seemed as living, moving, and formidable as they. Then my brain grew calmer, my imagination melted into dreaminess, and I fell into a deep sleep.

Chapter Nine

Ned Land's Anger

I DO NOT KNOW HOW LONG our sleep lasted, but it must have been a long time, for it rested us completely from our fatigues. I awoke first. My companions had not yet moved.

I had scarcely risen from my rather hard couch when I felt all my faculties clear, and looked about me.

Nothing was changed in the room. The prison was still a prison, and the prisoners prisoners. The steward, profiting by our sleep, had cleared the supper-things away. Nothing indicated an approaching change in our position, and I asked myself seriously if we were destined to live indefinitely in that cage.

This prospect seemed to me the more painful because, though my head was clear, my chest was oppressed. The heavy air weighed upon my lungs. We had evidently consumed the larger part of the oxygen the cell contained, although it was large. One man consumes in one hour the oxygen contained in 176 pints of air, and this air, then loaded with an almost equal quantity of carbonic acid, becomes unbearable.

It was, therefore, urgent to renew the atmosphere of our prison, and most likely that of the submarine boat also. Thereupon a question came into my head, 'How did the commander of this floating dwelling manage? Did he obtain air by chemical means, by evolving the heat of oxygen contained in chlorate of potassium, and by absorbing the carbonic acid with caustic potassium? In that case he must have kept up some relations with land in order to procure the materials necessary to this operation. Did he confine himself simply to storing up air under great pressure in reservoirs, and then let it out according to the need of his crew? Perhaps. Or did he use the more convenient, economical, and consequently more probable means of contenting himself with returning to breathe on the surface of the water like a cetacean, and of renewing for twenty-four hours his provision of atmosphere? Whatever his method might be, it seemed to me prudent to employ it without delay.

I was reduced to multiplying my respirations to extract from our cell the small quantity of oxygen it contained, when, suddenly, I was refreshed by a current of fresh air, loaded with saline odours. It was a sea breeze, life-giving, and charged with iodine. I opened my mouth wide, and my lungs became saturated with fresh particles. At the same time I felt the boat roll, and the iron-plated monster had evidently just ascended to the surface of the ocean to breathe like the whales. When I had breathed fully, I looked for the ventilator which had brought us the beneficent breeze, and before long, found it.

I was making these observations when my two companions awoke nearly at the same time, doubtless through the influence of the reviving air. They rubbed their eyes, stretched themselves, and were on foot instantly.

'Did monsieur sleep well?' Conseil asked me with his usual politeness.

'Very well, old fellow. And you, Mr Land?'

'Profoundly, Mr Professor. But if I am not mistaken, I am breathing a sea breeze.'

A seaman could not be mistaken in that, and I told the Canadian what had happened while he was asleep.

'That accounts for the roarings we heard when the supposed narwhal was in sight of the Abraham Lincoln.'

'Yes, Mr Land, that is its breathing.'

'I have not the least idea what time it can be, M. Aronnax, unless it be dinner time.'

'Dinner time, Ned? Say breakfast time at least, for we have certainly slept something like twenty-four hours.'

'I will not contradict you,' answered Ned Land, 'but dinner or breakfast, the steward would be welcome. I wish he would bring one or the other.'

'The one and the other,' said Conseil.

'Certainly,' answered the Canadian, 'we have a right to two meals, and, for my own part, I shall do honour to both.'

'Well, Ned, we must wait,' I answered. 'It is evident that those two men had no intention of leaving us to die of hunger, for in that case there would have been no reason to give us dinner yesterday.'

'Unless it is to fatten us!' answered Ned.

'I protest,' I answered. 'We have not fallen into the hands of cannibals.'

'One swallow does not make a summer,' answered the Canadian seriously. 'Who knows if those fellows have not been long deprived of fresh meat, and in that case these healthy and well-constituted individuals like the professor, his servant, and me——'

'Drive away such ideas, Mr Land,' I answered, 'and above all do not act upon them to get into a rage with our hosts, for that would only make the situation worse.'

'Anyway,' said the harpooner, 'I am devilishly hungry, and, dinner or breakfast, the meal does not arrive!'

'Mr. Land,' I replied, 'we must conform to the rule of the vessel, and I suppose that our stomachs are in advance of the steward's bell.'

'Well, then, we must put them right,' answered Conseil tranquilly.

'That is just like you, Conseil,' answered the impatient Canadian. 'You do not use up your bile or your nerves! Always calm, you would be capable of saying your grace before your Benedicite, and of dying of hunger before you complained.'

'What is the use of complaining?' asked Conseil.

'It does one good to complain! It is something. And if these pirates – I say pirates not to vex the professor, who does not like to hear them called cannibals – and if these pirates think that they are going to keep me in this cage where I am stifled without hearing how I can swear, they are mistaken. Come, M. Aronnax, speak frankly. Do you think they will keep us long in this iron box?'

'To tell you the truth I know no more about it than you, friend Land.'

'But what do you think about it?'

'I think that hazard has made us masters of an important secret. If it is the interest of the crew of this submarine vessel to keep it, and if this interest is of more consequence than the life of three men, I believe our existence to be in great danger. In the contrary case, on the first opportunity, the monster who has swallowed us will send us back to the world inhabited by our fellow-men.'

'Unless he enrols us amongst his crew,' said Conseil, 'and he keeps us thus——'

'Until some frigate,' replied Ned Land, 'more rapid or more skilful than the Abraham Lincoln, masters this nest of plunderers, and sends its crew and us to breathe our last at the end of his mainyard.'

'Well reasoned, Mr Land,' I replied. 'But I believe no proposition of the sort has yet been made to us, so it is useless to discuss what we should do in that case. I repeat, we must wait, take counsel of circumstances, and do nothing, as there is nothing to do.'

'On the contrary, Mr Professor,' answered the harpooner, who would not give up his point, 'we must do something.'

'What, then?'

'Escape.'

'To escape from a terrestrial prison is often difficult, but from a submarine prison, that seems to me quite impracticable.'

'Come, friend Ned,' said Conseil, 'what have you to say to master's objection? I do not believe an American is ever at the end of his resources.'

The harpooner, visibly embarrassed, was silent, a flight under the conditions hazard had imposed upon us was absolutely impossible. But a Canadian is half a Frenchman, and Ned Land showed it by his answer.

'Then, M. Aronnax,' he said, after some minutes' reflection, 'you do not guess what men ought to do who cannot escape from prison?'

'No, my friend.'

'It is very simple; they must make their arrangements to stop in it.'

'I should think so,' said Conseil; 'it is much better to be inside than on the top or underneath.'

'But after you have thrown your gaolers and keepers out?' added Ned Land.

'What, Ned? You seriously think of seizing this vessel?'

'Quite seriously,' answered the Canadian.

'It is impossible.'

'How so, sir? A favourable chance may occur, and I do not see what could prevent us profiting by it. If there are twenty men on board this machine they will not frighten two Frenchmen and a Canadian, I suppose.'

It was better to admit the proposition of the harpooner than to discuss it. So I contented myself with answering——

'Let such circumstances come, Mr Land, and we will see. But until they do I beg you to contain your impatience. We can only act by stratagem, and you will not make yourself master of favourable chances by getting in a rage. Promise me, therefore, that you will accept the situation without too much anger.'

'I promise you, professor,' answered Ned Land in a not very assuring tone; 'not a violent word shall leave my mouth, not an angry movement shall betray me, not even if we are not waited upon at table with desirable regularity.'

'I have your word, Ned,' I answered.

Then the conversation was suspended, and each of us began to reflect on his own account. I acknowledge that, for my own part, and notwithstanding the assurance of the harpooner, I kept no illusion. I did not admit the probability of the favourable occasions of which Ned Land had spoken. To be so well worked the submarine boat must have a numerous crew, and consequently, in case of a struggle, we should have to do with numbers too great. Besides, before aught else we must be free, and we were not. I did not even see any means of leaving this iron cell so hermetically closed. And should the strange commander of the boat have a secret to keep – which appeared at least probable – he would not allow us freedom of movement on board. Now, would he get rid of us by violence, or would he throw us upon some corner of the earth? All that was the unknown. All these hypotheses seemed to me extremely plausible, and one must be a harpooner to hope to conquer liberty again.

I understood, though, that Ned Land should get more exasperated with the thoughts that took possession of his brain. I heard him swearing in a gruff undertone, and saw his looks again become threatening. He rose, moved about like a wild beast in a cage, and struck the wall with his fist and foot. Moreover, time was going, hunger was cruelly felt, and this time the steward did not appear. If they had really good intentions towards us they had too long forgotten our shipwrecked condition.

Ned Land, tormented by the twinges of his robust stomach, became more and more enraged, and notwithstanding his promise I really feared an explosion when he would again be in the presence of the men on board.

Two more hours rolled on, and Ned's anger increased; he cried and called at the top of his voice, but in vain. The iron walls were deaf. The boat seemed quite still. The silence became quite oppressive.

I dare no longer think how long our abandonment and isolation in this cell might last. The hopes that I had conceived after our interview with the commander of the vessel vanished one by one. The gentle look of this man, the generous expression of his face, nobility of his carriage, all disappeared from my memory. I again saw this enigmatical personage such as he must necessarily be, pitiless and cruel. I felt him to be outside the pale of humanity, inaccessible to all sentiment of pity, the implacable enemy of his fellow-men, to whom he had vowed imperishable hatred.

But was the man going, then, to let us perish from inanition, shut up in this narrow prison, given up to the horrible temptations to which ferocious famine leads? This frightful thought took a terrible intensity in my mind, and imagination helping, I felt myself invaded by unreasoning fear. Conseil remained calm. Ned was roaring. At that moment a noise was heard outside. Steps clanged on the metal slabs. The bolts were withdrawn, the door opened, the steward appeared.

Before I could make a movement to prevent him the Canadian had rushed upon the unfortunate fellow, knocked him down, and fastened on his throat. The steward was choking under his powerful hand.

Conseil was trying to rescue his half-suffocated victim from the hands of the harpooner, and I was going to join my efforts to his, when, suddenly, I was riveted to my place by these words spoken in French:

'Calm yourself, Mr Land, and you, professor, please to listen to me.'

Chapter Ten

Nemo

THE MAN WHO SPOKE THUS was the commander of the vessel.

When Ned Land heard these words he rose suddenly. The almost strangled steward went tottering out on a sign from his master; but such was the power of the commander on his vessel that not a gesture betrayed the resentment the man must have felt towards the Canadian. Conseil, interested in spite of himself, and I stupefied, awaited the result of this scene in silence.

The commander, leaning against the angle of the table, with his arms folded, looked at us with profound attention. After some minutes of a silence which none of us thought of interrupting, he said in a calm and penetrating voice——

'Gentlemen, I speak French, English, German, and Latin equally well. I might, therefore, have answered you at our last interview, but I wished to know you first, and afterwards to ponder on what you said. The stories told by each of you agreed in the main, and assured me of your identity. I know now that accident has brought me into the presence of Mr Pierre Aronnax, Professor of Natural History in the Paris Museum, charged with a foreign scientific mission, his servant Conseil, and Ned Land of Canadian origin, harpooner on board the frigate Abraham Lincoln, of the United States Navy.'

I bent my head in sign of assent. There was no answer necessary. This man expressed himself with perfect ease, and without the least foreign accent. And yet I felt that he was not one of my countrymen. He continued the conversation in these terms:

'I daresay you thought me a long time in coming to pay you this second visit. It was because, after once knowing your identity, I wished to ponder upon what to do with you. I hesitated long. The most unfortunate conjuncture of circumstances has brought you into the presence of a man who has broken all ties that bound them to humanity. You came here to trouble my existence——'

'Unintentionally,' said I.

'Unintentionally,' he repeated, raising his voice a little. 'Is it unintentionally that the Abraham Lincoln pursues me in every sea? Was it unintentionally that you took passage on board her? Was it unintentionally that your bullets struck my vessel? Did Mr Land throw his harpoon unintentionally?'

'You are doubtless unaware,' I answered, 'of the commotion you have caused in Europe and America. When the Abraham Lincoln pursued you on the high seas everyone on board believed they were pursuing a marine monster.'

A slight smile curled round the commander's lips, then he went on in a calmer tone——

'Dare you affirm, M. Aronnax, that your frigate would not have pursued a submarine vessel as well as a marine monster?'

This question embarrassed me, for it was certain that Captain Farragut would not have hesitated. He would have thought it as much his duty to destroy such a machine as the gigantic narwhal he took it to be.

'You see, sir,' continued the commander, 'I have the right to treat you as enemies.'

I answered nothing, and for a very good reason; the unknown had force on his side, and it can destroy the best arguments.

'I have long hesitated,' continued the commander. 'Nothing obliges me to give you hospitality. I could place you upon the platform of this vessel, upon which you took refuge; I might sink it beneath the waters and forget that you ever existed. I should only be using my right.'

'The right of a savage, perhaps,' I answered, 'but not that of a civilized man.'

'Professor,' quickly answered the commander, 'I am not what is called a civilized man. I have done with society entirely for reasons that seem to me good; therefore I do not obey its laws, and I desire you never to allude to them before me again.'

This was uttered clearly. A flash of anger and contempt had kindled in the man's eyes, and I had glimpse of a terrible past in his life. He had not only put himself out of the pale of human laws, but he had made himself independent of them, free, in the most rigorous sense of the word, entirely out of their reach. Who, then, would dare to pursue him in the depths of the sea, when on its surface he baffled all efforts attempted against him? What armour, however thick, could support the blows of his spur? No man could ask him for an account of his works. God, if he believed in Him, his conscience, if he had one, were the only judges he could depend upon.

These reflections rapidly crossed my mind, whilst the strange personage was silent, absorbed, withdrawn into himself. I looked at him with terror mingled with interest, doubtless as Œdipus considered the Sphinx.

After a rather long silence the commander went on speaking.

'I have hesitated, therefore,' said he, 'but I thought that my interest might be reconciled with that natural pity to which every human being has a right. You may remain on my vessel, since fate has brought you to it. You will be free, and in exchange for this liberty, which after all will be relative, I shall only impose one condition upon you. Your word of honour to submit to it will be sufficient.'

'Speak, sir,' I answered. 'I suppose this condition is one that an honest man can accept?'

'Yes; it is this: It is possible that certain unforeseen events may force me to consign you to your cabin for some hours, or even days. As I do not wish to use violence, I expect from you, in such a case, more than from all others, passive obedience. By acting thus I take all the responsibility; I acquit you entirely, by making it impossible for you to see what ought not to be seen. Do you accept the condition?'

So things took place on board which were, at least, singular and not to be seen by people who were not placed beyond the pale of social laws.

'We accept,' I replied. 'Only I ask your permission to address to you one question – only one. What degree of liberty do you intend giving us?'

'The liberty to move about freely and observe even all that passes here – except under rare circumstances – in short, the liberty that my companions and I enjoy ourselves.

It was evident that we did not understand each other.

'Pardon me, sir,' I continued, 'but this liberty is only that of every prisoner to pace his prison. It is not enough for us.'

'You must make it enough.'

'Do you mean to say we must for ever renounce the idea of seeing country, friends, and relations again?'

'Yes, sir. But to renounce the unendurable worldly yoke that men call liberty is not perhaps so painful as you think.'

'I declare,' said Ned Land, 'I'll never give my word of honour not to try to escape.'

'I did not ask for your word of honour, Mr Land,' answered the commander coldly.

'Sir,' I replied, carried away in spite of myself, 'you take advantage of your position towards us. It is cruel!'

'No, sir, it is kind. You are my prisoners of war. I keep you when I could, by a word, plunge you into the depths of the ocean. You attacked me. You came and surprised a secret that I mean no man inhabiting the world to penetrate – the secret of my whole existence. And you think that I am going to send you back to that world? Never! In retaining you it is not you I guard, it is myself!'

These words indicated that the commander's mind was made up, and that argument was useless.

'Then, sir,' I answered, 'you give us the simple choice between life and death?'

'As you say.'

'My friends,' said I, 'to a question thus put there is nothing to answer. But no word of honour binds us to the master of this vessel.'

'None, sir,' answered the unknown.

Then in a gentler voice he went on——

'Now allow me to finish what I have to say to you. I know you, M. Aronnax. You, if not your companions, will not have so much to complain of in the chance that has bound you to my lot. You will find amongst the books which are my favourite study of work you have published on the *Great Submarine Grounds*.

I have often read it. You have carried your investigations as far as terrestrial science allowed you. But on board my vessel you will have an opportunity of seeing what no man has seen before. Thanks to me, our planet will give up her last secrets.'

I cannot deny that these words had a great effect upon me. My weak point was touched, and I forgot for a moment that the contemplation of these divine things was not worth the loss of liberty. Besides, I counted upon the future to decide that grave question, and so contented myself with saying——

'What name am I to call you by, sir?'

'Captain Nemo,' answered the commander. 'That is all I am to you, and you and your companions are nothing to me but the passengers of the Nautilus.'

The captain called, and a steward appeared. The captain gave him his orders in that foreign tongue which I could not understand. Then turning to the Canadian and Conseil——

'Your meal is prepared in your cabin,' he said to them. 'Be so good as to follow that man.'

My two companions in misfortune left the cell where they had been confined for more than thirty hours.

'And now, M. Aronnax, our breakfast is ready. Allow me to lead the way.'

I followed Captain Nemo into a sort of corridor lighted by electricity, similar to the waist of a ship. After going about a dozen yards a second door opened before me into a kind of dining-room, decorated and furnished with severe taste. High oaken sideboards, inlaid with ebony ornaments, stood at either end of the room, and on their shelves glittered china, porcelain, and glass of inestimable value. The plate that was on them sparkled in the light which shone from the ceiling, tempered and softened by fine painting. In the centre of the room was a table richly spread. Captain Nemo pointed to my seat.

'Sit down,' said he, 'and eat like a man who must be dying of hunger.'

The breakfast consisted of a number of dishes, the contents of which were all furnished by the sea; of some I neither knew the nature nor mode of preparation. They were good, but had a peculiar flavour which I soon became accustomed to. They appeared to be rich in phosphorus.

Captain Nemo looked at me. I asked him no questions, but he guessed my thoughts, and said——

'Most of these dishes are unknown to you, but you can eat of them without fear. They are wholesome and nourishing. I have long renounced the food of the earth, and I am none the worse for it. My crew, who are healthy, have the same food.

'Then all these dishes are the produce of the sea?' said I.

'Yes, professor, the sea supplies all my needs. Sometimes I cast my nets in tow, and they are drawn in ready to break. Sometimes I go and hunt in the midst of this element, which seems inaccessible to man, and run down the game of submarine forests. My flocks, like those of Neptune's old shepherd, graze fearlessly the immense ocean meadows. I have a vast estate there, which I cultivate myself, and which is always stocked by the Creator of all things.'

I looked at Captain Nemo with some astonishment, and answered——

'I can quite understand that your nets should furnish excellent fish for your table, and that you should pursue aquatic game in your submarine forests; but I do not understand how a particle of meat can find its way into your bill of fare.'

'What you believe to be meat, professor, is nothing but fillet of turtle. Here also are dolphins' livers, which you might take for ragout of pork. My cook is a clever fellow, who excels in preparing these various products of the sea. Taste all these dishes. Here is a conserve of holothuria, which a Malay would declare to be unrivalled in the world; here is cream furnished by the cetacea, and the sugar by the great fucus of the North Sea; and, lastly, allow me to offer you some anemone preserve, which equals that made from the most delicious fruits.'

Whilst I was tasting, more from curiosity than as a gourmet, Captain Nemo enchanted me with extraordinary stories.

'Not only does the sea feed me,' he continued, 'but it clothes me too. These materials that clothe you are wrought from the byssus of certain shells; they are dyed with the purple of the ancients, and the violet shades which I extract from the aplysis of the Mediterranean. The perfumes you will find on the toilette of your cabin are produced from the distillation of marine plants. Your bed is made with the softest wrack-grass of the ocean. Your pen will be a whale's fin, your ink the liquor secreted by the calamary. Everything now comes to me from the sea, and everything will one day return to it!'

'You love the sea, captain?'

'Yes, I love it. The sea is everything. It covers seven-tenths of the terrestrial globe. Its breath is pure and healthy. It is an immense desert where man is never alone, for he feels life quivering around him on every side. The sea is only the medium of a preternatural and wonderful existence; it is only movement and love; it is the infinite with life breathed into it, as one of your poets has said. And in reality, professor, Nature is manifested in it by her three kingdoms – mineral, vegetable, and animal. This last is largely represented by the four groups of zoophytes, by three classes of vertebrates, mammals, reptiles, and those innumerable legions of fish, an infinite order of animals that counts more than 13,000 species, of which a tenth only belongs to fresh water. The sea is the vast reservoir of Nature. It is by the sea that the globe has, so to speak, commenced, and who knows if it will not end by it? There is supreme tranquillity. The sea does not belong to despots. On its surface iniquitous rights can still be exercised, men can fight there, devour each other there, and transport all terrestrial horrors there. But at thirty feet below its level their power ceases, their influence dies out, their might disappears. Ah, sir, live in the bosom of the waters! There alone is independence! There I recognize no masters! There I am free!'

Captain Nemo stopped suddenly in the midst of this burst of enthusiasm which overflowed in him. Had he let himself be carried out of his habitual reserve? Had he said too much? During some moments he walked about much agitated. Then his nerves became calmer, his face regained its usual calm expression, and turning towards us——

'Now, professor,' said he, 'if you wish to visit the Nautilus, I am at your service.'

Chapter Eleven

The Nautilus

CAPTAIN NEMO ROSE, AND I followed him. A folding door, contrived at the back of the room, opened, and I entered a room about the same size as the one I had just left.

It was a library. High bookcases of black rosewood supported on their shelves a great number of books in uniform binding. They went round the room, terminating at their lower part in large divans, covered with brown leather, curved so as to afford the greatest comfort. Light movable desks, made to slide in and out at will, were there to rest one's book while reading. In the centre was a vast table, covered with pamphlets, amongst which appeared some newspapers, already old. The electric light flooded this harmonious whole, and was shed from four polished globes half sunk in the volutes of the ceiling. This room, so ingeniously fitted up, excited my admiration, and I could scarcely believe my eyes.

'Captain Nemo,' said I to my host, who had just thrown himself on one of the divans, 'you have a library here that would do honour to more than one continental palace, and I am lost in wonder when I think that it can follow you to the greatest depths of the ocean.'

'Where could there be more solitude or more silence, professor?' answered Captain Nemo. 'Did your study in the museum offer you as complete quiet?'

'No, and I must acknowledge it is a very poor one compared with yours. You must have from six to seven thousand volumes here.'

'Twelve thousand, M. Aronnax. These are the only ties between me and the earth. But the day that my Nautilus plunged for the first time beneath the waters the world was at an end for me. That day I bought my last books, my last pamphlets, and my last newspapers; and since then I wish to believe that men no longer think nor write. These books, professor are at your disposition, and you can use them freely.'

I thanked Captain Nemo, and went up to the library shelves. Books of science, ethics, and literature – written in every language – were there in quantities; but I did not see a single work on political economy amongst them; they seemed to be severely prohibited on board. A curious detail was that all these books were classified indistinctly, in whatever language they were written, and this confusion showed that the captain of the Nautilus could read with the utmost facility any volume he might take up by chance.

Amongst these works I remarked the *chef d'œuvres* of the ancient and modern masters – that is to say, all the finest things that humanity has produced in history, poetry, romance, and science, from Homer to Victor Hugo; from Xenophon to Michelet; from Rabelais to Madame Sand. But science, more particularly, was represented in this library; books on mechanics, ballistics, hydrography, meteorology, geography, geology, &c., held a no less important place than the works on natural history; and I understood that they formed the principal study of the captain. I saw there all the works of Humboldt, Arago, Foucault, Henry Sainte-Clare Deville, Chasles, Milne, Edwards, Quatrefages, Tyndall, Faraday, Berthelot, Abbé Secchi, Petermann, Commander Maury, Agassis, &c.; memoirs of the Académie des Sciences, the bulletins of different geographical societies, &c; and, in a good place, the two volumes which had perhaps procured me the relatively charitable welcome of Captain Nemo. Amongst the works of Joseph Bertrand, his book entitled, *Le Fondateur de l'Astronomie*, gave me a certain date; and as I knew that it had appeared during the course of 1865, I could conclude from that that the launching of the Nautilus did not take place at a later date. It was, therefore, three years, at the most, since Captain Nemo began his submarine existence. I hope, besides, that more recent works still will allow me to fix exactly the epoch; but I should have time to make that research, and I did not wish to delay any longer our inspection of the marvels of the Nautilus.

'Sir,' said I to the captain, 'I thank you for placing this library at my disposal. I see it contains treasures of science, and I shall profit by them.'

'This room is not only a library,' said Captain Nemo; 'it is a smoking-room too.'

'A smoking room?' cried I. 'Do you smoke here, then?'

'Certainly.'

'Then, sir, I am forced to believe that you have kept up relations with Havana?'

'No, I have not,' answered the captain. 'Accept this cigar, M. Aronnax; although it does not come from Havana, you will be pleased with it if you are a connoisseur.'

I took the cigar that was offered me; its shape was something like that of a *Londres*, but it seemed to be made of leaves of gold. I lighted it at a little brazier which was supported on an elegant bronze pedestal, and drew the first whiffs with the delight of an amateur who has not smoked for two days.

'It is excellent,' said I, 'but it is not tobacco.'

'No,' answered the captain. 'This tobacco comes neither from Havana nor the East. It is a sort of seaweed, rich in nicotine, with which the sea supplies me, but somewhat sparingly. If you do not reget the *Londres*, M. Aronnax, smoke these as much as you like.'

As Captain Nemo spoke he opened the opposite door to the one by which we had entered the library, and I passed into an immense and brilliantly lighted saloon. It was a vast four-sided room, with panelled walls, measuring thirty feet by eighteen, and about fifteen feet high. A luminous ceiling, decorated with light arabesques, distributed a soft, clear light over all the marvels collected in the museum. For it was, in fact, a museum in which an intelligent and prodigal hand had gathered together all the treasures of Nature and art with the artistic confusion of a painter's studio.

About thirty pictures by the first artists, uniformly framed and separated by brilliant drapery, were hung on tapestry of severe design. I saw there works of great value, most of which I had admired in the special collections of Europe, and in exhibitions of paintings. The different school of the old masters were represented by a Mad nna by Raphael, a Virgin by Leonardo da Vinci, a nymph by Correggio, an Assumption by Murillo, a portrait by Holbein, &c. The amazement which the captain of the Nautilus had predicted had already begun to take possession of me.

'Professor,' then said this strange man, 'you must excuse the unceremonious way in which I receive you, and the disorder of this room.'

'Sir,' I answered, 'without seeking to know who you are, may I be allowed to recognize in you an artist?'

'Only an amateur, sir. Formerly I liked to collect these works of art. I was a greedy collector and an indefatigable antiquary, and have been able to get together some objects of great value. These are my last gatherings from that world which is now dead to me. In my eyes your modern artists are already old; they have two or three thousand years of experience, and all masters are of the same age in my mind.'

'And these musicians?' said I, pointing to the works of Weber, Rossini, Mozart, Beethoven, Haydn, Meyerbeer, Hérold, Wagner, Au'er, Gounod, and many others, scattered over a large piano organ fixed in one of the panels of the room.

'These musicians,' answered Captain Nemo, 'are contemporaries of Orpheus, for all chronological differences are effaced in the memory of the dead; and I am dead, as much dead as those of your friends who are resting six feet under the earth.'

Captain Nemo ceased talking, and seemed lost in profound reverie. I looked at him with great interest, analysing in silence the strange expressions of his face.

Leaning on the corner of a costly mosaic table, he no longer saw me, and forgot my presence.

I respected his meditation, and went on passing in review the curiosities that enriched the saloon. They consisted principally of marine plants, shells, and other productions of the ocean, which must have been found by Captain Nemo himself. In the centre of the saloon rose a jet of water lighted up by electricity, and falling into a basin formed of a single tridacne shell, measuring about seven yards in circumference; it, therefore, surpassed in size the beautiful tridacnes which were given to Francis I of France by the Venetian Republic, and that now form two basins for holy water in the church of Saint Sulpice in Paris.

All round this basin were elegant glass cases, fastened by copper rivets, in which were classed and labelled the most precious productions of the sea that had ever been presented to the eye of a naturalist. My delight as a professor may be imagined. The division that contained the zoophyte presented very curious specimens of the two groups of polypi and echinodermes. In the first group of the tubipores were gorgones arranged like a fan, soft Syrian sponges, Molucca ises, pennatules, superb varieties of coral, and, in short, every species of those curious polypi of which entire islands are formed, which will one day become continents.

A conchyliologist at all nervous would certainly have fainted before other more numerous cases in which the specimens of molluscs were classified. I saw there a collection of inestimable value. Amongst these specimens I will quote from memory the elegant royal hammer-fish of the Indian Ocean, with its regular white spots standing out brightly on a red and brown ground; an imperial spondyle, bright-coloured, and bristling with spikes, a rare specimen in the museums of Europe, and the value of which I estimated at £800; a common hammer-fish from the Australian seas, which is only procured with difficulty; exotic buccardia from Senegal; fragile white bivalve shells that a breath might blow away like a soap-bubble; several varieties of the Java aspirgillum, a sort of calcareous tube, edged with leafy folds, much prized by amateurs; a whole series of trochi, some a greenish yellow, found in the American seas; others of a reddish brown, natives of Australian waters; others from the Gulf of Mexico, remarkable for their imbricated shells; stellari, found in the southern seas; and, last and rarest of all, the magnificent New Zealand spur.

Apart and in special apartments were spread out chaplets of pearls of the greatest beauty, which the electric light pricked with points of fire; pink pearls, torn from the pinna-marina of the Red Sea; green pearls from the haliotyde iris; yellow, blue and black pearls, the curious productions of different molluscs from every ocean, and certain mussels from the watercourses of the North; lastly, several specimens of priceless value, which had been gathered from the rarest pintadines. Some of these pearls were bigger than a pigeon's egg, and were worth more than the one which the traveller Tavernier sold to the Shah of Persia for 3,000,000 francs, and surpassed the one in the possession of the Imaum of Muscat, which I had believed to be unrivalled in the world.

It was impossible to estimate the worth of this collection. Captain Nemo must have spent millions in acquiring these various specimens, and I was asking myself from whence he had drawn the money to gratify his fancy for collecting, when I was interrupted by these words:

'You are examining my shells, professor. They certainly must be interesting to a naturalist, but for me they have a greater charm, for I have collected them all myself, and there is not a sea on the face of the globe that has escaped my search.'

'I understand, captain – I understand the delight of moving amongst such riches. You are one of those people who lay up treasures for themselves. There is not a museum in Europe that possesses such a collection of marine products. But if I exhaust all my admiration upon it, I shall have none left for the vessel that carries it. I do not wish to penetrate into your secrets, but I must confess that this Nautilus, with the motive power she contains, the contrivances by which she is worked, the powerful agent which propels her, all excite my utmost curiosity. I see hung on the walls of this room instruments the use of which I ignore.'

'When I told you that you were free on board my vessel, I meant that every portion of the Nautilus was open to your inspection. The instruments you will see in my room professor, where I shall have much pleasure in explaining their use to you. But come and look at your own cabin.'

I followed Captain Nemo, who, by one of the doors opening from each panel of the drawing-room, regained the waist of the vessel. He conducted me aft, and there I found, not a cabin, but an elegant room with a bed, toilette-table, and several other articles of furniture. I could only thank my host.

'Your room is next to mine,' said he, opening a door; 'and mine opens into the saloon we have just left.'

I entered the captain's room; it had a severe, almost monkish aspect. A small iron bedstead, an office desk, some articles of toilet – all lighted by a strong light. There were no comforts, only the strictest necessaries.

Captain Nemo pointed to a seat.

'Pray sit down,' he said.

I obeyed, and he began thus:——

Chapter Twelve

Everything by Electricity

'SIR,' SAID CAPTAIN NEMO, showing me the instruments hung on the walls of the room, 'here are the instruments necessary for the navigation of the Nautilus. Here, as in the saloon, I have them always before me, and they indicate my position and exact direction in the midst of the ocean. You are acquainted with some of them – the thermometer, for instance – which give the internal temperature of the vessel; the barometer, indicating the weight of the air, and foretelling changes in the weather; the hygrometer, for indicating the degree of dryness in the atmosphere; the storm-glass, the contents of which decompose at the approach of tempests; the compass, for guiding our course; the sextant, for taking latitude; chronometers, for calculating longitude; and, lastly, the glasses for day and night, which I use to examine the horizon when the Nautilus rises to the surface of the waves.'

'Yes,' I answered; 'I understand the usual nautical instruments. But I see others that doubtless answer the peculiar requirements of your vessel. That dial with a movable needle is a manometer, is it not?'

'Yes: by communication with the water it indicates the exterior pressure and gives our depth at the same time.'

'And these sounding-lines of a novel kind?'

'They are thermometric, and give the temperature of the different depths of water.'

'And these other instruments, the use of which I cannot guess?'

'Here I ought to give you some explanation, professor. There is a powerful, obedient, rapid, and easy agent which lends itself to all uses, and reigns supreme here. We do everything by its means. It is the light, warmth, and soul of my mechanical apparatus. This agent is electricity.'

'Yet, captain, you possess an extreme rapidity of movement which does not well agree with the power of electricity. Until now its dynamic force has been very restricted, and has only produced little power.'

'Professor,' answered Captain Nemo, 'my electricity is not everybody's, and you will permit me to withhold any further information.'

'I will not insist, sir; I will content myself with being astonished at such wonderful results. A single question, however, I will ask, which you need not answer if it is an indiscreet one. The elements which you employ to produce this marvellous agent must necessarily be soon consumed. The zinc, for instance, that you use – how do you obtain a fresh supply? You now have no communication with the land?'

'I will answer your question,' replied Captain Nemo. 'In the first place I must inform you that there exist, at the bottom of the sea, mines of zinc, iron, silver, and gold, the working of which would most certainly be practicable; but I am not indebted to any of these terrestrial metals. I was determined to seek from the sea alone the means of producing my electricity.'

'From the sea?'

'Yes, professor, and I was at no loss to find these means. It would have been possible, by establishing a circuit between wires plunged to different depths, to obtain electricity by the diversity of temperature to which they would have been exposed; but I preferred to employ a more practicable system.'

'And what was that?'

'You know the composition of sea-water? In 1,000 grammes of sea-water you find 96½ centigrammes of pure water, and about 2⅔ centigrammes of chloride of sodium; in addition, small quantities of the chlorides of magnesium and potassium, bromide of magnesium, sulphate of magnesia, sulphate and carbonate of lime. You see, then, that chloride of sodium forms a notable proportion of it. Now it is this sodium that I extract from sea-water, and of which I compose my ingredients. Mixed with mercury it takes the place of zinc for the voltaic pile. The mercury is never exhausted; only the sodium is consumed, and the sea itself gives me that. Besides, the electric power of the sodium piles is double that of the zinc ones.'

'I clearly understand, captain, the convenience of sodium in the circumstances in which you are placed. The sea contains it. Good. But you still have to make it, to extract it, in a word. And how do you do that? Your pile would evidently serve the purpose of extracting it; but unless I am mistaken, the consumption of sodium necessitated by the electrical apparatus would exceed the quantity extracted. The consequence would be that you would consume more of it than you would produce.'

'That is why I do not extract it by the pile, my dear professor. I employ nothing but the heat of coal.'

'Coal!' I urged.

'We will call it sea-coal if you like,' replied Captain Nemo.

'And are you able to work submarine coal-mines?'

'You shall see me so employed, M. Aronnax. I only ask you for a little patience; you have time to be patient here. Only remember I get everything from the ocean. It produces electricity, and electricity supplies the Nautilus with light – in a word, with life.'

'But not with the air you breathe.'

'I could produce the air necessary for my consumption, but I do not, because I go up to the surface of the water when I please. But though electricity does not furnish me with the air to breathe, it works the powerful pumps which store it up in special reservoirs, and which enable me to prolong at need, and as long as I like, my stay in the depths of the sea.'

'Captain,' I replied, 'I can do nothing but admire. You have evidently discovered what mankind at large will, no doubt, one day discover, the veritable dynamic power of electricity.'

'Whether they will discover it I do not know,' replied Captain Nemo coldly. 'However that may be, you now know the first application that I have made of this precious agent. It is electricity that furnishes us with a light that surpasses in uniformity and continuity that of the sun itself. Look now at this clock! It is an electric one, and goes with a regularity that defies the best of chronometers. I have divided it into twenty-four hours, like the Italian clocks, because there exists for me neither night nor day, sun nor moon, only this factitious light that I take with me to the bottom of the sea. Look! just now it is ten a.m.'

'Exactly so.'

'This dial hanging in front of us indicates the speed of the Nautilus. An electric wire puts it into communication with the screw. Look! just now we are going along at the moderate speed of fifteen miles an hour. But we have not finished yet, M. Aronnax,' continued Captain Nemo, rising, 'if you will follow me we will visit the stern of the Nautilus.'

I already knew all the anterior part of this submarine boat, of which the following is the exact division, starting from the centre of the prow: The dining-room, 15 feet long, separated from the library by a water-tight partition; the library, 15 feet long; the large saloon, 30 feet long, separated from the captain's room by a second water-tight partition; the captain's room, 15 feet; mine, 9 feet; and lastly, a reservoir of air of 20 feet that reached to the prow; total, 104 feet. The partitions had doors that were shut hermetically by means of indiarubber, assuring the safety of the Nautilus in case of a leak.

I followed Captain Nemo across the waist, and in the centre of the boat came to a sort of well that opened between two water-tight partitions. An iron ladder, fastened by an iron hook to the partition, led to the upper end. I asked the captain what it was for.

'It leads to the boat,' answered he.

'What! have you a boat?' I exclaimed in astonishment.

'Certainly, an excellent one, light and unsinkable, that serves either for fishing or pleasure trips.'

'Then when you wish to embark you are obliged to go up to the surface of the water.'

'Not at all. The boat is fixed to the top of the Nautilus in a cavity made for it. It has a deck, is quite water-tight, and fastened by solid bolts. This ladder leads to a man-hole in the hull of the Nautilus, corresponding to a similar hole in the boat. It is by this double opening that I get to the boat. The one is shut by my men in the vessel, I shut the one in the boat by means of screw pressure, I undo the bolts, and the little boat darts up to the surface of the sea with prodigious rapdity. I then open the panel of the deck, carefully closed before, I mast it, hoist my sail, take my oars, and am off.'

'But how do you return?'

'I do not return to it; it comes to me.'

'At your order?'

'At my order. An electric wire connects us. I telegraph my orders.'

'Really,' I said, intoxicated by such marvels, 'nothing can be more simple!'

After having passed the companion-ladder that led to the platform I saw a cabin about twelve feet long, in which Conseil and Ned Land were devouring their meal. Then a door opened upon a kitchen nine feet long, situated between the vast store-rooms of the vessel. There electricity, better than gas itself, did all the cooking. The wires under the stoves communicated with platinum sponges, and gave out a heat which was regularly kept up and distributed. They also heated a distilling apparatus, which, by evaporation, furnished excellent drinking water. A bath-room, comfortably furnished with hot and cold water taps, opened out of this kitchen.

Next to the kitchen was the berth-room of the vessel, eighteen feet long. But the door was closed, and I could not see how it was furnished, which might have given me an idea of the number of men employed on board the Nautilus. At the far end was a fourth partition, which separated this room from the engine-room. A door opened, and I entered the compartment where Captain Nemo – certainly a first-rate engineer – had arranged his locomotive machinery. It was well lighted, and did not measure less than sixty-five feet. It was naturally divided into two parts; the first contained the materials for producing electricity, and the second the machinery that moved the screw. I was at first surprised at a smell *sui generis* which filled the compartment. The captain saw that I perceived it.

'It is only a slight escape of gas produced by the use of the sodium, and not much inconvenience, as every morning we purify the vessel by ventilating it in the open air.'

In the meantime I was examining the machinery with great interest.

'You see,' said the captain, 'I use Bunsen's elements, not Ruhmkorff's – they would not have been powerful enough. Bunsen's are fewer in number, but strong and large, which experience proves to be the best. The electricity produced passes to the back, where it works by electromagnets of great size on a peculiar system of levers and cog wheels that transmit the movement to the axle of the screw. This one, with a diameter of nineteen feet and a thread twenty-three feet, performs about a hundred and twenty revolutions in a second.'

'What speed do you obtain from it?'

'About fifty miles an hour.'

Here was a mystery, but I did not press for a solution. How could electricity act with so much power? Where did this almost unlimited force originate? Was it in the excessive tension obtained by some new kind of spools? Was it by its transmission that a system of unknown levers could infinitely increase? (And by a remarkable coincidence, a discovery of this kind is talked of in which a new arrangement of levers produces considerable force. Can the inventor have met with Captain Nemo?)

'Captain Nemo,' I replied, 'I recognize the results, and do not seek to explain them. I saw the Nautilus worked in the presence of the Abraham Lincoln, and I know what to think of its speed. But it is not enough to be able to walk; you must see where you are going; you must be able to direct yourself to the right or left, above or below. How do you reach the great depths, where you find an increasing resistance, which is rated by hundreds of atmospheres? How do you return to the surface of the ocean, or maintain yourself at the proper depth? Am I indiscreet in asking you this question?'

'Not at all, professor,' answered the captain, after a slight hesitation. 'As you are never to leave this submarine boat, come into the saloon – it is our true study – and there you shall learn all you want to know about the Nautilus.'

Chapter Thirteen

Figures

A MOMENT AFTERWARDS we were seated on a divan in the saloon, with our cigars. The captain spread out a diagram that gave the plan of the Nautilus. Then he began his description in these terms.

'Here, M. Aronnax, are the different dimensions of the vessel you are in. It is a very elongated cylinder, with conical ends, much like a cigar in shape – a shape already adopted in London for constructions of the same sort. The length of this cylinder, from one end to the other, is exactly 232 feet, and its maximum breadth is 26 feet. It is, therefore, not altogether constructed by tenths, like your quick steamers, but its lines are sufficiently long, and its slope lengthened out to allow the displaced water to escape easily, and opposes no obstacle to its speed. These two dimensions allow you to obtain, by a simple calculaton, the surface and volume of the Nautilus. Its surface is 1,011 metres and 45 centimetres; its volume, 1,500 cubic metres and two-tenths, which is the same as saying that it is entirely immersed. It displaces 50,000 feet of water, or weighs 1,500 tons.

'When I made the plans for this vessel – destined for submarine navigation – I wished that when it was in equilibrium nine-tenths of it should be under water, and one-tenth only should emerge. Consequently, under these conditions, it only ought to displace nine-tenths of its volume, or 1,356 metres and 48 centimetres – that is to say, it only ought to weigh the same number of tons. I therefore did not exceed this weight in constructing it according to the above named dimensions.

'The Nautilus is composed of two hulls, one inside the other, and joined together by T-shaped irons, which make it very strong. Owing to this cellular arrangement it resists like a block, as if it were solid. Its sides cannot yield; they adhere spontaneously, and not by the closeness of their rivets; and the homogeneity of their construction, due to the perfect union of the materials, enables my vessel to defy the roughest seas.

'These two hulls are made of steel plates, the density of which is to water seven- to eight-tenths. The first is not less than five centimetres thick, and weighs: 94.96 tons. The second envelope, the keel, is 50 centimetres high and 25 wide, weighing by itself 62 tons; the machine, ballast, different accessories, the interior partitions and props weigh 961 tons, which, added to the rest, form the required total of 1,356.48 tons. Do you follow me?'

'Yes,' I replied.

'Then,' continued the captain, 'when the Nautilus is afloat in these conditions one-tenth is out of water. I have placed reservoirs of a size equal to this tenth capable of holding 150.72 tons, and when I fill them with water the vessel becomes completely immersed. These reservoirs exist in the lowest parts of the Nautilus. I turn on taps, they fill, and the vessel sinks just below the surface of the water.'

'Well, captain, but now we arrive at the real difficulty. I can understand your being able to keep just level with the surface of the ocean. But lower down, when you plunge below that surface, does not your submarine apparatus meet with a pressure from below, which must be equal to one atmosphere for every thirty feet of water, or one kilogramme for every square centimetre?'

'True, sir.'

'Then unless you fill the Nautilus entirely I do not see how you can draw it down into the bosom of the liquid mass.'

'Professor,' answered Captain Nemo, 'you must not confound statics with dynamics, or you will expose yourself to grave errors. There is very little work necessary to reach the lowest depths of the ocean, for bodies have a tendency "to sink". Follow my reasoning.'

'I am listening to you, captain.'

'When I wished to determine the increase in weight that must be given to the Nautilus to sink it, I had only to occupy myself with the reduction in volume which sea-water experiences as it becomes deeper and deeper.'

'That is evident,' said I.

'Now if water is not absolutely incompressible, it is, at least, very slightly compressible – in fact, according to the most recent calculations 0000436 in an atmosphere or in each thirty feet of depth. If I wish to go to the depth of 1,000 metres I take into account the reduction of volume under a pressure equivalent to that of a column of water of 1,000 metres – that is to say, under a pressure of 100 atmospheres. I ought, therefore, to increase the weight so as to weigh 1,513.79 tons instead of 1,507.2 tons. The augmentation will, consequently, only be 6.77 tons. Only that, Monsieur Aronnax, and the calculation is easy to verify. Now I have supplementary reservoirs capable of embarking 100 tons. I can, therefore, descend to considerable depths. When I wish to remount to the level of the surface, I have only to let out this water, and to entirely empty all the reservoirs, if I desire that the Nautilus should emerge one-tenth of its total capacity.'

To this reasoning, founded upon figures, I had nothing to object.

'I admit your calculations, captain,' I replied, 'and I should be foolish to dispute them, as experience proves them every day, but I foresee a real difficulty.'

'What is that, sir?'

'When you are at the depth of 1,000 yards the sides of the Nautilus support a pressure of 100 atmospheres. If, therefore, at this moment you wish to empty the supplementary reservoirs to lighten your vessel and ascend to the surface, the pumps must conquer this pressure of 100 atmospheres, which is that of 100 kilogrammes for every square centimetre. Hence a power——'

'Which electricity alone can give me,' hastened to say Captain Nemo. 'I repeat, sir, that the dynamic power of my machines is nearly infinite. The pumps of the Nautilus have prodigious force, which you must have seen when their columns of water were precipitated like a torrent over the Abraham Lincoln. Besides, I only use supplementary reservoirs to obtain middle depths of 1,500 to 2,000 metres, and that in order to save my apparatus. When the fancy takes me to visit the depths of the ocean at two or three leagues below its surface, I use longer means, but no less infallible.'

'What are they, captain?' I asked.

'That involves my telling you how the Nautilus is worked.'

'I am all impatience to hear it.'

'In order to steer my vessel horizontally I use an ordinary rudder, worked by a wheel and tackle. But I can also move the Nautilus by a vertical movement, by means of two inclined planes fastened to the sides and at the centre of flotation, planes that can move in every direction, and are worked from the interior by means of powerful levers. When these planes are kept parallel with the boat it moves horizontally; when slanted, the Nautilus, according to their inclination, and under the influence of the screw, either sinks according to an elongated diagonal, or rises diagonally as it suits me. And even when I wish to rise more quickly to the surface I engage the screw, and the pressure of the water causes the Nautilus to rise vertically like a balloon into the air.'

'Bravo! captain,' I cried. 'But how can the helmsman follow the route you give him in the midst of the waters?'

'The helmsman is placed in a glass cage jutting from the top of the Nautilus and furnished with lenses.'

'Capable of resisting such pressure?'

'Perfectly. Glass, which a blow can break, offers, nevertheless, considerable resistance. During some fishing experiments we made in 1864, by electric light, in the Northern Seas, we saw plates less than a third of an inch-thick resist a pressure of sixteen atmospheres. Now the glass that I use is not less than thirty times thicker.'

'I see now. But, after all, it is dark under water; how do you see where you are going?'

'There is a powerful reflector placed behind the helmsman's cage, the rays from which light up the sea for half a mile in front.'

'Ah, now I can account for the phosphorescence in the supposed narwhal that puzzled me so. May I now ask you if the damage you did to the Scotia was due to an accident?'

'Yes, it was quite accidental. I was sailing only one fathom below the surface when the shock came. Had it any bad result?'

'None, sir. But how about the shock you gave the Abraham Lincoln?'

'Professor, it was a great pity for one of the best ships in the American navy; but they attacked me and I had to defend myself! Besides, I contented myself with putting it out of the power of the frigate to harm me; there will be no difficulty in getting her repaired at the nearest port.'

'Ah, commander!' I cried with conviction, 'your Nautilus is certainly a marvellous boat.'

'Yes, professor,' answered Captain Nemo with real emotion, 'and I love it as if it were flesh of my flesh! Though all is danger on one of your ships in subjection to the hazards of the ocean, though on this sea the first impression is the sentiment of unfathomable depth, as the Dutchman Jansen has so well said, below and on board the Nautilus the heart of man has nothing to dread. There is no deformation to fear, for the double hull of this vessel is as rigid as iron; no rigging to be injured by rolling and pitching; no sails for the wind to carry away; no boilers for steam to blow up; no fire to dread, as the apparatus is made of iron and not of wood; no coal to get exhausted, as electricity is its mechanical agent; no collision to fear, as it is the only vessel in deep waters; no tempests to set at defiance, as there is perfect tranquillity at some yards below the surface of the sea! The Nautilus is the ship of ships, sir. And if it is true that the engineer has more confidence in the vessel than the constructor, and the constructor more than the captain himself, you will understand with what confidence I trust to my Nautilus, as I am at the same time captain, constructor and engineer!'

Captain Nemo spoke with captivating eloquence. His fiery look and passionate gestures transfigured him. Yes! he did love his vessel like a father loves his child!

But a question, perhaps an indiscreet one, came up naturally, and I could not help putting it.

'Then you are an engineer, Captain Nemo?'

'Yes, professor, I studied in London, Paris and New York when I was still an inhabitant of the world's continents.'

'But how could you construct this admirable Nautilus in secret?'

'I had each separate portion made in different parts of the globe, and it reached me through a disguised address. The keel was forged at Creuzot, the shaft of the screw at Penn and Co.'s, of London; the iron plates of the hull at Laird's, of Liverpool; the screw itself at Scott's, of Glasgow. Its reservoirs were made by Cail and Co., of Paris; the engine by the Prussian Krupp; the prow in Motala's workshop in Sweden; the mathematical instruments by Hart Brothers, of New York, &c.; all of these people had my orders under different names.'

'But how did you get all the parts put together?'

'I set up a workshop upon a desert island in the ocean. There, my workmen – that is to say, my brave companions whom I instructed – and I put together our Nautilus. When the work was ended, fire destroyed all trace of our proceedings on the island, which I should have blown up if I could.'

'It must have cost you a great deal.'

'An iron vessel costs £45 a ton. The Nautilus weighs 1,500 tons. It came, therefore, to £67,500, and £80,000 more for fitting up; altogether, with the works of art and collections it contains, it cost about £200,000.'

'One last question, Captain Nemo.'

'Ask it, professor.'

'You must be rich?'

'Immensely rich sir; and I could, without missing it, pay the English National Debt.'

I stared at the singular person who spoke thus. Was he taking advantage of my credulity? The future alone could decide.

Chapter Fourteen

The Black River

THE PORTION OF THE TERRESTRIAL globe covered by water is estimated at 3,832,558 square myriametres, or 38,000,000 hectares. This liquid mass comprehends 2,250,000,000 of cubic miles, and would form a sphere of a diameter of sixty leagues, the weight of which would be three trillions of tons.

To take in the idea of such a number we must remember that a trillion is to a thousand millions what a thousand millions are to unity – that is to say, there are as many thousand millions in a trillion as there are unities in a thousand millions. Now this liquid mass is about the quantity of water that all the rivers of the earth would pour out during forty thousand years. In the geological epochs the period of water succeeded the period of fire. The ocean was at first universal. They, by degrees in the silurian epoch, the summits of mountains appeared, islands emerged, disappeared under partial deluges, again showed themselves, united together formed continents, and at last lands were geographically placed as we see them now. Solid matter had conquered from liquid matter 37,657,000 square miles, or 12,916,000,000 of hectares.

The configuration of continents allows us to divide water into five great parts – the Arctic Frozen Ocean, the Antarctic Frozen Ocean, the Indian Ocean, the Atlantic Ocean, and the Pacific Ocean.

The Pacific Ocean extends from north to south between the two polar circles, and from west to east between Asia and America over an extent of 145° of longitude. It is the smoothest of all seas; its currents are wide and slow, its tides slight, its rains abundant. Such was the ocean that my destiny called upon me to go over under such strange conditions.

'Now, professor,' said Captain Nemo, 'we will, if you please, take our bearings and fix the starting-point of this voyage. It wants a quarter to twelve. I am going up to the surface of the water.'

The captain pressed an electric bell three times. The pumps began to drive water out of the reservoirs; the needle of the manometer marked by the different pressures the ascensional movement of the Nautilus, then it stopped.

'We have arrived,' said the captain.

We went to the central staircase which led up to the platform, climbed the iron steps, and found ourselves on the top of the Nautilus.

The platform was only three feet out of the water. The front and back of the Nautilus were of that spindle shape which caused it justly to be compared to a cigar. I noticed that its iron plates slightly overlaid each other, like the scales on the body of our large terrestrial reptiles. I well understood how, in spite of the best glasses, this boat should have been taken for a marine animal.

Towards the middle of the platform, the boat, half sunk in the vessel, formed a slight excrescence. Fore and aft rose two cages of medium height, with inclined sides, and partly inclosed by thick lenticular glasses. In the one was the helmsman who directed the Nautilus; in the other a powerful electric lantern that lighted up his course.

The sea was beautiful, the sky pure. The long vessel could hardly feel the broad undulations of the ocean. A slight breeze from the east rippled the surface of the water. The horizon was quite clear, making observation easy. There was nothing in sight – not a rock nor an island, no Abraham Lincoln, nothing but a waste of waters.

Captain Nemo took the altitude of the sun with his sextant to get his latitude. He waited some minutes till the planet came on a level with the edge of the horizon. Whilst he was observing not one of his muscles moved, and the instrument would not have been more motionless in a hand of marble.

'It is noon. Professor, when you are ready——'

I cast a last look at the sea, slightly yellowed by the Japanese coast, and went down again to the saloon.

There the captain made his point, and calculated his longitude chronometri-
cally, which he controlled by preceding observations of horary angles. Then he
said to me——

'M. Aronnax, we are in west longitude 137° 15′.'

'By what meridian?' I asked quickly, hoping that the captain's answer might
indicate his nationality.

'Sir,' he answered, 'I have different chronometers regulated on the meridians
of Paris, Greenwich, and Washington. But, in your honour, I will use the Paris
one.'

This answer taught me nothing. I bowed, and the commander continued——

'Thirty-seven degrees and fifteen minutes longitude west of the Paris
meridian, and thirty degrees and seven minutes north latitude – that is to say,
about three hundred miles from the coasts of Japan. Today, the 8th of
November, at noon, our voyage of exploration under the waters begins.'

'God preserve us!' I answered.

'And now, professor,' added the captain, 'I leave you to your studies. I have
given E.N.E. as our route at a depth of fifty yards. Here are maps on a large scale
on which you can follow it. The saloon is at your disposition, and I ask your
permission to withdraw.'

Captain Nemo bowed to me. I remained alone, absorbed in my thoughts. All
of them referred to the commander of the Nautilus. Should I ever know to what
nation belonged the strange man who boasted of belonging to none? This hatred
which he had vowed to humanity – this hatred which perhaps sought terrible
means of revenge, what had provoked it? Was he one of those misjudged *savants*,
a genius to whom '*on a fait du chagrin*,' according to an expression of Conseil's, a
modern Galileo, or one of those scientific men like the American Maury, whose
career has been broken by political revolutions? I could not yet say. I, whom
hazard had just cast upon his vessel – I, whose life he held in his hands, he had
received me coldly, but with hospitality. Only he had never taken the hand I
had held out to him. He had never held out his to me.

For a whole hour I remained buried in these reflections, seeking to pierce the
mystery that interested me so greatly. Then my eyes fell upon the vast
planisphere on the table, and I placed my finger on the very spot where the
given latitude and longitude crossed.

The sea has its large rivers like continents. They are special currents, known
by their temperature and colour. The most remarkable is known under the name
of the Gulf Stream. Science has found out the direction of five principal currents
– one in the North Atlantic, a second in the South Atlantic, a third in the
North Pacific, a fourth in the South Pacific, and a fifth in the South Indian
Ocean. It is probable that a sixth current formerly existed in the North Indian
Ocean, when the Caspian and Aral Seas, united to the great Asiatic lakes, only
formed one vast sheet of water.

At the point on the planisphere where my finger lay, one of these currents was
rolling – the Kuro-Scivo or Black River of the Japanese, which, leaving the Gulf
of Bengal, where the perpendicular rays of a tropical sun warm it, crosses the
Straits of Malacca, runs along the coast of Asia, turns into the North Pacific as
far as the Aleutian Islands, carrying with it the trunks of camphor-trees and
other indigenous productions, contrasting by the pure indigo of its warm waters

with the waves of the ocean. It was this current that the Nautilus was going to follow. I saw that it lost itself in the immensity of the Pacific, and felt myself carried along by it. Just then Ned Land and Conseil appeared at the door of the saloon.

My two companions were petrified at the sight of the marvels spread out before their eyes.

'Where are we – where are we?' cried the Canadian. 'At the Quebec Museum?'

'If monsieur allows me to say so,' replied Conseil, 'it is more like the Hôtel du Sommerard.'

'My friends,' said I, making them a sign to enter, 'you are neither in Canada nor France, but on board the Nautilus, and at more than twenty-five fathoms below the sea level.'

'We must believe what monsieur says,' replied Conseil, 'but really this saloon is enough to astonish even a Dutchman like me.'

'Marvel and look Conseil, for there is enough for such a good classifier as you to do here.'

There was no need for me to encourage Conseil. The worthy fellow, leaning over the cases, was already muttering words in the language of naturalists – Gasteropodes class, Buccinoides family, sea-snail genus, *Cypræa Madagascariensis* species, &c.

During this time Ned Land, who was not much interested in conchology, questioned me about my interview with Captain Nemo. Had I discovered who he was, from whence he came, whither he was going, to what depths he was dragging us? – in short, a thousand questions, to which I had not time to answer.

I told him all I knew, or rather all I did not know, and I asked him what he had heard or seen on his side.

'I have seen nothing, heard nothing,' answered the Canadian. 'I have not even perceieved the ship's crew. Is it by chance, or can it be electric too?'

'Electric!'

'Faith, any one would think so. But you, M. Aronnax,' said Ned Land, who stuck to his idea, 'can you tell me how many men there are on board? Are there ten, twenty, fifty, a hundred?'

'I know no more than you, Mr Land; it is better to abandon at present all idea of either taking possession of the Nautilus or escaping from it. This vessel is a masterpiece of modern industry, and I should regret not to have seen it. Many people would accept our position only to move amidst such marvels. The only thing to do is to keep quiet and watch what passes around us.'

'Watch!' exclaimed the harpooner, 'but there's nothing to watch; we can't see anything in this iron prison. We are moving along blindfolded.'

Ned Land had scarcely uttered these words when it became suddenly dark. The light in the ceiling went out, and so rapidly that my eyes ached with the change, in the same way as they do after passage from profound darkness to the most brilliant light.

We remained mute and did not stir, not knowing what surprise, agreeable or disagreeable, awaited us. But a sliding noise was heard. It was like as if panels were being drawn back in the sides of the Nautilus.

'It is the end of all things!' said Ned Land.

'Hydrometridæ family!' muttered Conseil.

Suddenly light appeared on either side of the saloon, through two oblong openings. The liquid mass appeared vividly lighted up by the electric effluence.

Two crystal panes separated us from the sea. At first I shuddered at the thought that this feeble partition might break, but strong copper bands bound it, giving an almost infinite power of resistance.

The sea was distinctly visible for a mile round the Nautilus. What a spectacle! What pen could describe it? Who could paint the effect of the light through those transparent sheets of water, and the softness of its successive gradations from the lower to the upper beds of the ocean?

The transparency of the sea is well known, and its limpidity is far greater than that of fresh water. The mineral and organic substances which it holds in suspension increase its transparency. In certain parts of the ocean at the Antilles, under seventy-five fathoms of water, the sandy bottom can be seen with surprising clearness, and the penetrating strength of the sun's rays only appears to stop at a depth of 150 fathoms. But in this fluid medium through which the Nautilus was travelling the electric light was produced in the very bosom of the waves. It was not luminous water, but liquid light.

In the hypothesis of Erhemberg, who believes in a phosphorescent illumination in the submarine depths, is admitted, Nature has certainly reserved to the inhabitants of the sea one of her most marvellous spectacles, and I could judge of it by the effect of the thousand rays of this light. On either side I had a window opening on these unexplored depths. The darkness in the saloon made the exterior light seem greater, and we could see the same as if the pure crystal had been the panes of an immense aquarium.

The Nautilus did not seem to be moving. It was because there were no landmarks. Sometimes however, the lines of water, furrowed by her prow, flowed before our eyes with excessive speed.

Lost in wonder we stood before these windows, and none of us had broken this silence of astonishment when Conseil said——

'Well, friend Ned, you wanted to look; well, now you see!'

'It is curious!' exclaimed the Canadian, who, forgetting his anger and projects of flight, was under the influence of irresistible attraction. 'Who wouldn't come for the sake of such a sight?'

'Now I understand the man's life,' I exclaimed. 'He has made a world of marvels for himself?'

'But I don't see any fish,' said the Canadian.

'What does it matter to you, friend Ned,' answered Conseil, 'since you know nothing about them?'

'I! A fisherman!' cried Ned Land.

And thereupon a dispute arose between the two friends, for each had some knowledge of fish, though in a very different way.

Everyone knows that fish come from the fourth and last class in the embranchment of vertebrates. They have been rightly defined as 'vertebrates with double circulation and cold blood, breathing through gills, and made to live in water.' They are composed of two distinct series: the series of bony fish – that is to say, those whose spines are made of cartilaginous vertebrate.

Perhaps the Canadian knew this distinction, but Conseil knew much more, and now that he had made friends with Ned, he could not allow himself to seem less learned than he. He accordingly said to him——

'Friend Ned, you are a killer of fish – a very skilful fisher. You have taken a great number of these interesting animals. But I wager you do not know how they are classified.'

'Yes, I do,' answered the harpooner seriously. 'They are classified into fish that are good for food and fish that are not.'

'That is a greedy distinction,' answered Conseil. 'But do you know the difference between bony and cartilaginous fish?'

'Perhaps I do, Conseil.'

'And the subdivision of these two grand classes?'

'I daresay I do,' answered the Canadian.

'Well, friend Ned, listen and remember! The bony fish are subdivided into six orders. Primo, the acanthopterygii, of which the upper jaw is complete, mobile with gills in the form of a comb. This order comprises fifteen families – that is to say, the three-fourths of known fish. Type: the common perch.'

'Pretty good eating,' answered Ned Land.

'Secundo,' continued Conseil, 'the abdominals, an order of fish whose ventral fins are placed behind the pectoral, without being attached to the shoulder-bones – an order which is divided into five families, and comprises most fresh-water fish. Type: the carp, roach, salmon, pike, &c.'

'Perch!' said the Canadian disdainfully; 'fresh-water fish!'

'Tertio,' said Conseil, 'the subrachians, with ventral fins under the pectoral, and fastened to the shoulder-bones. This order contains four families. Type: plaice, mud-fish, turbots, brills, soles, &c.'

'Excellent! – excellent!' cried the harpooner, who would only think of them from their eatable point of view.

'Quarto,' said Conseil, nowise confused, 'the apodes with long bodies and no ventral fins, covered with a thick and often sticky skin – an order that only comprises one family. Type: the eel, wolf-fish, sword-fish, lance, &c.'

'Middling! – only middling!' answered Ned Land.

'Quinto,' said Conseil, 'the liphiadæ, distinguished by the bones of the carpus being elongated, and forming a kind of arm, which supports the pectoral fins. Type: the angler, or fishing frog.'

'Bad! – bad!' replied the harpooner.

'Secto and lastly,' said Conseil, 'the plectognathes, which include those which have the maxillary bones anchylosed to the sides of the intermaxillaries, which along form the jaws – an order which has no real ventral fins, and is composed of two families. Type: the sun-fish.'

'Which any saucepan would be ashamed of!' cried the Canadian.

'Did you understand, friend Ned?' asked the learned Conseil.

'Not the least in the world, friend Conseil,' answered the harpooner. 'But go on, for you are very interesting.'

'As to the cartilaginous fish,' continued the imperturbable Conseil, 'they only include three orders.'

'So much the better,' said Ned.

'Primo, the cyclostomes, with circular mouths and gills opening by numerous holes – an order including only one family. Type: the lamprey.'

'You must get used to it to like it,' answered Ned Land.

'Secundo, the selachii, with gills like the cyclostomes, but whose lower jaw is mobile. This order, which is the most important of the class, includes two families. Types: sharks and rays.'

'What!' cried Ned; 'rays and sharks in the same order? Well, friend Conseil, I should not advise you to put them in the same jar.'

'Tertio,' answered Conseil, 'the sturiones, with gills opened as uusual by a single slit, furnished with an operaculum – an order which includes four genera. Type: the sturgeon.'

'Well, friend Conseil, you have kept the best for the last, in my opinion, at least. Is that all?'

'Yes, Ned,' answered Conseil; 'and remark that even when you know that you know nothing, for the families are subdivided into genera, sub-genera, species, varieties.'

'Well friend Conseil,' said the harpooner, leaning against the glass of the panel, 'there are some varieties passing now.'

'Yes! – some fish,' cried Conseil. 'It is like being at an aquarium.'

'No,' I answered, 'for an aquarium is only a cage, and those fish are as free as birds in the air.'

'Well, now, Conseil, tell me their names! – tell me their names!' said Ned Land.

'I?' answered Conseil; 'I could not do it; that is my master's business.'

And, in fact, the worthy fellow, though an enthusiastic classifier, was not a naturalist, and I do not know if he could have distinguished a tunny-fish from a bonito. The Canadian, on the contrary, named them all without hesitation.

'A balister,' said I.

'And a Chinese balister too!' answered Ned Land.

'Genus of the balisters, family of the scleroderms; order of the plectognaths,' muttered Conseil.

Decidedly, between them, Ned Land and Conseil would have made a distinguished naturalist.

The Canadian was not mistaken. A shoal of balisters with fat bodies, grained skins, armed with a spur on their dorsal fin, were playing round the Nautilus and agitating the four rows of quills bristling on either side of their tails. Nothing could be more admirable than their grey-backs, with stomachs, and gold spots that shone admist the waves. Anongst them undulated skates like a sheet abandoned to the winds, and with them I perceived, to my great joy, the Chinese skate, yellow above, pale pink underneath, with three darts behind the eye – a rare species, and even doubtful in the time of Lacepéde, who had never seen any except in a book of Japanese drawings.

For two hours a whole aquatic army escorted the Nautilus. Amidst their games and gambols, whilst they rivalled each other in brilliancy and speed, I recognized the green wrasse, the surmullet, marked with a double black stripe; the goby, with its round tail, white with violet spots; the Japanese mackerel, with blue body and silver head; brilliant, the azure fish, the name of which beggars all descriptions, gilt heads with a black band down their tails; aulostones with flute-like noses, real sea-woodcocks, of which some specimens attain a yard in length; Japanese salamanders; sea-eels, serpents six feet long with bright little eyes and a huge mouth bristling with teeth, &c.

Our admiration was excited to the highest pitch. Ned named the fish, Conseil classified them, and I was delighted with their vivacity and the beauty of their forms. It had never been my lot to see these animals living and free in their natural element. I shall not cite all the varieties that passed before our dazzled eyes, all that collection from the Japanese and Chinese seas. More numerous than the birds of the air, these fish swam round us, doubtless attracted by the electric light.

Suddenly light again appeared in the saloon. The iron panels were again closed. The enchanting vision disappeared. But long after that I was dreaming still, until my eyes happened to fall on the instruments hung on the partition. The compass still indicated the direction of N.N.E., the manometer indicated a pressure of five atmospheres, corresponding to a depth of 100 fathoms, and the electric log gave a speed of 15 miles an hour.

I expected Captain Nemo, but he did not appear. The clock was on the stroke of five. Ned Land and Conseil returned to their cabin, and I regained my room. My dinner was laid there. It consisted of turtle soup made of the most delicate imbricated hawksbill turtle, of a delicate white surmullet, slightly crimped, of which the liver, cooked by itself, made a delicious dish, and fillets of the emperor-holocanthus, the flavour of which appeared to me superior even to salmon.

I passed the evening reading, writing, and thinking. Then sleep overpowered me, and I stretched myself on my zostera couch and slept profoundly, whilst the Nautilus glided rapidly along the current of the Black River.

Chapter Fifteen

A Written Invitation

THE NEXT DAY, THE 9TH OF NOVEMBER, I awoke after a long sleep that had lasted twelve hours. Conseil came, as was his custom, to ask 'how monsieur had passed the night,' and to offer his services. He had left his friend the Canadian sleeping like a man who had never done anything else in his life.

I let the brave fellow chatter on in his own fashion, without troubling to answer him much. I was anxious about the absence of Captain Nemo during our spectacle of the evening before, and hoped to see him again that day.

I was soon clothed in my byssus garments. Their nature provoked many reflections from Conseil. I told him they were manufactured with the lustrous and silky filaments which fasten a sort of shell, very abundant on the shores of the Mediterranean, to the rocks. Formerly beautiful materials – stockings and gloves – were made from it, and they were both very soft and very warm. The crew of the Nautilus could, therefore, be clothed at a cheap rate, without help of either cotton-trees, sheep, or silkworms of the earth.

When I was dressed I went into the saloon. It was deserted.

I plunged into the study of the conchological treasures piled up in the cases. I ransacked in great herbals filled with the rarest marine plants, which, though dried up, retained their lovely colours. Amongst these precious hydrophytes I remarked vorticellæ, pavoniæ, vine-leaved caulerps, callibrichaceæ, delicate ceramies with scarlet tints, fan-shaped agari, acalephæ, like much-depressed mushrooms, which were for a long time classified amongst the zoophytes – in short, a perfect series of algæ.

The whole day passed without my being honoured with a visit from Captain Nemo. The panels of the saloon were not opened. Perhaps they did not wish us to get tired of such beautiful things.

The direction of the Nautilus kept N.N.E., its speed at twelve miles, its depth between twenty-five and thirty fathoms.

The next day, the 10th of November, the same desertion, the same solitude. I did not see one of the ship's crew. Ned and Conseil passed the greater part of the day with me. They were astonished at the inexplicable absence of the captain. Was the singular man ill? Did he mean to alter his plans about us?

After all, as Conseil said, we enjoyed complete liberty; we were delicately and abundantly fed. Our host kept to the term of his treaty. We could not complain, and, besides, the singularity of our destiny reserved us such great compensations that we had no right to accuse it.

That day I began the account of these adventures, which allowed me to relate them with the most scrupulous exactness, and, curious detail, I wrote it on paper made with marine zostera.

Early in the morning of November 11th, the fresh air spread over the interior of the Nautilus told me that we were again on the surface of the ocean to renew our supply of oxygen. I went to the central staircase and ascended it to the platform. It was 6 à.m. The weather was cloudy, the sea grey, but calm. There was scarcely any swell. I hoped to meet Captain Nemo there. Would he come? I only saw the helmsman in his glass case. Seated on the upper portion of the hull, I drank in the sea-breeze with delight.

Little by little the clouds disappeared under the action of the sun's rays. The clouds announced wind for all that day. But the wind was no concern to the Nautilus. I was admiring this joyful sunrise, so gay and reviving, when I heard someone coming up to the platform. I prepared to address Captain Nemo, but it was his mate – whom I had already seen during the captain's first visit – who appeared. He did not seem to perceive my presence, and with his powerful glass he swept the horizon, after which he approached the stair-head and called out some words which I reproduce exactly, for every morning they were uttered under the same conditions. They were the following:

'Nautron respoc lorni virch.'

What those words meant I know not.

After pronouncing them the mate went below again, and I supposed that the Nautilus was going to continue her submarine course. I therefore followed the mate and regained my room.

Five days passed thus and altered nothing in our position. Each morning I ascended to the platform. The same sentence was pronounced by the same individual. Captain Nemo did not appear.

I had made up my mind that I was not going to see him again, when on the 16th of November, on entering my room with Ned Land and Conseil, I found a note directed to me upon the table.

I opened it with impatient fingers. It was written in a bold, clear hand, of slightly Gothic character, something like the German types.

The note contained the following:

To Professor ARONNAX, on board the *Nautilus*.
November 16th, 1867.

Captain Nemo invites Professor Aronnax to a hunt which will take place tomorrow morning in the forest of the island of Crespo. He hopes nothing will prevent the professor joining it, and he will have much pleasure in seeing his companions also.

The Commander of the Nautilus
CAPTAIN NEMO.

'A hunt!' cried Ned.

'And in the forests of Crespo Island,' added Conseil.

'Then that fellow does land sometimes,' said Ned Land.

'It looks like it,' said I, reading the letter again.

'Well, we must accept,' replied the Canadian. 'Once on land we can decide what to do. Besides, I shall not be sorry to eat some fresh meat.'

I consulted the planisphere as to the whereabouts of the island of Crespo, and in 32° 40′ north lat. and 167° 50′ west long. I found a small island which was reconnoitred in 1801 by Captain Crespo, and which was marked in old Spanish maps as Rocca de la Plata, or 'Silver Rock'. We were then about 1,800 miles from our starting-point, and the course of the Nautilus, a little changed, was bringing us back towards the south-east. I pointed out to my companions the little rock lost in the midst of the North Pacific.

'If Captain Nemo does land sometimes,' I said, 'he at least chooses quite desert islands.'

Ned Land shrugged his shoulders without speaking, and he and Conseil left me. After supper, which was served by the mute and impassible steward, I went to bed, not without some anxiety.

The next day, November 17th, when I awoke, I felt that the Nautilus was perfectly still. I dressed quickly and went to the saloon.

Captain Nemo was there waiting for me. He rose, bowed, and asked me if it was convenient for me to accompany him.

As he made no allusion to his eight days' absence I abstained from speaking of it, and answered simply that my companions and I were ready to follow him.

'May I ask you, captain,' I said, 'how it is that, having broken all ties with earth, you possess forests in Crespo Island?'

'Professor,' answered the captain, 'my forests are not terrestrial forests but submarine forests.'

'Submarine forests!' I exclaimed.

'Yes, professor.'

'And you offer to take me to them?'

'Precisely.'

'On foot?'

'Yes, and dryfooted too.'

'But how shall we hunt? – with a gun?'

'Yes, with a gun.'

I thought the captain was gone mad, and the idea was expressed on my face, but he only invited me to follow him like a man resigned to anything. We entered the dining-room, where breakfast was laid.

'M. Aronnax,' said the captain, 'will you share my breakfast without ceremony? We will talk as we eat. You will not find a restaurant in our walk though you will a forest. Breakfast like a man who will probably dine very late.'

I did honour to the meal. It was composed of different fish and slices of holithuria, excellent zoophytes, cooked with different seaweeds, such as the *Porphyria laciniata* and the *Laurentia primafetida*. We drank clear water, and, following the captain's example, I added a few drops of some fermented liquor, extracted by the Kamschatchan method from a seaweed known under the name of *Rhodomenia palmata*. Captain Nemo went on eating at first without saying a word. Then he said to me——

'When I invited you to hunt in my submarine forests, professor, you thought I was mad. You judged me too lightly. You know as well as I do that man can live under water, providing he takes with him a provision of air to breathe. When submarine work has to be done, the workman, clad in an impervious dress, with his head in a metal helmet, receives air from above by means of pumps and regulators.'

'Then it is a diving apparatus?'

'Yes, but in one that enables him to rid of the indiarubber tube attached to the pump. It is the Rouquayrol Denayrouze apparatus, invented by two of your own countrymen, but which I have brought to perfection for my own use, and which will allow you to risk yourself in the water without suffering. It is composed of a reservoir of thick iron plates, in which I store the air under a pressure of fifty atmospheres. The reservoir is fastened on to the back by means of braces, like a soldier's knap-sack; its upper part forms a box, in which the air is kept by means of bellows, and which cannot escape except at its normal tension. Two indiarubber pipes leave this box and join a sort of tent, which imprisons the nose and mouth; one introduces fresh air, the other lets out foul, and the tongue closes either according to the needs of respiration. But I, who encounter great pressure at the bottom of the sea, am obliged to shut my head in a globe of copper, into which the two pipes open.'

'Perfectly Captain Nemo; but the air that you carry with you must soon be used up, for as soon as it contains fifteen per cent of oxygen, it is no longer fit to breathe.'

'I have already told you, M. Aronnax, that the pumps of the Nautilus allow me to store up air under considerable pressure, and under these conditions the reservoir of the apparatus can furnish breathable air for nine or ten hours.'

'I have no other objection to make,' I answered. 'I will only ask you one thing, captain. How do you light your road at the bottom of the ocean?'

'With the Ruhmkorff apparatus, M. Aronnax. It is composed of a Bunsen pile, which I do not work with bichromate of potassium, but with sodium. A wire is introduced, which collects the electricity produced, and directs it towards a particularly-made lantern. In this lantern is a spiral glass which contains a small quantity of carbonic gas. When the apparatus is at work the gas becomes luminous, and gives out a white and continuous light. Thus provided, I breathe and see.'

'But, Captain Nemo, what sort of a gun do you use?'

'It is not a gun for powder, but an air-gun. How could I manufacture gunpowder on board without either saltpetre, sulphur, or charcoal?'

'Besides,' I added, 'to fire under water in a medium 855 times denser than air, very considerable resistance would have to be conquered.'

'That would be no difficulty. There exist certain Felton guns, perfected in

England by Philip Coles and Burley, by the Frenchman Furcy and the Italian Landi, furnished with a peculiar system of closing, which can be fired under these conditions. But, I repeat, having no powder, I use air under great pressure, which the pumps of the Nautilus furnish abundantly.'

'But this air must be rapidly consumed.'

'Well, have I not my Rouquayrol reservoir, which can furnish me with what I need? All I want for that is a tap *ad hoc*. Besides, you will see for yourself, M. Aronnax, that during these submarine shooting excursions you do not use either much air or bullets.'

'But it seems to me that in the half-light, and amidst a liquid so much more dense than the atmosphere, bodies cannot be projected far, and are not easily mortal.'

'Sir, with these guns every shot is mortal, and as soon as the animal is touched, however slightly, it falls crushed.'

'Why?'

'Because they are not ordinary bullets. We use little glass percussion-caps, invented by the Austrian chemist Leniebroek, and of which I have a considerable provision. These glass caps, covered with steel, and weighted with a leaden bottom, are really little Leyden bottles in which electricity is forced to a very high tension. At the slightest shock they go off, and the animal, however powerful it may be, falls dead. I must add that these caps are not larger than the No. 4, and the charge of an ordinary gun could contain ten of them.'

'I will argue no longer,' I replied, rising from the table. 'The only thing left me is take my gun. Besides, where you go I will follow.'

Captain Nemo then led me aft of the Nautilus, and whilst passing the cabin of Ned and Conseil, I called my two companions, who followed me immediately. Then we came to a kind of cell, situated near the engine room, in which we were to put on our walking dress.

Chapter Sixteen

At the Bottom of the Sea

THIS CELL WAS, PROPERLY speaking, the arsenal and wardrobe of the Nautilus. A dozen diving apparatus, hung from the wall, awaiting our use.

Ned Land, seeing them, manifested evident repugnance to put one on.

'But, my worthy Ned,' I said, 'the forests of Crespo Island are only submarine forests!'

The disappointed harpooner saw his dreams of fresh meat fade away.

'And you, M. Aronnax, are you going to put on one of those things?'

'I must, Master Ned.'

'You can do as you please, sir,' replied the harpooner, shrugging his shoulders, 'but as for me, unless I am forced, I will never get into one.'

'No one will force you, Ned,' said Captain Nemo.

'Does Conseil mean to risk it?' said Ned.

'I shall follow monsieur wherever he goes,' answered Conseil.

Two of the ship's crew came to help us on the call of the captain, and we donned the heavy and impervious clothes made of seamless indiarubber, and constructed expressly to resist considerable pressure. They looked like a suit of armour, both supple and resisting, and formed trousers and coat; the trousers were finished off with thick boots, furnished with heavy leaden soles. The texture of the coat was held together by bands of copper, which crossed the chest, protecting it from the pressure of the water, and leaving the lungs free to act; the sleeves ended in the form of supple gloves, which in no way restrained the movements of the hands.

There was much difference noticeable between these perfected diving apparatus and the old, shapeless cork breastplates, sea-jackets, boxes, &c., in vogue during the eighteenth century.

Captain Nemo and one of his companions – a sort of Hercules, who must have been of prodigious strength – Conseil, and myself, were soon enveloped in these dresses. There was nothing left but to put our heads into the metallic globes. But before proceeding with this operation I asked the captain's permission to examine the guns we were to take.

One of the crew gave me a simple gun, the butt-end of which made of steel and hollowed in the interior, was rather large; it served as a reservoir for compressed air, which a valve, worked by a spring, allowed to escape into a metal tube. A box of projectiles, fixed in a groove in the thickness of the butt-end, contained about twenty electric bullets, which, by means of a spring, were forced into the barrel of the gun. As soon as one shot was fired another was ready.

'Captain Nemo,' said I, 'this arm is perfect and easily managed; all I ask now is to try it. But how shall we gain the bottom of the sea?'

'At this moment, professor, the Nautilus is stranded in five fathoms of water, and we have only to start.'

'But how shall we get out?'

'You will soon see.'

Captain Nemo put on his helmet. Conseil and I did the same, not without hearing an ironical 'Good sport' from the Canadian. The upper part of our coat was terminated by a copper collar, upon which the metal helmet was screwed. As soon as it was in position the apparatus on our backs began to act, and, for my part, I could breathe with ease.

I found when I was ready, lamp and all, that I could not move a step. But this was foreseen. I felt myself pushed along a little room contiguous to the wardrobe-room. My companions, tugged along in the same way, followed me. I heard a door, furnished with obturators, close behind us, and we were wrapped in profound darkness.

After some minutes I heard a loud whistling, and felt the cold mount from my feet to my chest. It was evident that they had filled the room in which we were with sea-water by means of a tap. A second door in the side of the Nautilus opened then. A faint light appeared. A moment after, our feet were treading the bottom of the sea.

And now, how could I retrace the impression made upon me by that walk under the sea? Words are powerless to describe such marvels. When the brush itself is powerless to depict the particular effects of the liquid element, how can the pen reproduce them?

Captain Nemo walked on in front, and his companion followed us some steps behind. Conseil and I remained near one another, as if any exchange of words had been possible through our metallic covering. I no longer felt the weight of my clothes, shoes, air-reservoir, nor of that thick globe in the midst of which my head shook like an almond in its shell.

The light which lighted up the ground at thirty feet below the surface of the ocean astonished me by its power. The solar rays easily pierced this water mass and dissipated its colour. One easily distinguished objects 120 yards off. Beyond that the tints faded into fine gradations of ultramarine, and became effaced in a vague obscurity. The water around me only appeared a sort of air, denser than the terrestrial atmosphere, but nearly as transparent. Above me I perceived the calm surface of the sea.

We were walking on fine even sand, not wrinkled, as it is on a flat shore which keeps the imprint of the billows. This dazzling carpet reflected the rays of the sun with surprising intensity. Shall I be believed when I affirm that at that depth of thirty feet I saw as well as in open daylight?

For a quarter of an hour I trod on this shining sand, sown with the impalpable dust of tinted shells. The hull of the Nautilus, looked like a long rock, disappeared by degrees; but its lantern, when night came, would facilitate our return on board. I put back with my hands the liquid curtains which closed again behind me, and the print of my steps was soon effaced by the pressure of the water.

I soon came to some magnificent rocks, carpeted with splendid zoophytes, and I was at first struck by a special effect of this medium.

It was then 10 a.m. The rays of the sun struck the surface of the waves at an oblique angle, and at their contact with the light, composed by a refraction as through a prism, flowers, rocks, plants, and polypi were shaded at their edges by the seven solar colours; it was a grand feast for the eyes this complication of tints, a veritable kaleidoscope of green, yellow, orange, violet, indigo, and blue – in a word, all the palette of an enthusiastic colourist.

Before this splendid spectacle Conseil and I both stopped. Variegated isis, clusters of pure tuffed coral, prickly fungi and anemones adhering by their muscular disc, made perfect flower-beds, enamelled with porphitæ, decked with their azure tentacles, sea-stars studding the sand, and warted asterophytons, like fine lace embroidered by the hands of Naïads, whose festoons waved in the gentle undulations caused by our walk. It was quite a grief to me to crush under my feet the brilliant specimens of molluscs which lay on the ground by thousands, the concentric combs, the hammerheads, the donaces, real bounding shells, the broques, the red helmets, the angel-winged strombes, the aphysies, and many other products of the inexhaustible ocean. But we were obliged to keep on walking, whilst above our heads shoals of physalia, letting their ultramarine tentacles float after them, medusæ, with their rose-pink opaline parasols festooned with an azure border, sheltered us from the solar rays, and panophyrian pelagies, which, had it been dark, would have showered their phosphorescent gleams over our path.

All these wonders I saw in the space of a quarter of a mile. Soon the nature of the soil changed; to the sandy plains succeeded an extent of slimy mud composed of equal parts of siliceous and calcareous shells. Then we travelled over meadows of seaweed so soft to the foot that they would rival the softest carpet made by man. And at the same time that verdure was spread under our feet, marine plants, of which more than two thousand species are known, were growing on the surface of the ocean. I saw long ribands of fucus floating, some globular and others tubulous; laurenciæ and cladostephi, of most delicate foliage, and some rhodomeniæ ánd palmatæ resembling the fan of a cactus. I noticed that the green plants kept near the surface, whilst the red occupied a middle depth, leaving to the black or brown hydrophytes the care of forming gardens and flower-beds in the remote depths of the ocean. The family of seaweeds produces the largest and smallest vegetables of the globe.

We had left the Nautilus about an hour and a half. It was nearly twelve o'clock; I knew that by the perpendicularity of the sun's rays, which were no longer refracted. The magical colours disappeared by degrees, and the emerald and sapphire tints died out. We marched along with a regular step which rang upon the ground with astonishing intensity; the slightest sound is transmitted with a speed to which the ear is not accustomed on the earth – in fact, water is a better conductor of sound than air in the ratio of four to one.

The ground gradually sloped downwards, and the light took a uniform tint. We were at a depth of more than a hundred yards, and bearing a pressure of ten atmospheres. But my diving apparatus was so small that I suffered nothing from this pressure. I merely felt a slight discomfort in my finger joints, and even that soon disappeared. As to the fatigue that this walk in such unusual harness might be expected to produce, it was nothing. My movements, helped by the water, were made with surprising facility.

At this depth of three hundred feet I could still see the rays of the sun, but feebly. To their intense brilliancy had succeeded a reddish twilight, middle term between day and night. Still we saw sufficiently to guide ourselves, and it was not yet necessary to light our Ruhmkorff lamps.

At that moment Captain Nemo stopped. He waited for me to come up to him, and with his finger pointed to some obscure masses which stood out of the shade at some little distance.

'It is the forest of Crespo Island,' I thought, and I was not mistaken.

Chapter Seventeen

A Submarine Forest

WE HAD AT LAST ARRIVED on the borders of this forest, doubtless one of the most beautiful in the immense domain of Captain Nemo. He looked upon it as his own, and who was there to dispute his right? This forest was composed of arborescent plants, and as soon as we had penetrated under its vast arcades, I was struck at first by the singular disposition of their branches, which I had not observed before.

None of those herbs which carpeted the ground – none of the branches of the larger plants, were either bent, drooped, or extended horizontally. There was not a single filament, however, thin, that did not keep as upright as a rod of iron. The fusci and llianas grew in rigid perpendicular lines, commanded by the density of the element which had produced them. When I bent them with my hand these plants immediately resumed their first position. It was the reign of perpendicularity.

I soon accustomed to this fantastic disposition of things, as well as to the relative obscurity which enveloped us. The soil of the forest seemed covered with sharp blocks difficult to avoid. The submarine flora appeared to me very perfect, and richer than it would have been in the Arctic or tropical zones, where these productions are less numerous. But for some minutes I involuntarily confounded the genera, taking zoophytes for hydrophytes, animals for plants. And who would not have been mistaken? The fauna and flora are so nearly allied in this submarine world.

I noticed that all these productions of the vegetable kingdom had no roots, and only held on to either sand, shell, or rock. These plants drew no vitality from anything but the water. The greater number, instead of leaves, shot forth blades of capricious shapes, comprised within a scale of colours – pink, carmine, red, olive, fawn, and brown.

'Curious anomaly, fantastic element,' said an ingenious naturalist. 'Where the animal kingdom blossoms the vegetable does not.'

Amongst these different shrubs, as large as the trees of temperate zones, and under their humid shade, were massed veritable bushes of living flowers, hedges of zoophytes, on which blossomed meandrina with tortuous stripes, yellow cariophylles with transparent tentacles, grassy tufts of zoantharia, and, to complete the illusion, the fish-flies flew from branch to branch like a swarm of humming-birds, whilst yellow lepisacomthi, with bristling jaws, dactylopteri, and monocentrides rose at our feet like a flight of snipes.

About one o'clock Captain Nemo gave the signal to halt. I, for my part, was not sorry, and we stretched ourselves under a thicket of alariæ, the long thin blades of which shot up like arrows.

This short rest seemed delicious to me. Nothing was wanting but the charm of conversation, but it was impossible to speak – I could only approach my large copper head to that of Conseil. I saw the eyes of the worthy fellow shine with contentment, and he moved about in his covering in the most comical way in the world.

After this four hours' walk I was much astonished not to find myself violently hungry, and I cannot tell why, but instead I was intolerably sleepy, as all divers are. My eyes closed behind their thick glass, and I fell into an unavoidable slumber, which the movement of walking had alone prevented up till then. Captain Nemo and his robust companion, lying down in the clear crystal, set us the example.

How long I remained asleep I cannot tell, but when I awoke the sun seemed sinking towards the horizon. Captain Nemo was already on his feet, and I was stretching myself when an unexpected apparition brought me quickly to my feet.

A few steps off an enormous sea-spider, more than a yard high, was looking at me with his squinting eyes ready to spring upon me. Although my dress was thick enough to defend me against the bite of the animal, I could not restrain a movement of horror. Conseil and the sailor of the Nautilus awoke at that moment. Captain Nemo showed his companion the hideous crustacean, and a blow from the butt-end of a gun killed it, and I saw its horrible claws writhe in horrible convulsions.

This accident reminded me that other animals, more to be feared, might haunt these obscure depths, and that my diver's dress would not protect me against their attacks. I had not thought of that before, and resolved to be on my guard. I supposed that this halt marked the limit of our excursion, but I was mistaken, and instead of returning to the Nautilus, Captain Nemo went on.

The ground still inclined and took us to greater depths. It must have been about three o'clock when we reached a narrow valley between two high cliffs, situated about seventy-five fathoms deep. Thanks to the perfection of our apparatus, we were forty-five fathoms below the limit which Nature seems to have imposed on the submarine excursions of man.

I knew how deep we were because the obscurity became so profound – not an object was visible at ten paces. I walked along groping when I suddenly saw a white light shine out. Captain Nemo had just lighted his electric lamp. His companion imitated him. Conseil and I followed their example. By turning a screw I established the communication between the spool and the glass serpentine, and the sea, lighted up by our four lanterns, was illuminated in a radius of twenty-five yards.

Captain Nemo still kept on plunging into the dark depths of the forest, the trees of which were getting rarer and rarer. I remarked that the vegetable life disappeared sooner than the animal. The medusæ had already left the soil, which had become arid, whilst a prodigious number of animals, zoophytes, articulata, molluscs, and fish swarmed there still.

As we walked I thought that the light of our Ruhmkorff apparatus could not fail to draw some inhabitants from these sombre depths. But if they did approach us they at least kept a respectful distance from the hunters. Several times I saw Captain Nemo stop and take aim; then, after some minutes' observation, he rose and went on walking.

At last, about four o'clock, this wonderful excursion was ended. A wall of superb rocks rose up before us, enormous granite cliffs impossible to climb. It was the island of Crespo. Captain Nemo stopped suddenly. We stopped at a sign from him. Here ended the domains of the captain.

The return began. Captain Nemo again kept at the head of his little band, and directed his steps without hesitation. I thought I perceived that we were not returning to the Nautilus by the road we had come. This new one was very steep, and consequently very painful. We approached the surface of the sea rapidly. But his return to the upper beds was not so sudden as to produce the internal lesions so fatal to divers. Very soon light reappeared and increased, and as the sun was already low on the horizon refraction edged the different objects with a spectral ring.

At a depth of ten yards we were walking in a swarm of little fish of every sort, more numerous than birds in the air, and more agile too. But no aquatic game worthy of a shot had as yet met our gaze.

At that moment I saw the captain put his gun to his shoulder and follow a moving object into the shrubs. He fired, I heard a feeble hissing, and an animal fell a few steps from us.

It was a magnificent sea-otter, a veritable enhydros, the only quadruped which is exclusively marine. This otter was five feet long, and must have been very valuable. Its skin, chestnut brown above and silvery underneath, would have made one of those beautiful furs so sought after in the Russian and Chinese markets; the fineness and lustre of its coat was certainly worth at least eight pounds. I admired this curious mammal – its rounded head and short ears, round eyes and white whiskers, like those of a cat, with webbed feet and claws and tufted tail. This precious animal, hunted and tracked by fishermen, is becoming very rare, and it takes refuge principally in the northern parts of the Pacific, where it is likily that its race will soon become extinct. Captain Nemo's companion took up the animal and threw it over his shoulders, and we continued our route.

During the next hour a plain of sand lay stretched before us. Sometimes it rose within two yards and some inches of the surface of the water. I then saw the reflection of our images above us, like us in every point, except that they walked with their heads downwards and their feet in the air.

The thick waves above us looked like clouds above our heads – clouds which were no sooner formed than they vanished rapidly. I even perceived the shadows of the large birds as they floated on the surface of the water.

On this ocassion I was witness to one of the finest gun-shots which ever made a hunter's nerve thrill. A large bird, with great breadth of wing, hovered over us. Captain Nemo's companion shouldered his gun and fired when it was only a few yards above the waves. The bird fell dead, and the fall brought it in reach of the skilful hunter's grasp. It was an albatross of the finest kind.

Our march was not interrupted by this incident. I was worn out by fatigue when we at last perceived a faint light half a mile off. Before twenty minutes were over we should be on board and able to breathe with ease, for it seemed to me that my reservoir of air was getting very deficient in oxygen, but I did not reckon upon a meeting which delayed our arrival.

I was about twenty steps behind Captain Nemo when he suddenly turned towards me. With his vigorous hand he threw me to the ground, whilst his companion did the same to Conseil. At first I did not know what to think of this sudden attack, but I was reassured when I saw that the captain lay down beside me and remained perfectly motionless.

I was stretched on the ground just under the shelter of a bush of algæ, when, on raising my head, I perceived enormous masses throwing phosphorescent gleams pass blusteringly by.

My blood froze in my veins. I saw two formidable dog-fish threatening us; they were terrible creatures, with enormous tails and dull and glassy stare, who threw out phosphorescent beams from holes pierced round their muzzles. Monstrous brutes which would crush a whole man in their jaws! I do not know if Conseil stayed to classify them. For my part, I noticed their silver stomachs and their formidable mouths bristling with teeth from a very unscientific point of view – more as a possible victim than as a naturalist.

Happily, these voracious animals see badly. They passed without perceiving us, brushing us with their brownish fins, and we escaped, as if by a miracle, this danger, certainly greater than the meeting of a tiger in a forest.

Half an hour after, guided by the electric light, we reached the Nautilus. The outside door had remained open, and Captain Nemo closed it as soon as we had entered the first cell. Then he pressed a knob. I heard the pumps worked inside the vessel. I felt the water lower around me, and in a few moments the cell was entirely empty. The inner door then opened, and we entered the wardrobe-room.

There our diving dresses were taken off, and, quite worn out from want of food and sleep, I returned to my room, lost in wonder at this surprising excursion under the sea.

Chapter Eighteen

Four Thousand Leagues under the Pacific

THE NEXT MORNING, THE 18th of November, I was perfectly recovered from my fatigue of the day before, and I went up to the platform at the very moment that the mate was pronouncing his daily sentence. It then came into my mind that it had to do with the state of the sea, and that it signified 'There is nothing in sight.'

And, in fact, the ocean was quite clear. There was not a sail on the horizon. The heights of Crespo Island had disappeared during the night. The sea, absorbing the colours of the solar prism, with the exception of the blue rays, reflected them in every direction, and was of an admirable indigo shade. A large wave was regularly undulating its surface.

I was admiring this magnificent aspect of the sea when Captain Nemo appeared. He did not seem to perceive my presence, and began a series of astronomical observations. Then, when he had ended his operation, he went and leaned against the cage of the watch-light and watched the surface of the ocean.

In the meantime about twenty sailors from the Nautilus, strong and well-built men, ascended upon the platform. They came to draw in the nets which had been out all night. These sailors evidently belonged to different nations, although they were all of the European type. I recognized, to a certainty, Irishmen, Frenchmen, some Sclaves, one Greek, or a Candiote. These men spoke very little, and only used the strange idiom of which I could not even guess the origin, so that I could not question them.

The nets were hauled in. They were a species of 'chaluts,' like those used on the Normandy coast, vast pockets which a floating yard and a chain marled into the lower stitches keep half open. These pockets, thus dragged along in their iron gauntlets, swept the bottom of the ocean, and took in all its products on their way. That day they brought in curious specimens from these fish-fields – lophiadæ, that from their comical movements have acquired the name of buffoons; black commersons, furnished with antennæ, undulating balisters, encircled with red bands, orthragorisci, with very subtle venom; olive-coloured lampreys, macrorhynci, covered with silver scales; trichiuri, with an electric power equal to that of the gymnotus and cramp-fish; scaly notopleri, with transverse brown bands; greenish cod, several varieties of gobies, &c.; and, lastly, several fish of larger size, a caranx with a prominent head more than a yard long, several fine bonitos, bedizened with blue and silver colours, and three magnificent tunnies, which, in spite of their speed, had not escaped the net.

I reckoned that the haul had brought in more than nine hundredweight of fish. It was a fine haul, but not to be wondered at. We should not want for food.

These different products of the sea were immediately lowered down by the panel leading to the storerooms, some to be eaten fresh, others to be preserved.

The fishing ended and the provision of air renewed, I thought that the Nautilus was going to continue its submarine excursion, and I was preparing to return to my room, when, without further preamble, the captain turned to me and said——

'Is not the ocean gifted with real life, professor? It is sometimes gentle, at other times tempestuous. Yesterday it slept as we did, and now it has awaked after a peaceful night.'

Neither 'Good morning' nor 'Good evening!' It was as though this strange personage was continuing a conversation already commenced with me.

'See now,' he said, 'it wakes under the sun's influence. It will now renew its diurnal existence. It is deeply interesting to watch the play of its organization. It possesses a pulse and arteries, it has its spasms, and I agree with the learned Maury, who discovered in it a circulation as real as the circulation of blood in animals.'

It was certain that Captain Nemo expected no answer from me, and it appeared to me useless to keep saying 'Evidently,' or 'You are right,' or 'It must be so.' He spoke rather to himself, taking some time between each sentence. It was a meditation aloud.

'Yes,' said he, 'the ocean possesses a veritable circulation, and in order to cause it, it sufficed the Creator of all things to multiply in it caloric, salt, and animalculæ. Caloric creates the different densities, the cause of currents and under-currents. Evaporation, which does not go on at all in hyperborean regions, and is very active in the equatorial zones, constitutes a permanent exchange between tropical and polar water. Besides, I have felt the perpendicular currents which form the real respiration of the ocean. I have seen the molecule of sea-water warmed on the surface, re-descend to the depths, reach its maximum of density at 2° below zero, then, cooling again, become lighter, and ascend again. You will see at the poles the consequences of this phenomenon, and you will understand why, according to the law of provident Nature, freezing can never take place except on the surface of the water!'

Whilst Captain Nemo was finishing his sentence I said to myself, 'The pole! Does the daring man intend to take us as far as there?'

In the meantime the captain had stopped talking, and was contemplating the element he so incessantly studied. Then he resumed.

'The salts,' said he, 'exist in a considerable quantity in the sea, professor, and if you were to take out all it contains in solution, you would make a mass of four million and a half square miles, which, spread over the globe, would form a layer more than ten yards deep. And do not think that the presence of this salt is due to a caprice of Nature. No. It makes sea-water less capable of evaporation, and prevents the wind taking off too great a quantity of vapour, which, when it condenses, would submerge the temperate zones. It has a great balancing part to play in the general economy of the globe!'

Captain Nemo stopped, rose, took several steps on the platform, and came back towards me.

'As to the infusoria, as to the hundreds of millions of animalculæ which exist by millions in a drop of water, and of which it takes 800,000 to weigh a milligramme, their part is not less important. They absorb the marine salts, they assimilate the solid elements of water, and, veritable manufacturers of calcareous continents, they make coral and madrepores, and then the drop of water deprived of its mineral element is lightened, mounts to the surface, absorbs there the salt left by evaporation, is weighted, sinks again, and takes back to the animalculæ new elements to absorb. Hence a double current, ascending and descending, always movement and life – life more intense than that of continents, more exuberant, more infinite, flourishing in every part of this ocean, element of death to man, they say, element of life to myriads of animals, and to me!'

When Captain Nemo spoke thus he was transfigured, and evoked in me extraordinary emotion.

'True existence is there,' added he, 'and I could conceive the foundation of nautical towns, agglomeration of submarine houses, which, like the Nautilus, would go up every morning to breathe on the surface of the water – free towns, if ever there were any, independent cities! And yet who knows if some despot——'

Captain Nemo finished his sentence by a violent gesture. Then, addressing himself directly to me as if to drive away some gloomy thought, he said——

'M. Aronnax, do you know how deep the ocean is?'

'I know at least, captain, what the principal soundings have taught us.'

'Could you repeat them to me, so that I might counter-register them if necessary?'

'Here are some that occur to me,' I answered. 'If I am not mistaken they have found an average depth of 8,200 metres in the North Atlantic, and 2,500 metres in the Mediterranean. The most remarkable soundings have been taken in the South Atlantic, near the 35th degree; and they have given 1,200 metres, 14,081 metres, and 15,149 metres – in short, it is estimated that if the bottom of the sea was levelled its average depth would be about five miles.'

'Well, professor,' answered Captain Nemo, 'we shall show you better than that, I hope. As to the average depth of this part of the Pacific, I can tell you that it is only 4,000 metres.'

That said, Captain Nemo went towards the panel and disappeared down the ladder. I followed him, and went into the saloon. The screw then began to work, and the log gave twenty miles an hour.

For days and weeks Captain Nemo was very sparing of his visits. I only saw him at rare intervals. His mate pricked the ship's course regularly on the chart, and I could always tell the exact route of the Nautilus.

Conseil and Land passed long hours with me. Conseil had related to his friend the marvels of our excursion, and the Canadian regretted not having accompanied us.

Almost every day, during some hours, the panels of the saloon were opened, and our eyes were never tired of penetrating the mysteries of the submarine world.

The general direction of the Nautilus was S.E., and it kept between 100 and 150 yards depth. One day, however – I do not know by what caprice – it reached the beds of water situated at 2,000 yards. On the 26th of November, at 3 a.m., the Nautilus crossed the tropic of Cancer by long. 172°. On the 27th it sighted the Sandwich Islands, where the illustrious Cook met his death on the 14th February 1779. We had then made 4,860 leagues from our starting-point. In the morning, when I arrived on the platform, I saw, two miles to the windward, Hawaii, the largest of the seven islands which form this archipelago. I clearly distinguished its cultivated border, the different chains of mountains which run parallel to the coast, and its volcanoes, the highest of which is the Mouna-Rea. Amongst other specimens brought up by the nets in this part of the ocean were several polypi of graceful form, which are peculiar to that region.

The Nautilus still kept a north-easterly direction. It crossed the equator on December 1st by long. 142°, and the 4th of the same month, after a rapid passage during which no particular incident happened, we sighted the group of the Marquesas. I perceived, at a distance of three miles, by 8° 57' south lat. and 139° 32' west long., the point Martin de Nouka-Hiva, the principal of this group, which belongs to France. I only saw the wooded mountains outlined on the horizon, for Captain Nemo did not like to draw near any land. There the nets brought in some fine specimens of fish – choryphenes with azure fins and golden tails, the flesh of which is without a rival in the world; hologymnoses, nearly destitute of scales, but of exquisite flavour; ostorhyncs with bony jaws and yellowish thasards, as good as bonitoes – all fish worthy of being classified in the pantries on board.

After leaving these charming islands protected by the French flag, from the 4th to the 11th of December the Nautilus sailed over 2,000 miles. This navigation was marked by the meeting of an immense shoal of calmars, curious molluscs, near neighbours to the cuttle. The French fishermen call them *ecornets*; they belong to the class of cephalopods and the family of the dibranches, that comprehends the cuttles and argonauts. These animals were particularly studied by the naturalists of antiquity, and they furnished numerous metaphors to the orators of the Agora, as well as excellent dishes for the tables of the rich citizens, if we can believe Athenæus, a Greek doctor who lived before Galen.

It was during the night between the 9th and 10th of December that the Nautilus met with the shoal of molluscs that are particularly nocturnal. They could be counted by millions. They were emigrating from the temperate to the warmer zones, following the track of herrings and sardines. We watched them through the crystal panes, swimming backwards with extreme rapidity, moving by means of their locomotive tube, pursuing fish and molluscs, eating the little ones, eaten by the big ones, and agitating, in indescribable confusion, the ten arms that Nature has placed on their heads, like a crest of pneumatic serpents. The Nautilus, notwithstanding its speed, sailed for several hours in the midst of these animals, and its nets drew in an innumerable quantity, amongst which I recognized the nine species that Orbigny has classified as belong to the Pacific Ocean.

It will be seen that during this voyage the sea was prodigal of its most marvellous spectacles. It varied them infinitely. It changed its scenes and grouping for the pleasure of our eyes, and we were called upon, not only to contemplate the works of the Creator amidst the liquid element, but to penetrate as well into the most fearful mysteries of the ocean.

During the day of the 11th December I was reading in the saloon. Ned Land and Conseil were looking at the luminous water through the half-open panels. The Nautilus was stationary; it was keeping at a depth of 1,000 yards, a region not much inhabited, in which large fish alone make rare appearances.

I was reading at that moment a charming book by Jean Macé, *Les Serviteurs de l'Estomac*, and I was learning the ingenious lessons it gives, when Conseil interrupted me.

'Will monsieur come here for a moment?' said he in a singular voice.

I rose, went to the window, and looked out. Full in the electric light an enormous black mass, immovable, was suspended in the midst of the waters. I looked at it attentively, trying to make out the nature of this gigantic cetacean. But an idea suddenly came into my mind.

'A vessel!' I cried.

'Yes,' replied the Canadian, 'a disabled ship sunk perpendicularly.'

Ned Land was right. We were close to a vessel of which the tattered shrouds still hung from their chains. The hull seemed to be in good order, and it could not have been wrecked more than a few hours; the vessel had had to sacrifice its mast. It lay on its side, had filled, and was heeling over to port. This skeleton of what it had once been was a sad spectacle under the waves, but sadder still was the sight of the deck, where corpses, bound with rope, were still lying. I counted five; one man was at the helm, and a woman stood by the poop holding an infant in her arms; she was quite young. I could clearly see her features by the light of the Nautilus – features which the water had not yet decomposed. In a last effort she had raised the child above her head, and the arms of the little one were round its mother's neck. The sailors looked frightful, and seemed to be making a last effort to free themselves from the cords that bound them to the vessel. The helmsman alone, calm, with a clear, grave face and iron-grey hair glued to his forehead, was clutching the wheel of the helm, and seemed, even then, to be guiding the vessel through the depths of the ocean!

What a scene! It struck us dumb, and our hearts beat faster at the sight of this wreck, photographed at the last moment, and I already saw, advancing towards it with hungry eyes, enormous sharks attracted by the human flesh!

The Nautilus just then turned round the submerged vessel, and I read on the stern 'Florida, Sunderland'.

Chapter Nineteen

Vanikoro

THIS TERRIBLE SPECTACLE inaugurated the series of maritime catastrophes which the Nautilus was to meet with on her route. Since it had been in more frequented seas we often perceived the hulls of ships – wrecked vessels which were rotting in the midst of the waters, and deeper down, cannons, bullets, anchors, chains, and other iron objects which were being eaten up by the rust.

We lived in the Nautilus our usual isolated lives, and on the 11th of December we sighted the archipelago of Pomotou, the ancient 'dangerous group' of Bougainville, which extends over a space of 500 leagues from the E.S.E. to W.N.W., between 13° 30′ and 23° 50′ south lat. and 125° 30′ and 151° 30′ west long., from Ducie Island to that of Lazareffe.

This archipelago covers an area of 370 square leagues, and is formed of sixty groups of islands, amongst which is the Gambier group, over which France rules. These islands are of coral formation. They slowly but continuously rise by the work of the polypi, which will one day join them together. Then this new island will be joined to the neighbouring archipelagoes, and a fifth continent will stretch from New Zealand and New Caledonia to the Marquesas.

The day that I developed this theory before Captain Nemo he answered me coldly——

'The earth does not want new continents, but new men!'

The hazards of its navigation had precisely conducted the Nautilus towards the island of Clermont-Tonnerre, one of the most curious of the group, which was discovered in 1822 by Captain Bell, of the Minerva. I could now study the madreporal system to which islands of this ocean are due.

Madrepores, which must not be mistaken for corals, have a tissue covered with a calcareous crust, and the modifications of its structure have made Mr Milne Edwards, my illustrious master, classify them into five sections. The little animalculæ which these polypi secrete live by millions at the bottom of their cells. It is their calcareous deposit which becomes rocks, reefs, and large and small islands. Here they form a ring surrounding a lagoon or small interior lake, which gaps put into communication with the sea. There they make barriers of reefs like those which exist on the coasts of New Caledonia and the different Pomotou Islands. In other places, such as Réunion and Maurice, they raise fringed reefs, high straight walls, near which the depths of the ocean are considerable.

As we were coasting at some cable-lengths only off the shore of the island of Clermont-Tonnerre I admired the gigantic work accomplished by these microscopical workmen. These walls are specially the work of madrepores, known as milleporas, porites, astræas, and meandrines. These polypi breed particularly in the rough beds on the surface of the sea, and consequently it is from their upper part that they begin their substructure, which sinks gradually with the debris of secretions which support them. Such is at least Mr Darwin's theory to that which gives for basis of madreporical works the summits of mountains or volcanoes that are submerged some feet below the level of the sea.

I could closely observe these curious walls, for the fathom line gave them perpendicularly more than 300 yards in depth, and our electric light made the calcareous matter shine brilliantly.

Replying to a question Conseil asked me as to how long it took these colossal barriers to grow, I astonished him much by telling him that learned men reckoned the growth to be one-eighth of an inch in a century.

'Then how long has it taken to raise these walls?' he said.

'Four hundred and ninety-two thousand years, Conseil. Besides, the formation of coal and the mineralizing of the forests buried by the deluge has taken a much longer time still.'

When the Nautilus returned to the surface of the ocean I could take in all the development of this low and wooded island of Clermont-Tonnerre. Its madreporal rocks were evidently fertilized by water-spouts and tempests. One day some grain, carried away from neighbouring land by a tempest of wind, fell on these calcareous layers, mixed with the decomposed detritus of fish and marine plants which formed vegetable soil. A cocoanut, pushed along by the waves, arrived on this new coast. The germ took root. The tree grew and stopped the vapour of the water. Streams were born, vegetation spread little by little. Animalculæ, worms, insects landed upon trunks of trees, torn away from other islands by the wind. Turtles came to lay their eggs. Birds built their nests in the young trees. In that manner animal life was developed, and attracted by verdure and fertility, man appeared. Thus these islands, the immense works of microscopical animals, were formed.

Towards evening Clermont-Tonnerre was lost in the distance, and the route of the Nautilus was changed perceptibly. After having touched the tropic of Capricorn, in long. 135°, it directed its course W.N.W., sailing up the whole tropical zone again. Although the summer sun was prodigal of its rays, we did not suffer at all from the heat, for at thirty or forty yards below the water the temperature did not rise above from ten to twelve degrees.

On the 15th of December we left to the east the bewitching archipelago of the Society Islands and the graceful Tahiti, the queen of the Pacific. I perceived in the morning the elevated summits of this island. Its waters furnished our tables with excellent fish, mackerel, bonitoes, and albicores, and some varieties of a sea serpent called munirophis.

The Nautilus had come 8,100 miles; 9,720 miles were registered by the log as we passed between the archipelago of Tonga-Tabou, where perished the crews of the Argo, the Port-au-Prince, and the Duke of Portland, and the Navigator archipelago, where Captain Langle, the friend of La Perouse, was killed. Then we sighted the archipelago Viti, where the natives massacred the crews of L'Union, and Captain Bureau, of Nantes, commander of L'Aimable Josephine.

This archipelago, which stretches over one hundred leagues from north to south, and ninety leagues from east to west, is comprised between 6° and 2° of S. lat. and 179° of west long. It is composed of a number of large and small islands and reefs, amongst which are the islands of Viti-Levou, of Vanona-Levou, and Kandubon.

It was Tasman who discovered this group in 1643, the same year that Torricelli invented the barometer and Louis XIV ascended the throne. I leave it to be imagined which of these facts was the more useful to humanity. Afterwards came Cook in 1714, d'Entrecasteaux in 1793, and lastly, Dumont d'Urville in 1827 unravelled all the geographical chaos of this archipelago.

The Nautilus approached Wailia Bay, the scene of the terrible adventures of Captain Dillon, who was the first to clear up the mystery of the shipwreck of La Perouse.

This bay, after several draggings, furnished us with abundance of excellent oysters. We ate them immoderately, opening them on our own table, according to the precept of Seneca. These molluscs belong to the species known under the name of 'estrea camelloso,' which is very common in Corsica. This Wailia bank must be considerable, and certainly without multiplied causes of destruction, the oysters would end by filling up the bays, as each contains two millions of eggs.

If Ned Land had not to repent of his greediness in this case, it was because the oyster is the only dish which never provokes indigestion. In fact, it takes at least sixteen dozen of these acephalous molluscs to furnish the quantity of azote necessary to the daily food of one man.

On the 25th of December the Nautilus sailed into the midst of the New Hebrides, which Quiros discovered in 1606, which Bougainville explored in 1768, and to which Cook gave its present name in 1773. This group is composed principally of nine large islands, that form a band of 120 leagues from N.N.W. to the S.S.E. between 15° and 2° south lat., and 164° and 168° long. We passed rather near to the island of Aurou, that at noon looked to me like a mass of green woods, surmounted by a peak of green height.

That day being Christmas Day, Ned Land seemed to me to regret that it could not be celebrated as the family fete dear to Protestant hearts.

I had not seen Captain Nemo for a week, when, on the 27th, in the morning, he entered the saloon, looking like man who had seen you five minutes before. I was occupied in tracing the route of the Nautilus on the planisphere. The captain approached, put his finger on a spot in the map, and pronounced this one word:——

'Vanikoro.'

This name was magical. It was the name of the islands upon which the vessels of La Perouse had been lost. I rose immediately.

'Is the Nautilus taking us to Vanikoro?' I asked.

'Yes, professor,' answered the captain.

'And can I visit these celebrated islands where the Boussole and Astrolabe were lost?'

'If you please, professor.'

'When shall we reach Vanikoro?'

'We are there now, professor.'

Followed by Captain Nemo I went to the platform, and from there I looked with avidity round the horizon.

To the N.E. emerged two volcanic islands of unequal size, surrounded by coral reefs measuring forty miles in circumference. We were in presence of Vanikoro Island, properly so called to which Dumont d'Urville gave the name of Ile de la Recherche; we were just in front of the little harbour of Vanou, situated in 16° 4' south lat. and 164° 3' east long. The land seemed covered with verdure from the shore to the summits of the interior, crowned by Mount Kapogo, 3,000 feet high.

The Nautilus, after having crossed the exterior ring of rocks through a narrow passage, was inside the reefs where the sea is from thirty to forty fathoms deep. Under the verdant shade of some mangroves I perceived several savages, who looked extremely astonished at our approach. Perhaps they took the long body advancing along the suface of the water for some formidable cetacean that they ought to guard themselves against. At that moment Captai Nemo asked me what I knew about the shipwreck of La Perouse.

'What everyone knows, captain,' I answered.

'And can you tell me what everone knows?' he asked in a slightly ironical tone.

'Easily.'

I then related what the last works of Dumont d'Urville had made known, of which the following is an abridgment: 'La Perouse and his second in command, Captain Langle, were sent by Louis XVI, in 1785, to make a voyage round the world. They equipped the corvettes, the Boussole and the Astrolabe, neither of which was again heard of.'

In 1791 the French Government, rightly uneasy about the fate of the two corvettes, equipped two large merchantmen, the Recherche and the Esperance, which left Brest on the 28th of September, under the orders of Bruni d'Entrecasteaux. Two months afterwards it was learnt, through the testimony of Bowen, captain of the Albermarle, that the debris of shipwrecked vessels had been seen on the coasts of New Georgia. But D'Entrecasteaux, ignoring this communication, which was rather uncertain, made for the Admiralty Islands, designated in a report of Captain Hunter's as the scene of La Perouse's shipwreck.

His search was fruitless. The Esperance and Recherche even passed before Vanikoro without stopping there, and, on the whole, this voyage was very unfortunate, for it cost the life of d'Entrecasteuax, of two of his mates, and several sailors of his crew.

It was an old Pacific seaman, Captain Dillon, who first found indisputable traces of the shipwreck. On May 15th, 1824, his ship, the Saint Patrick passed near the Island of Tikopia, one of the New Hebrides. There a Lascar, having hailed him in a pirogue, sold him the silver handle of a sword that had something engraved on it. The Lascar said that six years before, while he was staying at Vanikoro, he had seen two Europeans who belonged to ships wrecked many years before upon the reefs of the island.

Dillon guessed that he referred to the ships of La Perouse, the disappearance of which had troubled the entire world. He wished to reach Vanikoro, where, according to the Lascar, numerous debris of the wrecks were to be found; but contrary winds and currents prevented him. Dillon returned to Calcutta. There he interested the Asiatic Society and the East India Company in his search. A ship, to which they gave the name of the Recherche, was placed at his disposal, and he set out on the 23rd of January, 1827, accompanied by a French agent.

The Recherche, after touching at several points in the Pacific, anchored before Vanikoro on the 7th of July, 1827, in this same harbour of Vanou where the Nautilus is now floating. There he gathered together numerous remains of the wrecks – iron utensils, anchors, pulley-strops, swivel-guns, an 18 lb shot, debris of astronomical instruments, a piece of taffrail, and a bronze bell, bearing the inscription, *Bazin m'a fait*, the mark of the foundry of Brest Arsenal, about 1785. Doubt was no longer possible.

Dillon, to complete his information, remained upon the scene of the disaster till the month of October. Then he left Vanikoro, made for New Zealand, anchored at Calcutta on the 7th of April, 1828, and returned to France, where he was received very warmly by Charles X.

Dumont d'Urville, commander of the Astrolabe, had set sail, and two months after Dillon had left Vanikoro he anchored before Hobart Town. There he heard of the results obtained by Dillon, and, moreover, he learnt that a certain James Hobbs, mate on board the Union, of Calcutta, having landed on an island situated by 80° 18' south lat. and 156° 30' east long., had noticed bars of iron and red stuffs being used by the natives of the place. Durmont d'Urville was perplexed, and did not know if he ought to credit these reports, made by newspapers little worthy of confidence. However, he decided to go on Dillon's track.

On the 10th of February, 1828, the Astrolabe anchored before Tikopia, and took for guide and interpreter a deserter who had taken refuge on that island, set sail for Vanikoro, and sighted it on the 12th of February, coasted its reefs until the 14th, and on the 20th only anchored inside the barrier, in the harbour of Vanou.

On the 23rd several officers went round the island and brought back some unimportant debris. The natives, adopting a system of denials and evasions, refused to take them to the scene of the disaster. This suspicious conduct led to the belief that they had ill-treated the shipwrecked men, and, in fact, they seemed to fear that Dumond d'Urville and his companions were come to revenge La Perouse and his unfortunate companions.

However, on the 26th, decided by presents, and understanding that they had nothing to fear, they conducted the mate, M. Jacquinot, to the place of shipwreck.

There, in three to four fathoms of water, between the reefs of Pacou and Vanou, lay anchors, cannons, pigs of iron and lead, encrusted in the calcareous concretion. The longboat and the whaler from the Astrolabe were sent to this place, and, not without much fatigue, their crews succeeded in raising an anchor weighing 800 pounds, an 800 pound brass cannon, some pigs of lead, and two copper swivel guns.

Dumont d'Urville, by questioning the natives, learnt also that La Perouse, after having lost his two ships on the reefs of the island, had built a smaller vessel, only to be lost a second time – no one knew where. The commander of the Astrolabe then, under a thicket of mangroves, caused a cenotaph to be raised to the memory of the celebrated navigator and his companions. It was a simple quadrangular pyramid on a coral foundation, in which there was no iron to tempt the cupidity of the natives. Then Dumont d'Urville wished to depart, but his crew were worn out by the fevers of those unhealthy shores, and he was so ill himself that he could not get under sail before the 17th of March.

In the meantime the French Government, fearing that Dumont d'Urville was not acquainted with Dillon's movements, had sent the sloop Bayonnaise, commanded by Legoarant de Tromelin, who was stationed on the West Coast of America. He anchored before Vanikoro some months after the departure of the Astrolabe, found no new document, but saw that the savages had respected La Perouse's mausoleum. Such is the substance of what I told Captain Nemo.

'Then,' he said, 'they do not know where the third vessel, built by the shipwrecked men on the island of Vanikoro, perished?'

'No one knows.'

Captain Nemo answered nothing, and made me a sign to follow him to the saloon. The Nautilus sank some yards below the surface of the waves, and then the panels were drawn back. I rushed towards the window, and under the crustations of coral covered with fungi, syphonules, alcyons, madrepores, through myriads of charming fish – jinells, glyphisidons, pomphérides, diacopes, holocentres – I recognized certain objects which the drags could not bring up – iron stirrups, anchors, cannons, bullets, capstan fittings, the stem of a ship – all objects from shipwrecked vessels, now carpeted with living flowers. While I was looking upon these sad remnants Captain Nemo said to me in a grave voice——

'Commander La Perouse started on the 7th of December, 1785, with his ships the Boussole and the Astrolabe. He anchored first in Botany Bay, visited the Friendly Isles, New Caledonia, made for Santa Cruz, and touched at Namouka, one of the Hapai group. Then his ships arrived on the unknown reefs of Vanikoro. The Boussole, which went first, struck on the south coast. The Astrolabe went to help, and met with the same fate. The former ship was almost immediately destroyed; but the Astrolabe, sheltered by the wind, lasted some days. The natives received the shipwrecked men very well. They installed themselves on the island, and built a smaller vessel with the remains of the two larger ones. Some of the sailors chose to remain at Vanikoro. The others, weakened by illness, started with La Perouse. They directed their course towards the Solomon Islands. They all perished on the western coast of the principal island of the group, between Capes Deception and Satisfaction.'

'And how do you know that?' I exclaimed.

'This is what I found on the very spot of the last shipwreck.'

Captain Nemo showed me a tin box, stamped with the French arms, and corroded by the salt water. He opened it, and I saw a mass of papers, yellow but still readable. They were the instructions of the *Ministre de la Marine* to the Commander La Perouse, annotated on the margin in the handwriting of Louis XVI.

'Ah, that is a fine death for a sailor!' then said Captain Nemo; 'a coral tomb is a tranquil one, and may Heaven grant that my companions and I may never have another!'

Chapter Twenty

Torres Straits

DURING THE NIGHT BETWEEN the 27th and 28th of December the Nautilus left the neighbourhood of Vanikoro with excessive speed. Its direction was southwest, and in three days it cleared the 750 leagues that separate the group of La Perouse from the south-east point of Papua. Early on the morning of the 1st of January, 1863, Conseil joined me on the platform.

'Monsieur,' said the brave fellow, 'will monsieur allow me to wish him a happy New Year?'

'Why, any one would think, Conseil, that I was in Paris in my Jardin des Plantes study. Thank you for your good wishes, only I should like to ask you what you mean by "happy year" in our present circumstances? Will this year bring the end of our imprisonment, or will it see us continue this strange voyage?'

'I do not know quite what to say to monsieur,' answered Conseil. 'It is certain that we see curious things, and the last two months we have not had time to be dull. The last marvel is always the most astonishing, and if this rate of progress is maintained I do not know how it will end. My opinion is that we shall never find such another occasion.'

'Never, Conseil.'

'Besides, M. Nemo, who well justifies his Latin name, is not more troublesome than if he did not exist. I therefore think a happy year would be a year which would allow us to see everything.'

'To see everything, Conseil? That would perhaps take too long. But what does Ned Land think about it?'

'Ned thinks exactly the contrary to what I do,' answered Conseil. 'He has a positive mind and an imperious stomach. To look at fish and always eat it does not suffice him. The want of wine, bread, and meat scarcely agrees with the worthy Saxon, to whom beefsteaks are familiar, and who is not frightened at brandy or gin taken in moderation.'

'For my own part, Conseil, it is not that which torments me, and I accommodate myself very well to the food on board.'

'And so do I,' answered Conseil, 'and I think as much of remaining as Land does of taking flight. Therefore, if the year that is beginning is not a happy one for me it will be for him; or vice versa. By that means someone will be satisfied. In short, to conclude, I wish monsieur anything that would please him.'

'Thank you, Conseil; only I must ask you to put off the question of a New Year's present, and to accept provisionally a shake of the hand. That is all I have upon me.'

'Monsieur has never been so generous.'

And thereupon the worthy fellow went away.

On the 22nd of January we had made 11,340 miles, or 5,250 French leagues, from our point of departure in the Japanese seas. Before the prow of the Nautilus extended the dangerous regions of the coral sea on the N.E. coast of Australia. Our boat coasted at a distance of some miles the dangerous bank on which Captain Cook's ships were lost on June 10th, 1770. The vessel Cook was on struck on a rock, and if it did not go down it was, thanks to this circumstance, that a piece of coral, struck off by the shock, remained fixed in the half open hull.

I should have much liked to visit this reef 360 leagues long, against which the sea, always rough there, broke with a formidable intensity and a noise like the rolling of thunder. But at that moment the inclined planes of the Nautilus dragged us down to a great depth. I could see nothing of these high coral walls. I was obliged to content myself with different specimens of fish brought in by our nets. I remarked, amongst others, germons, a species of mackerel as large as tunny-fish, with bluish sides, striped with transverse bands, which disappear with the life of the animal. These fish accompanied us in shoals, and furnished our table with excessively delicate dishes. They also took a great number of greenish giltheads, about five inches long, tasting like the dorado fish, and flying pyrapeds, real submarine swallows, which in dark nights alternately strike the air and water with their phosphorescent gleams. Amongst the molluscs and the zoophytes I found in the meshes of the net several species of alcyonarians, echini, hammers, spurs, dials, cerites, and hyalleæ. The flora was represented by beautiful seaweeds, laminariæ and macrocystes, impregnated with the mucilage that transudes through their pores, and amongst which I founded an admirable *nemastoma geliniarois* that was classed amongst the natural curiosities of the museum.

Two days after crossing the coral sea, on the 4th of January, we sighted the Papuan coasts. On this occasion Captain Nemo informed me that it was his intention to get into the Indian Ocean by Torres Straits. His communication ended there. Ned Land saw with pleasure that this route would take him nearer to the European seas.

The Torres Straits are considered no less dangerous on account of the reefs with which they bristle than because of the savage inhabitants who frequent their shores. They separate New Holland from the large island of Papua, named also New Guinea.

Papua is 400 leagues long and 130 leagues wide, and has a surface of 40,000 geographical miles. It is situated between 0° 19′ and 10° 2′ south latitude, and between 128° 23′ and 146° 15′ longitude. At noon, whilst the mate was taking the sun's altitude, I perceived the summits of the Arfalxs mountains, rising by plains, and terminating in sharp peaks. This land, discovered in 1511 by the Portuguese Francisco Serrano, was successively visited by Don Jose de Meneses in 1526, by Grijalva in 1527, by the Spanish General Alvar de Saavedra in 1528, by Juigo Ortez in 1545, by the Dutchman Shouten in 1616, by Nicolas Sruick in 1753, by Tasman, Dampier, Fumel, Carteret, Edwards, Bougainville, Cook, Forrest, MacClure, by d'Entrecasteaux, in 1792, by Duperrey in 1823, and by Dumont d'Urville in 1827. 'It is the focus of the blacks who occupy all Malaysia,' says M. de Rienzi, and I little thought that the chances of this navigation were going to bring me in presence of the formidable Andamenes.

The Nautilus then entered the most dangerous straits on the globe, those that the boldest seamen dare scarcely cross, the straits that Louis Paz de Torres affronted when returning from the South Seas, and in which, in 1840, the stranded corvettes of Dumont d'Urville were on the point of being totally wrecked. The Nautilus itself, superior to all dangers of the sea, was going, however, to make the acquaintance of its coral reefs.

The Torres Straits are about thirty-four leagues wide, but it is obstructed by an innumerable quantity of islands, reefs, and rocks, which make its navigation almost impracticable. Captain Nemo consequently took every precaution to cross it. The Nautilus, on a level with the surface of the water, moved slowly along. Its screw, like the tail of a cetacean, slowly beat the billows.

Profiting by this situation, my two companions and I took our places on the constantly-deserted platform. Before us rose the helmsman's cage, and I am very much mistaken if Captain Nemo was not there directing his Nautilus himself.

I had spread out before me the excellent charts of the Torres Straits, taken by the hydrographical engineer, Vincendon Dumoulin, and the midshipman Coupvent Desbois – now an admiral – who made part of Dumont d'Urville's état-major during his last voyage round the world. They are, along with those of Captain King, the best charts for threading the maze of this narrow passage, and I consulted them with scrupulous attention.

Around the Nautilus the sea was furiously rough. The current of the waves, which was bearing from S.E. to N.W. with a speed of two and a half miles, broke over the coral reefs that emerged here and there.

'An ugly sea!' said Ned Land to me.

'Detestable indeed,' I answered, 'and one that is not suitable to such a vessel as the Nautilus.'

'That confounded captain must be very certain of his route,' answered the Canadian, 'for I see coral reefs which would break its keel in a thousand pieces if it only just touched them.!'

The situation was indeed dangerous, but the Nautilus seemed to glide off the dangerous reefs as if by enchantment. It did not exactly follow the routes of the Astrolabe and Zélée, for they proved fatal to Dumont d'Urville. It bore more northwards, coasted the Island of Murray, and came back south-west towards Cumberland Passage. I thought it was going to enter it, when going back N.W. it went amongst a large quantity of little-known islands and islets towards South Island and Mauvais Canal.

I was wondering if Captain Nemo, foolishly imprudent, was going to take his vessel into that pass where Dumont d'Urville's two corvettes were stranded, when he again changed his direction, and cutting straight through to the west, he steered for the Island of Bilboa. It was then three o'clock in the afternoon. The ebb tide was just beginning. The Nautilus approached this island, which I still think I see with its remarkable border of screw-pines. We were coasting at a distance of two miles.

Suddenly a shock overthrew me. The Nautilus had just touched a reef, and was quite still, laying lightly to port side.

When I rose I saw Captain Nemo and his second on the platform. They were examining the situation of the vessel, and talking in their incomprehensible dialect.

The situation was the following:—— Two miles on the starboard appeared the Island of Gilboa, the coast of which was rounded from N. to W.; like an immense arm towards the S. and E. some heads of coral rocks were jutting, which the ebb tide left uncovered. We had run aground, and in one of the seas where the tides are very slight, an unfortunate circumstance in the floating of the Nautilus; however, the vessel had in no wise suffered, its keel was so solidly joined; but although it could neither sink nor split, it ran the risk of being for ever fastened on to these reefs, and then Captain Nemo's submarine aparatus would be done for.

I was reflecting thus, when the captain, cool and calm, always master of himself, appearing neither vexed nor moved, came up.

'An accident!' I asked.

'No, an incident,' he answered.

'But an incident,' I replied, 'which will perhaps again force you to become an inhabitant of the land from which you flee.'

Captain Nemo looked at me in a curious manner, and made a negative gesture. It was as much as to say to me that nothing would ever force him to set foot on land again. Then he said——

'Besides, M. Aronnax, the Nautilus is not lost. It will yet carry you amid the marvels of the ocean. Our voyage is only just begun, and I do not wish to deprive myself so soon of the honour of your company.'

'But, Captain Nemo,' I replied, without noticing the irony of his sentence, 'the Nautilus ran aground at high tide. Now tides are not strong in the Pacific, and if you cannot lighten the Nautilus I do not see how it can be floated again.'

'Tides are not strong in the Pacific – you are right, professor,' answered Captain Nemo; 'but in Torres Straits there is a difference of five feet between the level of high and low tide. Today is the fourth of January, and in five days the moon will be at the full. Now I shall be very much astonished if this complaisant satellite does not sufficiently raise these masses of water, and render me a service which I wish to owe to her alone.'

This said, Captain Nemo, followed by his second, went down again into the interior of the Nautilus. The vessel remained as immovable as if the coral polypi had already walled it up in their indestructible cement.

'Well, sir?' said Ned Land, who came to me after the departure of the captain.

'Well, friend Ned, we must wait patiently for high tide on the ninth. It appears that the moon will be kind enough to set us afloat again.'

'Really?'

'Really.'

'And this captain is not going to weigh anchor, to set his machine to work, or to do anything to get the vessel off?'

'Since the tide will suffice,' answered Conseil simply.

The Canadian looked at Conseil, then shrugged his shoulders. It was the seaman who spoke in him.

'Sir,' he replied, 'you may believe me when I tell you that this piece of iron will never be navigated again, either on or under the sea. It is only fit to be sold by weight. I think, then, that the moment is come to part company with Captain Nemo.'

'Friend Ned,' I answered, 'I do not despair, like you, of this valiant Nautilus, and in four days we shall know what to think of these tides on the Pacific. Besides, the advice to fly might be opportune if we were in sight of the coasts of England or Provence, but in the Papuan regions it is another thing, and it will be quite time to resort to that extremity if the Nautilus does not succeed in getting off, which I should look upon as a grave event.'

'But still we might have a taste of land,' replied Ned Land. 'There is an island; on that island there are trees; under those trees are terrestrial animals, bearers of cutlets and roast beef, which I should like to be able to taste.'

'There friend Ned is right, said Conseil, 'and I am of his opinion. Could not monsieur obtain from his friend Captain Nemo the permission to be transported to land, if it was only not to lose the habit of treading the solid parts of our planet?'

'I can ask him,' I answered, 'but he will refuse.'

'Let monsieur risk it,' said Conseil, 'and then we shall know what to think about the captain's amiability.'

To my great surprise Captain Nemo gave the permission I asked for, and he gave it me very courteously, without even exacting from me a promise to come back on board. But a flight across the lands of New Guinea would have been very perilous, and I should not have advised Ned Land to attempt it. It was better to be a prisoner on board the Nautilus than to fall into the hands of the natives of Papua.

The longboat was put at our disposal the next morning. I did not seek to know if Captain Nemo would accompany us. I thought even that no man of the crew would be given to us, and that Ned Land alone would have the care of directing the vessel. Besides, land was not more than two miles distant, and it was only play to the Canadian to conduct this light boat amongst the lines of reefs so fatal to large ships.

The next day, January 5th, the boat, its deck taken off, was lifted from its niche, and launched from the top of the platform. Two men sufficed for this operation. The oars were in the boat, and we had only to take our place.

At eight o'clock, armed with guns and hatchets, we descended the sides of the Nautilus. The sea was pretty calm. A slight breeze was blowing from land. Conseil and I rowed vigorously, and Ned steered in the narrow passages between the breakers. The boat was easily managed, and fled along rapidly.

Ned Land could not contain his joy. He was a prisoner escaped from prison, and did not think of the necessity of going back to it again.

'Meat!' he repeated. 'We are going to eat meat, and what meat! Real game! – no bread, though! I don't say that fish is not a good thing, but you can have too much of it, and a piece of fresh venison, grilled over burning coals, would be an agreeable variation to our ordinary fare.'

'Gourmand!' said Conseil. 'He makes the water come into my mouth!'

'You do not know yet,' I said, 'if there is any game in these forests, or if the game will not hunt the hunter himself.'

'Well, M. Aronnax,' replied the Canadian, whose teeth seemed sharpened like the edge of a hatchet, 'but I will eat tiger – a loin of tiger – if there is not other quadruped on this island.'

'Friend Ned is alarming,' answered Conseil.

'Whatever animal it is,' replied Ned Land, 'whether it is one with four paws and no feathers or two paws and feathers, it will be saluted by my first shot.'

'Good,' I replied; 'you are already beginning to be imprudent.'

'Never fear, M. Aronnax,' answered the Canadian; 'row along; I only ask twenty-five minutes to offer you a dish or my sort.'

At half-past eight the boat of the Nautilus ran softly aground on a strand of sand, after having cleared the coral reef which surrounds the Island of Gilboa.

Chapter Twenty-One

Some Days on Land

TOUCHING LAND AGAIN MADE a great impression on me. Ned Land struck the ground with his foot as if to take possession of it. Yet we had only been, according to Captain Nemo's expression, the 'passengers of the Nautilus' for two months – that is to say, we had only been the captain's prisoners for two months.

In a very short time we were within a gun-shot of the coast. The soil was almost entirely madreporic, but certain dried-up beds of streams, strewed with granitic debris, demonstrated that this island was owing to a primordial formation. All the horizon was hidden by a curtain of admirable forests. Enormous trees, some 200 feet high, with garlands of creepers joining their branches, were real natural hammocks, which were rocked in the slight breeze. They were mimosas, ficus, casuarinas, teak-trees, hibiscus, pendanus, palm-trees, mixed in profusion; and under the shelter of their verdant vault, at the foot of their gigantic stype, grew orchids, leguminous plants, and ferns.

But without noticing all these fine specimens of Papuan flora, the Canadian abandoned the agreeable for the useful. He perceived a cocoanut tree, brought down some nuts, broke them, and we drank their milk and ate their kernel with a relish that protested against the ordinary fare of the Nautilus.

'Excellent!' said Ned Land.

'Exquisite!' answered Conseil.

'I do not think,' said the Canadian, 'that your Nemo would object to our taking back a cargo of cocoanuts on board.'

'I do not think so,' I answered, 'but he would not taste them himself.'

'So much the worse for him,' said Conseil.

'And so much the better for us,' replied Ned Land; 'there will be more left.'

'One word only, Land,' I said to the harpooner, who was beginning to ravage another cocoanut tree. 'Cocoanuts are good things, but before filling the boat with them I think it would be wise to see if the island does not produce some substance no less useful. Fresh vegetables would be well received in the kitchen of the Nautilus.'

'Monsieur is right,' answered Conseil, 'and I propose to reserve three places in our boat – one for fruit, another for vegetables, and the third for venison, of which I have not seen the slightest sample yet.'

'We should not despair of anything, Conseil,' answered the Canadian.

'Let us go on with our excursion,' I replied, 'and keep a sharp look-out. Although the island appears to be inhabited, it might contain individuals who would be easier to please then we on the nature of the game.'

'Ha! ha!' said Ned Land, with a very significant movement of the jaw.

'What is it, Ned?' cried Conseil.

'I am beginning to understand the charms of cannibalism,' answered the Canadian.

'What are you talking about, Ned?' replied Conseil. 'If you are a cannibal, I shall no longer feel safe with you in the same cabin! Shall I wake one day and find myself half devoured?'

'Friend Conseil, I like you very much, but not enough to eat you, unless I am obliged.'

'I do not trust to it,' answered Conseil. 'Well, let us start; we must really bring down some game to satisfy this cannibal, or one of these fine mornings monsieur will only find pieces of a servant to serve him.'

In such-like conversation we penetrated the sombre vaults of the forest, and for two hours walked about it in every direction.

Fortune favoured us in this search after edibles, and one of the most useful products of tropical zones furnished us with a valuable article of food which was wanting on board – I mean the bread-tree, which is very abundant in the Island of Gilboa, and I remarked there principally that variety destitute of seeds which bears in Malaysian the name of 'Rima'. This tree was distinguished from others by its straight trunk forty feet high; its summit, gracefully rounded and formed of large multilobe leaves, designated sufficiently to the eyes of a naturalist the artocarpus, which has been very happily naturalized in the Mascareigne Islands. From its mass of verdure stood out large globular fruit two and a half inches wide, with a rough skin in a hexagonal pattern – a useful vegetable, with which Nature has gratified the regions in which wheat is wanting, and which, without exacting any culture, gives fruit for eight months in the year. Ned Land knew this fruit well; he had eaten it before in his numerous voyages, and he knew how to prepare its edible substance. The sight of it excited his appetite, and he could contain himself no longer.

'Sir,' he said to me, 'may I die if I don't taste a little of that bread-fruit!'

'Taste, friend Ned – taste as much as you like. We are here to make experiments; let us make them.'

'It will not take long,' answered the Canadian; and with a burning-glass he lighted a fire of dead wood which crackled joyously.

During this time Conseil and I chose the best fruits of the artocarpus. Some were not ripe enough, and their thick skin covered a white but slightly fibrous pulp. There were a great number of others, yellow and gelatinous ready for gathering.

There was no kernel in this fruit. Conseil took a dozen to Ned Land, who placed them on a fire of cinders, after having cut them into thin slices, during which he kept saying——

'You will see, sir, how good this bread is!'

'Especially when one has been deprived of it for so long, Conseil.'

'It is better than bread,' added the Canadian; 'it is like delicate pastry. Have you never eaten any, sir?'

'No, Ned.'

'Well, then, prepare for something very good. If you don't return to the charge I am no longer the king of harpooners.'

In a short time the side exposed to the fire quite black. In the interior appeared a white paste and a sort of tender crumb, with a taste something like that of an artichoke.

It must be acknowledged this bread was excellent, and I ate it with great pleasure.

'Unfortunately,' I said, 'such paste will not keep fresh; and it appears useless to me to make any provision for the vessel.'

'Why sir,' cried Ned Land, 'you speak like a naturalist, but I am going to act like a baker. Gather some of the fruit, Conseil; we will take it on our return.'

'And how do you prepare it?' I asked.

'By making a fermented paste with its pulp, which will keep any length of time. When I wish to use it I will have it cooked in the kitchen on board; and, notwithstanding its slightly acid taste, you will find it excellent.'

'Then, Ned, I see that nothing is wanting to this bread.'

'Yes, professor,' answered the Canadian; 'we want fruit, or at least vegetables.'

'Let us seek the fruit and vegetables.'

When our gathering was over we set out to complete this terrestrial dinner. Our search was not a vain one, and towards noon we had made an ample provision of bananas. These delicious productions of the torrid zone ripen all through the year, and the Malaysians, who have given them the name of 'pisang,' eat them raw. With these bananas we gathered enormous 'jaks' with a very decided taste, savoury mangoes, and pineapples of an incredible size. But this gathering took up a great deal of our time, which there was no cause to regret.

Conseil watched Ned continually. The harpooner marched on in front and during his walk across the forest he gathered with a sure hand the excellent fruit with which to complete his provisions.

'You do not want anything more, Ned, do you?'

'Hum,' said the Canadian.

'Why, what have you to complain of?'

'All these vegetables cannot constitute a meal,' answered Ned; 'they are only good for dessert. There is the soup and the roast.'

'Yes,' said I. 'Ned had promised us cutlets, which seemed to me very problematic.'

'Sir,' answered the Canadian, 'our sport is not only not ended, but is not even begun. Patience! We shall end by meeting with some animal or bird, and if it is not in this place it will be in another.'

'And if it is not today it will be tomorrow,' added Conseil, 'for we must not go too far away. I vote to go back to the boat now.'

'What, already,' cried Ned.

'We must come back before night,' I said.

'What time is it?' asked the Canadian.

'Two o'clock at least,' answered Conseil.

'How the time does go on dry land!' cried Ned Land with a sigh of regret.

We came back across the forest, and completed our provision by making a razzia of palm cabbages, which we were obliged to gather at the summit of the trees, and little beans which I recognized as being the 'abrou' of the Malaysians, and yams of a superior quality.

We were overburdened when we arrived at the boat, yet Ned Land did not think his provisions sufficient. But fortune favoured him. At the moment of embarking he perceived several trees from twenty-five to thirty feet high, belonging to the palm species. These trees, as precious as the artocarpus, are justly counted amongst the most useful products of Malaysia. There were sago-trees, vegetables which grow without culture, and reproduce themselves like blackberries by their shoots and seeds. Ned Land knew how to treat these trees. He took his hatchet, and using it vigorously, he soon brought two or three sago-trees level with the ground, their ripeness being recognized by the white powder dusted over their branches.

I watched him more with the eyes of a naturalist than those of a famished man. He began by stripping the bark from each trunk, an inch thick, which covered a network of long fibres, forming inextricable knots, that a sort of gummy flour cemented. This flour was sago, an edible substance which forms the principal food of the Melanasian population. Ned Land was content for the time being to cut these trunks in pieces, as he would have done wood to burn, meaning to extract the flour later on, and to pass it through a cloth in order to separate it from its fibrous ligaments, to leave it to dry in the sun, and let it harden in moulds.

At least, at five o'clock in the evening, loaded with our riches, we left the shores of the island, and half an hour later reached the Nautilus. No one appeared on our arrival. The enormous iron cylinders seemed deserted. When the provisions were embarked I went down to my room. There I found my supper ready. I ate it, and then went to sleep.

The next day, January 6th, there was nothing new on board. No noise in the interior, not a sign of life. The canoe had remained alongside, in the very place where we had left it. We resolved to return to the Island of Gilboa. Ned Land hoped to be more fortunate than before from the hunting point of view, and wished to visit another part of the forest.

We set out at sunrise. The boat, carried away by the waves, which were flowing inland, reached the island in a few minutes. We landed, and thinking it was better to trust to the instinct of the Canadian, we followed Ned Land, whose long legs threatened to outdistance us. Ned Land went up the coast westward, and fording some beds of streams, he reached the high plain, bordered by the admirable forests. Some kingfishers were on the banks of the stream, but they would not let themselves be approached; their circumspection proved to me that these fowl knew what to think of bipeds of our sort, and I therefore concluded that, if the island were not inhabited, it was at least frequented by human beings. After having crossed some rich meadow land we reached the borders of a little wood, animated by the song and flight of a great number of birds.

'There are only birds yet,' said Conseil.

'But some of them are good to eat,' answered the harpooner.

'No, friend Ned,' replied Conseil, 'for I see nothing but simple parrots.'

'Friend Conseil,' answered Ned gravely, 'a parrot is the friend of those who have nothing else to eat.'

'And I may add,' I said, 'that this bird, well prepared, is quite worth eating.'

Under the thick foliage of this wood, a whole world of parrots were flying from branch to branch, only waiting for a better education to speak the human language. At present they were screeching in company with parroquets of all colours, grave cockatoos who seemed to be meditating upon some philosophical problem, whilst the dories, of a bright red colour, passed like a morsel of stamen carried off by the breeze, amidst kalaos of noisy flight, papouas, painted with the finest shades of azure, and a whole variety of charming, but generally not edible birds.

However, a bird peculiar to these lands, and which has never passed the islands of Arrow and the Papua Islands, was wanting to this collection. But fortune reserved me the favour of admiring it before long.

After having crossed a thicket of moderate thickness we found a plain again obstructed with bushes. I then saw a magnificent bird rise, the disposition of whose long tails forces them to fly against the wind. The undulating flight, the grace of their aerial curves, the play of their colours, attracted and charmed the eye. I had no trouble to recognize them.

'Birds of Paradise!' I cried.

'Order of sparrows, section of clystornores,' answered Conseil.

'Family of partridges?' asked Ned Land.

'I do not think so, Land. Nevertheless, I count on your skill to catch one of these charming productions of tropical nature.'

'I will try, professor, although I am more accustomed to handle the harpoon than the gun.'

The Malays, who carry on a great trade with these birds with the Chinese, have several means of taking them which we cannot employ. Sometimes they place nets on the summits of high trees that the birds of Paradise prefer to inhabit. Sometimes they catch them with a viscous birdlime, that paralyses their movements; they even poison the fountains that the birds generally drink from. We were obliged to fire at them while flying, which gave us few chances of hitting them, and, in fact, we exhausted in vain a part of our ammunition.

About 11 a.m. we had traversed the first range of mountains that form the centre of the island, and we had killed nothing. Hunger drove us on. The hunters had relied on the products of the chase, and they had done wrong. Fortunately, Conseil, to his great surprise, made a double shot, and secured breakfast. He brought down a white and a wood pigeon, which, quickly plucked and suspended to a skewer, were roasted before a flaming fire of dead wood. Whilst these interesting animals were cooking, Ned had prepared the fruit of the 'artocarpus,' then the pigeons were devoured to the bones, and pronounced excellent. Nutmegs, with which they are in the habit of stuffing their crops, flavours their flesh, and makes it delicious.

'It is like the fowls that eat truffles,' said Conseil.

'And now, Ned, what is there wanting?' I asked the Canadian.

'Some four-footed game. M. Aronnax,' answered Ned Land. 'All these pigeons are only side-dishes and mouthfuls, and until I have killed an animal with cutlets I shall not be content.'

'Nor I, Ned, until I have caught a bird of Paradise.'

'Let us go on with our hunting,' answered Conseil, 'but towards the sea. We have reached the first declivities of the mountains, and I think we had better regain the forest regions.'

It was sensible advice, and was followed. After an hour's walk we reached a veritable forest of sago-trees. Some inoffensive serpents fled at the sound of our footsteps. The birds of Paradise fled at our approach, and I really despaired of getting near them, when Conseil, who was walking on in front, suddenly stooped, uttered a cry of triumph, and came back to me, carrying a magnificent bird of Paradise.

'Ah, bravo! Conseil,' I exclaimed.

'Monsieur is very kind,' answered Conseil.

'No, my boy, that was a master stroke, not only to take one of the birds living, but to catch it simply by hand.'

'If master will examine it closely, he will see that my merit has not been great.'

'Why, Conseil?'

'Because this bird is as intoxicated as a quail.'

'Intoxicated?'

'Yes, intoxicated with the nutmegs he was devouring under the nutmeg-tree where I found him. See, friend Ned, see the monstrous effects of intemperance.'

'You need not grudge me the gin I've drunk the last two months!' answered the Canadian.

In the meantime I examined the curious bird. Conseil was not mistaken. The bird of Paradise, intoxicated by the spirituous juice, was powerless. It could not fly, and could hardly walk. But that did not make me uneasy. I left it time to get over the effects of its nutmegs.

This bird belonged to the finest of the eight species which are counted in Papua and the neighbouring islands. It was 'the large emerald,' one of the rarest. It measured nine inches in length, its head was relatively small, and its eyes, placed near the opening of the beak, were small too. But its colours were admirable; it had a yellow beak, brown legs and claws, nut-coloured wings, with purple borders, a pale yellow head and back of neck, emerald throat, and maroon breast. Two horned downy nets rose above the tail, that was prolonged by two very light feathers of admirable fineness, completing the effect of this marvellous bird, that the natives have poetically named 'bird of the sun.'

I much wished to be able to take this superb specimen back to Paris, in order that I might make a present of it to the Jardin des Plantes, which does not possess a single living one.

'Is it so rare, then?' asked the Canadian, in the tone of a hunter who does not care much for it as game.

'Very rare, my brave companion, and, above all, very difficult to take alive, and even dead these birds are the object of an important traffic. Hence the natives fabricate them as pearls and diamonds are fabricated.'

'What!' cried Conseil, 'they make false birds of Paradise?'

'Yes, Conseil.'

'Does monsieur know how the natives set about it?'

'Perfectly. These birds, during the eastern monsoon, lose the magnificent feathers which surround their tails, and which naturalists call subulate feathers. The false coiners gather up these feathers, which they skilfully fasten on to some poor parrot previously mutilated. Then they die the suture, varnish the bird, and send to the museums and amateurs of Europe the product of their singular industry.'

'Good!' said Ned Land; 'if they have not the bird they at least have its feathers, and as they don't want to eat it, I see no harm.'

But if my desires were satisfied by the possession of the bird of Paradise, the Canadian's were not yet. Happily, about two o'clock Ned Land killed a magnificent hog, one of those the natives call 'bari-outang.' The animal came in time to give us real quadruped meat, and it was well received. Ned Land was very proud of his shot. The hog, struck by the electric bullet, had fallen stone dead.

The Canadian soon skinned and prepared it after having cut out half-a-dozen cutlets to furnish us with grilled meat for our evening meal. Then we went on with the chase that was again to be marked by Ned and Conseil's exploits.

The two friends, by beating the bushes, roused a herd of kangaroos that fled away bounding on their elastic paws. But these animals did not take flight too rapidly for the electric capsule to stop them in their course.

'Ah, professor,' cried Ned Land, excited by the pleasure of hunting, 'what excellent game, especially stewed! What provisions for the Nautilus! Two, three, five down! And when I think that we shall eat all that meat, and those imbeciles on board will not have a mouthful!'

I think that in his delight the Canadian, if he had not talked so much, would have slaughtered the whole herd! But he contented himself with a dozen of these interesting marsupials, which, as Conseil informed us, form the first order of agrea-centiary mammals.

These animals were small. They belong to a species of kangaroo 'rabbits' that live habitually in the hollow of trees, and that are of extraordinary speed; but although they are of middling size, they, at least, furnish excellent meat.

We were very much satisfied with the result of our hunt. The delighted Ned proposed to return the next day to this enchanted island, which he wanted to clear of all its edible quadrupeds. But he reckoned without circumstances.

At 6 a.m. we returned to the shore. Our boat was stranded in its place. The Nautilus, like a long rock, emerged from the waves two miles from the island. Ned Land, without more delay, began to prepare the dinner. He understood all about cooking well. The cutlets 'bari-outang,' grilled on the cinders, soon scented the air with a delicious odour.'

But here I perceived that I am walking in the footsteps of the Canadian in delight before grilled pork. May I be pardoned as I have pardoned Ned Land and from the same motives? In short, the dinner was excellent. Two wood- pigeons completed this extraordinary bill of fare. The sago paste, the artocarpus bread, mangoes, half-a-dozen pineapples, and the fermented liquor of some cocoanuts delighted us. I even think that the ideas of my worthy companions were not so clear as they might be.

'Suppose we do not return to the Nautilus this evening,' said Conseil.

'Suppose we never return,' added Ned Land.

Just then a stone fell at our feet and cut short the harpooner's proposition.

Chapter Twenty-Two

Captain Nemo's Thunderbolt

WE LOOKED TOWARDS THE forest without rising, my hand stopping in its movement towards my mouth, Ned Land's completing its office.

'A stone does not fall from the sky,' said Conseil, 'without deserving the name of aërolite.'

A second stone, carefully rounded, which struck out of Conseil's hand a savoury pigeon's leg, gave still more weight to his observations.

We all three rose and shouldered our guns, ready to reply to any attack.

'Can they be monkeys?' asked Ned Land.

'Something like them,' answered Conseil; 'they are savages.'

'The boat,' said I, making for the sea. In fact, we were obliged to beat a retreat, for about twenty natives, armed with bows and slings, appeared on the skirts of the thicket that hid the horizon one hundred steps off.

Our boat was anchored at about sixty feet from us.

The savages approached us, not running, making most hostile demonstrations. It rained stones and arrows.

Ned Land did not wish to leave his provisions, notwithstanding the imminence of the danger. He went on tolerably fast with his pig on one side and his kangaroos on the other.

In two minutes we were on shore. It was the affair of an instant to land the boat with the provisions and arms, to push it into the sea, and to take the two oars. We had not gone two cables' length when a hundred savages, howling and gesticulating, entered the water up to their waists. I watched to see if their appearance would not attract some men from the Nautilus on to the platform.

But no. The enormous machine, lying off, seemed absolutely deserted. Twenty minutes after we ascended the sides; the panels were open. After we had made the boat fast we re-entered the interior of the Nautilus.

I went to the saloon, from whence I heard some chords. Captain Nemo was there, bending over his organ, and plunged into a musical ecstacy.

'Captain,' I said to him.

He did not hear me.

'Captain,' I repeated, touching his hand.

He shuddered and turned.

'Ha, it is you, professor?' he said to me. 'Well, have you had good sport? Have you botanized successfully?'

'Yes, captain,' answered I, 'but we have, unfortunately, brought back a troop of bipeds, whose neighbourhood appears to me dangerous.'

'What bipeds?'

'Savages.'

'Savages?' answered Captain Nemo in an ironical tone. 'And you are astonished, professor, that having set foot on one of the lands of this globe, you find savages there? Where are there no savages? Besides, those you call savages, are they worse than others?'

'But, captain——'

'For my part, sir, I have met with some everywhere.'

'Well,' I answered, 'if you do not wish to receive any on board the Nautilus, you will do well to take some precautions.'

'Make yourself easy, professor; there is nothing worth troubling about.'

'But these natives are numerous.'

'How many did you count?'

'A hundred at least.'

'M. Aronnax,' answered Captain Nemo, who had again placed his fingers on the organ keys, 'if all the natives of Papua were gathered together on that shore, the Nautilus would have nothing to fear from their attacks.'

The captain's fingers were then running over the keys of the instrument, and I noticed that he only struck the black keys, which gave to his melodies an essentially Scotch character. He had soon forgotten my presence, and was plunged into a reverie that I did not seek to dissipate.

I went up again on to the platform. Night had already come, for in this low latitude the sun sets rapidly, and there is no twilight. I could only see the island indistinctly. But the numerous fires lighted on the beach showed that the natives did not dream of leaving it.

I remained thus alone for several hours, sometimes thinking about the natives, but not otherwise anxious about them, for the imperturbable confidence of the captain gained upon me, sometimes forgetting them to admire the splendours of the tropical night. My thoughts fled to France in the wake of the zodiacal stars which in a few hours would shine there. The moon shone brilliantly amidst the constellations of the zenith. I then thought that this faithful and complaisant satellite would come back tomorrow to the same place to draw the waves and tear away the Nautilus from its coral bed. About midnight, seeing that all was tranquil on the dark waves, as well as under the trees on the shore, I went down to my cabin and went peacefully to sleep.

The night passed without misadventure. The Papuans were doubtless frightened by the very sight of the monster stranded in the bay, for the open panels would have given them easy access to the interior of the Nautilus.

At 6 a.m., on January 8th, I went up on the platform. The morning was breaking. The island soon appeared through the rising mists, its shores first, then its summits.

The natives were still there, more numerous than the day before, perhaps five or six hundred strong. Some of them, taking advantage of the low tide, had come on to the coral heads at less than two cables' length from the Nautilus. I easily recognized them. They were real Papuans of athletic stature, men of fine breed, with wide high foreheads, large, but not broad, and flat noses, and white teeth. Their woolly hair, dyed red, showed off their bodies, black and shining like those of the Nubians. From the cut and distended lobes of their ears hung bone chaplets. These savages were generally naked. Amongst them I remarked some women, dressed from the hips to the knees in a veritable crinoline of herbs, which hung to a vegetable waistband. Some of the chiefs had ornamented their necks with a crescent and collar of red and white glass beads. Nearly all were armed with bows, arrows, and shields, carrying on their shoulders a sort of net, containing the rounded stones which they threw with great skill from their slings.

One of these chiefs, rather near the Nautilus, was examining it attentively. He must have been a 'mado' of high rank, for he was draped in a plaited garment of banana-leaves, scalloped at the edges, and set off with brilliant colours. I could easily have shot this native, who was within short range, but I thought it better to wait for really hostile demonstrations. Between Europeans and savages it is better that the savages should make the attack.

During the whole time of low water these natives roamed about near the Nautilus, but they were not noisy. I heard them frequently repeat the word 'Assai,' and from their gestures I understood that they invited me to land, an invitation that I thought it better to decline.

So on that day the boat did not leave the vessel, to the great displeasure of

Ned Land, who could not complete his provisions. This skilful Canadian employed his time in preparing the meat and farinaceous substances he had brought from the Island of Gilboa. As to the savages, they returned to land about 11 a.m., as soon as the heads of coral began to disappear under the waves of the rising tide. But I saw their number considerably increase on the shore. It was probable that they came from the neighbouring islands, or from Papua proper. However, I had not seen a single native pirogue.

Having nothing better to do, I thought of dragging these limpid waters, under which was a profusion of shells, zoophytes, and marine plants. It was, moreover, the last day the Nautilus was to pass in these seas if it was set afloat the next day, according to Captain Nemo's promise.

I therefore called Conseil, who brought me a small light drag, something like those used in the oyster-fisheries.

'What about these savages?' Conseil asked me. 'They do not seem to me to be very cruel.'

'They are cannibals, however, my boy.'

'It is possible to be a cannibal and an honest man,' answered Conseil, 'as it is possible to be a gourmand and honest. One does not exclude the other.'

'Good, Conseil! I grant you there are honest cannibals, and that they honestly devour their prisoners. But as I do not care about being eaten, even honestly, I shall take care what I am about, for the commander of the Nautilus does not appear to be taking any precaution. And now to work.'

For two hours our dragging went on actively, but without bringing up any rarity. The drag was filled with Midas-ears, harps, melames, and particularly the finest hammers I ever saw. We also took some holothurias, pearl oysters, and a dozen small turtles, which were kept for the pantry on board.

But at the very moment when I expected it least I put my hand on a marvel – I ought to say on a natural deformity – very rarely met with. Conseil had just brought up the drag full of ordinary shells when all at once he saw me thrust my hand into the net, draw out a shell, and utter a conchological cry – that is to say, the most piercing cry that human throat can utter.

'Eh? what is the matter with monsieur?' asked Conseil, much surprised. 'Has monsieur been bitten?'

'No, my boy; and yet I would willingly have paid for my discovery with the loss of a finger.'

'What discovery?'

'This shell,' I said, showing the object of my triumph.

'It is simply an olive porphyry, genus olive, order of the pectinibranchidæ, class of gasteropods, sub-class of molluscs——'

'Yes, Conseil, but instead of this spiral being from right to left this olive turns from left to right!'

'Is it possible?' cried Conseil.

'Yes, my boy; it is a sinister shell.'

'A sinister shell!' repeated Conseil with a palpitating heart.

'Look at its spiral.'

'Ah, monsieur may believe me,' said Conseil, taking the precious shell with a trembling hand, 'I have never felt a like emotion!'

And there was cause for emotion! It is well known, as the naturalists have caused to be remarked, that dextrality is a law of Nature. The stars and their satellites in their rotatory movements go from right to left. Man oftener uses his right than his left hand, and consequently his instruments, apparatus, staircases, locks, watchsprings, &c., are put together so as to be used from right to left. Nature has generally followed the same law in the spiral of its shells; they are all dexter, with rare exceptions, and when it happens that their spiral is sinister amateurs pay their weight in gold.

Conseil and I were plunged in the contemplation of our treasure, and I was promising myself to enrich the museum with it, when a stone untowardly hurled by a native, broke the precious object in Conseil's hand.

I uttered a cry of despair! Conseil seized my gun, and aimed at a savage who was swinging his sling in the air about ten yards from him. I wished to stop him, but he had fired and broken the bracelet of amulets which hung upon the arm of the native.

'Conseil!' I cried—— 'Conseil!'

'What, does not monsieur see that this cannibal began the attack?'

'A shell is not worth a man's life,' I said.

'Ah, the rascal!' cried Conseil; 'I would rather he had broken my arm!'

Conseil was sincere, but I was not of his opinion. However, the situation had changed during the last few minutes, and we had not perceived it. About twenty pirogues then surrounded the Nautilus. These pirogues, hollowed in the trunks of trees, long, narrow, and well calculated for speed, were kept in equilibrium by means of double balances of bamboo, which floated on the surface of the water. They were worked by skilful paddlers, half naked, and their approach made me uneasy. It was evident that these Papuans had already had some relations with Europeans, and knew their ships. But what must they have thought of this long cylinder, without either masts or funnel? Nothing good, but they kept first at a respectful distance. However, seeing it did not move, they regained confidence by degrees and tried to familiarize themselves with it. Now it was precisely this familiarity which it was necessary to prevent. Our arms, which made no noise, could only produce an indifferent effect on these natives, who only respect noisy weapons. A thunderbolt without the rolling of thunder would not much frighten men, although the danger exists in the lightning and not in the noise.

At that moment the pirogues approached nearer the Nautilus, and a shower of arrows fell upon it.

'Why, it hails,' said Conseil, 'and perhaps poisoned hail.'

'I must tell Captain Nemo,' said I, going through the panel.

I went down to the saloon. I found no one there. I ventured to knock at the door of the captain's room.

A 'Come in!' answered me.

I entered, and found Captain Nemo occupied with a calculation where x and other algebraical signs were plentiful.

'I fear I am disturbing you,' said I.

'Yes, M. Aronnax,' answered the captain, 'but I think you must have serious reasons for seeing me.'

'Very serious; we are surrounded by the pirogues of the natives, and in a few minutes we shall certainly be assailed by several hundreds of savages.'

'Ah,' said Captain Nemo, tranquilly, 'so they are here with their pirogues?'

'Yes.'

'Well, all we have to do is to shut the panels.'

'Precisely, and I came to tell you.'

'Nothing is easier,' said Captain Nemo.

Pressing an electric bell he transmitted an order to the crew's quarters.

'That's done, sir,' said he after a few minutes; 'the boat is in its place, and the panels are shut. You do not fear, I imagine, that these gentlemen can break in walls which the balls from your frigate could not touch?'

'No, captain, but there exists another danger.'

'What is that, sir?'

'It is that tomorrow, at the same time, you will be obliged to open the panels to renew the air of the Nautilus.'

'Certainly, sir, as our vessel breathes like the cetaceans do.'

'Now, if at that moment the Papuans occupied the platform, I do not know how you could prevent them entering.'

'Then you believe they will get up on the vessel?'

'I am certain of it.'

'Well, let them. I see no reason for preventing them. These Papuans are poor devils, and I will not let my visit to Gilboa cost the life of one poor wretch.'

That said, I was going to withdraw, but Captain Nemo retained me, and invited me to take a seat near him. He questioned me with interest about our excursions on land and our sport, and he did not seem to understand the need for meat that impassioned the Canadian. Then the conversation touched upon divers subjects, and without being more communicative, Captain Nemo showed himself more amiable.

Amongst other things we spoke of the present position of the Nautilus, abandoned precisely in this strait, where Dumont d'Urville was nearly lost.

'He was one of your great seamen,' said the captain, 'one of your intelligent navigators, this d'Urville! He was the French Captain Cook. Unfortunate savant! after having braved the southern ice banks, the coral reefs of Oceania, and the cannibals of the Pacific, to perish miserably in a railway train! If that energetic man could think during the last seconds of his existence, you imagine what must have been his last thoughts!'

Whilst speaking thus Captain Nemo seemed moved, and I put this emotion to his credit.

Then, map in hand, we looked over again the works of the French navigator, his voyages of circumnavigation, his double attempt to reach the South Pole that led to the discovery of Adélie and Louis Philippe Lands; lastly, his hydrographical surveys of the principal Oceanian islands.

'What your d'Urville did on the surface I have done in the interior of the ocean,' said Captain Nemo, 'and more easily and completely than he. The Astrolabe and the Zélée, continually tossed above by the waves, could not be so good as the Nautilus, for it is a quiet study and really sedentary in the midst of the waters!'

'However, captain.' I said, 'there is one point of resemblance between the corvettes of Dumont d'Urville and the Nautilus.'

'What is that, sir?'

'The Nautilus is stranded like them.'

'The Nautilus is not stranded,' replied Captain Nemo coldly. 'The Nautilus is made to repose on the bed of the waters, and the difficult work, the manœuvres that d'Urville was obliged to have recourse to, to get his corvettes afloat again, I shall not undertake. The Astrolabe and Zélée nearly perished, but the Nautilus runs no risk. Tomorrow, at the said day and hour, the tide will quietly raise it, and it will recommence its navigation through the seas.'

'Captain,' I said, 'I do not doubt.'

'Tomorrow,' added the captain, rising—— 'tomorrow at 2.40 p.m. the Nautilus will be afloat again, and I will leave without damage Torres Straits.'

These words pronounced in a very curt tone, Captain Nemo bowed slightly. It was my dismissal, and I went back to my room.

There I found Conseil, who desired to know the result of my interview with the captain.

'My boy', I replied, 'when I seemed to think that his Nautilus was threatened by the natives of Papua, the captain answered me very ironically. I have, therefore, only one thing to say to you – have confidence in him, and go to sleep in peace.'

'Does monsieur require my services?'

'No my friend. What is Ned Land doing?'

'He is making a kangaroo pasty that will be a marvel!'

I was left alone. I went to bed, but slept badly. I heard the savages stamping about on the platform making a deafening noise. The night passed thus without the crew seeming to come out of their habitual inertia. They were not more anxious about their presence of these cannibals than the soldiers of an ironclad fortress would be about the ants that crawl over the iron.

I rose at 6 a.m. The panels had not been opened. The air, therefore, had not been renewed in the interior, but the reservoirs, filled ready for any event, sent some cubic yards of oxygen into the impoverished atmosphere of the Nautilus.

I worked in my room till noon without seeing Captain Nemo, even for an instant. There seemed to be no preparation for departure made on board.

I waited for some time longer, and then went into the saloon. The clock was at half-past two. In ten minutes the tide would be at its maximum, and if Captain Nemo had not made a boasting promise the Nautilus would be immediately set free. If not, many months would pass before it would leave its coral bed.

In the meantime several shocks were felt in the hull of the vessel. I heard its sides grate against the calcareous asperities of the coral.

At 2.35 p.m. Captain Nemo appeared in the saloon.

'We are going to start,' said he.

'Ah!' I said.

'I have given orders to have the panels opened.'

'What about the Papuans?'

'The Papuans?' answered Captain Nemo, slightly raising his shoulders.

'Will they not penetrate into the interior of the Nautilus?'

'How can they?'

'Through the panels you have had opened.'

'M. Aronnax,' answered Captain Nemo tranquilly, 'it is not so easy to enter the Nautilus through its panels, even when they are opened.'

I looked at the captain.

'You do not understand?' he asked.

'Not at all.'

'Well, come, and you will see.'

I went towards the central staircase. There Ned Land and Conseil, much puzzled, were looking at some of the crew, who were opening the panels, whilst cries of rage and fearful vociferations resounded outside.

The lids were opened on the outside. Seventy horrible faces appeared. But the first of the natives who put his hand on the balustrade, thrown backwards by some invisible force, fled, howling and making extraordinary gambols.

Ten of his companions succeeded him. Ten had the same fate.

Conseil was in ecstasies. Ned Land, carried away by his violent instincts, sprang up the staircase. But as soon as he had seized the hand-rail with both hands he was overthrown in his turn.

'Malediction!' he cried. 'I am thunderstruck.'

That word explained it all to me. It was no longer a hand-rail but a metal cable, charged with electricity. Whoever touched it felt a formidable shock, and that shock would have been mortal if Captain Nemo had thrown all the current of his apparatus into this conductor. It may be truly said that between his assailants and himself he had hung an electric barrier that no one could cross with impunity.

In the meantime the frightened Papuans had beaten a retreat, maddened with terror. We, half-laughing, consoled and frictioned the unfortunate Ned Land, who was swearing like one possessed.

But at that moment the Nautilus, raised by the last tidal waves, left its coral bed at that fortieth minute exactly fixed by the captain. Its screw beat the waves with magestic slowness. Its speed increased by degrees, and navigating on the surface of the ocean, it left safe and sound the dangerous passages of Torres Straits.

Chapter Twenty-Three

Aegri Somnia

THE FOLLOWING DAY, THE 10th of January, the Nautilus resumed its course under the water, but at a remarkable speed, which I could not estimate at less than thirty-five miles an hour. The rapidity of its screw was such that I could neither follow its turns nor count them.

When I thought that this marvellous electric agent, after having given movement, warmth, and light to the Nautilus, protected it likewise from exterior attacks, and transformed it into a holy ark, which no profane person could touch without being thunderstruck, my admiration was unbounded, and from the apparatus it ascended to the engineer who had created it.

We were speeding directly westward, and on January 11th we doubled Cape Wessel, situated in 135° long. and 10° north lat., which forms the eastern point of the Gulf of Carpentaria. The reefs were still numerous, but farther apart, and the Money Reefs on the larboard, and the Victoria Reefs on the starboard, situated in 130° long., and in the 10th parallel we were rigorously following.

The 13th of January Captain Nemo arrived in the sea of Timor and sighted the island of that name in longitude 122°. This island, the surface of which measures 16.255 square leagues, is governed by rajahs. These princes call themselves sons of crocodiles – this is to say, issues of the highest origin to which a human being can pretend. Their scaly ancestors swarm in the rivers of the islands, and are the objects of particular veneration. They are protected, spoiled, worshipped, fed, young girls are offered to them for pasture, and woe to the stranger who lays hands on one of these sacred lizards.

But the Nautilus had nothing to do with these ugly animals. Timor was only visible for an instant at noon, whilst the first officer took our bearings. I likewise only caught a glimpse of Kitti Island that forms a part of the group, and of which the women have a well-established reputation for beauty in Malaysian markets.

From this point the direction of the Nautilus in latitude was bent south-west. The prow was set for the Indian Ocean. Where was Captain Nemo's caprice going to take us to? Would he go up towards the coasts of Asia, or approach the shores of Europe? Both hardly probable resolutions for a man to take who was flying from inhabited continents. Would he then go down south? Would he double the Cape of Good Hope, Then Cape Horn, and push on to the Antarctic Pole? Would he afterwards return to the seas of the Pacific, where his Nautilus would find easy and independent navigation? The future would show us.

After coasting the reefs of Cartier, Hibernia, Seringapatam, and Scott, the last efforts of the solid element against the liquid element, on the 14th of January we were beyond all land. The speed of the Nautilus was singularly slackened, and very capricious in its movements; sometimes it swam amidst the waters, sometimes floated on their surface.

During this period of the voyage Captain Nemo made interesting experiments on the different temperatures of the sea at different depths. In ordinary conditions these experiments are only made by means of complicated instruments, and are often doubtful, whether made by thermometric sounding lines, the glasses of which often break under the pressure of the water, or by apparatus based on the variation of resistance in metals to electric currents. The results thus obtained cannot be sufficiently controlled. On the contrary, Captain Nemo went himself to seek the temperature in the different depths, and his thermometer put into communcation with the different liquid sheets gave him immediately and surely the degree he sought.

It was thus that, either by filling its reservoirs or descending obliquely by its inclined planes, the Nautilus successfully reached depths of three, four, five, seven, nine, and ten thousand metres, and the definitive result of these experiments was that the sea presented a permanent temperature of four and a half degrees at a depth of one thousand metres under all latitudes.

I followed these experiments with the most lively interest. Captain Nemo studied them with passion. I often asked myself to what end he made these observations. Was it for the good of his fellow-creatures? It was not probable, for one day his work must perish with him in some unknown sea unless he destined the results of his experiments for me. But that was to admit that my strange voyage would have a term, and this term I did not yet perceive.

However that may be, Captain Nemo told me of different calculations obtained by him which established the different evidence about the density of water in the principal seas of the globe. From that communication I drew some personal information which was not at all scientific.

It was during the morning of the 15th of January. The captain, with whom I was walking on the platform, asked me if I knew the different densities of sea-water. I answered in the negative, and added that rigorous observations were wanting to science on this subject.

'I have made those observations,' he said to me, 'and I can affirm that they are correct.'

'That may be,' I answered, 'but the Nautilus is a world in itself, and the secrets of its *savants* do not reach the earth.'

'You are right, professor,' he answered after a short silence; 'it is a world in itself. It is as much a stranger to the world as those planets that accompany this globe round the sun, and the world will never know the work of the *savants* in Jupiter and Saturn. Still, as chance has united our two lives, I give you the result of my observations.'

'I shall be glad to hear it, captain.'

'You know, professor, that sea-water is denser than fresh water, but that its density is not uniform. In fact, if I represent by one the density of fresh water, I find a twenty-eight-thousandth for the waters of the Atlantic, twenty-six-thousandth for those of the Pacific, a thirty-thousandth for those of the Mediterranean——'

'Ah,' thought I, 'he adventures into the Mediterranean.'

'An eighteen-thousandth for the waters of the Ionian Sea, and a twenty-thousandth for those of the Adriatic.'

Decidedly the Nautilus did not avoid the frequented seas of Europe, and I hence concluded that it would take us – perhaps before long – towards more civilized lands. I thought that Ned Land would learn this detail with very natural satisfaction.

We passed several days in making all sorts of experiments on the saltiness of the sea at different depths, on its electrification, coloration, transparency, and in all of them Captain Nemo displayed an ingenuity which was only equalled by his kindness towards me. Then, for some days, I saw him no longer, and again remained isolated on board.

On the 16th of January the Nautilus seemed to be sleeping at some yards only below the surface of the waves. Its electric apparatus was idle, and its immovable screw let it be rocked at the will of the currents. I supposed that the crew was occupied with interior reparations necessitated by the violence of the mechanical movements of the machine.

My companions and I were then witnesses of a curious spectacle. The panels of the saloon were open, and as the electric lantern of the Nautilus was not lighted, a vague obscurity reigned in the midst of the waters. The sky, which was stormy, and covered with thick clouds, only gave an insufficient light to the first depth of the ocean.

I was looking at the state of the sea under these conditions, and the largest fish only looked to me like half- formed shadows, when all at once the Nautilus was in broad light. I thought at first that the lantern had been relighted, and was projecting its electric brilliancy upon the liquid mass. I was mistaken, and after a rapid observation saw my error.

The Nautilus was floating amidst a phosphorescent layer, which in such obscurity became dazzling. It was produced by myriads of luminous animalculæ, the light of which was increased by being reflected against the metallic hull of the vessel. I then saw sheets of lightning amidst these luminous layers, like molten lead melted in a furnace, or metallic masses heated red hot, in such a manner that by opposition certain luminous portions made a shadow in this ignited medium, from which all shadow seemed as though it ought to be banished. No! it was not the calm irradiation of our habitual light. There was an unwonted vigour and movement in it. We felt that the light was living.

In fact, it was an infinite agglomeration of infusoria, of miliary 'noctiluques,' globules of diaphanous jelly, furnished with a filiform tentacle, of which 25,000 have been counted in 30 cubic centimetres of water. And their light was doubled by gleams peculiar to medusæ, asteriæ, and aureliæ, pholodestalles, and other phosphorescent zoophytes, impregnated with the greasy quality of organic matters decomposed by the sea, and perhaps by the mucus secreted by the fish.

During several hours the Nautilus floated among those brilliant sheets of water, and our admiration increased at seeing the large marine animals play among them like salamanders. I saw there amidst their fire that does not burn, elegant and rapid porpoises, indefatigable clowns of the sea, and istiophores three yards long, intelligent precursor of storms, the formidable sword of which struck against the glass of the saloon; and then appeared smaller fish, scombers, and others, which streaked the luminous atmosphere in their course.

This dazzling spectacle was enchanting! Perhaps some atmospheric condition augmented the intensity of the phenomenon. Perhaps some storm was going on above the waves, but at that depth of a few yards the Nautilus did not feel its fury, and was peacefully balancing itself amidst the tranquil waters.

Thus we went on our way, incessantly charmed by some new marvel. Conseil observed and classified his zoophytes, his articulates, his molluscs, and his fish. The days fled rapidly away, and I counted them no longer. Ned, according to his custom, tried to vary the fare on board. Veritable snails, we had become accustomed to our shell, and I affirmed that it is easy to become a perfect snail. This existence, then, appeared to us easy and natural, and we no longer thought of the different life that existed on the surface of the terrestrial globe, when an event happened to recall to us the strangeness of our situation.

On the 18th of January the Nautilus was in longitude 105°, in S. lat. 15°. The weather was threatening, the sea rough. The wind was blowing a strong gale from the east. The barometer, which had been going down for some days, announced an approaching war of the elements.

I had gone up on to the platform at the moment the first officer was taking his bearings. I expected as usual to hear the daily sentence pronounced. But that day it was replaced by another phrase not less incomprehensible. Almost immediately I saw Captain Nemo appear and sweep the horizon with a telescope.

For some minutes the captain remained immovable, without leaving the point inclosed in the field of his object-glass. Then he lowered his telescope and exchanged about ten words with his officer, who seemed to be a prey to an emotion that he tried in vain to suppress.

Captain Nemo, more master of himself, remained calm. He appeared, besides, to make certain objections, to which the officers answered by formal assurances – at least, I understood them thus by the difference of their tone and gesture.

I looked carefully in the direction they were observing without perceiving anything. Sky and water mixed in a perfectly clear horizon.

In the meantime Captain Nemo walked up and down the platform without looking at me, perhaps without seeing me. His step was assured, but less regular than usual. Sometimes he stopped, folded his arms, and looked at the sea. What was he seeking in that immense space? The Nautilus was then some hundreds of miles from the nearest coast.

The first officer had taken up his telescope again, and was obstinately interrogating the horizon, going and coming, stamping and contrasting with his chief by his nervous excitement.

This mystery must necessarily be soon cleared up, for, obeying an order of Captain Nemo's, the machine, increasing its propelling power, gave a more rapid rotatory movement to the screw.

At that moment the officer again attracted the captain's attention, who stopped his walk and directed his telescope towards the point indicated. He observed it for a long time. I, feeling very curious about it, went down to the saloon and brought up an excellent telescope that I generally used. Then leaning it against the lantern cage that jutted in front of the platform, I prepared to sweep all the line of sky and sea. But I had not placed my eye to it when the instrument was quickly snatched out of my hands.

I turned. Captain Nemo was before me, but I hardly knew him. His physiognomy was transfigured. His eyes shone with sombre fire under his frowning eyebrows. His teeth glittered between his firm set lips. His stiffened body, closed fists, and head set hard on his shoulders, showed the violent hatred breathed by his whole appearance. He did not move. My telescope, fallen from his hand, had rolled to his feet.

Had I, then, unintentionally provoked this angry attitude? Did the incomprehensible personage imagine that I had surprised some secret interdicted to the guests of the Nautilus?

No! I was not the object of this hatred, for he was not looking at me; his eyes remained fixed on the impenetrable point of the horizon.

At last Captain Nemo recovered his self-possession. His face, so profoundly excited, resumed its habitual calmness. He addressed some words in a foreign tongue to his officer, and then turned towards me again.

'M. Aronnax,' said he in a rather imperious tone, 'I require from you the fulfilment of one of the engagements that bind me to you.'

'What is that, captain?'

'To let yourself be shut up – you and your companions – until I shall think proper to set you at liberty again.'

'You are master here,' I answered, looking at him fixedly. 'But may I ask you one question?'

'No, sir, not one!'

After that I had nothing to do but obey, as all resistance would have been impossible.

I went down to the cabin occupied by Ned Land and Conseil, and I told them of the captain's determination. I leave it to be imagined how that communication was received by the Canadian. Besides, there was no time for any explanation. Four of the crew were waiting at the door, and they conducted us to the cell where we had passed our first night on board the Nautilus.

Ned Land wanted to expostulate, but for all the answer the door was shut upon him.

'Will monsieur tell me what this means?' asked Conseil.

I related what had happened to my companions. They were as astonished as I, and not more enlightened.

I was overwhelmed with reflections, and the strange look on Captain Nemo's face would not go out of my head. I was incapable of putting two logical ideas together, and was losing myself in the most absurd hypotheses, when I was aroused by these words of Ned Land:——

'Why, they have laid dinner for us!'

In fact, the table was laid. It was evident that Captain Nemo had given this order at the same time that he caused the speed of the Nautilus to be hastened.

'Will monsieur allow me to recommend something to him?' asked Conseil.

'Yes, my boy,' I replied.

'It is that monsieur should breakfast. It would be prudent, for we do not know what may happen.'

'You are right, Conseil.'

'Unfortunately,' said Ned Land, 'they have only given us the usual fare on board.'

'Friend Ned,' replied Conseil, 'what should you say if you had had no dinner at all?'

That observation cut short the harpooner's grumbling.

We sat down to dinner. The meal was eaten in silence. I ate little. Conseil forced himself to eat for prudence sake, and Ned Land ate as usual. Then, breakfast over, we each made ourselves comfortable in a corner.

At that moment the luminous globe that had been lighting us went out and left us in profound darkness. Ned Land soon went to sleep, and, what astonished me, Conseil went off into a heavy slumber. I was asking myself what could have provoked in him so imperious a need of sleep, when I felt heaviness creep over my own brain. My eyes, which I wished to keep open, closed in spite of my efforts. I became prey to painful hallucinations. It was evident that soporific substances had been mixed with the food we had just eaten. Imprisonment, then, was not enough to conceal Captain Nemo's projects from us; we must have sleep as well.

I heard the panels closed. The undulations of the sea, that of a slight rolling motion, ceased. Had the Nautilus, then, left the surface of the ocean? Had it again sunk to the motionless depth?

I wished to resist sleep. It was impossible. My breathing became weaker. I felt a deathlike coldness freeze and paralyse my limbs. My eyelids fell like leaden coverings over my eyes. I could not raise them. A morbid slumber, full of hallucinations, took possession of my whole being. Then the visions disappeared and left me in complete insensibility.

Chapter Twenty-Four

The Coral Kingdom

THE NEXT DAY I AWOKE with my faculties singularly clear. To my great surprise I was in my own room. My companions had doubtless been carried to their cabin without being more aware of it than I. They knew no more what had happened during the night than I, and to unveil the mystery I only depended on the hazards of the future.

I then thought of leaving my room. Was I once more free or a prisoner? Entirely free. I opened the door, went through the waist, and climbed the central staircase. The panels, closed the night before, were opened. I stepped on to the platform.

Ned Land and Conseil were awaiting me there. I questioned them; they knew nothing. They had slept a dreamless sleep, and had been much surprised to find themselves in their cabin on awaking.

As to the Nautilus, it appeared to us tranquil and mysterious as usual. It was floating on the surface of the waves at a moderate speed. Nothing on board seemed changed.

Ned Land watched the sea with his penetrating eyes. It was deserted. The Canadian signalled nothing fresh on the horizon – neither sail nor land. There was a stiff west breeze blowing, and the vessel was rolling under the influence of long waves raised by the wind.

The Nautilus, after its air had been renewed, was kept at an average depth of fifteen yards, so as to rise promptly, if necessary, to the surface of the waves, an operation which, contrary to custom, was performed several times during that day of January 19th. The second then went up on the platform, and the accustomed sentence was heard in the interior of the vessel.

Captain Nemo did not appear. Of the men on board I only saw the impassible steward, who served me with his usual exactitude and speechlessness.

About 2 p.m. I was in the saloon, occupied in classifying my notes, when the captain opened the door and appeared. I bowed to him. He returned it almost imperceptibly, without uttering a word. I went on with my work, hoping he would perhaps give me some explanation of the events that had occurred the previous night. He did nothing of the kind. I looked at him. His face appeared to me fatigued; his reddened eyelids showed they had not been refreshed by sleep; his physiognomy expressed profound and real grief. He walked about, sat down, rose up, took a book at random, abandoned it immediately, consulted his instruments without making his usual notes, and did not seem able to keep an instant in peace.

At last he came towards me and said——

'Are you a doctor, M. Aronnax?'

I so little expected such a question that I looked at him for some time without answering.

'Are you a doctor?' he repeated. 'Several of your colleagues have studied medicine – Gratiolet, Moquin, Sandon, and others.'

'Yes,' I said: 'I am doctor and surgeon. I was in practice for several years before entering the museum.'

'That is well.'

My answer had evidently satisfied Captain Nemo, but not knowing what he wanted, I awaited fresh questions, meaning to answer according to circumstances.

'M. Aronnax,' said the captain, 'will you consent to prescribe for a sick man?'

'There is someone ill on board?'

'Yes.'

'I am ready to follow you.'

'Come.'

I must acknowledge that my heart beat faster. I do not know why I saw some connection between the illness of this man of the crew and the events of the night before, and this mystery preoccupied me at least as much as the sick man.

Captain Nemo conducted me aft of the Nautilus, and made me enter a cabin situated in the crew's quarters.

There, upon a bed, a man of some forty years, with an energetic face and true Anglo-Saxon type, was reposing.

I bent over him. He was not only a sick man but a wounded one too. His head, wrapped in bandages, was resting on a double pillow. I undid the bandages, and the wounded man, looking with his large fixed eyes, let me do it without uttering a single complaint.

The wound was horrible. The skull, crushed by some blunt instrument, showed the brain, and the cerebral substance had sustained profound attrition. Clots of blood had formed in the wound the colour of wine-dregs. There had been both contusion and effusion of the brain. The breathing of the sick man was slow, and spasmodic movements of the muscles agitated his face. The cerebral phlegmasia was complete, and caused paralysis of movement and feeling.

I felt the pulse; it was intermittent. The extremities were already growing cold, and I saw that death was approaching without any possibility of my preventing it. After dressing the wound I bandaged it again, and turned towards Captain Nemo.

'How was this wound caused?' I asked.

'What does it matter?' answered the captain evasively. 'A shock of the Nautilus broke one of the levers of the machine, which struck this man. But what do you think of his condition?'

I hesitated to reply.

'You may speak,' said the captain, 'this man does not understand French.'

I looked a last time at the wounded man, then I answered——

'He will be dead in two hours.'

'Can nothing save him?'

'Nothing.'

Captain Nemo clenched his hand, and his eyes, which I did not think made for weeping, filled with tears.

For some time I still watched the dying man, whose life seemed gradually ebbing. He looked still paler under the electric light that bathed his deathbed. I looked at his intelligent head, furrowed with premature lines which misfortune, misery perhaps, had long ago placed there. I tried to learn the secret of his life in the last words that escaped from his mouth.

'You can go now, M. Aronnax,' said Captain Nemo.

I left the captain in the room of the dying man, and went back to my room much moved by this scene. During the whole day I was agitated by sinister presentiments. I slept badly that night, and, amidst my frequently-interrupted dreams, I thought I heard distant sighs and a sound like funeral chants. Was it the prayer for the dead murmured in that language which I could not understand?

The next morning I went up on deck. Captain Nemo had preceded me there. As soon as he perceived me he came to me.

'Professor,' said he, 'would it suit you to make a submarine excursion today?'

'With my companions?' I asked.

'If they like.'

'We are at your disposition, captain.'

'Then please put on your diving-dresses.'

Of the dying or dead there was no question. I went to Ned Land and Conseil and told them of Captain Nemo's proposal. Conseil accepted it immediately, and this time the Canadian seemed quite ready to go with us.

It was 8 a.m. At half-past we were clothed for our walk, and furnished with our breathing and lighting apparatus. The double door was opened, and accompanied by Captain Nemo, who was followed by a dozen men of the crew, we set foot at a depth of ten yards on the firm ground where the Nautilus was stationed.

A slight incline brought us to an undulated stretch of ground at about fifteen fathoms depth. This ground differed completely from any I saw during my first excursion under the waters of the Pacific Ocean. Here there was no fine sand, no submarine meadows, no seaweed forests. I immediately recognized this region of which Captain Nemo was doing the honours. It was the kingdom of coral.

In the embranchment of the zoophytes and the alcyon class, the order of gorgoneæ, isidiæ, and corollariæ are noticed. It is to the last that coral belongs – that curious substance that was by turns classified in the mineral, vegetable, and animal kingdoms. A remedy of the ancients, a jewel of modern times, it was not until 1694 that the Marseillais Peysonnel definitely placed it in the animal kingdom.

Coral is an assemblage of animalculæ, united on a polypier of a stony and breakable nature. These polypiers have a unique generator which produces them by gemmation, and they possess an existence of their own at the same time that they participate in the common life. It is, therefore, a sort of natural socialism. I knew the result of the last works made on this strange zoophyte, which mineralizes at the same time that it arborizes, according to the very just observation of naturalists; and nothing could be more interesting to me than to visit one of the petrified forests that Nature has planted at the bottom of the sea.

The Ruhmkorff apparatus were set going, and we followed a coral bank in process of formation, which, helped by time, would one day close in that portion of the Indian Ocean. The route was bordered by inextricable bushes formed by the entanglement of shrubs that the little white-starred flowers covered.

Sometimes, contrary to the land plants, these arborizations, rooted to the rocks, grew from top to bottom.

The light produced a thousand charming effects, playing amidst the branches that were so vividly coloured. It seemed to me as if the membraneous and cylindrical tubes trembled under the undulation of the waves. I was tempted to gather their fresh petals, ornamented with delicate tentacles, some freshly opened, others scarcely out, whilst light and rapid-swimming fish touched them slightly in passing like a flock of birds. But when my hand approached these living flowers, these animated sensitive plants, the whole colony was put on the alert. The white petals re-entered their red cases, the flowers vanished from my gaze, and the bushes changed into blocks of stony knobs.

Chance had brought me in presence of the most precious specimens of this zoophyte. This coral was as valuable as that found in the Mediterranean, on the coasts of France, Italy and Barbary. It justified by its brilliant tints the poetic names of 'Flower of Blood' and 'Froth of Blood' which commerce gives to its most beautiful productions. Coral is sold as high as £10 a pound, and in this place the liquid masses covered the fortune of a world of coral-dealers. This precious matter often mixed with the other polypiers, then formed the compact and inextricable compound called 'macciota,' on which I noticed several beautiful specimens of pink coral.

But soon the bushes contracted, and the arborizations increased. Real petrified thickets and long triforiums of fantastic architecture opened before our steps. Captain Nemo entered a dark gallery, the inclined plane of which led us down a depth of 100 yards. The light of our serpentines sometimes produced magical effects by following the rough outlines of the natural arches and pendants, like bushes, which it pricked with points of fire. Amongst the coralline shrubs I noticed other polypiers no less curious, melites and irises with articulated ramifications, also reefs of coral, some green, some red, like seaweed incrusted in their calcareous salts, which naturalists, after long discussion, have definitely classified in the vegetable kingdom. But, according to the remark of a thinker, 'This is perhaps the real point where life obscurely rises from its stony sleep, without altogether leaving its rude starting-point.'

At last, after two hours' walking, we reached a depth of about 150 fathoms – that is to say, the extreme limit that coral begins to form itself. But there it was no longer the isolated shrub nor the modest thicket of low brushwood. It was the immense forest, the great mineral vegetations, the enormous petrified trees, united by garlands of elegant plumarias, sea-bindweed, all decked off with colours and shades. We passed freely under their high branches lost in the depths of the water above, whilst, at our feet the tubipores, meandrines, stars, fungi, and caryo-phyllidæ formed a carpet of flowers strewed with dazzling gems.

It was an indescribable spectacle! Ah, why could we not communicate our sensations? Why were we imprisoned under these masks of metal and glass? Why were words between us forbidden? Why did we not at least live the life of the fish that people the liquid element, or rather that of the amphibians who, during long hours, can traverse as they like the double domain of land and water?

In the meantime Captain Nemo had stopped. My companions and I imitated him, and, turning round, I saw that his men had formed a semicircle round their chief. Looking with more attention, I noticed that four of them were carrying an object of oblong form on their shoulders.

We were then in the centre of a vast open space surrounded by high arborizations of the submarine forest. Our lamps lighted up the space with a sort of twilight which immoderately lengthened the shadows on the ground. At the limit of the open space darkness again became profound, and was only 'made visible' by little sparks reflected in the projections of the coral.

Ned Land and Conseil were near me. We looked on, and the thought that I was going to assist at a strange scene came into my mind. As I looked at the ground I saw that it was raised in certain places by slight excrescences incrusted with calcareous deposits, and laid out with a regularity that betrayed the hand of man.

In the centre of the open space, on a pedestal of rocks roughly piled together, rose a coral cross, which extended its long arms, that one might have said were made of petrified blood.

Upon a sign from Captain Nemo one of his men came forward, and at some feet distance from the cross began to dig a hole with a pickaxe that he took from his belt.

I then understood it all! This space was a cemetery; this hole a grave; this oblong object the body of the man who had died during the night! Captain Nemo and his men came to inter their companion in this common resting-place in the depths of the inaccessible ocean!

My mind was never so much excited before. More impressionable ideas had never invaded my brain! I would not see what my eyes were looking at!

In the meantime the tomb was being slowly dug. Fish fled hither and thither as their retreat was troubled. I heard on the calcareous soil the ring of the iron pickaxe that sparkled when it struck some flint lost at the bottom of the sea. The hole grew larger and wider, and was soon deep enough to receive the body.

Then the bearers approached. The body, wrapped in a tissue of white byssus, was lowered into its watery tomb. Captain Nemo, with his arms crossed on his chest, and all the friends of the man who had loved them, knelt in the attitude of prayer. My two companions and I bent religiously.

The tomb was then filled with the matter dug from the soil, and formed a slight excrescence.

When this was done Captain Nemo and his men rose; then, collecting round the tomb, all knelt again, and extended their hands in sign of supreme adieu.

Then the funeral procession set out for the Nautilus again, repassing under the arcades of the forest, amidst the thickets by the side of the coral-bushes, going uphill all the way.

At last the lights on board appeared. Their luminous track guided us to the Nautilus. We were back at one o'clock.

As soon as I had changed my clothes I went up on to the platform, and, a prey to a terrible conflict of emotions, I went and seated myself near the lantern-cage.

Captain Nemo joined me there. I rose and said——

'Then, as I foresaw, that man died in the night?'

'Yes, M. Aronnax,' answered Captain Nemo.

'And now he is resting by the side of his companions in the coral cemetery?'

'Yes, forgotten by everyone but us! We dig the grave, and the polypi take the trouble of sealing our dead therein for eternity?'

And hiding his face in his hands with a brusque gesture, the captain tried in vain to suppress a sob. Then he added——

'That is our peaceful cemetery, at some hundreds of feet below the surface of the waves!'

'Your dead sleep, at least, tranquil, captain, out of reach of the sharks!'

'Yes, sir,' answered Captain Nemo gravely, 'of sharks and men!'

Chapter Twenty-Five

The Indian Ocean

WE NOW COME TO THE SECOND part of our journey under the sea. The first ended with the moving scene in the coral cemetery, which left such a deep impression on my mind. Thus, in the midst of this great sea, Captain Nemo's life was passing even to his grave, which he had prepared in one of its deepest abysses. There, not one of the ocean's monsters could trouble the last sleep of the crew of the Nautilus, of those friends riveted to each other in death as in life. 'Nor any man either,' had added the captain. Still the same fierce, implacable defiance towards human society!

I could no longer content myself with the hypothesis which satisfied Conseil.

That worthy fellow persisted in seeing in the Commander of the Nautilus one of those unknown *savants* who return mankind's contempt for indifference. For him, he was a misunderstood genius, who, tired of earth's deceptions, had taken refuge in this inaccessible medium, where he might follow his instincts freely. To my mind, this hypothesis explained but one side of Captain Nemo's character.

Indeed, the mystery of that last night, during which we had been chained in prison, the sleep, and the precaution so violently taken by the captain of snatching from my eyes the glass I had raised to sweep the horizon, the mortal wound of the man, due to an unaccountable shock of the Nautilus, all put me on a new track. No; Captain Nemo was not satisfied with shunning man. His formidable apparatus not only suited his instinct of freedom, but, perhaps, also the design of some terrible retaliation.

At this moment, nothing is clear to me; I catch but a glimpse of light amidst all the darkness, and I must confine myself to writing as events shall dictate.

That day, the 24th of January 1868, at noon, the second officer came to take the altitude of the sun. I mounted the platform, lit a cigar, and watched the operation. It seemed to me that the man did not understand French; for several times I made remarks in a loud voice, which must have drawn from him some involuntary sign of attention, if he had understood them; but he remained undisturbed and dumb.

As he was taking observations with the sextant, one of the sailors of the Nautilus (the strong man who had accompanied us on our first submarine excursion to the Island of Crespo) came to clean the glasses of the lantern. I examined the fittings of the apparatus, the strength of which was increased a hundredfold by lenticular rings, placed similar to those in a lighthouse, and which projected their brilliance in a horizontal plane. The electric lamp was combined in such a way as to give its most powerful light. Indeed, it was produced *in vacuo*, which insured both its steadiness and its intensity. This vacuum economized the graphite points, between which the luminous arc was developed – an important point of economy for Captain Nemo, who could not easily have replaced them; and under these conditions their waste was imperceptible. When the Nautilus was ready to continue its submarine journey, I went down to the saloon. The panels were closed, and the course marked direct west.

We were furrowing the waters of the Indian Ocean, a vast liquid plain, with a surface of 1,200,000,000 of acres, and whose waters are so clear and transparent, that anyone leaning over them would turn giddy. The Nautilus usually floated between fifty and a hundred fathoms deep. We went on so for some days. To anyone but myself, who had a great love for the sea, the hours would have seemed long and monotonous; but the daily walks on the platform, when I steeped myself in the reviving air of the ocean, the sight of the rich waters through the windows of the saloon, the books in the library, the compiling of my memoirs, took up all my time, and left me not a moment of ennui or weariness.

For some days we saw a great number of aquatic birds, sea-mews or gulls. Some were cleverly killed, and, prepared in a certain way, made very acceptable water-game. Amongst large-winged birds, carried a long distance from all lands, and resting upon the waves from the fatigue of their flight, I saw some magnificent albatrosses, uttering discordant cries like the braying of an ass, and birds belonging to the family of the longipennates. The family of the totipalmates was represented by the sea-swallows, which caught the fish from the surface, and by numerous phætons, or lepturi; amongst others, the phæton with red lines, as large as a pigeon, whose white plumage, tintied with pink, shows off to advantage the blackness of its wings.

As to the fish, they always provoked our admiration when we surprised the secrets of their aquatic life through the open panels. I saw many kinds which I never before had a chance of observing.

I shall notice chiefly ostracions peculiar to the Red Sea, the Indian Ocean, and that part which washed the coast of tropical America. These fishes, like the tortoise, the armadillo, the sea hedgehog, and the crustacea, are protected by a breastplate which is neither chalky nor stony, but real bone. In some it takes the form of a solid triangle, in others of a solid quadrangle. Amongst the triangular I saw some an inch and a half in length, with wholesome flesh and a delicious flavour; they are brown at the tail, and yellow at the fins, and I recommend their introduction into fresh water, to which a certain number of sea-fish easily accustom themselves. I would also mention quadrangular ostracions, having on the back four large tubercles; some dotted over with white spots on the lower part of the body, and which may be tamed like birds; trigons provided with spikes formed by the lengthening of their bony shell, and which, from their strange gruntings, are called 'sea-pigs;' also dromedaries with large humps in the shape of a cone, whose flesh is very tough and leathery.

I now borrow from the daily notes of Master Conseil. 'Certain fish of the genus petrodon peculiar to those seas, with red backs and white chests, which are distinguished by three rows of longitudinal filaments; and some electrical, seven inches long, decked in the liveliest colours. Then, as specimens of other

kinds, some ovoides, resembling an egg of a dark brown colour, marked with
white bands, and without tails; diodons, real sea-porcupines, furnished with
spikes, and capable of swelling in such a way as to look like cushions bristling
with darts; hippocampi, common to every ocean; some pegasi with lengthened
snouts, which their pectoral fins, being much elongated and formed in the shape
of wings, allow, if not to fly, at least to shoot into the air; pigeon spatulæ, with
tails covered with many rings of shell; macrognathi with long jaws, an excellent
fish, nine inches long, and bright with most agreeable colours; pale-coloured
calliomores, with rugged heads; and plenty of chætodons, with long and tubular
muzzles, which kill insects by shooting them, as from an air-gun, with a single
drop of water. These we may call the fly-catchers of the seas.

'In the eighty-ninth genus of fishes, classed by Lacépède, belonging to the
second lower class of bony, characterized by opercules and bronchial membranes, I remarked the scorpæna, the head of which is furnished with spikes,
and which has but one dorsal fin; these creatures are covered, or not, with little
shells, according to the sub-class to which they belong. The second sub-class
gives us specimens of didactyles fourteen or fifteen inches in length, with yellow
rays, and heads of a most fantastic appearance. As to the first sub-class it gives
several specimens of that singular-looking fish appropriately called a "sea-frog,"
with large head, sometimes pierced with holes, sometimes swollen with
protuberances, bristling with spikes, and covered with tubercles; it has irregular
and hideous horns; its body and tail are covered with callosities; its sting makes a
dangerous wound; it is both repugnant and horrible to look at.'

From the 21st to the 23rd of January the Nautilus went at the rate of two
hundred and fifty leagues in twenty-four hours, being five hundred and forty
miles, or twenty-two miles an hour. If we recognized so many different varieties
of fish, it was because, attracted by the electric light, they tried to follow us; the
greater part, however, were soon distanced by our speed, though some kept their
place in the waters of the Nautilus for a time. The morning of the 24th, in 12° 5'
south latitude, and 94° 33' longitude, we observed Keeling Island, a madrepore
formation, planted with magnificent cacaos, and which had been visited by Mr
Darwin and Captain Fitzroy. The Nautilus skirted the shores of this desert island
for a little distance. Its nets brought up numerous specimens of polypi, and
curious shells of mollusca. Some precious productions of the species of
delphinulæ enriched the treasures of Captain Nemo, to which I added an astræa
punctifera, a kind of parasite polypus often found fixed to a shell. Soon Keeling
Island disappeared from the horizon, and our course was directed to the north-
west in the direction of the Indian Peninsula.

From Keeling Island our course was slower and more variable, often taking us
into great depths. Several times they made use of the inclined planes, which
certain internal levers placed obliquely to the water-line. In that way we went
about two miles, but without ever obtaining the greatest depths of the Indian
Sea, which soundings of seven thousand fathoms have never reached. As to the
temperature of the lower strata, the thermometer invariably indicated 4° above
zero. I only observed that, in the upper regions, the water was always colder in
the high levels than at the surface of the sea.

On the 25th of January, the ocean was entirely deserted; the Nautilus passed
the day on the surface, beating the waves with its powerful screw, and making
them rebound to a great height. Who under such circumstances would not have

taken it for a gigantic cetacean? Three parts of this day I spent on the platform. I watched the sea. Nothing on the horizon, till about four o'clock a steamer running west on our counter. Her masts were visible for an instant, but she could not see the Nautilus, being too low in the water. I fancied this steamboat belonged to the P.O. Company, which runs from Ceylon to Sydney, touching at King George's Point and Melbourne.

At five o'clock in the evening, before that fleeting twilight which binds night to day in tropical zones, Conseil and I were astonished by a curious spectacle.

It was a shoal of argonauts travelling along on the surface of the ocean. We could count several hundreds. They belonged to the tubercle kind which are peculiar to the Indian seas.

These graceful molluscs moved backwards by means of their locomotive tube, through which they propelled the water already drawn in. Of their eight tentacles, six were elongated, and stretched out floating on the water, whilst the other two, rolled up flat, were spread to the wind like a light sail. I saw their spiral-shaped and fluted shells, which Cuvier justly compares to an elegant skiff. A boat indeed! It bears the creature which secretes it without its adhering to it.

For nearly an hour the Nautilus floated in the midst of this shoal of molluscs. Then I know not what sudden fright they took. But as if at a signal every sail was furled, the arms folded, the body drawn in, the shells turned over, changing their centre of gravity, and the whole fleet disappeared under the waves. Never did the ships of a squadron manœuvre with more unity.

At that moment night fell suddenly, and the reeds, scarcely raised by the breeze, lay peaceably under the sides of the Nautilus.

The next day, 26th of January, we cut the equator at the eighty-second meridian, and entered the northern hemisphere. During the day, a formidable troop of sharks accompanied us, terrible creatures, which multiply in these seas, and make them very dangerous. They were 'cestracio philippi' sharks, with brown backs and whitish bellies, armed with eleven rows of teeth – eyed sharks – their throat being marked with a large black spot surrounded with white like an eye. There were also some Isabella sharks, with rounded snouts marked with dark spots. These powerful creatures often hurled themselves at the windows of the saloon with such violence as to make us feel very insecure. At such times Ned Land was no longer the master of himself. He wanted to go to the surface and harpoon the monsters, particularly certain smooth-hound sharks, whose mouth is studded with teeth like a mosaic; and large tiger-sharks nearly six yards long, the last named of which seemed to excite him more particularly. But the Nautilus, accelerating her speed, easily left the most rapid of them behind.

The 27th of January, at the entrance of the vast Bay of Bengal, we met repeatedly a forbidding spectacle, dead bodies floating on the surface of the water. They were the dead of the Indian villages, carried by the Ganges to the level of the sea, and which the vultures, the only undertakers of the country, had not been able to devour. But the sharks did not fail to help them at their funeral work.

About seven o'clock in the evening, the Nautilus, half immersed, was sailing in a sea of milk. At first sight the ocean seemed lactified. Was it the effect of the lunar rays? No; for the moon, scarcely two days old, was still lying hidden under the horizon in the rays of the sun. The whole sky, though lit by the sidereal rays, seemed black by contrast with the whiteness of the waters.

Conseil could not believe his eyes, and questioned me as to the cause of this strange phenomenon. Happily I was able to answer him.

'It is called a milk sea,' I exclaimed, 'a large extent of white wavelets often to be seen on the coasts of Amboyna, and in these parts of the sea.'

'But, sir,' said Conseil, 'can you tell me what causes such an effect? for I suppose the water is not really turned into milk.'

'No, my boy; and the whiteness which surprises you is caused only by the presence of myriads of infusoria, a sort of luminous little worm, gelatinous and without colour, of the thickness of a hair, and whose length is not more than the $7/1000$ of an inch. These insects adhere to one another sometimes for several leagues.'

'Several leagues!' exclaimed Conseil.

'Yes, my boy; and you need not try to compute the number of these infusoria. You will not be able; for, if I am not mistaken, ships have floated on these milk seas for more than forty miles.'

Towards midnight the sea suddenly resumed its usual colour; but behind us, even to the limits of the horizon, the sky reflected the whitened waves, and for a long time seemed impregnated with the vague glimmerings of an aurora borealis.

Chapter Twenty-Six

A Novel Proposal of Captain Nemo's

ON THE 28TH OF FEBRUARY, when at noon the Nautilus came to the surface of the sea, in 9° 4' north latitude, there was land in sight about eight miles to westward. The first thing I noticed was a range of mountains about two thousand feet high, the shapes of which were most capricious. On taking the bearings, I knew that we were nearing the Island of Ceylon, the pearl which hangs from the lobe of the Indian Peninsula.

Captain Nemo and his second appeared at this moment. The captain glanced at the map. Then, turning to me, said——

'The Island of Ceylon, noted for its pearl-fisheries. Would you like to visit one of them, M. Aronnax?'

'Certainly, captain.'

'Well, the thing is easy. Though if we see the fisheries, we shall not see the fishermen. The annual exportation has not yet begun. Never mind, I will give orders to make for the Gulf of Manaar, where we shall arrive in the night.'

The captain said something to his second, who immediately went out. Soon the Nautilus returned to her native element, and the manometer showed that she was about thirty feet deep.

'Well, sir,' said Captain Nemo, 'you and your companions shall visit the Bank of Manaar, and if by chance some fisherman should be there, we shall see him at work.'

'Agreed, captain!'

'By the by, M. Aronnax, you are not afraid of sharks?'

'Sharks!' exclaimed I.

This question seemed a very hard one.

'Well?' continued Captain Nemo.

'I admit, captain, that I am not yet very familiar with that kind of fish.'

'We are accustomed to them' replied Captain Nemo, 'and in time you will be too. However, we shall be armed, and on the road, we may be able to hunt some of the tribe. It is interesting. So, till tomorrow, sir, and early.'

This said in a careless tone, Captain Nemo left the saloon. Now, if you were invited to hunt the bear in the mountains of Switzerland, what would you say? 'Very well! tomorrow we will go and hunt the bear.' If you were asked to hunt the lion in the plains of Atlas, or the tiger in the Indian jungles, what would you say? 'Ha! ha! it seems we are going to hunt the tiger or the lion!' But when you are invited to hunt the shark in its natural element, you would perhaps reflect before accepting the invitation. As for myself, I passed my hand over my forehead, on which stood large drops of cold perspiration. 'Let us reflect,' said I, 'and take our time. Hunting otters in submarine forests, as we did in the Island of Crespo, will pass; but going up and down at the bottom of the sea, where one is almost certain to meet sharks, is quite another thing! I know well that in certain countries, particularly in the Andaman Islands, the negroes never hesitate to attack them with a dagger in one hand and a running noose in the other; but I also know that few who affront those creatures ever return alive. However, I am not a negro, and, if I were, I think a little hesitation in this case would not be ill-timed.'

At this moment, Conseil and the Canadian entered, quite composed, and even joyous. They knew not what awaited them.

'Faith, sir,' said Ned Land, 'your Captain Nemo – the devil take him! – has just made us a very pleasant offer.'

'Ah!' said I, 'you know?'

'If agreeable to you, sir,' interrupted Conseil, 'the commander of the Nautilus has invited us to visit the magnificent Ceylon fisheries tomorrow, in your company; he did it kindly, and behaved like a real gentleman.'

'He said nothing more?'

'Nothing more, sir, except that he had already spoken to you of this little walk.'

'Sir,' said Conseil, 'would you give us some details of the pearl-fishery?'

'As to the fishing itself,' I asked, 'or the incidents, which?'

'On the fishing,' replied the Canadian; 'before entering upon the ground, it is as well to know something about it.'

'Very well; sit down, my friends, and I will teach you.'

Ned and Conseil seated themselves on an ottoman, and the first thing the Canadian asked was——

'Sir, what is a pearl?'

'My worthy Ned,' I answered, 'to the poet, a pearl is a tear of the sea; to the Orientals, it is a drop of dew solidified; to the ladies, it is a jewel of an oblong shape, of a brilliancy of mother-of-pearl substance, which they wear on their fingers, their necks, or their ears; for the chemist, it is a mixture of phosphate and carbonate of lime, with a little gelatine; and lastly, for naturalists, it is simply a morbid secretion of the organ that produces the mother-of-pearl amongst certain bivalves.'

'Branch of mollusca,' said Conseil, 'class of acephali, order of testacea.'

'Precisely so, my learned Conseil; and, amongst these testacea, the earshell, the tridacnæ, the turbots, in a word, all those which secrete mother-of-pearl, that is, the blue, bluish, violet, or white substance which lines the interior of their shells, are. capable of producing pearls.'

'Mussels too?' asked the Canadian.

'Yes, mussels of certain waters in Scotland, Wales, Ireland, Saxony, Bohemia, and France.'

'Good! For the future I shall pay attention,' replied the Canadian.

'But,' I continued, 'the particular mollusc which secretes the pearl is the *pearl-oyster*, the *meleagrina margaritifera*, that precious pintadine. The pearl is nothing but a nacreous formation, deposited in a globular form, either adhering to the oyster-shell, or buried in the folds of the creature. On the shell it is fast; in the flesh it is loose; but always has for a kernel a small hard substance, maybe a barren egg, maybe a grain of sand, around which the pearly matter deposits itself year after year successively, and by thin concentric layers.'

'Are many pearls found in the same oyster?' asked Conseil.

'Yes, my boy. There are some pintadines a perfect casket. One oyster has been mentioned, though I allow myself to doubt it, as having contained no less than a hundred and fifty sharks.'

'A hundred and fifty sharks! exclaimed Ned Land.

'Did I say sharks?' said I, hurriedly. 'I meant to say a hundred and fifty pearls. Sharks would not be sense.'

'Certainly not,' said Conseil; 'but will you tell us now by what means they extract these pearls?'

'They proceed in various ways. When they adhere to the shell, the fishermen often pull them off with pincers; but the most common way is to lay the pintadines on mats of the seaweed which covers the banks. Thus they die in the open air; and at the end of ten days they are in a forward state of decomposition. They are then plunged into large reservoirs of sea-water; then they are opened and washed. Now begins the double work of the sorters. First they separate the layers of pearl, known in commerce by the name of bastard whites and bastard blacks, which are delivered in boxes of two hundred and fifty and three hundred pounds each. Then they take the parenchyma of the oyster, boil it, and pass it through a sieve in order to extract the very smallest pearls.'

'The price of these pearls varies according to their size?' asked Conseil.

'Not only according to their size,' I answered, 'but also according to their shape, their *water* (that is, their colour), and their lustre, that is, that bright and diapered sparkle which makes them so charming to the eye. The most beautiful are called virgin pearls or paragons. They are formed alone in the tissue of the mollusc, are white, often opaque, and sometimes have the transparency of an opal; they are generally round or oval. The round are made into bracelets, the oval into pendants, and, being more precious, are sold singly. Those adhering to the shell of the oyster are more irregular in shape, and are sold by weight. Lastly, in a lower order are classed those small pearls known under the name of seed-pearls; they are sold by measure, and are especially used in embroidery for church ornaments.'

'But,' said Conseil, 'is this pearl-fishery dangerous?'

'No,' I answered, quickly; 'particularly if certain precautions are taken.'

'What does one risk in such a calling?' said Ned Land; 'the swallowing of some mouthfuls of sea-water?'

'As you say, Ned. By the by,' said I, trying to take Captain Nemo's careless tone, 'are you afraid of sharks, brave Ned?'

'I!' replied the Canadian; 'a harpooner by profession? It is my trade to make light of them.'

'But,' said I, 'it is not a question of fishing for them with an iron swivel, hoisting them into the vessel, cutting off their tails with a blow of a chopper, ripping them up, and throwing their heart into the sea!'

'Then, it is a question of——'

'Precisely.'

'In the water?'

'In the water.'

'Faith, with a good harpoon! You know, sir, these sharks are ill-fashioned beasts. They must turn on their bellies to seize you, and in that time——'

Ned Land had a way of saying 'seize,' which made my blood run cold.

'Well, and you, Conseil, what do you think of sharks?'

'Me!' said Conseil. 'I will be frank, sir.'

'So much the better,' thought I.

'If you, sir, mean to face the sharks, I do not see why your faithful servant should not face them with you.'

Chapter Twenty-Seven

A Pearl of Ten Millions

THE NEXT MORNING AT four o'clock I was awakened by the steward, whom Captain Nemo had placed at my service. I rose hurriedly, dressed, and went into the saloon.

Captain Nemo was awaiting me.

'M. Aronnax,' said he, 'are you ready to start?'

'I am ready.'

'Then, please to follow me.'

'And my companions, captain?'

'They have been told, and are waiting.'

'Are we not to put on our diver's dresses?' asked I.

'Not yet. I have not allowed the Nautilus to come too near this coast, and we are some distance from the Manaar Bank; but the boat is ready, and will take us to the exact point of disembarking, which will save us a long way. It carries our diving apparatus, which we will put on when we begin our submarine journey.'

Captain Nemo conducted me to the central staircase, which led on to the platform. Ned and Conseil were already there, delighted at the idea of the 'pleasure party' which was preparing. Five sailors from the Nautilus, with their oars, waited in the boat, which had been made fast against the side.

The night was still dark. Layers of clouds covered the sky, allowing but few stars to be seen. I looked on the side where the land lay, and saw nothing but a dark line enclosing three parts of the horizon, from south-west to north-west. The Nautilus, having returned during the night up the western coast of Ceylon, was now west of the bay, or rather gulf, formed by the mainland and the island of Manaar. There, under the dark waters, stretched the pintadine bank, an inexhaustible field of pearls, the length of which is more than twenty miles.

Captain Nemo, Ned Land, Conseil, and I, took our places in the stern of the boat. The master went to the tiller; his four companions leaned on their oars, the painter was cast off, and we sheered off.

The boat went towards the south; the oarsmen did not hurry. I noticed that their strokes, strong in the water, only followed each other every ten seconds, according to the method generally adopted in the navy. Whilst the craft was running by its own velocity, the liquid drops struck the dark depths of the waves crisply like spats of melted lead. A little billow, spreading wide, gave a slight roll to the boat, and some samphire reeds flapped before it.

We were silent. What was Captain Nemo thinking of? Perhaps of the land he was approaching, and which he found too near to him, contrary to the Canadian's opinion, who thought it too far off. As to Conseil, he was merely there from curiosity.

About half-past five, the first tints on the horizon showed the upper line of coast more distinctly. Flat enough in the east, it rose a little to the south. Five miles still lay between us, and it was indistinct owing to the mist on the water. At six o'clock it became suddenly daylight, with that rapidity peculiar to tropical regions, which know neither dawn nor twilight. The solar rays pierced the curtain of clouds, piled up on the eastern horizon, and the radiant orb rose rapidly. I saw land distinctly, with a few trees scattered here and there. The boat neared Manaar Island, which was rounded to the south. Captain Nemo rose from his seat and watched the sea.

At a sign from him the anchor was dropped, but the chain scarcely ran, for it was little more than a yard deep, and this spot was one of the highest points of the bank of pintadines.

'Here we are, M. Aronnax,' said Captain Nemo. 'You see that enclosed bay? Here, in a month, will be assembled the numerous fishing-boats of the exporters, and these are the waters their divers will ransack so boldly. Happily, this bay is well situated for that kind of fishing. It is sheltered from the strongest winds; the sea is never very rough here, which makes it favourable for the diver's work. We will now put on our dresses, and begin our walk.'

I did not answer, and while watching the suspected waves, began with the help of the sailors to put on my heavy sea-dress. Captain Nemo and my companions were also dressing. None of the Nautilus' men were to accompany us on this new excursion.

Soon we were enveloped to the throat in indiarubber clothing; the air apparatus fixed to our backs by braces. As to the Ruhmkorff apparatus, there was no necessity for it. Before putting my head into the copper cap, I had asked the question of the captain.

'They would be useless,' he replied. 'We are going to no great depth, and the solar rays will be enough to light our walk. Besides, it would not be prudent to carry the electric light in these waters; its brilliancy might attract some of the dangerous inhabitants of the coast most inopportunely.'

As Captain Nemo pronounced these words, I turned to Conseil and Ned Land. But my two friends had already encased their heads in the metal cap, and they could neither hear nor answer.

One last question remained to ask of Captain Nemo.

'And our arms?' asked I; 'our guns?'

'Guns! what for? Do not mountaineers attack the bear with a dagger in their hand, and is not steel surer than lead? Here is a strong blade; put it in your belt, and we start.'

I looked at my companions; they were armed like us, and, more than that, Ned Land was brandishing an enormous harpoon, which he had placed in the boat before leaving the Nautilus.

Then, following the captain's example, I allowed myself to be dressed in the heavy copper helmet, and our reservoirs of air were at once in activity. An instant after we were landed, one after the other, in about two yards of water upon an even sand. Captain Nemo made a sign with his hand, and we followed him by a gentle declivity till we disappeared under the waves.

Over our feet, like conveys of snipe in a bog, rose shoals of fish, of the genus monoptera, which have no other fins but their tail. I recognized the Javanese, a real serpent two and a half feet long, of a livid colour underneath, and which might easily be mistaken for a conger eel if it was not for the golden stripes on its sides. In the genus stromateus, whose bodies are very flat and oval, I saw some of the most brilliant colours, carrying their dorsal fin like a scythe; an excellent eating fish, which, dried and pickled, is known by the name of *Karawade*; then some tranquebars, belonging to the genus apsiphoroides, whose body is covered with a shell cuirass of eight longitudinal plates.

The heightening sun lit the mass of waters more and more. The soil changed by degrees. To the fine sand succeeded a perfect causeway of boulders, covered with a carpet of molluscs and zoophytes. Amongst the specimens of these branches I noticed some placenæ, with thin unequal shells, a kind of ostracion peculiar to the Red Sea and the Indian Ocean; some orange lucinæ with rounded shells; rock-fish three feet and a half long, which raised themselves under the waves like hands ready to seize one. There were also some penopyres, slightly luminous; and lastly, some oculines, like magnificent fans, forming one of the richest vegetations of these seas.

In the midst of these living plants, and under the arbours of the hydrophytes, were layers of clumsy articulates, particularly some raninæ, whose carapace formed a slightly rounded triangle; and some horrible looking parthenopes.

At about seven o'clock we found ourselves at last surveying the oyster-banks, on which the pearl-oysters are reproduced by millions.

Captain Nemo pointed with his hand to the enormous heap of oysters; and I could well understand that this mine was inexhaustible, for Nature's creative power is far beyond man's instinct of destruction. Ned Land, faithful on his instinct, hastened to fill a net which he carried by his side with some of the finest specimens. But we could not stop. We must follow the captain, who seemed to guide himself by paths known only to himself. The ground was sensibly rising, and sometimes, on holding up my arm, it was above the surface of the sea. Then the level of the bank would sink capriciously. Often we rounded high rocks scarped into pyramids. In their dark tractures huge crustacea, perched upon their high claws like some war-machine, watched us with fixed eyes, and under our feet crawled various kinds of annelides.

At this moment there opened before us a large grotto, dug in a picturesque heap of rocks, and carpeted with all the thick warp of the submarine flora. At first it seemed very dark to me. The solar rays seemed to be extinguished by successive gradations, until its vague transparency became nothing more than drowned light. Captain Nemo entered; we followed. My eyes soon accustomed themselves to this relative state of darkness. I could distinguish the arches springing capriciously from natural pillars, standing broad upon their granite base, like the heavy columns of Tuscan architecture. Why had our incomprehensible guide led us to the bottom of his submarine crypt? I was soon to know. After descending a rather sharp declivity, our feet trod the bottom of a kind of circular pit. There Captain Nemo stopped, and with his hand indicated an object I had not yet perceived. It was an oyster of extraordinary dimensions, a gigantic tridacne, a goblet which could have contained a whole lake of holy water, a basin the breadth of which was more than two yards and a half, and consequently larger than that ornamenting the saloon of the Nautilus. I approached this extraordinary mollusc. It adhered by its byssus to a table of granite, and there, isolated, it developed itself in the calm waters of the grotto. I estimated the weight of this tridacne at 600 pounds. Such an oyster would contain thirty pounds of meat; and one must have the stomach of a Gargantua, to demolish some dozens of them.

Caption Nemo was evidently acquainted with the existence of this bivalve, and seemed to have a particular motive in verifying the actual state of this tridacne. The shells were a little open; the captain came near and put his dagger between to prevent them from closing; then with his hand he raised the membrane with its fringed edges, which formed a cloak for the creature. There, between the folded plaits, I saw a loose pearl, whose size equalled that of a cocoanut. Its globular shape, perfect clearness, and admirable lustre made it altogether a jewel of inestimable value. Carried away by my curiosity I stretched out my hand to seize it, weigh it, and touch it; but the captain stopped me, made a sign of refusal, and quickly withdrew his dagger, and the two shells closed suddenly. I then understood Captain Nemo's intention. In leaving this pearl hidden in the mantle of the tridacne, he was allowing it to grow slowly. Each year the secretions of the mollusc would add new concentric circles. I estimated its value at £500,000 at least.

After ten minutes Captain Nemo stopped suddenly. I thought he had halted previously to returning. No; by a gesture he bade us crouch beside him in a deep fracture of the rock, his hand pointed to one part of the liquid mass, which I watched attentively.

About five yards from me a shadow appeared, and sank to the ground. The disquieting idea of sharks shot through my mind, but I was mistaken; and once again it was not a monster of the ocean that we had anything to do with.

It was a man, a living man, an Indian, a fisherman, a poor devil who, I suppose, had come to glean before the harvest. I could see the bottom of his canoe anchored some feet about his head. He dived and went up successively. A stone held between his feet, cut in the shape of a sugar loaf, whilst a rope fastened him to his boat, helped him to descend more rapidly. This was all his apparatus. Reaching the bottom about five yards deep, he went on his knees and filled his bag with oysters picked up at random. Then he went up, emptied it, pulled up his stone, and began the operation once more, which lasted thirty seconds.

The diver did not see us. The shadow of the rock hid us from sight. And how should this poor Indian ever dream that men, beings like himself, should be there under the water watching his movements, and losing no detail of the fishing? Several times he went up in this way, and dived again. He did not carry away more than ten at each plunge, for he was obliged to pull them from the bank to which they adhered by means of their strong byssus. And how many of those oysters for which he risked his life had no pearl in them! I watched him closely, his manœuvres were regular; and, for the space of half an hour, no danger appeared to threaten him.

I was beginning to accustom myself to the sight of this interesting fishing, when suddenly, as the Indian was on the ground, I saw him make a gesture of terror, rise, and make a spring to return to the surface of the sea.

I understood his dread. A gigantic shadow appeared just above the unfortunate diver. It was a shark of enormous size advancing diagonally, his eyes on fire, and his jaws open. I was mute with horror, and unable to move.

The vocarcious creature shot towards the Indian, who threw himself on one side to avoid the shark's fins; but not its tail, for it struck his chest, and stretched him on the ground.

This scene lasted but a few seconds: the shark returned, and, turning on his back, prepared himself for cutting the Indian in two, when I saw Captain Nemo rise suddenly, and then, dagger in hand, walk straight to the monster, ready to fight face to face with him. The very moment the shark was going to snap the unhappy fisherman in two, he perceived his new adversary, and turning over, made straight towards him.

I can still see Captain Nemo's position. Holding himself well together, he waited for the shark with admirable coolness; and, when it rushed at him, threw himself on one side with wonderful quickness, avoiding the shock, and burying his dagger deep into its side. But it was not all over. A terrible combat ensued.

The shark had seemed to roar, if I might say so. The blood rushed in torrents from its wound. The sea was dyed red, and through the opaque liquid I could distinguish nothing more. Nothing more until the moment when, like lightning, I saw the undaunted captain hanging on to one of the creature's fins, struggling, as it were, hand to hand with the monster, and dealing successive blows at his enemy, yet still unable to give a decisive one.

The shark's struggles agitated the water with such fury that the rocking threatened to upset me.

I wanted to go to the captain's assistance, but, nailed to the spot with horror, I could not stir.

I saw the haggard eye; I saw the different phases of the fight. The captain fell to the earth, upset by the enormous mass which leant upon him. The shark's jaws opened wide, like a pair of factory shears, and it would have been all over with the captain; but, quick as thought, harpoon in hand, Ned Land rushed towards the shark and struck it with its sharp point.

The waves were impregnated with a mass of blood. They rocked under the shark's movements, which beat him with indescribable fury. Ned Land had not missed his aim. It was the monster's death-rattle. Struck to the heart, it struggled in dreadful convulsions, the shock of which overthrew Conseil.

But Ned Land had disentangled the captain, who, getting up without any wound, went straight to the Indian; quickly cut the cord which held him to his stone, took him in his arms, and, with a sharp blow of his heel, mounted to the surface.

We all three followed in a few seconds, saved by a miracle, and reached the fisherman's boat.

Captain Nemo's first care was to recall the unfortunate man to life again. I did not think he could succeed. I hoped so, for the poor creature's immersion was not long; but the blow from the shark's tail might have been his death-blow.

Happily, with the captain's and Conseil's sharp friction, I saw consciousness return by degrees. He opened his eyes. What was his surprise, his terror even, at seeing four copper heads leaning over him! And, above all, what must he have thought when Captain Nemo, drawing from the pocket of his dress a bag of pearls, placed it in his hands! This munificent charity from the man of the waters to the poor Cingalese was accepted with a trembling hand. His wondering eyes showed that he knew not to what superhuman beings he owed both fortune and life.

At a sign from the captain we regained the bank, and following the road already traversed, came in about half an hour to the anchor which held the canoe of the Nautilus to the earth.

Once on board, we each, with the help of the sailors, got rid of the heavy copper helmet.

Captain Nemo's first word was to the Canadian.

'Thank you, Master Land,' said he.

'It was in revenge, captain,' replied Ned Land, 'I owed you that.'

A ghastly smile passed across the captain's lips, and that was all.

'To the Nautilus,' said he.

The boat flew over the waves. Some minutes after, we met the shark's dead body floating. By the black marking on the extremity of its fins, I recognized the terrible melanopteron of the Indian Seas, of the species of shark properly so called. It was more than twenty-five feet long; its enormous mouth occupied one-third of its body. It was an adult, as was known by its six rows of teeth placed in an isosceles triangle in the upper jaw.

Conseil looked at it with scientific interest, and I am sure that he placed it, and not without reason, in the cartilaginous class, of the chondropterygian order, with fixed gills, of the selacian family, in the genus of the sharks.

Whilst I was contemplating this inert mass, a dozen of these voracious beasts appeared round the boat; and, without noticing us, threw themselves upon the dead body and fought with one another for the pieces.

At half-past eight we were again on board the Nautilus. There I reflected on the incidents which had taken place in our excursion to the Manaar Bank.

Two conclusions I must inevitably draw from it – one bearing upon the unparalleled courage of Captain Nemo, the other upon his devotion to a human being, a representative of that race from which he fled beneath the sea. Whatever he might say, this strange man had not yet succeeded in entirely crushing his heart.

When I made this observation to him, he answered in a slightly moved tone——

'That Indian, sir, is an inhabitant of an oppressed country; and I am still, and shall be, to my last breath, one of them!'

Chapter Twenty-Eight

The Red Sea

IN THE COURSE OF THE day of the 29th of January, the Island of Ceylon disappeared under the horizon, and the Nautilus, at a speed of twenty miles an hour, slid into the labyrinth of canals which separated the Maldives from the Laccadives. It coasted even the Island of Kiltan, a land originally madreporic, discovered by Vasco de Gama in 1499, and one of the nineteen principal islands of the Laccadive Archipelago, situated between 10 and 14° 30' north latitude, and 69° 50' 72" east longitude.

We had made 16,220 miles, or 7,500 (French) leagues from our starting-point in the Japanese Seas.

The next day (30th January), when the Nautilus went to the surface of the ocean, there was no land in sight. Its course was N.N.E., in the direction of the Sea of Oman, between Arabia and the Indian Peninsula, which serves as an outlet to the Persian Gulf. It was evidently a block without any possible egress. Where was Captain Nemo taking us to? I could not say. This, however, did not satisfy the Canadian, who that day came to me asking where we were going.

'We are going where our captain's fancy takes us, Master Ned.'

'His fancy cannot take us far, then,' said the Canadian. 'The Persian Gulf has no outlet: and if we do go in, it will not be long before we are out again.'

'Very well, then, we will come out again, Master Land; and if, after the Persian Gulf, the Nautilus would like to visit the Red Sea, the Straits of Bab-el-mandeb are there to give us entrance.'

'I need not tell you, sir,' said Ned Land, 'that the Red Sea is as much closed as the Gulf, as the Isthmus of Suez is not yet cut; and if it was, a boat as mysterious as ours would not risk itself in a canal cut with sluices. And again, the Red Sea is not the road to take us back to Europe.'

'But I never said we were going back to Europe.'

'What do you suppose then?'

'I suppose that, after visiting the curious coasts of Arabia and Egypt, the Nautilus will go down the Indian Ocean again, perhaps cross the Channel of Mozambique, perhaps off the Mascarenhas, so as to gain the Cape of Good Hope.'

'And once at the Cape of Good Hope?' asked the Canadian, with peculiar emphasis.

'Well, we shall penetrate into that Atlantic which we do not yet know. Ah! friend Ned, you are getting tired of this journey under the sea; you are surfeited with the incessantly varying spectacle of submarine wonders. For my part, I shall be sorry to see the end of a voyage which it is given to so few men to make.'

For four days, till the 3rd of January, the Nautilus scoured the Sea of Oman, at various speeds and at various depths. It seemed to go at random, as if hesitating as to which road it should follow, but we never passed the tropic of Cancer.

In quitting this sea we sighted Muscat for an instant, one of the most important towns of the country of Oman. I admired its strange aspect, surrounded by black rocks upon which its white houses and forts stood in relief. I saw the rounded domes of its mosques, the elegant points of its minarets, its fresh and verdant terraces. But it was only a vision! The Nautilus soon sank under the waves of that part of the sea.

We passed along the Arabian coast of Mahrah and Hadramaut, for a distance of six miles, its undulating line of mountains being occasionally relieved by some ancient ruin. On the 5th of February we at last entered the Gulf of Aden, a perfect funnel introduced into the neck of Bab-el-mandeb, through which the Indian waters entered the Red Sea.

On the 6th of February, the Nautilus floated in sight of Aden, perched upon a promontory which a narrow isthmus joins to the mainland, a kind of inaccessible Gibraltar, the fortifications of which were rebuilt by the English after taking possession in 1839. I caught a glimpse of the octagon minarets of this town, which was at one time, according to the historian Edrisi, the richest commercial magazine on the coast.

I certainly thought that Captain Nemo, arrived at this point, would back out again; but I was mistaken, for he did no such thing, much to my surprise.

The next day, the 7th of February, we entered the Straits of Bab-el-mandeb, the name of which, in the Arab tongue, means 'The gate of tears.'

To twenty miles in breadth, it is only thirty-two in length. And for the Nautilus, starting at full speed, the crossing was scarcely the work of an hour. But I saw nothing, not even the Island of Perim, with which the British Government has fortified the position of Aden. There were too many English or French steamers of the line of Suez to Bombay, Calcutta to Melbourne, and from Bourbon to the Mauritius, furrowing this narrow passage, for the Nautilus to venture to show itself. So it remained prudently below. At last, about noon, we were in the waters of the Red Sea.

I would not even seek to understand the caprice which had decided Captain Nemo upon entering the gulf. But I quite approved of the Nautilus entering it. Its speed was lessened: sometimes it kept on the surface, sometimes it dived to avoid a vessel, and thus I was able to observe the upper and lower parts of this curious sea.

On the 8th of February, from the first dawn of day, Mocha came in sight, now a ruined town, whose walls would fall at a gun-shot, yet which shelters here and there some verdant date-trees; once an important city, containing six public markets, and twenty-six mosques, and whose walls, defended by fourteen forts, formed a girdle of two miles in circumference.

The Nautilus then approached the African shore, where the depth of the sea was greater. There, between two waters clear as crystal, through the open panels we were allowed to contemplate the beautiful bushes of brilliant coral, and large blocks of rock clothed with a splendid fur of green algæ and fuci. What an indescribable spectacle, and what variety of sites and landscapes along these sandbanks and volcanic islands which bound the Libyan coast! But where these shrubs appeared in all their beauty was on the eastern coast, which the Nautilus soon gained. It was on the coast of Tehama, for there not only did this display of zoophytes flourish beneath the level of the sea, but they also found picturesque interlacings which unfolded themselves about sixty feet above the surface, more capricious but less highly coloured than those whose freshness was kept up by the vital power of the waters.

What charming hours I passed thus at the window of the saloon! What new specimens of submarine flora and fauna did I admire under the brightness of our electric lantern!

There grew sponges of all shapes, pediculated, foliated, globular, and digital. They certainly justified the names of baskets, cups, distaffs, elk's-horns, lion's-feet, peacock's-tails, and Neptune's-gloves, which have been given to them by the fishermen, greater poets than the *savants*.

Other zoophytes which multiply near the sponges consist principally of medusæ of a most elegant kind. The molluscs were represented by varieties of the calmar (which, according to Orbigny, are peculiar to the Red Sea); and reptiles by the virgata turtle, of the genus of cheloniæ, which furnished a wholesome and delicate food for our table.

As to the fish, they were abundant, and often remarkable. The following are those which the nets of the Nautilus brought more frequently on board:

Rays of a red-brick colour, with bodies marked with blue spots, and easily recognizable by their double spikes; some superb caranxes, marked with seven transverse bands of jet-black, blue and yellow fins, and gold and silver scales; mullets with yellow heads; gobies, and a thousand other species, common to the ocean which we had just traversed.

On the 9th of February, the Nautilus floated in the broadest part of the Red Sea, which is comprised between Souakin, on the west coast, and Koomfidah, on the east coast, with a diameter of ninety miles.

That day at noon, after the bearings were taken, Captain Nemo mounted the platform, where I happened to be, and I was determined not to let him go down again without at least pressing him regarding his ulterior projects. As soon as he saw me he approached, and graciously offered me a cigar.

'Well, sir, does this Red Sea please you? Have you sufficiently observed the wonders it covers, its fishes, its zoophytes, its parterres of sponges, and its forests of coral? Did you catch a glimpse of the towns on its borders?'

'Yes, Captain Nemo,' I replied; 'and the Nautilus is wonderfully fitted for such a study. Ah! It is an intelligent boat!'

'Yes, sir, intelligent and invulnerable. It fears neither the terrible tempests of the Red Sea, nor its currents, nor its sandbanks.'

'Certainly,' said I, 'this sea is quoted as one of the worst, and in the time of the ancients, if I am not mistaken, its reputation was detestable.'

'Detestable, M. Aronnax. The Greek and Latin historians do not speak favourably of it, and Strabo says it is very dangerous during the Etesian winds, and in the rainy season. The Arabian Edrisi portrays it under the name of the Gulf of Colzoum, and relates that vessels perished there in great numbers on the sandbanks, and that no one would risk sailing in the night. It is, he pretends, a sea subject of fearful hurricanes, strewn with inhospitable islands, and "which offers nothing good either on its surface or in its depths." Such, too, is the opinion of Arrian, Agatharcides, and Artemidorus.'

'One may see,' I replied, 'that these historians never sailed on board the Nautilus.

'Just so,' replied the captain, smiling; 'and in that respect moderns are not more advanced than the ancients. It required many ages to find out the mechanical power of steam. Who knows if, in another hundred years, we may not see a second Nautilus? Progress is slow, M. Aronnax.'

'It is true,' I answered; 'your boat is at least a century before its time, perhaps an era. What a misfortune that the secret of such an invention should die with its inventor!'

Captain Nemo did not reply. After some minutes' silence he continued——

'You were speaking of the opinions of ancient historians upon the dangerous navigation of the Red Sea.'

'It is true,' said I; 'but were not their fears exaggerated?'

'Yes and no, M. Aronnax,' replied Captain Nemo, who seemed to know the Red Sea by heart. 'That which is no longer dangerous for a modern vessel, well rigged, strongly built, and master of its own course, thanks to obedient steam, offered all sorts of perils to the ships of the ancients. Picture to yourself those first navigators venturing in ships made of planks sewn with the cords of the palm-tree, saturated with the grease of the sea-dog, and covered with powdered resin! They had not even instruments wherewith to take their bearings, and they went by guess amongst currents of which they scarcely knew anything. Under such conditions shipwrecks were, and must have been, numerous. But in our time, steamers running between Suez and the South Seas have nothing more to fear from the fury of this gulf, in spite of contrary trade-winds. The captain and passengers do not prepare for their departure by offering propitiatory sacrifices: and, on their return, they no longer go ornamented with wreaths and gilt fillets to thank the gods in the neighbouring temple.'

'I agree with you,' said I; 'and steam seems to have killed all gratitude in the hearts of sailors. But, captain, since you seem to have especially studied this sea, can you tell me the origin of its name?'

'There exist several explanations on the subject, M. Aronnax. Would you like to know the opinion of a chronicler of the fourteenth century?'

'Willingly.'

'This fanciful writer pretends that its name was given to it after the passage of the Israelites, when Pharaoh perished in the waves which closed at the voice of Moses.'

'A poet's explanation, Captain Nemo,' I replied; 'but I cannot content myself with that. I ask you for personal opinion.'

'Here it is, M. Aronnax. According to my idea, we must see in this appellation of the Red Sea a translation of the Hebrew word "Edom"; and if the ancients gave it that name, it was on account of the particular colour of its waters.'

'But up to this time I have seen nothing but transparent waves and without any particular colour.'

'Very likely; but as we advance to the bottom of the gulf, you will see this singular appearance. I remember seeing the Bay of Tor entirely red, like a sea of blood.'

'And you attribute this colour to the presence of a microscopic seaweed?'

'Yes; it is a mucilaginous purple matter, produced by the restless little plants known by the name of trichodesmia, and of which it requires 40,000 to occupy the space of a square .04 of an inch. Perhaps we shall meet some when we get to Tor.'

'So, Captain Nemo, it is not the first time you have overrun the Red Sea on board the Nautilus?'

'No, sir.'

'As you spoke a while ago of the passage of the Israelites, and of the catastrophe to the Egyptians, I will ask whether you have met with traces under the water of this great historical fact?'

'No, sir; and for a very good reason.'

'What is it?'

'It is, that the spot where Moses and his people passed is now so blocked up with sand, that the camels can barely bathe their legs there. You can well understand that there would not be water enough for my Nautilus.'

'And the spot?' I asked.

'The spot is situated a little above the Isthmus of Suez, in the arm which formerly made a deep estuary, when the Red Sea extended to the Salt Lakes. Now, whether this passage were miraculous or not, the Israelites, nevertheless, crossed there to reach the Promised Land, and Pharaoh's army perished precisely on that spot; and I think that excavations made in the middle of the sand would bring to light a large number of arms and instruments of Egyptian origin.'

'That is evident,' I replied; 'and for the sake of archaeologists let us hope that these excavations will be made sooner or later, when new towns are established on the isthmus, after the construction of the Seuz Canal; a canal, however, very useless to a vessel like the Nautilus.'

'Very likely; but useful to the whole world,' said Captain Nemo. 'The ancients well understood the utility of a communication between the Red Sea and the Mediterranean for their commercial affairs: but they did not think of digging a canal direct and took the Nile as an intermediate. Very probably the canal which united the Nile to the Red Sea was begun by Sesostris, if we may believe tradition. One thing is certain, that in the year 615 before Jesus Christ, Necos undertook the works of an elementary canal to the waters of the Nile, across the plain of Egypt, looking towards Arabia. It took four days to go up this canal, and it was so wide that two triremes could go abreast. It was carried on by Darius, the son of Hystaspes, and probably finished by Ptolemy II. Strabo saw it navigated; but its decline from the point of departure, near Bubastes, to the Red Sea was so slight, that it was only navigable for a few months in the year. This canal answered all commercial purposes to the age of Antoninus, when it was abandoned and blocked up with sand. Restored by order of the Caliph Omar, it was definitely destroyed in 761 or 762 by Caliph Al-Mansor, who wished to prevent the arrival of provisions to Mohammed-ben-Abdallah, who had revolted against him. During the expedition into Egypt, your General Bonaparte discovered traces of the works in the Desert of Suez; and surprised by the tide, he nearly perished before regaining Hadjaroth, at the very place where Moses had encamped three thousand years before him.'

'Well, captain, what the ancients dared not undertake, this junction between the two seas, which will shorten the road from Cadiz to India, M. Lesseps has succeeded in doing; and before long he will have changed Africa into an immense island.'

'Yes, M. Aronnax; you have the right to be proud of your countryman. Such a man brings more honour to a nation than great captains. He began, like so many others, with disgust and rebuffs; but he has triumphed, for he has the genius of will. And it is sad to think that a work like that, which ought to have been an international work, and which would have sufficed to make a reign illustrious, should have succeeded by the energy of one man. All honour to M. Lesseps!'

'Yes, honour to the great citizen!' I replied, surprised by the manner in which Captain Nemo had just spoken.

'Unfortunately,' he continued, 'I cannot take you through the Suez Canal; but you will be able to see the long jetty of Port Said after tomorrow, when we shall be in the Mediterranean.

'The Mediterranean!' I exclaimed.

'Yes, sir; does that astonish you?'

'What astonishes me is to think that we shall be there the day after tomorrow.'

'Indeed?'

'Yes, captain, although by this time I ought to have accustomed myself to be surprised at nothing since I have been on board your boat.'

'But the cause of this surprise?'

'Well! it is the fearful speed you will have to put on the Nautilus, if the day after tomorrow she is to be in the Mediterranean, having made the round of Africa, and doubled the Cape of Good Hope!'

'Who told you that she would make the round of Africa, and double the Cape of Good Hope, sir?'

'Well, unless the Nautilus sails on dry land, and passes above the isthmus——'

'Or beneath it, M. Aronnax.'

'Beneath it?'

'Certainly,' replied Captain Nemo, quietly. 'A long time ago Nature made under this tongue of land what man has this day made on its surface.'

'What! such a passage exists?'

'Yes; a subterranean passage, which I have named the Arabian Tunnel. It takes us beneath Suez, and opens into the Gulf of Pelusium.'

'But this isthmus is composed of nothing but quicksands?'

'To a certain depth. But at fifty-five yards only, there is a solid layer of rock.'

'Did you discover this passage by chance?' I asked, more and more surprised.

'Chance and reasoning, sir; and by reasoning even more than by chance. Not only does this passage exist, but I have profited by it several times. Without that I should not have ventured this day into the impassable Red Sea. I noticed that in the Red Sea and in the Mediterranean there existed a certain number of fishes of a kind perfectly identical – ophidia, fiatoles, girelles, and exocoeti. Certain of that fact, I asked myself was it possible that there was no communication between the two seas? If there was, the subterranean current must necessarily run from the Red Sea to the Mediterranean, from the sole cause of difference of level. I caught a large number of fishes in the neighbourhood of Suez. I passed a copper ring through their tails, and threw them back into the sea. Some months later, on the coast of Syria, I caught some of my fish ornamented with the ring. Thus the communication between the two was proved. I then sought for it with my Nautilus; I discovered it, ventured into it, and before long, sir, you too will have passed through my Arabian tunnel!'

Chapter Twenty-Nine

The Arabian Tunnel

THAT SAME EVENING, IN 21° 30′ north latitude, the Nautilus floated on the surface of the sea, approaching the Arabian coast. I saw Djeddah, the most important counting-house of Egypt, Syria, Turkey, and India. I distinquished clearly enough its buildings, the vessels anchored at the quays, and those whose draught of water obliged them to anchor in the roads. The sun, rather low on the horizon, struck full on the houses of the town, bringing out their whiteness. Outside, some wooden cabins, and some made of reeds, showed the quarter inhabited by the Bedouins. Soon Djeddah was shut out from view by the shadows of night, and the Nautilus found herself under water slightly phosphorescent.

The next day, the 10th of February, we sighted several ships running to windward. The Nautilus returned to its submarine navigation; but at noon, when her bearings were taken, the sea being deserted, she rose again to her waterline.

Accompanied by Ned and Conseil, I seated myself on the platform. The coast on the eastern side looked like a mass faintly printed upon a damp fog.

We were leaning on the sides of the pinnace, talking of one thing and another, when Ned Land stretching out his hand towards a spot on the sea, said——

'Do you see anything there, sir?'

'No, Ned,' I replied; 'but I have not your eyes, you know.'

'Look well,' said Ned, 'there, on the starboard beam, about the height of the lantern! Do you not see a mass which seems to move?'

'Certainly,' said I, after close attention; 'I see something like a long black body on the top of the water.'

And certainly before long the black object was not more than a mile from us. It looked like a great sandbank deposited in the open sea. It was a gigantic dugong!

Ned Land looked eagerly. His eyes shone with covetousness at the sight of the animal. His hand seemed ready to harpoon it. One would have thought he was awaiting the moment to throw himself into the sea, and attack it in its element.

At this instant Captain Nemo appeared on the platform. He saw the dugong, understood the Canadian's attitude, and addressing him, said——

'If you held a harpoon just now, Master Land, would it not burn your hand?'

'Just so, sir.'

'And you would not be sorry to go back, for one day, to your trade of a fisherman, and to add this cetacean to the list of those you have already killed?'

'I should not, sir.'

'Well, you can try.'

'Thank you, sir,' said Ned Land, his eyes flaming.

'Only,' continued the captain, 'I advise you for your own sake not to miss the creature.'

'Is the dugong dangerous to attack?' I asked, in spite of the Canadian's shrug of the shoulders.

'Yes,' replied the captain; 'sometimes the animal turns upon its assailants and overturns their boat. But for Master Land, this danger is not to be feared. His eye is prompt, his arm sure.'

At this moment seven men of the crew, mute and immovable as ever, mounted the platform. One carried a harpoon and a line similar to those employed in catching whales. The pinnace was lifted from the bridge, pulled from its socket, and let down into the sea. Six oarsmen took their seats, and the coxswain went to the tiller. Ned, Conseil, and I went to the back of the boat.

'You are not coming, captain?' I asked.

'No, sir; but I wish you good sport.'

The boat put off, and lifted by the six rowers, drew rapidly towards the dugong, which floated about two miles from the Nautilus.

Arrived some cables' length from the cetacean, the speed slackened, and the oars dipped noiselessly into the quiet waters. Ned Land, harpoon in hand, stood in the fore part of the boat. The harpoon used for striking the whale is generally attached to a very long cord, which runs out rapidly as the wounded creature draws it after him. But here the cord was not more than ten fathoms long, and the extremity was attached to a small barrel, which, by floating, was to show the course the dugong took under the water.

I stood, and carefully watched the Canadian's adversary. This dugong, which also bears the name of the halicore, closely resembles the manatee; its oblong body terminated in a lengthened tail, and its lateral fins in perfect fingers. Its difference from the manatee consisted in its upper jaw, which was armed with two long and pointed teeth, which formed on each side of diverging tusks.

This dugong, which Ned Land was preparing to attack, was of colossal dimensions; it was more than seven yards long. It did not move, and seemed to be sleeping on the waves, which circumstance made it easier to capture.

The boat approached within six yards of the animal. The oars rested on the rowlocks. I half rose. Ned Land, his body thrown a little back, brandished the harpoon in his experienced hand.

Suddenly a hissing noise was heard, and the dugong disappeared. The harpoon, although thrown with great force, had apparently only struck the water.

'Curse it!' exclaimed the Canadian, furiously; 'I have missed it!'

'No,' said I; 'the creature is wounded – look at the blood; but your weapon has not stuck in his body.'

'My harpoon! my harpoon!' cried Ned Land.

The sailors rowed on, and the coxswain made for the floating barrel. The harpoon regained, we followed in pursuit of the animal.

The latter came now and then to the surface to breathe. Its wound had not weakened it, for it shot onwards with great rapidity.

The boat, rowed by strong arms, flew on its track. Several times it approached within some few yards, and the Canadian was ready to strike, but the dugong made off with a sudden plunge, and it was impossible to reach it.

Imagine the passion which excited impatient Ned Land! He hurled at the unfortunate creature the most energetic expletives in the English tongue. For my part, I was only vexed to see the dugong escape all our attacks.

We pursued it without relaxation for an hour, and I began to think it would prove difficult to capture, when the animal, possessed with the perverse idea of vengeance, of which he had cause to repent, turned upon the pinnace and assailed us in its turn.

This manœuvre did not escape the Canadian.

'Look out!' he cried.

The coxswain said some words in his outlandish tongue, doubtless warning the men to keep on their guard.

The dugong came within twenty feet of the boat, stopped, sniffed the air briskly with its large nostrils (not pierced at the extremity, but in the upper part of its muzzle). Then taking a spring he threw himself upon us.

The pinnace could not avoid the shock, and half upset, shipped at least two tons of water, which had to be emptied; but thanks to the coxswain, we caught it sideways, not full front, so we were not quite overturned. While Ned Land, clinging to the bows, belaboured the gigantic animal with blows from his harpoon, the creature's teeth were buried in the gunwale, and it lifted the whole thing out of the water, as a lion does a roebuck. We were upset over one another, and I know not how the adventure would have ended, if the Canadian, still enraged with the beast, had not struck it to the heart.

I heard its teeth grind on the iron plate, and the dugong disappeared, carrying the harpoon with him. But the barrel soon returned to the surface, and shortly after the body of the animal, turned on its back. The boat came up with it, took it in tow, and made straight for the Nautilus.

It required tackle of enormous strength to hoist the dugong on to the platform. It weighed 10,000 lbs.

The next day, February 11th, the larder of the Nautilus was enriched by some more delicate game. A flight of sea-swallows rested on the Nautilus. It was a species of the Sterna nilotica, peculiar to Egypt; its beak is black, head grey and pointed, the eye surrounded by white spots, the back, wings, and tail of a greyish colour, the belly and throat white, and claws red. They also took some dozen of Nile ducks, a wild bird of high flavour, its throat and upper part of the head white with black spots.

About five o'clock in the evening we sighted to the north the Cape of Ras-Mohammed. This cape forms the extremity of Arabia Petræa, comprised between the Gulf of Suez and the Gulf of Acabah.

The Nautilus penetrated into the Straits of Jubal, which leads to the Gulf of Suez. I distinctly saw a high mountain, towering between the two gulfs of Ras-Mohammed. It was Mount Horeb, that Sinai at the top of which Moses saw God face to face.

At six o'clock the Nautilus, sometimes floating, sometimes immersed, passed some distance from Tor, situated at the end of the bay, the waters of which seemed tinted with red, an observation already made by Captain Nemo. Then night fell in the midst of a heavy silence, sometimes broken by the cries of the pelican and other night-birds, and the noise of the waves breaking upon the shore, chafing against the rocks, or the panting of some far-off steamer beating the waters of the Gulf with its noisy paddles.

From eight to nine o'clock the Nautilus remained some fathoms under the water. According to my calculation we must have been very near Suez. Through the panel of the saloon I saw the bottom of the rocks brilliantly lit up by our electric lamp. We seemed to be leaving the Straits behind us more and more.

At a quarter-past nine, the vessel having returned to the surface, I mounted the platform. Most impatient to pass through Captain Nemo's tunnel, I could not stay in one place, so came to breathe the fresh night-air.

Soon in the shadow I saw a pale light, half discoloured by the fog, shining about a mile from us.

'A floating lighthouse!' said someone near me.

I turned, and saw the captain.

'It is the floating light of Suez,' he continued. 'It will not be long before we gain the entrance of the tunnel.'

'The entrance cannot be easy?'

'No, sir; and for that reason I am accustomed to go into the steersman's cage, and myself direct our course. And now if you will go down, M. Aronnax, the Nautilus is going under the waves, and will not return to the surface until we have passed through the Arabian Tunnel.'

Captain Nemo led me towards the central staircase; half-way down he opened a door, traversed the upper deck, and landed in the pilot's cage, which it may be remembered rose at the extremity of the platform. It was a cabin measuring six feet square, very much like that occupied by the pilot on the steamboats of the Mississippi or Hudson. In the midst worked a wheel, placed vertically, and caught to the tiller-rope, which ran to the back of the Nautilus. Four light-ports with lenticular glasses, let in a groove in the partition of the cabin, allowed the man at the wheel to see in all directions.

This cabin was dark; but soon my eyes accustomed themselves to the obscurity, and I perceived the pilot, a strong man, with his hands resting on the spokes of the wheel. Outside, the sea appeared vividly lit up by the lantern, which shed its rays from the back of the cabin to the other extremity of the platform.

'Now,' said Captain Nemo, 'let us try to make our passage.'

Electric wires connected the pilot's cage with the machinery room, and from there the captain could communicate simultaneously to his Nautilus the direction and the speed. He pressed a metal knob, and at once the speed of the screw diminished.

I looked in silence at the high straight wall we were running by at this moment, the immovable base of a massive sandy coast. We followed it thus for an hour only some few yards off.

Captain Nemo did not take his eye from the knob, suspended by its two concentric circles in the cabin. At a simple gesture, the pilot modified the course of the Nautilus every instant.

I had placed myself at the port-scuttle, and saw some magnificent substructures of coral, zoophytes, seaweed, and fucus, agitating their enormous claws, which stretched out from the fissures of the rock.

At a quarter-past ten, the captain himself took the helm. A large gallery, black and deep, opened before us. The Nautilus went boldly into it. A strange roaring was heard round its sides. It was the waters of the Red Sea, which the incline of the tunnel precipitated violently towards the Mediterranean. The

Nautilus went with the torrent, rapid as an arrow, in spite of the efforts of the machinery, which, in order to offer more effective resistance, beat the waves with reversed screw.

On the walls of the narrow passage I could see nothing but brilliant rays, straight lines, furrows of fire, traced by the great speed, under the brilliant electric light. My heart beat fast.

At thirty-five minutes past ten, Captain Nemo quitted the helm; and, turning to me, said——

'The Mediterranean!'

In less than twenty minutes, the Nautilus, carried along by the torrent, had passed through the Isthmus of Suez.

Chapter Thirty

The Grecian Archipelago

THE NEXT DAY, THE 12TH OF FEBRUARY, at the dawn of day, the Nautilus rose to the surface. I hastened on to the platform. Three miles to the south the dim outline of Pelusium was to be seen. A torrent had carried us from one sea to the other. About seven o'clock Ned and Conseil joined me.

'Well, Sir Naturalist,' said the Canadian, in a slightly jovial tone, 'and the Mediterranean?'

'We are floating on its surface, friend Ned.'

'What!' said Conseil, 'this very night.'

'Yes, this very night; in a few minutes we have passed this impassable isthmus.'

'I do not believe it,' replied the Canadian.

'Then you are wrong, Master Land,' I continued; 'this low coast which rounds off to the south is the Egyptian coast. And you, who have such good eyes, Ned, you can see the jetty of Port Said stretching into the sea.'

The Canadian looked attentively.

'Certainly you are right, sir, and your captain is a first-rate man. We are in the Mediterranean. Good! Now, if you please, let us talk of our own little affair, but so that no one hears us.'

I saw what the Canadian wanted, and, in any case, I thought it better to let him talk, as he wished it; so we all three went and sat down near the lantern, where we were less exposed to the spray of the blades.

'Now, Ned, we listen; what have you to tell us?'

'What I have to tell you is very simple. We are in Europe; and before Captain Nemo's caprices drag us once more to the bottom of the Polar Seas, or lead us into Oceania, I ask to leave the Nautilus.'

I wished in no way to shackle the liberty of my companions, but I certainly felt no desire to leave Captain Nemo.

Thanks to him, and thanks to his apparatus, I was each day nearer the completion of my submarine studies; and I was re-writing my book of submarine depths in its very element. Should I ever again have such an opportunity of observing the wonders of the ocean? No, certainly not! And I could not bring myself to the idea of abandoning the Nautilus before the cycle of investigation was accomplished.

'Friend Ned, answer me frankly, are you tired of being on board? Are you sorry that destiny has thrown us into Captain Nemo's hands?'

The Canadian remained some moments without answering. Then crossing his arms, he said——

'Frankly, I do not regret this journey under the seas. I shall be glad to have made it; but now that it is made, let us have done with it. That is my idea.'

'It will come to an end, Ned.'

'Where and when?'

'Where I do not know – when I cannot say; or rather, I suppose it will end when these seas have nothing more to teach us.'

'Then what do you hope for?' demanded the Canadian.

'That circumstances may occur as well six months hence as now by which we may and ought to profit.'

'Oh!' said Ned Land, 'and where shall we be in six months, if you please, Sir Naturalist?'

'Perhaps in China; you know the Nautilis is a rapid traveller. It goes through water as swallows through the air, or as an express on the land. It does not fear frequented seas; who can say that it may not beat the coasts of France, England, or America, on which flight may be attempted as advantageously as here.'

'M. Aronnax,' replied the Canadian, 'your arguments are rotten at the foundation. You speak in the future, "We shall be there! we shall be here!" I speak in the present, "We are here, and we must profit by it."'

Ned Land's logic pressed me hard, and I felt myself beaten on that ground. I knew not what argument would now tell in my favour.

'Sir,' continued Ned, 'let us suppose an impossibility; if Captain Nemo should this day offer you your liberty, would you accept it?'

'I do not know,' I answered.

'And if,' he added, 'the offer he made you this day was never to be renewed, would you accept it?'

'Friend Ned, this is my answer. Your reasoning is against me. We must not rely on Captain Nemo's good-will. Common prudence forbids him to set us at liberty. On the other side, prudence bids us profit by the first opportunity to leave the Nautilus.'

'Well, M. Aronnax, that is wisely said.'

'Only one observation – just one. The occasion must be serious, and our first attempt must succeed; if it fails, we shall never find another, and Captain Nemo will never forgive us.'

'All that is true,' replied the Canadian. 'But your observation applies equally to all attempts at flight, whether in two years' time, or in two days. But the question is still this: If a favourable opportunity presents itself, it must be seized.'

'Agreed! and now, Ned, will you tell me what you mean by a favourable opportunity?'

'It will be that which, on a dark night, will bring the Nautilus a short distance from some European coast.'

'And you will try and save yourself by swimming?'

'Yes, if we were near enough to the bank, and if the vessel was floating at the time. Not if the bank was far away, and the boat was under the water.'

'And in that case?'

'In that case, I should seek to make myself master of the pinnace. I know how it is worked. We must get inside, and the bolts once drawn, we shall come to the surface of the water, without even the pilot, who is in the bows, perceiving our flight.'

'Well, Ned, watch for the opportunity; but do not forget that a hitch will ruin us.'

'I will not forget, sir.'

'And now, Ned, would you like to know what I think of your project?'

'Certainly, M. Aronnax.'

'Well, I think – I do not say I hope – I think that this favourable opportunity will never present itself.'

'Why not?'

'Because Captain Nemo cannot hide from himself that we have not given up all hope of regaining our liberty, and he will be on his guard, above all, in the seas, and in the sight of European coasts.'

'We shall see,' replied Ned Land, shaking his head determinedly.

'And now, Ned Land,' I added, 'let us stop here. Not another word on the subject. The day that you are ready, come and let us know, and we will follow you. I rely entirely upon you.'

Thus ended a conversation which, at no very distant time, led to such grave results. I must say here that facts seemed to confirm my foresight, to the Canadian's great despair. Did Captain Nemo distrust us in these frequented seas? or did he only wish to hide himself from the numerous vessels, of all nations, which ploughed the Mediterranean? I could not tell; but we were oftener between waters, and far from the coast. Or, if the Nautilus did emerge, nothing was to be seen but the pilot's cage; and sometimes it went to great depths, for, between the Grecian Archipelago and Asia Minor, we could not touch the bottom by more than a thousand fathoms.

Thus I only knew we were near the Island of Carpathos, one of the Sporades, by Captain Nemo reciting these lines from Virgil——

> Est in Carpathio Neptuni gurgite vates,
> Cæruleus Proteus,

as he pointed to a spot on the planisphere.

It was indeed the ancient abode of Proteus, the old shepherd of Neptune's flocks, now the Island of Scarpanto, situated between Rhodes and Crete. I saw nothing but the granite base through the glass panels of the saloon.

The next day, the 14th of February, I resolved to employ some hours in studying the fishes of the Archipelago; but for some reason or other, the panels remained hermetically sealed. Upon taking the course of the Nautilus I found that we were going towards Candia, the ancient Isle of Crete. At the time I embarked on the Abraham Lincoln, the whole of this island had risen in insurrection against the despotism of the Turks. But how the insurgents had fared since that time I was absolutely ignorant, and it was not Captain Nemo, deprived of all land communications, who could tell me.

I made no allusion to this event when that night I found myself alone with him in the saloon. Besides, he seemed to be taciturn and preoccupied. Then, contrary to his custom, he ordered both panels to be opened, and going from one to the other, observed the mass of waters attentively. To what end I could not guess; so, on my side, I employed my time in studying the fish passing before my eyes.

Amongst others, I remarked some gobies, mentioned by Aristotle, and commonly known by the name of sea-braches, which are more particularly met with in the salt waters lying near the Delta of the Nile. Near them rolled some sea-bream, half phosphorescent, a kind of sparus, which the Egyptians ranked amongst their sacred animals, whose arrival in the waters of their river announced a fertile overflow, and was celebrated by religious ceremonies. I also noticed some cheilines about nine inches long, a bony fish with transparent shell, whose lived colour is mixed with red spots; they are great eaters of marine vegetation, which gives them an exquisite flavour. These cheilines were much sought after by the epicures of ancient Rome; the inside, dressed with the soft roe of the lamprey, peacocks' brains, and tongues of the phenicoptera, composed that divine dish of which Vitellius was so enamoured.

Another inhabitant of these seas drew my attention, and led my mind back to recollections of antiquity. It was the remora, that fastens on to the shark's belly. This little fish, according to the ancients, hooking on to the ship's bottom, could stop its movements; and one of them, by keeping back Antony's ship during the battle of Actium, helped Augustus to gain the victory. On how little hangs the destiny of nations! I observed some fine anthiæ, which belong to the order of lutjans, a fish held sacred by the Greeks, who attributed to them the power of hunting the marine monsters from waters they frequented. The name signifies *flower*, and they justify their appellation by their shaded colours, their shades comprising the whole gamut of reds, from the paleness of the rose to the brightness of the ruby, and the fugitive tints that clouded their dorsal fin. My eyes could not leave these wonders of the sea, when they were suddenly struck by an unexpected apparition.

In the midst of the waters a man appeared, a diver, carrying at his belt a leathern purse. It was not a body abandoned to the waves; it was a living man, swimming with a strong hand, disappearing occasionally to take breath at the surface.

I turned towards Captain Nemo, and in an agitated voice exclaimed——'A man shipwrecked! He must be saved at any price!'

The captain did not answer me, but came and leaned against the panel.

The man had approached, and with his face flattened against the glass, was looking at us.

To my great amazement, Captain Nemo signed to him. The diver answered with his hand, mounted immediately to the surface of the water, and did not appear again.

'Do not be uncomfortable,' said Captain Nemo. 'It is Nicholas of Cape Matapan, surnamed Pesca. He is well known in all the Cyclades. A bold diver! water is his element, and he lives more in it than on land, going continually from one island to another, even as far as Crete.'

'You know him, captain?'

'Why not, M. Aronnax?'

Saying which, Captain Nemo went towards a piece of furniture standing near the left panel of the saloon. Near this piece of furniture, I saw a chest bound with iron, on the cover of which was a copper plate, bearing the cypher of the Nautilus with its device.

At that moment, the captain, without noticing my presence, opened the piece of furniture, a sort of strong box, which held a great many ingots.

They were ingots of gold. From whence came this precious metal, which represented an enormous sum? Where did the captain gather this gold from? And what was he going to do with it?

I did not say one word. I looked. Captain Nemo took the ingots one by one, and arranged them methodically in the chest, which he filled entirely. I estimated the contents at more than 4,000 lbs weight of gold, that is to say, nearly £200,000.

The chest was securely fastened, and the captain wrote an address on the lid, in characters which must have belonged to modern Greece.

This done, Captain Nemo pressed a knob, the wire of which communicated with the quarters of the crew. Four men appeared, and, not without some trouble, pushed the chest out of the saloon. Then I heard them hoisting it up the iron staircase by means of pulleys.

At that moment, Captain Nemo turned to me.

'And you were saying, sir?' said he.

'I was saying nothing, captain.'

'Then, sir, if you will allow me, I wish you goodnight.'

Whereupon he turned and left the saloon.

I returned to my room much troubled, as one may believe. I vainly tried to sleep – I sought the connecting link between the apparition of the diver and the chest filled with gold. Soon, I felt by certain movements of pitching and tossing, that the Nautilus was leaving the depths and returning to the surface.

Then I heard steps upon the platform; and I knew they were unfastening the pinnace, and launching it upon the waves. For one instant it struck the side of the Nautilus, then all noise ceased.

Two hours after, the same noise, the same going and coming was renewed; the boat was hoisted on board, replaced in its socket, and the Nautilus again plunged under the waves.

So these millions had been transported to their address. To what point of the Continent? Who was Captain Nemo's correspondent?

The next day, I related to Conseil and the Canadian the events of the night, which had excited my curiosity to the highest degree. My companions were not less surprised than myself.

'But where does he take his millions to?' asked Ned Land.

To that there was no possible answer. I returned to the saloon after having breakfast, and set to work. Till five o'clock in the evening, I employed myself in arranging my notes. At that moment – (ought I to attribute it to some peculiar idiosyncrasy) – I felt so great a heat that I was obliged to take off my coat of byssus! It was strange, for we were not under low latitudes; and even then, the Nautilus, submerged as it was, ought to experience no change of temperature. I looked at the manometer; it showed a depth of sixty feet, to which atmospheric heat could never attain.

I continued my work, but the temperature rose to such a pitch as to be intolerable.

'Could there be fire on board?' I asked myself.

I was leaving the saloon, when Captain Nemo entered; he approached the thermometer, consulted it, and turning to me, said——

'Forty-two degrees.'

'I have noticed it, captain,' I replied, 'and if it gets much hotter we cannot bear it.'

'Oh! sir, it will not get hotter if we do not wish it.'

'You can reduce it as you please, then?'

'No; but I can go further from the stove which produces it.'

'It is outward then!'

'Certainly; we are floating in a current of boiling water.'

'Is it possible!' I exclaimed.

'Look.'

The panels opened, and I saw the sea entirely white all round. A sulphurous smoke was curling amid the waves, which boiled like water in a copper. I placed my hand on one of the panes of glass, but the heat was so great that I quickly took it off again.

'Where are we?' I asked.

'Near the Island of Santorin, sir,' replied the captain, 'and just in the canal which separates Nea Kamenni from Pali Kamenni. I wished to give you a sight of the curious spectacle of a submarine eruption.'

'I thought,' said I, 'that the formation of these new islands was ended.'

'Nothing is ever ended in the volcanic parts of the sea,' replied Captain Nemo; 'and the globe is always worked by subterranean fires. Already, in the nineteenth year of our era, according to Cassiodorus and Pliny, a new island, Theia (the divine), appeared in the very place where these islets have recently been formed. Then they sank under the waves, to rise again in the year 69, when they again subsided. Since that time to our days, the Plutonian work has been suspended. But, on the 3rd of February 1866, a new island, which they named George Island, emerged from the midst of the sulphurous vapour near Nea Kamenni, and settled again on the 6th of the same month. Seven days after, the 13th of February, the Island of Aphroessa appeared, leaving between Nea Kamenni and itself a canal ten yards broad. I was in these seas when the phenomenon occurred, and I was able therefore to observe all the different phases. The Island of Aphroessa, of round form, measured 300 feet in diameter, and thirty feet in height. It was composed of black and vitreous lava, mixed with fragments of felspar. And lastly, on the 10th of March, a smaller island, called Reka, showed itself near Nea Kamenni, and since then, these three have joined together, forming but one and the same island.'

'And the canal in which we are at this moment?' I asked.

'Here it is,' replied Captain Nemo, showing me a map of the Archipelago. 'You see I have marked the new islands.'

I returned to the glass. The Nautilus was no longer moving, the heat was becoming unbearable. The sea, which till now had been white, was red, owing to the presence of salts of iron. In spite of the ship's being hermetically sealed, an insupportable smell of sulphur filled the saloon, and the brilliancy of the electricity was entirely extinguished by bright scarlet flames. I was in a bath, I was choking, I was broiled.

'We can remain no longer in this boiling water,' said I to the captain.

'It would not be prudent,' replied the impassive Captain Nemo.

An order was given; the Nautilus tacked about and left the furnace it could not brave with impunity. A quarter of an hour after we were breathing fresh air on the surface. The thought then struck me that, if Ned Land had chosen this part of the sea for our flight, we should never have come alive out of this sea of fire.

The next day, the 16th of February, we left the basin which, between Rhodes and Alexandria, is reckoned about 1,500 fathoms in depth, and the Nautilus, passing some distance from Cerigo, quitted the Grecian Archipelago, after having doubled Cape Matapan.

Chapter Thirty-One

The Mediterranean in Forty-Eight Hours

THE MEDITERRANEAN, THE blue sea *par excellence*, 'the great sea' of the Hebrews, 'the sea' of the Greeks, the 'mare nostrum' of the Romans, bordered by orange-trees, aloes, cacti, and sea-pines; embalmed with the perfume of the myrtle, surrounded by rude mountains, saturated with pure and transparent air, but incessantly worked by underground fires, a perfect battlefield in which Neptune and Pluto still dispute the empire of the world!

It is upon these banks, and on these waters, says Michelet, that man is renewed in one of the most powerful climates of the globe. But, beautiful as it was, I could only take a rapid glance at the basin whose superficial area is two millions of square yards. Even Captain Nemo's knowledge was lost to me, for this enigmatical person did not appear once during our passage at full speed. I estimated the course which the Nautilus took under waves of the sea at about six hundred leagues, and it was accomplished in forty-eight hours. Starting on the morning of the 16th of February from the shores of Greece, we had crossed the Straits of Gibraltar by sunrise on the 18th.

It was plain to me that this Mediterranean, enclosed in the midst of those countries which he wished to avoid, was distasteful to Captain Nemo. Those waves and those breezes brought back too many remembrances, if not too many regrets. Here he had no longer that independence and that liberty of gait which he had when in the open seas, and his Nautilus felt itself cramped between the close shores of Afria and Europe.

Our speed was now twenty-five miles an hour. It may be well understood that Ned Land, to his great disgust, was obliged to renounce his intended flight. He could not launch the pinnace, going at the rate of twelve or thirteen yards every second. To quit the Nautilus under such conditions would be as bad as jumping from a train going at full speed – an imprudent thing, to say the least of it. Besides, our vessel only mounted to the surface of the waves at night to renew its stocks of air; it was steered entirely by the compass and the log.

I saw no more of the interior of this Mediterranean than a traveller by express train perceives of the landscape which flies before his eyes; that is to say, the distant horizon, and not the nearer objects which pass like a flash of lightning.

In the midst of the mass of waters brightly lit up by the electric light, glided some of those lampreys, more than a yard long, common to almost every climate. Some of the oxyrhynchi, a kind of ray five feet broad, with white belly and grey spotted back, spread out like a large shawl carried along by the current. Other rays passed so quickly that I could not see if they deserved the name of eagles which was given to them by the ancient Greeks, or the qualification of rats, toads, and bats, with which modern fishermen have loaded them. A few milander sharks, twelve feet long, and much feared by divers, struggled amongst them. Sea-foxes eight feet long, endowed with wonderful fineness of scent, appeared like large blue shadows. Some dorades of the shark kind, some of which measured seven feet and a half, showed themselves in their dress of blue and silver, encircled by small bands which struck sharply against the sombre tints of their fins, a fish consecrated to Venus, the eyes of which are encased in a socket of gold, a precious species, friend of all waters, fresh or salt, an inhabitant of rivers, lakes, and oceans, living in all climates, and bearing all temperatures; a race belonging to the geological era of the earth, and which has preserved all the beauty of its first days. Magnificent sturgeons, nine or ten yards long, creatures of great speed, striking the panes of glass with their strong tails, displayed their bluish backs with small brown spots; they resemble the sharks, but are not equal to them in strength, and are to be met with in all seas. But of all the divers inhabitants of the Mediterranean, those I observed to the greatest advantage, when the Nautilus approached the surface, belong to the sixty-third genus of bony fish. They were a kind of tunny, with bluish black backs, and silvery breastplates, whose dorsal fins threw out sparkles of gold. They are said to follow in the wake of vessels whose refreshing shade they seek from the fire of the tropical sky, and they did not belie the saying, for they accompanied the Nautilus as they did in former times the vessel of La Perouse. For many a long hour they struggled to keep up with our vessel. I was never tired of admiring these creatures really built for speed – their small heads, their bodies lithe and cigar-shaped, which in some were more than three yards long, their pectoral fins and forked tail endowed with remarkable strength. They swam in a triangle, like certain flocks of birds, whose rapidity they equalled, and of which the ancients used to say that they understood geometry and strategy. But still they do not escape the pursuit of the Provençals, who esteem them as highly as the inhabitants of the Propontis and of Italy used to do; and these precious, but blind and foolhardy creatures, perish by millions in the nets of the Marseillaise.

With regard to the species of fish common to the Atlantic and the Mediterranean, the giddy speed of the Nautilus prevented me from observing them with any degree of accuracy.

As to marine mammals, I thought, in passing the entrance of the Adriatic, that I saw two or three cachalots, furnished with one dorsal fin, of the genus physetera, some dolphins of the genus globicephali, peculiar to the Mediterranean, the back part of the head being marked like a zebra with small lines; also, a dozen of seals, with white bellies and black hair, known by the name of *monks*, and which really have the air of a Dominican; they are about three yards in length.

As to zoophytes, for some instants I was able to admire a beautiful orange galeolaria, which had fastened itself to the port panel; it held on by a long filament, and was divided into an infinity of branches, terminated by the finest lace which could ever have been woven by the rivals of Arachne herself. Unfortunately, I could not take this admirable specimen; and doubtless no other Mediterranean zoophyte would have offered itself to my observation, if, on the night of the 16th, the Nautilus had not, singularly enough, slackened its speed, under the following circumstances.

We were then passing between Sicily and the coast of Tunis. In the narrow space between Cape Bon and the Straits of Messina, the bottom of the sea rose almost suddenly. There was a perfect bank, on which there was no more than nine fathoms of water, whilst on either side the depth was ninety fathoms.

The Nautilus had to manœuvre very carefully so as not to strike against this submarine barrier.

I showed Conseil, on the map of the Mediterranean, the spot occupied by this reef.

'But if you please, sir,' observed Conseil, 'it is like a real isthmus joining Europe to Africa.'

'Yes, my boy, it forms a perfect bar to the Straits of Libya, and the soundings of Smith have proved that in former times the continents between Cape Boco and Cape Furina were joined.'

'I can well believe it,' said Conseil.

'I will add,' I continued, 'that a similar barrier exists between Gibraltar and Ceuta, which in geological times formed the entire Mediterranean.'

'What if some volcanic burst should one day raise these two barriers above the waves?'

'It is not probable, Conseil.'

'Well, but allow me to finish, please, sir; if this phenomenon should take place, it will be troublesome for M. Lesseps, who has taken so much pains to pierce the isthmus.'

'I agree with you; but I repeat, Conseil, this phenomenon will never happen. The violence of subterranean force is ever diminishing. Volcanoes, so plentiful in the first days of the world, are being extinguished by degrees; the internal heat is weakened, the temperature of the lower strata of the globe is lowered by a perceptible quantity every century to the detriment of our globe, for its heat is its life.'

'But the sun?'

'The sun is not sufficient, Conseil. Can it give heat to a dead body?'

'Not that I know of.'

'Well, my friend, this earth will one day be that cold corpse; it will become uninhabitable and uninhabited like the moon, which has long since lost all its vital heat.'

'In how many centuries?'

'In some hundreds of thousands of years, my boy.'

'Then,' said Conseil, 'we shall have time to finish our journey, that is, if Ned Land does not interfere with it.'

And Conseil, reassured, returned to the study of the bank, which the Nautilus was skirting at a moderate speed.

There, beneath the rocky and volcanic bottom, lay outspread a living flora of sponges and reddish cydippes, which emitted a slight phosphorescent light, commonly known by the name of sea-cucumbers; and walking comatulæ more than a yard long, the purple of which completely coloured the water around.

The Nautilus having now passed the high bank in the Libyan Straits, returned to the deep waters and its accustomed speed.

From that time no more molluscs, no more articulates, no more zoophytes; barely a few large fish passing like shadows.

During the night of the 16th and 17th February, we had entered the second Mediterranean basin, the greatest depth of which was 1,450 fathoms. The Nautilus, by the action of its screw, slid down the inclined planes, and buried itself in the lowest depths of the sea.

On the 18th of February, about three o'clock in the morning, we were at the entrance of the Straits of Gibraltar. There once existed two currents: an upper one, long since recognized, which conveys the waters of the ocean into the basin of the Mediterranean; and a lower counter-current, which reasoning has now shown to exist. Indeed, the volume of water in the Mediterranean, incessantly added to by the waves of the Atlantic, and by rivers falling into it, would each year raise the level of this sea, for its evaporation is not sufficient to restore the equilibrium. As it is not so, we must necessarily admit the existence of an under-current, which empties into the basin of the Atlantic, through the Straits of Gibraltar, the surplus waters of the Mediterranean. A fact, indeed; and it was this counter-current by which the Nautilus profited. It advanced rapidly by the narrow pass. For one instant I caught a glimpse of the beautiful ruins of Hercules, buried in the ground, according to Pliny, and with the low island which supports it; and a few minutes later we were floating on the Atlantic.

Chapter Thirty-Two

Vigo Bay

THE ATLANTIC! A VAST sheet of water, whose superficial area covers twenty-five millions of square miles, the length of which is nine thousand miles, with a mean breadth of two thousand seven hundred – an ocean whose parallel winding shores embrace an immense circumference, watered by the largest rivers of the world, the St Lawrence, the Mississippi, the Amazon, the Plata, the Orinoco, the Niger, the Senegal, the Elbe, the Loire, and the Rhine, which carry water from the most civilized, as well as from the most savage countries! Magnificent field of water, incessantly ploughed by vessels of every nation, sheltered by the flags of every nation, and which terminates in those two terrible points so dreaded by mariners, Cape Horn, and the Cape of Tempests!

The Nautilus was piercing the water with its sharp spur, after having accomplished nearly ten thousand leagues in three months and a half, a distance greater than the great circle of the earth. Where were we going now? and what was reserved for the future? The Nautilus, leaving the Straits of Gibraltar, had gone far out. It returned to the surface of the waves, and our daily walks on the platform were restored to us.

I mounted at once, accompanied by Ned Land and Conseil. At a distance of about twelve miles, Cape St Vincent was dimly to be seen, forming the south-western point of the Spanish peninsula. A strong southerly gale was blowing. The sea was swollen and billowy; it made the Nautilus rock violently. It was almost impossible to keep one's footing on the platform, which the heavy rolls of the sea beat over every instant. So we descended after inhaling some mouthfuls of fresh air.

I returned to my room, Conseil to his cabin; but the Canadian, with a preoccupied air, followed me. Our rapid passage across the Mediterranean had not allowed him to put his project into execution, and he could not help showing his disappointment. When the door of my room was shut, he sat down and looked at me silently.

'Friend Ned,' said I, 'I understand you; but you cannot reproach yourself. To have attempted to leave the Nautilus under the circumstances would have been folly.'

Ned Land did not answer; his compressed lips, and frowning brow, showed with him the violent possession this fixed idea had taken of his mind.

'Let us see,' I continued; 'we need not despair yet. We are going up the coast of Portugal again; France and England are not far off, where we can easily find refuge. Now, if the Nautilus, on leaving the Straits of Gibraltar, had gone to the south, if it had carried us towards regions where there were no continents, I should share your uneasiness. But we know now that Captain Nemo does not fly from civilized seas, and in some days I think you can act with security.'

Ned Land still looked at me fixedly; at length his fixed lips parted, and he said, 'It is for tonight.'

I drew myself up suddenly. I was, I admit, little prepared for this communication. I wanted to answer the Canadian, but words would not come.

'We agreed to wait for an opportunity,' continued Ned Land, 'and the opportunity has arrived. This night we shall be but a few miles from the Spanish coast. It is cloudy. The wind blows freely. I have your word M. Aronnax, and I rely upon you.'

As I was still silent, the Canadian approached me.

'Tonight, at nine o'clock,' said he. 'I have warned Conseil. At that moment, Captain Nemo will be shut up in his room, probably in bed. Neither the engineer nor the ship's crew can see us. Conseil and I will gain the central staircase, and you, M. Aronnax, will remain in the library, two steps from us, awaiting my signal. The oars, the mast, and the sail, are in the canoe. I have even succeeded in getting in some provisions. I have procured an English wrench, to unfasten the bolts which attach it to the shell of the Nautilus. So all is ready, till tonight.'

'The sea is bad.'

'That I allow,' replied the Canadian; 'but we must risk that. Liberty is worth paying for; besides, the boat is strong, and a few miles with a fair wind to carry us, is no great thing. Who knows but by tomorrow we may be a hundred leagues away? Let circumstances only favour us, and by ten or eleven o'clock we shall have landed on some spot of *terra firma*, alive or dead. But adieu now till tonight.'

With these words the Canadian withdrew, leaving me almost dumb. I had imagined that, the chance gone, I should have time to reflect and discuss the matter. My obstinate companion had given me no time; and, after all, what could I have said to him? Ned Land was perfectly right. There was almost the opportunity to profit by. Could I retract my word, and take upon myself the responsibility of compromising the future of my companions.? Tomorrow Captain Nemo might take us far from all land.

At that moment a rather loud hissing told me that the reservoirs were filling, and that the Nautilus was sinking under the waves of the Atlantic.

A sad day I passed, between the desire of regaining my liberty of action, and of abandoning the wonderful Nautilus, and leaving my submarine studies incomplete.

What dreadful hours I passed thus! sometimes seeing myself and companions safely landed, sometimes wishing, in spite of my reason, that some unforeseen circumstance would prevent the realization of Ned Land's project.

Twice I went to the saloon. I wished to consult the compass. I wished to see if the direction the Nautilus was taking was bringing us nearer or taking us farther from the coast. But no; the Nautilus kept in Portuguese waters.

I must therefore take my part, and prepare for flight. My luggage was not heavy; my notes nothing more.

As to Captain Nemo, I asked myself what he would think of our escape; what trouble, what wrong it might cause him, and what he might do in case of its discovery or failure. Certainly I had no cause to complain of him; on the contrary, never was hospitality freer than his. In leavng him I could not be taxed with ingratitude. No oath bound us to him. It was on the strength of circumstances he relied, and not upon our word, to fix us for ever.

I had not seen the captain since our visit to the island of Santorin. Would chance bring me to his presence before our departure? I wished it, and I feared it at the same time. I listened if I could hear him walking in the room contiguous to mine. No sound reached my ear. I felt an unbearable uneasiness. This day of waiting seemed eternal. Hours struck too slowly to keep pace with my impatience.

My dinner was served in my room as usual. I ate but little, I was too preoccupied. I left the table at seven o'clock. A hundred and twenty minutes (I counted them) still separated me from the moment in which I was to join Ned Land. My agitation redoubled. My pulse beat violently. I could not remain quiet. I went and came, hoping to calm my troubled spirit by constant movement. The idea of failure in our bold enterprise was the least painful of my anxieties; but the thought of seeing our project discovered before leaving the Nautilus, of being brought before Captain Nemo, irritated, or (what was worse) saddened at my desertion, made my heart beat.

I wanted to see the saloon for the last time. I descended the stairs, and arrived in the museum where I had passed so many useful and agreeable hours. I looked at all its riches, all its treasures, like a man on the eve of an eternal exile, who was leaving never to return. These wonders of Nature, these masterpieces of Art, amongst which, for so many days, my life had been concentrated, I was going to abandon them for ever! I should like to have taken a last look through the windows of the saloon into the waters of the Atlantic: but the panels were hermetically closed, and a cloak of steel separated me from that ocean which I had not yet explored.

In passing through the saloon, I came near the door, let into the angle, which opened into the captain's room. To my great surprise, this door was ajar. I drew back, involuntarily. If Captain Nemo should be in his room, he could see me. But, hearing no noise, I drew nearer. The room was deserted. I pushed open the door, and took some steps forward. Still the monk-like severity of aspect.

Suddenly the clock struck eight. The first beat of the hammer on the bell awoke me from my dreams. I trembled as if an invisible eye had plunged into my most secret thoughts, and I hurried from the room.

There my eye fell upon the compass. Our course was still north. The log indicated moderate speed, the manometer a depth of about sixty feet.

I returned to my room, clothed myself warmly – sea boots, an otterskin cap, a great coat of byssus, lined with sealskin; I was ready, I was waiting. The vibration of the screw alone broke the deep silence which reigned on board. I listened attentively. Would no loud voice suddenly inform me that Ned Land had been surprised in his projected flight? A mortal dread hung over me, and I vainly tried to regain my accustomed coolness.

At a few minutes to nine, I put ear to the captain's door. No noise. I left my room and returned to the saloon, which was half in obscurity, but deserted.

I opened the door communicating with the library. The same insufficient light, the same solitude. I placed myself near the door leading to the central staircase, and there waited for Ned Land's signal.

At that moment the trembling of the screw sensibly diminished, then it stopped entirely. The silence was now only disturbed by the beatings of my own heart. Suddenly a slight shock was felt; and I knew that the Nautilus had stopped at the bottom of the ocean. My uneasiness increased. The Canadian's signal did not come. I felt inclined to join Ned Land and beg of him to put off his attempt I felt that we were not sailing under our usual conditions.

At this moment the door of the large saloon opened, and Captain Nemo appeared. He saw me, and, without further preamble, began in an amiable tone of voice——

'Ah, sir! I have been looking for you. Do you know the history of Spain?'

Now, one might know the history of one's own country by heart; but in the condition I was at the time, with troubled mind and head quite lost, I could not have said a word of it.

'Well,' continued Captain Nemo, 'you heard my question? Do you know the history of Spain?'

'Very slightly,' I answered.

'Well, here are learned men having to learn,' said the captain. 'Come, sit down, and I will tell you a curious episode in this history. – Sir, listen well,' said he; 'this history will interest you on one side, for it will answer a question which doubtless you have not been able to solve.'

'I listen, captain,' said I, not knowing what my interlocutor was driving at, and asking myself if this incident was bearing on our projected flight.

'Sir, if you have no objection, we will go back to 1702. You cannot be ignorant that your king, Louis XIV, thinking that the gesture of a potentate was sufficient to bring the Pyrenees under his yoke, had imposed the Duke of Anjou, his grandson, on the Spaniards. This prince reigned more or less badly under the name of Philip V, and had a strong party against him abroad. Indeed, the preceding year, the royal houses of Holland, Austria, and England, had concluded a treaty of alliance at the Hague, with the intention of plucking the crown of Spain from the head of Philip V, and placing it on that of an archduke to whom they prematurely gave the title of Charles III.

'Spain must resist this coalition; but she was almost entirely unprovided with either soldiers or sailors. However, money would not fail them, provided that their galleons, laden with gold and silver from America, once entered their ports. And about the end of 1702 they expected a rich convoy which France was escorting with a fleet of twenty-three vessels, commanded by Admiral Château Renaud, for the ships of the coalition were already beating the Atlantic. This convoy was to go to Cadiz, but the Admiral, hearing that an English fleet was cruising in those waters, resolved to make for a French port.

'The Spanish commanders of the convoy objected to this decision. They wanted to be taken to a Spanish port, and if not to Cadiz, into Vigo Bay, situated on the north-west coast of Spain, and which was not blocked.

'Admiral Château Renaud had the rashness to obey this injunction, and the galleons entered Vigo Bay.

'Unfortunately, it formed an open road which could not be defended in any way. They must therefore hasten to unload the galleons before the arrival of the combined fleet; and time would not have failed them had not a miserable question of rivalry suddenly arisen.

'You are following the chain of events?' asked Captain Nemo.

'Perfectly,' said I, not knowing the end proposed by this historical lesson.

'I will continue. This is what passed. The merchants of Cadiz had a privilege by which they had the right of receiving all merchandise coming from the West Indies. Now, to disembark these ingots at the port of Vigo, was depriving them of their rights. They complained at Madrid, and obtained the consent of the weak-minded Philip that the convoy, without discharging its cargo, should remain sequestered in the roads of Vigo until the enemy had disappeared.

'But whilst coming to this decision, on the 22nd of October 1702, the English vessels arrived in Vigo Bay, when Admiral Château Renaud, in spite of inferior forces, fought bravely. But seeing that the treasure must fall into the enemy's hands, he burnt and scuttled every galleon, which went to the bottom with their immense riches.'

Captain Nemo stopped. I admit I could not yet see why his history should interest me.

'Well?' I asked.

'Well, M. Aronnax,' replied Captain Nemo, 'we are in that Vigo Bay; and it rests with yourself whether you will penetrate its mysteries.'

The captain rose, telling me to follow him. I had had time to recover. I obeyed. The saloon was dark, but through the transparent glass the waves were sparkling. I looked.

For half a mile around the Nautilus, the waters seemed bathed in electric light. The sandy bottom was clean and bright. Some of the ship's crew in their diving dresses were clearing away half rotten barrels and empty cases from the midst of the blackened wrecks. From these cases and from these barrels escaped ingots of gold and silver, cascades of piastres and jewels. The sand was heaped up with them. Laden with their precious booty the men returned to the Nautilus, disposed of their burden, and went back to this inexhaustible fishery of gold and silver.

I understood now. This was the scene of the battle of 22nd of October 1702. Here on this very spot the galleons laden for the Spanish Government had sunk. Here Captain Nemo came, according to his wants, to pack up those millions with which he burdened the Nautilus. It was for him and him alone America had given up her precious metals. He was heir direct, without anyone to share, in those treasures torn from the Incas and from the conquered of Ferdinand Cortez.

'Did you know, sir,' he asked, smiling, 'that the sea contained such riches?'

'I knew,' I answered, 'that they value the money held in suspension in these waters at two millions.'

'Doubtless; but to extract this money the expense would be greater than the profit. Here, on the contrary, I have but to pick up what man has lost – and not only in Vigo Bay, but in a thousand other spots where shipwrecks have happened, and which are marked on my submarine map. Can you understand now the source of the millions I am worth?'

'I understand, captain. But allow me to tell you that in exploring Vigo Bay you have only been beforehand with a rival society.'

'And which?'

'A society which has received from the Spanish Government the privilege of seeking these buried galleons. The shareholders are led on by the allurement of an enormous bounty, for they value these rich shipwrecks at five hundred millions.'

'Five hundred millions they were,' answered Captain Nemo, 'but they are so no longer.'

'Just so,' said I; 'and a warning to those shareholders would be an act of charity. But who knows if it will be well received? What gamblers usually regret above all is less the loss of their money, than of their foolish hopes. After all, I pity them less than the thousands of unfortunates to whom so much riches well-distributed would have been profitable, whilst for them they will be for ever barren.'

I had no sooner expressed this regret, than I felt it must have wounded Captain Nemo.

'Barren!' he exclaimed, with animation. 'Do you think then, sir, that these riches are lost because I gather them? Is it for myself alone, according to your idea, that I take the trouble to collect these treasures? Who told you that I did not make a good use of it? Do you think I am ignorant that there are suffering beings and oppressed races on this earth, miserable creatures to console, victims to avenge? Do you not understand?'

Captain Nemo stopped at these words, regretting perhaps that he had spoken so much. But I had guessed that whatever the motive which had forced him to seek independence under the sea, it had left him still a man, that his heart still beat for the sufferings of humanity, and that his immense charity was for oppressed races as well as individuals. And I then understood for whom those millions were destined, which were forwarded by Captain Nemo when the Nautilus was cruising in the waters of Crete.

Chapter Thirty-Three

A Vanished Continent

THE NEXT MORNING, THE 19th of February, I saw the Canadian enter my room. I expected this visit. He looked very disappointed.

'Well, sir?' said he.

'Well, Ned, fortune was against us yesterday.'

'Yes; that captain must needs stop exactly at the hour we intended leaving this vessel.'

'Yes, Ned, he had business at his bankers.'

'His bankers!'

'Or rather his banking-house; by that I mean the ocean, where his riches are safer than in the chests of the State.'

I then related to the Canadian the incidents of the preceding night, hoping to bring him back to the idea of not abandoning the captain; but my recital had no other result than an energetically expressed regret from Ned, that he had not been able to take a walk on the battlefield of Vigo on his own account.

'However,' said he, 'all is not ended. It is only a blow of the harpoon lost. Another time we must succeed; and tonight, if necessary——'

'In what direction is the Nautilus going?' I asked.

'I do not know,' replied Ned.

'Well, at noon we shall see the point.'

The Canadian returned to Conseil. As soon as I was dressed, I went into the saloon. The compass was not reassuring. The course of the Nautilus was S.S.W. We were turning our backs on Europe.

I waited with some impatience till the ship's place was pricked on the chart. At about halfpast eleven the reservoirs were emptied, and our vessel rose to the surface of the ocean. I rushed towards the platform. Ned Land had preceded me. No more land in sight. Nothing but an immense sea. Some sails on the horizon, doubtless those going to San Roque in search of favourable winds for doubling the Cape of Good Hope. The weather was cloudy. A gale of wind was preparing. Ned raved, and tried to pierce the cloudy horizon. He still hoped that behind all that fog stretched the land he so longed for.

At noon the sun showed itself for an instant. The second profited by this brightness to take its height. Then the sea becoming more billowy, we descended, and the panel closed.

An hour after, upon consulting the chart, I saw the position of the Nautilus was marked at 16° 17′ longitude, and 33° 22′ latitude, at 150 leagues from the nearest coast. There was no means of flight, and I leave you to imagine the rage of the Canadian, when I informed him of our situation.

For myself, I was not particularly sorry. I felt lightened of the load which had oppressed me, and was able to return with some degree of calmness to my accustomed work.

That night, about eleven o'clock, I received a most unexpected visit from Captain Nemo. He asked me very graciously if I felt fatigue from my watch of the preceding night. I answered in the negative.

'Then, M. Aronnax, I propose a curious excursion.'

'Propose, captain?'

'You have hitherto only visited the submarine depths by daylight, under the brightness of the sun. Would it suit you to see them in the darkness of the night?'

'Most willingly.'

'I warn you, the way will be tiring. We shall have far to walk, and must climb a mountain. The roads are not well kept.'

'What you say, captain, only heightens my curiosity; I am ready to follow you.'

'Come then, sir, we will put on our diving dresses.'

Arrived at the robing-room, I saw that neither of my companions nor any of the ship's crew were to follow us on this excursion. Captain Nemo had not even proposed my taking with me either Ned or Conseil.

In a few moments we had put on our diving dresses; they placed on our backs the reservoirs, abundantly filled with air, but no electric lamps were prepared. I called the captain's attention to the fact.

'They will be useless,' he replied.

I thought I had not heard aright, but I could not repeat my observation, for the captain's head had already disappeared in its metal case. I finished harnessing myself, I felt them put an iron-pointed stick into my hand, and some minutes later, after going through the usual form, we set foot on the bottom of the Atlantic, at a depth of 150 fathoms. Midnight was near. The waters were profoundly dark, but Captain Nemo pointed out in the distance a reddish spot, a sort of large light shining brilliantly, about two miles from the Nautilus. What this fire might be, what could feed it, why and how it lit up the liquid mass, I could not say. In any case, it did light our way, vaguely, it is true, but I soon accustomed myself to the peculiar darkness, and I understood, under such circumstances, the uselessness of the Rumhkorff apparatus.

As we advanced, I heard a kind of pattering above my head. The noise redoubling, sometimes producing a continual shower, I soon understood the cause. It was rain falling violently, and crisping the surface of the waves. Instinctively the thought flashed across my mind that I should be wet through! By the water! in the midst of the water! I could not help laughing at the odd idea. But indeed, in the thick diving dress, the liquid element is no longer felt, and one only seems to be in an atmosphere somewhat denser than the terrestrial atmosphere. Nothing more.

After half an hour's walking the soil became stony. Medusæ, microscopic crustacea, and pennatules lit it slightly with their phosphorescent gleam. I caught a glimpse of pieces of stone covered with millions of zoophytes, and masses of seaweed. My feet often slipped upon this viscous carpet of seaweed, and without my iron-tipped stick I should have fallen more than once. In turning round, I could still see the whitish lantern of the Nautilus beginning to pale in the distance.

But the rosy light which guided us increased and lit up the horizon. The presence of this fire under water puzzled me in the highest degree. Was it some electric effulgence? Was I going towards a natural phenomenon as yet unknown to the *savants* of the earth? Or even (for this thought crossed my brain) had the hand of man aught to do with this conflagration? Had he fanned this flame? Was I to meet in these depths companions and friends of Captain Nemo whom he was going to visit, and who, like him, led this strange existence? Should I find down there a whole colony of exiles, who, weary of the miseries of this earth, had sought and found independence in the deep ocean? All these foolish and unreasonable ideas pursued me. And in this condition of mind, over-excited by the succession of wonders continually passing before my eyes, I should not have been surprised to meet at the bottom of the sea one of those submarine towns of which Captain Nemo dreamed.

Our road grew lighter and lighter. The white glimmer came in rays from the summit of a mountain about 800 feet high. But what I saw was simply a reflection, developed by the clearness of the waters. The source of this inexplicable light was a fire on the opposite side of the mountain.

In the midst of this stony maze, furrowing the bottom of the Atlantic, Captain Nemo advanced without hesitation. He knew this dreary road. Doubtless he had often travelled over it, and could not lose himself. I followed him with unshaken confidence. He seemed to me like a genie of the sea; and, as he walked before me, I could not help admiring his stature, which was outlined in black on the luminous horizon.

It was one in the morning when we arrived at the first slopes of the mountain; but to gain access to them we must venture through the difficult paths of a vast copse.

Yes; a copse of dead trees, without leaves, without sap, trees petrified by the action of the water, and here and there overtopped by gigantic pines. It was like a coal pit, still standing, holding by the roots to the broken soil, and whose branches, like fine black paper cuttings, showed distinctly on the watery ceiling. Picture to yourself a forest in the Hartz, hanging on to the sides of the mountain, but a forest swallowed up. The paths were encumbered with seaweed and fucus, between which grovelled a whole world of crustacea. I went along, climbing the rocks, striding over extended trunks, breaking the sea bind-weed, which hung from one tree to the other; and frightening the fishes, which flew from branch to branch. Pressing onward, I felt no fatigue. I followed my guide, who was never tired. What a spectacle! how can I express it? how paint the aspect of those woods and rocks in this medium – their underparts dark and wild, the upper coloured with red tints, by that light which the reflecting powers of the waters doubled? We climbed rocks, which fell directly after with gigantic bounds, and the low growling of an avalanche. To right and left ran long, dark galleries, where sight was lost. Here opened vast glades which the hand of man seemed to have worked; and I sometimes asked myself if some inhabitant of these submarine regions would not suddenly appear to me.

But Captain Nemo was still mounting. I could not stay behind. I followed boldly. My stick gave me good help. A false step would have been dangerous on the narrow passes sloping down to the sides of the gulfs; but I walked with firm step, without feeling any giddiness. Now I jumped a crevice the depth of which would have made me hesitate had it been among the glaciers on the land; now I ventured on the unsteady trunk of a tree, thrown across from one abyss to the other, without looking under my feet, having only eyes to admire the wild sites of this region.

There, monumental rocks, leaning on their regularly cut bases, seemed to defy all laws of equilibrium. From between their stony knees, trees sprang, like a jet under heavy pressure, and upheld others which upheld them. Natural towers, large scarps, cut perpendicularly, like a 'curtain', inclined at an angle which the laws of gravitation could never have tolerated in terrestrial regions.

Two hours after quitting the Nautilus, we had crossed the line of trees, and a hundred feet above our heads rose the top of the mountain, which cast a shadow on the brilliant irradiation of the opposite slope. Some petrified shrubs ran fantastically here and there. Fishes got up under our feet like birds in the long grass. The massive rocks were rent with impenetrable fractures, deep grottos, and unfathomable holes, at the bottom of which formidable creatures might be heard moving. My blood curdled when I saw enormous antennæ blocking my road, or some frightful claw closing with a noise in the shadow of some cavity. Millions of luminous spots shone brightly in the midst of the darkness. They were the eyes of giant crustacea crouched in their holes; giant lobsters setting themselves up like halberdiers, and moving their claws with the clicking sound of pincers; titanic crabs, pointed like a gun on its carriage; and frightful looking poulps, interweaving their tentacles like a living nest of serpents.

We had now arrived on the first platform, where other surprises awaited me. Before us lay some picturesque ruins, which betrayed the hand of man, and not that of the Creator. There were vast heaps of stone, amongst which might be traced the vague and shadowy forms of castles and temples, clothed with a world of blossoming zoophytes, and over which, instead of ivy, seaweed and fucus threw a thick vegetable mantle. But what was this portion of the globe which had been swallowed by cataclysms? Who had placed those rocks and stones like cromlechs of pre-historic times? Where was I? Whither had Captain Nemo's fancy hurried me?

I would fain have asked him; not being able to, I stopped him – I seized his arm. But shaking his head, and pointing to the highest point of the mountain, he seemed to say——

'Come, come along; come higher!'

I followed, and in a few minutes I had climbed to the top, which for a circle of ten yards commanded the whole mass of rock.

I looked down the side we had just climbed. The mountain did not rise more than seven or eight hundred feet above the level of the plain; but on the opposite side it commanded from twice that height the depths of this part of the Atlantic. My eyes ranged far over a large space lit by a violent fulguration. In fact, the mountain was a volcano.

At fifty feet above the peak, in the midst of a rain of stones and scoriæ, a large crater was vomiting forth torrents of lava which fell in a cascade of fire into the bosom of the liquid mass. Thus situated, this volcano lit the lower plain like an immense torch, even to the extreme limits of the horizon. I said that the submarine crater threw up lava, but no flames. Flames require the oxygen of the air to feed upon, and cannot be developed under water; but streams of lava, having in themselves the principles of their incandescence, can attain a white heat, fight vigorously against the liquid element, and turn it to vapour by contact.

Rapid currents bearing all these gases in diffusion, and torrents of lava, slid to the bottom of the mountain like an eruption of Vesuvius on another Terra del Greco.

There, indeed, under my eyes, ruined, destroyed, lay a town – its roofs open to the sky, its temples fallen, its arches dislocated, its columns lying on the ground, from which one could still recognize the massive character of Tuscan architecture. Further on, some remains of a gigantic aqueduct; here the high base of an Acropolis, with the floating outline of a Parthenon; there traces of a quay, as if an ancient port had formerly abutted on the borders of the ocean, and disappeared with its merchant vessels and its war galleys. Further on again, long lines of sunken walls and broad deserted streets – a perfect Pompeii escaped beneath the waters. Such was the sight that Captain Nemo brought before my eyes!

Where was I? Where was I? I must know, at any cost. I tried to speak, but Captain Nemo stopped me by a gesture, and picking up a piece of chalk stone, advanced to a rock of black basalt, and traced the word——

ATLANTIS.

What a light shot through my mind! Atlantis, the ancient Meropis of Theopompus, the Atlantis of Plato, that continent denied by Origen, Jamblichus, D'Anville, Malte-Brun, and Humboldt, who placed its disappearance amongst the legendary tales admitted by Posidonius, Pliny, Ammianus Marcellinus, Tertullian, Engel, Buffon, and D'Avezac. I had it there now before my eyes, bearing upon it the unexceptionable testimony of its catastrophe. The region thus engulfed was beyond Europe, Asia, and Libya, beyond the columns of Hercules, where those powerful people, the Atlantides, lived, against whom the first wars of ancient Greece were waged.

Thus, led by the strangest destiny, I was treading under foot the mountains of this continent, touching with my hand those ruins a thousand generations old, and contemporary with the geological epochs. I was walking on the very spot where the contemporaries of the first man had walked.

Whilst I was trying to fix in my mind every detail of this grand landscape, Captain Nemo remained motionless, as if petrified in mute ecstasy, leaning on a mossy stone. Was he dreaming of those generations long since disappeared? Was he asking them the secret of human destiny? Was it here this strange man came to steep himself in historical recollections, and live again this ancient life – he who wanted no modern one? What would I not have given to know his thoughts, to share them, to understand them! We remained for an hour at this place, contemplating the vast plain under the brightness of the lava, which was sometimes wonderfully intense. Rapid tremblings ran along the mountain caused by internal bubblings, deep noises distinctly transmitted through the liquid medium were echoed with majestic grandeur. At this moment the moon appeared through the mass of waters, and threw her pale rays on the buried continent. It was but a gleam, but what an indescribable effect! The captain rose, cast one last look on the immense plain, and then bade me follow him.

We descended the mountain rapidly, and the mineral forest once passed, I saw the lantern of the Nautilus shining like a star. The captain walked straight to it, and we got on board as the first rays of light whitened the surface of the ocean.

Chapter Thirty-Four

The Submarine Coal-mines

THE NEXT DAY, THE 20TH OF FEBRUARY, I awoke very late: the fatigues of the previous night had prolonged my sleep until eleven o'clock. I dressed quickly, and hastened to find the course the Nautilus was taking. The instruments showed it to be still towards the south, with a speed of twenty miles an hour, and a depth of fifty fathoms.

The species of fishes here did not differ much from those already noticed. There were rays of giant size, five yards long, and endowed with great muscular strength, which enabled them to shoot above the waves; sharks of many kinds, amongst others, a glaucus of fifteen feet long, with triangular sharp teeth, and whose transparency rendered it almost invisible in the water; brown sagræ; humantins, prism-shaped, and clad with a tuberculous hide; sturgeons, resembling their congeners of the Mediterranean; trumpet syngnathes, a foot and a half long, furnished with greyish bladders, without teeth or tongue, and as supple as snakes.

Amongst bony fish, Conseil noticed some blackish makairas, about three yards long, armed at the upper jaw with a piercing sword; other bright coloured creatures, known in the time of Aristotle by the name of the sea dragon, which are dangerous to capture on account of the spikes on their back; also some coryphænes, with brown backs marked with little blue stripes, and surrounded with a gold border; some beautiful dorades; and swordfish four-and-twenty feet long, swimming in troops, fierce animals, but rather herbivorous than carnivorous.

About four o'clock, the soil, generally composed of a thick mud mixed with petrified wood, changed by degrees, and it became more stony, and seemed strewn with conglomerate and pieces of basalt, with a sprinkling of lava and sulphurous obsidian. I thought that a mountainous region was succeeding the long plains; and accordingly, after a few evolutions of the Nautilus, I saw the southerly horizon blocked by a high wall which seemed to close all exit. Its summit evidently passed the level of the ocean. It must be a continent, or at least an island – one of the Canaries, or of the Cape Verde Islands. The bearings not being yet taken, perhaps designedly, I was ignorant of our exact position. In any case, such a wall seemed to me to mark the limits of that Atlantis, of which we had in reality passed over only the smallest part.

Much longer should I have remained at the window, admiring the beauties of sea and sky, but the panels closed. At this moment the Nautilus arrived at the side of this high perpendicular wall. What it would do, I could not guess. I returned to my room; it no longer moved. I laid myself down with the full intention of waking after a few hours' sleep; but it was eight o'clock the next day when I entered the saloon. I looked at the manometer. It told me that the

Nautilus was floating on the surface of the ocean. Besides, I heard steps on the platform. I went to the panel. It was open; but, instead of broad daylight, as I expected, I was surrounded by profound darkness. Where were we? Was I mistaken. Was it still night? No; not a star was shining, and night was not that utter darkness.

I knew not what to think, when a voice near me said——

'Is that you, professor?'

'Ah! captain,' I answered, 'where are we?'

'Under ground, sir.'

'Under ground!' I exclaimed. 'And the Nautilus floating still?'

'It always floats.'

'But I do not understand.'

'Wait a few minutes, our lantern will be lit, and if you like light places, you will be satisfied.'

I stood on the platform and waited. The darkness was so complete that I could not even see Captain Nemo; but looking to the zenith, exactly above my head, I seemed to catch an undecided gleam, a kind of twilight filling a circular hole. At this instant the lantern was lit, and its vividness dispelled the faint light. I closed my dazzled eyes for an instant, and then looked again. The Nautilus was stationary, floating near a mountain which formed a sort of quay. The lake then supporting it was a lake imprisoned by a circle of walls, measuring two miles in diameter, and six in circumference. Its level (the manometer showed) could only be the same as the outside level, for there must necessarily be a communication between the lake and the sea. The high partitions, leaning forward on their base, grew into a vaulted roof bearing the shape of an immense funnel turned upside down, the height being about five or six hundred yards. At the summit was a circular orifice, by which I had caught the slight gleam of light, evidently daylight.

'Where are we?' I asked.

'In the very heart of an extinct volcano, the interior of which has been invaded by the sea, after some great convulsion of the earth. Whilst you were sleeping, professor, the Nautilus penetrated to this lagoon by a natural canal, which opens about ten yards beneath the surface of the ocean. This is its harbour or refuge, a sure, commodious, and mysterious one, sheltered from all gales. Show me, if you can, on the coasts of any of your continents or islands, a road which can give such perfect refuge from all storms.'

'Certainly,' I replied, 'you are in safety here, Captain Nemo. Who could reach you in the heart of a volcano? But did I not see an opening at its summit?'

'Yes; its crater, formerly filled with lava, vapour, and flames, and which now gives entrance to the life-giving air we breathe.'

'But what is this volcanic mountain?'

'It belongs to one of the numerous islands with which this sea is strewn – to vessels a simple sandbank – to us an immense cavern. Chance led me to discover it, and chance served me well.'

'But of what use is this refuge, captain? The Nautilus wants no port.'

'No, sir; but it wants electricity to make it move, and the wherewithal to make the electricity – sodium to feed the elements, coal from which to get the sodium, and a coal-mine to supply the coal. And exactly on this spot the sea covers entire forests embedded during the geological periods, now mineralized, and transformed into coal; for me they are an inexhaustible mine.'

'Your men follow the trade of miners here, then, captain?'

'Exactly so. These mines extend under the waves like the mines of Newcastle. Here, in their diving dresses, pickaxe and shovel in hand, my men extract the coal, which I do not even ask from the mines of the earth. When I burn this combustible for the manufacture of sodium, the smoke, escaping from the crater of the mountain, gives it the appearance of a still active volcano.'

'And we shall see your companions at work?'

'No; not this time at least; for I am in a hurry to continue our submarine tour of the earth. So I shall content myself with drawing from the reserve of sodium I already possess. The time for loading is one day only, and we continue our voyage. So if you wish to go over the cavern, and make the round of the lagoon, you must take advantage of today, M. Aronnax.'

I thanked the captain, and went to look for my companions, who had not yet left their cabin. I invited them to follow me without saying where we were. They mounted the platform. Conseil, who was astonished at nothing, seemed to look upon it as quite natural that he should wake under a mountain, after having fallen asleep under the waves. But Ned Land thought of nothing but finding whether the cavern had any exit. After breakfast, about ten o'clock, we went down on to the mountain.

'Here we are, once more on land,' said Conseil.

'I do not call this land,' said the Canadian. 'And besides, we are not on it, but beneath it.'

Between the walls of the mountain and the waters of the lake lay a sandy shore, which, at its greatest breadth, measured five hundred feet. On this soil one might easily make the tour of the lake. But the base of the high partitions was stony ground, with volcanic blocks and enormous pumice stones lying in picturesque heaps. All these detached masses, covered with enamel, polished by the action of the subterraneous fires, shone resplendent by the light of our electric lantern. The mica dust from the shore, rising under our feet, flew like a cloud of sparks. The bottom now rose sensibly, and we soon arrived at long circuitous slopes, or inclined planes, which took us higher by degrees; but we were obliged to walk carefully among these conglomerates, bound by no cement, the feet slipping on the glassy trachyte, composed of crystal, felspar, and quartz.

The volcanic nature of this enormous excavation was confirmed on all sides, and I pointed it out to my companions.

'Picture to yourselves,' said I, 'what this crater must have been when filled with boiling lava, and when the level of the incandescent liquid rose to the orifice of the mountain, as though melted on the top of a hot plate.'

'I can picture it perfectly,' said Conseil. 'But, sir, will you tell me why the Great Architect has suspended operations, and how it is that the furnace is replaced by the quiet waters of the lake?'

'Most probably, Conseil, because some convulsion beneath the ocean produced that very opening which has served as a passage for the Nautilus. Then the waters of the Atlantic rushed into the interior of the mountain. There must have been a terrible struggle between the two elements, a struggle which ended in the victory of Neptune. But many ages have run out since then, and the submerged volcano is now a peaceable grotto.'

'Very well,' replied Ned Land; 'I accept the explanation, sir; but, in our own interests, I regret that the opening of which you speak was not made above the level of the sea.'

'But, friend Ned,' said Conseil, 'if the passage had not been under the sea, the Nautilus could not have gone through it.'

We continued ascending. The steps became more and more perpendicular and narrow. Deep excavations, which we were obliged to cross, cut them here and there; sloping masses had to be turned. We slid upon our knees and crawled along. But Conseil's dexterity and the Canadian's strength surmounted all obstacles. At a height of about thirty-one feet, the nature of the ground changed without becoming more practicable. To the conglomerate and trachyte succeeded black basalt, the first dispread in layers full of bubbles, the latter forming regular prisms, placed like a colonnade supporting the spring of the immense vault, an admirable specimen of natural architecture. Between the blocks of basalt wound long streams of lava, long since grown cold, encrusted with bituminous rays; and in some places there were spread large carpets of sulphur. A more powerful light shone through the upper crater, shedding a vague glimmer over these volcanic depressions for ever buried in the bosom of this extinguished mountain. But our upward march was soon stopped at a height of about two hundred and fifty feet by impassable obstacles. There was a complete vaulted arch overhanging us, and our ascent was changed to a circular walk. At the last change vegetable life began to struggle with the mineral. Some shrubs, and even some trees, grew from the fractures of the walls. I recognized some euphorbias, with the caustic sugar coming from them; heliotropes, quite incapable of justifying their name, sadly drooped their clusters of flowers, both their colour and perfume half gone. Here and there some chrysanthemums grew timidly at the foot of an aloe with long sickly-looking leaves. But between the streams of lava, I saw some little violets still slightly perfumed, and I admit that I smelt them with delight. Perfume is the soul of the flower, and sea flowers, those splendid hydrophytes, have no soul.

We had arrived at the foot of some sturdy dragon trees, which had pushed aside the rocks with their strong roots, when Ned Land exclaimed——

'Ah! sir, a hive! a hive!'

'A hive!' I replied, with a gesture of incredulity.

'Yes, a hive,' repeated the Canadian, 'and bees humming round it.'

I approached, and was bound to believe my own eyes. There, at a hole bored in one of the dragon trees, were some thousands of these ingenious insects, so common in all the Canaries, and whose produce is so much esteemed. Naturally enough, the Canadian wished to gather the honey, and I could not well oppose his wish. A quantity of dry leaves, mixed with sulphur, he lit with a spark from his flint, and he began to smoke out the bees. The humming ceased by degrees, and the hive eventually yielded several pounds of the sweetest honey, with which Ned Land filled his haversack.

'When I have mixed this honey with the paste of the artocarpus,' said he, 'I shall be able to offer you a succulent cake.'

'Upon my word,' said Conseil, 'it will be gingerbread.'

'Never mind the gingerbread,' said I; 'let us continue our interesting walk.'

At every turn of the path we were following, the lake appeared in all its length and breadth. The lantern lit up the whole of its peaceable surface which knew neither ripple nor wave. The Nautilus remained perfectly immovable. On the platform, and on the mountain, the ship's crew were working like black shadows clearly carved against the luminous atmosphere. We were now going round the highest crest of the first layers of rock which upheld the roof. I then saw that bees were not the only representatives of the animal kingdom in the interior of this volcano. Birds of prey hovered here and there in the shadows, or fled from their nests on the top of the rocks. There were sparrow hawks with white breasts, and kestrels, and down the slopes scampered, with their long legs, several fine fat bustards. I leave anyone to imagine the covetousness of the Canadian at the sight of this savoury game, and whether he did not regret having no gun. But he did his best to replace the lead by stones, after several fruitless attempts, he succeeded in wounding a magnificent bird. To say that he risked his life twenty times before reaching it, is but the truth; but he managed so well, that the creature joined the honey cakes in his bag. We were now obliged to descend towards the shore, the crest becoming impracticable. Above us the crater seemed to gape like the mouth of a well. From this place the sky could be clearly seen, and clouds, dissipated by the west wind, leaving behind them, even on the summit of the mountain, their misty remnants – certain proof that they were only moderately high, for the volcano did not rise more than eight hundred feet about the level of the ocean. Half an hour after the Canadian's last exploit we had regained the inner shore. Here the flora was represented by large carpets of marine crystal, a little umbelliferous plant very good to pickle, which also bears the name of pierce-stone, and sea-fennel. Conseil gathered some bundles of it. As to the fauna, it might be counted by thousands of crustacea of all sorts, lobsters, crabs, palæmons, spider crabs, chameleon shrimps, and a large number of shells, rockfish and limpets. Three-quarters of an hour later, we had finished our circuitous walk, and were on board. The crew had just finished loading the sodium, and the Nautilus could have left that instant. But Captain Nemo gave no order. Did he wish to wait until night, and leave the submarine passage secretly? Perhaps so. Whatever it might be, the next day, the Nautilus, having left its port, steered clear of all land at a few yards beneath the waves of the Atlantic.

Chapter Thirty-Five

The Sargasso Sea

THAT DAY THE NAUTILUS crossed a singular part of the Atlantic Ocean. No one can be ignorant of the existence of a current of warm water, known by the name of the Gulf Stream. After leaving the Gulf of Florida, we went in the direction of Spitzbergen. But before entering the Gulf of Mexico, about the forty-fifth degree of north latitude, this current divides into two arms, the principal one going towards the coast of Ireland and Norway, whilst the second bends to the south about the height of the Azores; then, touching the African shoe, and describing a lengthened oval, returns to the Antilles. This second arm – it is rather a collar than an arm – surrounds with its circles of warm water that portion of the cold, quiet, immovable ocean called the Sargasso Sea, a perfect lake in the open Atlantic: it takes no less than three years for the great current to pass round it. Such was the region the Nautilus was now visiting, a perfect meadow, a close carpet of seaweed, fucus, and tropical berries, so thick and so compact, that the stem of a vessel could hardly tear its way through it. And Captain Nemo, not wishing to entangle his screw in this herbaceous mass, kept some yards beneath the surface of the waves. The name Sargasso comes from the Spanish word 'sargazzo,' which signifies kelp. This kelp or varech, or berry-plant, is the principal formation of this immense bank. And this is the reason, according to the learned Maury, the author of 'The Physical Geography of the Globe,' why these hydrophytes unite in the peaceful basin of the Atlantic. The only explanation which can be given, he says, seems to me to result from the experience known to all the world. Place in a vase some fragments of cork or other floating body, and give to the water in the vase a circular movement, the scattered fragments will unite in a group in the centre of the liquid surface, that is to say, in the part least agitated. In the phenomenon we are considering, the Atlantic is the vase, the Gulf Stream the circular current, and the Sargasso Sea the central point at which the floating bodies unite.

I share Maury's opinion, and I was able to study the phenomenon in the very midst, where vessels rarely penetrate. Above us floated products of all kinds, heaped up among these brownish plants; trunks of trees torn from the Andes or the Rocky Mountains, and floated by the Amazon or the Mississippi; numerous wrecks, remains of keels, or ships' bottoms, side planks stove in, and so weighted with shells and barnacles, that they could not again rise to the surface. And time will one day justify Maury's other opinion, that these substances thus accumulated for ages, will become petrified by the action of the water, and will then form inexhaustible coal-mines – a precious reserve prepared by far-seeing Nature for the moment when man shall have exhausted the mines of continents.

In the midst of this inextricable mass of plants and seaweed, I noticed some charming pink halcyons and actiniæ, with their long tentacles trailing after them: medusæ, green, red, and blue, and the great rhyostoms of Cuvier, the large umbrella of which was bordered and festooned with violet.

All the day of the 22nd of February we passed in the Sargasso Sea, where such fish as are partial to marine plants and fuci find abundant nourishment. The next, the ocean had returned to its accustomed aspect. From this time for nineteen days, from the 23rd of February to the 12th of March, the Nautilus kept in the middle of the Atlantic, carrying us at a constant speed of a hundred leagues in twenty-four hours. Captain Nemo evidently intended accomplishing his submarine programme, and I imagined that that he intended, after doubling Cape Horn, to return to the Australian seas of the Pacific. Ned Land had cause for fear. In these large seas, void of islands, we could not attempt to leave the boat. Nor had we any means of opposing Captain Nemo's will. Our only course was to submit; but what we could neither gain by force nor cunning, I liked to think might be obtained by persuasion. This voyage ended, would he not consent to restore our liberty, under an oath never to reveal his existence? – an oath of honour which we should have religiously kept. But we must consider that delicate question with the captain. But was I free to claim this liberty? Had he not himself said from the beginning, in the firmest manner, that the secret of his life exacted from him our lasting imprisonment on board the Nautilus? And would not my four months' silence appear to him a tacit acceptance of our situation? And would not a return to the subject result in raising suspicions which might be hurtful to our projects, if at some future time a favourable opportunity offered to return to them.

During the nineteen days mentioned above, no incident of any note happened to signalize our voyage. I saw little of the captain; he was at work. In the library I often found his books left open, especially those on Natural History. My work on submarine depths, conned over by him, was covered with marginal notes, often contradicting my theories and systems; but the captain contented himself with thus purging my work; it was very rare for him to discuss it with me. Sometimes I heard the melancholy tones of his organ; but only at night, in the midst of the deepest obscurity when the Nautilus slept upon the deserted ocean. During this part of our voyage we sailed whole days on the surface of the waves. The sea seemed abandoned. A few sailing vessels, on the road to India, were making for the Cape of Good Hope. One day we were followed by the boats of a whaler, who, no doubt, took us for some enormous whale of great price; but Captain Nemo did not wish the worthy fellows to lose their time and trouble, so ended the chase by plunging under the water. Our navigation continued until the 13th of March; that day the Nautilus was employed in taking soundings, which greatly interested me. We had then made about 13,000 leagues since our departure from the high seas of the Pacific. The bearings gave us 45° 37' south latitude, and 37° 53' west longitude. It was the same water in which Captain Denham of the Herald sounded 7,000 fathoms without finding the bottom. There, too, Lieutenant Parker, of the American frigate Congress, could not touch the bottom with 15,140 fathoms. Captain Nemo intended by means of lateral planes placed at an angle of forty-five degrees with the water line of the Nautilus. Then the screw set to work at its maximum speed, its four blades beating the waves indescribable force. Under this powerful pressure the hull of the Nautilus quivered like a sonorous chord, and sank regularly under the water.

At 7,000 fathoms I saw some blackish tops rising from the midst of the waters; but these summits might belong to high mountains like the Himalayas or Mount Blanc, even higher; and the depth of the abyss remained incalculable. The Nautilus descended still lower, in spite of the great pressure. I felt the steel plates tremble at the fastenings of the bolts; its bars bent, its partitions groaned; the windows of the saloon seemed to curve under the pressure of the waters. And this firm structure would doubtless have yielded, if, as its Captain had said, it had not been capable of resistance like a solid block. In skirting the declivity of these rocks, lost under the water, I still saw some shells, some serpulæ and spinorbes, still living, and some specimens of asteriads. But soon this last representative of animal life disappeared; and at the depth of more than three leagues, the Nautilus had passed the limits of submarine existence, even as a balloon does when it rises above the respirable atmosphere. We had attained a depth of 16,000 yards (four leagues), and the sides of the Nautilus then bore a pressure of 1,600 atmospheres, that is to say, 3,200 pounds to each square two fifths of an inch of its surface.

'What a situation to be in!' I exclaimed. 'To overrun these deep regions where man has never trod! Look, captain, look at these magnificent rocks, these uninhabited grottoes, these lowest receptacles of the globe, where life is no longer possible! What unknown sights are here! Why should we be unable to preserve a remembrance of them?'

'Would you like to carry away more than the remembrance?' said Captain Nemo.

'What do you mean by those words?'

I mean to say that nothing is easier than to take a photographic view of this submarine region.'

I had not time to express my surprise at this new proposition, when, at Captain Nemo's call, an objective was brought into the saloon. Through the widely opened panel, the liquid mass was bright with electricity, which was distributed with such uniformity, that not a shadow, not a gradation, was to be seen in our manufactured light. The Nautilus remained motionless, the force of its screw subdued by the inclination of its planes: the instrument was propped on the bottom of the oceanic site, and in a few seconds we had obtained a perfect negative. I here give the positive, from which may be seen those primitive rocks, which have never looked upon the light of heaven; that lowest granite which forms the foundation of the globe; those deep grottoes, woven in the stony mass whose outlines were of such sharpness, and the border lines of which is marked in black, as if done by the brush of some Flemish artist. Beyond that again a horizon of mountains, an admirable undulating line, forming the prospective of the landscape. I cannot describe the effect of these smooth, black, polished rocks, without moss, without a spot, and of strange forms, standing solidly on the sandy carpet, which sparkled under the jets of our electric light.

But the operation being over, Captain Nemo said, 'Let us go up; we must not abuse our position, nor expose the Nautilus too long to such great pressure.'

'Go up again!' I exclaimed.

'Hold well on.'

I had not time to understand why the captain cautioned me thus, when I was thrown forward on the carpet. At a signal from the captain, its screw was shipped, and its blades raised vertically; the Nautilus shot into the air like a balloon, rising with stunning rapidity, and cutting the mass of waters with a sonorous agitation. Nothing was visible; and in four minutes it had shot through the four leagues which separated it from the ocean, and after emerging like a flying fish, fell, making the waves rebound to an enormous height.

Chapter Thirty-Six

Cachalots and Whales

DURING THE NIGHTS OF THE 13th and 14th of March, the Nautilus returned to its southerly course. I fancied that, when on a level with Cape Horn, he would turn the helm westward, in order to beat the Pacific seas, and so complete the tour of the world. He did nothing of the kind, but continued on his way to the southern regions. Where was he going to? To the pole? It was madness! I began to think that the captain's temerity justified Ned Land's fears. For some time past the Canadian had not spoken to me of his projects of flight; he was less communicative, almost silent. I could see that this lengthened imprisonment was weighing upon him, and I felt that rage was burning within him. When he met the captain, his eyes lit up with suppressed anger; and I feared that his natural violence would lead him into some extreme. That day, the 14th of March, Conseil and he came to me in my room. I inquired the cause of their visit.

'A simple question to ask you sir,' replied the Canadian.

'Speak, Ned.'

'How many men are there on board the Nautilus, do you think?'

'I cannot tell, my friend.'

'I should say that its working does not require a large crew.'

'Certainly, under existing conditions, ten men, at the most ought to be enough.'

'Well, why should there be any more?'

'Why?' I replied, looking fixedly at Ned Land, whose meaning was easy to guess. 'Because,' I added, 'if my surmises are correct, and if I have well understood the captain's existence, the Nautilus is not only a vessel: it is also a place of refuge for those who, like its commander, have broken every tie upon earth.'

'Perhaps so,' said Conseil; 'but, in any case, the Nautilus can only contain a certain number of men. Could not you, sir, estimate their maximum?'

'How, Conseil?'

'By calculation; given the size of the vessel, which you know, sir, and consequently the quantity of air it contains, knowing also how much each man expends at a breath, and comparing these results with the fact that the Nautilus is obliged to go to the surface every twenty-four hours.'

Conseil had not finished the sentence before I saw what he was driving at.

'I understand,' said I; 'but that calculation, though simple enough, can give but a very uncertain result.'

'Never mind,' said Ned Land, urgently.

'Here it is, then,' said I. 'In one hour each man consumes the oxygen contained in twenty gallons of air; and in twenty-four, that contained in 480 gallons. We must, therefore, find how many times 480 gallons of air the Nautilus contains.'

'Just so,' said Conseil.

'Oh,' I continued, 'the size of the Nautilus being 1,500 tons; and one ton holding 200 gallons, it contains 300,000 gallons of air, which divided by 480, gives a quotient of 625. Which means to say, strictly speaking, that the air contained in the Nautilus would suffice for 625 men for twenty-four hours.'

'Six hundred and twenty-five!' repeated Ned.

'But remember, that all of us, passengers, sailors, and officers included, would not form a tenth part of that number.'

'Still too many for three men,' murmured Conseil.

The Canadian shook his head, passed his hand across his forehead, and left the room without answering.

'Will you allow me to make one observation, sir?' said Conseil. 'Poor Ned is longing for everything that he cannot have. His past life is always present to him; everything that we are forbidden he regrets. His head is full of old recollections. And we must understand him. What has he to do here? Nothing; he is not learned like you, sir; and has not the same taste for the beauties of the sea that we have. He would risk everything to be able to go into a tavern in his own country.'

Certainly the monotony on board must seem intolerable to the Canadian, accustomed as he was to a life of liberty and activity. Events were rare which could rouse him to any show of spirit; but that day an event did happen which recalled the bright days of the harpooner. About eleven in the morning, being on the surface of the ocean, the Nautilus fell in with a troop of whales – an encounter which did not astonish me, knowing that these creatures, hunted to the death, had taken refuge in high latitudes.

We were seated on the platform, with a quiet sea. The month of October in those latitudes gave us some lovely autumnal days. It was the Canadian – he could not be mistaken – who signalled a whale on the eastern horizon. Looking attentively one might see its black back rise and fall with the waves five miles from the Nautilus.

'Ah!' exclaimed Ned Land, 'if I was on board a whaler now such a meeting would give me pleasure. It is one of large size. See with what strength its blow holes throw up columns of air and steam! Confound it, why am I bound to these steel plates?'

'What, Ned,' said I, 'you have not forgotten your old ideas of fishing?'

'Can a whale fisher ever forget his old trade, sir?' Can he ever tire of the emotions caused by such a chase?'

'You have never fished in these seas, Ned?'

'Never, sir; in the northern only, and as much in Behring as in Davis Straits.'

'Then the southern whale is still unknown to you. It is the Greenland whale you have hunted up to this time, and that would not risk passing through the warm waters of the equator. Whales are localized, according to their kinds, in certain seas which they never leave. And if one of these creatures went from Behring to Davis Straits, it must be simply because there is a passage from one sea to the other, either on the American or the Asiatic side.'

'In that case, as I have never fished in these seas, I do not know the kind of whale frequenting them.'

'I have told you, Ned.'

'A greater reason for making their acquaintance,' said Conseil.

'Look! Look!' exclaimed the Canadian, 'they approach; they aggravate me; they know that I cannot get at them!'

Ned stamped his feet. He had trembled, as he grasped an imaginary harpoon.

'Are these cetacea as large as those of the northern seas?' asked he.

'Very nearly, Ned.'

'Because I have seen large whales, sir, whales measuring a hundred feet. I have even been told that those of Hullamoch and Umgallick, of the Aleutian Islands, are sometimes a hundred and fifty feet long.'

'That seems to me to be an exaggeration. These creatures are only balænopterons, provided with dorsal fins; and, like the cachalots, are generally much smaller than the Greenland whale.'

'Ah!' exclaimed the Canadian, whose eyes had never left the ocean, 'they are coming nearer; they are in the same water as the Nautilus!'

Then returning to the conversation, he said——

'You spoke of the cachalot as a small creature. I have heard of gigantic ones. They are intelligent cetacea. It is said of some that they cover themselves with seaweed and fucus, and then are taken for islands. People encamp upon them, and settle there; light a fire,——'

'And build houses,' said Conseil.

'Yes, joker,' said Ned Land. 'And one fine day the creature plunges, carrying with it all the inhabitants to the bottom of the sea.'

'Something like the travels of Sinbad the Sailor,' I replied, laughing.

'Ah!' suddenly exclaimed Ned Land, 'it is not one whale: there are ten – there are twenty – it is a whole troop! And I not able to do anything! hands and feet tied!'

'But, friend Ned,' said Conseil, 'why do you not ask Captain Nemo's permission to chase them?'

Conseil had not finished his sentence when Ned Land had lowered himself through the panel to seek the captain. A few minutes afterwards the two appeared together on the platform.

Captain Nemo watched the troop of cetacea playing on the waters about a mile from the Nautilus.

'They are southern whales,' said he; 'there goes the fortune of a whole fleet of whalers.'

'Well, sir,' asked the Canadian, 'can I not chase them, if only to remind me of my old trade of harpooner?'

'And to what purpose?' replied Captain Nemo; 'only to destroy! We have nothing to do with whale oil on board.'

'But, sir,' continued the Canadian, 'in the Red Sea you allowed us to follow the dugong.'

'Then it was to procure fresh meat for my crew. Here it would be killing for killing's sake. I know that is a privilege reserved for man, but I do not approve of such a murderous pastime. In destroying the southern whale (like the Greenland whale, an inoffensive creature), your traders do a culpable action, Master Land. They have already depopulated the whole of Baffin's Bay, and are annihilating a class of useful animals. Leave the unfortunate cetacea alone. They have plenty of natural enemies, cachalots, swordfish, and sawfish, without your troubling them.'

The captain was right. The barbarous and inconsiderate greed of these fishermen will one day cause the disappearance of the last whale in the ocean. Ned Land whistled 'Yankee doodle' between his teeth, thrust his hands into his pockets, and turned his back upon us. But Captain Nemo watched the troop of cetacea, and addressing me, said——

'I was right in saying that whales had natural enemies enough, without counting man. These will have plenty to do before long. Do you see, M. Aronnax, about eight miles to leeward, those blackish moving points?'

'Yes, captain,' I replied.

'Those are cachalots – terrible animals, which I have sometimes met in troops of two or three hundred. As to *those*, they are cruel mischievous creatures; they would be right in exterminatng them.'

The Canadian turned quickly at the last words.

'Well, Captain,' said he, 'it is still time, in the interests of the whales.'

'It is useless to expose one's self, Professor. The Nautilus will disperse them. It is armed with a steel spur as good as Master Land's harpoon, I imagine.'

The Canadian did not put himself out enough to shrug his shoulders. Attack cetacea with blows of a spur! Who had ever heard of such a thing?

'Wait, M. Aronnax,' said Captain Nemo. 'We will show you something you have never yet seen. We have no pity for these ferocious creatures. They are nothing but mouth and teeth.'

Mouth and teeth! No one could better describe the macrocephalous cachalot, which is sometimes more than seventy-five feet long. Its enormous head occupies two thirds of its entire body. Better armed than the whale, whose upper jaw is furnished only with whalebone, it is supplied with twenty-five large tusks, about eight inches long, cylindrical and conical at the top, each weighing two pounds. It is in the upper part of this enormous head, in great cavities divided by cartilages, that is to be found from six to eight hundred pounds of that precious oil called spermaceti. The cachalot is a disagreeable creature, more tadpole than fish, according to Fredol's description. It is badly formed, the whole of its left side being (if we may say it), a 'failure,' and being only able to see with its right eye. But the formidable troop was nearing us. They had seen the whales and were preparing to attack them. One could judge beforehand that the cachalots would be victorious, not only because they were better built for attack than their inoffensive adversaries, but also because they could remain longer under water without coming to the surface. There was only just time to go to the help of the whales. The Nautilus went under water. Conseil, Ned Land, and I took our places before the window in the saloon, and Captain Nemo joined the pilot in his cage to work his apparatus as an engine of destruction. Soon I felt the beatings of the screw quicken, and our speed increased the battle between the cachalots and the whales had already begun when the Nautilus arrived. They did not at first show any fear at the sight of this new monster joining in the conflict. But they soon had to guard against its blows. What a battle! The Nautilus was nothing but a formidable harpoon, brandished by the hand of its captain. It hurled itself against the fleshy mass, passing through from one part to the other, leaving behind it two quivering halves of the animal. It could not feel the formidable blows from their tails upon its sides, nor the shock which it produced itself, much more. One cachalot killed, it ran at the next, tacked on the spot that it might not miss its prey, going forwards and backwards, answering to its helm, plunging when the cetacean dived into the deep waters, coming up with it when it returned to the surface, striking it front or sideways, cutting or tearing in all directions, and at any pace, piercing it with its terrible spur. What carnage! What noise on the surface of the waves! What sharp hissing, and what snorting peculiar to these enraged animals! In the midst of these waters, generally so peaceful, their tails made perfect billows. For one hour this wholesale massacre continued, from which the cachalots could not escape. Several times ten or twelve united tried to crush the Nautilus by their weight. From the window we could see their enormous mouths studded with tusks, and their formidable eyes. Ned Land could not contain himself, he threatened and swore at them. We could feel them clinging to our vessel like dogs worrying a wild boar in a copse. But the Nautilus, working its screw, carried them here and there, or to the upper levels of the ocean, without caring for their enormous weight, nor the powerful strain on the vessel. At length, the mass of cachalots broke up, the waves became quiet, and I felt that we were rising on the surface. The panel opened, and we hurried on to the platform. The sea was covered with mutilated bodies. A formidable explosion could not have divided and torn this fleshy mass with more violence. We were floating amid gigantic bodies, bluish on the back and white underneath, covered with enormous protuberances. Some terrified cachalots were flying towards the horizon. The waves were dyed red for several miles, and the Nautilus floated in a sea of blood. Captain Nemo joined us.

'Well, Master Land?' said he.

'Well, sir,' replied the Canadian, whose enthusiasm had somewhat calmed; 'it is a terrible spectacle, certainly. But I am not a butcher. I am a hunter, and I call this a butchery.'

'It is a massacre of mischievous creatures,' replied the captain; 'and the Nautilus is not a butcher's knife.'

'I like my harpoon better,' said the Canadian.

'Everyone to his own,' answered the captain, looking fixedly at Ned Land.

I feared he would commit some act of violence, which would end in sad consequences. But his anger was turned by the sight of a whale which the Nautilus had just come up with. The creature had not quite escaped from the cachalot's teeth. I recognized the southern whale by its flat head, which is entirely black. Anatomically, it is distinguished from the white whale and the North Cape whale by the seven cervical vertebræ, and it has two more ribs than its congeners. The unfortunate cetacean was lying on its side, riddled with holes from the bites, and quite dead. From its mutilated fin still hung a young whale which it could not save from the massacre. Its open mouth let the water flow in and out, murmuring like the waves breaking on the shore. Captain Nemo steered close to the corpse of the creature. Two of his men mounted its side, and I saw, not without surprise, that they were drawing from its breasts all the milk which they contained, that is to say, about two or three tons. The captain offered me a cup of the milk, which was still warm. I could not help showing my repugnance to the drink; but he assured me that it was excellent, and not to be distinguished from cow's milk. I tasted it, and was of his opinion. It was a useful reserve to us, for in the shape of salt butter or cheese it would form an agreeable variety from our ordinary food. From that day I noticed with uneasiness that Ned Land's ill-will towards Captain Nemo increased, and I resolved to watch the Canadian's gestures closely.

Chapter Thirty-Seven

The Iceberg

THE NAUTILUS WAS STEADILY pursuing its southerly course, following the fiftieth meridian with considerable speed. Did he wish to reach the pole? I did not think so, for every attempt to reach that point had hitherto failed. Again the season was far advanced, for in the antarctic regions, the 13th of March corresponds with the 13th of September of northern regions, which begin at the equinoctial season. On the 14th of March I saw floating ice in latitude 55°, merely pale bits of debris from twenty to twenty-five feet long, forming banks over which the sea curled. The Nautilus remained on the surface of the ocean. Ned Land, who had fished in the arctic seas, was familiar with its icebergs; but Conseil and I admired them for the first time. In the atmosphere towards the southern horizon stretched a white dazzling band. English whalers have given it the name of 'ice blink'. However thick the clouds may be, it is always visible, and announces the presence of an ice pack or bank. Accordingly, larger blocks soon appeared, whose brilliancy changed with the caprices of the fog. Some of these masses showed green veins, as if long undulating lines had been traced with sulphate of copper; others resembled enormous amethysts with the light shining through them. Some reflected the light of day upon a thousand crystal facets. Others shaded with vivid calcareous reflections resembled a perfect town of marble. The more we neared the south, the more these floating islands increased both in number and importance.

At the sixtieth degree of latitude, every pass had disappeared. But seeking carefully, Captain Nemo soon found a narrow opening, through which he boldly slipped, knowing that it would close behind him. Thus, guided by this clever hand, the Nautilus passed through all the ice with a precision which quite charmed Conseil; icebergs or mountains, ice-fields or smooth plains, seeming to have no limits, drift ice or floating ice-packs, or plains broken up, called *palchs* when they are circular, and streams when they are made up of long strips. The temperature was very low; the thermometer exposed to the air marked two or three degrees below zero, but we were calmly clad with fur, at the expense of the sea-bear and seal. The interior of the Nautilus, warmed regularly by its electric apparatus, defied the most intense cold. Besides, it would only have been necessary to go some yards beneath the waves to find a more bearable temperature. Two months earlier we should have had perpetual daylight in these latitudes; but already we had three or four hours of night, and by and by there would be six months of darkness in these circumpolar regions. On the 15th of March we were in the latitude of New Shetland and South Orkney. The captain told me that formerly numerous tribes of seals inhabited them; but that English and American whalers, in their rage for destruction, massacred both old and young; thus where there was once life and animation, they had left silence and death.

About eight o'clock on the morning of the 16th of March, the Nautilus, following the fifty-fifth meridian, cut the antarctic polar circle. Ice surrounded us on all sides, and closed the horizon. But Captain Nemo went from one opening to another, still going higher. I cannot express my astonishment at the beauties of these new regions. The ice took most surprising forms. Here the grouping formed an oriental town, with innumerable mosques and minarets; there a fallen city thrown to the earth, as it were, by some convulsion of Nature. The whole aspect was constantly changed by the oblique rays of the sun, or lost in the greyish fog amidst hurricanes of snow. Detonations and falls were heard on all sides, great overthrows of icebergs, which altered the whole landscape like a diorama. Often seeing no exit, I thought we were definitely prisoners; but instinct guiding him at the slightest indication, Captain Nemo would discover a new pass. He was never mistaken when he saw the thin threads of bluish water trickling along the ice-fields; and I had no doubt that he had already ventured into the midst of these antarctic seas before. On the 16th of March, however, the ice-fields absolutely blocked our road. It was not the iceberg itself, as yet, but vast fields cemented by the cold. But this obstacle could not stop Captain Nemo: he hurled himself against it with frightful violence. The Nautilus entered the brittle mass like a wedge, and split it with frightful crackings. It was the battering ram of the ancients hurled by infinite strength. The ice thrown high in the air, fell like hail around us. By its own power of impulsion our apparatus made a canal for itself; sometimes carried away by its own impetus it lodged on the ice-field, crushing it with its weight, and sometimes buried beneath it, dividing it by a simple pitching movement, producing large rents in it. Violent gales assailed us at the time, accompanied by thick fogs, through which, from one end of the platform to the other, we could see nothing. The wind blew sharply from all points of the compass, and the snow lay in such hard heaps that we had to break it with blows of a pickaxe. The temperature was always at five degrees below zero; every outward part of the Nautilus was covered with ice. A rigged vessel could never have worked its way there, for all the rigging would have been entangled in the blocked-up gorges. A vessel without sails, with electricity for its motive power, and wanting no coal, could alone brave such high latitudes. At length, on the 18th of March, after many useless assaults, the Nautilus was positively blocked. It was no longer either streams, packs, or ice-fields, but an interminable and immovable barrier, formed by mountains soldered together.

'An iceberg!' said the Canadian to me.

I knew that to Ned Land, as well as to all other navigators who had preceded us, this was an inevitable obstacle. The sun appearing for an instant at noon, Captain Nemo took an observation as near as possible, which gave our situation at 51° 30' longitude and 67° 39' of south latitude. We had advanced one degree more in this antarctic region. Of the liquid surface of the sea there was no longer a glimpse. Under the spur of the Nautilus lay stretched a vast plain, entangled with confused blocks. Here and there sharp points, and slender needles rising to a height of 200 feet; further on a steep shore, hewn as it were with an axe, and clothed with greyish tints; huge mirrors, reflecting a few rays of sunshine, half drowned in the fog. And over this desolate face of Nature a stern silence reigned, scarcely broken by the flapping of the wings of petrels and puffins.

Everything was frozen – even the noise. The Nautilus was then obliged to stop in
its adventurous course amid these fields of ice. In spite of our efforts, in spite of
the powerful means employed to break up the ice, the Nautilus remained
immovable. Generally, when we can proceed no further, we have return still
open to us; but here return was as impossible as advance, for every pass had
closed behind us; and for a few moments when we were stationary, we were
likely to be entirely blocked, which did, indeed, happen about two o'clock in
the afternoon, the fresh ice forming around its sides with astonishing rapidity. I
was obliged to admit that Captain Nemo was more than imprudent. I was on the
platform at that moment. The captain had been observing our situation for some
time past, when he said to me——

'Well, sir, what do you think of this?'

'I think that we are caught, captain.'

'So, M. Aronnax, you really think that the Nautilus cannot disengage itself?'

'With difficulty, captain; for the season is already too far advanced for you to
reckon on the breaking up of the ice.'

'Ah! sir,' said Captain Nemo, in an ironical tone, 'you will always be the
same. You see nothing but difficulties and obstacles. I affirm that not only can
the Nautilus disengage itself, but also that it can go further still.'

'Further to the south?' I asked, looking at the captain.

'Yes, sir; it shall go to the pole.'

'To the pole!' I exclaimed, unable to repress a gesture of incredulity.

'Yes,' replied the captain, coldly, 'to the antarctic pole – to that unknown
point from whence springs every meridian of the globe. *You* know whether I can
do as I please with the Nautilus!'

Yes, I knew that. I knew that this man was bold, even to rashness. But to
conquer those obstacles which bristled round the sough pole, rendering it more
inaccessible than the north, which had not yet been reached by the boldest
navigators – was it not a mad enterprise, one which only a maniac would have
conceived? It then came into my head to ask Captain Nemo if he had ever
discovered that pole which had never yet been trodden by a human creature?

'No, sir,' he replied; 'but we will discover it together. Where others have
failed, *I* will not fail. I have never yet led my Nautilus so far into southern seas;
but, I repeat, it shall go further yet.'

'I can well believe you, captain,' said I, in a slightly ironical tone. 'I believe
you! Let us go ahead! There are no obstacles for us! Let us smash this iceberg!
Let us blow it up; and if it resists, let us give the Nautilus wings to fly over it!'

'Over it, sir!' said Captain Nemo, quietly; 'no, not *over* it, but *under* it!'

'Under it!' I exclaimed, a sudden idea of the captain's projects flashing upon
my mind. I understood; the wonderful qualities of the Nautilus were going to
serve us in this superhuman enterprise.

'I see we are beginning to understand one another, sir,' said the captain, half
smiling. 'You begin to see the possibility – I should say the success – of this
attempt. That which is impossible for an ordinary vessel, is easy to the Nautilus.
If a continent lies beneath the pole, it must stop before the continent; but if, on
the contrary, the pole is washed by open sea, it will go even to the pole.'

'Certainly,' said I, carried away by the captain's reasoning; 'if the surface of
the sea is solidified by the ice, the lower depths are free by the providential law
which has placed the maximum of density of the waters of the ocean one degree

higher than freezing point; and, if I am not mistaken, the portion of this iceberg which is above the water, is as four to one to that which is below.'

'Very nearly, sir; for one foot of iceberg above the sea there are three below it. If these ice mountains are not more than 300 feet above the surface, they are not more than 900 beneath. And what are 900 feet to the Nautilus?'

'Nothing, sir.'

'It could even seek at greater depths that uniform temperature of sea-water, and there brave with impunity the thirty or forty degrees of surface cold.'

'Just so, sir – just so,' I replied, getting animated.

'The only difficulty,' continued Captain Nemo, 'is that of remaining several days without renewing our provision of air.'

'Is that all? The Nautilus has vast reservoirs; we can fill them, and they will supply us with all the oxygen we want.'

'Well thought of, M. Aronnax,' replied the captain, smiling. 'But not wishing you to accuse me of rashness, I will first give you all my objections.'

'Have you any more to make?'

'Only one. It is possible, if the sea exists at the south pole, that it may be covered; and, consequently, we shall be unable to come to the surface.'

'Good, sir! but do you forget that the Nautilus is armed with a powerful spur, and could we not sent it diagonally against these fields of ice, which would open at the shock.'

'Ah! sir, you are full of ideas today.'

'Besides, captain,' I added, enthusiastically, 'why should we not find the sea open at the south pole as well as at the north? The frozen poles and the poles of the earth do not coincide, either in the southern or in the northern regions; and until it is proved to the contrary, we may suppose either a continent or an ocean free from ice at these two points of the globe.'

'I think so too, M. Aronnax,' replied Captain Nemo. 'I only wish you to observe that, after having made so many objections to my project, you are now crushing me with arguments in its favour!'

The preparations for this audacious attempt now began. The powerful pumps of the Nautilus were working air into the reservoirs and storing it at high pressure. About four o'clock, Captain Nemo announced the closing of the panels on the platform. I threw one last look at the massive iceberg which we were going to cross. The weather was clear, the atmosphere pure enough, the cold very great, being twelve degrees below zero; but the wind having gone down, this temperature was not so unbearable. About ten men mounted the sides of the Nautilus, armed with pickaxes to break the ice around the vessel, which was soon free. The operation was quickly performed, for the fresh ice was still very thin. We all went below. The usual reservoirs were filled with the newly liberated water, and the Nautilus soon descended. I had taken my place with Conseil in the saloon; through the open window we could see the lower beds of the Southern Ocean. The thermometer went up, the needle of the compass deviated on the dial. At about 900 feet, as Captain Nemo had foreseen, we were floating beneath the undulating bottom of the iceberg. But the Nautilus went lower still – it went to the depth of four hundred fathoms. The temperature of the water at the surface showed twelve degrees, it was now only eleven; we had gained two. I need not say the temperature of the Nautilus was raised by its heating apparatus to a much higher degree; every manœuvre was accomplished with wonderful precision.

'We shall pass it, if you please, sir,' said Conseil.

'I believe we shall,' I said, in a tone of firm conviction.

In this open sea, the Nautilus had taken its course direct to the pole, without leaving the fifty-second meridian. From 67° 30' to 90°, twenty-two degrees and a half of latitude remained to travel; that is, about five hundred leagues. The Nautilus kept up a mean speed of twenty-six miles an hour – the speed of an express train. If that was kept up, in forty hours we should reach the pole.

For a part of the night the novelty of the situation kept us at the window. The sea was lit with the electric lantern; but it was deserted; fishes did not sojourn in these imprisoned water: they only found there a passage to take them from the antarctic ocean to the open polar sea. Our pace was rapid; we could feel it by the quivering of the long steel body. About two in the morning, I took some hours' repose, and Conseil did the same. In crossing the waist I did not meet Captain Nemo: I supposed him to be in the pilot's cage. The next morning, the 19th of March, I took my post once more in the saloon. The electric log told me that the speed of the Nautilus had been slackened. It was then going towards the surface; but prudently emptying its reservoirs very slowly. My heart beat fast. Were we going to emerge and regain the open polar atmosphere? No! A shock told me that the Nautilus had struck the bottom of the iceberg, still very thick, judging from the deadened sound. We had indeed 'struck,' to use a sea expression, but in an inverse sense, and at a thousand feet deep this would give three thousand feet of ice above us; one thousand being above the water-mark. The iceberg was then higher than at its borders – not a very reassuring fact. Several times that day the Nautilus tried again, and every time it struck the wall which lay like a ceiling above it. Sometimes it met with but 900 yards, only 200 of which rose above the surface. It was twice the height it was when the Nautilus had gone under the waves. I carefully noted the different depths, and thus obtained a submarine profile of the chain as it was developed under the water. That night no change had taken place in our situation. Still ice between four and five hundred yards in depth! It was evidently diminishing, but still what a thickness between us and the surface of the ocean! It was then eight. According to the daily custom on board the Nautilus, its air should have been renewed four hours ago; but I did not suffer much, although Captain Nemo had not yet made any demand upon his reserve of oxygen. My sleep was painful that night; hope and fear besieged me by turns: I rose several times. The groping of the Nautilus continued. About three in the morning, I noticed that the lower surface of the iceberg was only about fifty feet deep. One hundred and fifty feet now separated us from the surface of the waters. The iceberg was by degrees becoming an ice-field, the mountain a plain. My eyes never left the manometer. We were still rising diagonally to the surface, which sparkled under the electric rays. The iceberg was stretching both above and beneath into lengthening slopes; mile after mile it was getting thinner. At length, at six in the morning of that memorable day, the 19th of March, the door of the saloon opened, and Captain Nemo appeared.

'The sea is open!' was all he said.

Chapter Thirty-Eight
The South Pole

I RUSHED ON TO THE PLATFORM. Yes! The open sea, with but a few scattered pieces of ice and moving icebergs – a long stretch of sea; a world of birds in the air, and myriads of fishes under those waters, which varied from intense blue to olive green, according to the bottom. The thermometer marked three degrees centigrade above zero. It was comparatively spring, shut up as we were behind the iceberg, whose lengthened mass was dimly seen on our northern horizon.

'Are we at the pole?' I asked the captain, with a beating heart.

'I do not know,' he replied. 'At noon I will take our bearings.'

'But will the sun show himself through this fog?' said I, looking at the leaden sky.

'However little it shows, it will be enough,' replied the captain.

About ten miles south, a solitary island rose to a height of one hundred and four yards. We made for it, but carefully, for the sea might be strewn with banks. One hour afterwards we had reached it, two hours later we had made the round of it. It measured four or five miles in circumference. A narrow canal separated it from a considerable stretch of land, perhaps a continent, for we could not see its limits. The existence of this land seemed to give some colour to Maury's hypothesis. The ingenious American has remarked, that between the south pole and the sixtieth parallel, the sea is covered with floating ice of enormous size, which is never met with in the North Atlantic. From this fact he has drawn the conclusion that the antarctic circle encloses considerable continents, as icebergs cannot form in open sea, but only on the coasts. According to these calculations, the mass of ice surrounding the southern pole forms a vast cap, the circumference of which must be, at least, 2,500 miles. But the Nautilus, for fear of running aground, had stopped about three cables' length from a strand over which reared a superb heap of rocks. The boat was launched; the captain, two of his men bearing instruments, Conseil, and myself, were in it. It was ten in the morning. I had not seen Ned Land. Doubtless the Canadian did not wish to admit the presence of the south pole. A few strokes of the oar brought us to the sand, where we ran ashore. Conseil was going to jump on to the land, when I held him back.

'Sir,' said I to Captain Nemo, 'to you belongs the honour of first setting foot on this land.'

'Yes, sir,' said the captain; 'and if I do not hesitate to tread this south pole, it is because, up to this time, no human being has left a trace there.'

Saying this, he jumped lightly on to the sand. His heart beat with emotion. He climbed a rock, sloping to a little promontory, and there, with his arms crossed, mute and motionless, and with an eager look, he seemed to take possession of these southern regions. After five minutes passed in this ecstasy, he turned to us.

'When you like, sir.'

I landed, followed by Conseil, leaving the two men in the boat. For a long way the soil was composed of a reddish, sandy stone, something like crushed brick, scoriæ, streams of lava, and pumice stones. One could not mistake its volcanic origin. In some parts, slight curls of smoke emitted a sulphurous smell, proving that the internal fires had lost nothing of their expansive powers, though, having climbed a high acclivity, I could see no volcano for a radius of several miles. We know that in those antarctic countries, James Ross found two craters, the Erebus and Terror, in full activity, on the 167th meridian, latitude 77° 32′. The vegetation of this desolate continent seemed to me much restricted. Some lichens of the species unsnea melanoxantha lay upon the black rocks; some microscopic plants, rudimentary diatomas, a kind of cells, placed between two quartz shells; long purple and scarlet fucus, supported on little swimming bladders, which the breaking of the waves brought to the shore. These constituted the meagre flora of this region. The shore was strewn with molluscs, little mussels, limpets, smooth bucards in the shape of a heart, and particularly some clios, with oblong membraneous bodies, the head of which was formed of two rounded lobes. I also saw myriads of northern clios, one and a quarter inches long, of which a whale would swallow a whole world at a mouthful; and some charming pteropods, perfect sea butterflies, animating the waters on the skirts of the shore.

Amongst other zoophytes, there appeared on the high bottoms some coral shrubs, of that kind which, according to James Ross, live in the antarctic seas to the depth of more than 1,000 yards. Then there were little kingfishers, belonging to the species procellaria pelagica, as well as a large number of asteriads, peculiar to these climates, and starfish studding the soil. But where life abounded most was in the air. There thousands of birds fluttered and flew of all kinds, deafening us with their cries; others crowded the rocks, looking at us as we passed by without fear, and pressing familiarly close by our feet. There were penguins, so agile in the water, that they have been taken for the rapid bonitos, heavy and awkward as they are on the ground; they were uttering harsh cries, a large assembly, sober in gesture, but extravagant in clamour. Amongst the birds I noticed the chionis, of the long-legged family, as large as pigeons, white, with a short conical beak, and the eye framed in a red circle. Conseil laid in a stock of them, for these winged creatures, properly prepared, make an agreeable meat. Albatrosses passed in the air (the expanse of their wings being at least four yards and a half), and justly called the vultures of the ocean; some gigantic petrels, and some damiers, a kind of small duck, the under part of whose body is black and white; then there were a whole series of petrels, some whitish, with brown-bordered wings, others blue, peculiar to the antarctic seas, and so oily, as I told Conseil that the inhabitants of the Ferroe Islands had nothing to do before lighting them, but to put a wick in.

'A little more,' said Conseil, 'and they would be perfect lamps! After that, we cannot expect Nature to have previously furnished them with wicks!'

About half a mile further on, the soil was riddled with ruff's nests, a sort of laying ground, out of which many birds were issuing. Captain Nemo had some hundreds hunted. They uttered a cry like the braying of an ass, were about the size of a goose, slate colour on the body, white beneath, with a yellow line round their throats; they allowed themselves to be killed with a stone, never trying to escape. But the fog did not lift, and at eleven the sun had not yet shown itself. Its absence made me uneasy. Without it no observations were possible. How then could we decide whether we had reached the pole? When I rejoined Captain Nemo, I found him leaning on a piece of rock, silently watching the sky. He seemed impatient and vexed. But what was to be done? This rash and powerful man could not command the sun as he did the sea. Noon arrived without the orb of day showing itself for an instant. We could not even tell its position behind the curtain of fog; and soon the fog turned to snow.

'Till tomorrow,' said the captain, quietly, and we returned to the Nautilus amid these atmospheric disturbances.

The tempest of snow continued till the next day. It was impossible to remain on the platform. From the saloon, where I was taking notes of incidents happening during this excursion to the polar continent, I could hear the cries of petrels and albatrosses sporting in the midst of this violent storm. The Nautilus did not remain motionless, but skirted the coast, advancing ten miles more to the south in the half light left by the sun as it skirted the edge of the horizon. The next day, the 20th of March, the snow had ceased. The cold was a little greater, the thermometer showing two degrees below zero. The fog was rising, and I hoped that that day our observations might be taken. Captain Nemo not having yet appeared, the boat took Conseil and myself to land. The soil was still of the same volcanic nature; everywhere were traces of lava, scoriæ, and basalt; but the crater which had vomited them I could not see. Here, as lower down, this continent was alive with myriads of birds. But their rule was now divided with large troops of sea-mammals, looking at us with their soft eyes. There were several kinds of seals, some stretched on the earth, some on flakes of ice, many going in and out of the sea. They did not flee at our approach, never having anything to do with man; and I reckoned that there were provisions there for hundreds of vessels.

'Sir,' said Conseil, 'will you tell me the names of these creatures?'

'They are seals and morses.'

It was now eight in the morning. Four hours remained to us before the sun could be observed with advantage. I directed our steps towards a vast bay cut in the steep granite shore. There, I can aver that earth and ice were lost to sight by the numbers of sea-mammals covering them, and I involuntarily sought for old Proteus, the mythological shepherd who watched these immense flocks of Neptune. There were more seals than anything else, forming distinct groups, male and female, the father watching over his family, the mother suckling her little ones, some already strong enough to go a few steps. When they wished to change their place, they took little jumps, made by the contraction of their bodies, and helped awkwardly enough by their imperfect fin, which, as with the lamantin, their congener, forms a perfect forearm. I should say that, in the water, which is their element – the spine of these creatures is flexible – with smooth and close skin, and webbed feet, they swim admirably. In resting on the earth they take the most graceful attitudes. Thus the ancients, observing their soft and expressive looks, which cannot be surpassed by the most beautiful look a woman can give, their clear voluptuous eyes, their charming positions, and the poetry of their manners, metamorphosed them, the male into a triton and the female into a mermaid. I made Conseil notice the considerable development of the lobes of the brain in these interesting cetaceans. No mammal, except man, has such a quantity of cerebral matter; they are also capable of receiving a certain amount of education, are easily domesticated, and I think, with other naturalists, that, if properly taught, they would be of great service as fishing-dogs. The greater part of them slept on the rocks or on the sand. Amongst these seals, properly so called, which have no external ears (in which they differ from the otter, whose ears are prominent), I noticed several varieties of stenorhynchi about three yards long, with a white coat, bulldog heads, armed with teeth in both jaws, four incisors at the top and four at the bottom, and two large canine teeth in the shape of a 'fleur de lis'. Amongst them glided sea-elephants, a kind of seal, with short flexible trunks. The giants of this species measured twenty feet round, and ten yards and a half in length; but they did not move as we approached.

'These creatures are not dangerous?' asked Conseil.

'No; not unless you attack them. When they have to defend their young, their rage is terrible, and it is not uncommon for them to break the fishing-boats to pieces.'

'They are quite right,' said Conseil.

'I do not say they are not.'

Two miles further on we were stopped by the promontory which shelters the bay from the southerly winds. Beyond it we heard loud bellowings such as a troop of ruminants would produce.

'Good!' said Conseil; 'a concert of bulls!'

'No; a concert of morses.'

'They are fighting!'

'They are either fighting or playing.'

We now began to climb the blackish rocks, amid unforeseen stumbles, and over stones which the ice made slippery. More than once I rolled over at the expense of my loins. Conseil, more prudent or more steady, did not stumble, and helped me up, saying——

'If, sir, you would have the kindness to take wider steps, you would preserve your equilibrium better.'

Arrived at the upper ridge of the promontory, I saw a vast white plain covered with morses. They were playing amongst themselves, and what we heard were bellowings of pleasure, not anger.

As I passed near these curious animals, I could examine them leisurely, for they did not move. Their skins were thick and rugged, of a yellowish tint, approaching to red; their hair was short and scant. Some of them were four yards and a quarter long. Quieter, and less timid than their congeners of the north, they did not, like them, place sentinels round the outskirts of their encamp-ment. After examining this city of morses, I began to think of returning. It was eleven o'clock, and if Captain Nemo found the conditions favourable for observations, I wished to be present at the operation. We followed a narrow pathway running along the summit of the steep shore. At half past eleven we had reached the place where we landed. The boat had run aground bringing the captain. I saw him standing on a block of basalt, his instruments near him, his eyes fixed on the northern horizon, near which the sun was then describing a lengthened curve. I took my place beside him, and waited without speaking. Noon arrived, and, as before, the sun did not appear. It was a fatality.

Observations were still wanting. If not accomplished tomorrow, we must give up all idea of taking any. We were indeed exactly at the 20th of March. Tomorrow, the 21st, would be the equinox; the sun would disappear behind the horizon for six months, and with its disappearance the long polar night would begin. Since the September equinox it had emerged from the northern horizon, ·rising by lengthened spirals up to the 21st December. At this period, the summer solstice of the northern regions, it had begun to descend; and tomorrow was to shed its last rays upon them. I communicated my fears and observations to Captain Nemo.

'You are right, M. Aronnax,' said he; 'If tomorrow I cannot take the altitude of the sun, I shall not be able to do it for six months. But precisely because chance has led me into these seas on the 21st of March, my bearings will be easy to take, if at twelve we can see the sun.'

'Why, captain?'

'Because then the orb of day describes such lengthened curves, that it is difficult to measure exactly its height above the horizon, and grave errors may be made with instruments.'

'What will you do then?'

'I shall only use my chronometer,' replied Captain Nemo. 'If tomorrow, the 21st of March, the disc of the sun, allowing for refraction, is exactly cut by the northern horizon, it will show that I am at the south pole.'

'Just so,' said I. 'But this statement is not mathematically correct, because the equinox does not necessarily begin at noon.'

'Very likely, sir; but the error will not be a hundred yards, and we do not want more. Till tomorrow then!'

Captain Nemo returned on board. Conseil and I remained to survey the shore, observing and studying until five o'clock. Then I went to bed, not, however, without invoking, like the Indian, the favour of the radiant orb. The next day, the 21st of March, at five in the morning, I mounted the platform. I found Captain Nemo there.

'The weather is lightening a little,' said he. 'I have some hope. After breakfast we will go on shore, and choose a post for observation.'

That point settled, I sought Ned Land. I wanted to take him with me. But the obstinate Canadian refused, and I saw that his taciturnity and his bad humour grew day by day. After all I was not sorry for his obstinacy under the circumstances. Indeed, there were too many seals on shore, and we ought not to lay such temptation in this unreflecting fisherman's way. Breakfast over, we went on shore. The Nautilus had gone some miles further up in the night. It was a whole league from the coast, above which reared a sharp peak about five hundred yards high. The boat took with me Captain Nemo, two men of the crew, and the instruments, which consisted of a chronometer, a telescope, and a barometer. While crossing, I saw numerous whales belonging to the three kinds peculiar to the southern seas; the whale, or the English 'right whale,' which has no dorsal fin; the 'humpback', or balænopteron, with reeved chest, and large whitish fins which, in spite of its name, do not form wings; and the fin-back, of a yellowish brown, the liveliest of all the cetacea. This powerful creature is heard a long way off when he throws to a great height columns of air and vapour, which look like whirlwinds of smoke. These different mammals were disporting themselves in troops in the quiet waters; and I could see that this basin of the antarctic pole served as a place of refuge to the cetacea too closely tracked by the hunters. I also noticed long whitish lines of salpæ, a kind of gregarious mollusc, and large medusæ floating between the reeds.

At nine we landed; the sky was brightening, the clouds were flying to the south, and the fog seemed to be leaving the cold surface of the waters. Captain Nemo went towards the peak, which he doubtless meant to be his obervatory. It was a painful ascent over the sharp lava and the pumice stones, in an atmosphere often impregnated with a sulphurous smell from the smoking cracks. For a man unaccustomed to walk on land, the captain climbed the steep slopes with an agility I never saw equalled, and which a hunter would have envied. We were two hours getting to the summit of this peak, which was half porphyry and half basalt. From thence we looked upon a vast sea, which, towards the north, distinctly traced its boundary line upon the sky. At our feet lay fields of dazzling whiteness. Over our heads a pale azure, free from fog. To the north the disc of the sun seemed like a ball of fire, already horned by the cutting of the horizon. From the bosom of the water rose sheaves of liquid jets by hundreds. In the distance lay the Nautilus like a cetacean asleep on the water. Behind us, to the south and east, an immense country, and a chaotic heap of rocks and ice, the limits of which were not visible. On arriving at the summit, Captain Nemo carefully took the mean height of the barometer, for he would have to consider that in taking his observations. At a quarter to twelve, the sun, then seen only by refraction, looked like a golden disc shedding its last rays upon this deserted continent, and seas which never man had yet ploughed. Captain Nemo, furnished with a lenticular glass, which, by means of a mirror, corrected the refraction, watched the orb sinking below the horizon by degrees, following a lengthened diagonal. I held the chronometer. My heart beat fast. If th' disappearance of the half-disc of the sun coincided with twelve o'clock on th' chronometer, we were at the pole itself.

'Twelve!' I exclaimed.

'The South Pole!' replied Captain Nemo, in a grave voice, handing me the glass, which showed the orb cut in exactly equal parts by the horizon.

I looked at the last rays crowning the peak, and the shadows mounting by degrees up its slopes. At that moment Captain Nemo, resting with his hand on my shoulder, said——

'I, Captain Nemo, on this 21st day of March 1868, have reached the south pole on the ninetieth degree; and I take possession of this part of the globe, equal to one-sixth of the known continents.'

'In whose name, captain?'

'In my own sir!'

Saying which, Captain Nemo unfurled a black banner, bearing an N in gold quartered on its bunting. Then turning towards the orb of day, whose last rays lapped the horizon of the sea, he exclaimed——

'Adieu, sun! Disappear, thou radiant orb! rest beneath this open sea, and let a night of six months spread its shadows over my new domains!'

Chapter Thirty-Nine

Accident or Incident?

THE NEXT DAY, THE 22ND OF MARCH, at six in the morning, preparations for departure were begun. The last gleams of twilight were melting into night. The cold was great; the constellations shone with wonderful intensity. In the zenith glittered that wondrous Southern Cross – the polar bear of antarctic regions. The thermometer showed twelve degrees below zero, and when the wind freshened, it was most biting. Flakes of ice increased on the open water. The sea seemed everywhere alike. Numerous blackish patches spread on the surface, showing the formation of fresh ice. Evidently the southern basin, frozen during the six winter months, was absolutely inaccessible. What became of the whales in that time? Doubtless they went beneath the icebergs, seeking more practicable seas. As to the seals and morses, accustomed to live in a hard climate, they remained on these icy shores. These creatures have the instinct to break holes in the ice-fields, and to keep them open. To these holes they come for breath; when the birds, driven away by the cold, have emigrated to the north, these sea mammals remain sole masters of the polar continent. But the reservoirs were filling with water, and the Nautilus was slowly descending. At 1,000 feet deep it stopped; its screw beat the waves, and it advanced straight towards the north, at a speed of fifteen miles an hour. Towards night it was already floating under the immense body of the iceberg. At three in the morning I was awakened by a violent shock. I sat up in my bed and listened in the darkness, when I was thrown into the middle of the room. The Nautilus, after having struck, had rebounded violently. I groped along the partition, and by the staircase to the saloon, which was lit by the luminous ceiling. The furniture was upset. Fortunately the windows were firmly set, and had held fast. The pictures on the starboard-side, from being no longer vertical, were clinging to the paper, whilst those of the port-side were hanging at least a foot from the wall. The Nautilus was lying on its starboard-side perfectly motionless. I heard footsteps, and a confusion of voices; but Captain Nemo did not appear. As I was leaving the saloon, Ned Land and Conseil entered.

'What is the matter?' said I, at once.

'I came to ask you, sir,' replied Conseil.

'Confound it!' exclaimed the Canadian, 'I know well enough! The Nautilus has struck; and judging by the way she lies, I do not think she will right herself as she did the first time in Torres Straits.'

'But,' I asked, 'has she at least come to the surface of the sea?'

'We do not know,' said Conseil.

'It is easy to decide,' I answered. I consulted the manometer. To my great surprise it showed a depth of more than 180 fathoms. 'What does that mean?' I exclaimed.

'We must ask Captain Nemo,' said Conseil.

'But where shall we find him?' said Ned Land.

'Follow me,' said I, to my companions.

We left the saloon. There was no one in the library. At the centre staircase, by the berths of the ship's crew, there was no one. I thought that Captain Nemo must be in the pilot's cage. It was best to wait. We all returned to the saloon. For twenty minutes we remained thus, trying to hear the slightest noise which might be made on board the Nautilus, when Captain Nemo entered. He seemed not to see us; his face, generally so impassive, showed signs of uneasiness. He watched the compass silently, then the manometer; and going to the planisphere, placed his finger on a spot representing the southern seas. I would not interrupt him; but, some minutes later, when he turned towards me, I said, using one of his own expressions in the Torres Straits——

'An incident, captain?'

'No, sir; an accident this time.'

'Serious?'

'Perhaps.'

'Is the danger immediate?'

'No.'

'The Nautilus has stranded?'

'Yes.'

'And this has happened – how?'

'From a caprice of Nature, not from the ignorance of man. Not a mistake has been made in the working. But we cannot prevent equilibrium from producing its effects. We may brave human laws, but we cannot resist natural ones.'

Captain Nemo had chosen a strange moment for uttering his philosophical reflection. On the whole, his answer helped me little.

'May I ask, sir, the cause of this accident?'

'An enormous block of ice, a whole mountain, has turned over,' he replied. 'When icebergs are undermined at their base by warmer water or reiterated shocks, their centre of gravity rises, and the whole thing turns over. This is what has happened; one of these blocks, as it fell, struck the Nautilus, then, gliding under the hull, raised it with irresistible force, bringing it into beds which are not so thick, where it is lying on its side.'

'But can we not get the Nautilus off by emptying its reservoirs, that it may regain its equilibrium?'

'That, sir, is being done at this moment. You can hear the pump working. Look at the needle of the manometer; it shows that the Nautilus is rising, but the block of ice is rising with it; and until some obstacle stops its ascending motion, our position cannot be altered.'

Indeed, the Nautilus still held the same position to starboard; doubtless it would right itself when the block stopped. But at this moment who knows if we may not strike the upper part of the iceberg, and if we may not be frightfully crushed between the two glassy surfaces? I reflected on all the consequences of our position. Captain Nemo never took his eyes off the manometer. Since the fall of the iceberg, the Nautilus had risen about a hundred and fifty feet, but it still made the same angle with the perpendicular. Suddenly a slight movement was felt in the hold. Evidently it was righting a little. Things hanging in the saloon were sensibly returning to their normal position. The partitions were nearing the upright. No one spoke. With beating hearts we watched and felt the straightening. The boards became horizontal under our feet. Ten minutes passed.

'At last we have righted!' I exclaimed.

'Yes,' said Captain Nemo, going to the door of the saloon.

'But are we floating?' I asked.

'Certainly,' he replied; 'since the reservoirs are not empty; and, when empty, the Nautilus must rise to the surface of the sea.'

We were in open sea; but at a distance of about ten yards, on either side of the Nautilus, rose a dazzling wall of ice. Above and beneath the same wall. Above, because the lower surface of the iceberg stretched over us like an immense ceiling. Beneath, because the overturned block, having slid by degrees, had found a resting place on the lateral walls, which kept it in that position. The Nautilus was really imprisoned in a perfect tunnel of ice more than twenty yards in breadth, filled with quiet water. It was easy to get out of it by going either forward or backward, and then make a free passage under the iceberg, some hundreds of yards deeper. The luminous ceiling had been extinguished, but the saloon was still resplendent with intense light. It was the powerful reflection from the glass partition sent violently back to the sheets of the lantern. I cannot describe the effect of the voltaic rays upon the great blocks so capriciously cut; upon every angle, every ridge, every facet was thrown a different light, according to the nature of the veins running through the ice; a dazzling mine of gems, particularly of sapphires, their blue rays crossing with the green of the emerald. Here and there were opal shades of wonderful softness, running through bright spots like diamonds of fire, the brilliancy of which the eye could not bear. The power of the lantern seemed increased a hundredfold, like a lamp through the lenticular plates of a first-class lighthouse.

'How beautiful! how beautiful!' cried Conseil.

'Yes,' I said, 'it is a wonderful sight. Is it not, Ned?'

'Yes, confound it! Yes,' answered Ned Land, 'it is superb! I am mad at being obliged to admit it. No one has ever seen anything like it; but the sight may cost us dear. And if I must say all, I think we are seeing here things which God never intended man to see.'

Ned was right, it was too beautiful. Suddenly a cry from Conseil made me turn.

'What is it?' I askd.

'Shut your eyes, sir! do not look, sir!' Saying which, Conseil clapped his hands over his eyes.

'But what is the matter, my boy?'

'I am dazzled, blinded.'

My eyes turned involuntarily towards the glass, but I could not stand the fire which seemed to devour them. I understood what had happened. The Nautilus had put on full speed. All the quiet lustre of the ice walls was at once changed into flashes of lightning. The fire from these myriads of diamonds was blinding. It required some time to calm our troubled looks. At last the hands were taken down.

'Faith, I should never have believed it,' said Conseil.

It was then five in the morning; and at that moment a shock was felt at the bows of the Nautilus. I knew that its spur had struck a block of ice. It must have been a false manæuvre, for this submarine tunnel, obstructed by blocks, was not very easy navigation. I thought that Captain Nemo, by changing his course, would either turn these obstacles, or else follow the windings of the tunnel. In any case, the road before us could not be entirely blocked. But, contrary to my expectations, the Nautilus took a decided retrograde motion.

'We are going backwards?' said Conseil.

'Yes,' I replied. 'This end of the tunnel can have no egress.'

'And then?'

'Then,' said I, 'the working is easy. We must go back again, and go out at the southern opening. That is all.'

In speaking thus, I wished to appear more confident than I really was. But the retrograde motion of the Nautilus was increasing; and, reversing the screw, it carried us at great speed.

'It will be a hindrance,' said Ned.

'What does it matter, some hours more or less, provided we get out at last?'

'Yes,' repeated Ned Land, 'provided we do get out at last!'

For a short time I walked from the saloon to the library. My companions were silent. I soon threw myself on an ottoman, and took a book, which my eyes overran mechanically. A quarter of an hour after, Conseil, approaching me, said, 'Is what you are reading very interesting, sir?'

'Very interesting!' I replied.

'I should think so, sir. It is your own book you are reading.'

'My book?'

And indeed I was holding in my hand the work on the 'Great Submarine Depths'. I did not even dream of it. I closed the book, and returned to my walk. Ned and Conseil rose to go.

'Stay here, my friends,' said I, detaining them. 'Let us remain together until were are out of this block.'

'As you please, sir,' Conseil replied.

Some hours passed. I often looked at the instruments hanging from the partition. The manometer showed that the Nautilus kept a constant depth of more than three hundred yards; the compass still pointed to the south; the log indicated a speed of twenty miles an hour, which, in such a cramped space, was very great. But Captain Nemo knew that he could not hasten too much, and that minutes were worth ages to us. At twenty-five minutes past eight a second shock took place, this time from behind. I turned pale. My companions were close by my side. I seized Conseil's hand. Our looks expressed our feelings better than words. At this moment the captain entered the saloon. I went up to him.

'Our course is barred southward?' I asked.

'Yes, sir. The iceberg has shifted, and closed every outlet.'

'We are blocked up, then?'

'Yes.'

Chapter Forty

Want of Air

THUS, AROUND THE NAUTILUS, above and below, was an impenetrable wall of ice. We were prisoners to the iceberg. I watched the captain. His countenance had resumed its habitual imperturbability.

'Gentlemen,' he said, calmly, 'there are two ways of dying in the circumstances in which we are placed.' (This inexplicable person had the air of a mathematical professor lecturing to his pupils.) 'The first is to be crushed; the second is to die of suffocation. I do not speak of the possibility of dying of hunger, for the supply of provisions in the Nautilus will certainly last longer than we shall. Let us then calculate our chances.'

'As to suffocation, captain,' I replied, 'that is not to be feared, because our reservoirs are full.'

'Just so; but they will only yield two days' supply of air. Now, for thirty-six hours we have been under the water, and already the heavy atmosphere of the Nautilus requires renewal. In forty-eight hours our reserve will be exhausted.'

'Well, captain, can we be delivered before forty-eighty hours?'

'We will attempt it, at least, by piercing the wall that surrounds us.'

'On which side?'

'Sound will tell us. I am going to run the Nautilus aground on the lower bank, and my men will attack the iceberg on the side that is least thick.'

Captain Nemo went out. Soon I discovered by a hissing noise that the water was entering the reservoirs. The Nautilus sank slowly, and rested on the ice at a depth of 350 yards, the depth at which the lower bank was immersed.

'My friends,' I said, 'our situation is serious, but I rely on your courage and energy.'

'Sir,' replied the Canadian, 'I am ready to do anything for the general safety.'

'Good! Ned,' and I held out my hand to the Canadian.

'I will add,' he continued, 'that being as handy with the pickaxe as the harpoon, if I can be useful to the captain, he can command my services.'

'He will not refuse your help. Come, Ned?'

I led him to the room where the crew of the Nautilus were putting on their cork-jackets. I told the captain of Ned's proposal, which he accepted. The Canadian put on his sea costume, and was ready as soon as his companions. When Ned was dressed, I re-entered the drawing-room, where the panes of glass were open, and, posted near Conseil, I examined the ambient beds that supported the Nautilus. Some instants after, we saw a dozen of the crew set foot on the bank of ice, and among them Ned Land, easily known by his stature. Captain Nemo was with them. Before proceeding to dig the walls, he took the soundings, to be sure of working in the right direction. Long sounding lines were sunk in the side walls, but after fifteen yards they were again stopped by the thick wall. It was useless to attack it on the ceiling-like surface, since the iceberg itself measured more than 400 yards in height. Captain Nemo then sounded the lower surface. There ten yards of wall separated us from the water, so great was the thickness of the ice-field. It was necessary, therefore, to cut from it a piece equal in extent to the waterline of the Nautilus. There were about 6,000 cubic yards to detach, so as to dig a hole by which we could descend to the ice-field. The work was begun immediately, and carried on with indefatigable energy. Instead of digging round the Nautilus, which would have involved greater difficulty, Captain Nemo had an immense trench made at eight yards from the port quarter. Then the men set to work simultaneously with their screws, on several points of its circumference. Presently the pickaxe attacked this compact matter vigorously, and large blocks were detached from the mass. By a curious effect of specific gravity, these blocks, lighter than water, fled, so to speak, to the vault of the tunnel, that increased in thickness at the top in proportion as it diminished at the base. But that mattered little, so long as the lower part grew thinner. After two hours' hard work, Ned Land came in exhausted. He and his comrades were replaced by new workers, whom Conseil and I joined. The second lieutenant of the Nautilus superintended us. The water seemed singularly cold, but I soon got warm handling the pickaxe. My movements were free enough, although they were made under a pressure of thirty atmospheres. When I re-entered, after working two hours, to take some food and rest, I found a perceptible difference between the pure fluid with which the Rouquayrol engine supplied me, and the atmosphere of the Nautilus, already changed with carbonic acid. The air had not been renewed for forty-eight hours, and its vivifying qualities were considerably enfeebled. However, after a lapse of twelve hours, we had only raised a block of ice one yard thick, on the marked surface, which was about 600 cubic yards! Reckoning that it took twelve hours to accomplish this much, it would take five nights and four days to bring this enterprise to a satisfactory conclusion. Five nights and four days! And we have only air enough for two days in the reservoirs! 'Without taking into account,' said Ned, 'that, even if we get out of this infernal prison, we shall also be imprisoned under the iceberg, shut out from all possible communication with the atmosphere.' True enough! Who could then foresee the minimum of time necessary for our deliverance? We might be suffocated before the Nautilus could regain the surface of the waves? Was it destined to perish in this ice-tomb, with all those it enclosed? The situation was terrible. But every one had looked the danger in the face, and each was determined to do his duty to the last.

As I expected, during the night a new block a yard square was carried away, and still further sank the immense hollow. But in the morning when, dressed in my cork-jacket, I traversed the slushy mass at a temperature of six or seven degrees below zero, I remarked that the side walls were gradually closing in. The beds of water farthest from the trench, that were not warmed by the men's mere work, showed a tendency to solidification. In presence of this new and imminent danger, what would become of our chances of safety, and how hinder the solidification of this liquid medium, that would burst the partitions of the Nautilus like glass?

I did not tell my companions of this new danger. What was the good of damping the energy they displayed in the painful work of escape? But when I went on board again, I told Captain Nemo of this grave complication.

'I know it,' he said, in that calm tone which could counteract the most terrible apprehensions. 'It is one danger more; but I see no way of escaping it; the only chance of safety is to go quicker than solidification. We must be beforehand with it, that is all.'

On this day for several hours I used my pickaxe vigorously. The work kept me up. Besides, to work was to quit the Nautilus, and breathe directly the pure air drawn from the reservoirs, and supplied by our apparatus, and to quit the impoverished and vitiated atmosphere. Towards evening the trench was dug one yard deeper. When I returned on board, I was nearly suffocated by the carbonic acid with which the air was filled – ah! if we had only the chemical means to drive away this deleterious gas. We had plenty of oxygen; all this water contained a considerable quantity, and by dissolving it with our powerful piles, it would restore the vivifying fluid. I had thought well over it; but of what good was that, since the carbonic acid produced by our respiration had invaded every part of the vessel? To absorb it, it was necessary to fill some jars with caustic potash, and to shake them incessantly. Now this substance was wanting on board, and nothing could replace it. On that evening, Captain Nemo ought to open the taps of his reservoirs, and let some pure air into the interior of the Nautilus; without this precaution, we could not get rid of the sense of suffocation. The next day, March 26th, I resumed my miner's work in beginning the fifth yard. The side walls and the lower surface of the iceberg thickened visibly. It was evident that they would meet before the Nautilus was able to disengage itself. Despair seized me for an instant my pickaxe nearly fell from my hands. What was the good of digging if I must be suffocated, crushed by the water that was turning into stone? – a punishment that the ferocity of the savages even would not have invented! Just then Captain Nemo passed near me. I touched his hand and showed him the walls of our prison. The wall to port had advanced to at least four yards from the hull of the Nautilus. The captain understood me, and signed to me to follow him. We went on board. I took of my cork-jacket, and accompanied him into the drawing-room.

'M. Aronnax, we must attempt some desperate means, or we shall be sealed up in this solidified water as in cement.'

'Yes; but what is to be done?'

'Ah!, if my Nautilus were strong enough to bear this pressure without being crushed!'

'Well?' I asked, not catching the captain's idea.

'Do you not understand,' he replied, 'that this congelation of water will help us? Do you not see that, by its solidification, it would burst through this field of ice that imprisons us, as, when it freezes, it bursts the hardest stones? Do you perceive that it would be an agent of saftey instead of destruction?'

'Yes, captain, perhaps. But whatever resistance to crushing the Nautilus possesses, it could not support this terrible pressure, and would be flattened like an iron plate.'

'I know it, sir. Therefore we must not reckon on the aid of Nature, but on our own exertions. We must stop this solidification. Not only will the side walls be pressed together; but there is not ten feet of water before or behind the Nautilus. The congelation gains on us on all sides.'

'How long will the air in the reservoirs last for us to breathe on board?'

The captain looked in my face. 'After tomorrow they will be empty!'

A cold sweat came over me. However, ought I to have been astonished at the answer? On March 22nd, the Nautilus was in the open polar seas. We were at 26°. For five days we had lived on the reserve on board. And what was left of the respirable air must be kept for the workers. Even now, as I write, my recollection is still so vivid, that an involuntary terror seizes me, and my lungs seem to be without air. Meanwhile, Captain Nemo reflected silently, and evidently an idea had struck him; but he seemed to reject it. At last, these words escaped his lips——

'Boiling water!' he muttered.

'Boiling water?' I cried.

'Yes, sir. We are enclosed in a space that is relatively confined. Would not jets of boiling water, constantly injected by the pumps, raise the temperature in this part, and stay the congelation?'

'Let us try it,' I said, resolutely.

'Let us try, professor.'

The thermometer then stood at seven degrees outside. Captain Nemo took me to the galleys, where the vast distillatory machines stood that furnished the drinkable water by evaporation. They filled these with water, and all the electric heat from the piles was thrown through the worms bathed in the liquid. In a few minutes this water reached a hundred degrees. It was directed towards the pumps, while fresh water replaced it in proportion. The heat developed by the troughs was such that cold water, drawn up from the sea, after only having gone through the machines, came boiling into the body of the pump. The injection was begun, and three hours after the thermometer marked six degrees below zero outside. One degree was gained. Two hours later, the thermometer only marked four degrees.

'We shall succeed,' I said to the captain, after having anxiously watched the result of the operation.

'I think,' he answered, 'that we shall not be crushed. We have no more suffocation to fear.'

During the night the temperature of the water rose to one degree below zero. The injections could not carry it to a higher point. But as the congelation of the sea-water produces at least two degrees, I was at last reassured against the dangers of solidification.

The next day, March 27th, six yards of ice had been cleared, four yards only remaining to be cleared away. There was yet forty-eight hours' work. The air could not be renewed in the interior of the Nautilus. And this day would make it worse. An intolerable weight oppressed me. Towards three o'clock in the evening, this feeling rose to a violent degree. Yawns dislocated my jaws. My lungs panted as they inhaled this burning fluid, which became rarefied more and more. A moral torpor took hold of me. I was powerless, almost unconscious. My brave Conseil, though exhibiting the same symptoms and suffering in the same manner, never left me. He took my hand and encouraged me, and I heard him murmur, 'Oh! If I could only not breathe, so as to leave more air for my master!'

Tears came into my eyes on hearing him speak thus. If our situation to all was intolerable in the interior, with what haste and gladness would we put on our cork-jackets to work in our turn! Pickaxes sounded on the frozen ice-beds. Our arms ached, the skin was torn off our hands. But what were these fatigues, what did the wound matter? Vital air came to the lungs! we breathed! we breathed!

All this time, no one prolonged his voluntary task beyond the prescribed time. His task accomplished, each one handed in turn to his panting companions the apparatus that supplied him with life. Captain Nemo set the example, and submitted first to this severe discipline. When the time came, he gave up his apparatus to another, and returned to the vitiated air on board, calm, unflinching, unmurmuring.

On that day the ordinary work was accomplished with unusual vigour. Only two yards remained to be raised from the surface. Two yards only separated us from the open sea. But the reservoirs were nearly emptied of air. The little that remained ought to be kept for the workers; not a particle for the Nautilus. When I went back on board, I was half suffocated. What a night! I know not how to describe it. The next day my breathing was oppressed. Dizziness accompanied the pain in my head, and made me like a drunken man. My companions showed the same symptoms. Some of the crew had rattling in the throat.

On that day, the sixth of our imprisonment, Captain Nemo, finding the pickaxes work too slowly, resolved to crush the ice-bed that still separated us from the liquid sheet. This man's coolness and energy never forsook him. He subdued his physical pains by moral force.

By his orders the vessel was lightened, that is to say, raised from the ice-bed by a change of specific gravity. When it floated they towed it so as to bring it above the immense trench made on the level of the waterline. Then filling his reservoirs of water, he descended and shut himself up in the hole.

Just then all the crew came on board, and the double door of communication was shut. The Nautilus then rested on the bed of ice, which was not one yard thick, and which the sounding leads had perforated in a thousand places. The taps of the reservoirs were then opened, and a hundred cubic yards of water was let in, increasing the weight of the Nautilus to 1,800 tons. We waited, we listened, forgetting our sufferings in hope. Our safety depended on this last chance. Notwithstanding the buzzing in my head, I soon heard the humming sound under the hull of the Nautilus. The ice cracked with a singular noise, like tearing paper, and the Nautilus sank.

'We are off!' murmured Conseil in my ear.

I could not answer him. I seized his hand, and pressed it convulsively. All at once, carried away by its frightful overcharge, the Nautilus sank like a bullet under the waters, that is to say, it fell as if it was in a vacuum. Then all the electric force was put on the pumps, that soon began to let the water out of the reservoirs. After some minutes, our fall was stopped. Soon, too, the manometer indicated an ascending movement. The screw, going at full speed, made the iron hull tremble to its very bolts, and drew us towards the north. But if this floating under the iceberg is to last another day before we reach the open sea, I shall be dead first.

Half stretched upon a divan in the library, I was suffocating. My face was purple, my lips blue, my faculties suspended. I neither saw nor heard. All notion of time had gone from my mind. My muscles could not contract. I do not know how many hours passed thus, but I was conscious of the agony that was coming over me. I felt as if I was going to die. Suddenly I came to. Some breaths of air penetrated my lungs. Had we risen to the surface of the waves? Were we free of the iceberg? No; Ned and Conseil, my two brave friends, were sacrificing themselves to save me. Some particles of air still remained at the bottom of one apparatus. Instead of using it, they had kept it for me, and while they were being suffocated, they gave me life drop by drop. I wanted to push back the thing; they held my hands, and for some moments I breathed freely. I looked at the clock; it was eleven in the morning. It ought to be the 28th of March. The Nautilus went at a frightful pace, forty miles an hour. It literally tore through the water. Where was Captain Nemo? Had he succumbed? Were his companions dead with him? At the moment, the manometer indicated that we were not more than twenty feet from the surface. A mere plate of ice separated us from the atmosphere, could we not break it? Perhaps. In any case the Nautilus was going to attempt it. I felt that it was in an oblique position, lowering the stern, and raising the bows. The introduction of water had been the means of disturbing its equilibrium. Then, impelled by its powerful screw, it attacked the ice-field from beneath like a formidable battering-ram. It broke it by backing and then rushing forward against the field, which gradually gave way; and at last dashing suddenly against it, shot forward on the icy-field, that crushed beneath its weight. The panel was opened – one might say torn off – and the pure air came in in abundance to all parts of the Nautilus.

Chapter Forty-One

From Cape Horn to the Amazon

HOW I GOT ON TO THE PLATFORM, I have no idea; perhaps the Canadian had carried me there. But I breathed, I inhaled the vivifying sea-air. My two companions were getting drunk with the fresh particles. The other unhappy men had been so long without food, that they could not with impunity indulge in the simplest ailments that were given them. We, on the contrary, had no need to restrain ourselves; we could draw this air freely into our lungs, and it was the breeze, the breeze alone, that filled us with this keen enjoyment.

'Ah!' said Conseil, 'how delightful this oxygen is! Master need not fear to breathe it. There is enough for everybody.'

Ned Land did not speak, but he opened his jaws wide enough to frighten a shark. Our strength soon returned, and when I looked round me, I saw we were alone on the platform. The foreign seamen in the Nautilus were contented with the air that circulated in the interior; none of them had come to drink in the open air.

The first words I spoke were words of gratitude and thankfulness to my two companions. Ned and Conseil had prolonged my life during the last hours of this long agony. All my gratitude could not repay such devotion.

'My friends,' said I, 'we are bound one to the other for ever, and I am under infinite obligations to you.'

'Which I shall take advantage of,' exclaimed the Canadian.

'What do you mean?' said Conseil.

'I mean that I shall take you with me when I leave this infernal Nautilus.'

'Well,' said Conseil, 'after all this, are we going right?'

'Yes,' I replied, 'for we are going the way of the sun, and here the sun is in the north.'

'No doubt,' said Ned Land; 'but it remains to be seen whether he will bring the ship into the Pacific or the Atlantic Ocean, that is, into frequented or deserted seas.'

I could not answer that question, and I feared that Captain Nemo would rather take us to the vast ocean that touches the coasts of Asia and America at the same time. He would thus complete the tour round the submarine world, and return to those waters in which the Nautilus could sail freely. We ought, before long, to settle this important point. The Nautilus went at a rapid pace. The polar circle was soon passed, and the course shaped for Cape Horn. We were off the American point, March 31st, at seven o'clock in the evening. Then all our past sufferings were forgotten. The remembrance of that imprisonment in the ice was effaced from our minds. We only thought of the future. Captain Nemo did not appear again either in the drawing-room or on the platform. The point shown each day on the planisphere, and marked by the lieutenant, showed me the exact direction of the Nautilus. Now, on that evening, it was evident, to my great satisfaction, that we were going back to the north by the Atlantic. The next day, April 1st, when the Nautilus ascended to the surface, some minutes before noon, we sighted land to the west. It was Terra del Fuego, which the first navigators named thus from seeing the quantity of smoke that rose from the natives' huts. The coast seemed low to me, but in the distance rose high mountains. I even thought I had a glimpse of Mount Sarmiento, that rises 2,070 yards above the level of the sea, with a very pointed summit, which, according as it is misty or clear, is a sign of fine or of wet weather. At this moment, the peak was clearly defined against the sky. The Nautilus, diving again under the water, approached the coast, which was only some few miles off. From the glass windows in the drawing-room, I saw long seaweeds, and gigantic fuci, and varech, of which the open polar sea contains so many specimens, with their sharp polished filaments; they measured about 300 yards in length – real cables, thicker than one's thumb; and having great tenacity, they are often used as ropes for vessels. Another weed known as velp, with leaves four feet long, buried in the coral concretions, hung at the bottom. It served as nest and food for myriads of crustacea and molluscs, crabs and cuttle-fish. There seals and otters had splendid repasts, eating the flesh of fish with sea-vegetables, according to the English fashion. Over this fertile and luxuriant ground the Nautilus passed with great rapidity. Towards evening, it approached the Falkland group, the rough summits of which I recognized the following day. The depth of the sea was moderate. On the shores, our nets brought in beautiful specimens of seaweed, and particularly a certain fucus, the roots of which were filled with the best mussels in the world. Geese and ducks fell by dozens on the platform, and soon took their places in the pantry on board. With regard to fish, I observed especially specimens of the goby species, some two feet long, all over white and yellow spots. I admired also numerous medusæ, and the finest of the sort, the crysaora, peculiar to the sea about the Falkand Isles. I should have liked to preserve some specimens of these delicate zoophytes: but they are only like clouds, shadows, apparitions, that sink and evaporate, when out of their native element.

When the last heights of the Falklands had disappeared from the horizon, the Nautilus sank to between twenty and twenty-five yards, and followed the American coast. Captain Nemo did not show himself. Until the 3rd of April we did not quit the shores of Patagonia, sometimes under the ocean, sometimes at the surface. The Nautilus passed beyond the large estuary formed by the mouth of the Plata, and was, on the 14th of April, fifty-six miles off Uruguay. Its direction was northwards, and followed the long windings of the coast of South America. We had then made 1,600 miles since our embarkation in the seas of Japan. About eleven o'clock in the morning the tropic of Capricorn was crossed on the thirty-seventh meridian, and we passed Cape Frio standing out to sea. Captain Nemo, to Ned Land's great displeasure, did not like the neighbourhood of the inhabited coasts of Brazil, for we went at a giddy speed. Not a fish, not a bird of the swiftest kind could follow us, and the natural curiosities of these seas escaped all observation.

This speed was kept up for several days, and in the evening of the 9th of April we sighted the most westerly point of South America that forms Cape San Roque. But then the Nautilus swerved again, and sought the lowest depth of a submarine valley which is between this cape and Sierra Leone on the African coast. This valley bifurcates to the parallel of the Antilles, and terminates at the north by the enormous depression of 9,000 yards. In this place, the geological basin of the ocean forms, as far as the Lesser Antilles, a cliff of three and a half miles perpendicular in height, and at the parallel of the Cape Verde Islands, another wall not less considerable, that encloses thus all the sunk continent of the Atlantic. The bottom of this immense valley is dotted with some mountains, that give to these submarine places a picturesque aspect. I speak, moreover, from the manuscript charts that were in the library of the Nautilus – charts evidently due to Captain Nemo's hand, and made after his personal observations. For two days the desert and deep waters were visited by means of the inclined planes. The Nautilus was furnished with long diagonal broadsides which carried it to all elevations. But, on the 11th of April, it rose suddenly, and land appeared at the mouth of the Amazon River, a vast estuary, the embouchure of which is so considerable that it freshens the sea-water for the distance of several leagues.

The equator was crossed. Twenty miles to the west were the Guianas, a French territory, on which we could have found an easy refuge; but a stiff breeze was blowing, and the furious waves would not have allowed a single boat to face them. Ned Land understood that, no doubt, for he spoke not a word about it. For my part, I made no allusion to his schemes of flight, for I would not urge him to make an attempt that must inevitably fail. I made the time pass pleasantly by interesting studies. During the days of April 11th and 12th, the Nautilus did not leave the surface of the sea, and the net brought in a marvellous haul of zoophytes, fish and reptiles. Some zoophytes had been fished up by the chain of the nets; they were for the most part beautiful phyctallines, belonging to the actinidian family, and among other species the phyctalis protexta, peculiar to that part of the ocean, with a little cylindrical trunk, ornamented with vertical lines, speckled with red dots, crowning a marvellous blossoming of tentacles. As to the molluscs, they consisted of some I had already observed – turritellas, olive porphyras, with regular lines intercrossed with red spots standing out plainly against the flesh; odd pteroceras, like petrified scorpions; translucid hyaleas, argonauts, cuttle-fish (excellent eating), and certain species of calmars that naturalists of antiquity have classed amongst the flying-fish, and that serve principally for bait for cod-fishing. I had not an opportunity of studying several species of fish on these shores. Amongst the cartilaginous ones, petromyzons-pricka, a sort of eel, fifteen inches long, with a greenish head, violet fins, grey-blue back, brown belly, silvered and sewn with bright spots, the pupil of the eye encircled with gold – a curious animal, that the current of the Amazon had drawn to the sea, for they inhabit fresh waters – tuberculated streaks, with pointed snouts, and a long loose tail, armed with a long jagged sting; little sharks, a yard long, grey and whitish skin, and several rows of teeth, bent back, that are generally known by the name of pantouffles; vespertilios, a kind of red isosceles triangle, half a yard long, to which pectorals are attached by fleshy prolongations that make them look like bats, but that their horny appendage, situated near the nostrils, has given them the name of sea-unicorns; lastly, some species of balistæ, the curassavian, whose spots were of a brilliant gold colour, and the capriscus of clear violet, and with varying shades like a pigeon's throat.

I end here this catalogue, which is somewhat dry perhaps, but very exact, with a series of bony fish that I observed in passing belonging to the apteronotes, and whose snout is white as snow, the body of a beautiful black, marked with a very long loose fleshy strip; odontognathes, armed with spikes; sardines, nine inches long, glittering with a bright silver light; a species of mackerel provided with two anal fins; centronotes of a blackish tint, that are fished for with torches, long fish, two yards in length, with fat flesh, white and firm, which, when they are fresh, taste like eel, and when dry, like smoked salmon; labres, half red, covered with scales only at the bottom of the dorsal and anal fins; chrysoptera, on which gold and silver blend their brightness with that of the ruby and topaz; golden-tailed spares, the flesh of which is extremely delicate, and whose phosphorescent properties betray them in the midst of the waters; orange-coloured spares with a long tongue; maigres, with gold caudal fins, dark thorn-tails, anableps of Surinam, &c.

Notwithstanding this 'etcetera', I must not omit to mention fish that Conseil will long remember, and with good reason. One of our nets had hauled up a sort of very flat rayfish, which, with the tail cut off, formed a perfect disc, and weighed twenty ounces. It was white underneath, red above, with large round spots of dark blue encircled with black, very glossy skin, terminating in a bilobed fin. Laid out on the platform, it struggled, tried to turn itself by convulsive movements, and made so many efforts, that one last turn had nearly sent it into the sea. But Conseil, not wishing to let the fish go, rushed to it, and, before I could prevent him, had seized it with both hands. In a moment he was overthrown, his legs in the air, and half his body paralysed, crying——

'Oh! master, master! come to me!'

It was the first time the poor boy had not spoken to me in the third person. The Canadian and I took him up, and rubbed his contracted arms till he became sensible. The unfortunate Conseil had attacked a crampfish of the most dangerous kind, the cumana. This odd animal, in a medium conductor like water, strikes fish at several yards' distance, so great is the power of its electric organ, the two principal surfaces of which do not measure less than twenty-seven square feet. The next day, April 12th, the Nautilus approached the Dutch coast, near the mouth of the Maroni. There several groups of sea-cows herded together; they were manatees, that, like the dugong and the stellera, belong to the sirenian order. These beautiful animals, peaceable and inoffensive, from eighteen to twenty-one feet in length, weigh at least sixteen hundredweight. I told Ned Land and Conseil that provident Nature had assigned an important rôle to these mammalia. Indeed, they, like the seals, are designed to graze on the submarine prairies, and thus destroy the accumulation of weed that obstructs the tropical rivers.

'And do you know,' I added, 'what has been the result since men have almost entirely annihilated this useful race? That the putrified weeds have poisoned the air, and the poisoned air causes the yellow fever, that desolates these beautiful countries. Enormous vegetations are multiplied under the torrid seas, and the evil is irresistibly developed from the mouth of the Rio de la Plata to Florida. If we are to believe Toussenel, this plague is nothing to what it would be if the seas were cleared of whales and seals. Then, infested with poulps, medusæ, and cuttle-fish, they would become immense centres of infection, since their waves would not possess "these vast stomachs that God had charged to infest the surface of the seas."'

However, without disputing these theories, the crew of the Nautilus took possession of half a dozen manatees. They provisioned the larders with excellent flesh, superior to beef and veal. This sport was not interesting. The manatees allowed themselves to be hit without defending themselves. Several thousand pounds of meat were stored up on board to be dried. On this day, a successful haul of fish increased the stores of the Nautilus, so full of game were these seas. They were echneides belonging to the third family of the malacopterygiens; their flattened discs were composed of transverse movable cartilaginous plates, by which the animal was enabled to create a vacuum, and so to adhere to any object like a cupping-glass. The remora that I had observed in the Mediterranean belongs to this species. But the one of which we are speaking was the echeneis osteochera, peculiar to this sea.

The fishing over, the Nautilus neared the coast. About here a number of sea-turtles were sleeping on the surface of the water. It would have been difficult to capture these precious reptiles, for the least noise awakens them, and their solid shell is proof against the harpoon. But the echeneis effects their capture with extraordinary precision and certainty. This animal is, indeed, a living fishhook, which would make the fortune of an inexperienced fisherman. The crew of the Nautilus tied a ring to the tail of these fish, so large as not to encumber their movements, and to this ring a long cord, lashed to the ship's side by the other end. The echeneids, thrown into the sea, directly began their game, and fixed themselves to the breastplate of the turtles. Their tenacity was such, that they were torn rather than let go their hold. The men hauled them on board, and with them the turtles to which they adhered. They took also several cacouannes a yard long, which weighed 400 lbs. Their carapace covered with large horny plates, thin, transparent, brown, with white and yellow spots, fetch a good price in the market. Besides, they were excellent in an edible point of view, as well as the fresh turtles, which have an exquisite flavour. This day's fishing brought to a close our stay on the shores of the Amazon, and by nightfall the Nautilus had regained the high seas.

Chapter Forty-Two

The Poulps

FOR SEVERAL DAYS THE NAUTILUS kept off from the American coast. Evidently it did not wish to risk the tides of the Gulf of Mexico, or of the sea of the Antilles. April 16th, we sighted Martinique and Guadaloupe from a distance of about thirty miles. I saw their tall peaks for an instant. The Canadian, who counted on carrying out his projects in the Gulf, by either landing, or hailing one of the numerous boats that coast from one island to another, was quite disheartened. Flight would have been quite practicable, if Ned Land had been able to take possession of the boat without the captain's knowledge. But in the open sea it could not be thought of. The Canadian, Conseil, and I, had a long conversation on this subject. For six months we had been prisoners on board the Nautilus. We had travelled 17,000 leagues; and, as Ned Land said, there was no reason why it should not come to an end. We could hope nothing from the captain of the Nautilus, but only from ourselves. Besides, for some time past he had become graver, more retired, less sociable. He seemed to shun me. I met him rarely. Formerly, he was pleased to explain the submarine marvels to me; now, he left me to my studies, and came no more to the saloon. What change had come over him? For what cause? For my part, I did not wish to bury with me my curious and novel studies. I had now the power to write the true book of the sea; and this book, sooner or later, I wished to see daylight. Then again, in the water by the Antilles, ten yards below the surface of the waters, by the open panels, what interesting products I had to enter on my daily notes! There were, among other zoophytes, those known under the name of physalis pelagica, a sort of large oblong bladder, with mother-of-pearl rays, holding out their membranes to the wind, and letting their blue tentacles float like threads of silk; charming medusæ to the eye, real nettles to the touch, that distil a corrosive fluid. There were also annelides, a yard and a half long, furnished with a pink horn, and with 1,700 locomotive organs, that wind through the waters, and throw out in passing all the light of the solar spectrum. There were, in the fish category, some Malabar rays, enormous gristly things, ten feet long, weighing 600 pounds, the pectoral fin triangular in the midst of a slightly humped back, the eyes fixed in the extremities of the face, beyond the head, and which floated like weft, and looked sometimes like an opaque shutter on our glass window. There were American balistæ, which Nature has only dressed in black and white; gobies, with yellow fins and prominent jaw; mackerel sixteen feet long, with short-pointed teeth, covered with small scales, belonging to the albicore species. Then, in swarms, appeared grey mullet, covered with stripes of gold from the head to the tail, beating their resplendent fins, like masterpieces of jewellery, consecrated formerly to Diana, particularly sought after by rich Romans, and of which the proverb says, 'Whoever takes them does not eat them.' Lastly, pomacanthe dorees, ornamented with emerald bands, dressed in velvet and silk, passed before our eyes like Veronese lords; spurred spari passed with their pectoral fins; clupanodons fifteen inches long, enveloped in their phosphorescent light; mullet beat the sea with their large jagged tail; red vendaces seemed to mow the waves with their showy pectoral fins; and silvery selenes, worthy of their name, rose on the horizon of the waters like so many moons with whitish rays. April 20th, we had risen to a mean height of 1,500 yards. The land nearest us then was the archipelago of the Bahamas. There rose high submarine cliffs covered with large weeds, giant laminariæ and fuci, a perfect espalier of hydrophytes worthy of a Titan world. It was about eleven o'clock when Ned Land drew my attention to a formidable pricking like the sting of an ant, which was produced by means of large seaweeds.

'Well,' I said, 'these are proper caverns for poulps, and I should not be astonished to see some of these monsters.'

'What!' said Conseil; 'cuttle-fish, real cuttle-fish, of the cephalopod class?'

'No,' I said; 'poulps of huge dimensions.'

'I will never believe that such animals exist,' said Ned.

'Well,' said Conseil, with the most serious air in the world; 'I remember perfectly to have seen a large vessel drawn under the waves by a cephalopod's arm.'

'You saw that?' said the Canadian.

'Yes, Ned.'

'With your own eyes?'

'With my own eyes.'

'Where, pray, might that be?'

'At St Malo,' answered Conseil.

'In the port?' said Ned, ironically.

'No; in a church,' replied Conseil.

'In a church!' cried the Canadian.

'Yes; friend Ned. In a picture representing the poulp in question.'

'Good!' said Ned Land, bursting out laughing.

'He is quite right,' I said. 'I have heard of this picture; but the subject represented is taken from a legend, and you know what to think of legends in the matter of natural history. Besides, when it is a question of monsters, the imagination is apt to run wild. Not only is it supposed that these poulps can draw down vessels, but a certain Olaüs Magnus speaks of a cephalopod a mile long, that is more like an island than an animal. It is also said that the Bishop of Nidros was building an altar on an immense rock. Mass finished, the rock began to walk, and returned to the sea. The rock was a poulp. Another bishop, Pontoppidan, speaks also of a poulp on which a regiment of cavalry could manœuvre. Lastly, the ancient naturalists speak of monsters whose mouths were like gulfs, and which were too large to pass through the Straits of Gibraltar.'

'But how much is true of these stories?' asked Conseil.

'Nothing, my friends; at least of that which passes the limit of truth to get to fable or legend. Nevertheless, there must be some ground for the imagination of the story-tellers. One cannot deny that poulps and cuttle-fish exist on a large species, inferior, however, to the cetaceans. Aristotle has stated the dimensions of a cuttle-fish as five cubits, or nine feet two inches. Our fishermen frequently see some that are more than four feet long. Some skeletons of poulps are preserved in the museums of Trieste and Montpelier, that measure two yards in length. Besides, according to the calculations of some naturalists, one of these animals, only six feet long, would have tentacles twenty-seven feet long. That would suffice to make a formidable monster.'

'Do they fish for them in these days?' asked Ned.

'If they do not fish for them, sailors see them at least. One of my friends, Captain Paul Bos of Havre, has often affirmed that he met one of these monsters, of colossal dimensions, in the Indian seas. But the most astonishing fact, and which does not permit of the denial of the existence of these gigantic animals, happened some years ago, in 1861.'

'What is the fact?' asked Ned Land.

'This is it. In 1861, to the north-east of Tenerife, very nearly in the same latitude we are in now, the crew of the despatch-boat Alector perceived a monstrous cuttle-fish swimming in the waters. Captain Bouguer went near to the animal, and attacked it with harpoons and guns, without much success, for balls and harpoons glided over the soft flesh. After several fruitless attempts, the crew tried to pass a slip-knot round the body of the mollusc. The noose slipped as far as the caudal fins, and there stopped. They tried then to haul it on board, but its weight was so considerable that the tightness of the cord separated the tail from the body, and, deprived of this ornament, he disappeared under the water.'

'Indeed! is that a fact?'

'An indisputable fact, my good Ned. They proposed to name this poulp "Bouguer's cuttle-fish."'

'What length was it?' asked the Canadian.

'Did it not measure about six yards?' said Conseil, who, posted at the window, was examining again the irregular windings of the cliff.

'Precisely,' I replied.

'Its head,' rejoined Conseil, 'was it not crowned with eight tentacles, that beat the water like a nest of serpents?'

'Precisely.'

'Had not its eyes, placed at the back of its head, considerable development?'

'Yes, Conseil.'

'And was not its mouth like a parrot's beak?'

'Exactly, Conseil.'

'Very well! no offence to master,' he replied, quietly; 'if this is not Bouguer's cuttle-fish, it is, at least, one of its brothers.'

I looked at Conseil. Ned Land hurried to the window.

'What a horrible beast!' he cried.

I looked in my turn, and could not repress a gesture of disgust. Before my eyes was a horrible monster, worthy to figure in the legends of the marvellous. It was an immense cuttle-fish, being eight yards long. It swam crossways in the direction of the Nautilus with great speed, watching us with its enormous staring green eyes. Its eight arms, or rather feet, fixed to its head, that have given the name of cephalopod to these animals, were twice as long as its body, and were twisted like the furies' hair. One could see the 250 air holes on the inner side of the tentacles. The monster's mouth, a horned beak like a parrot's, opened and shut vertically. Its tongue, a horned substance, furnished with several rows of pointed teeth, came out quivering from this veritable pair of shears. What a freak of Nature, a bird's beak on a mollusc! Its spindle-like body formed a fleshy mass that might weigh 4,000 to 5,000 lbs; the varying colour changing with great rapidity, according to the irritation of the animal, passed successively from livid grey to reddish brown. What irritated this mollusc? No doubt the presence of the Nautilus, more formidable than itself, and on which its suckers or its jaws had no hold. Yet, what monsters these poulps are! what vitality the Creator has given them! what vigour in their movements! and they possess three hearts! Chance had brought us in presence of this cuttle-fish, and I did not wish to lose the opportunity of carefully studying this specimen of cephalopods. I overcame the horror that inspired me; and, taking a pencil, began to draw it.

'Perhaps this is the same which the Alector saw,' said Conseil.

'No,' replied the Canadian; 'for this is whole, and the other had lost its tail.'

'That is no reason,' I replied. 'The arms and tails of these animals are reformed by redintegration; and, in seven years, the tail of Bouguer's cuttle-fish has no doubt had time to grow.'

By this time other poulps appeared at the port light. I counted seven. They formed a procession after the Nautilus, and I heard their beaks gnashing against the iron hull. I continued my work. These monsters kept in the water with such precision, that they seemed immovable. Suddenly the Nautilus stopped. A shock made it tremble in every plate.

'Have we struck anything?' I asked.

'In any case,' replied the Canadian, 'we shall be free, for we are floating.'

The Nautilus was floating, no doubt, but it did not move. A minute passed. Captain Nemo, followed by his lieutenant, entered the drawing-room. I had not seen him for some time. He seemed dull. Without noticing or speaking to us, he went to the panel, looked at the poulps, and said something to his lieutenant. The latter went out. Soon the panels were shut. The ceiling was lighted. I went towards the captain.

'A curious collection of poulps?' I said.

'Yes, indeed, Mr Naturalist,' he replied; 'and we are going to fight them, man to beast.'

I looked at him. I thought I had not heard aright.

'Man to beast?' I repeated.

'Yes, sir. The screw is stopped. I think that the horny jaws of one of the cuttle-fish is entangled in the blades. That is what prevents our moving.'

'What are you going to do?'

'Rise to the surface, and slaughter this vermin.'

'A difficult enterprise.'

'Yes, indeed. The electric bullets are powerless against the soft flesh, where they do not find resistance enough to go off. But we shall attack them with the hatchet.'

'And the harpoon, sir,' said the Canadian, 'if you do not refuse my help.'

'I will accept it, Master Land.'

'We will follow you,' I said, and following Captain Nemo, we went towards the central staircase.

There, about ten men with boarding hatchets were ready for the attack. Conseil and I took two hatchets; Ned Land seized a harpoon. The Nautilus had then risen to the surface. One of the sailors, posted on the top ladder step, unscrewed the bolts of the panels. But hardly were the screws loosed, when the panel rose with great violence, evidently drawn by the suckers of a poulp's arm.

Immediately one of these arms slid serpent like down the opening, and twenty others were above. With one blow of the axe, Captain Nemo cut this formidable tentacle, that slid wriggling down the ladder. Just as we were pressing one on the other to reach the platform, two other arms, lashing the air, came down on the seaman placed before Captain Nemo, and lifted him up with irresistible power. Captain Nemo uttered a cry, and rushed out. We hurried after him.

What a scene! The unhappy man, seized by the tentacle, and fixed to the suckers, was balanced in the air at the caprice of this enormous trunk. He rattled in his throat, he was stifled, he cried, 'Help! help!' These words *spoken in French*, startled me! I had a fellow countryman on board, perhaps several! That heartrending cry! I shall hear it all my life. The unfortunate man was lost. Who could rescue him from that powerful pressure? However, Captain Nemo had rushed to the poulp, and with one blow of the axe had cut through one arm. His lieutenant struggled furiously against other monsters that crept on the flanks of the Nautilus. The crew fought with their axes. The Canadian, Conseil, and I, buried our weapons in the fleshy masses; a strong smell of musk penetrated the atmosphere. It was horrible!

For one instant, I thought the unhappy man, entangled with the poulp, would be torn from its powerful suction. Seven of the eight arms had been cut off. One only wriggled in the air, brandishing the victim like a feather. But just as Captain Nemo and his lieutenant threw themselves on it, the animal ejected a stream of black liquid. We were blinded with it. When the cloud dispersed, the cuttle-fish had disappeared, and my unfortunate countryman with it. Ten or twelve poulps now invaded the platform and sides of the Nautilus. We rolled pellmell into the midst of this nest of serpents, that wriggled on the platform in the waves of blood and ink. It seemed as though these slimy tentacles sprang up like the hydra's heads. Ned Land's harpoon, at each stroke, was plunged into the staring eyes of the cuttle-fish. But my bold companion was suddenly overturned by the tentacles of a monster he had not been able to avoid.

Ah! how my heart beat with emotion and horror! The formidable beak of a cuttle-fish was open over Ned Land. The unhappy man would be cut in two. I rushed to his succour. But Captain Nemo was before me; his axe disappeared between the two enormous jaws, and miraculously saved the Canadian, rising, plunged his harpoon deep into the triple heart of the poulp.

'I owed myself this revenge!' said the captain to the Canadian.

Ned bowed without replying. The combat had lasted a quarter of an hour. The monsters, vanquished and mutilated, left us at last, and disappeared under the waves. Captain Nemo, covered with blood, nearly exhausted, gazed upon the sea that had swallowed up one of his companions, and great tears gathered in his eyes.

Chapter Forty-Three

The Gulf Stream

THIS TERRIBLE SCENE OF the 20th of April none of us can ever forget. I have written it under the influence of violent emotion. Since then I have revised the recital; I have read it to Conseil and to the Canadian. They found it exact as to facts, but insufficient as to effect. To paint such pictures, one must have the pen of the most illustrious of our poets, the author of 'The Toilers of the Deep'.

I have said that Captain Nemo wept while watching the waves; his grief was great. It was the second companion he had lost since our arrival on board, and what a death! That friend, crushed, stifled, bruised by the dreadful arms of a poulp, pounded by his iron jaws, would not rest with his comrades in the peaceful coral cemetery! In the midst of the struggle, it was the despairing cry uttered by the unfortunate man that had torn my heart. The poor Frenchman, forgetting his conventional language, had taken to his own mother tongue, to utter a last appeal! Amongst the crew of the Nautilus, associated with the body and soul of the captain, recoiling like him from all contact with men, I had a fellow-countryman. Did he alone represent France in this mysterious association, evidently composed of individuals of divers nationalties? It was one of these insoluble problems that rose up unceasingly before my mind!

Captain Nemo entered his room, and I saw him no more for some time. But that he was sad and irresolute I could see by the vessel, of which he was the soul, and which received all his impressions. The Nautilus did not keep on in its settled course; it floated about like a corpse at the will of the waves. It went at random. He could not tear himself away from the scene of the last struggle, from this sea that had devoured one of his men. Ten days passed thus. It was not till the 1st of May that the Nautilus resumed its northerly course, after having sighted the Bahamas at the mouth of the Bahama Canal. We were then following the current from the largest river to the sea, that has its banks, its fish, and its proper temperatures. I mean the Gulf Stream. It is really a river, that flows freely to the middle of the Atlantic, and whose waters do not mix with the ocean waters. It is a salt river, saltier than the surrounding sea. Its mean depth is 1,500 fathoms, its mean breadth ten miles. In certain places the current flows with the speed of two miles and a half an hour. The body of its waters is more considerable than that of all the rivers in the globe. It was on this ocean river that the Nautilus then sailed.

This current carried with it all kinds of living things. Argonauts, so common in the Mediterranean, were there in quantities. Of the gristly sort, the most remarkable were the turbot, whose slender tails form nearly the third part of the body, and that looked like large lozenges twenty-five feet long; also, small sharks a yard long, with large heads, short rounded muzzles, pointed teeth in several rows, and whose bodies seemed covered with scales. Among the bony fish I noticed some grey gobies, peculiar to these waters; black giltheads, whose iris shone like fire; sirenes a yard long, with large snouts thickly set with little teeth, that uttered little cries; blue coryphænes, in gold and silver; parrots, like the rainbows of the ocean, that could rival in colour the most beautiful tropical birds; blennies with triangular heads; bluish rhombs destitute of scales; batrachoides covered with yellow transversal bands like a Greek τ; heaps of little gobies spotted with yellow; dipterodons with silvery heads and yellow tails; several specimens of salmon, mugilomores slender in shape, shining with a soft light that Lacépède consecrated to the service of his wife; and lastly, a beautiful fish, the American-knight, that, decorated with all the orders and ribbons, frequents the shores of this great nation, that esteems orders and ribbons so little.

I must add that, during the night, the phosphorescent waters of the Gulf Stream rivalled the electric power of our watch-light, especially in the stormy weather that threatened us so frequently. On May 8th, we were still crossing Cape Hatteras, at the height of the North Caroline. The width of the Gulf Stream there is seventy-five miles, and its depth 210 yards. The Nautilus still went at random; all supervision seemed abandoned. I thought that, under these circumstances, escape would be possible. Indeed, the inhabited shores offered anywhere an easy refuge. The sea was incessantly ploughed by the steamers that ply between New York or Boston and the Gulf of Mexico, and overrun day and night by the little schooners coasting about the several parts of the American coast. We could hope to be picked up. It was a favourable opportunity, notwithstanding the thirty miles that separated the Nautilus from the coasts of the Union. One unfortunate circumstance thwarted the Canadian's plans. The weather was very bad. We were nearing those shores where tempests are so frequent, that country of waterspouts and cyclones actually engendered by the current of the Gulf Stream. To tempt the sea in a frail boat was certain destruction. Ned Land owned this himself. He fretted, seized with nostalgia that flight only could cure.

'Master,' he said that day to me, 'this must come to an end. I must make a clean breast of it. This Nemo is leaving land and going up to the north. But I declare to you, I have had enough of the South Pole, and I will not follow him to the North.'

'What is to be done, Ned, since flight is impracticable just now?'

'We must speak to the captain,' said he; 'you said nothing when we were in your native seas. I will speak, now we are in mine. When I think that before long the Nautilus will be by Nova Scotia, and that there near Newfoundland is a large bay, and into that bay the St Lawrence empties itself, and that the St Lawrence is my river, the river by Quebec my native town – when I think of this, I feel furious, it makes my hair stand on end. Sir, I would rather throw myself into the sea! I will not stay here! I am stifled!'

The Canadian was evidently losing all patience. His vigorous nature could not stand this prolonged imprisonment. His face altered daily; his temper became more surly. I knew what he must suffer, for I was seized with nostalgia myself. Nearly seven months had passed without our having had any news from land; Captain Nemo's isolation, his altered spirits, especially since the fight with the poulps, his taciturnity, all made me view things in a different light.

'Well, sir?' said Ned, seeing I did not reply.

'Well, Ned! do you wish me to ask Captain Nemo his intentions concerning us?'

'Yes, sir.'

'Although he has already made them known?'

'Yes; I wish it settled finally. Speak for me, in my name only, if you like.'

'But I so seldom meet him. He avoids me.'

'That is all the more reason for you to go to see him.'

I went to my room. From thence I meant to go to Captain Nemo's. It would not do to let this opportunity of meeting him slip. I knocked at the door. No answer. I knocked again, then turned the handle. The door opened, I went in. The captain was there. Bending over his work table, he had not heard me. Resolved not to go without having spoken, I approached him. He raised his head quickly, frowned, and said roughly, 'You here! What do you want?'

'To speak to you, captain.'

'But I am busy, sir; I am working. I leave you at liberty to shut yourself up; cannot I be allowed the same?'

This reception was not encouraging; but I was determined to hear and answer everything.

'Sir,' I said, coldly, 'I have to speak to you on a matter that admits of no delay.'

'What is that, sir?' he replied, ironically. 'Have you discovered something that has escaped me, or has the sea delivered up any new secrets?'

We were at cross-purposes. But before I could reply, he showed me an open manuscript on his table, and said, in a more serious tone, 'Here, M. Aronnax, is a manuscript written in several languages. It contains the sum of my studies of the sea; and, if it please God, it shall not perish with me. This manuscript, signed with my name, complete with the history of my life, will be shut up in a little insubmersible case. The last survivor of all of us on board the Nautilus will throw this case into the sea, and it will go whither it is borne by the waves.'

This man's name! his history written by himself! His mystery would then be revealed some day.

'Captain,' I said, 'I can but approve of the idea that makes you act thus. The result of your studies must not be lost. But the means you employ seem to me to be primitive. Who knows where the winds will carry this case, and in whose hands it will fall? Could you not use some other means? Could not you, or one of yours——'

'Never, sir!' he said, hastily interrupting me.

'But I and my companions are ready to keep this manuscript in store; and, if you will put us at liberty——'

'At liberty?' said the captain, rising.

'Yes, sir; that is the subject on which I wish to question you. For seven months we have been here on board, and I ask you today, in the name of my companions, and in my own, if your intention is to keep us here always?'

'M. Aronnax, I will answer you today as I did seven months ago: Whoever enters the Nautilus must never quit it.'

'You impose actual slavery on us!'

'Give it what name you please.'

'But everywhere the slave has the right to regain his liberty.'

'Who denies you this right? Have I ever tried to chain you with an oath?'

He looked at me with his arms crossed.

'Sir,' I said, 'to return a second time to this subject will be neither to your nor to my taste; but, as we have entered upon it, let us go through with it. I repeat, it is not only myself whom it concerns. Study is to me a relief, a diversion, a passion that could make me forget everything. Like you, I am willing to live obscure, in the frail hope of bequeathing one day, to future time, the result of my labours. But it is otherwise with Ned Land. Every man, worthy of the name, deserves some consideration. Have you thought that love of liberty, hatred of slavery, can give rise to schemes of revenge in a nature like the Canadian's; that he could think, attempt, and try——'

I was silenced; Captain Nemo rose.

'Whatever Ned Land thinks of, attempts, or tries, what does it matter to me? I did not seek him! It is not for my pleasure that I keep him on board! As for you, M. Aronnax, you are one of those who can understand everything, even silence. I have nothing more to say to you. Let this first time you have come to treat of this subject be the last; for a second time I will not listen to you.'

I retired. Our situation was critical. I related my conversation to my two companions.

'We know now,' said Ned, 'that we can expect nothing from this man. The Nautilus is nearing Long Island. We will escape, whatever the weather may be.'

But the sky became more and more threatening. Symptoms of a hurricane became manifest. The atmosphere was becoming white and misty. On the horizon fine streaks of cirrus clouds were succeeded by masses of cumuli. Other low clouds passed swiftly by. The swollen sea rose in huge billows. The birds disappeared, with the exception of the petrels, those friends of the storm. The barometer fell sensibly, and indicated an extreme tension of the vapours. The mixture of the storm glass was decomposed under the influence of the electricity that pervaded the atmosphere. The tempest burst on the 18th of May, just as the Nautilus was floating off Long Island, some miles from the port of New York. I can describe this strife of the elements! for, instead of fleeing to the depths of the sea, Captain Nemo, by an unaccountable caprice, would brave it at the surface. The wind blew from the south-west at first. Captain Nemo, during the squalls, had taken his place on the platform. He had made himself fast, to prevent being washed overboard by the monstrous waves. I had hoisted myself up, and made myself fast also, dividing my admiration between the tempest and this extraordinary man who was coping with it. The raging sea was swept by huge cloud-drifts, which were actually saturated with the waves. The Nautilus, sometimes lying on its side, sometimes standing up like a mast, rolled and pitched terribly. About five o'clock a torrent of rain fell, that lulled neither sea nor wind. The hurricane blew nearly forty leagues an hour. It is under these conditions that it overturns houses, breaks iron gates, displaces twenty-four pounds. However, the Nautilus, in the midst of the tempest, confirmed the words of a clever engineer, 'There is no well-constructed hull that cannot defy the sea.' This was not a resisting rock; it was a steel spindle, obedient and movable, without rigging or masts, that braved its fury with impunity. However, I watched these raging waves attentively. They measured fifteen feet in height, and 150 to 175 yards long, and their speed of propagation was thirty feet per second. Their bulk and power increased with the depth of the water. Such waves as these at the Hebrides, have displaced a mass weighing 8,400 lbs. They are

they which, in the tempest of December 23rd 1864, after destroying the town of
Yeddo, in Japan, broke the same day on the shores of America. The intensity of
the tempest increased with the night. The barometer, as in 1860 at Réunion
during a cyclone, fell seven-tenths at the close of day. I saw a large vessel pass
the horizon struggling painfully. She was trying to lie to under half steam, to
keep up above the waves. It was probably one of the steamers of the line from
New York to Liverpool, or Havre. It soon disappeared in the gloom. At ten
o'clock in the evening the sky was on fire. The atmosphere was streaked with
vivid lightning. I could not bear the brightness of it; while the captain, looking
at it, seemed to envy the spirit of the tempest. A terrible noise filled the air, a
complex noise, made up of the howls of the crushed waves, the roaring of the
wind, and the claps of thunder. The wind veered suddenly to all points of the
horizon; and the cyclone, rising in the east, returned after passing by the north,
west, and south, in the inverse course pursued by the circular storms of the
southern hemisphere. Ah, that Gulf Stream! It deserves its name of the King of
Tempests. It is that which causes those formidable cyclones, by the difference of
temperature between its air and its currents. A shower of fire had succeeded the
rain. The drops of water were changed to sharp spikes. One would have thought
that Captain Nemo was courting a death worthy of himself, a death by
lightning. As the Nautilus, pitching dreadfully, raised its steel spur in the air, it
seemed to act as a conductor, and I saw long sparks burst from it. Crushed and
without strength, I crawled to the panel, opened it, and descended to the
saloon. The storm was then at its height. It was impossible to stand upright in
the interior of the Nautilus. Captain Nemo came down about twelve. I heard
the reservoirs filling by degrees, and the Nautilus sank slowly beneath the waves.
Through the open windows in the saloon I saw large fish terrified, passing like
phantoms in the water. Some were struck before my eyes. The Nautilus was still
descending. I thought that at about eight fathoms deep we should find a calm.
But no! the upper beds were too violently agitated for that. We had to seek
repose at more than twenty-five fathoms in the bowels of the deep. But there,
what quiet, what silence, what peace! Who could have told that such a
hurricane had been let loose on the surface of that ocean?

Chapter Forty-Four

From Latitude 47° 24′ to Longitude 17° 28′

IN CONSEQUENCE OF THE storm, we had been thrown eastward once more. All
hope of escape on the shores of New York or St Lawrence had faded away; and
poor Ned, in despair, had isolated himself like Captain Nemo. Conseil and I,
however, never left each other. I said that the Nautilus had gone aside to the
east. I should have said (to be more exact), the north-east. For some days, it
wandered first on the surface, and then beneath it, amid those fogs so dreaded by
sailors. What accidents are due to these thick fogs! What shocks upon these

reefs when the wind drowns the breaking of the waves! What collisions between vessels, in spite of their warning lights, whistles, and alarm bells! And the bottoms of these seas look like a field of battle, where still lie all the conquered of the ocean; some old and already encrusted, others fresh and reflecting from their iron bands and copperplates the brilliancy of our lantern.

On the 15th of May we were at the extreme south of the Bank of Newfoundland. This bank consists of alluvia, or large heaps of organic matter, brought either from the Equator by the Gulf Stream, or from the north pole by the counter-current of cold water which skirts the American coast. There also are heaped up those erratic blocks which are carried along by the broken ice; and close by, a vast charnel-house of molluscs or zoophytes, which perish here by millions. The depth of the sea is not great at Newfoundland – not more than some hundreds of fathoms; but towards the south is a depression of 1,500 fathoms. There the Gulf Stream widens. It loses some of its speed and some of its temperature, but it becomes a sea.

It was on the 17th of May, about 500 miles from Heart's Content, at a depth of more than 1,400 fathoms, that I saw the electric cable lying on the bottom. Conseil, to whom I had not mentioned it, thought at first that it was a gigantic sea-serpent. But I undeceived the worthy fellow, and by way of consolation related several particulars in the laying of this cable. The first one was laid in the years 1857 and 1858; but, after transmitting about 400 telegrams, would not act any longer. In 1863, the engineers constructed another one, measuring 2,000 miles in length, and weighing 4,500 tons, which was embarked on the Great Eastern. This attempt also failed.

On the 25th of May the Nautilus, being at a depth of more than 1,918 fathoms, was on the precise spot where the rupture occurred which ruined the enterprise. It was within 638 miles of the coast of Ireland; and at half past two in the afternoon, they discovered that communication with Europe had ceased. The electricians on board resolved to cut the cable before fishing it up, and at eleven o'clock at night they had recovered the damaged part. They made another point and spliced it, and it was once more submerged. But some days after it broke again, and in the depths of the ocean could not be recaptured. The Americans, however, were not discouraged. Cyrus Field, the bold promoter of the enterprise, as he had sunk all his own fortune, set a new subscription on foot, which was at once answered, and another cable was constructed on better principles. The bundles of conducting wires were each enveloped in gutta-percha, and protected by a wadding of hemp, contained in a metallic covering. The Great Eastern sailed on the 13th of July 1866. The operation worked well. But one incident occurred. Several times in unrolling the cable they observed that nails had been recently forced into it, evidently with the motive of destroying it. Captain Anderson, the officers, and engineers, consulted together, and had it posted up that if the offender was surprised on board, he would be thrown without further trial into the sea. From that time the criminal attempt was never repeated.

On the 23rd of July the Great Eastern was not more than 500 miles from Newfoundland, when they telegraphed from Ireland news of the armistice concluded between Prussia and Austria after Sadowa. On the 27th, in the midst of heavy fogs, they reached the port of Heart's Content. The enterprise was successfully terminated; and for its first despatch, young America addressed old

Europe in these words of wisdom so rarely understood – 'Glory to God in the highest, and on earth peace, goodwill towards men.'

I did not expect to find the electric cable in its primitive state, such as it was on leaving the manufactory. The long serpent, covered with the remains of shells, bristling with foraminiferæ, was encrusted with a strong coating which served as a protection against all boring molluscs. It lay quietly sheltered from the motions of the sea, and under a favourable pressure for the transmission of the electric spark which passes from Europe to America in .32 of a second. Doubtless this cable will last for a great length of time, for they find that the gutta-percha covering is improved by the sea-water. Besides on this level, so well chosen, the cable is never so deeply submerged as to cause it to break. The Nautilus followed it to the lowest depth, which was more than 2,212 fathoms, and there it lay without any anchorage; and then we reached the spot where the accident had taken place in 1863. The bottom of the ocean then formed a valley about 100 miles broad, in which Mont Blanc might have been placed without its summit appearing above the waves. This valley is closed at the east by a perpendicular wall more than 2,000 yards high. We arrived there on the 28th of May, and the Nautilus was then not more than 120 miles from Ireland.

Was Captain Nemo going to land on the British Isles? No. To my great surprise he made for the south, once more coming back towards European seas. In rounding the Emerald Isle, for one instant I caught sight of Cape Clear, and the light which guides the thousands of vessels leaving Glasgow or Liverpool. An important question then arose in my mind. Did the Nautilus dare entangle itself in the Mauch? Ned Land, who had appeared since we had been nearing land, did not cease to question me. How could I answer? Captain Nemo remained invisible. After having shown the Canadian a glimpse of American shores, was he going to show me the coast of France?

But the Nautilus was still going southward. On the 30th of May, it passed in sight of the Land's End, between the extreme point of England and the Scilly Isles, which were left to starboard. If he wished to enter the Mauch he must go straight to the east. He did not do so.

During the whole of the 31st of May, the Nautilus described a series of circles on the water, which greatly interested me. It seemed to be seeking a spot it had some trouble in finding. At noon, Captain Nemo himself came to work the ship's log. He spoke no word to me, but seemed gloomier than ever. What could sadden him thus? Was it his proximity to European shores? Had he some recollections of his abandoned country? If not, what did he feel? Remorse or regret? For a long while this thought haunted my mind, and I had a kind of presentiment that before long chance would betray the captain's secrets.

The next day, the 1st of June, the Nautilus continued the same process. It was evidently seeking some particular spot in the ocean. Captain Nemo took the sun's altitude as he had done the day before. The sea was beautiful, the sky clear. About eight miles to the east, a large steam vessel could be discerned on the horizon. No flag fluttered from its mast, and I could not discover its nationality. Some minutes before the sun passed the meridian, Captain Nemo took his sextant, and watched with great attention. The perfect rest of the water greatly helped the operation. The Nautilus was motionless; it neither rolled nor pitched.

I was on the platform when the altitude was taken, and the captain pronounced these words – 'It is here.'

He turned and went below. Had he seen the vessel which was changing its course and seemed to be nearing us? I could not tell. I returned to the saloon. The panels closed, I heard the hissing of the water in the reservoirs. The Nautilus began to sink, following a vertical line, for its screw communicated no motion to it. Some minutes later it stopped at a depth of more than 420 fathoms, resting on the ground. The luminous ceiling was darkened, then the panels were opened, and through the glass I saw the sea brilliantly illuminated by the rays of our lantern for at least half a mile round us.

I looked to the port side, and saw nothing but an immensity of quiet waters. But to starboard, on the bottom appeared a large protuberance, which at once attracted my attention. One would have thought it a ruin buried under a coating of white shells, much resembling a covering of snow. Upon examining the mass attentively, I could recognize the ever thickening form of a vessel bare of its masts, which must have sunk. It certainly belonged to past times. This wreck, to be thus encrusted with the lime of the water, must already be able to count many years passed at the bottom of the ocean.

What was this vessel? Why did the Nautilus visit its tomb? Could it have been aught but a shipwreck which had drawn it under the water? I knew not what to think, when near me in a slow voice I heard Captain Nemo say——

'At one time this ship was called the Marseillais. It carried seventy-four guns, and was launched in 1762. In 1778, on the 13th of August, commanded by La Poype-Vertrieux, it fought boldly against the Preston. In 1779, on the 4th of July, it was at the taking of Grenada, with the squadron of Admiral Estaing. In 1781, on the 5th of September, it took part in the battle of Comte de Grasse, in Chesapeake Bay. In 1794, the French Republic changed its name. On the 16th of April, in the same year, it joined the squadron of Villaret Joyeuse, at Brest, being entrusted with the escort of a cargo of corn coming from America, under the command of Admiral Van Stabel. On the 11th and 12th Prairal of the second year, this squadron fell in with an English vessel. Sir, today is the 13th Prairal, the 1st of June 1868. It is now seventy-four years ago, day for day on this very spot, in latitude 47° 24', longitude 17° 28', that this vessel, after fighting heroically, losing its three masts, with the water in its hold, and the third of its crew disabled, preferred sinking with its 356 sailors to surrendering; and nailing its colours to the poop, disappeared under the waves to the cry of "Long live the Republic!"'

'The Avenger!' I exclaimed.

'Yes, sir, the Avenger! A good name!' muttered Captain Nemo, crossing his arms.

Chapter Forty-Five

A Hecatomb

THE WAY OF DESCRIBING THIS unlooked-for scene, the history of the patriot ship, told at first so coldly, and the emotion with which this strange man pronounced the last words, the name of the Avenger, the significance of which could not escape me, all impressed itself deeply on my mind. My eyes did not leave the captain; who, with his hand stretched out to sea, was watching with a glowing eye the glorious wreck. Perhaps I was never to know who he was, from whence he came, or where he was going to, but I saw the man move, and apart from the *savant*. It was no common misanthropy which had shut Captain Nemo and his companions within the Nautilus, but a hatred, either monstrous or sublime, which time could never weaken. Did this hatred still seek for vengeance? The future would soon teach me that. But the Nautilus was rising slowly to the surface of the sea, and the form of the Avenger disappeared by degrees from my sight. Soon a slight rolling told me that we were in the open air. At that moment a dull boom was heard. I looked at the captain. He did not move.

'Captain?' said I.

He did not answer. I left him and mounted the platform. Conseil and the Canadian were already there.

'Where did that sound come from?' I asked.

'It was a gun shot,' replied Ned Land.

I looked in the direction of the vessel I had already seen. It was nearing the Nautilus, and we could see that it was putting on steam. It was within six miles of us.

'What is that ship, Ned?'

'By its rigging, and the height of its lower masts,' said the Canadian, 'I bet she is a ship of war. May it reach us; and, if necessary, sink this cursed Nautilus.'

'Friend Ned,' replied Conseil, 'what harm can it do to the Nautilus? Can it attack it beneath the waves? Can it cannonade us at the bottom of the sea?'

'Tell me, Ned,' said I, 'can you recognize what country she belongs to?'

The Canadian knitted his eyebrows, dropped his eyelids, and screwed up the corners of his eyes, and for a few moments fixed a piercing look upon the vessel.

'No, sir,' he replied; 'I cannot tell what nation she belongs to, for she shows no colours. But I can declare she is a man of war, for a long pennant flutters from her main mast.'

For a quarter of an hour we watched the ship which was steaming towards us. I could not, however, believe that she could see the Nautilus from that distance; and still less, that she could know what this submarine engine was. Soon the Canadian informed me that she was a large armoured two-decker ram. A thick black smoke was pouring from her two funnels. Her closely-furled sails were stopped to her yards. She hoisted no flag at her mizen-peak. The distance prevented us from distinguishing the colours of her pennant, which floated like a thin ribbon. She advanced rapidly. If Captain Nemo allowed her to approach, there was a chance of salvation for us.

'Sir,' said Ned Land, 'if that vessel passes within a mile of us I shall throw myself into the sea, and I should advise you to do the same.'

I did not reply to the Canadian's suggestion, but continued watching the ship. Whether English, French, American, or Russian, she would be sure to take us in if we could only reach her. Presently a white smoke burst from the fore part of the vessel; some seconds after the water, agitated by the fall of a heavy body, splashed the stern of the Nautilus, and shortly afterwards a loud explosion struck my ear.

'What! they are firing at us!' I exclaimed.

'So please you, sir,' said Ned, 'they have recognized the unicorn, and they are firing at us.'

'But,' I exclaimed, 'surely they can see that there are men in the case?'

'It is, perhaps, because of that,' replied Ned Land, looking at me.

A whole flood of light burst upon my mind. Doubtless they knew now how to believe the stories of the pretended monster. No doubt, on board the Abraham Lincoln, when the Canadian struck it with the harpoon, Commander Farragut had recognized in the supposed narwhal a submarine vessel, more dangerous than a supernatural cetacean. Yes, it must have been so; and on every sea they were now seeking this engine of destruction. Terrible indeed! if, as we supposed, Captain Nemo employed the Nautilus in works of vengeance. On the night when we were imprisoned in that cell, in the midst of the Indian Ocean, had he not attacked some vessel? The man buried in the coral cemetery, had he not been a victim to the shock caused by the Nautilus? Yes, I repeat it, it must be so. One part of the mysterious existence of Captain Nemo had been unveiled; and, if his identity had not been recognized, at least, the nations united against him were no longer hunting a chimerical creature, but a man who had vowed a deadly hatred against them. All the formidable past rose before me. Instead of meeting friends on board the approaching ship, we could only expect pitiless enemies. But the shot rattled about us. Some of them struck the sea and ricochetted, losing themselves in the distance. But none touched the Nautilus. The vessel was not more than three miles from us. In spite of the serious cannonade, Captain Nemo did not appear on the platform; but, if one of the conical projectiles had struck the shell of the Nautilus, it would have been fatal. The Canadian then said, 'Sir, we must do all we can to get out of this dilemma. Let us signal them. They will then, perhaps, understand that we are honest folks.'

Ned Land took his handerchief to wave in the air; but he had scarcely displayed it, when he was struck by an iron hand, and fell, in spite of his great strength, upon the deck.

'Fool!' exclaimed the captain, 'do you wish to be pierced by the spur of the Nautilus before it is hurled at this vessel?'

Captain Nemo was terrible to hear; he was still more terrible to see. His face was deadly pale, with a spasm at his heart. For an instant it must have ceased to beat. His pupils were fearfully contracted. He did not *speak*, he *roared*, as, with his body thrown forward, he wrung the Canadian's shoulders. Then, leaving him, and turning to the ship of war, whose shot was still raining around him, he exclaimed, with a powerful voice, 'Ah, ship of an accursed nation, you know who I am! I do not want your colours to know you by! Look! and I will show you mine!'

And on the fore part of the platform Captain Nemo unfurled a black flag, similar to the one he had placed at the south pole. At that moment a shot struck the shell of the Nautilus obliquely, without piercing it; and, rebounding near the captain, was lost in the sea. He shrugged his shoulders; and addressing me, said shortly, 'Go down, you and your companions, go down!'

'Sir,' I exclaimed, 'are you going to attack this vessel?'

'Sir, I am going to sink it.'

'You will not do that?'

'I shall do it,' he replied, coldly. 'And I advise you not to judge me, sir. Fate has shown you what you ought not have seen. The attack has begun; go down.'

'What is this vessel?'

'You do not know? Very well! so much the better! its nationality to you, at least, will be a secret. Go down!'

We could but obey. About fifteen of the sailors surrounded the captain, looking with implacable hatred at the vessel nearing them. One could feel that the same desire of vengeance animated every soul. I went down at the moment another projectile struck the Nautilus, and I heard the captain exclaim——

'Strike, mad vessel! Shower your useless shot! And then, you will not escape the spur of the Nautilus. But it is not here that you shall perish! I would not have your ruins mingle with those of the Avenger!'

I reached my room. The captain and his second had remained on the platform. The screw was set in motion, and the Nautilus, moving with speed, was soon beyond the reach of the ship's guns. But the pursuit continued, and Captain Nemo contented himself with keeping his distance.

About four in the afternoon, being no longer able to contain my impatience, I went to the central staircase. The panel was open, and I ventured on to the platform. The captain was still walking up and down with an agitated step. He was looking at the ship, which was five or six miles to leeward.

He was going round it like a wild beast, and drawing it eastward, he allowed them to pursue. But he did not attack. Perhaps he still hesitated? I wished to mediate once more. But I had scarcely spoken, when Captain Nemo imposed silence, saying——

'I am the law, and I am the judge! I am the oppressed, and there is the oppressor! Through him I have lost all that I loved, cherished, and venerated – country, wife, children, father, and mother. I saw all perish! All that I hate is there! Say no more!'

I cast a last look at the man of war, which was putting on steam, and rejoined Ned and Conseil.

'We will fly!' I exclaimed.

'Good!' said Ned. 'What is this vessel?'

'I do not know; but whatever it is, it will be sunk before night. In any case, it is better to perish with it, than be made accomplices in a retaliation, the justice of which we cannot judge.

'That is my opinion too,' said Ned Land, coolly. 'Let us wait for night.'

Night arrived. Deep silence reigned on board. The compass showed that the Nautilus had not altered its course. It was on the surface, rolling slightly. My companions and I resolved to fly when the vessel should be near enough either to hear us or to see us; for the moon, which would be full in two or three days, shone brightly. Once on board the ship, if we could not prevent the blow which threatened it, we could, at least we would, do all that circumstances would allow. Several times I thought the Nautilus was preparing for attack; but Captain Nemo contented himself with allowing his adversary to approach, and then fled once more before it.

Part of the night passed without any incident. We watched the opportunity for action. We spoke little, for we were too much moved. Ned Land would have thrown himself into the sea, but I forced him to wait. According to my idea, the Nautilus would attack the ship at her waterline, and then it would not only be possible, but easy to fly.

At three in the morning, full of uneasiness, I mounted the platform. Captain Nemo had not left it. He was standing at the fore part near his flag, which a slight breeze displayed above his head. He did not take his eyes from the vessel. The intensity of his look seemed to attract, and fascinate, and draw it onward more purely than if he had been towing it. The moon was then passing the meridian. Jupiter was rising in the east. Amid this peaceful scene of nature, sky and ocean rivalled each other in tranquillity, the sea offering to the orbs of night the finest mirror they could ever have in which to reflect their image. As I thought of the deep calm of these elements, compared with all those passions brooding imperceptibly within the Nautilus, I shuddered.

The vessel was within two miles of us. It was ever nearing that phosphorescent light which showed the presence of the Nautilus. I could see its green and red lights, and its white lantern hanging from the large foremast. An indistinct vibration quivered through its rigging, showing that the furnaces were heated to the uttermost. Sheaves of sparks and red ashes flew from the funnels, shining in the atmosphere like stars.

I remained thus until six in the morning, without Captain Nemo noticing me. The ship stood about a mile and a half from us, and with the first dawn of day the firing began afresh. The moment could not be far off when, the Nautilus attacking its adversary, my companions and myself should for ever leave this man. I was preparing to go down to remind them, when the second mounted the platform, accompanied by several sailors. Captain Nemo either did not, or would not, see them. Some steps were taken which might be called the signal for action. They were very simple. The iron balustrade around the platform was lowered, and the lantern and pilot cages were pushed within the shell until they were flush with the deck. The long surface of the steel cigar no longer offered a single point to check its manœuvres. I returned to the saloon. The Nautilus still floated; some streaks of light were filtering through the liquid beds. With the undulations of the waves the windows were brightened by the red streaks of the rising sun, and this dreadful day of the 2nd of June had dawned.

At five o'clock, the log showed that the speed of the Nautilus was slackening, and I knew that it was allowing them to draw nearer. Besides, the reports were heard more distinctly, and the projectiles, labouring through the ambient water, were extinguished with a strange hissing noise.

'My friends,' said I, 'the moment is come. One grasp of the hand, and may God protect us!'

Ned Land was resolute, Conseil calm, myself so nervous that I knew not how to contain myself. We all passed into the library; but the moment I pushed the door opening on to the central staircase, I heard the upper panel close sharply. The Canadian rushed on to the stairs, but I stopped him. A well known hissing noise told me that the water was running into the reservoirs, and in a few minutes the Nautilus was some yards beneath the surface of the waves. I understood the manœuvre. It was too late to act. The Nautilus did not wish to strike at the impenetrable cuirass, but below the waterline, where the metallic covering no longer protected it.

We were again imprisoned, unwilling witnesses of the dreadful drama that was preparing. We had scarcely time to reflect; taking refuge in my room, we looked at each other without speaking. A deep stupor had taken hold of my mind: thought seemed to stand still. I was in that painful state of expectation preceding a dreadful report. I waited, I listened, every sense was merged in that of hearing! The speed of the Nautilus was accelerated. It was preparing to rush. The whole ship trembled. Suddenly I screamed. I felt the shock, but comparatively light. I felt the penetrating power of the steel spur. I heard rattlings and scrapings. But the Nautilus, carried along by its propelling power, passed through the mass of the vessel, like a needle through sailcloth!

I could stand it no longer. Mad, out of my mind, I rushed from my room into the saloon. Captain Nemo was there, mute, gloomy, implacable; he was looking through the port panel. A large mass cast a shadow on the water; and that it might lose nothing of her agony, the Nautilus was going down into the abyss with her. Ten yards from me I saw the open shell through which the water was rushing with the noise of thunder, then the double line of guns and the netting. The bridge was covered with black agitated shadows.

The water was rising. The poor creatures were crowding the ratlins, clinging to the masts, struggling under the water. It was a human ant heap overtaken by the sea. Paralysed, stiffened with anguish, my hair standing on end, with eyes wide open, panting, without breath, and without voice, I too was watching! An irresistible attraction glued me to the glass! Suddenly an explosion took place. The compressed air blew up her decks, as if the magazines had caught fire. Then the unfortunate vessel sunk more rapidly. Her topmast, laden with victims, now appeared; then her spars, bending under the weight of men; and last of all, the top of her mainmast. Then the dark mass disappeared, and with it the dead crew, drawn down by the strong eddy.

I turned to Captain Nemo. That terrible avenger, a perfect archangel of hatred, was still looking. When all was over, he turned to his room, opened the door, and entered. I followed him with my eyes. On the end wall beneath his heroes, I saw the portrait of a woman still young, and two little children. Captain Nemo looked at them for some moments, stretched his arms towards them, and kneeling down burst into deep sobs.

Chapter Forty-Six

The Last Words of Captain Nemo

THE PANELS HAD CLOSED on this dreadful vision, but light had not returned to the saloon: all was silence and darkness within the Nautilus. At wonderful speed, a hundred feet beneath the water, it was leaving this desolate spot. Whither was it going? To the north or south? Where was the man flying to after such dreadful retaliation? I had returned to my room, where Ned and Conseil had remained silent enough. I felt an insurmountable horror for Captain Nemo. Whatever he had suffered at the hands of these men, he had no right to punish thus. He had made me, if not an accomplice, at least a witness of his vengeance. At eleven the electric light reappeared. I passed into the saloon. It was deserted. I consulted the different instruments. The Nautilus was flying northward at the rate of twenty-five miles an hour, now on the surface, and now thirty feet below it. On taking the bearings by the chart, I saw that we were passing the mouth of the Manche, and that our course was hurrying us towards the northern seas at a frightful speed. That night we had crossed two hundred leagues of the Atlantic. The shadows fell, and the sea was covered with darkness until the rising of the moon. I went to my room, but could not sleep. I was troubled with dreadful nightmare. The horrible scene of destruction was continually before my eyes. From that day, who could tell into what part of the North Atlantic basin the Nautilus would take us? Still, with unaccountable speed. Still in the midst of these northern fogs. Would it touch at Spitzbergen, or on the shores of Nova Zembla? Should we explore those unknown seas, the White Sea, the Sea of Kara, the Gulf of Obi, the Archipelago of Liarrov, and the unknown coast of Asia? I could not say. I could no longer judge of the time that was passing. The clocks had been stopped on board. It seemed, as in polar countries, that night and day no longer followed their regular course. I felt myself being drawn into that strange region where the foundered imagination of Edgar Poe roamed at will. Like the fabulous Gordon Pym, at every moment I expected to see 'That veiled human figure, of larger proportions than those of any inhabitant of the earth, thrown across the cataract which defends the approach to the pole.' I estimated (though, perhaps, I may be mistaken) – I estimated this adventurous course of the Nautilus to have lasted fifteen or twenty days. And I know not how much longer it might have lasted, had it not been for the catastrophe which ended this voyage. Of Captain Nemo I saw nothing whatever now, nor of his second. Not a man of the crew was visible for an instant. The Nautilus was almost incessantly under water. When we came to the surface to renew the air, the panels opened and shut mechanically. There were no more marks on the planisphere. I knew not where we were. And the Canadian, too, his strength and patience at an end, appeared no more. Conseil could not draw a word from him; and fearing that, in dreadful fit of madness, he might kill himself, watched him with constant devotion. One morning (which date it was I could not say), I had fallen into a heavy sleep towards the early hours, a sleep both painful and unhealthy, when I suddenly awoke. Ned Land was leaning over me, saying, in a low voice, 'We are going to fly.'

I sat up.

'When shall we go?' I asked.

'Tomorrow night. All inspection on board the Nautilus seems to have ceased. All appear to be stupified. You will be ready, sir?'

'Yes; where are we?'

'In sight of land. I took the reckoning this morning in the fog – twenty miles to the east.'

'What country is it?'

'I do not know; but whatever it is, we will take refuge there.'

'Yes, Ned, yes. We will fly tonight, even if the sea should swallow us up.'

'The sea is bad, the wind violent, but twenty miles in that light boat of the Nautilus does not frighten me. Unknown to the crew, I have been able to procure food and some bottles of water.'

'I will follow you.'

'But,' continued the Canadian, 'if I am surprised, I will defend myself; I will force them to kill me.'

'We will die together, friend Ned.'

I had made up my mind to all. The Canadian left me. I reached the platform, on which I could with difficulty support myself against the shock of the waves. The sky was threatening; but, as land was in those thick brown shadows, we must fly. I returned to the saloon, fearing and yet hoping to see Captain Nemo, wishing and yet not wishing to see him. What could I have said to him? Could I hide the involuntary horror with which he inspired me? No. It was better that I should not meet him face to face; better to forget him. And yet——. How long seemed that day, the last that I should pass in the Nautilus. I remained alone. Ned Land and Conseil avoided speaking, for fear of betraying themselves. At six I dined, but I was not hungry; I forced myself to eat in spite of my disgust, that I might not weaken myself. At half past six Ned Land came to my room, saying, 'We shall not see each other again before our departure. At ten the moon will not be risen. We will profit by the darkness. Come to the boat; Conseil and I will wait for you.'

The Canadian went out without giving me time to answer. Wishing to verify the course of the Nautilus, I went to the saloon. We were running N.N.E. at frightful speed, and more than fifty yards deep. I cast a last look on these wonders of Nature, on the riches of art heaped up in this museum, upon the unrivalled collection destined to perish at the bottom of the sea, with him who had formed it. I wished to fix an indelible impression of it on my mind. I remained an hour thus, bathed in the light of that luminous ceiling, and passing in review those treasures shining under their glasses. Then I returned to my room.

I dressed myself in strong sea clothing. I collected my notes, placing them carefully about me. My heart beat loudly. I could not check its pulsations. Certainly my trouble and agitation would have betrayed me to Captain Nemo's eyes. What was he doing at this moment? I listened at the door of his room. I heard steps. Captain Nemo was there. He had not gone to rest. At every moment I expected to see him appear, and ask me why I wished to fly. I was constantly on the alert. My imagination magnified everything. The impression became at last so poignant that I asked myself if it would not be better to go the captain's room, see him face to face, and brave him with look and gesture.

It was the inspiration of a madman; fortunately I resisted the desire, and stretched myself on my bed to quiet my bodily agitation. My nerves were somewhat calmer, but in my excited brain I saw over again all my existence on board the Nautilus; every incident, either happy or unfortunate, which had happened since my disappearance from the Abraham Lincoln – the submarine hunt, the Torres Straits, the savages of Papua, the running ashore, the coral cemetery, the passage of Suez, the island of Santorin, the Cretan diver, Vigo Bay, Atlantis, the iceberg, the south pole, the imprisonment in the ice, the fight among the poulps, the storm in the Gulf Stream, the Avenger, and the horrible scene of the vessel sunk with all her crew. All these events passed before my eyes like scenes in a drama. Then Captain Nemo seemed to grow enormously, his features to assume superhuman proportions. He was no longer my equal, but a man of the waters, the genie of the sea.

It was then half past nine. I held my head between my hands to keep it from bursting. I closed my eyes, I would not think any longer. There was another half hour to wait, another half hour of a nightmare, which might drive me mad.

At that moment I head the distant strains of the organ, a sad harmony to an undefinable chaunt, the wail of a soul longing to break these earthly bonds. I listened with every sense, scarcely breathing; plunged, like Captain Nemo, in that musical ecstacy, which was drawing him in spirit to the end of life.

Then a sudden thought terrified me. Captain Nemo had left his room. He was in the saloon, which I must cross to fly. There I should meet him for the last time. He would see me, perhaps speak to me. A gesture of his might destroy me, a single word chain me on board.

But ten was about to strike. The moment had come for me to leave my room, and join my companions.

I must not hesitate, even if Captain Nemo himself should rise before me. I opened my door carefully; and even then, as it turned on its hinges, it seemed to me to make a dreadful noise. Perhaps it only existed in my own imagination.

I crept along the dark stairs of the Nautilus, stopping at each step to check the beating of my heart. I reached the door of the saloon, and opened it gently. It was plunged in profound darkness. The strains of the organ sounded faintly. Captain Nemo was there. he did not see me. In the full light I do not think he would have noticed me, so entirely was he absorbed in the ecstacy.

I crept along the carpet, avoiding the slightest sound which might betray my presence. I was at least five minutes reaching the door, at the opposite side, opening to the library.

I was going to open it, when a sigh from Captain Nemo nailed me to the spot. I knew that he was rising. I could even see him, for the light from the library came through to the saloon. He came towards me silently, with his arms crossed, gliding like a spectre rather than walking. His breast was swelling with sobs; and I heard him murmur these words (the last which ever struck my ear)——

'Almighty God! enough! enough!'

Was it a confession of remorse which thus escaped from this man's conscience?

In desperation I rushed through the library, mounted the central staircase, and following the upper flight reached the boat. I crept through the opening, which had already admitted my two companions.

'Let us go! let us go!' I exclaimed.

'Directly!' replied the Canadian.

The orifice in the plates of the Nautilus was first closed, and fastened down by means of a false key, with which Ned Land had provided himself; the opening in the boat was also closed. The Canadian began to loosen the bolts which still held us to the submarine boat.

Suddenly a noise within was heard. Voices were answering each other loudly. What was the matter? Had they discovered our flight? I felt Ned Land slipping a dagger into my hand.

'Yes,' I murmured, 'we know how to die!'

The Canadian had stopped in his work. But one word many times repeated, a dreadful word, revealed the cause of the agitation spreading on board the Nautilus. It was not we the crew were looking after!

'The maëlstrom! the maëlstrom!' I exclaimed.

The maëlstrom! Could a more dreadful word in a more dreadful situation have sounded in our ears! We were then upon the dangerous coast of Norway. Was the Nautilus being drawn into this gulf at the moment our boat was going to leave its sides? We knew that at the tide the pent up waters between the islands of Ferroe and Loffoden rush with irresistible violence, forming a whirlpool from which no vessel ever escapes. From every point of the horizon enormous waves were meeting, forming a gulf justly called the 'Navel of Ocean,' whose power of attraction extends to a distance of twelve miles. There, not only vessels, but whales are sacrificed, as well as white bears from the northern regions.

It is thither that the Nautilus, voluntarily or involuntarily, had been run by the captain.

It was describing a spiral, the circumference of which was lessening by degrees, and the boat, which was still fastened to its side, was carried along with giddy speed. I felt that sickly giddiness which arises from long continued whirling round.

We were in dread. Our horror was at its height, circulation had stopped, all nervous influence annihilated, and we were covered with cold sweat, like a sweat of agony! And what noise around our frail bark! What roarings repeated by the echo miles away! What an uproar was that of the waters broken on the sharp rocks at the bottom, where the hardest bodies are crushed, and trees worn away, 'with all the fur rubbed off,' according to the Norwegian phrase!

What a situation to be in! We rocked frightfully. The Nautilus defended itself like a human being. Its steel muscles cracked. Sometimes it seemed to stand upright, and we with it!

'We must hold on, said Ned, 'and look after the bolts. We may still be saved if we stick to the Nautilus——'

He had not finished the words, when we heard a crashing noise, the bolts gave way, and the boat, torn from its groove, was hurled like a stone from a sling into the midst of the whirlpool.

My head struck on a piece of iron, and with the violent shock I lost all consciousness.

Chapter Forty-Seven

Conclusion

THUS ENDS THE VOYAGE UNDER the seas. What passed during that night – how the boat escaped from the eddies of the maëlstrom – how Ned Land, Conseil, and myself ever came out of the gulf, I cannot tell.

But when I returned to consciousness, I was lying in a fisherman's hut, on the Loffoden Isles. My two companions, safe and sound, were near me holding my hands. We embraced each other heartily.

At that moment we could not think of returning to France. The means of communication between the north of Norway and the south are rare. And I am therefore obliged to wait for the steamboat running monthly from Cape North.

And among the worthy people who have so kindly received us, I revise my record of these adventures once more. Not a fact has been ómitted, not a detail exaggerated. It is a faithful narrative of this incredible expedition in an element inaccessible to man, but to which Progress will one day open a road.

Shall I be believed? I do not know. And it matters little, after all. What I now affirm is, that I have a right to speak of these seas, under which, in less than ten months, I have crossed 20,000 leagues in that submarine tour of the world, which has revealed so many wonders.

But what has become of the Nautilus? Did it resist the pressure of the maëlstrom? Does Captain Nemo still live? and does he still follow under the ocean those frightful retaliations? Or, did he stop after that last hecatomb?

Will the waves one day carry to him the manuscript containing the history of his life? Shall I ever know the name of this man? Will the missing vessel tell us by its nationality that of Captain Nemo?

I hope so. And I also hope that this powerful vessel has conquered the sea at its most terrible gulf, and that the Nautilus has survived where so many other vessels have been lost! If it be so – if Captain Nemo still inhabits the ocean, his adopted country, may hatred be appeased in that savage heart! May the contemplation of so many wonders extinguish for ever the spirit of vengeance! May the judge disappear, and the philosopher continue the peaceful exploration of the sea! If his destiny be strange, it is also sublime. Have I not understood it myself? Have I not lived ten months of this unnatural life? And to the question asked by Ecclesiastes 3,000 years ago, 'That which is far off and exceeding deep, who can find it out?' two men alone of all now living have the right to give an answer——

CAPTAIN NEMO AND MYSELF.